As _____ into
the so _____ mb
and fi _____ she
tried to withdraw her fingers, which were caught fast, dragging herself down until her helmet bobbed within a centimeter of the surface.

She extended her other hand to stop herself. It, too, sank in, and her helmet made contact. Now she screamed. She sank deeper and deeper, drawn by what force, she didn't know. She could no longer turn her head, could see nothing but the uniform, grainy color of the surface material. She felt Kamanov's hand on her, tugging at her life-support backpack.

"*I fear it is too late, Estrellita,*" exclaimed the Russian, "*I have become stuck, as well. Try to relax. Breathe evenly.*"

She stiffened. "Piotr, I can see light! It's brightening up in here! I don't know what it means, but . . ."

"*Yes,*" the scientist asked her, *what is happening?*"

"My helmet's broken through, like coming up through muddy water! It's hollow, and we've got company! Weird company!"

Half a dozen creatures were anchored by their feet (or whatever they stood on). They looked, more than anything else, like giant golden-brown cockroaches. Cockroaches her own size. Cockroaches with guns pointed at her.

Another being caught her astonished eye, of slender build, covered from head to foot either with soft scales fringed at the edges, or stubby feathers. It raised a hand and spoke to her in Spanish over her suit radio.

"*A good afternoon to you, Major Reille y Sanchez. As you've no doubt surmised by now, you and your party were expected.*"

**THE NOVEL THAT WON THE FREEDOM
BOOK OF THE YEAR AWARD**

FORGE OF THE ELDERS

L. NEIL SMITH

Forge of the Elders

This is a work of fiction. All the characters and events portrayed in this book are fictional, and any resemblance to real people or incidents is purely coincidental.

A Baen Books Original Omnibus

Baen Publishing Enterprises
P.O. Box 1403
Riverdale, NY 10471
www.baen.com

ISBN: 0-671-31982-5

Cover art by Bob Eggleton

First paperback printing, April 2001

Library of Congress Cataloging-in-Publication Number
99-086216

Distributed by Simon & Schuster
1230 Avenue of the Americas
New York, NY 10020

Production by Windhaven Press, Auburn, NH
Printed in the United States of America

CONTENTS

BOOK I
First Time the Charm
~1~

BOOK II
Second to One
~219~

BOOK III
Third Among Equals
~421~

ACKNOWLEDGMENTS

My personal thanks to Mr. Frank Harris at Kahr Arms, 630 Route 303, Blauvelt, NY 10913—and to Tom Creasing, my friend and attorney, who made it all happen—for their invaluable aid in making make-believe a little more real. Also, the lyrics at the top of Chapter Forty-Four are from the folk song "Cumberland Mountain Deer Chase" as sung and played by Uncle Dave Macon.

BOOK I:

FIRST TIME THE CHARM

THIS BOOK IS DEDICATED, with affection and admiration, to the memory of Karl Hess, who wields the Hammer of Volund at the Forge of Liberty.

PROLOGUE:
The House of Eneri Relda

A fountain sparkled in the broad, tiled courtyard of the hillside villa, cooling the afternoon breeze and sprinkling the sandaled feet of a lean-muscled young man seated before it. His sleeveless tunic, its decorative metallic border just reaching his knees, was the lightest in his wardrobe. As always, Eichra Oren wondered in an absent way how the air could remain so warm after passing across the Inland Sea from the Ocean of Sand where it had been born.

At his master's feet, also enjoying the cool spray, Oasam, a heavily furred white dog, grinned into the slanting sunlight, sniffing with contented curiosity at the hot, scent-laden air from the countryside beyond the villa. A colored bird chirped in a wicker cage hung from a mimosa tree nearby.

As on countless previous occasions, Eichra Oren listened (as absently as he wondered about the wind) to his mother regaling guests in the Original Language with oft-told tales of life before the Continent was Lost. From an unobtrusive corner, a lyrist, hired for the day, counterpointed the burbling of the fountain, weaving notes between the woman's words. More dignified than beautiful in the flowing

1

drapery of her girlhood, she was much respected by those
who considered themselves honored to hear the old stories once again from the lips of Eneri Relda, one of the
remaining few who had lived them.

Although he still felt bone-weary as he sipped his bowl
of wine, the young man centered his thoughts—couched
in a Successor Tongue he had only yesterday been asked
to learn—less upon the perilous task he had just performed than upon whatever he might be required to do
next. Eichra Oren was skilled and enjoyed most aspects
of his trade. A short, broad-bladed sword, the badge of
his profession—representing all those things about it he
enjoyed least—leaned in its unembellished scabbard against
the graceful stuccoed archway leading through the villa's
atrium to the cobbled street beyond.

Of a sudden, he heard insistent shrilling behind his eyes.
Others heard it, as well. The lyre-playing creature paused
to brush its bristly mandibles with claws enameled in the
latest fashion. A guest ruffled its feathers, stretched its
flightless wings, and scratched its powdered beak with a
scaled foot. Another splayed its glistening tentacles over
the courtyard tile, turning its awkward, giant, colorfully
striped shell to peer at the tunic-clad figure with a giant,
placid eye. Eichra Oren's mother gave him a brief, irritated
scowl, then resumed her story. Glancing at his wristwatch,
he swore a soft oath in the Original Language.

His dog looked up, remarking, "Boss, there goes the
doorbell—what'll you bet it's a snake on a bicycle?"

ONE
The Golden Apple

The answer, once they had it, had only generated more questions.

As usual.

Regrettably, they were a people for whom it had become difficult—because they'd been taught the hard way—to ask and answer questions.

"Front and center, EVA team, you're about to earn your pay."

The familiar voice crackling over the intraship comsystem was that of Brigadier General Horatio Z. Gutierrez, commonly referred to as "the Captain" by virtue of his appointment as expedition commander.

"Aye, aye, Commodore!"

The source of this facetious reply was the team's geologist, Dr. Piotr Kamanov, one of a few token Russians participating in what, in due course, would be advertised at home—provided they could stake a claim to anything resembling success out here—as an international undertaking. It was accompanied by a characteristic grin, and a wicked twinkle which contrasted with the icy and penetrating blue of the eyes that had produced it, neither of which the remark's intended recipient was present to appreciate, separated, as the two men were, by 250 centimeters of hard vacuum and a pair of aluminum-epoxy-graphite bulkheads.

From several others who were present, a ripple of nervous laughter followed. Despite the technical fact that he rated it, Gutierrez, a career Aerospace Force officer, had admonished them all, with an identical grin, just after the voyage had begun, that any crewperson addressing him by that irredeemably naval title would be immediately ejected from the air lock. Since this was precisely the fate now awaiting the EVA team, perhaps it had seemed worth the risk.

"Major?" Technical Sergeant Toya Pulaski whispered. "The EVA team's about buttoned up—everyone but Dr. Kamanov, of course—would you like some help with your suit-seals?"

The gloves, with their knurled lock-rings, were the hardest part to finish by yourself. Pulaski was one member of the EVA team who wouldn't be venturing outside with the others. To anyone who'd given it a thought (no one ever had), it wouldn't have seemed in character for the hesitant-voiced young woman who offered every appearance, deceptive though it must be, of frail timidity. It was her job to see that those suiting up got through their checklists without skipping items that might cost them their lives.

"What?"

In many ways a perfect contrast to Pulaski, Marine Corps Major Estrellita Reille y Sanchez, the EVA team's nominal leader, blinked and shook her head at her subordinate, a bit chagrined to be caught wool-gathering at a crucial moment. The multilayered bulk of the vacuum-armor enveloping and disguising her full, feminine form (one of several differences between the major and the less-endowed sergeant) failed as yet to conceal her thick, wavy red hair, trimmed just short of shoulder-length. Giving the fabric an overly positive tug, she pulled the suit's upper torso flap down over the waist ring and reached for the soft helmet which the yellowed NASA manuals labeled "communications carrier," but which everybody else called a "Snoopy cap."

"No thank you, Sergeant, I believe I can manage."

Reille y Sanchez faced the forward bulkhead, every meter of which was bedecked with storage lockers, shelf grating, and gear attachment points. The bulkhead stood between her and, across a narrow gap of empty space, the flight deck of the refitted and rechristened shuttle *Honorable Robert Dole*. Once the property of NASA, it now served as flagship to the little fleet it was a part of. The major's small, space-booted feet were tucked into nylon stirrups projecting from the curved wall of the cargo bay passenger insert, a twelve-faceted cylinder, four meters by fifteen, which had been home to more people, for a longer time, than she liked to think about even now, when at long last they'd reached their destination. Her sense of smell alone, she felt, would never be the same for having made this journey.

Others, flight crews, scientists, engineers, mining and ag specialists, refinery technicians, the Vietnamese-American physician whose name she always had to struggle to remember—Rosalind Nguyen—forty-two individuals, had been just as cramped, dirty and uncomfortable. This and the other two eighty-year-old vessels, the *Honorable John McCain* and the *Honorable Orrin Hatch*, had never been intended for flights of this duration, let alone interplanetary travel. They were fourteen souls per shuttle, seven forward in crew quarters, seven aft in Hell for 349 days, 11 hours, 7 minutes. She was grateful that consumables were stored in an emptied auxiliary fuel tank, fastened in Earth orbit under the flattened belly of each ship.

Tucking an intransigent auburn strand into her cap, the major settled the phones over her ears, plugging their leads into a receptacle just under the gasketed neck-rim of her suit. Peering over the rim, she adjusted her oxygen flow and reached for her gloves, detaching them from the bulkhead with a ripping noise. The nylon thumb loops fastened to her cooling undergarment had already begun irritating the soft webbing of her thumb, but the gloves went on without a hitch. She snapped the lock-rings together and turned them from the OPEN position to CLOSED without Pulaski's help, smoothing the cuffs back over her wrists.

She reached for the bulky helmet which invariably reminded her of a gumball machine she'd been fascinated

with as a child. It still stood, she imagined, in a dusty corner
of the grimy Trailways station in the central Texas town
where she'd been born. One of her earliest memories was
of wondering what it had looked like, full of the multicolored spheres it had been placed there to dispense by the
McQueenie Kiwanis or some other long-gone local pillar
of a now-defunct establishment.

Reille y Sanchez had never seen a gumball, let alone
tasted one. This had failed to strike her, even then, as any
great personal tragedy. In a global civilization reeling into
the second quarter of an already ragged twenty-first century, small children everywhere had at least been as equal
as possible in their deprivation. At that age (twenty years
ago, she mused; she must have been all of eight or nine
the last time she'd been home) she couldn't appreciate the
desperate situation in detail, but even then she'd understood, to some small degree, how a nation locked into a
collapsing international economy couldn't spare resources
on trivialities.

She wondered why she was thinking about it now. Perhaps it was something to do with that same nation's
eleventh-hour gamble (things hadn't improved since she'd
grown up) employing obsolete machinery, mothballed for
decades, which had never been that good to begin with,
to explore and exploit the swirling belt of flying mountains
circling between Jupiter and Mars. . . .

"Major?"

Before she was entirely aware of it, the air lock
ready-light had turned green and the lid swung aside. She
squeezed into a compartment beyond the bulkhead, allowing herself to be sealed in. Across from the hatch she'd
come through, another led to the crew compartment
mid-deck. Her helmet brushed a third hatch, pierced with
a tiny porthole like the others, leading outside.

She just had room to extract her EAA Witness, a high-
capacity semiautomatic pistol of Czech design and Italian
manufacture chambered for 11.43x23mm Lenin (the original ".45 ACP" designation having been dropped when all
American gun companies were nationalized) from an insulated pocket on her right thigh and give it a final check.
It was an awkward task with the gloves, despite the special

oversized trigger guard, yet one she'd been reluctant to perform in front of the others. When she'd satisfied herself that the chamber was loaded, the magazine full and locked in the grip, and three spares were in their places in her left thigh pocket, she reholstered the weapon, smoothing the Velcroed flap. Clanking and hissing noises faded as the machinery which made them reclaimed precious oxygen from the compartment, replacing it with nothingness.

Instead of looking up, as might be expected, into the starry depths of space (Gutierrez was preparing a hasty getaway and a view of the major's real destination, a kilometer aft, was blocked by the bulk of the passenger insert, the cowled OMS pods, and the tail assembly of the shuttle), Reille y Sanchez peered back through the thick transparency at her companions, soon to follow, she hoped, despite a mixture of less than enthusiastic expressions—nervousness, anxiety, uneuphemized terror—on their lens-distorted features. She wondered how her features looked to them.

Again before she knew it, this being a calculated result of countless Earthside simulations and endless drilling afterward in space, which had taught her body what to do while rendering it independent (in these matters, at least) of her mind, she'd observed the second ready-light, opened the overhead hatch, and was outside the free-falling craft with the lock dogged shut behind her. Nylon tether clipped in place and space-gloved fingers laced into one of several handholds at the rear of the flight deck, she waited for the rest of her team to emerge. Through paired windows high in the after bulkhead, she could discern human-shaped silhouettes. Too much yellow glare interfered to make out whose they were.

The air lock hatch swung open. First came Kamanov, his tanned, handsome face framed in his helmet, his grin belying not only the birthdate in his dossier (the geologist would turn seventy before his feet touched the Earth again), but the silver of his beard, mustache, and thick, unruly hair. Nor was the major ever altogether unaware of the Russian's broad shoulders and flat stomach, even concealed beneath the unflattering bulk of his suit. Clipping his tether to a ringbolt, he pivoted in "midair" and dogged the hatch. With a gentle kick at the stubby cylinder of the lock, he floated up beside her, giving her a friendly pat on the arm before turning his attention back where he'd come from.

This expedition, the major thought, represented a triumph of some kind for senior citizenry. After Kamanov came Colonel Vivian Richardson, the seams in her black face softened by reflections in her visor, just as the salt-and-pepper of her close-cropped hair was hidden by her cap. Expedition second-in-command and captain of the *Hatch*, she was also Gutierrez's emotional surrogate, since he wouldn't be obeying his strong personal inclination to accompany them on the initial EVA. Displaying none of Kamanov's athletic grace, Richardson closed the hatch (she'd often wished that someone had chosen a different name for the expedition's second vessel) and joined them aft of the flight deck, well out of the way of the air lock.

As they waited, the major squinted against what seemed to her a blinding glare. It was less actual light, she'd been informed, than a moonlit night back on Earth. At the *Dole's* stern, the inexplicably featureless surface of a miniature planet shone like a golden apple in the sun. Training for this expedition, no one had been able to tell her why the astronomers had taken so long discovering 5023 Eris, bright as it was compared to most bodies like it, nor why it displayed this particular shade of yellow. The odd color had drawn them, that and a spectrographic signature rich in hydrocarbons, lifestuff which promised to make establishing themselves here possible. Observations made closer at hand every day told them the hue was that of the same residual minerals which lent color to the fallen leaves of autumn. Yet the answer, once they had it, only generated more questions, and they were a people for whom it had become difficult—because they'd been taught the hard way—to ask and answer questions.

The expedition's political officer, Arthur Empleado, was the last to squeeze out through the lock, his sweat-beaded scalp glistening through his thinning hair. To the major, he looked incomplete, somehow, insecure without the complement of "associates" who normally followed him everywhere, an oddly assorted lot of, well . . ."thugs" wasn't quite the right word. He looked uncomfortable without them, even through the vacuum suit he was bundled up in. Like

Kamanov he was a civilian, rare among the crew. Short-winded and overweight like most of his professional brethren, he had nothing else in common with the perpetually youthful geologist.

Clever of Gutierrez, Reille y Sanchez thought, and daring, to place all of his rotten eggs in one dangerous basket. Expendables (including the major herself as chief of security) would take first risk. For many reasons (not the least an undeniable yearning for every personal advantage that footnotes in their records like "heroic" and "historic" might earn them) none of them could do a damned thing about it.

Empleado joined them at the bulkhead. Now it was time to make their mark on history, whether for the greater glory of their individual dossiers, their nation's honor, or perhaps a hungry world. Even if the bay doors hadn't been spread wide—superconducting solar panels sucking up the feeble sunlight—the major's team was at the wrong spot to look back along the foreshortened hull and read the blue block letters stenciled there, a meter high. Each of them already knew what they spelled out. Once the team had tethered itself together and begun drifting aft of the shuttle's stubby, swept-back wings—propelled by the reaction pistol their leader accepted from Kamanov, who helped her plug the rabbit-eared device into her backpack—the letters would be legible.

First they'd see the flag decaled on the fuselage to the left of the lettering, the same familiar banner a dozen generations of Americans had known, with thirteen horizontal stripes of red and white and a blue field in the upper left-hand quarter. Yet, rather than staggered rows of five-pointed stars, one for each state in the Union, the field contained a stylized yellow hammer and sickle.

And the lettering would say:

AMERICAN SOVIET SOCIALIST REPUBLIC

The United World Soviet—what Madison Avenue, on the air and in the pages of *American Truth*, would be calling (as their Russian predecessors had, three quarters of a century earlier) the "Cosmic Collective"—had come to the

Asteroid Belt. Or at least its latest, and in whispered opinion, most important dominion had.

TWO
The Catwalk

"Holy Mother of God!"

The words slipped unbidden from Richardson's lips into the open mike of her carrier. It occurred to the major that, whatever nominal allegiance they all owed to Marxist doctrine, by some coincidence each of her team, even the black American colonel and the Russian geologist (whose grandparents, in an earlier ambience of *glasnost*, had partaken of a sanctioned Orthodox revival) had been brought up Catholic.

"5023 Eris does appear rather impressive, does she not, for all that she is a very small asteroid," Kamanov responded with a grin, *"and a somewhat minor deity."*

"Belay that chatter!" Gutierrez interrupted from the flagship, unable to avoid nautical jargon even at a time like this. *"Keep the frequency clear!"* More than merely cost, it was security that had precluded television. The only eyes following this expedition for mankind as a whole were those of the KGB.

"Quite so." Empleado sounded no nearer to the major than the general. *"How unfortunate were it a religious oath*

11

that were the first words relayed to the United Peoples of the World Soviet."

"Not to mention," Kamanov suggested, *"your many and varied superiors, Comrade Political Officer?"*

In the privacy of her helmet, the major smiled. The Russian had raised a sore and complex point. Marxism's first century had been notable for its undisguised hostility toward religion which, despite an official easing of positions, still colored Eastern attitudes. You were free to believe what you liked without sanction, even manifest your belief openly, but never expect to rise in the bureaucracy if you exercised that freedom. In the West, with the Savior born again to lead the revolution, the situation differed. Representing an organization ostensibly subordinate to Moscow, Empleado must reflect that hierarchy's policy. A member of KGB America, he must act on principles diametrically opposed. It was what came of serving too many masters at once, she thought, and no more than he deserved.

Bereft of moral support from his "corporals four," Empleado refused Kamanov the dignity of an answer, which was how he usually played it anyway. At less than a meter's distance, the peculiar surface of 5023 Eris loomed before them like a wall, curvature unnoticed, the evidence of their senses in dire conflict. Eyes told them they were about to take an endless plunge down its flat, featureless face. Bodies, long since adjusted to the sensations of free fall, told them no such thing. Even worse, the wall appeared (and perhaps was) every bit as slick as their polished visors, affording not the slightest hand- or foothold.

"Doctor—" the major's part was to pretend to ignore the byplay between Kamanov and Empleado, civilian loyalty and discipline being the concern of the KGB, not the Marines "—if you'd assist?"

They'd anticipated difficulty and were prepared. Swimming closer to what appeared a boundless palisade of yellow-green plastic, Reille y Sanchez drew a five-centimeter steel ring from a Kevlar bag. Made from half-centimeter stock welded to a seven-centimeter steel disk, a dozen of these makeshifts had been fabricated in a sparse facility inboard the *McCain* by a grumbling machinist, when their instruments began giving them foreboding hints about the real nature of their destination. The major let the reaction pistol drift on the long plastic tube which fed gas from her backpack. Peeling a thin, circular polyethylene cover from the underside of the disk, she exposed a surface coated with a descendant of cyanoacrylic "crazy" glue. Extending her arm, she placed the disk in contact with the asteroid's glossy surface. Within heartbeats, nothing short of explosives might have removed it.

Kamanov, floating beside her, spring-latched a plastic hook into the ring and shook out paired nylon lines attached to it. Reille y Sanchez reclaimed the reaction pistol, pressed the trigger, and let it pull her a few meters to the left. Kamanov remained where he was. The slender lines slipped through her gloved fingers until she reached the spot, indicated by the tautness of the lines, where she intended anchoring a second adhesive piton.

That task accomplished and the free ends of the lines snapped into place, the major hung parallel to the surface as Richardson pulled closer on the single line to which they were all attached, seized an anchored line in each hand, brought her knees to her chin and performed an awkward somersault, pressing her booted feet against the asteroid and standing "up," held "down" by the lines.

The vice-commander was followed by Empleado, requiring assistance from both women, and afterward by the major. For a moment, Reille y Sanchez stood where she'd alighted, struggling against warnings from her kinesthetic sense to reorient herself, to see herself standing on the surface of a planet, looking up at a trio of winged spaceships hanging a kilometer overhead. As she knew it would, something readjusted itself inside her head with a mental *pop!* She was aware of watching Kamanov, a hand wrapped around each line, shuffling toward them from the other end of the odd catwalk they'd just built.

With Empleado's more-or-less useless help—they could all hear the man's labored breathing, and his helmet visor had begun to opaque with condensation—the colonel attached a scrap of colored fabric to one line: red, white, blue, and yellow. "*I claim this world*," she announced to her comrades and the universe, "*for humankind, on behalf of American Soviet Socialism and the United World Soviet!*"

"We copy that, EVA team, and are relaying it back to Earth," Gutierrez informed them, *"America, and, uh, the United World Soviet, have landed on 5023 Eris!"*

During this ragtag bit of ceremony, the major searched within herself for a feeling of achievement, finding only weary awareness of how much still had to be accomplished during this EVA. It was more than possible, should they fail to produce results, should some disaster, foreseen or unforeseen, befall them, that "humankind" would never hear those words. The expedition was being conducted in secrecy rivaling that enshrouding pre-Soviet American development of the atomic bomb. It wouldn't be reported until some spectacular discovery or success could be reported with it. Earth was poor and hungry, much of its populace homeless and hopeless. While its present rulers were less responsive to public pressure than the state which had constructed the shuttles, it would nevertheless be prudent to justify the enormous expenditure this undertaking represented before announcing that such an expenditure had been made.

The major's companions relaxed a bit, marking a conclusion. The next item on their agenda was a secure mooring for the three space vehicles themselves, each the size of an airliner. Detailed radar survey, as the expedition approached 5023 Eris, had informed them that the asteroid's composition, whatever unknown circumstances had created it, was more or less uniform. Under a polymerized surface only centimeters deep lay a radio-opaque core, presumably of accreted metal and hydrocarbons. It made slight difference where they attached their docking equipment.

A dozen words from Gutierrez, and an orange flash from the air lock of the *Hatch*—an atmosphere would have conveyed the dull boom of gunfire—warned the major that those inboard were ready for the next stage. In a long moment, during which she watched several spacesuited forms around the *Hatch*'s engine-mounted tail, another nylon line drifted into view, its many kinks elongating until they disappeared, propelled by a huge-bored Webley line-throwing gun at a tangent to the asteroid's surface.

"Got it!" Richardson, who happened to be nearest, caught the line as it snaked between the pitons they'd secured. She

handed it to the major, who tucked an end through the ring behind her. Reille y Sanchez pulled, a clumsy Empleado winding slack around his hand and elbow, until a heavier line jerked into view.

"*Easy,*" Reille y Sanchez shouted to no one in particular. "*Keep it taut! That thing weighs enough, even out here, to break bones!*"

The latter line, like those of the makeshift catwalk, was also paired, consisting of a doubled-over single length of nylon passing through a steel-and-plastic pulley which could be clipped to a ring. Seemingly of its own accord, the wheel began turning. Soon, attached to one side of the line like someone's washing, a bulky cargo hove into view. Shouting instructions into her mike, the major guided the object to a safe landing. Except for its size—the base of the device was a meter in diameter—it was identical in every respect to the pitons they'd just glued to the asteroid's surface, fabricated by the same man, by the same means.

Not trusting Empleado, the major summoned Kamanov to hold it while she peeled off the protective sheeting. Together they placed it two meters from the second of the smaller rings, at right angles to the nylon catwalk, waiting for the cyanoacrylate to set.

"*One down, my dear major,*" the geologist sighed wearily, "*and too many more to go!*"

Unclipping the pulley and retracing Kamanov's steps, they squeezed past the colonel and the sweating KGB officer, approached the first piton, snapped the pulley on, and took delivery of a second giant attachment. In minutes, they'd glued it on a line paralleling the smaller devices. A third parcel was the concern of Richardson and her dubious assistant, a trestle-base like a miniature, truncated Eiffel Tower, to be set between the two giant rings. The major and the geologist had their own task, but kept an eye on the operation as they lifted their feet, reversed positions relative to the asteroid and, not without trepidation, let the reaction pistol pull them up the face of 5023 Eris toward a new location. There they anchored a small ring, received the pulley via the line attaching them to the other explorers, and hauled in a third large ring from the *Hatch*. This and the initial large ring would anchor a second shuttle. The first and second rings would hold the first spacecraft that landed.

It was when they'd floated over the catwalk, to a point on the opposite side where they intended to prepare a berth for the third shuttle, that they ran into trouble. As Reille y Sanchez placed the last small ring, it sank into the solid-looking surface, taking her thumb and fingers with it. Without a sound, without thinking, she tried to withdraw her fingers, which were caught fast, dragging herself down until her helmet bobbed within a centimeter of the surface.

She let the reaction pistol float and extended her other hand to stop herself. It, too, sank in, and her helmet made contact. The spherical transparency before her face met the surface over a sharp-edged circular area the color and consistency of butterscotch pudding.

Now, she screamed. At the slightest motion, she sank deeper and deeper, drawn by what force, she didn't know. She could no longer turn her head, could see nothing but the uniform, grainy color of the surface material. Short of breath despite an ample oxygen supply, she felt Kamanov's hand on her, tugging at her life-support backpack. She presumed he'd snatched her reaction pistol, their one hope, and was firing it away from the asteroid. If so, it was without effect. Whatever energy acted on her, it was many times stronger than that minuscule thrust.

"*I fear it is too late, Estrellita,*" exclaimed the Russian, using her first name for the first time in the three years they'd known each other, "*I have become stuck, as well, at the elbow. Try to relax. Breathe evenly. I can see the shuttles. I have the pulley in my hand. I believe they intend to pull us up with the* Hatch's *reaction motors.*"

By now, her helmet was half-imbedded in the treacherous wall. Light around her face grew dimmer. Whatever the shuttle was doing, it made no difference. She felt strain where Kamanov gripped her suit. Breathe evenly, he'd advised. In her phones, she heard the geologist's breath coming in shorter, more painful-sounding gasps. The pull between shuttle and asteroid must be terrific, his merely human body part of the linkage. At the moment, however, she was more concerned about a drop in her suit pressure, an ominous hiss from the vicinity of her helmet collar.

"*No good, Doc!*" It was the *Hatch*. "*We're slacking off! Looks like the ship was being pulled in with you!*"

Kamanov remained silent, releasing a lungful of air. "*Thank you, Hatch. I confess your slacking off is something of a relief.*"

"*Roger that. Your suits'll keep you going a while. We'll get you out!*"

"Estrellita," Kamanov squeezed her shoulder, "*did you hear?*"

It was now dark. She took a breath. "Yes, Piotr, I heard. I can't see a thing, and I think my suit's leaking."

A long pause was followed by a sigh. "*It is an ill wind which blows no good to anyone. You need not worry about your suit, you are now covered with the surface material. As for myself, I shan't be able to see much longer. I have kept my face clear until now, but I believe I dislocated my shoulder when the* Hatch *attempted to pull us out. Looking back is a strain. The* Hatch *has performed an OMS burn, and resumed its original station.*"

"Running out on us, the rats!"

The geologist chuckled. "*Precisely.*"

The major shook her head inside her helmet, drops of perspiration burning in her eyes. Not being able to see the muck she was imbedded in was much better. She began calming down. "And to think we left Earth and came two hundred million klicks to die in quicksand."

"*Hush,*" Kamanov's answer was gentle. "*Do not say it, even—especially if it is true. The Commodore will dig us out, somehow.*"

"Richardson and Empleado," she struggled to remain conversational. "Did they—" She stiffened. "Piotr, I can see light! It's brightening up in here! I don't know what it means, but . . ."

"*Yes,*" the scientist asked her, "*what is happening?*"

"My helmet's broken through, like coming up through muddy water! The radar was wrong, Piotr! Underneath this epoxy or whatever, it's—"

"*What is it?*"

"It's hollow, and we've got company! Weird company!"

The major didn't exaggerate, as she knew he'd soon see for himself. The asteroid coating must be radio-opaque, for it was no more than centimeters thick. Two or three meters before her—below her, thinking of the asteroid's center as "down"—was another wall, or floor, of the plastic-covered mesh lawn furniture used to be made of, the open spaces between the wires not quite large enough for an ungloved fist.

This wasn't what had seized and held her attention. Between her and the wall half a dozen creatures were anchored by their feet (or whatever they stood on) so it appeared she looked down on them from above. The little rural Texas girl inside her squirmed. They looked, more than anything else, like giant golden-brown cockroaches. Cockroaches her own size. Cockroaches with gun belts and guns pointed at her.

Another being caught her astonished eye, smaller, of more slender build, apparently unclothed, but covered from head to foot either with soft scales fringed at the edges, or stubby feathers. Like the insect-things, it wore a weapons belt, although whatever device it carried there remained holstered. The creature lay supine on the mesh, she knew somehow, as a courtesy, that she might examine it full length. It raised a "hand," fingers spread to display translucent webbing, and spoke to her in Spanish over her suit radio.

"*A good afternoon to you, Major Reille y Sanchez. Or perhaps I may be privileged to address you as 'Estrellita,' a most charming and beautiful name. Welcome to what you call 'Fifty-Twenty-Three Eris.' I'm Aelbraugh Pritsch, administrative assistant to the Proprietor. As you've no doubt surmised by now, you and your party were expected.*"

THREE
The Proprietor's Assistant

"I, uh . . ."

Even had her state of mind permitted it, Reille y Sanchez hadn't, in fact, had time to surmise anything. Before she could reorder her thoughts to speak, the feather-scaled thing preempted her.

"And here, unless I'm greatly mistaken, is the distinguished Dr. Piotr Kamanov." Without perceptible effort, the creature had switched to a language both humans shared, standard English—with a fussy, pedantic accent. She realized in a corner of her mind that it sounded like an actor in those old talking gorilla movies which, despite their marginal legality, she, like most of her generation, had somehow managed to see while growing up. Or that gold-plated robot, what was its name? *"Good afternoon to you, sir."*

She glanced at the spot the bird or lizard thing had indicated. It seemed, for once, that the geologist was as speechless with amazement as she was. His helmet bubble, a gloved hand, and the toes of both his boots thrust from the ceiling like one of his fossils, embedded in a matrix of yellow silt. The major shook her head in disbelief: Kamanov was winking at her!

With a grunt, the entity climbed to its feet, which were built, she noticed through a lucid tunnel in her bewilderment, like those of a parrot, with two long toes in front and another pair jutting backward where the heel should be. It was hard deciding if its appearance was more birdlike or reptilian. Its overall color lay somewhere between silver-gray and lavender. Veins in its scales (or were they feathers?) were bright red. Its body color shaded gradually from its human-looking shoulders, along broad, oddly jointed arms, to hands with delicate, powdery white fingers.

The creature's chest was stooped (how scholarly, she thought), tapering to a paunch. Its hips, for all that they supported an ordinary holster belt, reminded her of allosaurs or tyrannosaurs in the San Antonio museum and children's books. The legs supporting them, heavily muscled under the feathers (or were they scales?) appeared mammalian, but bent in the wrong places. The feet, as she'd observed, were birdlike, except that they ended in round toes with flat black nails like those of the fingers.

Aelbraugh Pritsch's scarlet-crested head was unquestionably that of a sapient being, with shrewd amber eyes under the same domed shape that afforded volume for her own capable brain. The face was as flat as any human face, with a pair of small nostril-holes beneath the eyes. A flattened beak, no more than a triangle of black horn scalloped twice along its bottom edge, met a mammalian-looking lower lip. As the thing spoke, the major watched for teeth, but wasn't surprised to see none. The tongue, too, was black, and looked as if it would be dry to the touch.

"*My associates—*" the alien indicated the insect beings "*—whose names, I regret to confess, are impossible even for me to pronounce. They will assist you. Please don't be alarmed at their formidable appearance.*"

A couple of the living nightmares raised pairs of many-jointed arms to lift the major down. Despite herself, she shrank away.

"*I assure you, Major, they're quite as civilized as you or I. Their drawn weapons were merely a precaution,*" *occasioned by the rather fearsome reputation of your own species. But don't underestimate them, whatever you do. Their reflexes are a bit slower than yours or mine, but they're a remarkably hardy folk, singularly difficult to dispatch, in particular with firearms such as you wear. They'd wreak havoc before they expired, and my employer would be most distressed with me if you should happen to be damaged."*

Shoving revulsion aside, Reille y Sanchez cooperated, only half hearing what the entity said. She could see now that its companions were more like marine crustaceans, giant lobsters, than giant roaches. What made accepting them most difficult was that they lacked anything like a face. The carapace covering the—the word was "thorax" she recalled—was ridged, made up of plates like samurai armor, showing hints of green on the high spots. The pattern seemed to vary with the individual. Golden-brown shaded to black at the edges of each segment. Below the thorax a lobsterlike tail seemed disproportionately small.

She never made an accurate count of the limbs. An upper pair of arms ended in mutually opposed chitin-covered fingers. Several middle sets boasted serrated claws. The weapons swinging at their sides were stubby cylinders, fifteen centimeters long, half that in diameter, attached to stirrup-shaped handles. Despite her resolve, she felt grateful when they released their hold on her. Looking into their compound eyes, their only identifiable facial feature, she managed a ragged, "Th-thank you."

Together, using claws, the creatures snapped out a faultless "shave-and-a-haircut," conveying several messages at once. She was welcome, they appreciated her courtesy under trying circumstances. They were intelligent creatures, not trained monsters, and they'd done their homework when it came to twenty-first-century humanity. Their impossibly long, slender antennae (each creature seemed to have several pairs) waved in what even she could tell was meant to be a comical manner. Aelbraugh Pritsch chuckled.

Standing upright (whatever that meant where gravity was an ill-remembered ghost) she reoriented herself the second time that day. The meshed platform was a huge shallow basket suspended, on cables too light for their impressive length, from half a dozen massive green columns, each a klick apart, three or four meters in diameter, blending without embellishment into the ceiling. The surface of the mesh was tacky enough that her bootsoles stayed where she put them (accustomed to Velcro inboard the shuttles, she knew to keep one foot on the floor at all times) without inhibiting movement. Reille y Sanchez watched another pair of crustaceans assist Kamanov from what now appeared to be the ceiling. He grimaced as his shoulder was moved, tears forming in the corners of his eyes, but was silent until they set him on his feet.

The geologist addressed Aelbraugh Pritsch: *"Tell me, sir—or perhaps 'madame'—can our people hear us?"* Kamanov's voice came by radio and air-conduction. By the way their suits hung, the place had plenty of atmosphere. What particular gases, the major thought, was another matter.

Aelbraugh Pritsch raised feathery brows, bent its arms at misplaced elbows, and turned up webbed palms in a shrug. *"It would be 'sir,' Dr. Kamanov, were my species given to honorifics in our own languages, which we are not. I'm a reproductive male. And to answer your question, I regret to inform you that you aren't being heard. The canopy's designed, among its other functions, to filter harmful and unwanted energies. This precludes communication in the radio wavelengths, which haven't been employed by our civilization for . . . well, for rather a long time."*

The chief of military security had an imaginative flash of condensers, tubes, and other early components petrified in the geological strata of some far-off planet. "We're to be held," she stated, "incommunicado?"

Aelbraugh Pritsch blinked, looked at its—his—hands, turned one over and placed it in the other. *"Great Egg, no! On the contrary, you're free to do anything you wish, within bounds of my employer's propriety. I'll order an antenna—is that correct, or is it aerial?—exserted through the canopy, if you insist. I suggest patience, since your colleagues, Col. Richardson and Mr. Empleado, will join us in a moment, along with Corporals Wise, Roo, Hake, and Betal, who've been sent to 'dig you out.' In due course, a matter of mere hours, your entire group will be invited in, spacecraft and all, if it should be their desire.*"

The major opened her mouth to reply, but the being snapped his digits. "*That reminds me: feel free to remove your helmets! I'm a bureaucrat by inclination, an execrable host. Your suits are stuffy. Our atmosphere's the same as you're accustomed to, twenty percent oxygen, most of the rest nitrogen. It contains less trace lead and carbon monoxide than you may feel comfortable with, having poured so much into the air of your homeworld.*"

The humans glanced at one another, shrugging at the same time, Kamanov with a grimace of pain. Reille y Sanchez pushed fabric out of the way to unlock her helmet ring, only to discover that it had been damaged and wouldn't detach from her suit. For his part, Kamanov made a half-hearted attempt to remove his helmet with one hand, and gave it up. His left arm floated useless.

"*Dear me, I'm remiss again!*" their host exclaimed. "*Allow me, I'm rather good with primitive mechanics. The major first, I believe is the custom.*"

With the assistance of the nimble-fingered being and two crustaceans standing nearby at parade-rest, Reille y Sanchez's helmet was soon free, its sealing ring warped, accounting for the leak she'd experienced. She set it on the mesh and strode to Kamanov, boots making tearing noises like Velcro. With the aliens, she removed the geologist's helmet, revealing a pale, sweaty countenance. His eyes still twinkled.

"Are you okay, Doctor?" she asked, admiring and alarmed. If she felt the way he looked, she'd be lying down by now, or throwing up.

Kamanov bit his lip, then let it go. "You were calling me 'Piotr,' when we thought we were going to die."

She frowned. "Okay, Piotr-when-we-thought-we-were-going-to-die, you don't look well. I think your shoulder's dislocated."

He began to nod and stopped himself. "I am afraid so." With this, the geologist's body slackened, his knees bent, his arms began floating to a half-horizontal position. His eyes were still alert, but his companion knew he was in shock and not far from unconsciousness.

"First Nest!" Aelbraugh Pritsch exclaimed, failing to suppress a canarylike trill of alarm. "I didn't realize he'd been injured! He must be seen to immediately! Section chief, a vehicle!" One of the crustaceans clacked claws and reached to its belt with armored fingers. Making more noises, somewhere between those of a dozen sets of castanets and a pan full of frying bacon, it communicated with someone or something somewhere else, received an answer composed of the same noises, switched off, and made noises at the bird-being. Aelbraugh Pritsch turned to the major. "A vehicle will be here any moment, to take your friend to the surface below to be looked after."

"We have a medical doctor," Reille y Sanchez protested, "aboard the—"

"It will require an hour, I believe the interval's called, to get her here. If my information's correct, Major, Dr. Kamanov isn't a young being. He could die of shock, however superficial his injury."

The woman shrugged. "What do we do when the vehicle gets here?"

Aelbraugh Pritsch thought, then examined Kamanov without touching him, peering into the collar of his suit. "The important thing is what we do beforehand. Like me, you're endothermic creatures. Dr. Kamanov is warmed by his suit. His isn't an open wound, no fluid loss must be staunched. In absence of gravity, his circulatory system—"

"*Kamanov? Reille y Sanchez? Is that you?*"

The interrupting voice was Empleado's. True to Aelbraugh Pritsch's word, the hands and helmets of what turned out to be the expedition's political officer and second-in-command weren't long emerging from the substance of the ceiling. Beyond those first few, fearful words, Empleado was as speechless and shaken when finally freed from the matrix as the geologist and the major had been, content to be led aside by gentle claws and armored fingers as they all turned their attention to the colonel.

Richardson was in much worse condition, paralyzed and pale despite her complexion, unconscious despite wide-open eyes—until the bird being's assistants began reaching for her arms and legs.

"Get back all of you! Don't touch me! Don't touch me!"

With a screech, Richardson burst into a blurred flurry of furious motion, slapping hysterically at the creatures' manipulators, kicking at them with her heavy boots. The startled and dismayed crustaceans exploded from around her like pins in a bowling alley, adding their sizzling expostulations to the woman's shouts of terror and warning. No one, human or otherwise, dared approach her without risk of serious injury.

"Blessed Hatching," declared Aelbraugh Pritsch, almost unheard above the stream of noise and abuse, "can't you do something about her, Major?"

Reille y Sanchez shook her head without speaking, keeping wary eyes on the colonel while trying to watch the injured Kamanov, as well. Windmilling her limbs, the black woman slipped, unassisted, from the ceiling. Any one of those wild kicks might have sent her spinning in any direction, transforming her into a deadly, bone-breaking human missile. Instead, still flailing, she began settling toward the mesh below amidst screams and curses which filled the air about her and reverberated painfully in the major's suit communicator. Kamanov seemed inert, oblivious to it all.

By the time Richardson reached the mesh, she had a glove off, a tiny gun in her hand, and was swinging the black eye of its outsized suppressor back and forth at a variety of targets, failing to exclude her shipmates. The major thought she glimpsed the dull gleam of a hollowpoint deep in the chamber at the rear of the suppressor and short barrel—which she recognized as that of a double-action Kahr K9 9mm, a favorite of all the covert agencies—but it may have been her imagination.

The bird-being and his party knew what the weapon was. They scattered, ducked, and flinched, no less enthusiastic in their effort to avoid being shot than the humans, including Empleado, who found themselves on the wrong end of Richardson's little pistol. Briefly, from behind a pair of hunched-over crustaceans, Reille y Sanchez considered drawing her own Witness and putting an end to this insane display. Before she could act, however, despite his own physical difficulties, Kamanov had come to sudden life and somehow managed to slip behind the colonel and seize the Kahr K9 before it went off.

Exhaling a deep-throated moan into her suit mike, Richardson slumped into the relaxed posture which, in the absence of gravity, meant she was truly unconscious. As everyone else relaxed, as well, Reille y Sanchez noticed that, this time, the woman's eyes were closed.

"Major?" Reille y Sanchez almost jumped, despite Aelbraugh Pritsch's mild tone. With Empleado's help, the crustaceans were attending the colonel and the geologist. "I'll order that aerial run out, now. The vehicle's on its way. You can let your people know what's happened."

She nodded, watching the orders carried out. Despite her experience of darkness in the center of the ceiling, it seemed to transmit abundant sunlight of an eerie yellow-green character. No wonder she and Kamanov had been expected! She could make out, she realized with astonishment, fuzzy-edged silhouettes of her would-be rescuers, Empleado's four musclemen, who'd be the next to come through unless they exercised extraordinary care.

She glanced down, wondering about the vehicle. Under her feet, through the supporting mesh, she noticed a sight which severely tested her recent reorientation. The thick green columns seemed to reach into a nether region an infinite distance away, lost in shadows and obscuring haze. Gravity or not, a fall of at least a kilometer awaited before one encountered, at whatever velocity, the real surface of the asteroid. Nor, she became aware, was the bottom of the basket entirely flat and floorlike. Where she'd emerged, she'd just missed dropping into a long central depression worked into its shape, as if it were made to nest a piece of enormous, oddly-shaped equipment. This provoked a laugh: it was just right to cradle one of the shuttles!

One of the crustaceans handed her a stiff copper lead terminating in an ordinary alligator clamp. It took a moment to find the right place to clip it on her suit. Following the wire with her eyes, she observed that it had been thrust through the substance of the ceiling. She should have watched how that was done, she admonished herself. On the other hand, there was too much to be watched all at once.

Meantime, a soft humming from below announced the arrival of the vehicle. She'd have to hurry not to be left behind. She recited the names of three misunderstood and martyred socialist statesmen who, according to her schoolbooks, had made America what it was today:

"*Dole, McCain, Hatch*? General Gutierrez, this is Major Reille y Sanchez. Do you copy?"

FOUR
White Gloves,
Trousers Optional

"Have you seen the ones," hissed a voice which had been born to gossip, "that look like giant spiders?"

Aerospace Force Brigadier General Horatio Z. Gutierrez looked up from the tiled floor he stared at into the small, porcine eyes of Arthur Empleado, KGB(ASSR). Having been brought up properly, he promptly glanced away again. Pacing this brightly lit area for what seemed hours, worried about his friend, preoccupied with a dozen other trains of thought, he was vaguely aware that he'd been wondering, all along, why a corridor should be forty meters wider than the suburban streets of Walton Beach, the Florida-panhandle bedroom community for nearby Humphrey Field (also known as Engels Auxiliary #9) where he and his family had lived the last six years. Despite Empleado's audible enthusiasm, the general's concerns of the moment didn't include a zoological catalog of the inhabitants of 5023 Eris.

The general opened his mouth. "Art, don't—"

"Spiders have eight legs, Comrades," another voice interrupted before he could finish. "These have six, although appendage-counting's the last item one thinks of in their presence. I take it you don't mean the major's friends, Arthur. Toya says they're marine crustaceans."

The portal Gutierrez paced in front of (no human architect would have designed a door two meters high and five wide) had evaporated without a sound. Rosalind Nguyen stood before him, incongruous and unmedical in hospital-like surroundings wearing her frayed and faded ship-suit. Like his own, it had served during the months they'd traveled to this place, only to discover that someone—something—had gotten here first. Already it seemed days, rather than six short hours, since two of his people had dissolved into the surface. Two more had been lost before rescue could be mobilized and one victim had relayed an alien invitation to come in from the cold of interplanetary space. He'd refused to consider it without the return of the major, the colonel, and Empleado, their unfettered presence serving as assurance—frail, since the aliens intended keeping Kamanov, ostensibly to treat his injuries—that they weren't walking ("sinking" might be a better term, or "being sucked") into a trap.

Handing him the first of many new riddles, the major had returned under her own power, Empleado and a catatonic Richardson in tow. In the view of nonhuman therapists, the latter wouldn't regain sanity in their company. Rising from the muck she'd vanished into, the major had used a reaction pistol to pull her party to the waiting shuttle. The bird-being who named himself "the Proprietor's assistant" had apologized for the inconvenience, explaining that his group on 5023 Eris possessed no spacecraft. But if that were true, how the flaming hell had they gotten here? Asked the question (in more diplomatic tones), Aelbraugh Pritsch had begged Gutierrez to hold his inquiries for the Proprietor. One of many items on the general's crowded mental agenda was an appointment with that individual an hour hence.

"Sir." Dr. Nguyen didn't wait for an answer from Empleado, whose four oddly assorted henchmen stood nearby as usual, trying unsuccessfully to look like casual loungers. "You can see Dr. Kamanov, now. I assured myself they did a good job with him."

Gutierrez blinked down into her exotic features. Neither he nor Empleado was a big man, but both loomed over the little Vietnamese. This silly mission, he thought—remembering that it was a good thought to keep to himself—consisted of every obsolete loser and disposable misfit the ASSR could find room for (an iconoclastic brigadier, for example, who never kept his mouth shut at inopportune times), but it also included, by accident he was sure, some of the most beautiful women he'd ever known. It was a toss-up, he'd long since decided, whether the doctor, with her delicate face and flawless skin, or the major, with her striking combination of Irish and Mexican attractions, was easier on the eyes.

As always on such occasions, he reminded himself of the darkly beautiful woman he'd wed thirty-two years ago, more Indian than Spanish in appearance, whom he loved with whatever heart and soul the service left him, and with whom he'd raised eight splendid children. His second eldest, Danny, happened to be a junior officer aboard the *McCain*. As always on such occasions, he tried not to think of his eldest, blown to radioactive vapor in a recent, less-than-successful attempt to bestow the benefits of American Marxism upon the benighted denizens of South Africa who had jettisoned their Marxist government and were determined to keep it that way.

"Thanks, Doctor," he answered, "I'll see him now." Followed by Empleado, who left his sinister cohort behind, he headed for the wall where the door had been, too conscious of his dignity in the presence of the KGB to approach it with caution. He hoped the damn thing would remember to go away before he broke his nose on it.

"Horatio!" At the sight of his old friend, Kamanov propped himself up on an elbow. He lay on a platform extruded from the floor, as far as the general could see, which grew more resilient the closer it came to the skin. He was covered, in homely contrast, by a worn blanket from one of the shuttles.

"Pete." The general glanced around the chamber, failing to find a flat surface (except for the floor and the bed) or a straight edge. The room's plan was kidney-shaped. Soft light glowed from every centimeter of the low, domed ceiling. A meter away, in a sort of corner where a sort of chair had been created the same way as the bed, Pulaski, whom Dr. Nguyen often drafted as an assistant, sat at rigid attention. To the general's surprise, Kamanov smoked one of the Cuban cigars which had seemed almost an appendage back in the premission planning days in Florida. Near one wall lay the twisted cellophane of its wrapper. Gutierrez stooped to pick it up. "I'm surprised," he observed, "they let you smoke that thing in here."

"Leave it, my friend, it is an experiment—they seem content to let me go to hell in my own way; notice that no trace of smoke or even of the odor remains—and the sergeant and I have been watching that wrapper creep toward the wall at a rate of about fifty centimeters per hour."

"What?"

"In an otherwise seamless surface, a fine line runs about the room a centimeter up the curve where floor turns into wall. This is what caught my eye: subduction, as on Earth, one tectonic plate flowing under another. The surfaces are self-sweeping, dust and litter carried by the 'current' to disappear into the crack. The same mechanism provides a certain tackiness, allowing firm footing in almost nonexistent gravity. You, too, would slowly slide across the room if you stood motionless. Unless, like this nightstand, you wore small spikes which penetrate the surface, placing you in contact with the substrate. The surface then flows around you. Fascinating."

The general shrugged. "Ven Kamanov draws final breath," he intoned in a theatrical accent, "he vill dictate notes about it." He turned to the little sergeant, bestowing an imperative glance on Empleado, as well. "Take ten, Pulaski." She jittered out into the relative sanctuary of the corridor, perhaps unaware of the four awaiting her outside. There had been some kind of trouble between her and one of Empleado's men earlier in the voyage, although Major Reille y Sanchez had taken care of it and he didn't know the details. The KGB man gave his head a microscopic shake, intending to stay through Gutierrrez's conversation with the Russian. The American let out an exasperated breath and, despite the fact it had never been raised,

changed the subject. "Glad to see you looking well. Rosalind
said you'd pulled your arm out of the socket trying to rescue the major."

Kamanov grinned. "What man with testosterone in his
blood would not?" His eyebrows suggested he excluded
Empleado from that category—and that, if no one else did,
he'd hold the man responsible for the behavior of his
underlings. Assuming a frozen expression, Empleado sat in
the seat vacated by Pulaski, feet flat on the floor, arms
folded in front of him. The general remained standing.

"Trying to rescue myself, as well," Kamanov continued.
"It was the *Hatch* that did the pulling. You know, the sound
of a shoulder separating is worse than any pain." He shivered, shaking his head. "It's like the idea of sliding down
a fifty-meter razorblade into a barrel of vodka." Across the
room, Empleado squirmed. "Thanks to the dextrous
manipulators of our esteemed hosts, however, I now feel
fit and hale. I wish they would find it in whatever they
use to encourage circulation to let me out of this place."
He brushed the blanket from his shoulder. No scar or
inflammation could be seen. "We have arrived, Horatio. I
have work. And many, many questions to ask."

"Like everybody else aboard Earth's three best—and
only—spaceships!"

"Except," Kamanov glanced at Empleado to observe
whether he'd caught the general's unpatriotic complaint,
"that everybody else, *tovarich*, has had the advantage of
seeing all that has happened so far with his own eyes. While
I have been occupied thus far—what is the expression?
Making zees?"

Grinning, Gutierrez told Kamanov about the major's return.
"The landing went pretty much as planned. Instead of mooring to the rings Corporal Owen manufactured, we used RCS
thrusters, sinking into the surface as you did. Our hosts had
suspended docking cradles to support the shuttles—made
up in advance! That's something I want to know more about,
Pete. We were expected, as soon as we left Earth under strict
secrecy and radio silence. Like everything else about this
place, it gives me a creepy feeling."

"And the colonel?" Kamanov asked. "I am told she is
not here, in the infirmary, where they might help her."

"You're told correctly. Your multilegged doctors are afraid they'll drive her down even deeper, and I think they may be right. She's limp as a dishrag now, has been since you took her gun away—with one exception. She threw another fit when the shuttles were settling through the roof. Bloodied several noses, including mine, broke one wrist, not her own, and damned near ruined a couple of the crewmen for life."

"This reminds me, Comrade Doctor Kamanov." It was Empleado, speaking up for the first time. "Whatever became of Col. Richardson's weapon after you took it away? And the silencer? I haven't seen it since."

"An excellent question, Comrade Political Officer, but you ask it of the wrong individual. You tell me where they took my trousers, which I would like very much to have, and I will tell you where Col. Richardson's gun has gone." The Russian dismissed the KGB man and let his head swing from side to side. "I have seen this sort of thing before, Horatio. After a great fire or an earthquake. So have you, I suspect, in combat."

"It's like she's asleep," Gutierrez nodded, "only we can't wake her up. Rosalind says it's a simple retreat from reality, because she can't stand talking to Big Bird out there, or the sight of giant bugs with guns, or something."

"Possibly the worst case of culture shock on record, my friend. Our first contact with a nonterrestrial intelligence. Some will be affected worse than others. Some, like you and I, may even be immune. How is the rest of our little party standing up to it?"

The general shrugged. "Certainly no more reactions as bad as Vivian's, but there's something like a flu bug, ugliness at both ends, going around. I suspect it's partly relief after being cooped up for so long, and partly tension on account of what we've found here. Or what's found us. We've already had to break up a couple of fistfights."

"You may eventually have to restrain me, if they will not let me out of here. You have seen everything. I missed by passing out like a schoolgirl. What is it like outside?"

"You've seen sequoia forests in California." Gutierrez shrugged. "It's like that, moist without feeling humid. Somber, but not depressing like you'd expect. The asteroid's covered with huge plants, Pete. I'm not sure they're trees. Thousands of them, a kilometer tall and the same distance apart, not arranged in any regular pattern. Remember the redwoods tunneled out for Model Ts? Some of these could accommodate a freight train. They spread at the top, fusing into an airtight, self-repairing canopy that forms the artificial upper surface of this place. It fills the area below with a diffuse yellowy-green light, and retains, probably even manufactures, oxygen and water vapor for a worldwide shirtsleeve environment."

Kamanov nodded again. "This much I managed to learn from Rosalind and Toya. As I understand it, even yet we are not on the surface?"

"Within a dozen meters. They use more than the surface of this world, Pete. The hanging baskets—they're down with us now, by the way—weren't invented for our benefit. This area of the asteroid's full of platforms, catwalks, what you might call 'treehouses,' all the way to the canopy. A dozen living and working environments for use by at least as many species."

Again Kamanov glanced at Empleado, but for what reason, besides polite acknowledgement of his existence or an unconscious effort to include him in the conversation, Gutierrez couldn't guess. "Tell me about them."

"You saw Aelbraugh Pritsch, a kind of bird or reptile. And the lobsters, soldiers of some kind. The place reminds me of a cross between a paleontology exhibit and a cartoon where the animals wear trousers."

"White, three-fingered gloves." Kamanov chuckled. "In cartoons, trousers are optional. I have seen the insect folk, the ones who fixed my shoulder."

"Okay, so far I've seen a big rubber flower, yellow and red, and a walking quilt made of gray plastic covered with a half-invisible film that's silvery at an angle. I wouldn't have known it was intelligent, except that it was pushing a cart with wheels roweled like a vaquero's spurs. Now I know why—the creeping floor. It offered me a cup of coffee in perfectly unaccented Spanish."

"Coffee?" Kamanov's expression was almost greedy.

"Something that smelled like coffee, and a doughnut! I turned it down, politely as I could, until Dr. Nguyen tests a sample. It wasn't easy. I could use a cup of real coffee. Have you eaten?"

Kamanov made a sour face. "Rations, from the ships."

"Probably all to the good. I asked this blanket creature why—call it 'she'—with all the mechanized wonders surrounding us, she was stuck pushing a cart. She replied that in convalescent circumstances, the 'human' touch was more to be desired than efficiency. That's what she was providing."

"Hmmm."

"Hmmm, indeed." Gutierrez was reluctant, but needed his friend's advice. "There's more. While I had her attention, I asked after the Proprietor, what he's like, what species he belongs to. A long pause, during which I'm sure she stared at me with an expression of profound pity and amazement, although I don't know how I know it. I certainly didn't know what part of her to watch in order to see it. She said, in words approaching religious awe, that the Proprietor's one of the 'Elders.' Pete, I've got a bad feeling—"

"One bad feeling at a time, Horatio. What happened after you docked?"

"The *Dole* was last. We were met at the platform by a squadron of wingless aircraft like the one that brought you here."

The icy blue eyes twinkled. "Tell me what that was like. I missed it."

Gutierrez sighed. "Like an amusement-park ride, flattened spheres four meters in diameter, each a different color. Open tops, padded floors and walls. No controls, no seats, either, I suppose because they accommodate a variety of species with equal discomfort. I thought they had antigravity, but they turned out to be fanless hovercraft, operating, so Aelbraugh Pritsch said, by ion exchange. I didn't tell him I don't know what that means, but I asked him other questions. He gave up and told me I should see his boss, which I'm planning to do in about twenty minutes."

"I see." The Russian scratched his chin thoughtfully. "We could always send Arthur in your place." He grinned at Empleado, who ignored him.

Gutierrez shoved his hands in his pockets, looked first

at Empleado, then at Kamanov. "Aelbraugh Pritsch told me
an odd thing before he shut his beak and referred further
inquiries to the Proprietor. I thought I'd figured it out.
Despite how well they're established here, the place has
a new feel to it, as if they'd just arrived themselves. Having
read some science fiction, I figured it was sort of an
advance base for an interstellar expedition. You know, a
galactic federation of races from many different worlds?"

"And?" Kamanov raised bushy white eyebrows.

"I offered my deduction to Aelbraugh Pritsch," his friend
told him, "who replied, 'But General, we're all from the
planet you call Earth.'"

FIVE
The Proprietor

"Take my side arm, sir," the major offered. "I can always draw another from the armorer."

The redheaded Marine officer pulled her Witness from the synthetic Webb weapons belt slanting across her hips, let the muzzle roll backward, past her extended thumb as the pistol pivoted about her trigger finger, and executed a practiced, casual wrist-snap which ended with the automatic's broad backstrap thrust toward her superior.

"Careful, sir, there's one up the spout."

Irritable with preoccupation, and a little short of breath, Gutierrez shook his head. He and Reille y Sanchez hastened down a maze of identical roofless corridors, trying to keep up with Aelbraugh Pritsch, who was faster on those parrotlike feet of his than he looked. Overhead, beyond a screen of overhanging foliage, for the first time since they'd arrived on 5023 Eris, they could have seen the yellow "sky" darken as the asteroid rotated into night—corridor walls glowed to make up the deficit—but neither of them looked up to see the change.

"Thank you, Estrellita," he puffed. "I understand that you're paid to be paranoid. I'll even grant that paranoids live longer. But I don't think going armed to this meeting would be a very auspicious way to start official relations with the Proprietor. Do you?"

Life was difficult enough, he thought. Nothing about this expedition was going according to plan. Their shuttlecraft were parked inside the asteroid, more or less, instead of out, which saved on valuable consumables, but involved them with an advanced technology they didn't understand, meaning that they required local cooperation to get back outside, which placed them at the mercy of their hosts.

Vivian Richardson, his vice-commander and captain of one of the three shuttles, had become, well, not a vegetable, exactly, since she appeared to be subject to unpredictable outbursts of violence. The fact that, over the many months the voyage had lasted, he'd come to believe the colonel was a covert KGB observer (in a manner of speaking Empleado's second-in-command, as well as his own) made things nice and complicated. Hell, maybe Empleado was *her* second-in-command.

Worst of all, any claim they made here would now be disputed. One item of news he hadn't discussed with Kamanov, and not just because Empleado had insisted on hanging around, was the detailed report he'd radioed Earthward soon after his three spacecraft had been bedded down, via the antenna provided by their hosts. Also the resulting orders he'd received from Washington, and certain conspicuous differences between them and the equivalent orders Moscow might have issued.

"I guess not, sir." With reluctance she didn't bother disguising, she flipped the grip of the pistol back into her palm in a maneuver known for two centuries in her part of the country as the "road agent's spin," shucking the 11.43x23mm Lenin into its Kevlar holster and refastening the flap. As Gutierrez struggled to remember what it was he'd asked her, he realized the holster was balanced neatly by the big wire-cutting Bowie she wore at the offside of her waist in a matching scabbard. "But it might be a good deal safer, sir," she added, earning her pay. "Isn't anyone going with you, sir, not even our political officer or one of his four—?"

"Hoods? I had that out with Art not five minutes ago."

The general dropped his heels, out of breath and suddenly heedless of how the dinosaurlike bird-being outdistanced them. "I won't repeat the same argument with you. Thanks, Estrellita, for caring, but I was invited to this party by myself. I'll go by myself and fill Arthur in later, for the edification of his bosses. He needn't worry about my leaving anything out. The crime that got me sent here was saying too much, not too little."

He resumed his forward motion, but not the previous pace. Beside him, Reille y Sanchez nodded, but offered no immediate reply, first of all, he suspected, because he was correct in his assessment of the political realities, and she knew it. Second, because she probably didn't wish to contemplate whatever crime had gotten her volunteered for this expedition. Third, he thought, there was always the possibility that even Estrellita had bosses outside the normal chain of command to report to. Instead, she seemed to wait for what felt to him like the regulation decent interval for changing the subject in conversations with a superior officer.

"As you will, sir. I'll be back at the *Dole*." She tossed him a salute and turned to go.

"You do that, Major. On your way, look in on Dr. Kamanov. He's restive in durance vile and considers you decorative."

For that matter, he thought, watching the rakish slant of her pistol belt as she retreated down the corridor, her fighting knife slapping at her thigh, so do I. Enjoying a reflexive moment of guilty feelings about his wife, he began taking longer strides, pivoting to follow the Proprietor's assistant around a corner. That obviously impatient individual now awaited him at the end of a passage where it T-junctioned with yet another.

"You mustn't be late, General," the avian fussed when twenty such strides had brought him even. The man resisted an urge to rub his eyes, seeing motion, or thinking he saw it, near the base of the birdlike being's neck, a flash of turquoise and perhaps the slender whip of a reptilian tail. "At the end of this passage a pressure door and a flight of stairs lead to the Proprietor's quarters. Don't be alarmed to find them awash with a colorless, odorless liquid."

Gutierrez stopped again. "What?"

"Oxygenated fluorocarbon. Some of our staff here substitute it for the marine environment they're naturally adapted to. My security party, for example, the individuals you call 'lobster people'?" The bird entity gave the flapped holster an unconscious pat where it hung at his belt. Gutierrez experienced a momentary doubt about having rejected Reille y Sanchez's side arm. Hadn't officers and diplomats once worn ceremonial swords on occasions like this?

"Yes?" the man asked, struggling to gather up loose ends of thought and recapture the subject at hand. Maybe Vivian wasn't the only victim suffering from culture shock. "What about them?"

"You may have noticed the protective membrane they all wear," replied Aelbraugh Pritsch. "In some respects, it's like your own spacesuits, I'd venture to guess, devised to retain moisture, temperature, and pressure necessary for their survival. Off duty, they inhabit quarters similar to those of the Proprietor."

Gutierrez hadn't noticed, now he mentioned it, and couldn't blame Pete or the major for failing to take in this minor detail earlier. There was just too much here, all at once, to see and wonder about. What did Aelbraugh Pritsch do, for instance, about the way his gun belt seemed to crush the feathers at what should have been his waist? Pressure, too? That hinted at an even more advanced technology than he'd imagined. It did explain the silvery appearance of the quilt-thing he'd seen himself. "I take it your boss isn't one of these lobster people?"

"Dear me, no!" The creature actually clucked like the barnyard fowl he resembled. "Great Egg, the Proprietor's no crustacean! Like them, he simply happens to have evolved in a saline medium. The artificial liquid I referred to permits him to remain comfortable, while others, land-evolved organisms such as you and I, may confer with him under more convenient circumstances than water would afford."

More confused than ever, Gutierrez shook his head. "I don't get you."

"You will, General, here we are."

This passageway terminated in a dead end. The oval

panel before them was the first real door Gutierrez had seen in this place, and fifteen centimeters thick. At Aelbraugh Pritsch's touch it swung aside on heavy hinges, allowing a faint scent of iodine to waft outward. Within a well-lit roofed-over chamber, a steep flight of plastic-coated stairs disappeared into a clear, mirror-surfaced liquid.

"Down there?" Recognizing a pressure lock when he saw one, Gutierrez laid a reluctant hand on the door-frame, turning to confront his strange guide with an expression, more than skeptical, which he wondered if the nonhuman could read. "What the hell do I wear, scuba gear?"

There it was again, that blue-green flash amidst the powdery gray-white of scaly feathers. Aelbraugh Pritsch blinked at him. "If you refer to mechanical breathing apparatus, not at all, sir. The liquid's fully charged with oxygen, every bit as breathable as air, and rather pleasant to the tactile senses. Nor will it damage anything you wear or carry with you, even the most primitive electronics. In that sense, it's quite inert. However, I do advise you to exhale completely before you take your first breath, as an uncomfortable cramping, owing to bubbles trapped in the respiratory system, may otherwise result."

The general braced both hands against the door-frame, like the family dog, he realized, reluctant to be bathed. His ostensible purpose was to lean in for a better look. "Let me get this straight: I'm supposed to walk down those stairs, duck my head, take a breath, and—"

The Proprietor's assistant raised a long, slender, admonitory finger. "Remembering to exhale thoroughly first."

This time Gutierrez blinked. "Remembering to—remind me to take you sky-diving some time. You're not coming along?"

The dinosauroid's scaly plumage fluffed out around his body, as if in alarm. In vain, Gutierrez watched for another glimpse of the turquoise-colored symbiote or parasite, wondering why it seemed so important. "Oh, no, sir! Not at all. This interview is to be private. Besides, I've other business to attend."

"I'll bet you do." Feeling a good deal less jocular than he hoped he sounded, he trod down the steps. "Well, my GI insurance is paid up. Here goes nothing!" He entered the liquid, which surprised him with its warmth where it lapped his ankles, his knees, his thighs up to the crotch, the waist, and at last his chest. It wasn't entirely odorless, but the odor wasn't entirely unpleasant. With all the trepidation in the world, he exhaled hard and ducked his head.

A moment passed.

A small string of bubbles rose to the surface.

Unable to overcome a lifetime of reflex, Gutierrez crashed back up through the wave-chopped liquid without having taken a breath of the stuff, coughing, his lungs aching for no reason he knew.

"Do keep trying, General, please!" Aelbraugh Pritsch stood, a single amber eye peeking around the door at the top of the stairs. Another pair of eyes, black and tiny in their turquoise settings, glittered down at Gutierrez from the feathered creature's shoulder. The avian's voice echoed in the bare-walled chamber as he raised it over the man's spluttering. "The first breath's the hardest!"

Gutierrez wiped liquid, not entirely tasteless, from his eyes. "That's what they told the guy in the gas chamber!" Nevertheless, he set his jaw, exhaled, and took two steps in a single, inexorable bound, surprised to find himself breathing. As with water, he discovered he was quite nearsighted. It gave him a shut-in, claustrophobic feeling. Hand on the rail beside him, he approached another door, placed his free hand as he'd seen his guide do upstairs, let it swing before him, and stepped through.

It closed behind him, plunging him into darkness.

For more than a moment, this time, he regretted having turned down Estrellita's offer of her pistol. No expression he could think of was adequate to describe the utter blackness that enveloped him, after the cheerful glare of the pressure chamber upstairs. He was blinded, cloaked in silence as absolute as the darkness. Adjusted now to the surrounding liquid, its smell, its taste, its temperature, his sensory deprivation was complete. Nameless fear of the unknown rode his spine in waves which threatened to paralyze his mind altogether.

Concentrate! he ordered himself. What is there left to feel? The floor still retained its tackiness. The liquid medium in which he stood was less dense than water.

Faint currents he could feel running through it didn't prevent him from maintaining an upright posture. When thirty seconds had crawled by, he began to make out blue-gray outlines. This wasn't an empty room; something was moving around him! Panic almost overtook him before he realized that the moving objects were marine plants, undulating with the gentle motion of the liquid.

Despite his fear, Gutierrez stepped forward, slowed by the fluorocarbon which made it all seem even more like the nightmare it was beginning to remind him of. Another slow-motion step. In the distance, blurred and exaggerated by refraction, he could make out the faint sparkle of colored lights. They twinkled at the far end of the chamber like pilots on a console, winking on and off at apparent random, appearing, disappearing, replaced by others which winked on and off in turn. They formed a pattern, he thought, like faraway Chinese lanterns strung on a line, bobbing in a breeze.

A few more steps brought him closer, but not to any better understanding of what they were. Darkness seemed to lift by stages as his eyes adjusted. The room, more and more visible in shades of gray-on-gray, began to assume dimensions: a ceiling low and oppressive overhead, enclosing walls more palpable than seen. Humped amorphous shadow-forms lurked about him. The blackest, most shapeless lay ahead. The chill he felt wash through his body had nothing to do with temperature.

Without warning, the darkest of the shadows pivoted before him with a low moan and a grating noise. Moved by a reflex he hadn't known he possessed, he slapped at his thigh, feeling liquid stream between his outstretched fingers, clawing for the weapon he wasn't carrying. A tangled mass of thick, writhing, fleshy ribbons squirmed toward his unprotected face, each illuminated along its undulating length by row after row of the bioluminescent spots he'd first seen a moment before.

A deep voice boomed. "You are the human leader, General Horatio Z. Gutierrez?"

The general gulped the sour taste of panic, prevented from mindless flight by nothing more than the density of the liquid around his body. He opened his mouth, only to discover that whatever knack speech required in this medium, he didn't have it. In front of him, the thrashing horror grated closer, the obscene mobility of that portion nearest him somehow limited by a grotesque, massive object at the rear.

Unbidden, the surrealistic image came to him of landed eels: horrible, slimy, maddened by barbed hooks in their tongues, squirming to regain the water, yet cruelly fastened by their tails to a granite tombstone grinding across the bank behind them.

Above the unthinkable junction where the tentacles found root, a pair of cold, golden, luminescent eyes regarded him, englobed in glassy corneal spheres and slitted, like those of a jungle cat. Behind them, the meter-thick tube of the monster's gigantic body disappeared into a vaster spiral-coiled shell that might have garaged a small automobile.

Somehow, Gutierrez found his voice, deepened by the liquid medium he forced it into.

"You're . . . the Proprietor?"

SIX
Beer and Sympathy

A tentacle-tip stabbed toward a wall.

Illumination sprang up in a sudden flood, making Gutierrez blink. Before him, across the diameters of eyes the proverbial size of dinner plates, vast pupils shrank to fine, black vertical lines.

"Forgive me for not having done that sooner. You're rather earlier than expected, General Gutierrez, doubtless at the urging of my overly punctilious assistant, and I'm afraid you startled me. I'm descended from abyssal species, you know, and in any event, like you, would enjoy my dark, quiet hour of contemplation."

"I startled you," Gutierrez gulped, "the Proprietor?"

"'If you prick us, do we not bleed? If you tickle us, do we not laugh?'" A respiratory organ two hundred centimeters long and forty in diameter seemed to generate a colossal, godlike chuckle, rattling the man's teeth. "I'm a simple tradesman, my boy, no distinguished military hero like yourself, with nerves of steel. The individual who refers to me as 'the Proprietor' possesses an unfortunate predilection for the melodramatic. Also, I suspect he thinks it looks good on his résumé. Everybody else calls me Mister

Thoggosh, for the excellent reason that it happens to be my name."

Nerves of steel. Now that the danger was past, another humiliating wave of panic swept through the man's body, this one worst of all. This, he thought, must be what Vivian's been feeling—maybe even what Art feels all the time. "I'm pleased," he lied, attempting to control his bodily functions, "to meet you."

"Do try to relax," the giant told him. "I realize I'm something of a spectacle for anyone who's never seen the like, but I assure you I'm quite an ethical being. I wouldn't dream of eating you."

Gutierrez found himself muttering an inane, "That's nice . . ."

"And before we start, my boy, the next time you come to see me, by all means wear your side arm. Everybody here carries personal weapons. You appear quite unclothed without yours."

Gutierrez suddenly wished for a chair, although most of his weight was supported by the liquid filling the room. Growing calmer, he glanced around. In one corner, suspended on light, decorative cords between floor and ceiling, hung a cage about the right size for a small parrot. Through the bars, he could see, "perched" in "midair," a brightly-striped, spiny fish, trilling an undistracting, if not exactly musical, song.

"I'll, er, try to remember."

If there is a next time, he thought. His recent, peremptory orders from Earth intruded themselves into the forefront of his mind, although it wasn't as if he'd forgotten them. He tried to breathe deeply. The floor directly in front of Mister Thoggosh, an area three meters wide by two across, was set aside as a desk, dappled with buttons and lights, handy to the giant being's sinuous manipulators. Behind the technicolor house-sized horror lay an unnaturally broad door (now he understood the infirmary's architecture) flanked by a pair of large, upright boxes resembling stereo speakers. Gutierrez realized he hadn't been listening to Mister Thoggosh, but to their output, balanced so the sound seemed to emanate from the great mollusc.

Mister Thoggosh noticed him noticing. "Your surmise

is correct, my boy. My species is quite mute, incapable of uttering a sound, although our hearing's rather keen. For reasons peculiar to our evolutionary history, we communicate by what would no doubt strike you as telepathy, although, in point of plain fact, it's rather less romantic than that. You'd understand better if I told you that, had you worn your spacesuit to this meeting, I might be able to speak with you directly."

Gutierrez peered at the monster. "Natural radio?"

"I assure you, sir, your vocal ability to compress and rarify the medium about you at will is no less marvelous to me. We're all beings, are we not, of infinite wonderment?"

Mister Thoggosh chuckled, his many tentacles twining a complex pattern. Gutierrez couldn't estimate the number of those writhing limbs, but he remembered that a squid (which his host resembled) had ten, while a nautilus (which he also resembled) had more, he thought. One of them lashed across the "desk" and touched a colored light. A wave of pressure passed through the fluid. Gutierrez glanced toward the ceiling, where an object—a plastic-coated wire chair—sank to the floor beside him.

"Will you be seated, General?" Mister Thoggosh asked him. "I prefer eyes at a level. And, as I suspect this conversation will continue rather a long while, I'd be more comfortable if I felt you were."

"Thanks." Gutierrez sat.

"And so, my boy," Mister Thoggosh began, "contact has at long last occurred between humanity and another sapience, just as your species dreamed of for so many centuries. And on your first real deep-space voyage, at that. Yet none of you seems much prepared to celebrate it."

The general grunted. "Mister Thoggosh, before this goes any further, I have an important—an official—message to relay to you from my superiors. I haven't been looking forward to it."

"A moment, sir." Two of the mollusc's tentacles were longer than the others. Instead of tapering to slender ends, they possessed splayed tips. Mister Thoggosh laid one across his "desk," crossing the other over it. "Do you care for refreshment? I'm having beer. This liquid we steep ourselves in has its uses, but it will dehydrate the tissues."

"Beer?" Gutierrez felt his eyebrows rise. At the rate they were getting exercised here, he thought, they'd eventually take up residence at the back of his neck. Suddenly, to his even greater astonishment, one of his host's tentacles separated from his body with a plop, and began swimming like a snake toward a wall on the right.

"Surely, General, you can't imagine yours the only culture, in a universe far wider than you know, to have discovered fermentation."

Open-mouthed, the human watched the mollusc's disembodied limb wriggle through the handle of a round-cornered door (inside, a light came on), remove a pair of containers, and place them on a tray.

"Not," Mister Thoggosh told him, "by at least five hundred million years."

At the desk, the tentacle wound itself about a small gold-colored metal accessory, piercing the top of a container and bringing it, with a slender plastic tube trailing behind, to the general. Mister Thoggosh reached for his own beer and reclaimed his wandering limb.

"This, for example, and at the risk of sounding like your legendary Captain Nemo, is brewed from a variety of kelp native to the waters off the landmass you call New Mexico. Or is it Old Mexico?"

With another tentacle, Mister Thoggosh inserted the tube where Gutierrez knew his mouth must be.

"Or perhaps it was California. In any event," the mollusc sighed (no other word could describe it), "I find it very satisfactory. My only regret is that I can't invite you to smoke, a fascinating habit. This liquid carries heat away too quickly and won't support combustion."

The songfish warbled in its cage. Gutierrez sampled the exotic beverage, surprised to discover he agreed with that individual's evaluation of it. He admitted as much.

"I'm highly gratified to hear it," Mister Thoggosh replied. "And now, my boy, if I may help you: you've been instructed to inform me—that is, whoever's 'in charge' among my party—that this asteroid, indeed every celestial body and the entire volume of space within the 'Solar System,' is the property of Earth, under the authority of your United World Soviet, as 'the common heritage of all mankind.'"

Gutierrez's jaw dropped. The beer-tube floated free. "How—?"

Tentacles lifted and spread in a shrug. "It must certainly have occurred to you by now that our command of English, Spanish, Russian, and quite a number of other human languages results from the fact that your planet, in certain frequencies, is quite the brightest—or, rather, the loudest— object in the Solar System."

"Yes, but—"

"Further reflection would make it clear that the computative sophistication requisite to sort this tangle of signals out from one another—and, in a word, 'decode' those languages—empowers us, by necessary implication, to comprehend them *whatever* enciphering may have been imposed upon them. It isn't so much that we set out to break your rather childish codes, General, our apparatus simply removes interference, be it from solar radiation or our own machinery."

Gutierrez reached for his siphon. "Which is how you knew we were coming, the names of some of the people onboard the shuttles—and the rest of my message."

It was as if the mollusc sighed again. "Sir, you've my profoundest sympathies. The spectrographic signature of this little world signifies to any observer a concentration of resources highly desirable to the prospective colonist expected to support himself as soon as possible. Moreover, the planetoid describes an orbit which carries it near quite a variety of other such bodies. To your American Soviet Socialist Republic, as it is to us, 5023 Eris is perfectly conceived as a base for science and exploitation. Thus you're ordered to evict us, no allowance being made by those with the power to command you for the priority of our claim, or the fact that you possess no means whatever of carrying out that order."

Now that it had been mentioned, Gutierrez found himself wishing for a cigarette, although he'd given up the habit a quarter of a century earlier. "Well," he told the mollusc, "at least all my cards are on the table. I ought to thank you. I was dreading it."

Mister Thoggosh emitted a chuckle. "As I would in your place, my boy. Permit me to put my cards on the table, as well. Let us discuss what alternatives present themselves, before you try to carry out that preposterous command. First, we'll dispose of this 'common heritage' nonsense: that a body lies within the same stellar system as your United World Soviet scarcely means that you own it. I gather that this pernicious doctrine was first promulgated to prevent the assertion of private property claims in space, in effect assuring a Marxist revolution there before your species had even arrived on a permanent basis."

Gutierrez raised his eyebrows significantly, but patriotically refrained from comment. The chuckle became Olympian before the great mollusc managed to get it back under control.

"Do forgive me, sir, I beg you. Where was I? Oh yes: those penalized most by this doctrine nevertheless felt compelled, for some reason, to accept it, to their eventual fatal disadvantage. Now, it's being used to assert a property claim—a collective one, your own—in the face of our having arrived here first. In short, those you call your superiors wish to retain their pie and consume it at the same time."

It was probable, the general realized, given government control of education and the media, that the Proprietor was better informed regarding Earth's recent history than any member of the expedition, with the possible exception of Piotr Kamanov. In his profession, Gutierrez couldn't help understanding how eventual American acceptance of United Nations treaties governing such unclaimed territories as Antarctica, the ocean floor, and outer space (after earlier periods of rejection) had deprived it of resources and defenses appropriate to the late twentieth century, and disproportionately influenced subsequent political events. It was one of the things that made him a dangerous liability to the ASSR.

"Cake," he corrected, "although I wouldn't want to go on record agreeing with you about that."

The mollusc waved a negligent limb. "For reasons that will become more and more obvious as you get to know us better, my boy, this isn't going onto any sort of record.

However, I do sympathize with your dilemma. One grows accustomed to free speech, and the casual opinions I've just expressed would get you sentenced to Siberia, would they not?"

"Labrador." Gutierrez grinned. "We Americans take care of our own."

Great pupils widened in what the human believed was a smile. The mouth, probably a great parrot-jawed beak, wasn't visible, even if it were capable of expressing Mister Thoggosh's feelings.

"Labrador." That being shuddered. "I'm not overly fond of the cold, being a creature of tropical waters. In fact, General, I come equipped with a full complement of prejudices. I confess that I'm disposed to regard this Marxism of yours, indeed collectivism of any sort, as a manifestation of primitivity; a pitiable, aberrational phase in the otherwise progressive development of any culture which it nevertheless appears all intelligent species must go through. They do grow out of it eventually, provided they survive its immediate, disastrous economic and ethical consequences."

Mister Thoggosh stirred. "Which brings us to the nub of the situation, and to words I don't mind telling you I've dreaded saying quite as fully as you dreaded conveying your superiors' message to me.

"I, too, have principals, General, investors I must answer to. Not to mention employees who traveled here with me in good faith. I'm not a free agent. My policy will be to remain amiable as long as your superiors permit me, but we'll not be dispossessed, whatever consequences we're forced to bear. We pursue important business here, touching deeply upon our civilization's most ancient and fundamental values and beliefs."

"I wanted to ask—" Gutierrez began.

"I trust you'll not regard me as persisting with perverse mysteriousness if, for the nonce, our business here remains unspecified."

Believing he was being dismissed, the general rose.

"You've your imperatives, as well," his host conceded, "and we may soon confront each other in mortal conflict. Yet I'm reminded, in all courtesy, that, whereas I know exactly who and what you are—to the extent those things can be known about anyone—you've still many unanswered questions about me and my associates."

Gutierrez sat down again.

"Will you have another beer, while I anticipate some of those questions? Has anyone informed you, for example, that we aren't the extraterrestrials of your folklore?"

"Yes, thanks. Aelbraugh Pritsch told me you were from Earth—"

"But he didn't bother to elaborate upon what must seem to you a remarkable assertion." A snorting noise came from the speakers behind Mister Thoggosh. "How very like him. There are times I—but I suppose it's best to start at the beginning."

Gutierrez took a sip of his second beer, nodding agreement.

"We are, indeed, from Earth, sir," the mollusc told him, sampling his own beverage. "Not from the Earth you know, but from what you'd no doubt regard as another dimension."

"I'm familiar with the phrase," the human replied, "although I never understood what it means."

"You're refreshingly forthright, sir. Indeed, it's been truly said that 'To know what you know, and to know what you don't know, is to know.' In this instance, it means an alternative branching of historical probability. I haven't the time or temperament, nor, I suspect, have you the patience at the moment, for a lecture on metaphysics. Let it stand, then, that my people discovered long ago that each choice which reality offers us, in a wider reality, is resolved in every possible way it can be."

Gutierrez resisted the urge to wrinkle his brow and scratch his head. "Would you like to try that again?"

"To be certain," Mister Thoggosh replied. "In this continuum, you accept my offer of kelp beer. In another, altogether separate from our particular consciousness yet somehow nearby, your counterpart refuses. In a third, my counterpart was niggardly and never made the offer."

He took a draw on his own beer.

"Farther out upon the bell curve of ultimate reality, you and I never had this meeting. Human beings never came to 5023 Eris. At the farthest extreme known or conceivable, the 'Big Bang' never happened and a universe was stillborn. In this context, in addition to its other manifold attractions, 5023 Eris presents us with something of a conundrum. Its counterpart fails to appear in our version of reality."

"I—" Gutierrez tried to interrupt.

"But I digress." Mister Thoggosh ignored him. "You see, General, in my version of prehistory, exactly as in your own, during what your scientists term the late Cambrian Period, the dominant life-form on Earth was a small and unprepossessing ancestor of mine, called a 'nautiloid.' This, you must understand, was five hundred million years before anything even remotely resembling human beings evolved."

Gutierrez nodded. "I think I follow you."

"I should hardly have expected otherwise, my boy. In your prehistory, with perhaps a single exception, none of the ocean animals developed high intelligence and, in due course, they were supplanted by other forms, culminating in your own."

He raised a tentacle-tip, "Ah, but in mine . . ."

In its cage, the striped fish trilled a mindless melody.

SEVEN
Rumors of War

They reminded him of embattled prairie Conestogas.

Only in this case, they were surrounded by jungle, and were merely three well-worn orbiters—spaceships only by the most generous courtesy—lowered to the crumbling gray-brown surface where they lay now, cradled in plastic-coated wire mesh baskets. And a triangular configuration was as close as they could get to a circle.

Nestled within, what was beginning to be the human campsite on 5023 Eris occupied the space left by the shuttles' backswept, stubby wings, which served as tents of a sort. They might be needed, thought Piotr Kamanov. The asteroid's organic canopy enclosed more than enough volume to support rain, and the humidity had been increasing since sundown.

In the jungle, beyond the geologist's night-shortened vision, something rustled leaves, some kind of animal life, he guessed, brought along to balance the great plants. Approaching the camp, he took his time, squeezing between the blunt nose of the *McCain* and the scorched tail of the *Hatch*, not overly anxious to rejoin his fellow voyagers. He'd bidden his nonhuman well-wishers what he hoped was a temporary farewell as one of their electrostatic craft, apparently the only mechanized transport on the asteroid, had left him on the ground to return "upstairs," walking the remaining distance, a matter of five hundred meters, to the human enclave. Rosalind and Toya had descended with him, but he'd urged them to hurry ahead on the strong, swift legs of youth, so he could be alone to think.

Kamanov's arm hung in the sling he'd be wearing, if he obeyed doctors' orders, another couple of days. It no longer pained him, and hadn't from the moment he'd been placed in the care of the insect-surgeons a level up in the series of complex structures built under the canopy. It wasn't his injury which filled him now with a feeling of weary sickness.

It was news from home.

"Pete!" Kamanov watched his friend Horatio rise on stiff knees, a malady of middle age he identified with. The general was hunkered by a tiny fire of branches and huge fallen leaves. As new as the alien colony appeared, the ground between here and where they'd dropped him already had a scattering of debris he associated with forests. Among their other uses, the growths were creating soil for the miniature planet.

His geologist's eye noted that the fire was built on an upcropping of iron-bearing rock, an obvious accretion feature on a world mostly composed of carbonaceous chondrites. He was also aware that there was no objective need for such a fire. No one was cold, no one was cooking, but he understood the primeval necessity. Toya huddled near, despite the mild temperature, as did others from the three shuttle complements.

"Horatio." Not quite recovered from his ordeal, Kamanov leaned, a bit short of energy, against the mesh basket under a shuttle wingtip. He waited for Gutierrez, but didn't wait to speak, nor bother keeping his voice down, despite the presence, beneath the wing, of a dozen figures curled in makeshift sleeping bags. "What is this nonsense they speak of at the infirmary, that we are about to declare war on our hosts?"

Two or three recumbent figures stirred. A faint, general muttering passed through the camp. Gutierrez shrugged as he met his friend and took his arm. "I guess I shouldn't be surprised that their grapevine's as good as ours. It's orders, Pete, straight out of an old B-movie: Earth versus slave-warriors of the Elder race."

"Orders?" Kamanov halted halfway from the center of the little compound, only pretending to catch his breath. Having become an old man, he'd long since discovered, offered one excuse after another for stealing time to think. He turned to look at his American friend, this time lowering his voice. "Washington's or Moscow's?"

Gutierrez blinked, deadpan, "Should it make a difference?"

Meaning, Kamanov knew, should you admit in front of this many witnesses that it does? Beyond the firelit circle he heard noises again, as if squirrels were rummaging for acorns among dried leaves. He took another breath, dropping to a whisper. "When they are such exceptionally stupid orders, commanding me, if I can, to murder—or be murdered by—sapient beings I have grown in so short a time to like and respect."

Gutierrez looked him in the eye, but refrained from contradicting him. For an American in this part of the twenty-first century, that alone represented fervent agreement with a politically dangerous opinion. They resumed walking. Within a few steps, they stood beside the fire, which threw grotesque, wavering shadows onto the flanks of the surrounding orbiters. The general thrust both hands into his pants pockets.

"If I'd known earlier they were going to release you so soon, I'd have stopped for you on the way back from my talk with Mister Thoggosh."

Kamanov surveyed the scene about the fire. Despite the relaxed postures and exotic setting, it had the look of a meeting, Empleado taking part, along with Estrellita sitting at attention. He often had to think twice before recalling that the redhead was *Spetznaz*, and a military security officer, at that, although at the moment she looked every centimeter of it. Several others added their silhouettes to the eerie shadows, Lieutenant Colonel Juan Sebastiano, captain of the *McCain*, Major Jesus Ortiz, Richardson's erstwhile second-in-command, C. C. Jones, supposedly the expedition's news correspondent, Carlos Alvarez, the cook, and young Danny Gutierrez, a mere second lieutenant but the general's son. Rosalind Nguyen was absent—catching up on needed sleep or checking on her charges, among them Richardson, Gutierrez's missing-but-accounted-for second-in-command— while Toya Pulaski, her occasional assistant, sat with her forearms on her knees, staring into the fire, stirring it with the meter-long skeleton of a gigantic leaf.

Watching everything and everybody from scattered points somewhere in the nearby darkness were Empleado's crew of KGB enforcers, blocky Demene Wise, Broward Hake, the oily one, the deceptively charming Roger Betal, and sinister Delbert Roo.

"The Proprietor?" Kamanov asked.

"None other. Pull up a rock. I'd just started filling everybody in, so I won't have to do much back-tracking on your account."

Kamanov found space, as usual—although he didn't notice it, himself—between a pair of handsome young women, the major and Lt. Lee Marna, a husky blond life-support tech from the *McCain*. Stretching full length on the ground, he cradled his head in his good hand. Campfire and flickering shadows sent his memories back a lifetime, to red-neckerchiefed childhood outings with the Young Soviet Pioneers.

Horatio must be right about the speed of informal communication among their hosts; this would be an attribute of all intelligent life. But most of what he thought of as "grapejuice" he'd squeezed a drop at a time from his own doctor and her aide, not their new acquaintances. As Gutierrez spoke, Kamanov understood that it had been hours since he'd returned from conferring with the alien leader, soaked in rapidly evaporating fluid but otherwise intact. Naturally, Gutierrez had been required to report Earthside, via a kilometer-long antenna lead, before talking to anyone, even the local KGB. This surely would have rankled Arthur.

But the geologist was most startled to learn that, following this initial report, each and every one of the expedition's half dozen department heads had been privately summoned to the mike as individuals, apparently to receive specific, highly classified orders direct from Washington.

"I was telling Pete," Gutierrez continued, "this Mister Thoggosh is the one Aelbraugh Pritsch called the Proprietor. And before you ask, we didn't go into it: beyond informing me he had stockholders to consider, I've no idea what authority he exercises. You have to see him to believe him. He calls himself a nautiloid, sort of a giant squid in a big colorful snail shell. He's preoccupied with some kind of search on this asteroid, but from what little he said, it looks more like a religious exercise than anything else."

He described the great mollusc as best he could, the medium in which he lived, something of his dissertation on alternative probability. It took several tries, with Kamanov's help, before everyone understood that, even in their own version of reality, nonsapient creatures similar to Mister Thoggosh had been supreme on Earth far longer than humans—even mammals, Kamanov told them—had so far existed. Conveying the length of time involved, hundreds of millions of years, they were almost required to start over.

"Such organisms dominate Upper Paleozoic strata," the geologist added, "but may be found, in one morphology or another, from the Cambrian through the Jurassic. Unless, of course, one includes the famous chambered and paper nautiluses, in which case they survive even today. They are a hardy form, vulnerable only to whatever mysterious force exterminated the dinosaurs." He shrugged, not an easy gesture with his stiff shoulder. "But why listen to me—it is not my specialty—when we enjoy the fortuitous presence of an amateur, but competent, paleobiologist."

Gutierrez frowned a question. No such specialty appeared on the roster. The major and several others looked to the general. His son glanced from Toya to the blond lieutenant and back again, there being little about Toya to hold his interest. Like his henchmen, Empleado glared suspiciously at everyone, frustrated, it seemed to the Russian, that he couldn't glare suspiciously at himself, as well. In the silence, Kamanov heard that rustling again, from outside the encampment. He could tell from their expressions that the others heard it, too.

"Toya is perhaps too modest to inform you of the fine conversation we enjoyed on this very topic in the infirmary. An intrepid fossil hunter and collector in her girlhood, she remains a part-time delver into the past even now. She identified those beings—whom most of you Americans, through ideologically colored glasses, seem anxious to view as soldier-slaves—as descendants of sea-scorpions."

Empleado gave the Russian a sharp glance which he may have believed no one else noticed. KGB or not, however, he'd learned that there was little he could do to restrain the geologist.

"How about it, Pulaski?" Sebastiano stroked his goatee. "A zinky for your thoughts." Faces turned to look at the girl. The expression, originally meaning debased American coins of the lowest denomination, was now applied in common currency to kopecks, as well, just as dollars and rubles were often and interchangeably called "ferns," in reference to unsecured banknotes once issued by the long-defunct Federal Reserve system. Toya kept her eyes on the fire and cleared her throat as her thin, nervous hands wrung the end of the fire-stirring stick she held.

"On Earth—our Earth, sir—sea-scorpions were crustaceans which, in normal history, followed nautiloids as the dominant life-form. The soldiers evolved from them, as we did from primates." This evoked muttered comments, nothing intelligible enough to reply to. She stopped, her small supply of courage consumed by what had been, for her, a terrible effort.

"You see." Kamanov smiled. "Not so difficult." To Gutierrez: "What did I tell you?"

Gutierrez looked down at the fire with a hand over his mouth. The geologist had no way of knowing that the general was torn, as he'd been for his entire acquaintance with Kamanov, between exasperation and amusement at his friend's instinct for treating women of all shapes and ages in a manner which attracted them like a magnet. That the attraction was quite mutual had no doubt made his life very interesting. Kamanov turned to Pulaski. "Explain the rest of your remarkable theory, if you will, Toya."

"Doctor Kamanov!" she protested in a hoarse whisper, blushing and pleased by his encouragement, if not by his having made her the center of attention. "I'm so embarrassed!"

"Not as much as I have embarrassed me," the reclining Kamanov lifted his good hand, palm up, in a half-shrug, "by not thinking of it myself." The casual motion assumed more ominous proportions, exaggerated in a huge serpentine shadow on the fuselage behind him.

Grinning into the flames, Sebastiano peered at Kamanov where he lay between the two good-looking women. "We can all see how embarrassed you are, Pete." He looked around the fire. "Poor guy must've had something else on his mind at the time."

In the laughter that followed, Pulaski reddened further. "I, that is, Captain, they . . ." Her voice trailed off in bashful paralysis.

"What the hell's wrong with you, Pulaski?" snapped the major. "Spit it out!" Estrellita must be as nervous as everyone else, Kamanov observed. She was usually a good deal more patient with the shy little sergeant.

A fist-sized flying something swooped through the dark overhead, underlit by the fire, and disappeared again into the jungle.

"What Toya is trying to say, Major—" Kamanov ran fingers through his shaggy white hair, as if even he found her idea staggering "—and I remind you it is her idea, is that we see here creatures not from one alternative world but from several, perhaps dozens."

"What?" Marna, the life-support specialist, let her jaw drop.

Danny whistled, then cut it off.

"Hundreds," the embarrassed girl stammered into the ground. "I've seen beings descended, like we are from simians, the way Mister Thoggosh is from nautiloids, from cartilaginous vertebrates like sharks." Her eyes jerked away, toward the shadows beneath the nose of the *Hatch*. The night-flapper had confirmed Kamanov's theory about animal life on the asteroid. As the evening cooled, he surmised, whatever he'd heard earlier was being attracted to the warmth of the fire. Pulaski shivered, huddling closer to the coals.

"Do not forget," he added, trying to distract Toya from

her fear, "those who patched me up. All who see them believe they might be insects."

Gutierrez agreed with what he heard. "How about the ever-popular Aelbraugh Pritsch? Nobody seems to know what he's descended from. I'd be surprised if he does, himself."

"Some flightless avian, I'd guess, or dinosaur, sir. I'm not certain which, or that it even matters, given the warm-blood hypothesis." Toya had surprised everyone but Kamanov by speaking up again. As she warmed to her subject, some of her shyness seemed to slough away. "I'd be surprised if there weren't at least one true fish species, living in the same environment as Mister Thoggosh. Of course, I've seen two or three creatures I couldn't recognize at all. Sir."

"What gets me," Reille y Sanchez sounded calmer, yet still edgier than Kamanov was used to finding her, "is that every individual, all these other species, refer to the nautiloids, molluscs, cephalopods, whatever they are, as 'Elders.' With a deference I'm beginning to find—"

"The nautiloids," Gutierrez interrupted, "do give the impression of being wise and ancient. Mister Thoggosh certainly did."

"Wise and ancient," Empleado snorted, "when their notion of terraforming consists of planting this runaway kudzu and letting it do all the work?"

Kamanov sat up. "Arthur, even someone with your obligations appreciates the absurdity of the labor theory of value. The point is—how did you call it, super kudzu? You Americans have such a flair for phrases. Whatever you call the stuff, it works. The plant is gene-designed to germinate in the airless cold of space, grow to a predetermined—"

"Enough biology, Comrade Scientist," put in Empleado, "the point is, what do we do about these molluscs? Goddamn it, they're individualists!"

"Goodness." Kamanov widened his eyes in mock horror. "How shocking!"

"And even worse," the KGB man added, "they're capitalists!"

Kamanov laughed out loud. Empleado's men glowered. Gutierrez exhaled. "Down, Pete. Funny thing about that,

Art. Mister Thoggosh described himself to me as a merchant-explorer. Yet when I tried to follow up on that, to make some accommodation between us, he regretted, on behalf of his fellow Elders, that in all conscience he couldn't trade with us. Not as representatives of the United World Soviet."

"We have become," Kamanov grinned, "the kind of kids our mothers warned us not to play with."

Gutierrez glared at Kamanov. "Lay off, Pete. 5023 Eris is rich in resources. I thought we might work them, sell the results in exchange for a claim. But the Elders didn't travel to this dreary place, Mister Thoggosh informed me, at great peril and expense—underline expense—with trade in mind. Whatever they find here for themselves will, they anticipate, just pay a fraction of their costs."

"They came," agreed Kamanov, "for a more important purpose—"

"Which they won't—" continued Gutierrez.

"—perhaps cannot—" Kamanov interrupted.

"—reveal," Gutierrez finished with annoyance in his voice. "In any case, he explained—or he thought he was explaining—in the matter of trade, their ethics forbid them to receive stolen property."

"Meaning what?" Reille y Sanchez raised her eyebrows, then: "Did anybody else hear that? Some kind of scrabbling under the ship?"

"A peculiar attitude," agreed Sebastiano, "for a self-admitted capitalist. I heard it, too, Major, and I don't like it."

The general shook his head. "I've been hearing it all night, myself. Little animals, I guess. You'll find this even more peculiar, Juan." Gutierrez glanced at Empleado. "And try to remember Mister Thoggosh said it, not me. That's all—stolen property—he says any collectivist society, founded on 'theft, brutality, coercive central planning, and murder,' has to trade."

The resulting silence lasted several heartbeats.

"Then there will indeed be war." The Russian geologist was sober at last. "Although, as with many another war in human history, no one on either side seems to want it."

EIGHT
Texas Marxism

"Comrade Doctor Kamanov." Empleado folded his arms. "The Earth is hungry. We must have what we came for, whatever the cost."

Kamanov shook his head. "This must be a very popular view, Comrade Thought Policeman, among your colleagues back on Earth who are at no personal risk of any kind."

"He's right," Lee Marna muttered, almost to herself. "What chance do we have? They're millions of years ahead of us."

Reille y Sanchez snorted. "It'll be more even than that, Lieutenant. Sure they've got a head start. If you believe this Thoggosh, of a few hundred million years." She slapped the scabbard on her hip. "But a man with a rifle can be killed with a knife, so I figure a thing with a deathray can be killed with a rifle. We aren't savages to be cowed by technology, no matter how much it looks like magic. From what the general says, I've got an idea they take a long view and their progress is slow. Soviet humanity's way behind, but we're capable of catching up!"

"Spoken as a true daughter of the Lone Star People's

63

Republic." Kamanov grinned. "And valid, provided we can steal enough of their magical technology, soon enough. For what it is worth, however, both sides always believe a fight will be more even than first appears to be the case."

"There's something in what she says." Gutierrez wrinkled his brow, suspended between a tactical need for truth and a political necessity to weigh his words. "I gathered that most of the Elders, including Mister Thoggosh and, no doubt, his fastidious assistant, have little stomach for war. In fact, they seem to abhor the prospect."

"War is bad for nautiloids," Kamanov misquoted a saying from the previous century, "and other living things."

"That seems to be the attitude. Also, it's bad for business."

"One would expect such a craven attitude," Empleado sneered, "from a—"

"Warmongering capitalist?" Kamanov supplied with his sweetest smile. Empleado glared back and clenched his fists. In the shadows, his men tensed.

Gutierrez ignored them both. "Worst of all, from their point of view, it may interfere with the all-important—"

Kamanov interrupted once again, "—albeit unstated—"

By now, Gutierrez was used to interruptions, "—necessity which brought Mister Thoggosh and his people here in the first place."

"I shall be in the minority, so let me be first," offered Kamanov, "to echo the opinion of Mister Thoggosh. Do you not realize, in its current pitiable condition, that the United World Soviet must learn to tolerate the Elders, if only for the sake of regaining what it lost by conquering the world?"

Around the fire there were actual gasps. "I warn you," Empleado snarled as his corporals took a step forward, "I tire of your sarcastic revisionism. You Russians are all alike, making a world united under scientific socialism sound like the worst thing that could have happened—what's that?"

They all heard it that time, dry leaves blown in a breeze. Yet there wasn't any breeze. The principal result, quite agreeable to Kamanov, was that the women on either side of him moved closer.

He went on. "It is certainly the worst thing that ever

happened to scientific socialism. Deny, Arthur, that no Marxist nation ever managed to survive without—let us be kind and say 'inputs'—from non-Marxists. Always they import innovations they cannot generate for themselves. Endless supplies of foodstuffs. Most important, price information essential to planning. Was this not why the Union of Soviet Socialist Republics was compelled so long to suffer—with a smile—the independent existence of the United non-Soviet States of America?"

"I'm KGB, you fool!" All four corporals were a step closer to the fire. Empleado was furious. "Stop this slanderous sedition, now!"

"On the contrary, Comrade Inquisitor, if it be sedition, let me make the most of it. We Russians are all alike? Yes: horrified at the way Americans became what they are, with scarcely a shot fired! 'Scientific socialism,' like Negro slavery before the cotton gin, was used up by expansionism, discredited by universal failure, convicted of a hundred million murders! Even Europe, with its penchant for preserving and parading every mistake ever made by the human race, had finally given up on this one! Those suffering its tender ministrations looked forward eagerly to its imminent demise!"

Dark-faced, Empleado opened his mouth, thought better of it, and closed it again. His hands appeared restless, as if he didn't know what to do with them. Suddenly, he exploded, leaping atop Kamanov, fingers around the older man's throat. With one arm restrained, the geologist seemed helpless. Before Gutierrez or any of the other men could move, the women acted, prying Empleado off and throwing him half across the fire, half into it. Amidst a shower of sparks he scrambled backward, clothes smoldering, and lay red-faced and panting, eyes filled with murderous hatred.

Demene Wise rushed forward to help his superior to his feet, brushing nervously at Empleado's jacket. A large, square-headed, broad-shouldered figure, cursed with jowls twenty years before his time, Wise's effeminate movements seemed even more grotesque in contrast to his solid stature. Growling, Empleado pushed him away. A more determined movement toward the geologist on the part of

Broward Hake, a short, compact man with a round, slick head, was stopped cold by Major Reille y Sanchez, with a shake of her head and a subtle gesture of her hand toward her holster.

"Go ahead, Arthur." Kamanov levered himself up. "Take your notebook from your pocket. Get it all down. I promise not to go too fast for you. America is a tail wagging the dog. It is regarded by onlookers everywhere as typical of your character that, once you Americans adopted Communism, you strove to become the biggest and best Communists of all. This, you may be interested to know, is referred to, everywhere but in America, as 'Texas Marxism.' "

"Pete—" Gutierrez began, then let it go.

Kamanov wheeled on him. "What has perhaps not occurred to Washington, Horatio, what they will not admit, will be uppermost in the minds of those in Moscow who have lived for generations with the shortcomings of an unworkable theory. Will they countenance throwing away this contact with a superior technology? And another likelihood which no one appears to have considered: people being what they are, wise and ancient to the contrary, it is inevitable that there are factions on the other side who will welcome this conflict."

"They'll see us as interlopers," Reille y Sanchez agreed, "or vermin, better off exterminated before we cause real trouble."

"More to the point," added Kamanov, "I suspect yet another motive behind Washington's sudden enthusiasm for the shedding of our blood."

"What's that?" asked Gutierrez, who'd been examining his own dark suspicions in this regard all day.

"How can your countrymen not fear that the Elders' antisocial, unconventional, but demonstrably practical social and economic ideas may contaminate an Earth just united—and still rather uncomfortably so—under a shared hegemony with mine? We all know what we are, do we not? What is our value to the United World Soviet? We are simply the most expendable individuals they could find. Would they not perhaps welcome a massacre here, whatever the outcome?"

Several of them shook their heads. Reille y Sanchez put

her face in her hands. With a resigned expression, the general pointed to the EAA Witness at her waist. "How many of those damned things," he asked her, "did we bring with us?" No response. "Major, I asked you a question!"

Reille y Sanchez started violently. "Twelve, sir, 'Pistol, 11.43x23mm Lenin, service, officers, for the use of'!" Now she looked up with something resembling a game grin. "Sorry, sir. Also an assortment of H&K 11mm signal flare launchers which might serve as incendiaries. Our main battery's a dozen semiauto carbines with bayonets in 7.62x39mm Russian. Commercial-issue Ruger Mini-30s, sir, old; none of that new trash from the nationalized plants. Same number of Remington twelve-gauge riot guns, also semiauto, also with bayonets, also very old. They might prove more effective in this jungle than the carbines. I wish they were Czech AKs, or at least selective fire."

"There it is again!" Empleado had calmed down enough to exchange sheepish expressions with Kamanov, who was prepared to write the whole performance off, his own as well as Empleado's, to whatever tensions had caused the earlier fights among the crew as well as Richardson's illness. But now the political officer's eyes widened. The geologist knew from previous conversations that Empleado was city born and bred, unaccustomed to normal noises in the countryside. The KGB man started to get up. "We'll get flashlights and see what the hell that is!"

"Let's finish this first, Art." Relief was audible in the general's voice that things were returning to as close to normal as they ever were. "Then you can hunt snipe to your heart's content." Gutierrez squinted at the major. "Do we need bayonets in the middle of the twenty-first century?"

"The general," she answered with diplomacy, "perhaps because he's Aerospace, sir, has less reason to be enthusiastic about bayonets than I do. I like bayonets. They're quiet and don't run out of ammo."

"Right," Sebastiano agreed, patting a pistol-shaped bulge under his suit which didn't appear on the major's list. "But I wish we had a dozen RPGs." Behind him, Ortiz was nodding agreement.

"I wish . . ." Gutierrez shook his head, not for the first

time wondering why the shuttles' meager capacity had been used sending hundreds of kilos of weapons, ammunition, and accessories to what was supposed to be an uninhabited worldlet. "I wish we'd picked another goddamned asteroid."

Around the fire, not one failed to nod, agreeing with the general. His son reached out to touch him, but was restrained by military discipline. Even Reille y Sanchez rubbed first the inner, then the outer corners of her eyes with thumb and forefinger; a seasoned Marine officer, Kamanov thought, attempting to deny the tears that many of her comrades also felt like shedding.

He climbed to his feet. "While some prepare for war, Horatio," he asked, "might not others see what can be done to salvage peace?"

The general turned to his friend. "What've you got in mind, Pete?"

"I have no orders," the geologist shook his head, "from Washington or Moscow. I will speak with Mister Thoggosh." He went to his second selling point before Gutierrez considered the first. "It could buy us time."

"We don't know these things," Reille y Sanchez asserted, nerves in her voice again. "They might take hostages!" She softened her voice, putting a hand on Kamanov's arm. "I know it sounds crazy, but listen, Piotr, please?"

"Some of us came prepared for contingencies." The Russian fumbled in his ship-suit pocket. "'Peace through superior firepower.' Or, if you prefer, chance favors the ready trigger finger."

The general's eyes widened. "What in the name of God is *that*?"

Holding a large-framed revolver in one hand, the geologist grinned. "Better to ask in the name of Harry Callahan, Horatio. This is a .44 magnum, certainly this world's most powerful handgun, and it could blow my hand right off—had I not practiced assiduously before we left. A Smith and Wesson model 629, stainless steel, its little barrel not quite eight centimeters—three imperialist inches—long. Highly pocketable, do you not think?"

Gutierrez scowled at what looked like a small piece of artillery to him. The short barrel was thick-walled, the weapon's front sight inset with orange plastic, the rear sight outlined in white. The handle was of wraparound neoprene, the overall finish a wirebrushed silver. Hollowpoints, also silvery and notch-toothed at their front edges, gleamed at him from the four visible cavernous chamber-mouths. Kamanov handed him the revolver. Low gravity or not, the gun's weight seemed immense.

"You'll shoot your eye out," he muttered, handing it back. "How in—Callahan's—name did you get that thing past security?"

Reille y Sanchez leaned forward, whether to hear his explanation, bearing on her efficiency, or to drool over his Smith & Wesson, the geologist couldn't tell. Her hair smelled nice, so he didn't care.

"Innocent Horatio," Kamanov smiled, "lovely Estrellita. A geologist's tools are among those items least susceptible to X-ray or metal detection. Besides, comrades, I am Russian. My people have lived with, and in spite of, 'security' for a century and a half. There is an old Georgian proverb— Soviet Georgian—'Do not annoy Babushka with instructions on extracting—' Rosalind! Vivian! How good to see you!" Kamanov spread his arms in delighted invitation, "Come sit by the fire and join the conversation!"

Heads turned as two figures took substance from the shadows, becoming Rosalind Nguyen and Vivian Richardson. The physician led the taller, heavier woman by the arm, murmuring occasional assurances which were audible, but not intelligible, to the others. The colonel walked in a gingerly manner, half leaning on Dr. Nguyen as if it were her legs which had been injured, rather than her mind. From time to time she stumbled, or hesitated over apparent obstructions which wouldn't have been noticed by anybody else.

As she and her doctor drew near the fire, a dazed, exhausted look could be seen on the Aerospace Force officer's face, as if she'd just been awakened—which, in fact, she had—from a deep, drugged sleep. Looking repeatedly to Dr. Nguyen, her expression was childlike in its reliance on the smaller woman and in its fear of the surrounding night.

Beaten to the social punch again, Gutierrez nodded

rather than echoing the geologist. Dr. Nguyen smiled at them both. "We're just taking a little walk. I'm not sure whether we're up to much, yet, in the way of conversation. What was that you started to say about annoying your grandmother?"

"'With instructions,'" the geologist finished, "'on extracting yolk from eggshell.'" He grinned. "I did not claim it was a sensible proverb."

"What a peculiar turn of phrase." Something slithered from the shadows under the *McCain*, fleshy, elongated, its surface glistening in the firelight. Toya and Marna yelped rather than screamed. Danny seized a burning branch from the fire, holding it aloft in the hand that wasn't wrapped around a pistol like the major's. In that instant, three other guns snapped level in one motion—Kamanov's revolver, the major's Witness, and a Glock 9mm Sebastiano had been concealing—muzzles locked on the object like quivering compass needles on a magnet. The four KGB men assumed similar postures a heartbeat later. A voice arose from the apparition, filtered and artificial in tone. "Good evening, humans. Set your primitive weapons aside. For the moment, I intend you no harm."

"What is this," Empleado demanded from behind the line of his underlings, "an evolved snake of some kind?"

Kamanov lowered his gun, trying to ignore the way his heart pounded, as if at any moment it would smash through his rib cage. He took several deep breaths. "No, Arthur, it is one of those separable tentacles Horatio told us about. I do not believe this one belongs to Mister Thoggosh."

"How perceptive, Doctor." The tentacle moved, sidewinderlike, between shuttle and fire. As it drew closer, its filmy covering became discernable. At its base, Kamanov also saw a flat three-by-fivish object between plastic and flesh, correctly guessing it to be a thin-film audio communicator. "Permit this extension of myself to introduce me. I am Semlohcolresh."

For once, Kamanov looked to someone else to take the lead. It was his friend Horatio's place, he thought, to receive guests.

"How do you do?" Gutierrez somehow overcame the

feeling of absurdity in addressing a disembodied append-
age. "I gather you know Dr. Kamanov, Col. Richardson,
Col. Sebastiano, Mr. Empleado, Major Ortiz, Mr. Jones,
Dr. Nguyen, Major Reille y Sanchez, Lieutenant Marna,
Lieutenant Gutierrez, Sergeant Pulaski, Corporals Alvarez,
Roo, Betal, Hake, and Wise, and myself. How can we help
you?"

The tentacle squirmed and twisted. "You'll excuse my
eavesdropping. You're correct about the existence of a
faction among us who hope for an excuse to employ violence against you."

Gutierrez and Kamanov glanced at one another. Almost
forgotten in the midst of the alien intrusion, and unnoticed
by everyone but her physician, Richardson had stiffened
all over, bone-breaking tension singing through her muscles.
Dr. Nguyen's shouted warning preceded the hideous noise
Richardson made by only a fraction of a second.

Shaking the little Vietnamese off as if she were an unwanted,
flimsy garment, the black woman shoved her aside, bowled
through the line of individuals confronting Semlohcolresh,
and snatched the weapon from Danny Gutierrez's hand.
Sebastiano dived to tackle her at the ankles, but with the
speed and agility of determined insanity, Richardson side-
stepped. He crashed into Danny, knocking him onto the
ground.

Richardson raised the Witness just as Gutierrez and
Kamanov shouted at her. She turned for a moment, a
betrayed, bewildered look on her face, unconsciously swinging the pistol's muzzle toward them. As they sprang aside,
with a different sort of shout, she swung the muzzle back
toward the disembodied appendage and pulled the trigger
twice. The double detonation shocked and deafened the
camp, dazzling vision with a yellow-orange ball of fire which
blossomed at the automatic's muzzle.

In that instant, a blue sizzling bolt of energy leaped from
the filmy covering of the limb, exploding halfway between
the tentacle and the woman, consuming both bullets before
they reached their target. Richardson's weapon bucked with
recoil. Two distinct metallic clinks marked the places on
the *McCain*'s hull where her spent brass struck before it
fell to the ground.

Screaming with frustrated rage, she leaped between two shuttles, pistol in hand, vanishing into the dark. Gutierrez pointed toward where his son and Sebastiano were occupied untangling themselves. "You two," he shouted, "after her! Arthur, your men, too!" All seven followed her between the craft and out into the night.

"Some among us," Semlohcolresh continued as if nothing had happened, "believe your species corrupt beyond salvage. I'd say that what we've just witnessed confirms it. I, too, regard your species' eradication as an act of mercy toward you and a positive benefit to the rest the universe.

"Thus it will be me, not my overly tolerant colleague Thoggosh, whom you'll have to convince, if there's to be peace between us."

NINE
Words of Iron

"Aha!"

Tucking the big revolver into the sling holding his injured arm, Kamanov spoke across the campfire to Gutierrez. "Horatio, this is an opportunity such as I had hoped for when I told you I wished to see about keeping the peace." He glanced about at the "circled" shuttles, grinning at a random thought. "Shall we not have a friendly powwow, Semlohcolresh?"

It seemed to Kamanov that the others around the fire were holding their breaths. With the nautiloid's harsh words ringing in his memory, Gutierrez raised his shoulders and dropped them. "Take your best shot, Pete. Just try and keep in mind who the Indians are, here."

"'We have met the Indians and they is us,'" the geologist winked at the general and laughed, "to paraphrase the philosopher. I shall remember, my friend, never fear." He turned. "Semlohcolresh, I accept you as a being of your word. Let us withdraw to a quiet place where you will allow me to try some of that convincing you mentioned."

In response, the tentacle made a sinister humping motion like an obscene gigantic inchworm, its remote alien voice crackling through the anxious stillness among the humans. "As you wish, Dr. Kamanov, although I warn you, I hold little hope that—"

"Then you will also allow me to do the hoping for both of us, at least for the time being." The geologist sprang to his feet, showing no sign of his earlier injury or weariness. "Where would you feel most comfortable conducting a long conversation?"

Gutierrez and the others couldn't hear whatever reply the entity made as the unlikely pair shuffled off across the leaf-strewn forest floor. They passed between two of the grounded spacecraft and into the mysterious surrounding jungle darkness. "We can converse as we convey ourselves, if you find that suitable, Dr. Kamanov. My personal quarters aren't far from here, and we'll continue the discussion we've begun, once you and this extension of myself have arrived."

"Indeed." The Russian followed the serpentine organ over a slight rise and through the trees. "Will I, too, be expected to immerse myself in—"

The tentacle halted on the trail. "On the contrary, Doctor, you'll not be put to such a thoughtless inconvenience in my house. For reasons of my own, having to do with my position relative to others of my kind, with whom I presently find myself in disagreement, it's my wish to convey, to everyone concerned, every impression of cordiality, hospitality, and a sincere willingness to negotiate with you humans."

Kamanov grunted understanding and their walk resumed. Dodging a low-hanging branch which tore at his sling, he raised his bushy eyebrows, a gesture lost in the darkness, even had his odd companion been prepared to understand it. "Every impression, you say?"

"Every truthful impression, I assure you, sir. Kindly do me the courtesy not to mistake the firmness of my opinion—regarding a proper and pragmatic course—for a pathological eagerness on my part to initiate or even witness the gratuitous slaughter of other sapients. The position I've taken was arrived at after much thoughtful reflection, and not without a measure of ethical and emotional discomfort."

"I see. You mean killing us will hurt you," Kamanov

chuckled; having no idea where they were headed, he was careful to keep an eye on the glistening surface of the tentacle's silvery plastic covering as the limb squirmed through the underbrush, "more than it hurts me or my cosapients."

"I mean that—excuse me, Doctor, here we are."

The artificial forest, never very heavy, had opened onto a broad, well-manicured, grassy surface. At the back of this clearing, a long, low, half-cylindrical structure lay, where yellowish light shone from small, round windows. Kamanov suspected the building was filled with liquid of some kind. A few pale white globe lamps, hanging from tree branches, shed their own soft light over a dark, ripple-surfaced pool.

"These are the grounds of my quarters," Semlohcolresh continued. "I'm resting at the moment at the bottom of the decorative body of salt water you see before us. I'm quite an old organism, Dr. Kamanov, older than you can imagine. I'm inclined to pamper myself, and have never much cared, in any event, for the artificial sensation of liquid fluorocarbon. Now I'll summon refreshment. There are chairs beside the water which I believe you'll find comfortable."

The tentacle gathered itself and plopped over the side, into the water. Kamanov lowered himself into one of the sturdy, yielding chairs at the pool-edge. Before he was fully aware of it, a creature of a variety he hadn't seen before— in the dim light he had a fleeting impression of many glittering compound eyes, a hard carapace, thin, coarse hair, and an uncounted number of spindly legs—had appeared at his elbow proffering an engraved metal tray holding a number of colorful bottles and a variety of empty drinking containers. The Russian chose a tall, transparent glass and something that looked and smelled like vodka.

He nodded at the creature. "Thank you, very much."

"*Your courtesy's appreciated, Doctor.*" Semlohcolresh's voice came, still filtered and distant, from a patch fastened to the creature's carapace. "*However, this is a bright and well-trained animal, not an intelligent being. The species is known scientifically as* Leru obilnaj."

Kamanov sipped his drink. It tasted like vodka, too, to

the extent vodka tasted like anything. Between where he
sat and the forest edge, he made out the pleasant twinkling of ordinary fireflies. "Your people are capable," he
asked, "of drawing that line?"

The fireflies winked out and disappeared. A deep,
bone-felt rumbling vibrated the chair Kamanov sat in and
the ground beneath his feet, agitating the surface of the
water. It was joined, first by a mechanical hissing, then by
a long series of gurgling splashes as the center of the pool
seemed to hump upward two meters and became a streaming dome of striped and colored calcium at the base of
which, facing Kamanov, lay two huge, luminous golden eyes,
set over a tangle of wet, thick, fleshy tentacles.

Kamanov felt belated sympathy for his friend Gutierrez,
as the first human on 5023 Eris to confront such a monster.
And the general had done it without any warning or preparation. Kamanov's earlier feeling of absurdity at the prospect
of addressing one of these creatures now turned to barely
controlled horror.

"Yours are not?" Semlohcolresh stretched a sinuous limb
across the shimmering surface of the pool to take a strangely
shaped glass from the leru's tray. The nautiloid spoke through
yet another thin-film communicator, this time fastened somewhere on himself. "Tell me, then, Dr. Kamanov, on what
foundation your science of ethics reposes? Take care, lest
you confirm my opinion of your kind."

In the distance, one by one, the fireflies seemed to
recover their courage and begin twinkling again. Sipping
his drink, trying to quiet a yammering subconscious and
recover his own courage, the geologist took his time replying. "If you have observed my species with the conscien-
tiousness you claim, Semlohcolresh, then you know perfectly
well that we have not as yet developed a science of ethics. This does not mean that we have, as you also claim,
corrupted ourselves beyond salvaging, so that our eradication represents an act of mercy. It indicates only that we
are a younger species than your own. Surely there must
have been a time, sir, however long ago, when your people
had developed no ethical science. Would your extermina-
tion, at the behest of an elder race, have constituted a
positive benefit to the rest of the universe?"

The Russian became aware of a metallic, chipping noise, as if someone were striking a cinderblock with the tines of a steel fork. After a moment, he understood that this was the sound of a nautiloid chuckling to itself. Almost at the same time, another noise distracted him. "Semlohcolresh, is there someone or something in the woods behind us?"

"Yes, Dr. Kamanov, there is. I believe it's your Col. Richardson, who appears to be peering at us from behind a tree. My instruments tell me that she's in a highly agitated state. And almost as well armed as yourself. Do you think she's dangerous?"

Kamanov shook his head, now free to shift the heavy revolver in his sling to a more comfortable position. He had an odd sensation, as if a pistol were being pointed at the back of his neck. "I do not know. Vivian has not been well. There are searchers looking for her. I trust that they will find her and take her back."

"So I see. I hope you're right. I'll continue to monitor her location and activity, in any event. Now, where was I? Ethics: you may be aware," his host informed him, "that we cannot cover our figurative ears to exclude undesirable and distracting conversation. That facet of our 'hearing' is electronic in character, and can, at times, be very sensitive. You'd entertain a different opinion of your own race, Dr. Kamanov, were you compelled, as we have been, to incorporate dense shielding molecules in our environmental canopy, to shut out the incessant, disgusting, wheedling—"

Kamanov raised a warning hand. "Sir, it would be foolish to judge the unique collection of heroic human beings—your guests on 5023 Eris—by the sniveling signals you receive from Earth, which is now embarrassed by its heroes, and has discarded them."

It was as if the giant mollusc hadn't heard him. "—of the puny territorial agglomerations of collective subsapient incompetence, and huddled cowardice which bluster and threaten those they fail to cajole, imagining themselves unanswerable powers in a universe they haven't even begun—"

"And more foolish still," Kamanov insisted, "to underestimate them."

A surprised-sounding Semlohcolresh choked himself off in the midst of his tirade. "Why do you say that?"

"Take my friend Horatio," the geologist replied, "most heroic of the lot. He appears no more than an aging bureaucrat. Yet, as celebrated leader of the infamous Redhawk Squadron at Kearnysville, Long Beach, and Fort Collins, in refutation of the fashionable view that airpower is inefficacious in quelling popular insurrection, he was responsible for crushing the remaining opposition to the ascendency of the ASSR. That he now questions the wisdom of his achievement, as I do, does not diminish its remarkability."

"If I take your meaning, you warn me that this general of yours is a more formidable opponent than you believe we estimate him to be." Semlohcolresh paused, resting on the water in thought or at a loss for words, the Russian wasn't certain which. "Dr. Kamanov, I find these inappropriate words for a self-styled man of peace."

"As a student of history, Semlohcolresh," the geologist sipped his drink, wondering how marine organisms like the nautiloids had invented distillation, "I am a man of peace who nevertheless understands that a visible willingness and ability to wage war can often preserve the peace. It was a wide lack of this understanding which gave Marxism—an inferior philosophy by every measure of such things—its victory over America, although the latter was superior by all of the same measures."

"Agreed," the nautiloid replied, "but willingness and ability at what cost, or rather, what practical limit can there be to such a cost?"

Kamanov shrugged. "The one limit that makes sense, Semlohcolresh, the willingness of individuals—as individuals—to pay the cost. It cannot be by group decision or coercion. I know, for I am also a social being who nevertheless understands that civilization depends upon the individual for its very existence, whereas the individual is capable of doing fairly well without civilization. And it was widespread lack of this understanding which doomed those few Americans who, even understanding the relationship between war and peace, misunderstood the relationship between the individual and civilization, coming to believe that defense of the latter required imitating Marxism's disregard for the former."

"By the Predecessors, a civilized analysis!" In the center of the pool, tentacles stirred, splashing their owner with water. For the first time, Kamanov noticed that the nautiloid wasn't wearing any sort of protective covering, but was content simply to keep himself moist in the cool evening air. "And the result?"

"What any rational observer would expect. Taxed to a subsistence level, where no real hope for individual advancement was possible, bound hand and foot by ten million laws rendering any difference between their culture and its opposition academic, when the time came, no one was left in America who had anything to gain by defending it."

"This might," the nautiloid offered, "have been foreseen."

Kamanov shook his head, beginning to feel weary again. "I am sure some did foresee it. Perhaps I flatter myself, Semlohcolresh, that, for the rest of us, it represents wisdom won the hard way, never soon to be forgotten. Even so, it is rare wisdom, for my conclusions are not much shared, even today. A species may be young or old. It may have learned little of the universe or much, and, to be certain, its individual members may share in that knowledge and benefit by it, or not. Yet I have an idea that, at some fundamental level, individual beings stay much the same over millions of years. Tell me, if you will, how long did it take your people to discover these things for themselves?"

"Such persistence." In the pool, the creature seemed to heave a sigh. "Despite contrary expectations, you begin to interest me after all, Doctor."

Kamanov sat up, voice sharp. "It was never any part of my intention, Semlohcolresh, to amuse you! Nor to defend my species, like a lawyer, against your blanket accusations, for that would acknowledge a right, to which you have merely arrogated yourself, to judge them!" Startled by Kamanov's tone, the serving animal shrieked and ran off toward the dwelling.

With an abrupt, angry gesture, Kamanov set his half-finished glass on the pool surround and arose, turning on a heel to face the human encampment. As if struck by a final thought, he paused. "I am disappointed, Semlohcolresh! It was my understanding that you nautiloids were rugged individualists! Scheming capitalists! This was the basis for my conviction that we could bargain with one another! Believe me, on such a splendid evening, I would far rather be with a female of my own species."

Semlohcolresh lifted one of his long, spatulate tentacles into the air, his voice as emotional as electronics allowed. "Wait, Doctor! There may be justice in what you say, I confess it, do you hear me? At least insofar as your present understanding of us permits. Do please sit down."

Kamanov heard the same slithery whisper as when Semlohcolresh had reached across the pool for a drink. He felt a feathery tentacle touch on his shoulder. Still facing away from the pool, he allowed himself a small, self-satisfied grin before he turned back, exhibiting great reluctance, and sat again. He had the feeling once more that a gun was being pointed at him. "Tell me, is Col. Richardson still back there in the trees?"

"Not unless she's well shielded by minerals or vegetation. It's possible, my instruments are limited in range and penetration. But she appears to have left us. Your searchers are also gone."

"Very well." Kamanov tried to disregard that eerie feeling, with only partial success. "Enlighten me, then, O Elder. Answer the question I have asked you three times. Wisdom cannot grow in a vacuum. A species which has learned as much as yours must have a great deal of mayhem and bloodshed somewhere in its background. How long did it take you to arrive at an idea of ethics which would not insult the word 'science'?"

Relieved, the nautiloid lowered his long arm, summoned the leru back, and accepted another drink. "And if I were to say that it took us a million years, would that make you feel precocious? It took, in fact, even more time than that before the ideas you've just expressed came to be universally agreed upon, although their origins may be discovered among what remains of our earliest faltering attempts at civilization."

"So you, too," the human nodded, "are a student of history."

"Yes. And, as I'm certain you've discovered for yourself, Dr. Kamanov, the great tragedy of sapient history, one of them anyway, is that ethical innovations, unlike technical ones, take rather a long time to make their value apparent to their potential recipients."

"Nor," Kamanov agreed, "is progress along those lines ever assured, the way it often seems with technology. People will speak, without thinking, of the swings of a pendulum, but more often it seems like a dance consisting of one step forward and two steps back."

"A great pity, too," Semlohcolresh told him in an absent, musing tone. "I suspect, Dr. Kamanov, that the respective histories of our species might have turned out rather different had it been the other way around."

Kamanov threw back his shaggy head and laughed, slapping the arm of his chair with his good hand, frightening the leru again, and almost upsetting his half-finished drink. "So your civilization, too, my friend, has skeletons in its ethical closet! This was my point from the beginning, if you will recall." He leaned forward and peered into the luminous golden disks floating in the center of the pool. "Now, old mollusc, at last I believe we have a basis for understanding one another!"

"Dr. Kamanov," the nautiloid said, "you are indeed a dangerous being."

TEN
Sarajevo, Mon Amour

Against her better judgment, Reille y Sanchez kept a hand on the multicolored line drawing her toward the pulley attached to a branch overhead. It was that or fall a hundred meters. Yet common sense told her that her fingers would be shredded in seconds unless she let go. The only thing that kept them wrapped around the line, braided from strands of a dozen different colors, was her experience that common sense didn't count for much on 5023 Eris.

Bright-winged life fluted and rustled amid the litter of dew-damp leaves into which she rose. No other sapience (she entertained doubts about her own, hanging like a spider on someone else's thread) was in sight. Among its other notable events, last night had brought an invitation—and accompanying map—from Mister Thoggosh to visit a power plant turning garbage into energy, the appendage sent by the merchant-explorer had explained, on the principle by which quasars burned so fiercely in the extragalactic depths. She had no credentials for representing the humans as a technician, but was keeping the appointment as a tactician, with the idea of future seizure or destruction of the plant, which might even the odds should it come, as Washington intended, to open conflict.

She gasped; at the last moment the line writhed in her fingers, half of it unbraiding, passing over the pulley, while the other half remained in her hand below the rim. At the infirmary level where Piotr had spent his brief recuperation, she'd found what resembled ski tows, although she didn't know it. She had never engaged in a sport limited to the *nomenklatura*—the upper class of her supposedly classless society—and to special mountain troops. Her instructions had included the color combination to look for. She'd seized a line, been yanked aloft, and carried a kilometer before arriving at the high point of her journey, the pulley she now passed beneath.

Past the pulley, the line somehow reintegrated and she felt the descent begin. Nearer the surface, it carried her in a new direction and deposited her within walking distance of the plant. For reasons she couldn't explain—she'd never been afraid of heights—she already dreaded the return. Her watch said she'd arrived early. Taking her time along a forest path, she kicked through dead leaves like a child on her reluctant way to school, marveling at how quickly this once cold, airless rock circling so far from the sun had come to resemble, in its weird way, the wild reaches of her own planet.

If, she thought—then stopped thinking, certain what the object was, the moment she saw it. That didn't keep her from stepping closer, kneeling, clearing off the debris that failed to hide it. Under a bush, half-buried in dead vegetation, lay the equally dead body of Piotr Kamanov.

She sat on her haunches pondering items she must attend to in correct order. Alone, her first problem was that she mustn't leave the body to the next random idiot who stumbled over it, perhaps without her reasons for leaving it as it was. She needed, however, to inform Gutierrez and summon the doctor, what was her name?

Standing, she saw the building where she was to meet Aelbraugh Pritsch, a quonset-like structure in a clearing, surrounded by large bins, actually input chutes for raw materials. She wondered what he'd do when she didn't show up.

Glancing about, she also wondered how much damage a bullet would do the canopy keeping the asteroid covered with its blanket of air. She couldn't see all the way to the artificial sky anyway, couldn't risk killing some intelligence up there among the branches. Instead she chose a nearby tree—super kudzu, Piotr had called it— drew her Witness, aimed at the massive trunk, fired three quick shots, three spaced apart, and three more quick ones. Absently pleased that the slugs had all struck within a handspan at sixty meters, she swapped the partial magazine for a full one and bent to retrieve spent cases where they'd arced, glittering, into the brush. It took an effort to stop, thinking that such tidiness hardly mattered, and another to start over when the realization hit her, once again, that this murder would begin the fight which had dominated conversation since yesterday. They'd need to conserve brass.

"Major, what's— Oh, my!"

She whirled at a familiar voice. "Mr. Pritsch, you've got to go to the camp! Ask the general and the doctor to come. I can't, somebody's got to stay with—understand?"

"Aelbraugh Pritsch, Major, the whole name, together. This is beyond belief." The creature looked at her a long while before speaking again, his voice strained and thoughtful. "I believe I do understand. You can't trust me with the body. I expect you're wondering this very minute whether your message will ever arrive at what you call the camp."

Although she shook her head in polite denial, she'd wondered exactly that. Many of her fellow humans would blame his people for this. Suspecting the nonhumans might be inclined to preventive countermeasures, she intended to stay here, holding her weapon. "Just get my boss, please. I'll never ask you for another favor as long as I live."

The feathered biped nodded, stepped around her, and vanished down the trail the way she'd just come. She rubbed a hand over her face, ran the same hand through her auburn hair, took a breath, and sat. Her watch said it was half an hour—although it felt much longer—when Gutierrez and Dr. Nguyen arrived, with Pulaski. The sergeant took a look and disappeared into the undergrowth, retching. The major and the general stood by in a silent state of delayed shock. The doctor, kneeling, made the traditional arcane gestures. At last she stood, pronouncing the geologist officially dead.

"A blow to the head, I presume to subdue him, then he was strangled. As you can see, neither the person who did it is immediately apparent, nor whatever weapons were used by him or her."

"Or it," the general muttered between clenched teeth, fighting an urge to imitate Pulaski. Knowing him, the major guessed the only thing keeping him in control was the terrible anger she could read on his face. "Did he have any warning," he asked Dr. Nguyen, "any chance to defend himself?"

She sawed Kamanov's S&W revolver from his jacket pocket, catching its rear sight and the knurling of its hammer in the fabric. She handed it to him. "Six unfired .44 magnum caliber cartridges in the cylinder." From the opposite pocket, she pulled the tiny Kahr K9 autopistol with its long KGB suppressor, taken from Richardson. It, too, was fully loaded. "That's as far as my forensic expertise extends, I'm afraid." She looked around to see that they weren't overheard. "Something else: peculiar marks on the throat."

Looking where the doctor pointed, the major saw a row of indentations resembling the tracks left by a hermit crab in beach sand. Pulaski, having just returned, seemed fit enough to volunteer an opinion. "They look like marks," she offered, "from the tentacle of a squid or octopus."

"Let us hope you're mistaken." Aelbraugh Pritsch, having fetched the general and the doctor, had hurried off on another errand. He returned now with four sea-scorpions, sounding horrified. Even the expressionless lobster beings were agitated. "It would appear you're not. May forces of randomness aid us, those are markings which the tentacles of an Elder leave behind!"

Gutierrez looked at the avian as he spoke. "I was afraid you'd say that. Rosalind, this is his bailiwick. Back home, we'd have an inquest, but it's up to him to say what happens next. You and Toya go along and represent us, whatever turns out to be customary."

Aelbraugh Pritsch blinked affirmation. "Sir, your cooperation's greatly appreciated. Each of us understands that our situation, already tense, has taken a sudden turn for the worse."

"Thanks to unwanted interference from Washington." Gutierrez ignored Pulaski's scandalized gasp. The doctor's mouth was a grim line. Reille y Sanchez remained silent, curious to see what the general had in mind.

"How very generous of you, sir," the creature replied. "Shall we say, then, that a truce, however momentary and uneasy, still holds between beings who, sadly enough, were formerly just hosts and guests?"

"Gracious hosts and grateful guests," Gutierrez insisted. "Yes, Aelbraugh Pritsch, tell your employer it does, until we find out who did this to my friend. After that, well, I suppose that'll depend."

"Yes." The avian gave him a nod which almost amounted to a bow, then, an afterthought, extended a slim hand. "I suppose so." The humans watched him direct his guard in the use of what could only be recording equipment, small antenna-covered devices scanning the area around the body and pathways leading away in both directions. Afterward, the aliens helped Nguyen and Pulaski carry the remains back to the infirmary at ground level for examination by both sides. In this gravity, it constituted a burden only in a moral sense.

When the departing company was lost among the trees, Gutierrez turned to the major. "It must seem pretty grotesque to Aelbraugh Pritsch. I tell you, Estrellita, from a military viewpoint, to the poor asshole obeying them in the field, our orders are grotesque. Generous, he called me, for acknowledging the truth! The generosity of the helpless, the opposite of noblesse oblige!"

"Sir?" She wasn't sure whether he was talking to her or to himself, using her presence as an excuse. It was a difficulty of her trade. She didn't know how to respond, whether to stand at attention or slouched with her hands—which she never knew what to do with anyway—in her pockets.

"You still don't get it, do you? He doesn't want our blood on his hands! He's grateful I'm trying to prevent it!

Forty-two lunatics issuing orders to their numerical and technological superiors, our only weapons a comical collection of obsolete pistols, rifles, and shotguns. *Bayonets!* You saw what happened when Vivian shot at Semlohcolresh. What are their professionals like?" Staring at the .44 magnum as if he'd never seen it before, he shoved it in his suit at the waist. He unscrewed the suppressor and tucked the Kahr 9mm in his jacket pocket, thrust his hands in his pants pockets, and began shambling up the trail.

The major followed, a light breeze blowing the faint scent of magnolias toward them. In her mind, she reviewed their meager inventory. This, at least, was something she could deal with. "The ammo situation's even worse, sir. We brought no more than a token, a few dozen rounds per gun."

"Even that was sent," he told her, "against my better judgment."

The ground became uneven, her reply had to wait until they threaded their way down a miniature ravine. "We'll just let the enemy supply us, sir."

Eyes on his footing, he shook his head. "We can't afford an enemy, Estrellita. Few of our personnel—scientists, engineers—have the training or temperament for war. I'm nothing but a retired pilot myself. Being kicked upstairs isn't the same as a promotion for merit. Against us is an unknown force of unknown size, undetermined capability, and enormous versatility. We might be seeing them at their worst, roughing it, with what they consider only the bare necessities."

She agreed with his facts, but this wasn't the attitude she'd expected. The astonished Marine fought a humiliating urge to tears. Stumbling, she began to mutter at the rough going until she realized again that perhaps only weeks ago, this had been a cold, airless crater-scarred waste. "I hadn't considered the possibility, sir, I don't know what to say."

He stopped to smile. "I never know what not to say. Between us we might've made one decent officer. One thing I know, we must believe the evidence of our eyes. The Elders possess more numerous and potent weapons than we do, and they're armed to the mandibles all the time."

He resumed walking. She was surprised and hurried to catch up, almost turning her ankle where the ground dropped away. "Another aspect, sir, if you'll permit an observation from one of our professionals."

He didn't look up. "And what might that be, Major?"

"Sir, we're speaking of personal weapons."

"And you think they have something even nastier in reserve?"

"That isn't it, sir. They're like Sikhs or Moros, accustomed to handling their own weapons on an everyday basis, as familiar with them as we are with—I don't know what. That's worse news than any number or power—"

The general nodded. "We can't all be like you, Major, and with all due respect, maybe it's just as well. Peace is balanced on a knife edge. Before this is over, you'll see it tilted this way and that, from one instant to the next, by all kinds of conflicting forces and differing—"

"I thought it was just us and the—"

"More deadly, I think, than our dispute with the Elders, are frictions between, let's say, ideologues and pragmatists on both sides. I don't imply there's a reason to prefer one or the other; ideology's an ugly word because one in particular gave a bad name to the rest. It's just that it won't be fun to deal with while we're trying to find out what happened to Pete."

They reached the point where the tow line had dropped her and went past, still headed toward the camp. The general wanted to walk. It was a pleasant day for it, if they could have avoided thinking about current events. "I meant to ask, sir, how will we find out what happened?"

He stopped to lean against something like a birch tree. "I'd say it was Arthur's job, but he wasn't sent here as a detective, and I doubt he has any talent for it, being no more than a glorified . . ."

She swallowed. "Hall monitor, sir?"

Pushing away from the tree, he grinned. "You said it, Major, not me. 'Of the dead—and the KGB—speak nothing but good.' How brave a quarter of a billion miles makes us." He stopped again and turned. "Look, you're in military charge of this mission, I'm in overall command, sheriff and mayor, respectively. Whatever they decide back home about who does the investigating—you realize we'll have to ask?—it won't hurt if the two of us talk it over."

She smiled back. "I'm game, sir." This was more like it. Maybe he'd just been shocked with grief, forced to struggle the past half hour to refocus his reasoning power. "How do we begin?"

"By thinking out loud," he replied, resuming his former pace. "First we review a list of our shipmates, whom we must now regard as suspects."

"Yes, sir." This time she was ready and kept up without difficulty. For a man beyond his prime, she thought, his breath short from desk jobs and a little fat from a lifetime of flying, he made good time in the woods. She was a little out of breath, herself. "Also the nautiloids and their allies."

"We'll get to them. Given the effect this is likely to have, our best bet's someone who agrees with Washington and wants to provoke a fight. In no special order, consider Rosalind Nguyen, whose only known allegiance—known to me, that is—is to her patients. I've studied her dossier, so have you: personal background tragic, but far from unique; granddaughter of southeast Asian 'boat people' who fled halfway around the world to escape the rising tide, only to discover that their place of refuge . . . well, you know."

Without answering, she pushed a branch aside, ducked under another. The path had all but disappeared.

"Given official attitudes toward such refugees," he continued, "if she has a talent besides medicine, it's for survival. As a doctor, she can be presumed to oppose Washington's policy here, but keeps her opinion to herself, a talent I never had much luck cultivating. Her real position's unknown."

"Probably unknowable, sir."

They stepped over a stream, no more than a trickle centimeters wide, leaving heel marks in the soft ground. "Who next? Well, Toya's the descendant of refugees, too. Her ancestors were escaping Cossacks."

"I like Toya, sir," the major offered, "she's an overgrown Girl Scout. Any loyalties she has are to the ASSR. Deep down, I think she loves learning for its own sake. She'll never love anything more tangible."

"Like a man?" Following the stream, they arrived at a tiny cataract, stood watching the water, and went on. "Pretty rough for somebody you like. Can't say I disagree. From various inarticulate grunts—that's what we're reduced to—I'd guess she'd rather study the Elders than fight them."

"Yes, sir." She sneezed, then sneezed again violently. They'd wandered into a streamside grove of giant ferns. Spores drifting from the undersides of the broad fronds dusted their uniforms. "Sorry, sir."

They pushed through the plants and took a moment to slap at their clothing. "Bless you, Estrellita, are you all right?"

"Of course I am, sir, what were you saying?"

"I was saying, again, 'Of the dead—and the KGB—speak nothing but good.' But we can't allow that to limit us. It's with friend Arthur that we begin getting to the really interesting suspects. Hell, he might have killed Pete last night in front of all of us, if you and Marna hadn't pulled him off."

"Tension, sir." Reille y Sanchez shrugged. "That's what Piotr thought. Art's like anyone who belongs to the KGB." She wasn't sure why she dared such honesty with a superior. "Willingly, I mean. Not very deep inside, he's a power junkie, and likes the idea of going head-to-head with the Elders. It represents a good gamble, an obvious path to power."

"Promotions come most quickly in wartime," Gutierrez suggested, "and in the terms you state, power can be seized most easily. Hmmm. I never thought of Arthur as that sincere and open a fellow. I do remember his fingers around Pete's throat, however, and I'm putting him at the top of the list, along with those four flunkies of his. Any one of those mutants might have done it at Art's order while he was somewhere else, providing himself with an alibi. What do you make of Vivian?"

The general didn't know that she'd had to pull Hake off Pulaski early in the trip, adding to the difficulty of an already difficult situation, and making Toya her friend for life. She wasn't sure she wanted a friend for life. At the time, Empleado had expressed the opinion that she should have let his corporal have the girl. It wouldn't have done her lasting damage, he'd maintained. On the contrary, it might have made a woman out of a wallflower. It certainly would have prevented certain frictions created by the black eye the major had inflicted on Hake and his consequent loss of face. Demene Wise, by contrast, apparently couldn't get it up for anything female, and Delbert Roo, she was certain, couldn't get it up for anything human, whereas Roger Betal simply couldn't get it up. But Gutierrez had asked about Richardson.

The major inhaled. "On the assumption that her illness is fake? I wondered about that, myself. She's a good suspect, sir, loyal to the ASSR and covertly, but not very covertly—well, I just hope it's the *American* branch of the KGB."

He laughed. "You're a cynic, Estrellita! I was proud of myself for spotting her as Art's understudy, but the international wrinkle hadn't occurred to me."

"It's my job, sir. She'd like to fight for the same reasons Arthur does. In addition, she's black, and she's a woman."

"Too deep for me, Estrellita," Gutierrez replied. "What's being black and female have to do with it? I'm at a loss—"

"Beg pardon, sir, but you aren't in a position, if I may speak freely—"

"Major, that's what we're here for. We're not going to figure this out if we hold anything back."

"It's just that—" she colored from discomfiture "—socialism's been a bit relaxed about the equality it promised for women and minorities. I've heard it said— Piotr said it was originally a Russian saying—that socialist equality means women are perfectly free to do a man's job as long as they hurry home to cook dinner."

He laughed. "So, if anything, she'd be more volatile than Art. She could be our killer, even if she's genuinely flipped out."

"You can bet," she agreed, "it enters into the picture."

"I'll take your word. Okay, next suspect. How about me?"

ELEVEN
Fangs and Claws

"You, sir, a suspect?"

"Or you. How would either of us stack up to anyone who doesn't know our minds from the inside? What would I say is my primary loyalty? The Aerospace Force? My family? How would they deal with it when I answered that each takes precedence over the other depending on the circumstances? It's illogical, but it's true."

They were startled by a droning overhead. Three meters above them, on two pairs of half-meter transparent wings, hovered a dragonfly straight out of Reille y Sanchez's childhood dinosaur books.

What would I say, he thought, is my view of the little war I'm about to fight? As a career soldier, I'd say I'm used to obeying orders. By the same indications Pulaski manifests, those around me know that I also think that deliberately making enemies of the Elders is about the dumbest order I've ever been given. As long as I do my duty, am I responsible for their inferences? Of course I am, this is the ASSR, isn't it?

Lost in reflection, they walked in silence for a few heartbeats, Gutierrez scrambling for what must surely be firmer ground than his own muddy thoughts. "I guess you look forward to a fight, Major, the same way a dog looks forward to dog food. Then again, I'd probably be safe guessing that with any Marine, from the lowliest boot to the commanding general herself."

Estrellita grinned, yet seemed to remain dedicated to the socialist ideal (one she fell short of only a little less often than he did) of taking orders and keeping her mouth shut.

"Okay, if you don't like that direction, we'll pick someone else. Say, that life-support technician at the fire last night. You do realize that somewhere along the line, we're going to have to compile a sort of criminal dossier on every one of the members of this expedition?"

"Yes, sir." She was obviously relieved at the change of subject. "We need to supplement the, er, uninformative records we have."

He nodded. "There are lots of them I don't know nearly as well as some we've already considered. Right now, to my professional embarrassment, I can't seem to remember anything significant about Lieutenant Marna. I know I must have examined her records."

"Otherwise," Reille y Sanchez agreed, "she wouldn't have been approved for the mission. Lieutenant Marna, sir, Life Support. You can't remember everything. Going by the evidence of last night, she doesn't want to fight, although that could always be a pose. Isn't it peculiar, sir, that an unwillingness to fight for the ASSR constitutes reasonable doubt where murder's concerned? All traitors are innocent. But unless we find reason to place her higher on the list, her real thoughts are likely to remain unknown."

What Reille y Sanchez hadn't said, he reflected grimly, was that this was true of everyone here. Anyone who'd lived all of his life under Marxism. They'd become a civilization of accomplished liars. "That reminds me, Estrellita, your job, as you say: what do you think are the chances the KGB sent us another operative, somebody less conspicuous than Vivian?"

"Triple redundancy, sir?"

"Quadruple," he told her wearily. "You've made me realize the Russians must have someone here, as well."

"Maybe we should rethink this whole thing, sir. After all, there's an excellent likelihood the killer's someone other than a member of our expedition."

"Yes, God help us, I think that's altogether the best likelihood. It also represents a prolonged nightmare to any human investigator. Set aside the political and military complications which are enough, by themselves, to do us all in. The Elders, if Mister Thoggosh is to be believed—"

"I think he should, sir, insofar as it's practical."

"So do I—their culture's very ancient and complex. It's lasted half a billion years, a hundred thousand times longer than the Pyramids. At the gut level, I can't get a handle on a number like that, let alone half a billion. And we haven't even scratched the surface. Between us, we can't agree about their companion-species, whether the lobsters, or Aelbraugh Pritsch, are partners, conscripts, retainers, draft animals, slaves, pets . . ."

"I see what you mean, sir. And there are only three entities we know anything about: Aelbraugh Pritsch, Mister Thoggosh, now this Semlohcolresh."

He nodded. "You've got the picture. And all we know about them is what they've volunteered. If Mister Thoggosh can be believed—"

"Excuse me, sir, I hate to contradict myself, but if there's a chance Mister Thoggosh is the murderer, why should we believe him?"

"A point well taken. His interests lie unabashedly with himself, his investors and employees, and with this mysterious search of his. In general I'd say that wherever what he tells us doesn't buy him anything, we'll grant him credibility. We have to start somewhere."

"Which logically implies," Reille y Sanchez mused, "that he informed you truthfully, that he opposes the whole idea of any destructive—"

"Say, rather, 'unprofitable.' "

"Very well, any unprofitable conflict."

"Between you and me," he told her, "I always wondered, and mostly kept it to myself, why capitalists get characterized as warmongers." She turned, her expression curious, fearful. "Back home," he answered her unspoken thoughts, "I'd be treading on thin ice, if this were any ordinary situation. It isn't, and we're not back home. We have to understand the Elders if we're to survive here, let alone find out who killed Pete. Between making money and war, the choice is clear and mutually exclusive. It's more profitable to sell things to people than to kill them, and those occupied with the former are usually too busy to bother with the latter."

"My God, sir, where did you ever hear a thing like that? You've got to be more careful—what if I were Arthur?"

"Oh, I remember reading it somewhere," he grinned, "and instantly agreeing with it. Probably in one of the old comic books I collected as a kid, illegal as hell, but like cockroaches, they were everywhere."

"But think, sir! Capitalism and war go together like—"

"Bicycles and windshield wipers? Oh, doubtless some people make money at the start of every war, selling things to governments on both sides. But there couldn't be any war without governments. And whatever short-term profit you make comes at a risk of seeing your business controlled or seized by one of those governments, and with an even chance of winding up on the wrong side and losing everything."

Now the warm breeze carried a homelier odor than magnolia blossoms in their direction, one he recognized as sage and sunshine, mountain wildflowers and cattle. They emerged from the trees into a yellow meadow, broken at intervals by the huge trunks of the canopy, walking around it to avoid several large, somehow prehistoric-looking mammals grazing there.

"Major, believe me, I'm not engaging in heresy for its own sake, here. It's just that Semlohcolresh contradicted Mister Thoggosh, implying that certain unspecified tenets of enlightened nautiloid self-interest make killing humans morally imperative."

She shook her head, frightened, yet fascinated by his reasoning. "If Semlohcolresh is the murderer—"

"About the best guess anybody's made so far."

"I agree, sir. Then why should we believe anything he tells us?"

"There it is in a nutshell. Both Elders say they value profit and self-interest above all. One claims that this precludes war, while the other claims it demands it. Yet Semlohcolresh has no sensible motive for murder unless he's the one telling the truth! It occurs to me the easiest approach might be to learn more about this nautiloid philosophy. I've never been sure whether a people's character shapes their beliefs, or their beliefs shape their character—"

"Or both."

"Or neither. At the moment, I can think of arguments for either case—that's the trouble with intellectualism—and until now, I haven't really cared. With the limited goal of exposing a murderer, it might not matter: either might provide us the clue we need to unravel this mess. On the other hand—or would it be the other tentacle?—if the Elders are really after something religious here, all bets are off."

"I'm not sure I follow you, sir."

"Estrellita, religious motivation, even that of my own wife, has always been a mystery to me, more unfathomable and profound than anything we've encountered here. The one thing I like about Marxism was its original attitude toward religion."

" 'Was,' sir?"

"Just another politician's pose. I've done more serious reading than illicit comics, and Pete was right. Marxism had run its course at the end of the last century. Organized religion, too. Both twitched with death-throes which the West mistook for vitality. An alliance was the only way to prolong their precarious existence, and both pursued it with the ardor of young lovers whose families had been feuding for generations."

Reentering the jungle at the opposite edge of the meadow brought them into territory which Gutierrez thought he was beginning to recognize. They must be nearing the shuttles and the human encampment. It had been a much longer walk than he expected.

"Well, their bastard offspring," he continued, "so-called 'liberation theology,' spelled doom for the West. Or, as Pete suggested, maybe for the whole world. So much for Marx and religion. I understand my own culture, but what'll I do with a totally alien set of religious motivations? My official education left a lot to be desired, Estrellita. I'm afraid my only hope lies in even more illegal literature— the murder mysteries I used to read, waiting on alert with my squadron."

"And what do they tell you, sir?"

"Well, sometimes they held that the truth could best be determined by considering the character, not of the murderer, but of the victim. Pete was a charming and urbane gentleman whom everybody liked. Despite his age he was a ladies' man and, in his last hours, our self-appointed peace negotiator. It struck me the first moment I knew that he was dead that he was the last person on this expedition who deserved to die. Still, experience tells me that this is the way with murder. And maybe with death in general."

"You're thinking of your eldest son, sir?"

"But I'm not talking about him. First and foremost, Pete was moved by an innocent and limitless curiosity. I don't think he ever wanted anything more sinister or more demanding of anyone than simply to be permitted to learn everything he could about, well, these new beings we've discovered here, for example. Aside from that, he was something of a cynic in his own cheerful way. I was never sure he had any loyalty to anything, except the old-fashioned concept of individual autonomy, and his notion, at least, of decency. That's why he opposed the idea of conflict on this asteroid so bitterly and was never afraid to say so."

Hearing an odd noise, Gutierrez turned to Reille y Sanchez, placing both his hands on her shoulders. "What is this, Estrellita, tears?"

"It's nothing, sir. I'll be all right in a minute."

He shook his head with sympathy and surprise. "Shed some for me while you're at it. I wish I could afford them, myself."

Embarrassed, the major searched through her pockets, failing to find whatever she was looking for. Gutierrez produced a fold of tissues which she accepted, dabbing at her eyes and finally giving in and blowing her nose. "I'm sorry, sir, I . . . it isn't very—"

"Macho? Look, Estrellita, I loved Pete Kamanov like a brother. I'll miss him more than I ever missed my own brothers. He was the only completely happy individual I ever knew, and a good man to have around, just to remind you that happiness like that is possible. If it's the last thing I do, I'm going to find the son of a bitch who killed him, whatever species or gender it turns out to be, and make him pay for it."

Reille y Sanchez nodded agreement. Gutierrez thought he saw the white flank of a shuttlecraft among the trees. Very near home base now, they were beginning to hear familiar, human-sounding noises—although they were still too far away to make out individual voices—and smell the smoldering ghost of last night's campfire.

"And now it occurs to me," the general told her, "that Pete's character might be the key in a different way. I always talked too much about the wrong things, and felt guilty about my lack of caution. Well, maybe we should forget caution altogether. Maybe we should adopt, at least for the duration, the same unflinching scientific attitude he always displayed toward the bitter truth, whatever it turned out to be. Even if it doesn't prove to be of any practical use, it somehow strikes me as the only fitting monument to him. What do you say?"

The major took a deep breath, straightening her shoulders. "The bitter truth, whatever it turns out to be."

He grinned, restraining himself from kissing her or giving her a manly punch on the shoulder. Either would have served.

"Okay, the only sensible motive for Pete's murder was to provoke trouble between us and the nautiloids."

She stuffed the tissues into a jacket pocket. "The problem with the general's analysis, if you'll pardon me for saying so, sir, is that it fails to narrow the field."

He laughed. "You're right. Probably plenty of fools on both sides would like to start trouble." He paused a moment in thought. "You know, I remember once seeing pictures of a sperm whale covered with battle-scars like those on Pete's throat. It looked like the surface of the Moon. On the whale, the craters had been produced by suction organs, tooth-edged, I think, on the undersides of the tentacles of some very large squid. According to Aelbraugh Pritsch, the equivalent nautiloid organs are vestigial, the way fangs and claws are with us, although, as I noticed during my visit with Mister Thoggosh, they're far from altogether absent."

"Yes, sir?"

"Pete had a good idea about something else." He pulled the revolver from his pocket and gazed at it before continuing. "In nature, animals with plenty of spines and stingers never bother you if you leave them alone. We humans are too evolved for spines and stingers, and much too civilized to carry personal weapons even if the authorities permitted it. Now the same authority wants us to drive the Elders off this asteroid—do or die—and our friend Semlohcolresh thinks he has to wipe us out before we try. I lose my boy when we nuke South Africa to save it, and someone strangles Pete before he can make peace. It's funny, Estrellita, the more atrophied and ineffectual our natural defenses get, and the weaker we become as individuals, the blood thirstier we all seem to be as a collective."

Before the major could reply, they broke through the trees and were only a few meters from the *Hatch*, *Dole*, and *McCain*, sitting in their wire cradles. The camp had spread beyond the triangular circle of the shuttles. Several individuals were cutting and stacking wood, an incongruous task to be performing, the general thought, in their silver-gray ship-suits. A guitar-harmonica duet was being played somewhere out of sight. Sebastiano, Ortiz, and several of their crew members sat on the ground with their legs folded like cinematic Indians. Heavyset and naked to the waist, Corporal Owen, the machinist, seemed to be washing his underwear in a large plastic tub.

Closer to where their commander and the Marine major had emerged from the vegetation, Empleado and his four assorted assistants appeared to be waiting. The general had always privately thought that Delbert Roo was the one to keep a wary eye on. Little and wiry, the half Chinese, half Australian leprechaun seemed to have an almost magical talent for hurting things. Dr. Nguyen and Pulaski had returned to the camp and were standing with another figure, not a member of the expedition, not even human, but nevertheless no stranger to any of them.

"General Gutierrez! Major Reille y Sanchez!" Aelbraugh

Pritsch had been waiting for them impatiently. "I'm afraid I've the most distressing information to convey to you!"

The music halted without even a crash. Sebastiano and his group stopped talking and arose, almost as a man. As they approached, Gutierrez noticed that each and every one seemed to have drawn a weapon, probably on the colonel's authorization, from the expedition armory. In addition to his own unauthorized side arm, which he now wore openly in a holster, Sebastiano carried one of the heavy Remington riot guns, as did Ortiz.

The general sighed. "You're just in time, Aelbraugh Pritsch. I've been experiencing such a shortage of distressing information lately. What is it now?"

The avian's feathers rustled, and he fluttered nervous hands. The little reptile he seemed to carry with him all the time was nowhere in sight, which Gutierrez interpreted as a bad sign.

"Well, General, you see, as you might expect, the Elders have developed a reasonably advanced science of criminal forensics."

"That makes sense," offered Reille y Sanchez, "considering that they've had half a billion years to do it."

"What?" Aelbraugh Pritsch blinked, his pupils changing size, a sign of fear, Gutierrez knew, in many birds. "Oh, yes, Major, I see what you mean. In any event, as I gather you humans are able do with fingerprints, we've methods of identifying the specific individual who left . . . well, who made the marks on Dr. Kamanov's body."

The general tensed. "And?"

"And on behalf of Mister Thoggosh, and with considerable trepidation on my own part, I don't mind telling you, I've come to report the results of the postmortem examination to you humans. Dr. Nguyen and Sergeant Pulaski were there as witnesses, and—"

"And the apparent murderer," Sebastiano interrupted impatiently, "was Semlohcolresh, that Elder who, more than any of the others, favored war between our species. Now tell General Gutierrez the rest of it, Aelbraugh Pritsch, and get it over with."

"I, er, that is, as the Proprietor's assistant, as spokesbeing for the Elders and their associated species,

I confess shamefacedly and deeply regret that I've also to report, and with even more trepidation, I might add, that our colleague—"

"Semlohcolresh," the lieutenant colonel interrupted again, unconsciously fingering the safety of his semiautomatic shotgun, "seems to be conveniently among the missing!"

TWELVE
Ampersand and Asterisk

"Well, Juan, this is interesting."

Lethal hardware was everywhere. Gutierrez was more than a little annoyed that weapons had been issued to so many. The major could tell by the set of his lips as Sebastiano, to whom it was also obvious, stepped forward, indicating that what he wanted to say wasn't intended for everybody.

"In the general's absence," the *Hatch*'s captain whispered, "I thought it wise to give Big Bird, here, some protection." His eyebrows indicated the KGB nearby. "Considering the traditional fate, sir, of the bearer of bad news?"

Gutierrez gave him a grudging nod. The avian hadn't heard what passed between them. He was attempting to explain himself to an angry crowd. " . . . sincere belief that Semlohcolresh may have been the victim of foul play."

A dozen voices dropped to a sneer, an eerie effect Reille y Sanchez thought. Empleado left his underlings and approached Gutierrez. "General, must we waste time listening to this? Does this thing actually expect us to accept excuses for not handing a murderer over?"

"Art," replied the general, "I want you to—"

"Twenny ferns," Broward Hake interrupted in an accent which, with the rise of the ASSR, had fallen out of fashion in his native Texas, "says this Semlohcolresh

102

slimed his way back t'someplace where real people never evolved!"

The avian's hands fluttered like independent organisms. "General, help me! No matter how I explain the situation, your people won't understand!"

"Understand—just a minute." Hake had opened his mouth again, but Gutierrez spoke before he got a word out. "Arthur, listen up!"

Empleado's head snapped toward Gutierrez. "General?"

"Tell your Neanderthals if I'm interrupted again, it isn't going to help that they belong to the KGB. Do I make myself clear, Art?"

Empleado gulped and looked resentful. "Yes, General."

"Now, Aelbraugh Pritsch, you wanted us to understand something?"

"Yes, sir, I do. Regrettably, I can't explain a pivotal scientific fact when those I wish to explain it to lack the background to comprehend it."

"This," Gutierrez asked, "is leading somewhere?"

"General, it isn't our custom to keep secrets we can't profit by. Your technical education, that of your people, was to begin with the major's visit to our power plant. Mister Thoggosh even intended to show you the dimensional translation machinery which brought us to 5023 Eris."

"Intentions," he shook his head, "are the only thing cheaper than talk."

"Splendid! Is that original, sir, or is it—" replied the bird-being. "Never mind, to the point: in the absence of sufficient technical education, how can you appreciate the extreme difficulty, the overwhelming danger—"

"Not to mention the expense?"

"—the hideous expense interdimensional travel represents? I can't get your people to understand. Perhaps they won't understand. No one crosses world-lines casually or secretly."

"Why not?" Roger Betal had an accent, too, similar to Hake's, although he and the major had a nation of ancestral origin in common. She'd learned to keep track of what the man did, rather than what he said. He could be agreeable, say anything to win a friend or avoid a fight, but when she'd made the mistake of accepting his invitation to a movie near the base where they'd been training, she'd seen him beat a vagrant half to death because the poor man had touched his uniform with dirty hands. Afterward, he'd relied on his credentials to avoid formal charges. Gutierrez gave him a glare, but left it at that, probably because he was curious about the answer.

"Because too much energy is expended. There are manifestations. It would be like taking off from Cape Canaveral without being seen or heard."

"To the extent any of us believes you, Aelbraugh Pritsch," Empleado sneered, "you've just managed to make things worse!"

The avian turned to focus his amber eyes on the KGB man. "I'm afraid that I fail to understand *your* meaning, this time, sir."

"Yes, Arthur," echoed the general, "meaning what?"

"That these beasts," Empleado's face was red and his fists were clenched, "are conspiring! If Semlohcolresh didn't escape this asteroid to avoid the consequences of his crime, then his fellow creatures must be helping him to remain in hiding!"

"He's holed up," Hake seconded the motion, "and the rest are covering up!" Muttering, especially from Empleado's other three hirelings, agreed.

The major watched as the exasperated avian changed tactics. "General, I appeal to you." He spread his hands. "Whatever the truth, whoever killed Dr. Kamanov, don't you see that these events will plunge your entire Solar System, and all of us along with it, into war? I'm sure everybody, on every side, realizes one and only one thing can prevent such a catastrophe."

"Discovering," Gutierrez agreed, "whoever killed Pete Kamanov."

"Guilty or not," a cynical Sebastiano hissed under his breath, "as long as it's soon." Assenting noises were heard from others.

"Precisely," the avian replied, the major hoped to the general rather than the colonel. "Justice must be arrived at in a manner satisfactory to all."

"No small matter in itself," Gutierrez observed.

"The more reason both sides," the avian turned to plead

with all the humans, "must cooperate in trying to achieve it."

"This is bullshit!" Demene Wise complained. "Chicken shit!" amended Delbert Roo. "Parrot shit!" Wise tossed back. Nasty laughter from the other thugs wasn't shared this time by most of the humans.

"Look at him!" Reille y Sanchez startled herself by shouting. She strode forward, pointing a finger at Aelbraugh Pritsch. "Don't you morons understand that what you're hearing in his voice isn't fear for himself?"

"Estrellita," Gutierrez tried to interrupt, "what are you—"

"Sir, I've been thinking over what you said, about their not wanting our blood on their hands." Gutierrez gestured for her to go on. She turned to the stirring of voices around them. "'The same principle that powers quasars!' Have you thought about that? That nautiloid stopped two bullets before they reached their target, 11.43x23mm Lenin, traveling just over the speed of sound! They could wipe us off this rock at any second! Instead, the idea seems to upset them more than if their *own* lives were on the line!"

In the silence following her outburst, Gutierrez seized the initiative. "Okay," he told the avian, "I may regret it, but I'm assuming you're on the up and up." Breaking precedent himself, the usually loquacious being nodded and Gutierrez went on. "If you're handling this mess for your— the nautiloids, somebody'll have to take charge of it for us. I'm an obvious candidate, or Art, but it'll have to be confirmed by higher authority before we start." He turned. "Juan, I want Washington on the line five minutes ago."

"Aye, aye, Commodore!" Grinning, Sebastiano jogged toward the flagship. "One long-distance call, coming up!"

"General?" It was Rosalind Nguyen, carrying a small beaker of dark brown liquid. "May I speak with you a moment?"

Twenty minutes later, having seen Aelbraugh Pritsch off and attended to a few matters around camp, Gutierrez followed Sebastiano aboard the *Dole*, squeezing through the hatch, and climbed up to the rear of the command deck. He settled the phones over his ears, bending the slender microphone pipette until it was in place before his lips.

"Ampersand, this is Asterisk on Scramble Six. We've got a situation here, over."

Nearby, Reille y Sanchez was reminded of the lonely distance separating them from home. It would take over seventeen minutes for his words to reach Earth—where the duty tech at Canaveral would have to summon a responsible officer, probably in Washington, adding to the delay— and another seventeen to receive a reply. Gutierrez would like to spell their "situation" out this first time, she thought, but ASSR security measures forbade it. Unable to think of anything that could be done in the intervening time, they waited, Empleado fidgeting beside her. It was seventy-seven minutes later, by her watch, when a voice like crackling cellophane filtered into the general's phones and, at the same time, through a speaker on the panel.

"Asterisk, this is Ampersand. Scramble Six negatively secure. Go Scramble Nine or end transmission, over."

Surprised murmurs swept the deck. Gutierrez shook his head, a gesture of frustration lost over an audio link of over three hundred million kilometers. "Ampersand, Asterisk. Scramble Nine is no good, either, repeat, negatively good. Our, er, hosts can unscramble anything we can scramble, over." The general turned to those around him, giving them an ironic grin. "Three ways to do anything." He didn't need to finish the old army joke, they knew he meant the right way, the wrong way, and the government way. Experience indicated that there wasn't much difference between the latter two. "Would somebody like to make some real coffee while we wait?"

The suggestion was greeted with enthusiasm. Sometime during the long walk the general and the major had taken, Mister Thoggosh had sent a generous supply of roasted whole beans to the camp. His people apparently had the habit, too. Corporal Owen had cobbled up a drip device using laboratory filters and discarded food containers, but, wary of foreign substances, not to mention a murder already committed, Sebastiano had made everyone wait for Dr. Nguyen's analysis and Gutierrez's subsequent permission before brewing any.

This time the voice of Earth was impatient and peremptory. *"Asterisk, this is Ampersand. It isn't your 'hosts' we're*

*concerned with. Leaders of the United World Soviet, here
in the ASSR and in the USSR, have been kept up to date on
your mission and are conferring around the clock. Go
Scramble Nine immediately. Give us a telemetry update on
the sideband while you're at it, over."*

On the command deck, the aggregate eyebrow level was
raised a meter by the brief message. Beside the general,
Sebastiano, a set of phones pressed to one ear, made adjustments and examined readouts. He glanced for confirmation
at a tech standing in an identical posture on the side away
from his boss, then back at the general, lifting a circled
thumb and forefinger.

"Ampersand," Gutierrez told his mike, "this is Asterisk.
Roger telemetry on sideband at—" Sebastiano scribbled a
figure on a pad velcroed to the panel. "—128 to 1. Going
Scramble Nine as ordered in four seconds on my mark.
Mark, one, two, three. Ampersand, this is Asterisk on
Scramble Nine, do you still copy, over?"

"Around the clock?" Empleado's eyebrows were highest of all, making up in an odd way for his baldness. It
would be thirty-four minutes before they heard from Earth
again. Almost two hours wasted, the major thought, on
conversation which had so far been worth less than two
minutes. "Presumably our leaders differ on what Marxist
conduct demands in this instance."

Gutierrez turned from the console. "You bet your ass
they differ! Can't you see it, Congress and Politburo,
President and Premier, dithering themselves to death, while
the real negotiation—"

Empleado interrupted. "General, I—"

"Stow it, Art." He shot a glance at Reille y Sanchez. She
was reminded of their bargain: the truth, no matter what.
"Everyone knows about the Banker, Arthur. Why pretend it's
a deep, dark secret? It's what Pete said, we Americans, in
the Russian view, haven't lived with Marxism long enough.
Moscow—the Banker, his people—are bound to be more
'realistic and flexible' than Washington, especially when matters of ideology conflict with common sense. Moscow wants
peace with the Elders, to get their technology, no matter what."

"General, I—"

"Art, you're repeating yourself. Can I have another cup

of coffee? Thanks, Major. You know, Pete once told me that to his people, Marxism's like the old man who lived with a family for years in an overcrowded apartment in Leningrad. He was filthy, smelled bad, his personal habits would've disgusted Rasputin. No one in the family liked him much, but no one had the courage to tell him to get out. Finally, the wife confronted her husband, saying that he must tell his uncle to leave.

"'*My* uncle?' the husband replied, 'I thought he was *your* uncle!'"

"Sir, I was going to say—" Empleado paused as if expecting another interruption, seeming almost disappointed when it didn't happen. "—in the interest of survival, that our leaders, whose expedition this is supposed to be, may decide they can do without the advice of the world capital."

Gutierrez nodded. It was a surprising analysis, thought the major, considering the source. Like many Americans, she was aware that, for some time, Washington had only been paying lip service to Moscow.

"And now it's time," Sebastiano said, reminding her of Kamanov's remark about Texas Marxism, "to show the world who's the biggest and best Marxist power?"

Half an hour went by. "*Asterisk, this is Ampersand.*" A different voice, someone with more authority, or the shifts had changed at the Cape. "*We copy you five by five on Scramble Nine, voice and telemetry. Now why the hell are you breaking radio silence? It better be good, over.*"

"Hasn't it been good for you?" Gutierrez fought annoyance the one way he knew. "Strike that, Ampersand. We've had a series of, ah, events, here. We've lost Col. Richardson." He cleared his throat. "Not dead, repeat, negatively dead, just . . . misplaced. She collapsed on landing and had to be sedated. Under therapy, she went berserk and escaped with a gun after trying unsuccessfully, repeat, unsuccessfully, to kill one of the Elders. We have parties out. Negative results so far." He gave his next words careful thought. "That's the short subject. Our feature presentation is that Dr. Kamanov, our geologist, appears to have been strangled to death by one of the nautiloids, an individual named Semlohcolresh, now negatively present, over."

Finding one of the jump seats behind the control seats,

Reille y Sanchez dozed off, thinking that this kind of communication always gave her a feeling of not knowing what to do with herself once the last few words had been said. She could see that the general felt that way. Somewhere among such thoughts she lost track of time and was awakened, with sore back and stiffened muscles, by the radio.

"*Asterisk, this is Ampersand,*" came yet another faceless voice. "*For this you broke radio silence? What the fuck do you mean, negatively present? We don't understand why you broke fucking radio silence! Kamanov was nonessential personnel. Demand that the killer be turned over to you and execute it, SOP, over.*"

"Ampersand, it isn't that easy—I mean, this is Asterisk. You idiots invented this lingo." Struggling with anger again, Gutierrez took deep breaths to prevent the words he wanted to say from escaping. He'd noticed before that the higher somebody's authority, the worse language he used on his subordinates. "Semlohcolresh, the apparent killer, repeat, apparent, subsequently disappeared and is negatively available. His people swear they don't know where he is. They suggest that he, too, may be a victim of some kind of violence, over."

This time, rather than fall asleep and wake up with a useless body, the major decided to spend the lag time walking around the camp.

"Cancer stick?" Danny Gutierrez grinned, a slim cylinder between his lips. The trailing wisp had an unmistakable, welcome aroma. Somewhere, somehow, someone had scrounged some cigarettes, maybe the same way as the coffee. Yet she remembered what the general had said: as far as Mister Thoggosh knew, humans from her Earth were the only sapients anywhere, anywhen, dumb enough to have invented smoking.

She took one—for her part, she didn't know a Marine, anywhere, anywhen, who wouldn't—South African, as it turned out, Kendalls, when it was offered with the wrist-flick she'd never seen any non-American imitate successfully. Something sparked in the boy's hand, an emergency fire-lighter from one of the shuttle kits, knurled carbide thumb-wheel in a brass fixture which held what was called flint and a short length of fluffy cotton cord. It had been screwed onto an aluminum reservoir from arctic survival lip-gloss. Corporal Owen's handiwork. Reille y Sanchez bent over the tiny flame and drew smoke into her lungs.

"Thanks, Lieutenant." She exhaled. "Coffee and cigarettes. My life is complete. Feels like rain. How can that be?"

The air was warm, damp and as close as if they were indoors. In a way, they were. The yellow sky, of course, was artificial and never seemed to change. She found it getting on her nerves. Where she came from, sky that color meant tornadoes.

The lieutenant blinked, puppy-bashful in a more normal manner than Pulaski's habitual shyness, the supply of small talk which protected him from good-looking female officers who outranked him used up. "Dr. Kamanov said it's a matter of volume. There are buildings on Earth where it rains. Before he—he expected it to happen before this."

In that instant they heard a noise they might have described as a *ping*, if it hadn't been loud enough to deafen. Their attention, focused on the sky, was seized by the appearance, not quite overhead, more in the direction of the power plant, of a violet pinpoint bright enough to throw faint shadows on the grayish flank of the shuttle beside them.

"What the fu—sorry, Major!" Reille y Sanchez grinned despite a brief, dizzy feeling, as if her heart fluttered or a tremor lifted the ground under her feet. Of course that might well have been the nicotine.

The violet spot began pulsing, suddenly throwing off a ring of brilliant blue. At the fifth pulse, another ring swelled outward, emerald green, and at the tenth, another, yellow-gold, contrasting with the indifferent mustard of the sky it was projected on. Each ring was broader than the preceding one, with no space visible between them. Fascinated by the display, Reille y Sanchez had lost count of the pulses, although each was accompanied by the fluttery sensation which made it difficult to breathe. An orange ring took its place outside the others. It was hard to judge its size. She estimated it was nine or ten times the diameter of the moon as seen from Earth. It was joined by a ring of ruby red, its far edge hidden by the serried jungle horizon.

In the beginning, the rings pulsed together. Now they began to slip out of phase until, like a multicylindered engine, the sense of vibration spread evenly from moment to moment into a disturbing, low-throated growl. Reille y Sanchez felt her ears ringing. She was forced to concentrate to get her breath. The look on Danny's face, a softened version of the general's, was a mixture of fear and curiosity, probably identical to her own.

Without warning, another *ping* reverberated through the air. In a rush from the center, the rings suddenly reversed colors, violet outermost, shrank inward, and vanished. Before the major could decide what color of residual dazzle had imprinted itself on her retina, a blinding flash of lightning eradicated it. An ordinary peal of thunder followed. Rain began to fall as if directed downward at them through a fire hose. They ducked beneath the wing of the *Dole* to watch their fellow travelers, as enthralled as they had been at the aerial display, scrambling for cover.

"So that's what weather-making machinery's like." Danny, his earlier shyness forgotten, thrust thumb and forefinger into a breast pocket, extracting the pack of Kendalls. "Very impressive. Another cigarette, Major?"

She let him light it for her, and stood beside him, breathing smoke and watching the rain. When she returned to the flagship's command deck, it was in time to see the elder Gutierrez shaken out of sleep the same way she'd been. He'd slept through the spectacular beginning of the storm, but was alert the moment a voice issued from the radio.

"*Asterisk, this is Ampersand. This is a fucking stall and you ought to know it, Gutierrez—Ampersand—I mean Asterisk! Why haven't you ordered those vermin off the asteroid? Why haven't you ordered them to produce the killer? What's wrong with you, anyway, Asterisk? Over.*"

Rubbing an arm, the general lumbered to the mike, not bothering with the headphones. "Ampersand, this is Asterisk. I tried to explain last time. You didn't listen. These beings are five hundred million years ahead of us. They vaporize bullets and generate power with something so far beyond

fusion I don't know how to ask what it is, let alone how it
works. I'm in no position to order anybody to do anything.
We're outgunned and living on favors. I'm looking into the
murder, cooperating with what passes for authority here. I
called, SOP as you say, to see who you want to head the
investigation. We have an official of the American KGB—
no, I can't remember his damned code name—also any
unofficial 'representative' you may have aboard. Major
Estrellita Reille y Sanchez, in charge of military security,
might be a logical choice, considering the circumstances,
over."

Surprised and pleased to have been mentioned, the
major watched Gutierrez during the next endless lag, preparing himself for a counterblast. Instead, what they heard
was: "Stand by, Asterisk, over."

"Ampersand," the general keyed his mike, "this is
Asterisk, over." The hiss of empty airwaves filled head-
phones and speakers. "Ampersand," he insisted, "this is
Asterisk, do you copy, over?"

"Asterisk, this is Ampersand." Gutierrez jumped as the
reply coincided with his futile attempt to elicit it. "Negative your recommen—Jorge, what the fuck did you say the
code name was? I dunno, how the fuck can I remember
what you never told me, I'm just the fucking messenger
boy! Well, fuck you and your pet iguana! Strike that, Asterisk. Orders from Washington, highest priority: the political officer's passed over without prejudice."

This, thought Reille y Sanchez, despite the fact that
Empleado, at least until this afternoon, wholeheartedly supported ASSR policy. She wondered if it meant Washington knew something about him she didn't. She also
wondered how it might have gone if the number two KGB
officer hadn't lost her mind. Maybe Washington itself wasn't
sure, judging by what came next.

"For purposes of investigation, you'll place in charge
Major Estrellita Reille y Sanchez, field appointment to full
colonel, effective immediately, Russian KGB. Do you copy,
Asterisk? Never mind, don't answer that, maintain radio
silence. This is Ampersand, over and out."

THIRTEEN
Agent of Exultation

Rain roared on the overhead windows aft of the flagship's flight deck, reminding Reille y Sanchez of the semitropical monsoons which had often interrupted training in north Florida. There, it had been possible to stand in the sunshine and see a wall of falling water coming toward you. Here, amplified by the drumlike structure of the shuttle, it was more like being in a war zone during a firefight.

She tried to keep her mind on the ramifications of her new assignment. Although it wasn't her responsibility—doubly, now that she'd been conscripted into the KGB—her first thought was for the hardware and electronics in the cargo bay. Designed for vacuum, incredible temperatures, and lots of Gs, it had never been intended to get wet.

The doors were lined with superconducting solar collectors, the only new technology aboard. They lay open as they did in space, epoxy graphite clamshells in two sections which had once given this vehicle-type the nickname "Polish Bomber." The largest such structures ever fabricated for flight, they were controlled from a console near the aft windows. Closed, they were secured with thirty-two

113

latches which had proven no more reliable on the outward journey than anything else they were equipped with.

Others were thinking, as well. She joined what turned into a rush, clambering down the "primary interdeck access" to the middeck with Betal, Empleado, and the general, shouldering out through the crew hatch. The crews of the other shuttles had the same idea. Those within the containers jostled through the tiny airlocks into the bays. Shivering almost immediately, her ship-suit soaked, her thick auburn hair limp and streaming into her eyes, she emerged to climb another, cruder ladder of lashed branches onto the rain-slick starboard wing of the *Dole*. Her clothing already seemed impossibly heavy with the weight of absorbed water. Danny Gutierrez and Broward Hake were behind her, looking bedraggled.

Meters away, small figures struggled over the equally slippery airliner-sized hulls of the *McCain* and *Hatch*, heedless, in the light gravity, of the danger of falling or that they stood on "No Step" areas. Reille y Sanchez made out the drenched forms of Lee Marna and Rosalind Nguyen: thumb-sized drops struck, hundreds to the meter, atomizing themselves into a knee-deep coarse mist through which the lieutenant and the physician seemed to be wading.

The idea was to help the eighty-year-old motors close the doors and fasten the recalcitrant latches. Reille y Sanchez brushed a hand across her eyes, noticing how the ends of her fingers were wrinkled and pale. As she labored beside Owen, Pulaski (less fragile than she appeared), and other comrades, her holster slapping on her thigh through wet trousers, she abruptly remembered that her Spetznaz training had carried with it the reserve status of a KGB officer. At the time, she'd regarded it as purely ceremonial, and had never taken it seriously. Now she knew better as she tried to catch a breath from an atmosphere that seemed solid with rain.

From this perspective, it was suddenly absurd that she'd wondered whether Richardson served Washington or the Banker (why did they call him that?) and his Moscow cutthroats. Like most people, Reille y Sanchez detested *all* KGB, American or Russian. Now she feared that, having worked for them even in an emergency like this, she might not be allowed to quit. What was perhaps worse, certain ugly inferences—and uglier nicknames than Polish Bomber—seemed appropriate when a woman carried KGB credentials. She'd always been proud that her Marine rank and responsibilities had never had anything to do, as far as she knew, with her gender.

With Owen and Pulaski, she'd climbed to the flight-deck roof, standing over windows she'd been standing under earlier. A dozen people, including Gutierrez and his son, Delbert Roo and Demene Wise, had taken up positions along the wing root, working with a few brave souls perched atop the passenger insert. Across the camp, she saw Sebastiano bossing the same job from the roof of the *Hatch*. Aboard the *Dole*, those along the wing lifted. She felt rather than heard the whining of the elderly motors. The door rose with a series of jerks, a torrent sluicing down the curved photovoltaics, into the bay.

Those on the container seized the door, careful where they placed their hands, supporting it as it descended. Unsure whether she was helping, Reille y Sanchez held the front edge, as others at the tail fin, Empleado and Betal among them, held the rear. Someone shouted something, but she couldn't hear. Deafened by rain on the door, she tried to ignore the goosebumps covering her everywhere, tried not to ask herself what had caused them, dirty weather or dirtier politics. Her breath was visible when she exhaled.

The starboard door was down at last. Grinning at Pulaski and the machinist, she imitated them as she slid her feet carefully to the port side of the roof and prepared to be of what assistance she could. Thinking back to the EVA which had gotten her here, she realized the one good thing you could say about space was that it was dry.

Gutierrez had never really asked where she stood on the issues. He'd assumed she'd do her duty, possibly be one of the most vocal in favor of Washington's war. Scattered among the land mines in that assumption were reasons to feel complimented, she supposed. But she recognized other, dangerous possibilities inherent in her perceived bias and conflict of—

Someone shouted again—Sebastiano, pointing at the

sky—and at the same time she realized they'd managed to
shut the second door. From inside the bay, she could hear
somebody hammering at the stubborn latches. Reille y
Sanchez stepped back, nearly losing her footing as she
stumbled into Pulaski, who staggered against Corporal
Owen, who fell from the roof, almost floating in the asteroidal gravity to land with a disgusting splash in the mud.
He stood, wiping himself off with the edge of a broad
hand—the rain was doing a better job of it—laughing.

Meanwhile, Reille y Sanchez looked in the direction
Sebastiano had pointed, straining to hear, above the bumble
and splatter of the rain, the keening of one of the electric aircraft that had brought many of them here. The
encampment was about to have a visitor, and she was
curious to see how a species five hundred million years old
avoided getting wet in weather like this. As it materialized
from the mist and began settling toward the streaming,
muddy ground, she could see some object projecting from
the blue metallic doughnut-shape which hadn't been in
evidence when she'd ridden a machine exactly like it from
the cradle of plasticized mesh down to the infirmary.
Aelbraugh Pritsch appeared to be holding a bright yellow,
exceedingly large, and otherwise ordinary umbrella, attempting to keep not only his own feathers dry, but the forms
of two other occupants, one of whom might not have appreciated the gesture.

It was a nautiloid, not just a tentacular extension. From
the avian's bearing, Reille y Sanchez guessed that it was
Mister Thoggosh in the flesh—and massive coiled shell—
glistening within a covering of silvery-transparent plastic.
The general's description, vivid as it had been, failed to
convey how big and colorful the giant mollusc was. The
grooved, candy-striped dome of his shell bulged
shoulder-high from the open compartment of the vehicle,
and several tentacles, draped casually over the side, perhaps to allow more room for his fellow passengers, touched
ground before the undersurface of the machine.

The third rider was human, unfamiliar at this distance
in the rain. She hadn't been aware that anyone was missing from the camp. As the machine squelched into the
circle formed by the shuttles, a section of one side tucked

itself away. Protected and concealed by the umbrella, the bipeds clambered from the vehicle, leaving the nautiloid. To her astonishment, Reille y Sanchez watched a large, white, shaggy dog jump from the machine to follow those beneath the umbrella, although it made no effort to stay out of the rain.

Creeping along the sealed door, she slid off onto the starboard wing, found the makeshift ladder at the same moment as the general and the political officer, and soon stood with them beneath the fuselage, up to her ankles in mud, waiting for those beneath the umbrella. Aelbraugh Pritsch folded the contrivance. Standing beside the bird-being was a young man she'd never seen before, certainly not on the journey to 5023 Eris.

"General Gutierrez, Mr. Empleado," Aelbraugh Pritsch intoned, "Colonel Reille y Sanchez, late of the ASSR Marines. I congratulate you on your promotion, Colonel, and present my friend and associate, Eichra Oren."

Somehow, by a miracle of transportation or simple determination, Mister Thoggosh had extricated himself from the aircraft without help and joined them under the wing of the shuttle. Behind him, between the two vehicles, his heavy shell had left a deep groove in the mud, rapidly being eradicated by the rain. Introductions started again to include the Proprietor, with whom Reille y Sanchez managed to shake appendages without flinching. The strange man smiled and put out a hand. When it got to her, she unconsciously counted the fingers—the usual five—before taking it.

"Colonel, I'm pleased to meet you." For some reason he wore nylon running shoes, an obnoxious red-and-green Hawaiian shirt, and a pair of faded Levis. Of average height, well-muscled but a little thin, he was blond, tanned, and blue-eyed. His voice, deep and mellow, wasn't that of the kid surfer from a long-gone era he resembled. He had that inward look of a combat veteran on temporary leave. In one hand he carried a leather case a meter long, half again as wide as her hand, five centimeters thick. "This," he indicated the dog, "is Sam. Sam, Col. Reille y Sanchez."

The dog barked, its own voice deeper and more powerful than she'd expected. For a moment she was afraid the animal would try to shake itself dry in the shelter beneath the wing—not that it would have made much difference to her uniform—or jump up and put its paws on her. Instead it sat, mud and all, and raised its right paw to her.

"I'm pleased," she took the paw, delighted, "to meet you, Sam."

"Glad to hear it, Colonel," Sam replied. "You're very beautiful, if a bit wet. May I call you Estrellita?"

In the stunned silence that followed, the Proprietor's assistant, unaware of the shock the humans were coping with, went on. "As a *p'Nan* debt assessor of great reputation, exercising his talents on behalf of the Proprietor, Eichra Oren will be your opposite number, Col. Reille y Sanchez."

"I see," she lied.

The avian paused, listening to something. Sam and Eichra Oren turned their heads to look at Mister Thoggosh. "The Proprietor, unable to communicate owing to his lack of requisite organs, asks me to explain that this means Eichra Oren will act as our investigator into the mystery of Dr. Kamanov's unfortunate demise."

"Lieutenant," Gutierrez picked his son out of the crowd gathering around them, "go inboard and patch one of the ATUs into the middeck intercom for Mister Thoggosh. That's a portable transceiver," he explained, "over which he can broadcast to the audio system. You might inform him that Eichra Oren's sudden appearance on 5023 Eris represents something of a mystery in itself."

"As well it might," the avian replied, "if you're unaware of the significance of this storm and the display preceding it. I believe I said earlier that interdimensional travel, by means of which Eichra Oren has just arrived, occurs with rather spectacular side effects. And by the way, the Proprietor can hear you perfectly well."

"That's right." The general nodded, addressing Mister Thoggosh. "You did say your hearing was good, didn't you?"

"Indeed," the Proprietor's voice came from several sources, relayed through the unit plugged in by the younger Gutierrez, "I'm surprised that you remember, General, considering all you've been through. Aelbraugh Pritsch, having presented Eichra Oren, we'll retire and leave our old friends to become acquainted with our new friends. Eichra Oren, Sam, confer with me at your convenience, if you will."

The nautiloid began to turn his ponderous shell and point himself back toward the aircraft, with Aelbraugh Pritsch behind him.

"Just a minute!" Empleado squeezed between Reille y Sanchez and the general. "You've only managed to make things worse—again!"

The mollusc paused, causing his assistant to stumble into him. "You're speaking to me, sir?" Aelbraugh Pritsch replied. "I'm afraid I don't know what you're talking about. Perhaps by well-meaning inadvertence—"

"I'm not speaking to Tweetybird." Empleado's tone was nasty. "Or to this ventriloquist and his trained mutt! If this Oren's as human as he looks, he won't be doing any investigating for anybody. It's my duty to claim him by virtue of the fact that he's a civilian. Otherwise, he belongs to the general and Maj—Colonel Reille y Sanchez. I don't know where he came from, but he's a citizen of the United World Soviet whether he knows it—or wants to be—or not, and must therefore contribute to the general human welfare and obey the lawful orders of all duly constituted human authority."

Mister Thoggosh waved a tentacle, preliminary to speaking. "Excuse me," Eichra Oren interrupted. He faced the KGB officer. "Mr. Empleado—Art—isn't this doctrine the basis for several violent disputes now taking place between the remaining nations of Earth?" Without waiting for an answer, he turned to the general. "Including the one, sir, that squandered the life of your oldest son not long ago?" In the embarrassed silence, someone hidden in the crowd laughed at the frustrated Empleado.

"I might have anticipated this," sighed the Proprietor. "I suppose it's best to initiate Eichra Oren's tenure with a declaration of his independence. As a p'Nan debt assessor, certified by the market he serves and the sword he carries, he's immune to the laws, customs, and authority of the American Soviet Socialist Republic, the Union of Soviet Socialist Republics, the United World Soviet, and both versions of the KGB. I assure you he comes well-equipped to enforce any status he wishes to claim in that regard."

"We'll see about that!" Empleado seized Eichra Oren's arm as his four enforcers elbowed their way through the crowd. It was a mistake. Empleado, a perplexed look on his face, discovered he was holding his own arm instead of Eichra Oren's. The latter had tossed his case to Reille y Sanchez, who caught it automatically. Something heavy rattled inside.

Noncombatants, including Empleado, evaporated from beneath the wing. Broward Hake aimed broad, hardened knuckles at the side of the stranger's head, only to find his best punch captured in the man's left hand where it landed without a sound. At the same time, Delbert Roo launched a back-kick at Eichra Oren's kidney. It arrived in the man's other cupped palm. Eichra Oren spread his arms wide, as if to fling the unwanted energy away, tossing Roo and Hake a full dozen meters in different directions where they landed, with a spectacular double splash, in the mud.

Reille y Sanchez thought that Eichra Oren was the most beautiful thing she'd ever seen. Despite his unnatural speed and power, the strange warrior wasn't exerting himself, showed no sign of sweating, no shortness of breath, and his hair hardly stirred from its well-combed place.

She wished Gutierrez would do something, but the general seemed to be watching the fight with personal interest. From the way he bobbed and grimaced, raising his own fists and muttering, it was plain he wasn't siding with Empleado's men. His son Danny was shouting openly, taking the same side as his father, as did Marna.

Mister Thoggosh allowed his separable tentacle to wander to the other side of the camp, where it climbed onto the wing of the *Hatch*, perhaps affording him a better view. Aelbraugh Pritsch might have been expected to be fluttering nervously, exclaiming how dreadful it all was. Instead, the avian stood calm, his furled umbrella tucked beneath one winglike arm, as if the outcome were already certain. Anybody else's dog would be leaping, barking, joining the fray; Sam sat where he was, as calmly as Aelbraugh Pritsch, apparently watching the fight with intelligent interest.

Sebastiano grinned each time one of Empleado's four absorbed punishment. Empleado's face became grimmer with each setback they suffered. Undismayed or unobservant, Roger Betal and Demene Wise closed in. There was a lot of yelling from the fighters who fancied themselves martial artists, mixed with grunts of exertion and occasional screams of pain. It was difficult to hear them above the yelling from the crowd.

"Go Meany!" she presumed, was for Demene Wise. Someone chanted Hake's name over and over again. It didn't make a bad cheer, at that, even if it did sound a bit Orwellian. "Punch him, Roger, put his lights out!" "Sic him, Del!" seemed a bit more to the point, given what she knew of Delbert Roo. It was foolhardy to be standing anywhere near Corporal Owen. Eyes glued on the fighting men, he swung his massive fists in unconscious sympathy, jabbing and punching the air, endangering everyone within a meter of his reach.

A flurry of movement was hidden in a confusion of shoulders and elbows. Eichra Oren stepped back, having somehow braided one assailant's fingers. The victim stared at the bizarre result, an inescapable, anatomically impossible pattern, in dumb astonishment. Reille y Sanchez suspected it would require a surgeon's help to rearrange Betal's fingers.

Rosalind Nguyen had disappeared when the first blow was struck. Now she was back again, ducking through the crew hatch of the *Dole*, carrying the squarish zippered-nylon container which served her as the black bag of medical tradition.

Almost as an afterthought, Eichra Oren disabled Wise with a feathery toe-brush to the knee, the crack of the broken joint echoing through the camp. As earlier, at the sight of Kamanov's body, Pulaski ran behind one of the landing gear assemblies to throw up.

That didn't end the matter. Hake and Roo were back, advancing on the investigator, short knives with blackened blades appearing like magic in their fists. Eichra Oren's response resembled dancing more than fighting. Each movement of their feet threw sprays of mud into the crowd. Each of them, except for Eichra Oren, was plastered with mud, soaked to the bone. Reille y Sanchez was fascinated, watching his undisturbed face and fathomless eyes, believing she saw the same frightening exultation she'd seen before, in the line of duty, among the outlawed and legendary Penitentes of her native southwest. It was as if the lovely, lethal dance he performed were a religious exercise, putting him in touch with another reality. Suddenly the lower half of Hake's face looked like a bloody ruin, but it was only his nose that was bleeding.

Or maybe it was something sickening, she thought with a shudder which surprised her. Maybe what moved him to ecstasy was the idea of hurting, of killing, or even of being killed. This, too, she was familiar with, from the classrooms, training fields, and barracks where she'd obtained her own training. Then he laughed, shattering the illusion as he bobbed and whirled through stylized motions, keeping up a conversation with his opponents, too quiet for her to hear, as if instructing them. She shivered, clutching the leather case to her breasts, terrified and fascinated all at once. Perhaps that was exactly what he was doing.

Water streamed off the ships in a tangle of rivulets, treacherous miniature gulleys through which they splashed and stumbled as they fought. Eichra Oren elbowed his first opponent, Hake, into semiconsciousness. Roo was faster and came closest to scoring a blow, almost landing a heel in Eichra Oren's solar plexus. It was hard to follow the movements of either man, so fast were they. Compared to the others, it was like watching the same tape at different speeds. The newcomer took a step back, leaned in and gave Roo's forehead no more than a tap of his forefinger. Roo dropped to the mud and lay still—although no more so than three dozen horrified observers. As Eichra Oren turned his back, Hake, lying on his back in the mud, fumbled in his pocket and produced a gun, another of the little K9s like the one Richardson had carried. He raised it toward the investigator.

Reille y Sanchez almost tossed Eichra Oren his case. "Don't!" he shouted, at Hake not her, a gleaming weapon of his own materializing in his hand. He hadn't even turned to see Hake. Now he did.

"Watch!" He raised whatever he carried, no bigger than

a .25 auto, pointed it between the *Dole* and the *McCain* at a hillock just outside the camp. With an odd, muffled explosion, brief-lived smoke blossomed at the muzzle. The hillock vanished with a louder noise and a more impressive explosion. Where it had been, there now lay a deep, elliptical trench, the size of a human grave, into which water from the camp had already begun draining. Hake's mouth hung open. Climbing painfully to his feet, he dropped his pistol into the mud beside him, where it was quickly retrieved by Sebastiano.

"The little one hurried me," Eichra Oren told those around him, his eyes going to those of Reille y Sanchez. "I didn't have time to measure the touch. I apologize for having had to kill him."

From somewhere outside the camp, a shot rang like a thunderclap. Hake's arms stiffened and he collapsed again, face-first, legs crossed at the ankles, a ragged exit wound between his shoulder blades mingling carmine with the wet soil. The bullet had passed within a centimeter of Eichra Oren.

"A .45!" Sebastiano cried. Reille y Sanchez agreed.

"Richardson's still out there, somewhere!" the general added. "Juan, pick three people and go after her—and don't forget to duck!"

FOURTEEN
Horn of Unicorn

Empleado refused to let them bury Hake and Roo in the hole Eichra Oren had blasted from the ground. Instead, a handful of unlucky noncoms was given the task of digging a double grave out of crumbling carbonaceous chondrite and sticky mud. In a way, they were lucky; the rain had stopped. However the sky was beginning to dim; nightfall had come to 5023 Eris.

Reille y Sanchez had just returned from a long, fruitless couple of hours searching for Richardson. The first shift, just before hers, had discovered a spent cartridge case, 11.43x23mm Lenin, in the trees close to the camp, but no trace of the missing woman. By the time the newly fledged KGB colonel was back from what she increasingly regarded as a futile expenditure of manpower, Dr. Nguyen had repaired Demene Wise's shattered knee as best she could.

It had been a bloody mess in the most literal sense. The physician had spent her two hours picking bone splinters from the wound before calling for sutures and bandages. Why Pulaski was able to assist her without getting sick was a mystery. The joint would never be the same, that being the way of knees, but in his own way, Wise was lucky, too.

In this gravity he'd be ambulatory long before a similar recovery would have been possible on Earth. Eichra Oren would have to begin watching his back.

At least the so-called *p'Nan* debt assessor had saved Dr. Nguyen the time and energy involved in healing Roger Betal's "injury" which, given present technology and the minimal resources available, might otherwise have been as badly wasted as in the search for Richardson. Reille y Sanchez had watched him before returning what she presumed was a cased sword and leaving on her hopeless quest. He'd squatted beside the man, still conscious but far gone in shock and pain. Eichra Oren's ecstatic concentration had returned for a moment. Placing his hands over Betal's, he'd moved them in a complex pattern impossible for the eye to follow, as if casting a spell. When he lifted them, Betal's fingers had unlaced from one another. The KGB bully had sighed, a look of beatific gratitude on his face, and passed out.

Now Eichra Oren had a friend for life, she realized—and a couple of problems. Wise, despite his name, was too stupid to learn from experience, however painful. He'd pursue the man who'd crippled him, not giving up this side of the grave—probably his own. Betal, however, was a classic authoritarian: once beaten properly, he'd be loyal forever. On second thought, she grinned to herself. Maybe Eichra Oren's problems were self-canceling.

Changing to fresh clothes aboard the *Dole* for the second time that day—Richardson's, even the rank tabs were right—she found him sitting among empty crates under the starboard wing of the *McCain*, drinking coffee with the doctor who rose and left them, making noises about checking on her patients. The mysterious case lay across his legs. Sam, at his knee, grinned up at her, but his expression, like a dolphin's, seemed a permanent feature. The man lifted a thermos bottle. "Home is the hunter, and my fellow—or is it competitive?—investigator. Would you like some coffee?"

She smiled, taking a small crate on the opposite side of a large crate from his own. "Nothing I'd like better. This is comfortable, like a sidewalk café, complete with a billion-dollar aluminum-graphite awning. Let's leave it 'fellow investigator' as long as we can, shall we? Is your combat technique something special, or can anybody do it where you're from?"

"Wherever that is," he poured coffee for her into a paper cup, voicing her unspoken thought, "because God, or someone more acceptably Marxist, forbid that there may be any more at home like me?"

She took a sip. "Look, I don't care if you agree with your boss's condescendingly negative opinion of Marxism or not. I'm just trying to have a nice, polite, diplomatic conversation—"

"While obtaining whatever data you can persuade me to part with?" He leaned against the tire of the shuttle, shifted the leather case, and crossed his legs at the ankles (she thought it was like watching a cat stretch), grinning as he looked her over from beneath annoyingly raised eyebrows. "Fair enough, fair Colonel, if you return the favor. What would you like to know? The pocket arm I carry is fusion-powered—you'd call it a 'steam pistol'—with a coaxial laser pointer. Its power plant is about the size of a thimble, far beyond any current Soviet or American capability, and would serve the energy needs of all three of your spacecraft for a—"

She shook her head. Being a trained and experienced warrior herself, she was fascinated, astonished, by virtually every aspect of the man's appearance on 5023 Eris, but, at least for now, she'd leave the engineering questions to somebody else. "I know something about martial arts. Did you kill Roo by projecting your *ki* into him?"

"Nothing so romantic." He laughed. "Plain old hydrostatic shock."

More engineering, a phenomenon associated with high-velocity bullets. "What I really wondered, is it something specially devised with the help of the Elders? They're so advanced—"

Eichra Oren laughed again, not in an unkindly way. He did that a lot, she realized, the same open, unguarded laughter as during the fight. For some reason she found it more terrifying than the even greater mysteries he represented. "Art's pathetic leg-breakers," he explained, "were doomed the moment they initiated force against me,

Estrellita. Once committed, the poor devils never stood a chance."

"But they—"

"I know how they're carried on your expedition roster. Wise is supposedly a mining technician, Betal a structural engineer. Hake and Roo were agricultural equipment operators."

From the beginning, like everyone else, Reille y Sanchez had known that the four worked for Empleado. In fact they were—had been—exactly what they seemed to be, even to someone as naive as Pulaski: tough, highly trained KGB enforcement agents.

"Their failure was by no means their fault," Eichra Oren went on, "this I swear to you." By now, the strange exultation she'd twice seen in his eyes seemed to have faded altogether. In her judgment, he seemed apologetic, ashamed of himself, of the amazing thing he'd done—four to one, two armed with knives—afraid the survivors might be punished on his account. "Nor the fault of those—the Union of Soviet Socialist Republics, isn't it, or is it still sometimes called Russia?—who trained them."

She managed to summon up an official KGB frown far sterner than she actually felt. "What do you mean?"

"Their school of martial arts is simply more primitive than mine."

"How much," she thought of the two hundred thousand millennia nautiloid culture had existed, "more primitive?"

"Give or take a century or two, maybe fifteen thousand years. Like the Aztecs fighting your Spetznaz—did I say that right?—instead of Hernan Cortez. Only much worse."

They sat for a long moment in silence.

"Just who are you, anyway, Eichra Oren?" she demanded, reflecting on his weird talent and what kept striking her as the impossibility of his existence. "And more important from a strategic and tactical viewpoint, where the hell did you come from, all of a sudden?"

He spread his hands in a half-shrug, opening his mouth to speak.

"While I'm indulging myself," she interrupted, "asking questions that'll never be answered, what are the Elders searching for on Eris?" With a chill running up her spine, she realized she'd been saving the most frightening question for last. "What sort of terrible thing is it that an advanced people like the Elders need so desperately?"

"On our first date?" He took case in hand and arose from the crate he was sitting on. "My dear Colonel, I'm shocked. But I'll tell you what: I'm overdue to check in with the entity you call my boss. Until I do, believe it or not, I won't know a great deal more about all of this than you do. I'll leave Sam with you. Maybe he can answer some of your questions. All except that last one, that's—what's the expression?—'classified.' You're right, you'll probably never know the answer. Sam, remember you're with a lady and on your best behavior." With that, Eichra Oren turned and strode away from the shuttle, out into the jungle, and was gone.

"Swell: my first act as a KGB agent." She put her elbows on the makeshift table, chin in hands, glaring at the animal as it sat with its tongue hanging out through an idiot grin. "Interrogating a furry ventriloquist's dummy!"

The dog turned his head toward her. "Estrellita, my lovely, I'll be nice if you will. That's what he meant, 'best behavior.' He always accuses me of being a wise guy, if that's the idiom. Me, I think my sense of humor's fifteen thousand years more advanced than his, give or take a century or two."

"So you *can* talk!" She glanced around, remembering the relay carried by Semlohcolresh's separable tentacle, suspecting some kind of practical joke. On the other hand, how reasonable was the idea of a giant squid running this entire show? By comparison, a talking dog seemed downright mundane.

"No," Sam replied, "it's your imagination. The strain you're under. You're cracking up."

"That I can believe." Coming to a decision, she stood. "But cracking up or not, he said you'd answer my questions. Only let's take a walk, so I can enjoy my schizophrenia in privacy." They followed the route Eichra Oren had, slipping between two shuttles—she checked the contents of the chamber and magazine of her Witness, mindful of another colonel, whose uniform she wore—far enough into the trees so she could still see by half a dozen lights Sebastiano had strung around the camp.

"'Wise guy' is the correct idiom," she told the dog when they were out of human earshot, "although it's a bit dated. Your English is actually very good. So is Eichra Oren's. He also knows a lot about Earth's current and not-so-current history."

"Why shouldn't he?" Sam asked. "That's where we both come from."

Reille y Sanchez found a spot at the base of one of the giant growths where the ground was fairly dry despite the recent rain. She kept her pistol in her lap. "Yes, but what I've learned here—almost the only thing I've learned—is that there's Earth and then again there's Earth. Which version are you and Eichra Oren from?"

Sam stretched and lay down on the ground. "That's an assumption, isn't it, that he and I are from the same Earth? You don't know, Estrellita, maybe I'm from the Planet of the Dogs."

She chuckled. "Like Aelbraugh Pritsch is from the Planet of the Birds?"

"Birdbrains," he corrected, "and you're from the Planet of the Apes. But no, in this case your assumption's correct. It's an Earth where, for uncounted millennia, no sapient—including Eichra Oren, although I seem to be the cynical and worldly member of the firm—has ever known domination by, or of, another sapient. That's what scares you about him, Estrellita."

"What?"

"Didn't think I'd noticed, did you? I'm a dog, remember? I can smell fear. It smells like shit. You're frightened whenever he laughs. But, speaking of shit, with your political education, you've no way of realizing that it's merely the uncalculated laughter of a free individual, something you've never had a chance to see. Or be."

"There's a much simpler explanation than that, Sam." She took a deep breath. "Shit's all I seem to be wading through on my way to the truth. 'Uncounted millennia,' you say. Eichra Oren says 'fifteen thousand years.' On my Earth, fifteen thousand years ago, people were pretty much limited to stone knives and bear skins. What makes your Earth so different?"

Sam took several moments to answer. Deeper among the trees, Reille y Sanchez thought she saw fireflies winking. "Look," he told her, "suppose one of your space shuttles accidentally landed on some primitive island where people are still limited to stone knives and bear skins. There are still places like that on your Earth, aren't there?"

She nodded. "I suppose so. Jungles in New Guinea, maybe."

"All right, now suppose for some reason you had to explain fully and accurately where you'd come from and how you'd gotten there. The natives' view of the universe revolves around magic and mythology. It doesn't include things like science or spaceflight. They don't even know the world is round. You'd have to do a lot of preliminary educating before you got around to things like airfoils and rocket engines, wouldn't you?"

"Yes, you would." She frowned. "What're you driving at, Sam?"

"New Guinea primitives mightn't like what you tell them. They might get scared and burn you at the stake or shrink your head or something. I'm trying to warn you, Estrellita, that a full and accurate understanding of, well, of Eichra Oren's origin, or mine, requires that you unlearn a lot that's taken for granted—mistakenly—by your own civilization."

This time it was her turn for a long, thoughtful pause. I'm having this conversation, she told herself, with a big white shaggy animal. "Sam, I've been trying to cut down on burning people—and dogs—at the stake. It causes cancer. And I've given up shrinking heads for Lent. Will you please tell me what this is leading up to?"

"Simply that Eichra Oren's the descendent of an ancient civilization."

"That much I've managed to gather on my own, thank you."

Sam sat up. "Yes? Well, it's a civilization which existed on your very own alternate version of Earth, Estrellita. By a long, indirect route, he and I come from exactly the same place you do. Unfortunately, it happens to be a civilization none of your historians ever heard of and your archaeologists would maintain never existed." Observing her confused expression, he added, "Any questions, so far?"

"Sure. Lots. At the moment, I find the most important is this: is it at all smart to believe any of this nonsense you're telling me? Let me rephrase that: how can one tread safely between intellectual flexibility and foolish gullibility?"

"Between having an open mind and holes in your head?" he asked. "In my off moments, I've often pondered that never-ending conflict, myself."

She grinned at the dog and started, from reflex, to reach down and pat him on the head, stopping herself only at the last moment. "Most of all," she told him, "I wonder about myself, my own potential for both of those attributes. Would I have believed Galileo when he told me what he'd just seen through his telescope? Or William Harvey, claiming that the human heart is merely a mechanical pump?"

"Or whoever it was in your culture " Sam suggested, "who discovered that most human evils are caused by invisible plantlife?"

"Louis Pasteur." She nodded. "On the other hand, would I have been able to spot Piltdown Man or the Giant of Cardiff as hoaxes, or would I have been taken in with the rest of the crowd? Would I have dismissed truly revolutionary and valuable information as . . . as—"

"Having been decanted from a cracked pot?"

"Pretty good, Sam. You know, I remember reading somewhere that Sir Isaac Newton believed in astrology and numerology. He once conducted 'scientific' experiments with what he thought was the powder of ground unicorn horn. What was it you said? An Earth where, for uncounted millennia, no sapient being has dominated, or been dominated by, another sapient being? My Earth, Sam, the distant past, that's what you were talking about. And you're right, it does scare me. It also sounds a lot like powdered horn of unicorn."

"There's your answer, Estrellita, don't believe me. See for yourself. Excuse me." He reached up with a hind foot, scratched behind one ear, and Reille y Sanchez was reminded all over again what sort of creature she was discussing politics with. "You came to the right place for it."

"Well," she answered, giving it visible consideration. She'd meant her remark about unicorn horn, but maybe this was a way to draw him out. "I haven't seen any evidence of military discipline among the Proprietor's people—so many different weird and wonderful creatures. They don't seem to display anything resembling the legendary capitalist corporate loyalty. As far as I can tell, there isn't any clear-cut hierarchy of authority, no official table of organization, not even much of the minimal social pecking order I'd expect to see among intelligent and competitive beings."

"No distemper, worms, or rabies, either."

"Have it your way. Obviously you and Eichra Oren share the Elders' peculiar philosophy. Or is that an assumption, too? But it also means you're sitting ducks—you know that idiom?—for anybody better organized. You have no sense of internal security, no solidarity which would tend to protect you or your company secrets."

"Right again, Estrellita, try it for yourself. None of the Elders, nor any of their many associated species, will demonstrate even the slightest reluctance to tell you anything and everything you want to know."

She shifted the Witness in her lap, then discovered that some ground dampness was beginning to creep through her clothing after all. She decided to stick it out for a few more minutes. "The single exception being the precise reason or reasons for their presence on the asteroid to begin with, apparently at the order or suggestion or request, I can't tell which, of the one identifiable authority figure, the so-called Proprietor."

"The big fat bum."

She leaned forward, concentrating. "And even that secret, I'm inclined to agree with General Gutierrez, seems to have religious undertones about it which make me doubt the value of ferreting it out."

"Didn't one of your own greatest philosophers once observe that one man's theology is another man's belly laugh?"

"Wait," she held up a hand, "let me think. I'll make a

bet with you, Sam. If the people here turn out to be anything, it'll be too goddamned cooperative, won't they? As the expedition's—and Earth's—official investigator, I'll find myself in the worst imaginable position, inundated with more information than I can evaluate. That kind of generosity might be a clever tactic, in itself, mightn't it?"

Sam grinned and wagged his tail. "You say that with what sounds like grudging admiration."

"It's true," she replied distractedly, still thinking, then shifted her focus back to here and now. "But it's also true that I pride myself on being a practical, efficient type at heart, afflicted with very little unbridled imagination or useless curiosity." She leaned back against the tree.

"Anyway," he suggested, "that's what you've always wanted to believe about yourself."

"Sam! I thought you were going to be nice if I was."

"A point, Estrellita, but I can smell other things besides fear, you know. Intelligence. Curiosity. Imagination. They smell nice. You reek of them, if you don't mind my saying so."

She crossed her arms. "That's a hell of a compliment. I'll just have to take immediate and stern measures to control them."

"Do that, Estrellita, it'll be interesting to watch. I'll—" He lifted his head, ears perked rigid. "But you'll have to excuse me, I'm being paged. 'His master's voice' and all that. Can you find your way back?"

"Thanks, I'm a sapient, too, you know." A bit stiff from dampness, she climbed to her feet. He grinned, turned, and ran off into the jungle.

But not *very* sapient, she thought, I hardly found out anything I wanted to know, especially about where Eichra Oren came from. Shrugging to herself, always the practical, efficient type, she simply added the task of discovering more about the mystery man to a long list of other chores she saw, in her incurious, unimaginative way, looming ahead of her.

FIFTEEN
The Empty Millennia

To sleep, perchance *not* to dream—if she was lucky.

Now, in Vivian Richardson's continuing absence, the expedition's second-highest-ranking officer, Reille y Sanchez remembered that she rated a better place to toss and turn: a folding cot and sleeping bag—one of three available— in the relative privacy and luxury of the crew deck, either aboard the *Dole* or the *McCain*.

After being outdoors so much the last couple of days, her skin crawled at thought of the alternative. For most of the past year, eight hours a "day," she'd occupied thirty vertical centimeters between folding bunks arranged in a stack of six in the cargo bay insert, inboard the former vessel. Even as she strode alone through the trees on her way back to the camp, the idea of wedging herself once again into such confinement, of breathing air exhaled by others, of smelling their smells, gave her a feeling of suffocation.

Entering the lighted area around the shuttles, she brightened in more than a literal sense at a third possibility. She could follow the example of many of the crew who'd scrounged blankets and bags and were sleeping under the wings and hulls of the spacecraft. The idea appealed to her. She'd gotten almost nothing in the way of rest during the previous period of darkness, with Semlohcolresh's unexpected visit to the camp and the subsequent flap over the disappearance of the expedition's second-in-command. A few minutes, here and there, was all she'd had, sitting propped against the tandem-tired nose-gear of the *Hatch*, Witness in hand.

Glancing down now at the same kilo of Czech steel and plastic hanging in her numb, aching fingers, she smiled sheepishly to herself. She was exhausted and becoming careless, forgetful. She slid the weapon into its holster, fastening the flap. At that, she thought, it hadn't been bad last night, all things considered, particularly after the three-hundred-odd worse nights which had preceded it. It was warm enough outside that she shouldn't need much in the way of bedding. Maybe she could still find something fresh in the *Dole*'s emergency stores.

After a brief search, equipped with a lightweight silver-and-red plastic "space blanket" and a cup of tea courtesy of Corporal Owen's welding torch, Reille y Sanchez settled in under what was being called the "girl's wing" of the flagship, between Marna and Pulaski. She was too worn out for any conversation and grateful that both young women were already sound asleep (the latter, she observed, with her thumb in her mouth again, as had been her unconscious habit throughout most of the journey to the asteroid). As tired as Reille y Sanchez was, disturbing thoughts and vivid images kept circling inside her head. Her mind wouldn't shut itself off.

Among other things, until now, she hadn't really had time to feel the full loss of Piotr Kamanov. For most of her life, all of the people around her had been just like she was: sober, literal-minded, duty-oriented. She'd never met a man quite like the geologist, who seemed to live life simply for the fun of it. She knew now that she'd miss him very badly; his silly joking, his habit of collecting and redistributing strange stories and ideas, his astonishing lack of respect for authority and established wisdom.

Most of all, she couldn't get the Russian's stupid, senseless death out of her troubled mind, the horrifying sight of him, silent and slack-faced for the first time since she'd met him. She could think of a hundred individuals for whom the world would have been better off, had they died in his place. Now more than ever she understood that the general was right. The solution to their bizarre situation—to her own in particular—lay in somehow learning to think the way Kamanov had.

But Reille y Sanchez was a soldier. This sort of morbid preoccupation was unusual for the no-nonsense, action-oriented Marine officer, and she knew it. Finishing her tea, Reille y Sanchez set the cup aside, along with what she realized (with a small start of surprise) was her grieving. Likewise, she abandoned the speculation over the reliability of Sam and Eichra Oren which had filled her mind before these thoughts of Kamanov had intruded, and simply promised herself that she'd try her best to evaluate the amazing information they'd given her as objectively she could—tomorrow.

"Colonel?"

In a shorter time than seemed possible, the butterscotch-colored light of day had returned to the human encampment and sought out Reille y Sanchez where she lay, sweating under her plastic blanket, twitching occasionally in her sleep and mumbling to herself.

"Pulaski?" Blinking, Reille y Sanchez sat up, stiff and sore in every muscle, her mouth tasting like her idea of some nameless, ancient evil. Her right hip seemed particularly painful, as if she'd slept on a big rock. Pushing the blanket aside, she discovered that she'd fallen asleep still wearing her knife-and-pistol belt.

"Yes, ma'am. It's 0600, as near as anybody can figure, and I wondered if you'd like some coffee." The sergeant held a steaming cup under her nose, constructed neither of paper nor plastic, but of something somewhere between metal and ceramic, probably another gift from the strangely generous creatures Washington wanted them to kill. The colonel's initial nausea at the aroma was immediately smothered in a wave of irresistible craving. She took a sip and swallowed.

"Thanks—stick around. You're just the person I want to see."

"Me, Colonel?"

Reille y Sanchez struggled to her feet, brushing at her uniform with one hand while she held onto her cup with the other. "No, Pulaski, me colonel, you sergeant." She grinned self-consciously. It wasn't as bad as one of Kamanov's, but at least she was trying. "Get yourself some coffee, if you want, while I go inside for PTA drill." She watched the girl blush, as she always did, at the figure of speech, peculiar to the female Marine Corps, which stood for those parts of her anatomy she intended giving a cursory rinse. The A stood for armpits. "We're going to talk over all these ancient matters you're supposed to know so much about."

Pulaski actually threw her a salute. "Yes, ma'am."

Minutes later, they were sitting back outdoors in sunshine which came, surprisingly strong, through the asteroid canopy. For a bench, Pulaski had commandeered a fair-sized log, fated for this evening's fire. They were somewhat startled to be watching their commander, stripped to the waist and sweating, laboriously cutting kindling with the almost useless saw-toothed back of a big hollow-handled knife exactly like her own.

Adversity must be good for some people, Reille y Sanchez thought. The man seemed a lot less flabby than she recalled from their pre-voyage physical training. Brigadier General Gutierrez was being assisted by Second Lieutenant Gutierrez (if the younger man had been a Marine, he'd still be in the brig for losing his pistol to Richardson, but the Aerospace Force was infamous for gentle discipline), the first she'd ever seen them like this, father and son. It was a pleasant picture. For some reason, it made her want to cry.

"Let me see," declared the expedition's amateur paleontologist, answering the first question Reille y Sanchez had asked her. "I think the oldest known fully human remains are about a quarter of a million years old. They were discovered a long time ago, somewhere in the British Isles. I don't remember exactly where or when."

"How about," the colonel asked, "the oldest known civilization?"

Pulaski frowned. "In what sense do you mean 'civilization'?"

"I don't know, Toya, what *do* I mean?" No "ma'am" when answering questions in her field, observed Reille y Sanchez, who hated the word, let alone being called by it. I'll have to remember that. "Houses, buildings, cities? Doesn't 'civilization' mean cities?"

Pulaski blinked. "The most ancient known cluster of habitations which might—generously—be called a city, are about eight thousand years old. They were located somewhere in the Middle East, the so-called 'cradle of civilization,' before that whole area got slagged in '23."

Reille y Sanchez reflected without self-pity that these were items she might have learned about if she'd had anything resembling a normal growing up. Instead, on the basis of aptitudes she'd unknowingly demonstrated in written and athletic tests at the age of eight or nine, she'd been selected for special attention, taken from her family—tearfully proud to let their daughter go—and enrolled in a strictly supervised Soviet-American training academy.

She and her school had been interested in preparing her for a career as an officer. At the time, she'd have regarded any other kind of knowledge as useless mental clutter, possibly of mild interest but essentially irrelevant. This had certainly included subjects like paleontology, archaeology, and all but *military* history. If she'd ever heard anything about it, she'd have promptly forgotten it, having no way of knowing that such information might someday prove critical to her survival, not to mention her career.

Later, of course, she'd done some casual reading, a paperback purchased at a terminal or base exchange, shoved as an afterthought into a duffel bag. The hurry-up-and-wait life led by any professional soldier affords plenty of time for casual reading. A surprising number of thick-necked, dog-faced grunts of her own acquaintance might easily have qualified for doctorates, based on this sort of casually acquired information, if they'd given a damn, which they didn't. Now, thanks to Pulaski, who more or less fit into the same category, Reille y Sanchez had been supplied with new data and some refreshed memories.

"Thanks, Toya, that's about what I thought. And now I wonder why it's never occurred to anyone to ask one simple, highly disturbing question."

"Colonel?"

Better than "ma'am." Come to think of it, a lot better. "Well, if the oldest known human remains are two hundred fifty thousand years old, and the oldest known civilization only about eight thousand, what, in the sacred name of the martyred Geraldo Rivera was *Homo sapiens* doing with himself during the intervening two hundred forty-two thousand years?"

Pulaski had an odd, frightened expression on her face. "I don't believe I follow you, ma'am."

The colonel was too deep in concentration to be annoyed at this relapse. "Sure you do, Toya, look: it required only eighty centuries for mankind to step from your sun-baked adobe villages, somewhere in the Middle East, to the crater-marked surface of the Moon, right?"

"Right—" A dismayed look on the girl's face indicated a suspicion that, by some tricky, characteristically military twisting of logic, her answer might somehow get her into trouble. Reille y Sanchez knew from her own experience that such a suspicion, although groundless on this occasion, was as soundly rooted in reality as the great trees surrounding the encampment. "I mean, yes, Colonel."

"Relax, Toya, and answer this: could it actually have taken poor old *Homo sap* each of the preceding two hundred forty-two millennia to claw his way up from animal subsistence on the blood-soaked veldt of Africa to those damned adobe villages?"

"That's colorful, Colonel." The sergeant swallowed, still uncomfortable. "But not very, um, scientific—I mean I don't believe I ever thought much about it before."

Reille y Sanchez laughed. "That's what I was warned you'd say, as a representative of established science. Well, it occurred to me to ask that question, rather it was asked *for* me last night. And now, either I can't leave it alone, or it won't leave me alone. Could our species, the supposedly human race, possibly be as slow-witted as that empty, accusing quarter of a million years seems to imply?"

"I, er—" Pulaski closed her mouth, thinking.

"If that were truly so, how could they have survived all of those long, danger-filled tens of thousands of years in tooth-and-nail competition with what would, by logical comparison, have been vastly more intelligent species, like turtles, parakeets, garden snails—"

Pulaski giggled. "And giant ground sloths?"

"I think, Toya," Reille y Sanchez laughed again, "that you've got the idea. No matter how hard I try—no matter how the contrary proposition flies in the face of accepted scientific evidence—I can't bring myself to believe we're that dumb. I never thought of myself as an optimist regarding human nature, but there it is."

"There what is, Estrellita?" A shadow fell across the women. Gutierrez stood before them bare-chested, toweling himself off, his shirt still tucked in and hanging from the waist. Across the campsite, Danny was stacking kindling under a shuttle wingtip.

The colonel eyed the general's hands, covered with painful-looking blisters, broken and weeping. "I suppose I could be wrong," she mused. "Still, two hundred forty-two thousand years. What if people were doing something more ambitious, something nobler, with all that spare time?"

"Like what?" Pulaski asked.

"What are you two talking about?" demanded the general.

Pulaski looked up, visibly embarrassed by his naked, hairy torso, and even more, the colonel thought, by his not-unpleasant male-animal odor. "Anthropology, sir, and prehistory." Together, the women explained what they'd been discussing.

He nodded, folding his legs beneath him and sitting on the ground. "So the question is: what if people were accomplishing something all that time—besides bashing cave bears, saber-toothed tigers, and each other over the heads and subsisting as the fur-clad stone-tooled Alley Oops you see in museum dioramas? Well, what about it?"

Reille y Sanchez took up where she'd left off. "Okay, why is it archaeologists and paleontologists, even when they're violating all accepted academic precedent looking for it—"

"Which, for the most part," Pulaski interrupted, surprising even herself, "they're decidedly not—"

"Why can't they find any physical trace of it?" the colonel finished.

"For the excellent reason . . ." The general thrust his arms into the sleeves of his shirt, pulled it around his shoulders, and closed the zipper halfway. From the way his uniform hung, Reille y Sanchez guessed that he was still carrying the weapons left behind by Kamanov and Richardson. " . . . that the poor, ignorant, tenured schmucks've been looking in all the wrong places!"

Reille y Sanchez opened her mouth. She closed it.

"Don't look surprised," he said. "I've been doing some snooping on my own, as I said I would, among the asteroid's better-informed inhabitants. For instance, I had a long, interesting talk with Eichra Oren yesterday, while some of you were out looking for Vivian. Funny kind of investigator. He answers more questions than he asks. He suggested they'd be better off—archaeologists and paleontologists—if they'd drill for evidence of archaic civilization beneath the South Polar icecap. They might even find something rewarding by randomly dragging the bottom of the Indian Ocean."

"For what?" both women demanded of the man.

"For what, sir?" Pulaski added, after a moment, in a small voice.

Gutierrez grinned. "For physical evidence of a prehistoric civilization which it appears Mother Nature—or maybe it was Auntie Evolution—once shoved off the edge of a continental shelf."

Pulaski began nodding, understanding something Reille y Sanchez hadn't caught yet. "Tens of thousands of years ago," the girl declared, staring off at the treetops as if she were talking to herself, "what we regard as our hospitable home-continent of North America was every bit as uninhabitable as the surface of the Moon."

"The whole thing was covered," agreed Gutierrez, "from the Arctic Sea, almost to the Gulf of Mexico, by an ice sheet—as hard as it may be to imagine it—three kilometers thick in places."

They're both right, the colonel realized, remembering colored maps and artists' renderings from science and geographic magazines which, long after she'd left the academy and its narrow concerns, never failed to fascinate her. "The North and South Poles," she volunteered, "were in different places only a few thousand years ago."

He clapped his palms together. "As usual—*sonofabitch*, look at those blisters, will you? I didn't realize I'd done that! So much for healthy physical labor! I was about to say, you've hit the nail on the head, Estrellita. And at the same time—well, you tell it, Sergeant. About Antarctica during the same period. It's your hobby, after all." He stared down at his hands and shook his head.

Pulaski smiled a shy smile. The general, too, had made a friend. "Well, sir—ma'am—the fossil record demonstrates that today's ice-bound Antarctica was, by contrast, a dry, warm, heavily forested environment, even though, on all the Earth, it's now the bleakest and most barren."

"Right." In his enthusiasm, the general couldn't resist interrupting. "At least according to Eichra Oren, it wasn't in the so-called 'Fertile Crescent' of the Middle East that the human race built its first real civilizations. In a sense, if you believe him, that's where they were forced, later on, to begin climbing to the stars all over again."

"I don't know, sir, if it's smart to believe everything we're told." Again Reille y Sanchez faced the dilemma of open-mindedness and gullibility. "What you're saying, what Eichra Oren maintains, is that civilization began in Antarctica, the least hospitable—"

He nodded. "Back, to paraphrase George Harrison, when it was fab. I don't know whether we can believe Eichra Oren either, Estrellita, but it's fascinating to think about. Everything about Mister Thoggosh's new deputy seems mysterious and unbelievable. But Eichra Oren says his immediate ancestors once lived there."

"On that little frozen-over continent?"

"Not that little, really. And only recently frozen over. Soviet science states—correctly, according to Eichra Oren—that human beings first arose as a sapient species in nearby southern Africa. Somehow, some of them managed to cross the water and made history for thousands of years—history which would have been lost to us forever if we hadn't met Eichra Oren—and learned and grew as a people. Which accounts for at least a part of your missing two hundred forty-two thousand years, Estrellita. I gather these people spent a chunk of it building themselves a fairly impressive civilization, in every way comparable to the civilization achieved, oh, say by our European ancestors during the early Industrial Revolution."

Pulaski looked concerned. "But what became of them, sir?"

"Well, Toya, in a sense, nothing. Here we are, aren't we?"

Reille y Sanchez shook her head. "You mean to say, sir, that these ancient people we're just hearing about for the first time happen to be our ancestors, too?"

He stood up, grunting just a little. "By a more indirect route than they're Eichra Oren's, but yes. Our remote ancestors. Now, if you ladies will excuse me, I'm going to go find a Band-aid or nine."

"Our remote ancestors." Toya sighed.

"From the Lost Continent," the colonel answered, "of Antarctica."

SIXTEEN
Method, Motive, Opportunity

"I'm sorry," the rubber flower told her, "Tl°m°nch°l is out of the office. I'm Llessure Knarrfic, his, er—excuse me, please."

Reille y Sanchez wondered what this being had evolved from. Impossibly thin greenish fingers, six or seven to a hand (of which there were four), clattered over a circular keyboard set in the top of the desklike piece of furniture behind which the lower half of the peculiar sapient was hidden.

The "office" was a roofless cubicle she'd found after wandering a maze of similar corridors for what seemed hours. Overhead, a Fresnel lens two meters square focused the canopy's diffuse sunlight on the desk's occupant. Nearby, a humidifier hissed, adding to the tropical heat and moisture of what already seemed like a greenhouse.

From the general's description, Reille y Sanchez had imagined something like a big talking sunflower with petals around a "have-a-nice-day" face. This thing looked more like a pale green chrysanthemum with a blossom larger than a soccer ball. No eyes or other features could be seen, nor could she tell where the being's clear, androgynous voice was coming from. Beneath the blossom, a stalk or torso of the same color branched at intervals to produce the arms before it disappeared behind the desk. Now, symbols appeared on a screen no thicker than cardboard, standing at one end of that desk.

"There it is, according to this glossary of the human language, I'm Tl°m°nch°l's 'secretary or receptionist.' Can I help you, Col. Sanchez?"

This Tl°m°nch°l (at least it sounded like that to Reille y Sanchez) was one of the sea-scorpions, sapient crustaceans brought here by the Elders. Decorative frames on every wall except the one which had dilated to admit her made the colonel suspect this creature or its boss, head of the "giant bugs with guns," perceived light in different frequencies than human beings. Significant areas of the pictures seemed an empty, dull gray.

"Reille y Sanchez," the colonel corrected, "mine works differently than most human names, there's really more than one human language. Ask Aelbraugh Pritsch, he speaks lovely Spanish. You can tell me where Tlumunchul is, or when he's likely to be back."

The chrysanthemum made a noise, clearing whatever it used for a throat. "That's Tl°m°nch°l, Colonel Reille y Sanchez. Most sapients find his name, along with the rest of his language, difficult to pronounce and won't even try. He's busy somewhere, doing something I'm not supposed to talk about with you newcomers—"

Reille y Sanchez nodded. "The Elders' mysterious search for whatever?"

"I'm afraid," Llessure Knarrfic replied, ignoring the remark, "I don't know when he'll be back. Would you care to leave a message?"

"Sure. I'd like to speak with Tlemenchel about Piotr Kamanov's death. He's the Proprietor's security chief, therefore my 'opposite number.' He's also the first nonhuman I happened to see here. I've never investigated a murder before, and I'm trying to be methodical."

"That's Tl°m°nch°l, Colonel Reille y Sanchez. I'll give him the message. Will there be anything else?"

"I'll—hold on a minute, one more thing, if you don't mind." Excusing herself, Reille y Sanchez walked around the desk. Tucked beneath it were two pairs of fairly ordinary legs and feet, fairly ordinary considering that she'd expected to see a pot full of dirt. "That'll be all, thanks. I'm going to look up Aelbraugh Pritsch, and can be reached there, wherever 'there' is."

"Oh, fudge," answered the flower. "I'm afraid that you'll be disappointed again. Aelbraugh Pritsch happens to be *with* Tl°m°nch°l, as we speak."

Reille y Sanchez suppressed the first response that came to mind. "I'm afraid 'oh fudge' doesn't say it. Surprise the next human you talk to: check your glossary under sexual intercourse and bodily elimination."

"I will," the petals constituting Llessure Knarrfic's face seemed to spread, "and thank you, Col. Reille y Sanchez!"

"Don't mention it." She grinned, walked out through the wall, and stopped the next sapient she ran into.

By chance—or perhaps not—Tl°m°nch°l's office was near the infirmary (at least on the more-or-less random course Reille y Sanchez was following) where, it felt like such a long time ago, Kamanov had been taken for his shoulder injury. "Ran into" was more than a figure of speech. The "walking quilt" Gutierrez had told them of, who dispensed refreshments, came close to running the colonel over with its pushcart.

"Oops! Excuse me," were the colonel's first, reflexive words, "I'm Estrellita Reille y Sanchez. Have you seen Aelbraugh Pritsch or Tliminchil around anywhere? I need to speak with one of them."

"Greetings, Estrellita Reille y Sanchez, Colonel in Fullity of Kaygeebee, I have pleasure to be Remaulthiek and regret to inform you that both worthy sapients after whom you inquire—and it is pronounced Tl°m°nch°l—are at this time occupied in righteous and sacred undertakings which are not to be discussed with homosapienses. May I do something to recompense the debt of civility which this may otherwise create between us? You would, perhaps, delight to ingest caffeine infusion and a doughnut?"

Reille y Sanchez smiled. It was difficult to dislike these beings, even when they looked like GI-issue mummy bags wrapped in Saran Wrap. "Thanks—let me get this one straight: Remaulthiek?—the coffee smells wonderful, and I will have a doughnut. You haven't created any debt. If these were ordinary circumstances, I'd just mind my own business. But I need to talk to somebody among your people, the nonhomosapienses, who knows something."

Beside the cart, she watched Remaulthiek treat itself—herself, the general had decided—using a flexible corner of her blanket-shape to dissolve a doughnut in a cup of coffee, sipping the mess through a large-caliber straw thrust through her protective wrapper. As with Llessure Knarrfic, there was no expressive face to go by, no familiar body language, but Remaulthiek seemed to be pondering the request.

"Something, if I may ask, about what, Estrellita Reille y Sanchez?"

"I had definite ideas about that, earlier," the colonel replied, "detective-type questions about Semlohcolresh, Mister Thoggosh, the Elders' culture in general. Now, I'd settle for practically anything. What have you got in mind?"

"Please, if you wish it, to follow me."

Disposing of the cup and leaving the cart, the entity waddled toward a corridor wall and through, the colonel following. As the wall closed behind them, they encountered an insectile being, perhaps one of the surgeons who'd worked on Kamanov. It stood as tall as Reille y Sanchez, and was different from the sea-scorpions. For one thing, it wasn't wearing the transparent plastic affected by them and Remaulthiek. Instead, it wore a garment made of hundreds of centimeter-wide strips of fluorescent orange-and-green fabric. It seemed to be examining a sheaf of papers on a clipboard.

"Remaulthiek," it rasped, apparently making sounds by rubbing vestigial wing-cases together under its clothing, "you never sicken, nor are you easily injured. What service may I do you?"

"Dlee Raftan Saon," intoned the quilt-being, "though denied in kindness, I pay a debt of civility. Estrellita Reille y Sanchez, in Kaygeebee Full Colonelness, wishes to ask, of somebody who knows something, detective-type questions about Semlohcolresh, Mister Thoggosh, the Elders' culture, practically anything in general. Estrellita Reille y Sanchez, Dlee Raftan Saon, Restorer-of-Health, who knows much about many things."

Reille y Sanchez put out a hand. "Thank you, Remaulthiek, and for the, er, caffeine infusion and doughnut."

Remaulthiek bent a corner, touching her hand. "You are welcome, Estrellita Reille y Sanchez. I have savored the sweet scent of your naming and return to my occupation." With that, she walked through the wall.

Through its tattered, dazzling attire, the insect extended a bristly limb which the colonel accepted without examining closely. "Sit, my dear, while I finish these confounded records. May I call you Estrellita? Then we'll sneak out of this sweetshop—correct?—no? 'Sweatshop,' then, for a bit and a bite of talk, or is it the other way round? No matter. Tell me, this is your wish, to ask questions? It's difficult with Remaulthiek, her species communicates with pheromones and I've never quite trusted their translating software."

She sat, although she wasn't sure whether she'd chosen a tall bench or a low table. "You're actually speaking English, whereas Remaulthiek . . . how about Llessure Knarrfic, Tlomonchol's secretary, does it—"

"It's Tl°m°nch°l, Estrellita, and she. Llessure Knarrfic's quite as irresistibly feminine, in her specific way—that's a pun—as your charming self. There are many differing theories on the evolution of sapience. One I agree with claims it's impossible in life-forms not divided into sexes. I might add, it wouldn't be much fun." The physician flipped papers back over the clipboard and set it on another piece of furniture. "I happen to be male, and of so remarkably advanced an age that my enthusiastic interest in the opposite sex is seldom taken seriously by females of my species until it's too late for the little darlings. Shall we go to lunch?"

With the colonel hanging dubiously on one of his four available arms, they strolled down the corridor, entering what she guessed was a cafeteria. Around the walls of an area large enough for basketball, she saw waist-high counters heaped with steaming dishes, dishes at room temperature, dishes on ice. Much of what was offered looked and smelled appealing after shipboard rations. Other selections, those still squirming in their stainless warmers, made her want to run to the nearest bathroom (God alone knew what that was like) with both hands over her mouth. "*Gagh* is best served live," she remembered someone saying.

"I didn't realize," exclaimed the doctor, noting her reaction, "that this would be an ordeal. A moment's thought—here, find us an isolated table. Having treated one of your species, I've an idea of your requirements and can guess your preferences." He gave her arm a pat. "Perhaps by the window?"

Gulping her revulsion, she set a course for the indicated spot, closed her eyes, navigated by memory through a gauntlet of occupied tables laden with stuff which set her stomach churning.

Like any place where hundreds gather to eat together, the room was filled with chatter. Like any place where those hundreds were all foreigners, it consisted of incomprehensible gabble. Here, where Reille y Sanchez was the only human, the whooping, screeching, and buzzing of dozens of life-forms around her made it sound like a weird combination of cabinet factory and sheet-metal shop, set in the middle of a jungle (which it was) populated by noisy insects and tropical birds. The table she chose had potted ferns on either side—for a moment she worried that they might be sapient—sparing her further visual unpleasantness. She thanked whoever had designed the ventilation system that she couldn't smell most of what the others here seemed to be enjoying.

"You haven't found a seat." Dlee Raftan Saon arrived at her heels with a tray. "Don't you know how?" He set tray on table, eliciting a pinging noise. "Dlee Saon," he told it, "Reille y Sanchez." Chairs sprouted, one obviously for human use, the other an uncomfortable-looking rack resembling an upside-down director's chair. The table chimed until he fed it copper-colored coins.

Hitching her weapons belt, she sat. "Dlee—Doctor, I can't let you pay for lunch! Especially since I probably won't be able to eat it."

"Come, Estrellita, I know you haven't any money. You repay me with your delectable presence." Arranging himself on his rack, he slid the tray toward her. "See what I've chosen: uncooked greens in sweet, savory sauce. Muscle protein from a herbivorous mammal, minced, boiled in its own lipids until uniform in color and texture. Ground graminid kernels, leavened, heated until brown. Sliced tubers, also boiled in lipids, lightly salted. Coffee, seldom a wrong guess for any sapient. A bit short on certain essentials, but no one meal accomplishes everything. How have I done?"

She laughed, suddenly hungry. "Salad, hamburger with bun, fries? Doc, pass the ketchup. What're you having, ants? I haven't had any ants since survival school. I wonder what Tlamanchal's secretary over there is eating. And don't bother, I know I can't pronounce it."

"That's twice you've said that, Estrellita." His blue-green faceted eyes glittered in his heart-shaped, toast-colored face. She thought he looked like a mantis, although the swell of the skull (did insects have skulls?) behind his eyes was enormous. Hands at the ends of two-elbowed arms were like the armored gloves of a knight. The vestigial wings she'd guessed at lay under strips of colored cloth at the back of his neck, no bigger than the silver dollars her mother had once hidden under the basement floor. His antennae, jointed like a gooseneck lamp, made him look like a cartoon bug. "Must be something amiss with Knarrfic's software, too. She isn't Tl°m°nch°l's secretary, but his employer, under contract to Mister Thoggosh."

"That makes me feel better." She tried a bite of the burger. It tasted more like lamb than beef, and was delicious. More than that, she didn't want to know. "The only two nonhuman females I've met here, so far, and both of them menials? That doesn't speak well—"

Dlee Raftan Saon looked up from his food, live insects in a bowl with slick, in-tilted sides so they couldn't get out onto the table. The utensil in one of his hands was a spoon with a lid like a beer stein. Another was a miniature whisk broom. "My dear, you're mistaken. Remaulthiek's a wealthy being. Long ago, she did a great wrong by our standards, I don't know what. It was the decision of the debt assessor she engaged that she succor, not those who become ill or injured, but those who love them and wait in anguish to hear their fate. She comes here for the same reason we all have, as Mister Thoggosh's employees, investors, or both. Unlike most, she brings with her the necessity to pay the moral debt she incurred." He took a sip of coffee. "There are others you may consult about such matters. I'm best qualified to advise you on biology. How may I help?"

"Just being here with you," she blinked at the change of subjects, "adds to my knowledge. There's a basic logic to investigation, the discovery of 'method, motive, and opportunity,' but here, that isn't enough. I don't know what motivates nonhumans. I need to know more about the Elders, physical facts, as you say. And maybe I can pick up pointers from this—debt assessor?—Eichra Oren, if you tell me about the way he works. He's no doubt adding to his knowledge of my culture as we speak."

"I see." He sat a while, thinking. Reille y Sanchez paid attention to her lunch. "To begin with your first question, our esteemed benefactors are water-breathing creatures."

She nodded. "Although they're capable, in certain circumstances, of existing in the same environment as land sapients."

"For limited periods of time," Dlee Raftan Saon agreed, "and primarily by virtue of the almost nonexistent gravity on this asteroid, which makes up for a lack of buoyancy. In the water, you know, they can fill those awkward shells of theirs with air, rising and falling like, like—"

"Like submarines?" She raised her eyebrows.

"They propel themselves at great velocities, like submarines, employing respiratory siphons like the nonsapient octopi you know. By contrast, on land, in full gravity, their shells weigh hundreds, sometimes even thousands of— I don't recall the name of your unit of measure."

Reille y Sanchez swallowed coffee. "Kilograms. Or pounds."

"Depending on their age," he finished, "for they continue growing all their lives. That may be one reason they live so long."

She wanted to ask how long, but stuck to immediate business. "I've noticed that, exposed to air, like other aquatic species here, they wear a kind of spacesuit, practically invisible, which, I suppose, in addition to supplying breathable liquid, keeps their gills and other tissues moist. But I also know that, on some occasions, simply sitting in shallow water, out of direct sunlight, and splashing their gills seems to be sufficient."

Dlee Raftan Saon pushed his bowl aside, pouring coffee for both of them from a carafe. "In his personal quarters, Mister Thoggosh compromises all these possibilities, steeping himself in an oxygenated chemical which air-breathers like ourselves are able to survive in, although they may not like it much."

"General Gutierrez took a swim with Mister Thoggosh the first day we were here." She grinned. "It sounded like quite an experience."

"It's an expensive, somewhat experimental medium. Mister Thoggosh's use of the substance identifies him as progressive and forward-thinking. The fact is, he's one of the most radical individuals among the Elders."

"None of us," the colonel replied, "had enough data to appreciate that."

He leaned toward her. "We've been studying your species—are you going to finish your tubers?—a popular form of entertainment. As our computers sort your broadcasts, we've been catching up on thousands of years of history, one thrilling episode after another. I can tell you Mister Thoggosh is like your early aviation pioneers, radio tinkerers, women's suffragists. If it's new, he's interested. Semlohcolresh is more representative of Elders in general, which is why this asteroid venture is Mister Thoggosh's enterprise, not theirs. Fortunately, his enthusiasms invariably prove profitable."

"He's—" she searched for the hated epithet, "an entrepreneur?"

"Yes. For example, that chemical stuff makes it possible for members of more than one species to meet face-to-face, something he finds essential. It accounts, in part, for many of his past competitive—"

"Dlee Raftan Saon, I might have known! Colonel, here you are!"

She turned toward a voice she recognized. What she saw

was a tentacle wheeling toward them on a metal contrivance, like a snake on a bicycle.

"I heard you seek my friend, Tulominchel—confound it, I'll never be able to pronounce his name!—and my assistant. They're occupied, as indeed I am, but perhaps this surrogate will do. May it join you?"

SEVENTEEN
The Lost Continent

"Just in time," Dlee Raftan Saon exclaimed. "Estrellita asks after the biology of your species, with an eye toward learning what constitutes a motive for murder among the Elders."

The limb wheeled to the table, taking a position between them. "Aside from wealth," it asked, "the universal motive? I'll be of what assistance I can, Raftan. What would you like to know, Colonel?"

She shook her head. "I'm poking around at random, satisfying personal curiosity. Biology seemed the best place to start. You might tell me more about the nautiloid separable tentacle."

"As you wish, Colonel." The extension of Mister Thoggosh made up and down motions at its small end, nodding, as it explained unabashedly, "In primitive species of cephalopods, it was a sexual organ, which swam away from the male, carrying sperm to the female."

"This, too," added Dlee Raftan Saon, "is true of species familiar to humans. The 'Stone Age' precursors of Mister Thoggosh's people, for some reason, altered their sexual practices rather late in evolutionary history, to direct fertilization, rather than—"

"Doctor, I—"

"Just," Mister Thoggosh pointed out, "as happened with ancestors of human beings. Shortly after being driven out of the increasingly scarce trees by bigger, stronger monkeys, in an Africa going through a prolonged drought cycle, they, too, switched—from rear to frontal cop—"

"Mister Thoggosh, I—"

"You're discomfitted, Colonel, yet you did ask. But then your species is rather easily embarrassed. Your own Mark Twain observed that you're the only organisms who blush—or need to. Or was that H. L. Mencken? Do I fail to employ the language with sufficient clinical detachment?"

"You're both doing fine." She rubbed her hands over her face. "It's just me; too many surprises, too close together. Please go on."

"Very well," replied the physician, pouring himself more coffee. "With prehumans and their molluscoid equivalent, this small change caused greater changes, behavioral and physical, either accelerating development of speech in both species or being greatly influenced by it."

"Students of evolution," the tentacle offered, "have never been entirely certain which. Raftan, I wish I'd attended this lecture in person. That coffee smells good."

The doctor nodded. "Next time, you'll know better." He turned to Reille y Sanchez. "It's one of those aphid-and-egg things, Estrellita, impossible to say which came first. The result was the same in both instances. Intimate personal relations became, well, more intimate and personal, because they became more verbal. Thus, with the ancestors of the Elders, the sperm-bearing tentacle became an evolutionary redundancy."

"As you see," the tentacle gave a ripple, showing itself off, a display that struck her as somewhat obscene, considering the topic, "it didn't atrophy away. Evolution's conservative. Instead, it underwent metamorphosis, changing relatively quickly—in the geological scheme of things."

"By stages," explained Dlee Raftan Saon, "it became a remote-controlled general-purpose manipulator. Needing something to be controlled by, its existence encouraged the evolution of greater intelligence, as speech or the possession of thumbs may have done with your species."

Mister Thoggosh, or his general-purpose manipulator, went on: "Its first new function, paleobiologists believe, was as a decoy, expendably sent into harm's way to appease predators, as a lizard's tail is sacrificed. The theory derives from the fact that, among the primitive species, it grows back in time for the next mating season. In later species found in the fossil record, that process was accelerated."

If I stop for a second, thought Reille y Sanchez, her attention momentarily wandering, to consider how weird this conversation really is, I'll end up running through the woods like Richardson.

" . . . confers survival advantages," the doctor was saying, "and would never have evolved had the species from which the Elders sprang not been unique in another—"

"Raftan," the tentacle waved an admonitory tip, "I believe we stray from the immediate interests of the colonel."

Dlee Raftan Saon saw her expression. "I'm afraid we have. What else should we discuss, my dear?"

She cleared her throat. "Tell me about Eichra Oren. It was a surprise, meeting another human here. Where does he come from?"

Something, not the table, began beeping. "If you'll both excuse me," the doctor declared, rising, "it's back to indentured servitude. Estrellita." He bent over her hand and brushed it with his complex mouth-parts. It gave her a chill, not because he was an insect, but because the gesture, although she'd never seen the late geologist do it, somehow reminded her of Kamanov. "I've savored, to put it Remaulthiek's poetic way, the sweet scent of your naming. Come see me any time you wish, as long as you make it soon."

She felt herself blush like Toya. "Thank you, Dlee Raftan Saon, I will." Making his way among the crowded tables, he departed. She turned to the tentacle, which left the wheeled contraption to twine itself around the seat abandoned by the doctor. "You were telling me about Eichra Oren."

"So I—" Part of the noise she'd noticed must have been recorded music, for now they heard, all about them, Paul McCartney's "Yesterday," presumably sorted from a welter of signals received from Earth. It was good to hear, but must have been a South African or Swiss broadcast, possibly NeoIsraeli or PRC, because such music had been illegal—which didn't mean she hadn't enjoyed it all her life—before she was born. "Someone's noticed your presence, Colonel, and altered the entertainment program in your honor. I suppose we'll have to sit and listen politely to that outlandish racket. Then I suggest we find a place to converse without so much interference. You're aware that Eichra Oren's descended from ancient Antarcticans in your own continuum."

"Yes." Outside, morning had begun acquiring tints of jungle afternoon. Exotic birds fluttered from branch to branch amid giant orchids. Mosses and ferns filled the area between the great trees. She fought back tears evoked by the "outlandish racket." Was it possible that she, of all people, was homesick? "That's what he told the general, something about a great seafaring people wiped out by a sudden change of climate."

"Indeed," the Proprietor replied, apparently unaware of her struggle. "In their time, thousands of years ago, the Antarcticans built complex, efficient ocean-going ships, constructed, if you'll believe it, entirely of wood. Some boasted hundreds of sails, on masts of sixty or seventy meters. Often they had crews consisting of several hundred men and women—there, it's over with at last. Shall we leave, Colonel, before they honor you once more with something even more unbearable?"

Reille y Sanchez raised her eyebrows. "Women?"

The tentacle somehow conveyed a shrug. "A wise arrangement for those planning voyages lasting years. They knew the compass and sextant, although they were still at something of a loss regarding the calculation of longitude at sea. In this respect they were rather like the navies of your own civilization, well into the nineteenth century. I suggest we go to my office for further discussion. I'll have the rest of me meet us there."

Reille y Sanchez wasn't looking forward to her first dip in fluorocarbon. They followed Dlee Raftan Saon's footsteps out, the sound system blaring Sousa's "Stars and Stripes Forever." "That's more to my liking," exclaimed the tentacle wheeling beside her. "The subtleties! The intricacy! You people *can* produce real music, after all!"

"What was that," she had to shout, "about nineteenth-century navies?"

"Without offense," the voice suggested, "it occurs to me that you're unschooled in your own history. Mind you, I shouldn't want to give you the impression the Antarcticans were supernaturally skilled mariners. They did attain estimable heights of navigational proficiency, exploring and mapping most of what was then the Earth's surface. It's in this respect, although you may not be aware of it, that they were like the navy of your own British Empire at about the time of the Napoleonic—excuse me."

One of the lobster people stopped them just outside, apparently to talk business. Wondering if it was Tl°m°nch°l, Reille y Sanchez tried not to be conspicuous as she also tried to hear what was being said.

"Yes, Subbotsirrh, what is it?"

"English? Very well—and it's pronounced S°bb°ts°rrh. About these drilling equipment invoices . . ." Whatever S°bb°ts°rrh needed, it didn't take long. Mister Thoggosh and Reille y Sanchez were soon strolling down the corridor again, in the direction, she assumed, of his office.

"Now, what was it we were discussing? Navigation?"

"My British Empire," she replied. "Mister Thoggosh, I'm just a soldier. An American soldier. You know more about my world than I do. You even speak the language better. Everybody here does."

"My dear Colonel, unlike stupidity, ignorance is a curable condition. And unlike British mercantilists, the Antarcticans were basically free traders. As with many another such culture throughout sapient history, they welcomed innovation, and were in the initial stages of inventing mass production and the steam engine. Yet for all that, they were helpless when an incredible worldwide disaster—yes, what is it, Nellus?"

Again he was interrupted, this time by a furry animal which would have been taller than Reille y Sanchez had it not walked with a stoop. Its long, whiskered muzzle ended in a restless nose. Behind it lashed a hairless tail. It spoke a language consisting of squeaks and whistles.

"Colonel, this is Nellus Glaser, proprietor of the restaurant we just left. He wishes to know if you found your meal satisfactory."

Preoccupied with other matters, she had to think to remember what she'd just eaten. "I had no idea it was a private establishment. I assumed—I didn't see any signs. But yes," she grinned, "absolutely the best burger and fries I've ever had on another planet."

The tentacle emitted whistles and squeaks. So did Nellus Glaser, passing a handful of something metallic to it. It extended and dropped coins in her palm. "The signs are in radio frequencies you aren't equipped to perceive. Your fellow mammal wishes you to accept lunch as his guest. He asks whether he may quote you about the food."

"I guess it won't do any harm." She looked at the money in her hand, the amount Dlee Raftan Saon had fed into the table. "This is the doctor's. But ask him not to mention it to the general or Mr. Empleado."

"I wondered," replied the tentacle, "whether KGB officers made a habit of commercial endorsements. Keep the coins as souvenirs. Raftan would be pleased." More shrill communication took place. The cafeteria owner shook hands with Reille y Sanchez, and they were on their way down the corridor again. "I'm not certain what you assumed, but I refuse to attempt explaining the complex division-of-investment economy we've brought to 5023 Eris, until you understand more basic facts about us. What were we talking about?"

"Worldwide disaster. Shifting poles and the change in climate."

"Someone's been curing your ignorance already. Yes, the Earth precessed—wobbled in orbit—and the treacherous poles began wandering again."

"Again?"

"They've done so on many previous occasions. As long as continents drift, they'll do so again. Timing—whether or not a people has achieved sufficient sophistication to withstand such an event—has made all the difference in the survival or extinction of many sapient species. The poles' inconstancy is written in alternating magnetic patterns laid down, like your ferromagnetic musical recordings, in the great stone pillows of extruded lava at the bottommost abysses of Earth's deepest—what is it, this time?"

In that moment she came closest to imitating Richardson, paralyzed by primordial fear, even her saw-backed knife and Witness forgotten on her hips. Before them, on eight legs, not six, was a hairy presence the size of the proverbial Buick. Its overall color was straw gold, mottled with black which ran in stripes down its flying-buttress legs. The leglets—she couldn't remember what they were called—guarding the mandibles looked like a pair of brooms. The face—four visible eyes set in a horizontal line, two large between two smaller—was a painted-looking red. The giant spider hissed and bubbled at the Proprietor's surrogate.

"Moltchirtber," Mister Thoggosh told her, "my friend and chief engineer. Moltchirtber, forgive my snapping at you, dear. My talk with this lady's been much interrupted. May I present Col. Estrellita Reille y Sanchez?"

Please, God, she thought, or whoever has the duty, don't let it want to shake hands.

"Kindly accept apologies," the spider replied in an impatient but human-sounding voice, "for not beginning this in English. All of you vertebrates look alike to me—a bit frightening, actually—and I wasn't aware you were one of our recent guests. Mister Thoggosh, your integrated presence is urgently required at Shaft Thirteen, where we've experienced an equipment breakage. No casualties, this time, thanks be to Aelbraugh Pritsch's Cosmic Egg, but when we return home, a drilling manufacturer I know will be consulting his debt assessor, or my name's not Moltchirtber!"

"Tell them I'll be there, at once," he answered as the spider turned and sped away. "Colonel, we must alter our plans. We can continue to converse, if you care to accompany me." Reversing directions, they hurried along the corridor until they came to a spot on the wall which let them outside where an aircraft was waiting. As they climbed in—no pilot, no visible controls—Reille y Sanchez was out of breath. The machine lifted them a hundred meters and zoomed forward. Mister Thoggosh went on as before.

"As far as the Antarctican disaster's concerned, on a

planetary scale, the degree of shift was small, probably
not noticeable to an observer on some neighboring world.
For Earth's inhabitants, it was a cataclysm. One day it
began snowing in what had been the semitropics. It didn't
stop again, winter or summer, for two hundred years. The
first snowfall compressed under a load of new precipi-
tation into steely ice which crushed their greatest artifacts to powder, destroying every trace of their once-great
civilization. Dying of the cold or fleeing from it, they were
decimated, scattered. The little remaining evidence of their
existence was scraped, by the slowly flowing glaciers, off
the edges of the continent, into the surrounding oceans."

The craft tilted, giving them a view of the human
encampment. She waved at Toya, at the center, but the
machine was silent, and the girl didn't look up. With its
stale wood smoke and latrine smells, the place was hardly
a model of rustic charm. Surprised when he didn't land to
let her off, she thought Mister Thoggosh was polite not
to mention it. "Surely," she asked a question which had
puzzled her, "archaeologists would find something left."

"Outside their cities, Colonel, lost forever beneath
miles—pardon—kilometers of ice, they worked primarily
in wood, again much like nineteenth-century Britain. After
all these millennia, little remains. From time to time, an
inexplicable bit of stone or glasswork may show up, like
an orphan, among the remnants of later civilizations, no
more than a token of its creators' former greatness.

"There, if you look closely, you may see our destination,
that deforested rise and a cluster of low buildings.

"The question naturally arises, could such a disaster
repeat itself? If so, how much of today's human civilization would be left after fifteen thousand years? Certainly
nothing identifiable of nineteenth-century Britain will survive. What would, neglected for a period of a hundred fifty
centuries? Brace yourself for landing, Colonel. Out in the
countryside, this thing believes it's a jeep."

"But something survived. What about Eichra Oren?"

"People being sturdier than artifacts, some Antarcticans
escaped. For a variety of reasons, their choice of avenues
appeared more limited than it was. They falsely believed
Australia an uninhabitable wasteland. It's said they had

enemies in Africa, on whom a superstitious few among them blamed the catastrophe. If it ever truly existed, which I myself doubt, that culture also perished, for no trace of it remains. Thus it was to the southern tip of India the refugees came, with little more than the clothing they wore."

Mister Thoggosh had been correct about the landing. They bumped down in a trampled field sloping upward to become the ridge he'd mentioned. Aelbraugh Pritsch met them, comically attired in a workman's hard hat, a fireman's heavy coat, and a pair of odd boots, all of it, including what parts of him were visible, covered with dirt as if he'd been doing demolition work. Before the voluble avian could get a word out, another aircraft landed virtually on top of them. Mister Thoggosh climbed out. His tentacle slithered over the side of the machine Reille y Sanchez sat in, and integrated with its owner.

"Regrettably, we lack data," he went on as if he'd been with her all along, "for the next fifteen thousand years. Our ethnographers base their surmises on legends and linguistics. The Antarcticans may have been ancestral to certain wanderers who, migrating north and westward, perhaps for fear of something they no longer remembered clearly, came to dominate Europe, North America, and your modern world. Now, my dear, I must hand you off, in a manner of speaking, to my assistant, and attend a smaller disaster of my own."

"But you haven't explained Eichra Oren!"

"So I haven't. One thing we know with certainty: by coincidence, during this period, interdimensional translation was being invented by those among us who called themselves 'natural philosophers.' Conducting a monumental cross-probability survey of your Earth and several others, they 'collected' and saved a single shipload of glacial refugees.

"Eichra Oren's a descendent of these so-called 'Appropriated Persons.'"

EIGHTEEN
The Cage of Freedom

"Do please come in, Col. Reille y Sanchez."

Delightedly, Aelbraugh Pritsch led the human female to the construction office, a self-fabricating structure which the Proprietor had ordered planted when this location was selected. A light but thoroughly depressing drizzle was falling, no doubt due to Eichra Oren's recent arrival and its effects on the closed environment of the asteroid. Perhaps the atmosphere required readjusting. They climbed an uncovered flight of stairs to a deck where he manipulated the knob of a crude mechanical entrance.

"I'm afraid I must begin by anticipating your first question and refusing to say precisely what we're attempting to accomplish on this site. We can speak of anything else you wish. I spend an increasing amount of time here, so I've arranged things to my own taste and comfort. One item still sorely lacking is a humor door, although I'm not certain the place merits it."

The bits of fur over her eyes climbed her forehead. "A humidor? Isn't it humid enough already?"

"Humor. Door. Customary in the dwellings of my people, Colonel. It entertains a visitor with a riddle or a joke as

163

he waits for the occupants to answer. Or lets him down gently if they're not home or simply don't wish to be intruded upon. No house is properly a home without one. Perhaps before the next consignment—but no, I'm not sure we'll be here long enough to justify the expense. Nevertheless, I'm quite proud of what I've accomplished in these rustic conditions. May I offer you something to drink?"

Inside, it was all one large, high-ceilinged room, although it was difficult to find a level expanse larger than a desk. The building consisted of little besides stairs, landings, and lofts. He found broad, flat expanses as boring as his guest might have found a room painted a uniform gray.

"Not at the moment, thanks. As I explained to Dlee Raftan Saon and Mister Thoggosh, I'm trying to learn what I can of nautiloid biology. The doctor said something about the evolution of the Elders that intrigued me, but he got interrupted and didn't finish. It was about some other attribute, besides the separable tentacle, that made the Elders what they are?"

Stripping off his coat, hat, and boots near the entrance—his symbiote poked its blue-green head from his feathers for its first breath of fresh air in hours—he extracted a hot, wet cloth from the greeting bowl, refraining from offering one to the human. He led her to the room's center where, under a screen which kept him from singeing himself and protected his symbiote from even greater tragedy, a brazier of heated stones was glowing.

"Colonel, you'll find that padded swing comfortable. I'll perch here and get a little of this mud off my face. Grooming in the company of others is a custom of my people, so if you don't mind that I do it, I won't mind that you don't do it. You're sure I can't offer you something? That, I believe, is the custom of your people."

She sat and let her legs dangle, settling against the backrest. "Maybe later, if you don't mind. I just ate."

"I've been thinking it over." He took a place on a nearby perching rack and began toweling his face. "I can't imagine what Raftan referred to unless—of course! One takes it so much for granted. The Elders' ancestors were powerful 'electric fish.' They're still capable of generating a respectable current. You're familiar with eels, skates, rays, other aquatic nonsapients that do this with special cells in their nervous systems?"

She nodded. "Yes, I am. I hadn't noticed anything like that with the nautiloids, maybe because of the transparent— unless—that isn't how Semlohcolresh vaporized Col. Richardson's bullets, is it?"

He lowered the towel and looked at her. "Dear me, no. I don't know what you saw, but it was doubtless part of the technology built into his protective covering. The Elders are many orders of magnitude less powerful than that, Colonel. Such an ability often serves more than the simple purpose of defense. As with many modern species, it helped primitive molluscs to navigate, to remain in formation within schools, and in, er, finding and courting mates. The Elders generate a sort of biological radio energy little different in principle."

"I see." The human bobbed her head up and down, completely out of timing with the swing, which he discovered got on his nerves. "The famous nautiloid telepathy General Gutierrez told us about?"

Knowing that her disturbing lack of rhythm wasn't her fault, he tried to keep irritability out of his voice. The creatures were so sensitive. "The Elders are telepathic only in the sense that their fields are undetectable by other species unaided by technology. They employ them to control their remote tentacles and communicate with one another. The latter is limited to relatively short distances, analogous to those covered by our voices. Species employing sound-communications seem 'telepathic' to the Elders."

She exposed her fangs, something he struggled, against the racing of his heart—his symbiote buried its jewel-scaled head deep in his feathers—to remember had evolved into an expression of cordiality among these creatures. His species lacked fangs altogether, although they were as predatory in their heritage as humans. "Radio. Unless they can turn it off, doesn't that make it hard to think or get a night's sleep without distractions?"

"How very perceptive, Colonel," he chuckled. "Knowing no more than you do, you've put a foreclaw on a pivotal fact of history. Unlike a human being, the nautiloid encounters unique difficulties whenever he seeks solitude or quiet. He must confine himself within the sanctuary of a well-grounded shelter of metallic mesh, a basic amenity the species lacked for millions of years."

"One would think," she suggested, again nodding out of rhythm, "that the evolutionary result would be some sort of ultimate collectivism. Organisms like that might even develop a species-wide group-mind."

"True." He gave his symbiote's face a swipe, put the soiled towel aside on a dish for the purpose, and rose from his perch, hungry after the morning's work and wondering what he could do about it politely. "That's where the Elders might have found themselves, in a state of nature. However, it's equally true that the first imperative of evolution is diversity."

She stopped swinging. "I thought it was survival of the fittest."

"Survival of the *fit*, Colonel. The implications are worlds apart. Bereft of the vital aspect of diversity, the Elders might have died out. In their barbaric past, privacy-deprivation was a dreaded punishment, much like imprisonment in your culture, which I believe practices solitary confinement, its precise opposite. The Proprietor says one has only to experience collectivism of the mind to hate all forms of collectivism. Artificial privacy was his culture's most historically important invention, fully equivalent to your invention of the wheel."

Again the female bared her fangs, his heart began to flutter, and his symbiote dived for cover. "Did they ever get around to inventing the wheel?"

"An aquatic species had small use for the wheel until, like your astronauts, they began to explore the land. Its early remnants are seen at paleontological, rather than archaeological sites. But the invention of privacy is older. In a sense, it allowed them to invent individualism itself. Over five hundred million years, they've refined it to an amazing degree."

"Oh?" The fangs disappeared, which he knew wasn't a good sign, although he felt relieved. Ignoring a growling stomach, he sat again.

"Indeed. They've no authority you'd recognize, having discovered—being compelled to discover, over and over, through a long, bloody history—that, of the many things that may be said of it, foremost is that authority is always established for the opposite reasons its advocates claim."

"That's anarchy!" He was momentarily gratified, not without a pang of guilt, to see so fearsome a creature terrified at something he'd merely said. "What protects them from chaos? What holds their society together?"

He raised a hand. "Calm yourself, Colonel. The Elders, and those like my people who've learned from them, practice 'p'Na,' an ethical conceit vastly older than humankind, which has proven stable and workable. Although adept at self-defense and ruthless in its application, they believe the most heinous violation of p'Na is to interfere without justification in the lives of innocent sapients."

She opened her mouth, but he didn't give her a chance. "I've studied you enough to know that the word 'interference' takes on what may seem strange connotations to you, employed by someone such as myself, taught by the Elders. Their customary measure of unethical interference is the use of force in the absence of force initiated by another."

She nodded, mollified. "There are other ways to interfere with people."

"Indeed, there are. The least aesthetic, in their view, is the most insidiously attractive, consisting of an attempt, invariably well-meaning, to save others, willing or otherwise, from the effects of 'the Forge of Adversity.' By this they mean everyday vicissitudes that educate the individual, or what you mean by the process of natural selection that educates entire species."

He cast an eye toward the stasis-preserver at another level of the room and rose again. His symbiote slithered out and raced upstairs in anticipation. "If you'll excuse me, Colonel, it's been a long morning. I'm going to get something to eat. Do you still wish nothing?"

"I'll take something to drink." She put her feet on the floor, arose with him, and followed him upstairs to watch him place spiced, frozen grubs into an oiled pan. Sitting at the edge of the counter, his symbiote watched, too. When the grubs were sizzling nicely on the element, he began making a pot of coffee. "You know," declared the female, "we have a name for what you call the Forge of Adversity:

Social Darwinism. It was used to justify inhumane treatment of workers by antisocial industrial criminals and robber barons."

He gave the pan a shake before replying. "And like the phrase, 'that's anarchy!', Colonel, its function in your language is to prevent further consideration of whatever you don't want to consider further—the opposite of the way words ought to be used. Could you give the matter further consideration, you'd see at once that such a philosophy informs us, in a manner verifiable by science, that our suffering may mean something after all, in a universe that otherwise doesn't seem to make sense very often."

She took a step backward, raising her voice. "But it's so cruel!"

"Far from being cruel," he turned, missing his symbiote—it had fled to a cupboard, where its slender, projecting tail gave it away—feeling himself tremble as he answered and striving to keep it from his voice, "it's a deal more than religion or the state was ever able to deliver upon."

This, of course, evoked a flood of expostulation. Her passion rattled him, but she was ill-prepared to evaluate, let alone accept, any answers he offered; neither facts established by science nor validated by the experience (vicarious on his part, he admitted) of two million centuries. Gratified that she had no way of knowing how nervous she made him, he poured two large cups of coffee and a tiny one, offering her a variety of condiments, shuffled food from the pan, and gathered utensils. Still arguing, they returned to swing and perch. He placed a small plate on an end table for his symbiote, which glanced at them, picked up a feather-fine fork, and began to eat.

"What you refer to as 'Scientific Socialism,'" Aelbraugh Pritsch told her between bites, "has nothing to do with science. It consists, instead, of unexamined emotions and a desperate political need to justify the wholesale abuse and slaughter of billions of sapients by means of some imaginary—and, at its roots, purely mystical—'greater good.' The Proprietor warned me of this. Even after this much discussion, Colonel, I can see that the concept of the Forge remains unclear because you don't wish to understand it."

Holding the cup to warm her hands, she sipped her coffee. "Wait," she demanded, "didn't you say any well-meaning attempt to protect another sapient, willing or otherwise, from everyday natural selection deprives the individual and his species of education and constitutes the least aesthetic form of unethical interference?"

"That isn't precisely what I said," he set his empty plate aside, taking his own cup, "but it will do for purpose of this discussion."

"Okay, then," she went on, "wouldn't it be more consistent to let them run around naked and hungry, killing each other, being eaten by predators, and dying of diseases we found cures for centuries ago?"

He blinked. "More consistent with what? Who do you mean by 'them'?"

"More consistent than protecting people from the Forge of Adversity, as we obviously do in both our societies, by means of education, an industrial economy, and humane— or whatever you call it—medicine?"

He put his cup down. "I see. It would help if you limited yourself to one question at a time. Regrettably, your upbringing's left you ignorant of logic, let alone a profit-and-loss system of distribution and allocation and the voluntary division of labor. Such systems require an exchange of values. Life becomes easier, but none of the system's benefits arrive without thought and effort which are themselves part of the workings of the Forge."

"And as usual," she sneered, "the rich get richer while we dismiss the poor as unfit. There isn't much difference between your views and those of so-called intellectuals that we were warned about in school—Nietzsche, Stirner, Rand, others nobody reads any more, except a few South Africans or NeoIsraelis."

He chuckled. "Or a billion Chinese. The ideas you speak of aren't frequently broadcast, and my acquaintance with them is slight. But to the extent I'm familiar with them, I believe I detect within them an element of gratuitous contempt for others—life is difficult enough already—as if their originators weren't entirely certain of themselves or their ideas."

She raised her eyebrows. "Contempt? I call it class hatred."

"I imagine you would, but even I overstate the case, in particular where Rand is concerned. One is certain of that which he earns for himself. One with certainty possesses self-esteem. One possessed of self-esteem relates to others in a mutually satisfactory manner. Our culture, harsh as it may seem, makes possible more tolerance, respect, and love than any collective striving to shield those poor enfeebled creatures huddled within it. What yours 'protects' them from is a benevolent regard for others with foundations in reality, and the opportunity to grow beyond difficulty. Whatever else the concept of the Forge is, it precludes such stultifying interference. Do you care for more coffee?"

"I'm about coffeed out, thanks. Aelbraugh Pritsch, such an opportunity exists," she objected, "in our society, as long as its only object is to do things for others, rather than for yourself."

"The limitation," he countered, spreading his hands, "imposed at bayonet point or through guilt feelings, denies sapients any genuine motivation for growth. It steals from them the chance to transcend themselves, for their own sake, in both an individual and evolutionary sense. It denies them justifiable self-esteem, the cornerstone of any sane being's existence."

She stood, jamming her hands in her pockets. "But what about the needs of the community, of society or the nation? Aren't they larger than any single individual and worthy of self-sacrifice?"

Looking up, he shook his head. "Colonel, if your interest lies with the group, consider that it consists of nothing but individuals. What else exists for it to consist of? And it's from individuals that its survival, all of its growth and progress, derive. Where else could they come from? Suppress the individual, and you suppress the group, defeating your original purpose."

The human began to answer before what he'd said began to register. When it did, she closed her mouth, a puzzled expression distorting her features. At that, it was better than when she smiled. When she did speak, she wondered aloud whether his ideas mightn't represent a viewpoint biologically peculiar to the Elders, therefore not applicable to humans or any other species.

"Colonel, you're a military officer. You've been indoctrinated all your life in a centuries-old tradition of collectivism imposed, against your natural inclination, with gun, whip, and fist. But understand: centuries are an eye-blink. Already your faulty values begin to devour you, or you wouldn't be here. They run counter to billions of years of evolution. Any species which practices them consistently will eventually render itself extinct—as I gather your species is in process of doing. Fortunately for us all, collectivism and self-sacrifice are impossible to practice consistently."

Turning her back, she gazed into the glowing stones. "I admit none of us is perfect. Nobody ever said it's easy to measure up to what's right all the time." She turned to face him. "I was simply trying to understand your Elders, wondering whether this selfishness they've made a virtue of might not be, well, an instinct with them."

"So they aren't culpable for what you see as a moral failure? No, *p'Na* is by no means an instinct. Few beings evolve to sapience without having lost all such inbuilt guides. But it consists of something almost as—"

"Hey, birdbrain," a third voice demanded, "ask her when the last time was she screwed her father!"

"What?" Aelbraugh Pritsch leaped up, filled with alarm and unsure, in the interest of continued survival, which direction he should watch. Behind him, half a level up from perch, swing, and brazier, the front door swung aside, pushed by a damp, black nose.

"Mammalshit!" muttered his symbiote, setting its little cup down and diving back into his feathers. "It's that dog, again!"

NINETEEN
Crystal Music

The nose was only the beginning. Following behind it, its owner, then the Proprietor, entered the office, halting on the landing above the lounging area where Aelbraugh Pritsch and Reille y Sanchez had been talking for the past half hour. A damp, cold draft and a wisp of fog sneaked in with them before they shut the door.

"I expect," the Elder told the colonel, "lest you give up on us as hopelessly barbaric, that Oasam's remark may require as radical a readjustment as we've just performed on our atmosphere. With your assistance, gentlebeings?"

The Proprietor dragged himself perilously close to the edge of the steps, rising on the ends of his tentacles as on tiptoe. Aelbraugh Pritsch thought he resembled a grotesque spider, but his employer was never conscious of his dignity when he wanted something concrete accomplished, preferring to leave such aesthetic considerations to others. Reille y Sanchez hurried to help while his assistant assisted from behind, straining under the rough-surfaced, massive shell. It would have been an impossible task on Earth, given the mollusc's enormous weight. Here on the asteroid, half-floating the bulky Elder down a narrow flight of stairs

was much like handling a fiber carton greater than one's
own height and width, but empty.

Acting as host, the avian started another pot of coffee
brewing and resumed the perch he'd occupied. Reille y
Sanchez went back to the padded swing, Sam lying on the
floor at her knee.

The Proprietor trundled into place between them.
"Given the broad individual variation inevitably—and
happily—found among all sapients," he continued for the
human female's benefit, "I suspect that some few among
your number, Colonel, would perceive nothing untoward
in seeking reproductive converse with a parent—"

"*Mister Thoggosh!*"

"Aha! Enlighten me, then: does the shocked disgust in
which you audibly and visibly regard such a proposition
represent an instinctive reaction on your part, indelibly
imprinted on your genetic material?"

She didn't answer. Aelbraugh Pritsch gave puzzled
thought to what his own answer might have been, grateful he hadn't been asked. Had he been capable, he might
have blushed as furiously as she was doing now.

The Proprietor supplied his own reply. "I suspect the
contrary. As my assistant indicated, it's something else, is
it not? Something very powerful which must be reckoned
with, if—as all reflective beings must—we aspire to know
ourselves and act in accordance with our natures?"

"Alternatively," offered Aelbraugh Pritsch, "whenever one
believes it necessary or advantageous to act against his
nature, it's prudent, to say the least, to do so advisedly."

"If I follow you," Reille y Sanchez frowned, "you're saying this *p'Na* business isn't instinctive, as I suggested, but,
like the human distaste for incest, merely a longstanding
social prohibition?"

The nautiloid waved a tentacle in a negative gesture.
"The word 'merely' doesn't enter into it. All sapient species, even your own, have a distaste for incest, grounded
not in instinct, but in experience at a level of reality so
fundamental it can't be denied without terrible consequences."

"And *p'Na?*"

"Your species hasn't had the equivalent experience, yet,

in those areas of reality which bear on it. It took mine millions of years to reach our present level of understanding. But given time—provided you manage to live through the terrible consequences you now suffer out of ignorance— you, too, will create a concept so like *p'Na* as to be indistinguishable from it. It's a necessity for survival, both for individuals and whole species."

"Then maybe what I'm trying to do here isn't a total loss," she replied, "though it's a strange way to investigate a murder. The general maintains that the key to understanding you people—which he regards as a necessity for our survival—is through your most fundamental beliefs. That's why I started with basic biology."

At a signal from the heating element in the kitchen, Aelbraugh Pritsch got up to pour coffee for himself, his symbiote, Oasam, and the Proprietor—Reille y Sanchez having turned him down again—bringing it to the nautiloid in a wide-bottomed flask with a long, flexible sipping tube. Sam, as he recalled, preferred his coffee in a shallow bowl or saucer, with milk. He set it on the floor beside the dog. Mammals.

"The general," Mister Thoggosh told her, "is an astute individual, Colonel. It's exactly what Eichra Oren's doing with your party now, examining your most fundamental beliefs. Very well, let's discuss mine. Although customarily derived from first principles, for your purposes the first tenet is this: if, for whatever reason, one of us should injure another, the *p'Nan* system requires that he make appropriate restitution to the victim of his act." He glanced at Aelbraugh Pritsch and Sam. "Would you say that sums it up?"

"Why, yes, sir." The avian nodded.

The dog yawned. "I hear enough of this stuff at home."

The human shrugged. "It seems straightforward and comprehensible. Human ethics say the same thing: 'An eye for an eye and a tooth for a tooth.' "

"But you only have so much jaw-room," Sam sat up, "and did you ever ask yourself what you'd do with a spare eye?"

"Oasam, don't confuse her." The Elder smiled at her, although Aelbraugh Pritsch knew she might not have been aware of it. "Estrellita, I speak of a thing distinct from

Biblical retribution. Its opposite, in fact. The next logical, customary step may not be quite so comprehensible. If restitution can't possibly be made, our sense of justice—and, in a manner you may find difficult to appreciate, our sense of humor—demands that, in its place, the responsible party offer up his one irreplaceable asset."

"His life, of course. It still sounds pretty Biblical to me."

"I believe we'll eventually persuade you of the difference. Although, of course, it may come to his life, in the end. If, for example, he's caused a wrongful death, or otherwise created an unpayable moral debt. Rather than payment, think of it as a token of acknowledgement of that debt."

"Mister Thoggosh, that isn't quite as incomprehensible as you may think it is," she replied. "Aside from what you said about your sense of humor—which I admit I didn't get at all, and which I won't ask you to explain just now—in some ways it resembles the Japanese custom of *seppuku*, with which I'm reasonably familiar."

"Ah, the picturesque intestine-cutting ceremony. The spectacular rending of viscera." He raised a tentacle. "I trust you won't be too disappointed with us to learn that our custom is to avoid gratuitous suffering, where possible. And there are significant differences on our part regarding motivation. The *samurai* strives to meet what he imagines are the expectations of his ancestors. Unlike him, or your advocates of capital punishment for that matter, we're all too well aware that our deadly ritual restores nothing owed the damaged party. We recognize that it doesn't—that it can't—ever put back what was lost or damaged."

"That's the point," added Aelbraugh Pritsch. "It's an unpayable debt, and only an unpayable debt, which can create this rare and peculiar situation. I spoke of the importance to the Elders, as well as those they've influenced, of self-esteem. We speak now of an attempt to regain or repair it, before the end, through an ultimate display, on the part of those who create unpayable moral debts, of a willingness to make up for such mistakes, were it logically possible—which, in these circumstances, it isn't."

"Well." Reille y Sanchez shook her head in confusion. "That certainly muddies things up nicely."

At her feet, Sam permitted himself an undoglike chuckle.

"I'll try again," the Proprietor told her, interrupting whatever reply Aelbraugh Pritsch intended making. "Although this dramatic phenomenon is often referred to as the ultimate restitution, it's never actually considered to be the restitution itself, which, in cases like this, is acknowledged by everyone to be impossible by its very nature."

"So why," asked the colonel, "try?"

"Well, in a sense, the individual in question is concerned with payment of a debt which he also believes he owes himself. In that sense, his death represents a place-holder, a token, a customarily-accepted substitute, however unsatisfactory, for the more desirable restitution which could be made in less restrictive circumstances. Moreover, most individuals, however culpable, recognize the importance of not creating yet another debt by imposing the burden of doing the right thing on another being."

"*What?*"

"Please understand, Colonel," Aelbraugh Pritsch leaned forward on his perch and spread his hands to her, "that this is much more than mere lofty theorizing. You wished to know about our culture, and such considerations have previously been known—"

"On more than one occasion," the Proprietor interposed.

"—to have interrupted the otherwise stately progress of the Elders' cultural history." The avian glanced at his employer, then back at Reille y Sanchez. "Given current events, a notorious example arises in the mind."

"Here it comes," warned Sam.

"Yes," Mister Thoggosh agreed. "It seems that certain scientists among us—perhaps 'natural philosophers' is a better translation—devised a novel and intriguing application for the then newly invented and otherwise useless curiosity of dimensional translation."

The human female nodded. "So I've been told."

Aelbraugh Pritsch turned to the Proprietor. "I mentioned this to her already, sir, since it was during the period which happened to coincide with the Antarctican disaster. She knows they'd begun collecting life-forms from divergent branches of history."

"I see," the mollusc answered with a hint of annoyance

before continuing. "Now here's something you've not been told, for I don't believe my assistant is aware of this detail. It's well known that many nonsapient species, what you call pack rats, for example, and several bright species of squid, like collecting colorful, shiny objects. Natural philosophers had long known that virtually all creatures advanced beyond the gobble-it-raw-before-it-can-gobble-you stage appear to be partial to such objects, as well, although they tend to carry the fascination further than nonsapients."

"Diamonds are a girl's best friend." She smiled.

"You'll be gratified to know," the Proprietor replied, "that the same is true of females of my species. Now, as luck would have it, the deliberate cutting or faceting of certain brilliantly colorful artificial gemstones creates a brief but unmistakable, very subtle and complex piezoelectric impulse in certain radio frequencies. It happens, as you know, that we're natural transmitters and receivers of such waves. Thus we were sensitive to these piezoelectric gem-cutting impulses."

"Hold on," she asked, "you mean you could actually 'hear' these things being cut? From a distance?"

"In fact," he answered with an affirmative gesture of a tentacle, "their generation for pleasure was something of a musical art early in our history. The philosophers, remembering that, reasoned that such gemstones might be deliberately scattered to good effect throughout an area about to be studied. The effort, however, would aid scientific, rather than aesthetic values."

"I get it." The colonel grinned. "It might safely be assumed that any resulting electronic impulses would signify the presence of sapient life-forms, since nonsapients which found the gemstones would merely collect them, not cut them. Pretty neat."

The Proprietor chuckled. "As you say, pretty neat, indeed. With relatively little effort, the philosophers could reliably detect the presence of tool-making species in virtually any of the many universes of alternative probability which they purposed exploring. And it was in this way that, not just human beings, but many other intelligent species were discovered and subsequently 'sampled' by our dimensional translators."

"Including," Aelbraugh Pritsch nodded, "my own."

Sam lifted his head. "And that, lovely Estrellita, was only the beginning of the bad news."

"Oh?"

"Oasam's quite correct," Mister Thoggosh told her. "All good things have finite limits. There immediately ensued a prolonged and general debate, lasting hundreds of years, concerning the nature of what had been done and the fate of those it had been done to. At times, it came close to splitting our ancient culture down the middle."

"Like one of the gems," she suggested.

"Yes, but one would scarcely have termed it musical."

"During this time, as you may imagine," added Aelbraugh Pritsch, "every effort was expended to extend the lives of the individuals under debate."

"Yes," finished the Proprietor, "and, in the end, after much searching, they arrived at an answer which, however unpleasant its implications, they all agreed was preferable to the ongoing argument. It was decided that the tenets and precepts of *p'Na* were supreme. It was agreed—for reasons I shan't elaborate—that, according to those tenets and precepts, all rights derive from sapience. Despite their unenviably primitive estate, the collected beings—'Appropriated Persons' as they came to be called—were nonetheless sapient. That was the reason they'd been collected in the first place."

She nodded, "I take it this was bad news for the scientists?"

"You take it correctly," the Proprietor confirmed. "*p'Na* had to be applied equally to 'savage' sapients as well as civilized molluscs. This being so, their involuntary collection had been a forbidden act, constituting the grossest possible violation of an intelligent life-form's rights. Given universal recognition of the 'Forge of Adversity' concept, this was true even when it happened to save their lives, as it may have with the Antarctican humans my assistant told you about. The result was the unintentional creation of an enormous and so far unpaid debt."

Mister Thoggosh fell silent. As it became apparent he was through talking for the moment, Aelbraugh Pritsch took up the story. "This dismaying—and retroactively obvious—

realization on their part resulted in unprecedented trauma, a fatal discontinuity in the lives of a normally placid and far-seeing people. At stake was their ancient civilization, everything it stood for, their leisurely view of things. To this day, that discontinuity and its astonishing aftermath are an embarrassment. To many, being the long-lived species they are, it is recent history, but history they feel uncomfortable remembering, despite its generally beneficial outcome."

The human female set her feet on the floor and leaned forward, directing a gently toned question at the Proprietor, who still seemed lost in memory or contemplation. "How was the debt paid?"

Mister Thoggosh blinked and looked back at her. "Owing to the amount of time that had passed, as well as the immense difficulty and danger of interdimensional travel, the philosophers were physically unable to replace their living 'samples.' That, of course, did nothing to remove the burden of obligation from their figurative shoulders. There could be no statute of limitations on seeing that right was done. And this time, given the circumstances, expense didn't come into the picture."

"I see. And?"

"Nor were any other potentially negative effects on our society to be taken into account. At the time, it was generally predicted that the slow, inexorable progress of science might be measurably retarded. Nevertheless, such an irreplaceable loss of talent all at once was an unavoidable price that had to be paid."

"I think you lost me somewhere. What loss of talent? What happened?"

"Why, what else? In the most ancient and honored tradition of *p'Na*, those individuals who considered themselves most responsible for the ethical travesty, the physicists, specimen collectors, and their various associates, all suicided honorably."

TWENTY
The Great Restitution

"I've been higher than this," Reille y Sanchez told him, "on Earth, in the Rockies and Sierras, and here on 5023 Eris. But I don't think I remember being more intimidated by the height."

Eichra Oren nodded. They stood alone together on a balcony of the plastic-covered mesh the Elders seemed to use for everything here, half a kilometer from the surface. It was attached to the massive trunk of one of the giant trees which had created and held up the canopy.

Below, in the gathering twilight, they could see the site Mister Thoggosh wouldn't tell her about, laid out like a miniature model. Whatever adjustment had been made to the atmosphere, following the disturbance of his arrival, it had been correct. The air around them was warm for this late in the day, drier than it had been, she said, since the Soviet American expedition had landed. And at this altitude, there was a fair breeze which, he observed with interest, put color in her face and ruffled her thick auburn hair.

"I've heard it said heights aren't impressive unless something in your field of vision—like this tree—establishes an unbroken perspective, from bottom to top." He didn't relish standing close to the flimsy-looking rail himself, although he thought it unlikely that a fall of that distance, in this gravity, would injure. "But you didn't climb up here to discuss the weather or the altitude. Sam mentioned you'd been talking to Mister Thoggosh and Aelbraugh Pritsch about the Great Restitution."

"Sam told me how to find you. I thought you two were in constant touch. It's that radio thing the Elders do, isn't it?" She turned from the dizzying view to face him. "I didn't climb up here to talk about that, either. I'm trying to figure out what makes them tick. One minute I think I understand them, and the next, somebody throws something at me that confuses me all over again." She indicated the broad-bladed sword with its wire-wrapped handle and heavy brass-colored pommel and guard, leaning in its scabbard beside him. "You're human, but you also know the nautiloid culture. I decided to ask you why all those scientists killed themselves."

"I see." He turned—finding it hard to look into her eyes and think at the same time—to gaze out at the darkening landscape. "It might help to tell you about others, perhaps objectively less guilty, who *didn't* kill themselves. In a way, it was much harder for them. They'd supported the research, benefitted from the knowledge it produced, so they felt a measure of responsibility."

"What did they do?"

"To most of the Elders, the beings they called 'Appropriated Persons' were alien, repugnant creatures. Nevertheless, and although they had no moral obligation in my opinion—supposedly that of an expert—thousands personally adopted nonnautiloid sapients with the objective of bringing them fully into the culture. Appropriated Persons would enjoy exactly the same status as the Elders themselves. It couldn't have been easy, not after two hundred million years of being the only people they knew about. As I say, it may have been harder than for those who took an easier way out. Even so, it happened faster than anyone, including the Elders, expected. The process was already well underway by the time the decision was arrived at formally."

She stepped closer. "I don't think I follow you."

He turned back, equally unable to keep his eyes off her. "Well, it may be significant to you that the complete non-existence of anything resembling politics helped in a major way. There wasn't anything to interfere with what would have been a complicated process to plan—one that happened anyway, without anyone planning it. For example, they spoke of providing collectees with an education in any one of thousands of different fields. By the time anybody got around to it, they discovered the opportunity was already being provided by private parties through the market process."

"But why? I mean, aside from the restitution we've been talking about, why would anybody want to do something like that?"

He shrugged. "Why not? If you're an Elder, and you've a job that can be done better by a human or an avian or a sea-scorpion than another Elder, that's who you hire. If they need education first, technical or academic, you provide it if you want the job done badly enough. One way or another, the Elders were making their former 'victims' a remarkable, openhanded gift, giving away everything it had taken them millions of years to learn. But they didn't look at it that way. Once the decision was made, once it was discovered that the decision was irrelevant, many said special care should be exercised to avoid *injuring* the beneficiaries inadvertently."

Her eyes widened, and she spread her hands, palms up. "Now I'm really lost. Injuring them? By educating them, giving them work?"

"Your culture has an expression about killing with kindness. The Elders were worried that Appropriated Persons might become helpless, dependent welfare recipients. Remember, they had a long history, during which they'd made every possible mistake a people can make and live to tell about it. So they concocted all sorts of complicated plans. An Appropriated Person's education, they decided, should be as self-directed as possible. Productive employment should be offered as soon as Appropriated Persons qualified for it. Under their voluntarist—what you call 'laissez-faire'—economy, these measures, they felt, would prevent a welfare mentality."

She opened her mouth and closed it again. He was aware that, from her Marxist viewpoint, there were so many things wrong with what he'd said she didn't know where to begin answering it. He laughed. "Before any of it was thought out, it was already done, out of self-interest. Cortical implants, keyed to the Elders' frequencies, allowed others to share the 'telepathy.' Soon, other life-forms acquired the artificial equivalent of separable tentacles, a convenience as necessary as clothing in your culture. In my case, it's an energetic, long-haired dog with a lopsided grin, the remote I'd have if I'd been born a thinking mollusc, instead of a naked— Sam says, *sometimes* thinking—ape. The integration of Appropriated Persons into the Elders' world was swifter and smoother than anybody expected and, in time, they simply became *persons*."

"Okay." Reille y Sanchez nodded. "That explains something Aelbraugh Pritsch said about the nautiloids benefitting as much as those they were trying to recompense. In the end, their economy wound up with more manpower— beingpower—and more consumers."

He shook his head. "There's more. In addition to whatever culture Appropriated Persons brought with them— plenty, even if they were less advanced than the Elders—the climate encouraged cross-fertilization. New ideas, inventions, businesses sprang up overnight. The stubbornest Elder came to see that civilization had become—stagnant isn't the word—sluggish, before the 'victims' arrived.

"In the end—if such processes ever truly end—the Elders never abandoned *p'Na*. They'd learned the hard way, over a span of five hundred million years, and it was *p'Na* that had made everything else possible. But in other ways, they soon found themselves strangers in their own land, in as much need of reeducation as the adoptees, and surprised to be exploring a brand-new culture they'd all built together quite by accident."

She raised her eyebrows. "And none of this violated the *p'Nan* principle of the Forge of Adversity?"

"On the contrary," he explained, "to the Elders it represented payment of a vast and terrible debt, to people they saw as having been brutally kidnaped. Which, of course, is why the scientists killed themselves. Do you have any more questions, Col. Reille y Sanchez?"

She ran a self-conscious thumb around the top of her pistol belt before resting her palm on the pommel of her knife, "You could call me Estrellita. And since you invite it, this may be a minor mystery on the grand scale, but it's irritating. I'd resolved to speak with you or Sam about it, anyway."

"And what might that be . . . Estrellita?" He wondered whether she knew how beautiful her name was. Or how beautiful she was, for that matter.

"Well," she began, "you call him 'Oasam' sometimes, or often just 'Sam.'"

He nodded. "And sometimes 'Otusam,' as well."

"Okay, that raises a couple of questions. It must only be coincidence that he resembles the Samoyed breed you may not even be familiar with. After all, his name's a word in Antarctican or some other language unknown today on Earth. My Earth, anyway. I don't understand why or how everybody gives him three different names, and I don't know whether I'll ever have the chance to acquire sufficient vocabulary in your native language to . . ."

She stopped, apparently embarrassed. He smiled. "And it never occurred to you, in this connection, to make count of the various names and titles by which different people address you in different contexts, former Major and now Colonel Estrellita Reille y Sanchez?"

She smiled back at him. "I've noticed that, on principle, he's as disrespectful as he can possibly be to the Elders. The Proprietor, however, appears to have a well-developed sense of humor, and as a consequence—"

"Mister Thoggosh enjoys Sam's sassiness. Sam's especially merciless with Aelbraugh Pritsch, often referring to him as the Proprietor's *spare* separable tentacle. The fellow can be pretty humorless, and more than a little pompous, even if he's harmless. Aelbraugh Pritsch enjoys it less than Mister Thoggosh, who encourages it because he thinks it's healthy. Sam—"

"Aha! That's why my ears were burning!" They turned to the spiral stairs wrapped around the tree, now almost lost in the dimness, by way of which they'd each climbed here in the first place. "Despite the beautiful Estrellita's undisguised astonishment—as well as her initial scornful disbelief—regarding talking dogs, I can speak as well for myself as any beneficiary of cortical augmentation, thank you, ma'am."

Eichra Oren laughed. Reille y Sanchez frowned. "Cortical augmentation? You started to say something about that."

He nodded. "A sophisticated surgical process performed in utero, common in our society. I also meant to tell you, when you mentioned Samoyeds, that Sam's descended from animals aboard the Antarctican refugee ship you were told about when it departed the Lost Continent. Your Samoyeds probably descend from the ones who weren't Appropriated. In his case, augmentation had the effect of enhancing a suitable brain with the aid of electronics, until it was raised to the qualitative level of human sapience."

"Hell of a mouthful, right?" Sam grinned up at her. "Looked at differently, I'm a powerful cybernetic system riding around inside a doggy's body. Not too bad a deal, let me tell you, for either the computer or the doggy. Do you know what a gentleman's gentleman is?"

She put her fingers to her temples. "You make my head ache, both of you. Do you know how deep a person has to reach for vocabulary as illegal as that and almost two centuries out of date? 'A gentleman's gentleman.' That's a butler or a valet, isn't it? So what?"

"So I'm a sapient's sapient. Look, Boss, she's still thinking, can she really be talking to, and getting answers from, a hound? If this poochie's as Elderblessedly brilliant as he sounds, why is he content to act as a lowly, if rather insubordinate, servant? And she's thinking, how can such a thing be possible in a civilization founded on self-interest?"

She dropped her hands and laughed. "Wrong. I'm thinking I now have you in a logical trap. What I ask is, if you're a sapient being yourself, where the hell's *your* separable tentacle?"

Eichra Oren folded his arms and leaned against the trunk, grinning in the shadows. Sam sat and panted. It had been a long climb, even for him. "You'll be surprised to learn that I wonder about that myself, at what you might call a philosophical level. I'm considered an independent being by the Elders, who define that status, somewhat circularly, in terms of possession of sapience itself. What troubles me more is whether my intelligence is real or artificial and, in my more ironic moments, whether it makes any difference."

"I don't know what you mean," Reille y Sanchez admitted.

"If he means anything at all," suggested Eichra Oren. "This is his poor, confused little canine genius routine. He's extremely fond of human females, and it nearly always gets to them."

"Boss, this is serious! And before she gets the wrong idea, you'd better explain that I like human females because, back home, they always have canine female companions. What I wonder is if I'd be a different individual if my cybernetic component had been implanted, say, in the nervous system of that little blue-green lizard Aelbraugh Pritsch carries with him."

"I suspect," Reille y Sanchez looked at Eichra Oren, "what he wonders about is why, regardless of his status as independent sapient, he feels most comfortable as your companion. I'll bet he even feels a little lost on those occasions when you're not together. Most of all, he wonders how much of his contentment with his lot is real, and how much was programmed into him."

"Watch out," warned Eichra Oren, "I think she's got you, Sam."

Sam sighed. "I've looked through all the programming and every one of my circuit diagrams myself, many times. I've never found a satisfactory answer to any of those questions."

"Meanwhile," she went on, "regardless of the reason, he remains fondly loyal to you, a noble individual he feels deserving of nothing but fond loyalty. He sees himself, possibly with justification, as squire to a famous and formidable knight, although, talking to him, it sometimes seems he thinks of you as *his* appendage, rather than the other way around. Maybe that's the secret of his peculiar contentment. What do you think, Mr.

Famous *p'Nan* Debt Assessor—whatever that title actually means?"

"I think," Eichra Oren pushed himself from the tree and stood erect, "I'm not the only one who's formidable, and that whoever killed your friend Kamanov is in a great deal of trouble."

"I think," Sam added, "that it's getting late and I'd better get back to the surface and finish my errands. If you two can get along without me." He started down the stairs. "Don't do anything I wouldn't!"

Eichra Oren ignored the dog's advice and took a step closer to her. It was nearly dark. "As for my title, as close as English gets to the concept, I'm simply a kind of ethical bill collector."

She took a step closer to him. "Meaning you collect bills ethically, or you collect ethical bills?"

"Emphasis on the latter." He closed all but the last centimeters of distance between them. "I'm a debt assessor, employed most of the time by the parties I end up collecting from. I provide logical answers to questions regarding what you might call the balance of moral accounts. It usually comes down to a simple matter of settling honest disputes of fact or intention between individuals of good will. On occasion, clients want to be certain of the proper course ahead of time, before they act; I'll admit I've a good deal fewer clients of that sort than I might wish. In any case, once the equation's calculated, I prescribe a course of action to restore the balance, and sometimes act directly to restore it, myself."

"Pretty words." Reille y Sanchez cast a significant glance toward the sword, its handle gleaming in the day's last light where it leaned against the rail. The expression on her face wasn't revulsion. "Which mean you function as judge, jury, and executioner."

"Does spreading the responsibility," he countered, shrugging, "really lessen it?" Although there wasn't enough light to see her clearly by, he turned to face her directly, seized her by the upper arms, pulling her close against him. She, with more training in martial arts than the art of love, raised her forearms reflexively, trying to break the hold.

Before her body knew she wasn't being attacked, he'd

released her shoulders, taking her by the wrists instead,
bending her arms, not roughly, behind her back where he
held them crossed and pinned as he kissed her in the warm
dark. It wasn't a thing commonly done among his people.
He'd studied it for this assignment and was curious. After
a startled instant of resistance, her mouth softened under
his and opened. She closed her eyes—he could feel her
lashes on his cheek—and relaxed against his arms.

Nighttime had come to Eris once again.

TWENTY-ONE
Pleasure Before Business

Eichra Oren felt a tautness in his body, a singing in his nerves and muscles, a pleasure that was almost pain. Within the circle of his arms, Estrellita trembled and a tear escaped from the long sweep of her lashes. He released her wrists, keeping his arms around her. "Is it possible," he whispered, "that this incurs a moral debt on my part?"

"I hope—" Her voice came in a rusty croak. She inhaled and began over. "If you're apologizing, Eichra Oren, I, er, deny the debt."

He kissed her again. When some time had passed, he told her, "For the first time I regret the structure of my language. I haven't a shorter name for you to call me by. 'Eichra' and 'Oren' mean nothing, separate from one another. You've a beautiful name—I meant to tell you that before—and appropriate, since you're beautiful, yourself."

She buried her face against him, her shoulders worked, he felt dampness through his clothing, although she made no sound. He laid the palm of a hand along her cheek and gently turned her head to see her eyes. "You're crying," he told her, and felt like an idiot for stating the obvious.

"You don't know," she answered bitterly. "I'm far from

beautiful inside! I'm a Marine officer, a trained killer, and now I'm—"

"And by the same standard, what am I?" he demanded. "The blood of a thousand sapients is on my hands." In the darkness, she heard the whisper of an aircraft as it rose level with the balcony. He turned her so that she stood facing it. "Come," he told her, "we'll steal a few hours and see what you and I are like inside. My wager is that you're beautiful that way, as well."

Without waiting for an answer, he lifted her in his arms, carried her to the rail, set her in the machine, then climbed in beside her. Pilotless, the electrostat slipped sideways from the balcony, gaining altitude. Half reclining in the bottom of the craft, she brushed tears from her cheeks with a sleeve. "You've forgotten your sword."

He shook his head. "I can't forget it, Estrellita, but I can leave it behind for a while. It'll be there when I come back. Unfortunately."

One arm beneath her shoulders, he leaned over to place his mouth on hers again. His other hand operated the release of her weapons belt. Knife and pistol slid to the floor with a dull clunk. He took the toggle of her suit zipper, pulled it down between her breasts to the waist. She wrapped her arms around his neck and clung to him as the aircraft swooped toward the night-black canopy.

Later, she faced him cross-legged, holding his hands in hers, palms up. They rested on bare flesh; her uniform, which couldn't be said to be lying discarded in a corner only because there were no corners, had been discarded nonetheless. A soft light glowed from beneath the compartment rim. She looked at his hands, which she said seemed perfectly ordinary to her, and at the same time, perfectly extraordinary, then up into his eyes.

"A thousand sapients."

As naked to her as she was to him, he looked at his hands as if they were strange to him, then met her eyes by a more circuitous route than she'd taken, having decided she was very beautiful, indeed. "It doesn't happen every day," he told her. "Most of the time, I'm an arbiter in small matters of rights or property, rather than life. Often my presence will be requested to witness a personal or business agreement, or a potentially disputed event."

"In your official capacity?" she asked.

He smiled, enjoying the feel of the night around them. "I've no official capacity, Estrellita, only a customary one. Occasionally, a client will ask the most awful and fascinating question ever put to me. It's always an uncomfortable moment, and it's long established in formula: 'Am I allowing my existence to continue in ignorance of some irreversible breach I've unknowingly committed, some irrevocable restitution I've neglected to make?' "

With a frown, she repeated the words, " 'Am I allowing my existence to continue in ignorance of some irreversible breach I've unknowingly committed, some irrevocable restitution I've neglected to make?' "

"Have a care," he warned, reaching to brush a strand of hair from her eyes. She ducked her head, caressed his palm with her cheek and kissed it. "Once the words are spoken in earnest, they can't be taken back. I've no choice but to find an answer and recommend action to be taken in consequence. Sometimes—it's never pleasant—I must take the action myself. In your terms, my profession combines aspects of a rabbi, policeman, psychiatrist, lawyer, accountant, referee, father-confessor, judge, family doctor, philosopher, and, in ultimate resort, executioner."

She released his hand, leaned back against the side of the vehicle and straightened her legs across his thighs. "I get around, for a twenty-nine-year-old former virgin. A rabbi, a cop, a shrink, a lawyer, an accountant, a referee, a priest, a judge, a doctor, a philosopher, and an executioner, all in one day?"

"You've an excellent memory, Estrellita." He let his hands travel the length of her legs, enjoying her soft, flawless skin and the muscles lying beneath it. "And not as good an opinion of yourself as you deserve. It's true that, because of that last aspect, my work brings me, on rare occasion, into violent contact with others—what individual would be willing to trust me in small matters if I hadn't proven myself reliable in large ones?—or at least it presents its more physically active moments."

She laughed, pulling herself forward into his lap and wrapping her legs around his waist. "And what do you call this?"

He let his mouth and hands wander before he answered. "A splendid spirit of cooperation between two investigators. In fact, I'm ready to cooperate all over again, if you are." He moved and she settled lower in his lap.

She sighed, closed her eyes, and enjoyed a pleasant shudder. "So you are! No, don't turn out the lights. This time I want to see your face."

For an hour they were oblivious to anything but one another. Afterward he set the 'stat on a random course among the trees where lights twinkled here and there and she saw things strange and wonderful to her. They skimmed, at a modest distance, past a party of Aelbraugh Pritsch's species, celebrating the first hatching on the asteroid with traditional percussion music which must have sounded to an unaccustomed ear like an industrial accident. In their midst, a great arachnid held the equivalent of bagpipes to spiracles along its abdomen, adding to the racket.

Another pass took them by an off-duty drilling crew of sea-scorpions and cartiloids, no doubt discussing the latest failure as they shared a titanic keg of beer. Aboard the aircraft, their own talk returned to his profession. She expressed surprise that a species wise and ancient as the Elders needed someone like him, in her words, to maintain order.

"Wise and ancient they may be," he replied, "but the Elders are no angels. Their history embraces every good or evil which we, mere butterflies to them, ever conceived in our paltry million years. They've seen five *hundred* million, and they've long memories. They regard a certain amount of crime as thermodynamically inevitable. It may even measure a culture's health."

She raised her eyebrows. "Crime as a sign of health?"

He nodded. "There's no surer sign that a culture's sickly and on the edge than lack of gumption among its crime-prone members. No matter how much progress is made, it'll always be easier to steal something than to earn it. That's why theft will exist, as Mister Thoggosh says, 'for as long as stars of the nth generation continue to fuse hydrogen.' No matter what happens, it'll always be easier to destroy something—"

"And even easier," she added, "just to threaten its destruction."

"Statements of equal relevance to the phenomena of entropy and extortion. The Elders are optimistic; they feel both facts have more to do with the way the universe is constructed than with the behavior of sapients living in it. However, there'll always be people capable of reasoning only as far as those facts and no further. And of making criminal plans predicated on them."

"Which is why you still need police?"

"On the contrary, Estrellita, I'm no policeman. The persistence of crime reveals too much about the origin of authority. In what way could it have begun, other than by some gang threatening a farmer's crops—and the farmer with them—unless he agreed to part with a portion in order to protect the rest? That's the relationship between death and taxes."

"Anarchist! Lenin warned us about you." She laughed and shook her head. "And none of the younger species ever give the Elders an argument?"

"The Elders detest appealing to seniority for validation. Still, over the last hundred million years they've seen this process many times among many different species, beginning with their own. It's also characteristic of them that they're inclined to blame the farmer for inventing agriculture which, by its nature, rendered him helpless in the first place."

"Maybe farmers invented authority to protect them from gangs."

"Authority's always supposed, by history revised after the fact, to have arisen to prevent or punish acts which, in truth, sustain it. How long could authority continue if it were effectively forbidden to steal what others earn, to destroy—or threaten to destroy—what others create?"

"I won't answer," this time her mouth and hands did the wandering, "until you tell me how long I have to wait until you make love to me again."

He laughed. "Keep doing that, and—damn!" His implant shrilled, and for the first time the 'stat faltered in its flight.

They were in no danger, the warning was advisory, intended to protect the colony's only means, however imperfect, of returning to the home continuum. "Look," he told her, pointing over the rim of the craft, "it's the dimensional translator!"

It was the largest building on 5023 Eris. He tried to look at it as she must be seeing it. It could have been a particle accelerator, a raceway, or an athletic field. His layman's knowledge of the Elders' ultimate triumph in physics rendered him little less ignorant of its operation than she was. Its foundation, surrounded by jungle, was an enormous isolation field a hundred meters square, inset with a wheel-rim construction almost as large, split into truncated wedges seven meters wide, marching around the rim. Half a dozen pathways met at a hexagon in the center where he and Sam had materialized not long ago amid artificial lightning and a howling storm.

"Pretty," was her only comment. "You're easily distracted, Eichra Oren." She pulled him down, back to the center of the compartment as the craft steered past the installation and away. It was only a minute before she had his full attention again. After a considerably longer interval, their conversation returned, as it always must, given the kind of people they were, to their responsibilities.

"Sometimes I'm compelled—" He stroked her head, which lay against his thigh.

"Employing the least," she grinned, "of your many amazing abilities—"

"I'm compelled, as you suggest, to assist some clients with that sword which constitutes my badge of . . . there isn't a word for it in your language. 'Office,' 'authority' won't do at all. I said earlier, this is only in the uncommon instance of those few who, for one reason or another, happen to be—perhaps less morally capable—of making the ultimate restitution themselves."

She sat up and turned to face him. "So you force them?"

"On the contrary, Estrellita, no one's forced to the ultimate restitution. It's not even remotely related to capital punishment. But it'll happen that, in the course of collecting lesser debts, or defending my life trying to do so, I'm called on to collect a life. If they've time under such circumstances, even unwilling clients are sometimes grateful for my assistance. If not, their families or associates seldom fail to express a measure of gratitude."

She shook her head. "Sounds crazy to me."

He put a hand on her shoulder, where it displayed a tendency to explore elsewhere. "In a trade society, unwillingness or inability to pay a debt is the worst disgrace imaginable, spoken of afterward, often for millennia, to the detriment of the defaulter's interests. It doesn't happen much."

Despite martial skills, advanced weaponry, and sword of—"office" wasn't the word—Eichra Oren was more in his own mind and in those of others than a bloody-handed executioner. Trouble came when he tried explaining it to someone with Estrellita's background. He pointed out that Earth's barbaric past—not to mention its barbaric present—had plenty of that type. "They do nothing to maintain the moral elevation of cultures they infest. I gather some of these butchers even torture. That kind of savagery, like taxation or slavery, has been absent from our society for millions of years."

She laid a hand on his cheek. "I believe you're not a torturer. Every time you touch me you tell me what you are."

He shrugged. "I'm one of a handful of individuals . . ."

She interrupted. "Unusually capable individuals, Mister Thoggosh told me, upon which all civilization depends. His exact words."

"He generously exaggerates the qualities of all who work with him. I'd say, due to my basic character, as well as to later training, I'm able to take the process of moral reasoning to a conclusion regardless of what may happen as a consequence."

"And no one," she confirmed, "ever benefits from your, er, services unless they contract and pay for them voluntarily?"

"That's absolutely—" He frowned. "Damn, it's more complicated than that. They may, indeed, come to require them as the inevitable result of a chain of events which they initiated by choice."

She nodded. "Like saying a burglar or mugger or rapist

dying at the hands of his victim has chosen a complicated way of committing suicide?"

"What else? I'm grateful that, rather than being feared or hated or avoided because of the more sanguinary aspects of my profession, I'm honored out of proportion with my talents or accomplishments."

"You're like a celebrated surgeon," she told him, "one of those rare and valued individuals practicing a profession who are able to do it competently."

He shook his head. "It's seen as having little to do with me. As with your burglar, responsibility lies with the one who came to need my services. I'm seen by everyone, and see myself, as the instrument of his will. Also, despite its fascination, situations which end in bloodshed are rare. In the ordinary course of my profession, I'm more concerned with those who *aren't* criminals. It's the fervently held wish of the ordinary individual never, by accident, ignorance, or even by appearance, to become such. It's my function to help them any way I can, consistent with principle, to fulfill that wish."

"Don't do *me* any favors!" She laughed, but there was a nervous tone beneath it. "What about those who won't volunteer?"

"There are always those," he mused, "who for one reason or another are not so particular about maintaining their moral status."

"Sociopaths."

"I've heard the word," he told her. "I disbelieve it has a real referent. The Elders are concerned with the consequences of an individual's acts. The reasons he may present for them are considered secondary, if they're considered at all."

Her eyes widened. "No extenuating circumstances? No mercy?"

"I didn't say that, Estrellita. Putting accountability first, they feel, is responsible for the longevity of their culture and the level of peace, freedom, and prosperity within it."

She looked at her hands. "You didn't answer about non-volunteers."

"As one of your own philosophers once put it, life becomes impossible for them. No one will trade with them—hire, house, clothe, feed them—no matter what they offer. They wander the land becoming more ragged each day until, from desperation, they turn back—to find me following them."

She shivered and wrapped her arms around herself.

"You're right," he told her, "that few moral cripples such as these are grateful to me. So, out of a prudent regard for survival, let alone my reputation, in addition to pursuing philosophy and logic, I've become proficient at the martial arts."

"Be *good* at it, Eichra Oren." She placed her hands either side of his face. "Be as good as you are at making a girl feel decent about herself for a few minutes for the first time in her life!"

She wept again for a little while, and they made love all through the remainder of the night.

TWENTY-TWO
Mass Insanity

Daylight brought them back to reality and the human encampment.

They'd stopped, high among the trees, to dress and reaccouter themselves aboard the aircraft, wash and eat breakfast at a little balcony café run by one of the "rat-things" Estrellita said she'd seen earlier with Mister Thoggosh. Now the electrostat hovered over the shuttles. Beneath their feet, it felt as reluctant as they were about landing. Lost in thought, Eichra Oren turned as she said his name. "Speaking as a cooperating investigator," she asked, "what are you planning to do now?"

He grinned. "After I've caught up on my sleep? I've talked to almost all your people. I'll check in with Sam and start on mine."

"'Check in with Sam,' he says. Are you claiming that dog of yours wasn't eavesdropping electronically on us all night?"

"Hope you're not disappointed." The electrostat settled with a bump outside the triangular "circle" of spacecraft. He rose, tucking his recovered sword under his arm. "I locked out everything except that alarm, never having cared much for an audience. Oops, here's your general. You're sure we shouldn't have landed in the trees and let you walk in by yourself?"

"I believe you're trying to be a gentleman, unless you're worried about your own reputation. I just realized I know nothing—well, practically nothing—of Antarctican customs." She smiled and touched his cheek. "I'm not ashamed of anything I do with you, Eichra Oren. If anybody gave me any grief about it, I'd resign my commission and join the nautiloid foreign legion, just to be with you."

As the side of the craft shrank into itself and they alighted, the only humans who seemed to notice their arrival were Arthur Empleado and one of his surviving henchmen, Roger Betal, who slipped from between two of the shuttles and approached them. "Well, Colonel," asked the KGB man, "did you enjoy your dirty little interlude with this race traitor?"

Estrellita stiffened. Beside her, Eichra Oren was mystified to find himself despised. To the extent he understood it, the man's expression spoke of an ugly concept the Antarctican found devoid of meaning and, at the same time, infuriating. He stepped forward.

"Arthur," Estrellita demanded before Eichra Oren could reply, "I've hardly pulled my new rank on anybody yet, and it's about time. You justify your insubordinate innuendo, or you're in real trouble."

"There are limits to anyone's authority, Colonel," Empleado sneered, "and apparently more than one way to abuse it. What else but 'race traitor' is it reasonable to call a human who willingly works for these inhuman, regressive, individualistic monsters? Ruthlessly exploitive capitalists, striving selfishly for personal profit? Isn't he committing a crime against the collective interests of his own, naturally altruistic species? And what do you call one of us who, er, collaborates with him—all night?"

"Stop!" This time, Eichra Oren wouldn't be interrupted. His warning had an effect, since they'd all seen what had happened the last time he'd shouted. He stepped toward Empleado until he could see the pores on the man's nose, but didn't touch him. "Nothing would give me greater pleasure than to make you eat those words and your teeth along with them. I may yet, but for the time being, I'm the closest thing to a detective the Elders have produced—or needed to—and they've asked me to investigate a murder, using my own judgment. That's exactly what I'm doing."

"Roger!" Sweating profusely, Empleado appealed to his underling for support. Betal grinned at his boss, then at Eichra Oren, shrugged, and made no other move. Empleado gulped. Eichra Oren turned to face a small crowd beginning to filter out of the camp and gather around.

"I haven't refused to discuss my background with anyone interested enough to ask. For my part, I mistrust translation software. I'd risk offending my cosapients—" He glared at Empleado. "That's you—by breaking off this delightful conversation and asking to borrow a dictionary to look up the words you just threw at the colonel, except that I'm feeling too good this morning, and I don't want to start being sick to my stomach!"

At last, he turned to Reille y Sanchez. "Sorry, Estrellita, I thought something like this might happen."

She shook her head. "I told you what I thought already. Don't worry about it. Are you going back to—"

"I'm going for a walk, then to speak with some of Mister Thoggosh's people, as I said. The electrostat will find its own way home. I'll be back toward evening to see you."

Looking around self-consciously, she smiled, then stood on tiptoe and kissed him on the cheek. "I'll look forward to it."

He turned, heading for the jungle, where he'd been vaguely aware a shaggy dog was waiting for him. "Good speech, Boss. Have a good time last night?"

"Not you, too, Sam!" They walked together into the leaves, Eichra Oren swatting absently at random stalks with his sheathed sword. "I doubt that I've gotten any closer to understanding what motivates them. It must be something other than mere loyalty or affection such as we feel toward one another or my mother or Mister Thoggosh. They're strange, alien beings, although they look human enough if one goes by outward appearance. From time to time they even manifest what I'm forced to admit is evidence that they're capable of rational thought and behavior. Simply getting here in these primitive rockets of theirs represents a respectable feat—like sailing around the Earth in a washtub."

"Therefore," the dog answered, taking up the man's tone, "and despite all evidence to the contrary, they presumably fit somewhere into that broad class of entities with which we personally identify, sapient organisms."

Eichra Oren ducked to avoid brushing a dew-damp fern frond. Or maybe it was still wet from yesterday's rain. "Presumably. And yet their inexplicable everyday behavior, their unfathomable thoughts and feelings, their hostile attitude toward me before they knew anything about me . . ."

"Well, that's what you're good at, Boss, solving mysteries."

He pondered the elaborate metal handle of the sword. "Yes? Well, I've tried to adopt the long view of the Elders. I've considered the possibility that these people are bent on suicide, that they're some recent, nonviable mutation yet to be weeded out by natural selection."

They went on for a while, in silence. Finally, Eichra Oren spoke. "Sam, they're more alien than any of the nonhuman species we've grown up with, lived among, been ourselves a part of, all of our lives. Even the best of them, Gutierrez, Pulaski, the doctor, are preoccupied with a bizarre, dangerous, difficult, and not even particularly interesting, game of winning and holding power."

Sam looked up at his human. "And the lovely Estrellita—*your* lovely Estrellita?"

He shook his head. "I don't know, Sam. Her worst of all, maybe. Or maybe I'm just more sensitive where she's concerned. At first, try as I might, even with the help of Mister Thoggosh and the data you were gathering, I couldn't deduce the rules governing this pointless, painful competition. In the absence of contradictory evidence, its only purpose seemed to be to determine which of them gets to tell the others what to do."

"What connection does that have—" The dog stopped to scratch behind an ear. The man shrugged, waiting for the dog to finish. "With investigating a murder?"

"Well, it seems like a lot of trouble to go to, just to win

a prize consisting of being stuck with an unnecessary and objectionable task. Running other people's lives must be very unpleasant. It must take up time and energy more purposefully and pleasurably spent thousands of other ways. It's like holding an arm-wrestling contest where the winner gets to clean out the septic tank—"

Sam grinned. "Or gets to pick everybody else's nose."

"You're disgusting." Eichra Oren frowned. "Furthermore, it's impossible to accomplish without *damaging* those lives. I asked about that, over and over again. Sam, this revolting pursuit of power represents the only joy and satisfaction these people ever seem to derive from their lives. Their one consistent emotion is anger at everything and everybody, especially themselves."

"And they never wonder if that isn't connected with the game they play?"

"None of them came even close to understanding what I was getting at. Like you, they wanted to know what it had to do with my investigation. I tried, without success, to warn them that a *p'Nan* debt assessor isn't equivalent to any of the roles they're familiar with, that this was a necessary part of my work, that I had to weigh this strange behavior pattern, establish its dimensions and extent, integrate it into my other deductions."

"And?"

"Nothing. You want to know the most mysterious and frustrating facet of this mindless, self-destructive, sacrificial obedience I've observed being practiced among the members of the expedition?"

Sam sniffed at the base of a tree. "No."

"Good, I'll tell you." He stopped walking to concentrate on what he was saying, despite the fact that the dog yawned conspicuously. "The game is rigged so that you can never win the prize that *would* be worth winning: control over your own life. A few individuals back on Earth seem to have won permanently, and the perpetual losers feel they owe everything to them. One thing's clear; at their current, laughable level of technology, Earth's authorities are far too distant to account for the observed phenomenon. How could they offer a credible threat to the lives or safety of the members of this expedition they've all but abandoned?"

If a dog had been capable of shrugging, Sam would have shrugged. "The general and his friends have to go back sometime."

The man nodded. "They should. They've a lot of house-cleaning to do. But they won't. I'm tempted to regard it as a perversion. Three billion years evolving a brain to run your own affairs, and then you meekly, eagerly, hand them over to somebody whose credentials aren't superior knowledge or wisdom—"

"Simply the brute power," Sam replied, sitting on his haunches, "to beat you up and kill you if you won't."

Eichra Oren protested, "Any rational, feeling individual may be motivated readily enough to act against his interests or will by sufficiently dire threats. He can be moved by personal fear of physical injury or death to himself or someone he cares for. It's a historically common phenomenon. Yet this primitive, if understandable, motivation doesn't seem to be the pivotal factor. Taken by itself, it can't be the primary driving force behind this sickening phenomenon of 'obedience to authority.'"

"You'll find authority itself," a new voice interposed, "an even more difficult phenomenon to grasp, nothing more than one incomprehensible act of obedience piled on another, into pyramids."

They whirled to see a large, glistening snake. "Mister Thoggosh?"

"In the tentacle, if not in the flesh. Good morning, Eichra Oren, Sam. Having discussed it at length with several of them, after all's said and done, I'm still no closer to understanding it, myself. It's often seemed to me that unthinking obedience ought be physically impossible. Had such a suicidal behavior pattern ever begun to develop at any time in evolutionary history, it should have been immediately self-extinguishing."

"Go on," urged Eichra Oren, "I'm listening."

"Well, suppose an individual became deranged, perhaps through some near-fatal illness or injury, so that it seemed rational to him to demand that other people obey his every command. Wouldn't the majority rise up, immediately and spontaneously, and put the would-be dictator out of their misery? It would be easy, he's sick or injured. Yet, here we are, face-to-face with the nth generation of victims of power, confronted, as it were, with the tangible consequence of an impossible mass insanity, well-established on this version of Earth for thousands of years."

"What's even worse," Sam told the appendage, "is the embarrassing fact that it's *this* particular Earth."

"That's right, isn't it? Had your own forebears, both of you, not been Appropriated—"

"Rescued," the man insisted, "but you're right, these aliens could have been my descendants. Which means their culture, to dignify it in a way it doesn't deserve, somehow evolved from the remnants of my own."

"Perhaps it was the pole-reversal," the mollusc mused, "rearrangement of worldwide patterns of glaciation, the overwhelming cataclysm that resulted in the Loss of the Continent."

Eichra Oren nodded, mentally inventorying recently acquired information about Earth's history since the Loss. "I wonder if the story wasn't passed down as the sinking of Atlantis. Perhaps it scarred the survivors so badly, those who weren't rescued by the Elders, that it became the source of this mass aberration. But blast it all, where does a hypothesis like that get us? Whatever else it's worth, it doesn't tell us a thing about what happened to Semlohcolresh, or who killed Kam—"

"*I did it!*" The wild-eyed, torn, disheveled apparition springing from the bushes was hardly recognizable as human, let alone the human who'd been Vivian Richardson. Her suit, dirty and wet, was tattered. Through the rents, her skin was bruised and cut by days spent as an animal in hiding. Her hair was full of woods-debris. Her hands, extended in front of her in a rigid triangle, were full of large-bore service automatic.

"I did it!" she screamed. "I sawed that fucking monster's slimy arm off and strangled the shit out of that revisionist bastard with it! Now I'm gonna do you! All of you!" Nervously, she shifted her weight from foot to foot, pointing the gun first at Eichra Oren, then at the tentacle, even at Sam, and back at Eichra Oren.

"What became of Semlohcolresh?" the Antarctican stepped forward and asked in a firm, gentle voice.

"Down the Dumpster, and who wants to know?" Still shifting side to side, she, too, came a few steps forward. Deep in her skull, her eyes were red with veining, ringed with blue-black circles. "Who the hell're you, white boy? I don't know you!" Keeping her right hand on the pistol grip, she rocked the hammer back with her left thumb.

"Dumpster?" Mister Thoggosh demanded. "What's she talking about?"

Sam told him, "I think she's talking about the manual waste inports on your mass-energy converter."

"How in blazes could she know how to work the mass-energy converter? I hadn't shown any of them the power plant yet."

"I don't think it matters." Sam watched Eichra Oren, his eyes locked on Richardson's, extend a hand for her gun as the other crept to his waist. "Easy enough. The input looks like one of their own waste-disposal systems—how many different ways can you build a trash bin?—and the rest is automated. Garbage in, gigawatts out."

"Give me the weapon," Eichra Oren told her. "There's food, and you'll be dry and warm. No one will hurt you."

"Damn straight nobody's gonna hurt me!" She lifted the Witness a bare centimeter, sighting it on his face. "I did it! I did it! Let's—"

Behind him, a double explosion erupted. She was lifted off her feet, thrown against a tree where she hit with an ugly noise, and slid to the ground, a pair of close-spaced scarlet blossoms soaking her uniform. A second noise, a snapped twig, caught his attention and he whirled. Sebastiano came from the undergrowth, followed by young Gutierrez and two others. "I see you found her," the shuttle captain observed. "Did you have to shoot her?"

"I didn't." He discovered that, unaware, he'd drawn his little weapon and pointed it at the motionless figure on the ground. He stepped to her and pried the weapon from her cold, dead fingers.

"I did." From another direction, Reille y Sanchez strode onto the path, her own pistol smoking in her hand. "Another half second, she'd have fired."

Eichra Oren rose. "Thanks, Estrellita, but probably not

with this." Putting his own weapon away, he grasped the serrations on the Witness's slide and pulled it back until it locked, then held it out for her to examine. "Empty. She was out of ammunition."

TWENTY-THREE
The Fatal Question

"What now?"

"What?" Reille y Sanchez looked up from the path she and Eichra Oren followed, away from the encampment, through the jungle toward the Elders' establishment. They'd been going through the formalities associated with Richardson's confession and death for several hours. Now they had free time and had decided, without discussion, to spend it together.

"What's customary among your people?" he asked, shuffling beside her with his sword tucked beneath one arm and his hands in his pants pockets. "What'll you do now?"

She shrugged. "Oh, paperwork. I have to get a report ready for the general to send back to Earth."

He nodded without looking up. "To the KGB?"

"Yes, that's who I'm working for. Why?"

Taking his sword in one hand, with the other he held a leafy branch out of the way to let her through and followed. They crossed a little stream she said she recognized and began working their way along its low bank toward whatever source it flowed from. "Curiosity. I've no paperwork to do. The Elders are wary of it. If they weren't, after five hundred million years, their entire Earth would be buried under glaciers made of wood pulp or plastic instead of ice. Also, I've no one to report to. The surrogate of Mister Thoggosh was present and, in general, my clients are either satisfied with my work or not."

She stopped to face him, laying a hand on his arm and looking into his eyes. "Will you and Sam be going home now, to that other Earth?"

"Will you, Estrellita?" He covered her fingers with his free hand, shaking his head. "Nothing's been resolved here, you know. Your authorities still dispute our claim. Your orders to drive us off, however futile and inconsiderate of your survival, are still in effect. And, as Aelbraugh Pritsch would be the first to tell you, dimensional translation's too expensive and spectacular in its side effects to be used casually, even to get us back. Remember what happened last time."

She smiled. "The rain."

"The rain." They resumed walking until they came to the little waterfall that broke the course of the stream not far from the sprawling roots of an enormous canopy tree, thirty or thirty-five meters in diameter. "So I guess we're stuck here for the duration," he concluded, "whatever that turns out to be. Or until sufficient reasons accumulate to use the translator." He turned to look at her. "It could be quite a long while."

Again she smiled, shyly this time. "Is that so terrible?"

"It's why we're here, you and I, in this spot. I wanted to show you something." He reached into a pocket and handed her an object, knowing it would look to her like an undersized golf ball, complete to color and texture. "It's my office and personal quarters, Estrellita. At least it will be in a few days. You'd call it a seed, with engineered genes. Don't drop it, or it'll try to take root."

He took the object from her, stepped to the tree, reached as high as he could and touched it to the trunk. When he took his hand away, it stayed in place. "When it's mature, it'll cantilever out over the stream, and I can fall asleep listening to the waterfall. We're exactly half-way between your camp and the Elders' settlement, which sort of describes my position, as well. While I'm here,

I'll act as liaison between humans and nonhumans on the asteroid."

"Good," she replied, finding a mossy place near the base of the tree to sit down, "you can begin with me."

He smiled back self-consciously and joined her where she sat, propping sword and scabbard against the tree beside him and taking her hand. "Why, I believe I have. This report you'll make, part of its purpose will be to wrap up the loose ends?"

"Loose ends? There aren't any." Keeping his hand, she ticked off the fingers of her other hand. "Method: after she struck him down, Richardson strangled Piotr with one of Semlohcolresh's tentacles. She probably shot the nautiloid. Her gun wasn't empty then, she'd just taken it from Danny Gutierrez. Semlohcolresh would have been an easy mark. He wasn't wearing a protective suit. Opportunity: it was pitch dark. According to Sebastiano and others searching for Richardson, Semlohcolresh and Piotr were alone at the pool. Motive: Richardson was crazy."

Eichra Oren took her hand in both of his. "Estrellita, life consists of little besides loose ends. Sometimes that's the only thing that gives survivors a reason for going on."

"All right, if you're so smart," she retorted, "give me an example of a loose end."

He nodded. "I'll give you a good one. Your people in their camp should have heard the shot you mentioned, if that's how Semlohcolresh died. Your pistols are loud. I found that out this morning."

"Because the bullet went right by you, silly. Semlohcolresh's pool was almost a klick from the camp. The forest would have absorbed the sound. Next loose end, please."

"Motive." He shook his head. "Crazy's too easy, Estrellita, and at the same time, it's too hard."

She rolled her eyes and answered with exasperation. "Is this going to be some more of your deep philosophical and psychological ponderings? What do you mean, too hard?"

"In the sense that it violates parsimony, the principle of the fewest variables. What you call least reactance or Occam's Razor. A lone Soviet individual striking on her own? After everything I've learned about your people, I find that hard to believe. There's a perfect motive still lying around unused, Estrellita, a single reason for that particular double murder that makes sense in the light of everything else."

"And that is?" she asked in mock resignation.

"What it always was, to provoke conflict between the humans and the Elders. Therefore it must have been done on orders from your ASSR leaders. I've learned enough about affairs on Earth to know that Moscow had no wish to antagonize Mr. Thoggosh and his people."

She turned where she sat and faced him, taking both of his hands. "Now that you mention it, I do have a few unanswered questions of my own, mostly making certain I understand what the nautiloids and their friends seem to imply about their way of looking at things."

He raised his eyebrows. "We're still talking about motive?"

"In a way." She nodded. "Given the nautiloids' five hundred million year advantage, everybody but the government assumes we'll be wiped out the instant hostilities begin. But from what I've seen for myself, from what they've told me, I see what I think could be a fatal weakness on their part, if it came to conflict. I could hardly believe it myself, at first, it sounds so childish and naive. It appears your Elders can't use weapons of mass destruction."

"You're entirely correct, Estrellita, they can't." He paused, then added, "We can't."

She laughed gently. "Do you mean to tell me that all these gun-toting monsters are effectively disarmed by what's supposed to be a purely selfish, individualistic philosophy? They're prohibited from using fission or fusion bombs, even high explosives or hand grenades, no matter how desperate the circumstances?"

"Antimatter bombs, too. I'm not so sure about hand grenades. It must seem strange and contradictory to you. For their part, I imagine they can hardly believe it necessary to explain such an elementary matter of ethics to a person who represents herself as a reasoning being. The use of such nondiscriminating weapons is monstrous, Estrellita. No value it can possibly achieve can outweigh the values it destroys. The Elders aren't pacifists, as you know. But this would inevitably involve, in their view, inflicting injury or death on innocent individuals who are not party to whatever dispute's being settled. Will this, too, be in your report?"

She shrugged, and for the first time there was unhappiness on her face. "I don't see how I can avoid it. The Elders are aware of any number of politically dangerous facts. United or not, the World Soviet's very fragile, and that knowledge alone, in the hands of an enemy, could damage it beyond repair. Now I've learned a hidden vulnerability of the Elders, and you know I have. For the sake of your culture's survival, you'll try to keep it from the ASSR. With what the two of us know together—mutual, horrifying discoveries—we might even bring about the thermonuclear war which, until our arrival on this asteroid, everybody thought had been avoided."

"Peace, through bloodless capitulation?"

"It was almost bloodless. There are always a few who can't see the handwriting on the wall; it took people like Horatio Gutierrez to deal with them. It cost so much of so many, and now we can destroy it, all by ourselves. Wouldn't that be something to be proud of?"

He couldn't think of anything to say before she went on.

"As a result of those discoveries, I'd come to a decision. I'm a Marine, a veteran, proud to have earned my rank the hard way in a man's world. And I'm KGB, whether I like it or not. My opinion of agents willing to use sex as a weapon has always been low. I was happy it hadn't ever been required of me. To be completely truthful, Eichra Oren, I'd managed to fall in love with a mysterious stranger—no, don't say anything—and part of that happiness is that I slept with him for its own sake, outside the line of duty."

He sat up. "Why is all of this in the past-perfect tense?"

She wouldn't meet his eyes. "Because I'd hoped, without much basis, that after this mess was over with, something more might come of you and me. With all my heart, Eichra Oren, I loathed the idea of cheapening the first feelings like this I've ever had. But even though I made the decision despising myself, I could conceive of no option except to kill you!"

"Your duty to obey authority," he reflected, placing a hand on her shoulder. "And now?"

"Loathsome as it would have been, the task didn't appear difficult. We'd begin right now, making love. I'd pretend to be as relaxed and open toward you as I was last night." She reached to her belt and drew her fighting knife. "When your relaxation appeared complete," she raised it to his chin, "when you seemed off your guard—" the point touched his skin, indented it, "I'd discover I can't take your life!" She hurled the knife into the ground, where the blade stuck, and turned her back.

They were both silent for a long time, then Eichra Oren sighed. "For my part, Estrellita, I couldn't have made love to you this afternoon, because I've something I must tell you. Although I don't want to. Like you, I've pondered hard over this turn of events, always coming to the same miserable conclusion. The problem's my inability to understand my fellow beings, including most of all a beautiful, intelligent, accomplished young woman whom I've come in only a short time to love deeply.

"And to condemn."

She snapped around to face him. "Condemn? Why—"

He turned his hands over in an expression of helplessness. "Why would anyone betray what they value? Why would they destroy something—someone—they admire? Can it be, as they tell me, that they're obligated to obey some other sapient? Despite whatever education and intelligence I have, I've been unable to discover an answer that satisfies me, or any alternative to what must be done. Loathing myself, as you say you did, I'm forced to speak now, Estrellita, because *you* murdered Piotr Kamanov and Semlohcolresh."

Her eyes widened, and she didn't quite stop the gasp this provoked.

"I became suspicious," he continued, "when Dlee Raftan Saon told me you'd mentioned a nautiloid habit of venturing unprotected into the air to converse with land beings. You mentioned it again, just now. No such habit exists. Semlohcolresh's dislike for liquid fluorocarbon and protective suits was a personal eccentricity, as was lying in shallow water, splashing his gills. You could only have seen it when he and Kamanov conversed, the night they were both killed. It was you who strangled Kamanov, acting on orders from the American KGB which you were given in secret as a department head, before you received your official, public promotion."

She protested, "But how could you—"

"I lack direct evidence of this last surmise. The Elders listen to your transmissions and understand any encrypted message, but they couldn't recognize orders couched in terms of your previous missions: 'Do what was done on such-and-such a date in such-and-such a place.' Washington's objective was to provoke trouble. You pursued that objective, despite the fact that you liked and respected Kamanov. He was chosen to die because that might help alter Moscow's attitude, and even the murder weapon was chosen to maximize hostility between the species. I'll never be certain whether the murder of Semlohcolresh was your own idea, and that makes me sick."

"Eichra Oren, I—"

"I'll never know all of the details, and you needn't supply them. Kamanov started home through the jungle and you knocked him out. At the pool you shot Semlohcolresh with the silenced pistol from the Russian's pocket, replaced when you cut off Semlohcolresh's limb and finished Kamanov. Afterward, in the late night or early morning before your visit, you dragged the Elder's body to the matter-converter, easy in this gravity, and disposed of it, so it would look like Semlohcolresh killed Kamanov and ran away. You didn't know that Richardson had watched every step of the process. She was crazy enough to claim your deeds for her own. My suspicion was confirmed when you shot her, knowing that Mister Thoggosh was protected and that I'm quite able to take care of myself."

"I didn't know." She let her head fall to his shoulder and began to cry softly. "I only wanted to . . ."

He stroked her hair. "At that, you might have gotten away with it, but you didn't think of everything, my love. You'd seen Sam, who has a mind of his own. You'd seen Aelbraugh Pritsch's reptile companion. I don't know why it didn't occur to you that they're modeled on the nautiloid separable tentacle, a semi-independent being with complex nerve bundles, and therefore—like Sam—some independent intelligence. While you cut off one of his ordinary tentacles, Semlohcolresh's separable tentacle survived the death of its owner, Estrellita. It crawled into the jungle and lived long enough to identify you, by your red hair."

Not denying it, she sat back and looked at him, her expression that of a trusting child. Tears streamed down her cheeks without a sound to accompany them. Her voice was formal, as he'd specified, and in earnest. "God help me, Eichra Oren, am I allowing my existence to continue in ignorance of some irreversible breach I've unknowingly committed, some irrevocable restitution I've neglected to make?"

His tone was equally disconsolate as he reached behind him for his sword. "I wish I had a god to help me, Estrellita, because I lied. Separable limbs only survive their owners by a few seconds. That of Semlohcolresh was never found."

She smiled through her tears. "I love you, Eichra Oren. I've never said that to a man before. I more or less expected, maybe I even hoped, that things would turn out this way." She touched his arm. "I hate the idea of that sword of yours. So, having seen you fight four men at once, I'm going to make another sort of restitution, in advance, to you. Someday you'll be grateful that I didn't make this easy for you, that you didn't have a choice."

She was pulling the trigger as her weapon leveled on his body. Before his conscious mind could interfere, his unconscious mind responded. Holding her gun hand by the wrist, he paralyzed it with a touch, pressing her carotid arteries with the thumb and forefinger of his other hand. Whether her heart and mind were in the effort, her body struggled to survive. The effort was futile; his grip was steel. Estrellita relaxed and breathed her last breath.

Afterward, he held her pistol to his temple for a long while, but he never pulled the trigger.

TWENTY-FOUR
p'Na

They watched him from over half a kilometer away.

Eichra Oren was a tiny figure sitting on the tree balcony—where Sam had left him and a happy Estrellita only the previous evening—staring out over the landscape at his soul. Mister Thoggosh had come to the encampment, "in the flesh," to help his *p'Nan* debt assessor explain to General Gutierrez what had happened, but he'd wound up helping Sam, while the dog's companion climbed those spiral stairs to be alone.

"No, sir," the mollusc told the human, "it doesn't make him feel a bit better that, thanks to her, it was an act of self-defense. Col. Reille y Sanchez never had a chance to know that, in addition to the incredible reflexes she counted on, Eichra Oren had already responded consciously to principle. He understands that, in order to fulfill a function he long ago willingly accepted, he'd have had to assist her to make the ultimate restitution sooner or later. Whether he cared for her or not, as I gather he did rather deeply, wouldn't have made any difference."

The general shook his head. They sat outside the circled shuttles in the waning light of late afternoon, Gutierrez on an improvised log bench, the Proprietor beside him on the ground. Nearby, the Elder's electrostat seemed to be waiting patiently. "She was morally wrong," replied the human, "because it was her duty to kill someone she cared for. He was morally right because it was his duty to kill someone he cared for. What's the difference?"

Mister Thoggosh raised a tentacle. "The difference, General, is that, having acted morally, he'll eventually get over the horror, whereas Reille y Sanchez, acting on immoral orders, and without the benefit of his philosophy, would never have. There's all the difference in the world—in several worlds—between acting against your own judgment on someone else's orders and committing what perhaps amounts to the same physical act for the sake of principle. He'll live and go forward because he acted consistently with what he believes."

Gutierrez folded his arms in front of his chest. "What he believes? Killing someone over a philosophical point?"

"Perhaps I used a word carelessly. In his view, in my own, *p'Na* is a fundamental feature of the material universe, no different from the operation of gravity—although quite distinct from foolish artificial laws made up by primitive sapients—and subject to the same process of verification. *p'Na* required, for the debt Col. Reille y Sanchez owed the sapients she murdered, that she make restitution. As a law of nature, this would be true whether she accepted it or not, although the question she asked, her token attempt to kill Eichra Oren, demonstrated her acceptance of her fate."

The general shook his head. "And there he is, without her."

The Elder pulled himself around to look the human in the eye. "Not by any act on Eichra Oren's part, but because of a chain of events which she began, of which he was but the final, inevitable link. From your expression, if I've learned to read it correctly, you fail to find that satisfying."

Gutierrez nodded; anger, disgust, and resignation coloring his tone. "You could say that, Mister Thoggosh."

"Then consider: it could also be surmised that he acted according to another principle. Ultimately, despite the pain it cost him, Eichra Oren acted because an abomination like socialism—any sort of collectivism—must be eradicated, if for no other reason than its power to corrupt love, such as he and Estrellita found too late."

Gutierrez rubbed his chin in thought. "The colonel was accused, tried, sentenced, and executed according to the laws—"

"Customs," the nautiloid insisted.

"Of the world she committed her crimes on." He stood. "Forgive me, sir, if I limit myself to that when I report to the KGB."

"I shall, General, I shall, indeed." With a tentacle, he indicated the electrostat he'd come in. "Now, I've brought some refreshment along, will you join me? I'm having beer."

BOOK II:

SECOND TO ONE

THIS BOOK IS DEDICATED to Rob and Laura
Arbury, Dave Blackmon, Ken Flurchick,
Michael Szeszny, and Kitty Woldow, for reasons
that will be obvious to each of them when they
recall the summer of '88.

TWENTY-FIVE
Cold Fusion

"Enter, Comrade Admiral! Sit! Have some vodka!"

Nikola Deshovich lifted a hairy hand, the stub of a cigar protruding between its first and second fingers. Inboard the *USSR Lavrenti Pavlovich Beria* he alone smoked, for who had the power to forbid it? Known as "the Banker"—for his habit of settling old political debts "with interest"—he was the absolute, undisputed master of the Soviet Union and, more recently, of the United World Soviet, as well. The air in the little room was blue and foul.

To hear Deshovich speak, thought Admiral Ghasil Mubakkir, was a sensual delight. He had a way of spacing words, pausing at unexpected intervals, that compelled. His voice was deep, with a hint of velvet which massaged and reassured, although it could turn cold and toneless when that served. Now he indicated the opposite bulkhead where a chair could be unfolded. He occupied another which would have been hideously uncomfortable beneath his great mass under ordinary circumstances. With an inward sigh, Mubakkir reflected that these were hardly ordinary circumstances. He dropped an unreturned salute and attempted to relax from the reflexive military posture

221

he'd assumed on knocking at the door of the one real passenger accommodation inboard the *Beria*, the cabin which, by rights, should have been his own.

"No vodka, thank you, sir."

The cabin wasn't spacious, nor particularly cramped. Deshovich appeared to fill it (the admiral didn't have to guess his mass at two hundred kilos, it was on the manifest), leaving room for two chairs, a small table on which a bottle stood with two glasses, and the cot, covered by a rumpled quilt, which had served as an acceleration couch during a liftoff that must have seemed unendurable to the man.

Mubakkir conspicuously kept his gaze from lingering over a curvaceous form the bedclothes failed to conceal, apparently still fast asleep. He unfolded a chair because it was easier than refusing and sat, trying not to crease his snow-white uniform trousers. He was known throughout the services for remaining crisp and spotless even in the heat of maneuvers where others found themselves soot-blackened, oil-stained, and streaked with sweat. It set an example for subordinates who whispered that if the Old Man were ever wounded in battle, he'd somehow manage to bleed neatly.

"I'm on duty."

The fact was that he never availed himself of luxuries within easy reach of his rank. As a rising young Third World officer in the corrupt navy of a decaying world power, it had given him an edge on the competition. It had nothing to do with his religious background. Mubakkir had one God, Marx, and at the moment Deshovich was His prophet. The admiral was no saint; he merely felt he was lucky that his one vice, in which he indulged himself fully, was also his solemn obligation: *command*.

"Don't mind if I do," Deshovich laughed heartily. Despite his great size, he conveyed an impression of fastidious dexterity. His thick hair and gray-shot beard were trimmed. His black silk pajama suit was cut as nicely as the admiral's uniform. "Until my own duty recommences, I'm simply cargo," he laid a hand across his middle, "bereft that I won't experience the weightlessness I was rather looking forward to. Well, leaving nine tenths of Earth's gravity behind represents considerable relief in itself. It also serves to keep things—bottles, glasses, one's skeletal calcium—in their places. I'm grateful to our Bureau of Suppressed Technologies that, instead of the better part of a year, the voyage will last only days. To think that America might have had cold fusion decades ago!"

"It gored too many well-fed oxen," Mubakkir agreed, "petrol cartels and power collectives, so they buried it and discredited its discoverers."

"So much for free enterprise!" The Banker laughed again. "Is this what gravity will be like when we arrive? Tell me, Comrade Admiral, what have you learned of events at our destination?"

Mubakkir watched him pour four fingers of Stolichnaya, sprinkling black pepper over the liquid surface. The gesture was pure affectation, he was too young to have lived through the harsh times when it was needed to counter the poisons of inept distillery, but it served a purpose, just like the admiral's sparkling uniforms, warning underlings and rivals that, despite generations of détente, glasnost, and perestroika, Deshovich's guiding spirit, summonable at need, was that of a Djugashvili.

"We lack detail, sir. According to reports from the mission commander, an Aerospace brigadier named Gutierrez, the interplanetary expedition of the American Soviet Socialist Republic arrived at the asteroid 5023 Eris less than a week ago and has already suffered five fatalities in an original complement of only forty-two. A Russian national on loan from Moscow University appears to have been murdered."

Deshovich took a sip of vodka, puffed his cigar only to find that it had gone out, relit it, and took another drink. "Careless of Gutierrez. Still, I suppose these things are to be expected under the circumstances . . ."

"Yes, sir: humans in space for the first time in half a century, in three refitted eighty-year-old NASA shuttles . . ."

"*Honorable John McCain, Honorable Orrin Hatch*, and *Honorable Robert Dole*, for three pioneers of the American Sovietization." He shook his head. "No, Admiral, I meant the property claim being made by these aliens—"

"Not aliens, sir." Mubakkir shifted on his chair uneasily.

"Molluscs, referred to politely as 'the Elders,' from another version of Earth, who came to the asteroid across lines of alternative probability. Imagine a long-tentacled squid in an automobile-sized snail shell—"

"*You* imagine it!" Deshovich raised a hand, palm out. "I haven't had breakfast yet."

Mubakkir blinked. "5023 Eris is carbonaceous chondrite, sir, promising for settlement. The Elders have equipped it with an atmosphere under a sort of canopy supported by giant treelike plants. The reports mention thick vegetation and abundant moisture."

"The sort of thing giant snails might like," Deshovich grunted.

"Yes, sir. In any case, one of them was killed, too, on illegal orders from the American KGB, by a Marine major later breveted to full colonel in *our* KGB, to investigate the very murder she'd committed!"

Deshovich shook his head, half amused, half disgusted. "I've spoken with Intelligence about that. Some of them are now searching the Tunguska region of Siberia for pieces of an alien spacecraft which may have exploded there in 1908."

Mubakkir suppressed a rueful grin. Elsewhere, he knew, heads had rolled rather more dramatically for issuing that illegal order. One purpose of this mission was to mend fences with these living fossils who, despite a quaint, incomprehensible ethical philosophy, had brought along thermonuclear matter-energy converters like kerosene lanterns to a picnic. An economically crippled United World Soviet needed technology like that—and anything else its leader could pry loose.

Sensing the admiral's distraction, Deshovich cleared his throat. "You've taken over from American Mission Control?"

Mubakkir nodded. "We're timing our replies so the expedition will think we're transmitting from Earth."

"Excellent. By the way, Admiral, if you wished to dispose of something aboard this vessel, how would you go about it?"

"Sir?" Mubakkir tried not to look surprised at the change of subject. "An air lock, I suppose. At this acceleration, it would—"

"Air lock, you say?" With a broad hand, Deshovich reached to flip back a corner of the duvet. Beneath it, her features obscured by a fall of dark, silky, waist-length hair, lay the naked body of a young girl, flesh white with the pallor of death. Between her hips and knees, the sheet was soaked with blood. "My secretary seems to have had an accident during dictation. Get her out quietly and have this cleaned up."

The admiral swallowed hard, but said nothing.

"And summon me another girl from the pool. A blonde this time, I think."

TWENTY-SIX
Absent Friends

Less than a week, he thought, and already five graves.

Lieutenant Colonel Juan Sebastiano stared grimly at the low mounds of carbonaceous soil covering the earthly remains (if "earthly" was the word) of five members of the expedition of which he suddenly found himself second in command, that of the American Soviet Socialist Republic to the asteroid 5023 Eris. The only thing missing to set the appropriate tone, he thought, was the oppressive drizzly overcast of their first couple of days here.

Their hosts, however, the giant molluscs who claimed this place by virtue of previous occupancy, had adjusted its atmosphere. Rain would now fall at night when it wouldn't represent an inconvenience. At present, without producing shadows, a diffuse golden glow seeped through overhead to tumble down a series of small craters overlapping in broad natural stairsteps, across the newly spaded ground.

Lush undergrowth surrounded the forlorn gravesite beneath sequoia-dwarfing plants supporting the world-enveloping organic canopy. "Super kudzu," Dr. Kamanov had called them. The asteroid was covered, more densely than any closeups of the Moon or Mars Sebastiano had studied during training, with impact features of all sizes, cloaked in vegetation. They textured the land in unpredictable ways. General Gutierrez had begun using a thesaurus to find synonyms of "hill" and "ridge" for reports which would probably never be transmitted back to Earth now.

Poor old Kamanov.

Sebastiano drew on an unfiltered, unsanctioned cigarette which his boss's son, Second Lieutenant Danny Gutierrez, had smuggled inboard the *McCain*, one of three old NASA shuttles that had borne them hundreds of millions of klicks deeper into space than Soviet Man had ever ventured before. He guessed that made them all heroes of some kind. To the ASSR they were no more than expendable veterans of various small conflicts it was politically unpragmatic to commemorate. Or they were incompetent (or *overly* competent) bureaucrats, or officers who couldn't keep their opinions to themselves, or enlisted personnel who insisted on remaining individuals—in short, nonteam players, well worth disposing of even if they discovered nothing of value out here among the debris of a broken planet.

Or a planet that had never been.

A blue-gray wisp from the cigarette's front end irritated the colonel's nose. It was nothing, he supposed, to what the back end must be doing to his lungs. He'd given up the habit years ago, in fighter school. Since then he'd struggled for physical and mental survival through three brushfire wars, each bloodier, each emptier of meaning and purpose, than the last. But it had taken these five incredibly stupid, wasteful deaths—and certain attendant complications which had only aggravated tensions over conflicting claims to the asteroid—to get him started smoking again.

Kamanov occupied the grave on the far left. Like most members of the expedition, Sebastiano had grown fond of the old man over the year-long voyage and the longer training period before that. More in love with life and fuller of it than anyone the colonel had ever known, as mission geologist Kamanov had been among a small group on loan from the Russians—this was billed as a cooperative venture, after all, on behalf of a new and fragile United World Soviet held together at this moment in history by wishful thinking and gunship diplomacy. He'd been horribly murdered to make a political point which seemed more obscure to Sebastiano with every day that passed.

In the next grave lay Delbert Roo, carried on the expedition roster as a mining-equipment operator, but in reality a KGB enforcer who'd drawn his last breath without learning (except in that last astonished fraction of a second) that there were individuals he wasn't free to terrorize and torture as he wished.

Broward Hake, in the third grave, had been Roo's colleague in thuggery. He was dead due to a regrettable mistake, the .45 caliber pistol bullet that had finished him having been meant for someone else.

Colonel Vivian Richardson, in the fourth grave, had been the mission's original vice-commander and possibly an agent of the Russian KGB—as opposed to the American KGB which was openly represented on the expedition. She'd died the same as Hake, or at least by a projectile of the same caliber, suggesting to Sebastiano that there might be some justice in an otherwise uncaring universe, since she'd been the one who'd shot the man.

At the end of the dismal row was a fifth grave, that of Marine Corps Major Estrellita Reille y Sanchez, a lovely redhead—lovely no longer—who'd started the whole mess against her better judgment, having been given certain unpleasant tasks to perform whether she wanted them or not. Her life had been choked off in its twenty-ninth year as Kamanov's had in his sixty-ninth. In Sebastiano's opinion it had been too soon for either of them. Life was too short, no matter how long it lasted.

There should have been a sixth grave for Semlohcolresh, that irascible old slug. (Technically, he and his fellow monsters—make that "sapient living fossils"—were descendants of Silurian-era molluscs.) There might have been, too, if his culture's burial customs were anything like humanity's. Sebastiano didn't know what the nautiloids, with their exotic philosophy, considered decent under the circumstances, but in any case it was academic. The squidlike body of Semlohcolresh, along with its multicolored Volkswagen-sized shell, had been dissolved into its constituent nuclei in the matter-energy converter his people—and the nightmare menagerie they'd brought with them across cosmic lines of probability from countless versions of Earth—used to power their colony here.

"Colonel?"

Behind him Sebastiano heard a footfall, then the polite, apologetic cough of someone he outranked. It was Major Jesus Ortiz, newly appointed captain of the *Hatch*. Sebastiano dropped his cigarette, slowly pivoted his bootsole on it, and turned from contemplation of the graves.

"What's up, Maje?"

"Could you come back to the *Dole*, Juan, ASAP? Mission Control's on the horn and they don't sound happy. The general's asking for you. He looks worried."

The Banker! Sebastiano shuddered. It can only be the Banker!

But he nodded and, following the major, headed in the direction of the campsite where the shuttles rested in a triangle which, more and more, seemed to him like the circled wagons of frightened pioneers in hostile Indian territory.

TWENTY-SEVEN
Laika

The Banker! The idea sent chills down the spine of General Horatio Gutierrez. It could only be the Banker! "I don't know, Juan." He shrugged, attempting to appear calm. "They just said to have all hands stand by for a message from 'the highest authority.'"

Surrounded by an array of switches and lights bewildering to anyone who lacked the training they shared, he watched Sebastiano lower himself into the lefthand seat, a position the colonel normally occupied aboard the *McCain*. This was the *Dole*, flagship of the expedition. Sebastiano adjusted the microphone tube of his Snoopy cap, the communications carrier he'd just jammed over his head.

Juan looked like a daredevil astronaut, Gutierrez always thought. His teeth shone white against a dark complexion. Almost as tall sitting down as the general was standing up, he sported a diabolical strip of Castillian beard and a nose that was pure Aztec. The confident movement of his slender fingers across the controls spoke of a competence rare these days in America or anywhere in the world—except, it was rumored, Switzerland, South Africa, NeoIsrael, and maybe the PRC. Who could ever tell about the PRC?

Standing behind him, Gutierrez twisted his neck for the fifth time in as many minutes to peer at the portside audio panel, waiting, he realized sourly, like the little dog to hear his master's voice. Through a window he saw a glint of copper rising in a graceful arc from one of many antenna penetrations in the fuselage to a great pseudotree which supported, and finally became, the atmospheric canopy a kilometer overhead. It would be some time, however, before his chance came to listen or to speak, and even then, given the vast distance involved, no real conversation with Earth would be possible. From Earth's viewpoint, it was an ideal situation: Gutierrez and his people were in a position only to receive orders and acknowledge them.

Three hundred million kilometers, he thought. At the moment, nearly two astronomical units lay between Earth and the asteroid, meaning it was twice as far from humanity's home to 5023 Eris as it was from the Earth to the Sun. At a walking pace of six and a half klicks an hour, he figured, stabbing buttons on his calculator watch as if literally killing time, it was a stroll of 5,308 years, almost the totality of written history—*human* history; from now on he'd have to add that modifier. Running at top speed, the fastest man alive might have shortened it to 1,416 years (the span since Moslems had begun praying toward Mecca), had he been able to keep the pace and had there been someplace to set his feet in all of that vast black emptiness. An auto cruising at 100 KPH might have made the trip in three and a half centuries, an airliner, ten times fleeter, in only thirty-five years.

Three hundred million kilometers. Lightlike energies crossed the vacuum at 300,000 klicks a second. It would require seventeen minutes for signals to arrive at the asteroid from their point of origin and seventeen more for an answer to be heard on Earth, making it an astonishing thirty-four minutes from "How are you?" to "I'm fine, thanks, and yourself?"

Three hundred million kilometers. In a sense, time and place had chosen one another. This was as close as Earth and Eris ever got. That wouldn't always be so—very little is ever *always* so—the two bodies whirled about the Solar primary at their own individual velocities, like hands on an

analog clock. Given that model, it was now 03:15. Before
now, and in time to come, when they were on opposite
sides of the giant fusion furnace at the center of the system, the distance would double to four units and it would
be a quarter past nine. Had this been the case at present,
another target would have been selected for the ASSR's
first (and now probably last) interplanetary mission and
things might have turned out differently.

For the tenth time, Gutierrez checked the row of toggles
on the audio panel, making sure the system would relay
signals to speakers throughout the ship, to others set up
in the campsite outside, and to the remaining pair of
shuttles. His attention was focused forward but he could
hear, and feel through the deck, the flight deck filling up
with curious and worried comrades.

In a corner by the life-support controls, Arthur
Empleado of the American KGB kept to himself. Or maybe
others were avoiding him. Dark as Sebastiano, older, not
nearly as well-muscled nor as tall, he'd begun to acquire
a paunch. In another five years his widow's peak would
disappear and he'd be bald. The general thought he looked
naked deprived of the goons who'd been his shadows the
past year. One of them didn't want any more to do with
him. Two were dead. A third nursed a ruined knee inboard
one of the other spacecraft, which housed a makeshift
infirmary.

Gutierrez looked for Rosalind Nguyen in what was
becoming a crowd. The *Dole*'s command deck wasn't roomy.
It was like a party in a shoebox. Even "Rubber Chicken"
Alvarez, cook, garbage disposer, and self-appointed clown,
was here. Gutierrez wondered whether his cooking or his
practical jokes had won him the nickname. Where was
Rosalind? It struck him that with Estrellita gone, the Vietnamese physician was the best-looking woman on 5023 Eris.
The unbidden thought made him feel guilty, not only
toward his wife of thirty years (that always happened when
he thought of other women), but toward poor, dead Reille
y Sanchez. For refuge he resumed his earlier ruminations,
reflecting that the interceptor he'd waged war in might have
brought him here in a mere eleven years, had it been able
to carry enough fuel for the voyage and had there been

something for its engines to breathe. As it was, the ancient shuttles they'd inherited, another order of magnitude faster, had managed the task for him and the others in a little under a year.

"General?" Tech Sergeant Toya Pulaski, amateur paleobiologist (and as it turned out, they'd needed one), handed him a cup. An odd girl, nervous and plain, she'd figured out what was happening here before any of the beings who knew had gotten around to explaining it. The coffee was a gift from those who were at once their hosts and the source of half their troubles. The other half originated with the voices they were waiting to hear on the radio.

"Thanks, Toya. Hullo, Eichra Oren, Sam." Gutierrez sipped coffee. He'd become aware that beside him stood the only human here who hadn't arrived in one of the shuttles, one of an unknown number of nonnautiloids the Elders had brought with them from various alternative realities. At his knee, as usual, sat a large, white, shaggy dog, its black-lipped grin resembling a Samoyed's.

Eichra Oren was not a large man. Something about the way he carried himself made up for that. He practiced an almost magical martial art that resembled interpretive dancing and produced truly horrifying results. Born into a culture gone from Earth for fifteen millennia, he chose to wear faded denims and Hawaiian shirts among his ship-suited fellow humans, perhaps to make his civilian status as plain to them as possible. He was aboard the *Dole* today as an observer for the Elders.

At last a voice issued from the radio, filtered and hissing from a voyage across unimaginable distance, yet still carrying the precise, compelling tones for which its owner was famous: *"Official message to officers and crew of the interplanetary expedition of the American Soviet Socialist Republic."*

"The Banker!" The hoarse whisper issued from an aft crewstation. It must be Empleado, Gutierrez thought, if only because of his penchant for stating the obvious. Eichra Oren looked a question.

"Nikola Deshovich," Gutierrez told him, "the real power now on Earth."

"Under him," somebody quipped, "the KGB compounds your fractures daily."

Deshovich was going on: *"Those who have been your national leaders, now retired in the light of events on Eris 5023, are enjoying a well-deserved rest in contemplative isolation."*

Eichra Oren raised an eyebrow. "Meaning they've been jailed or killed?"

Gutierrez nodded. "Because of what Deshovich and his cronies regard as their bungling of the situation here."

The man shook his head, "All that, from just 'in the light of.'"

The general put a finger to his lips. "There's more."

"... while suitable candidates for their replacement are sought. I, as Chief Executive, have undertaken to fulfill their responsibilities, as much for the sake of the people of the American Soviet Socialist Republic as for the United World Soviet as a whole."

Sebastiano wrenched around in his seat, looking up as if to say, *Here comes the real message!* Gutierrez gave him the same librarian's signal he'd given Eichra Oren and took another drink of coffee.

"Clearly, my first task is to deal with counterrevolutionary contamination of Marxist thought arising from your leaders' incautious fraternization with certain indigenous reactionary elements, which now threatens to impair our long-held mutual goal of an enlightened, ideologically unified Cosmic Collective."

So the old dream, a System-wide Soviet, was still alive. Gutierrez shook his head. And he was going to be the fall guy. Yet if it weren't for his "incautious fraternization," they'd all have starved or suffocated by now. Much of the expedition's equipment, as well as many of its personnel, had proven less than adequate.

Sebastiano grinned openly at Eichra Oren. "Bad enough your Elders are individualists," he offered, "they're capitalists, too!"

Eichra Oren shrugged as if to say it wasn't his fault, although everyone knew he shared the nautiloids' peculiar philosophy. Seeing it enforced (not quite the same as enforcing it) was his profession.

Unaware of Sebastiano's commentary, Deshovich went on: "... *unless a way can be devised by which mankind may benefit sufficiently from contact with these so-called 'Elders' to justify the attendant risks, I have ordered that the expedition be reported lost and its personnel declared dead.*"

So, Gutierrez thought, he wants his cake while thinking up a way to eat it, too. The edict provoked a harsh buzz of angry surprise. Sebastiano spoke a few words of gutter Spanish, echoed in English and other languages, including Russian. There was derisive shouting from outside the ship.

"*Quiet!*" The general's family and friends were part of a public about to be told he was dead. He felt pain and realized he'd set his jaw hard enough to break a tooth. Veins pulsed in his forehead and neck. He frowned at his cup, trying to breathe deeply and listen to the radio at the same time.

"... *on penalty of death, to send no further transmissions, which will be jammed in any event, nor to return to Earth. Do not acknowledge this transmission. Message ends.*"

Leaning awkwardly over Sebastiano's chair, Gutierrez bent the colonel's mike toward his own lips. At the same time, he stretched an arm behind him, letting the last few drops of coffee slip over the rim of his cup.

"Message received and understood," he told the Banker, disobeying the man's final order. As coffee splattered to the deck after its long fall in one-tenth gravity, he added, "Before signing off for good, I want you to hear this: I hereby rechristen this spacecraft, *Laika!*"

TWENTY-EIGHT
Out on Elba

"You can't *say* that!"

Empleado pushed through the small crowd gathered around the general. The KGB agent's expression was frightened, but his face was red with fury. When he spoke, Gutierrez saw little gobbets of saliva burst from his lips.

"You're talking to the goddamned *Banker*! Don't you realize—"

"You're losing it, Art." Ortiz, who'd replaced Richardson as captain of the *Hatch*, was the one man in the expedition shorter than its commander. Broad as he was short, scuttlebutt had it that his great-great-grandfather had been a Yaqui chieftain. The general straightened and turned toward him, but didn't interrupt. "What can Deshovich do to us that hasn't been done already—maroon us on an asteroid?"

"He could—" Empleado stopped, jaw hanging. People laughed at him, a sound he couldn't have heard much since beginning his career. He closed his mouth, realizing for the first time, perhaps, that the Banker's threats were empty: Earth's only spacegoing vessels were right here. And apparently it hadn't dawned on him before now that he was cut off from his source of power. Around him, more faces broke into appreciative grins. Even Pulaski was enjoying his discomfiture in her sheepish way. They couldn't get home, was the thought they all shared—all but the KGB man—but on the other hand, home couldn't get *them*, either.

For Gutierrez, among others, it meant a war was over before it started. The last time he'd been summoned to the radio this way, he'd been ordered by his now-"retired" leaders to use his forty-two-person "force," mostly scientific and technical personnel with little or no combat training, to drive the nautiloids off the asteroid. The fact that this would pit a handful of shotguns, rifles, and side arms, obsolete even on Earth, against pocketable nuclear plasma weapons half a billion years more advanced hadn't counted with the politicians who didn't have to live with the consequences.

One of those consequence was visible about him now, automatic pistols in flapped military holsters slapping the legs of engineers and laboratory types who'd never even handled a gun before. Better acquainted with such lethal hardware, Sebastiano not only carried a nonregulation Glock 9mm instead of the official EAA Witness the American military issued (his privilege as a command-level officer), but leaning against the console beside him was a twelve-gauge semiautomatic Remington shotgun from which he'd become inseparable the past couple of days.

Even Gutierrez, to his astonishment, found himself lugging not one but *two* handguns, picked up when their owners had no further use for them. At the time he'd been less concerned with self-defense than with keeping dangerous toys out of careless hands.

The stainless, short-barreled Smith & Wesson .44 magnum (even more nonregulation, if possible, than Juan's Glock) had been Kamanov's, smuggled like the cigarettes he knew his son Danny was responsible for. The Kahr K9 was evidence that Richardson had been KGB. They were known to favor the tiny pistol: 630 Route 303, Blauvelt, NY 10913, it said, stamped on the pistol at a time when there had still been separate states—and private gun companies. Both weapons dragged at his pockets. If it weren't for the one-piece garment he wore, they'd have pulled his pants down. Tired of the weight, he was somehow reluctant to give it up. It was the first time in his life, the aging fighter pilot thought, he'd relied on any weapon costing less than a hundred million dollars. Somehow, he felt more secure now.

Behind him, he heard Eichra Oren clear his throat. "Excuse me, General, I'm afraid I lack a referent. Would you mind explaining the significance of the name 'Laika'?"

Before Gutierrez could respond, there was another interruption. "Why is this man on the command deck," Empleado demanded, glaring at Eichra Oren, "armed with a dangerous weapon? He isn't a member of this expedition!"

Displacement activity. The behaviorist phrase welled up in the general's memory, heard at a leadership seminar he'd been required to attend years ago and remembered because of his fondness for cats. Empleado complained about an edged weapon when he was surrounded by guns, attacking Eichra Oren the same way a cat washes itself furiously when you catch it up to no good. Only now did Gutierrez consciously notice the sword hanging at Eichra Oren's thigh. It should have been the first thing anyone noticed about him. Somehow it never was.

"You know as well as I do, Art," he didn't try to hide his exasperation, "that Eichra Oren is serving as an observer for the Elders. That 'dangerous weapon' is his badge of office and he's never without it." He was tempted to ask what good a nondangerous weapon would be. "Try thinking of it as a naval officer's saber. It's the same kind of thing."

"Yes, General," Empleado was unmollified, "but unlike the unsharpened butterknives affected by our Navy, this is more than a ceremonial accessory!"

The remark, Gutierrez knew, was meant for Ortiz, recently transferred from the Navy to Aerospace. But Art was correct, in a minor, nitpicking sort of way. The Elders had no concept of divided powers. Not only did Eichra Oren serve as a policeman and judge, but as an executioner, killing with his hands and a tiny fusion-powered pistol as well as with the more conspicuous sword.

Summoned as what he termed a *"p'Nan* moral debt

assessor" when it appeared that Semlohcolresh had murdered Kamanov, he'd completed his task quickly and with greater success than even he might have wished, when he'd collected on the unpayable moral debt that murder creates by taking the life of Reille y Sanchez, with whom, Gutierrez knew, Eichra Oren had by then fallen in love. The whole thing was tragically dumb, but it had served to delay a suicidal little war it now looked like they wouldn't have to fight. Whatever else he'd said, the Banker hadn't mentioned those earlier orders.

The Elders' envoy had been briefed on present-day Earth before arrival. Gutierrez had been impressed over the past few days with their sources of information, along with whatever technique the man had applied not only to learn the facts, but English, Spanish, and Russian, as well. It appeared, however, that there were gaps in his understanding of human history and culture.

"At the beginning of space exploration," Gutierrez turned to Eichra Oren, determined to ignore Empleado if he couldn't outargue him, "we'd been putting small things into orbit. America managed to send up rats or mice, recovered for later examination, or maybe that was just the plan. In any case, the Russians, not to be outdone, sent up a big payload with a little sled dog named Laika. All over the world, everybody thought that was quite a feat—until the Russians admitted that they couldn't get her down again and had never intended to. She died slowly, of suffocation."

"I see." Eichra Oren frowned. Controlling his scabbard with one hand, he reached to give his dog a reassuring pat. "And this new leader—"

"*Self-appointed* leader!" Whoever interrupted immediately withdrew into the crowd. Gutierrez suspected it was Danny.

"Self-appointed leader, then," Eichra Oren agreed. "As far as he knows—"

"*Or cares!*" Gutierrez didn't even bother to look. Smuggler, seditionist, where in God's name had he and the boy's mother gone—on second thought, given recent experience, maybe they'd brought the kid up right, after all.

Eichra Oren was persistent. "As far as he knows or cares, he's stranded his own people here forever, until your consumables run out and you die just like that little dog, of suffocation, starvation, or the cold of space."

Gutierrez nodded. He knew that Eichra Oren had voluntarily marooned himself on this asteroid, at least for the time being, a necessity to which he'd been resigned from the beginning. Even so advanced a species as the Elders, with an evolutionary head start of five hundred million years and an equivalent technological lead, found travel between alternate universes difficult and dangerous. "Or left to whatever mercy a bunch of alien monsters—meaning the people you work for—offer us. Whether he knows that we won't suffocate or freeze—"

"Thanks to the way," Eichra Oren raised his eyebrows toward the canopy a kilometer overhead which lent a yellowish tint to everything beneath it, "the Elders have terraformed this place?"

"You still don't get the point," Gutierrez told the Antarctican. "I've only just seen it, myself. I'm not sure I knew myself why I held that little rechristening ceremony. Simple defiance, maybe. But look: it was a small thing, one poor little husky bitch. People get used to hearing of all kinds of evil happening to other people and they never seem to learn much from it. But animals—I've never been a great animal lover, Eichra Oren, but what happened with that little dog, the calculated coldbloodedness of it, should have told us all we needed to know about socialism."

"*General!*" Empleado gasped.

"The 'us' is figurative, of course," Gutierrez was unrelenting, "it was long before my time. I always thought there should have been bonfires in the streets the next day, the works of Marx, all kinds of leftist magazines and books, set ablaze by those who wrote and edited and published them—and now had reason to know better. That should have been followed by the collapse of America's most successful homegrown socialists, the Democrats and Republicans. But there weren't, it wasn't, and it was the last clear warning we ever got."

"*General!*"

"Sorry, Art, there's nobody to tattle to any more." Gutierrez turned to Eichra Oren. "When I was a kid, there was a cartoon that showed up in the underground papers called *Out On Elba*. It was set on an island only a couple of meters across, and only had a couple of characters."

Eichra Oren smiled. "All there was room for, probably."

"Probably." Gutierrez smiled back, mostly at the childhood memory. "The main character was the 'Little Corporal,' pudgy, with a face that reminded you of a snail. You know, *escargot*? He was supposed to represent power put in its place, but you sort of felt sorry for him. His only companion was a pig with a crown who was supposed to be a reincarnated Louis XIV."

"I get it," Sebastiano put in. "King of the Franks!"

Gutierrez watched the colonel struggle from the embrace of the command chair. "I hadn't thought of that, Juan. Louis the Pig was so fat that his feet wouldn't touch the ground, and he wasn't very good company. Always mumbling '*L'Etat c'est moi*.' The Little Corporal would watch ships on the horizon and wish he were a seagull so he could escape. He once said 'Exile, like the Academy Award, is a great honor. It only *seems* unbearable because you can't share it with all the little people who made it possible.'"

There was no outright laughter this time, but he got appreciative smiles, those of machinist Corporal Owen and life-support officer Lieutenant Lee Marna among them. Sedition appeared to be contagious. Eichra Oren grinned at Empleado, addressing Gutierrez. "Maybe there are exceptions."

Empleado reddened again. "General, I demand that you disarm this loudmouth immediately and eject him from the ship!"

Gutierrez laughed. "You disarm him, Art, I'd like to see that!"

"General!" Roger Betal, the former thug who now avoided his KGB boss, pushed in excitedly. Beside him was Staff Sergeant C. C. Jones, mission information officer (provided that any of this was ever made public), stringer for *American Truth*, and former network anchorman, retired when he'd suddenly begun speaking with a slur.

Gutierrez had all but forgotten Jones over the past few days. He'd opposed his being in the expedition in the first place. Twenty years ago, with the USA in the last throes of becoming the ASSR, Gutierrez had commanded the famous "Redhawk Squadron," suppressing guerilla resistance. He and Jones had argued over some bright lights—as useful to enemy snipers as to a TV crew—during nighttime efforts to disarm a bomb placed in one of his interceptors where it sat on a runway apron. Gutierrez had won the argument by knocking out the lights—and Jones' teeth—with a fire extinguisher.

". . . giant centipede!" Betal was saying. Gutierrez decided he'd better pay attention. "It just walked into camp! It says it wants to talk to you, Eichra Oren!" The assessor was responsible for Betal's disaffection, having won the man's admiration by humiliating him in unarmed combat.

Eichra Oren raised a hand before Empleado could speak. "I was just going anyway. That's my old friend Scutigera outside." To Gutierrez, Sebastiano, and Ortiz: "General, Colonel, Major. Coming, Sam?"

"Gladly." The dog bared its teeth at Empleado. "Some of the company around here *stinks*!"

TWENTY-NINE
Insider Trading

Stooping out through the oval portside crew-hatch at the middeck of the *Dole*, Eichra Oren clambered over the upturned edge of the plastic-coated wire mesh basket in which the shuttle and its fleetmates had been lowered to the surface. As his feet touched the ground, he discovered that his friend Scutigera was the center of considerable—if ambivalent—attention.

Most of the humans huddled beneath the stubby wings of their spacecraft, all eyes turned toward Scutigera. Nor was it difficult for him to dominate the scene, even without moving a limb. Nine meters from his rounded, intelligent-looking head with its pair of huge, glittering compound eyes, to the final segment of his tapered body, he took up even more space than that implied, since his graceful antennae and many of his fifteen pairs of slender legs were longer yet.

Eichra Oren had always thought Scutigera a handsome being. His legs and antennae were banded in contrasting shades of brown, his body patterned with what the newcomers would have termed "racing stripes." Beneath his head he bore three pairs of jaws, the rearmost vestigial (his remote ancestors had wielded poisoned fangs), the others specialized for manipulation. His people were the largest land sapients Eichra Oren knew of (and his knowledge was extensive), but they were subtle and accomplished technologists, producing, long before their first contact with the Elders, everything from nuclear steam turbines to watches with moving parts invisible to the naked human eye.

"Well, old crustacean," Sam spoke first, an attention—getter in itself for the dazed humans clustered under the spacecraft. Some, in a setting which afforded one shock after another, hadn't yet heard about his artificially enhanced intelligence. "You still know how to make an entrance!"

Adroit for a creature his size, Scutigera slewed his first few segments around and let his antenna-tips patter greetings along Sam's muzzle and then Eichra Oren's cheeks. Several beneath the shuttle wings groaned and turned away. From within the giant sapient came a low, cultivated voice, speaking the language of ancient, lost Antarctica. "Oasam, my furry and infuriating friend, as I have told you on many previous occasions, I am an arthropod, not a crustacean. How would you enjoy being called a reptile?"

"Some of my best friends—" Sam used the trilling tongue of a world in which warmblooded dinosaurs had survived global catastrophe to become Earth's sapient race "—are reptiles." If he sounded pleased with himself, it was because they were no more reptilian than Scutigera was crustacean.

"Hopeless," the centipede complained, still in the language of the Lost Continent. "Well, my warmest greetings, Eichra Oren. Kindly inform me of the health and happiness of your esteemed mother, Eneri Relda. And why haven't you sent this beast to obedience school?"

"He wouldn't go." Eichra Oren grinned up at the inhuman face hovering above his own. "My mother is well, happy, and busy, as usual. This is a surprise, old friend; I wasn't even aware you were in this universe until I received your signal just now." He tapped the side of his head where, as with all sapients associated with the Elders, sophisticated electronics had been implanted on his cortex, similar to the device which raised Sam's intelligence from that of an unusually bright dog to that of a human being.

"I am a partner in the enterprise." Scutigera waved meters of antenna in a shrug. "How could I deprive myself of one of Mister Thoggosh's adventures? They're inevitably diverting—at my age a greater consideration than you might imagine—and almost always indecently profitable. Speaking of our mutual molluscoid associate, he would appreciate your presence in his chambers at your earliest convenience. I came, supposing that you might prefer riding with me to risking life and limb in one of his flying bagels."

In fact he preferred the electrostatic aerocraft Scutigera mentioned, but visiting with his old comrade was a pleasant prospect. They'd shared many an adventure, but it was long since they'd seen each other. "American culture," he chuckled, "is getting to be a—what's the word, Sam, for an enthusiasm pursued *en masse?*"

" 'Fad.' " The dog rolled his eyes in appeal to Scutigera. "Too lazy to access his own implant—and if it's all the same to you, I'll walk."

"There's a stop I want to make," the man declared, "about halfway between here and Mister Thoggosh's residence."

Scutigera bent several legs, lowering his front quarters to assist as Eichra Oren clambered astride the first segment behind the arthropod's head. Smoothly polished, toast-colored chitin made a precarious perch. Resting his sword across his thighs, the man waved to his fellow humans as the arthropod's first stride, rippling through the ranks of his many legs like a kick through a chorus line, whisked them out of the camp and plunged them into the jungle surrounding it. Sam trotted along beside them, not quite forced to break into a lope. In addition to being the largest land sapients Eichra Oren knew of, Scutigera's people were among the swiftest, their present breathtaking pace representing no more than a stately crawl to the giant.

"I observe," Scutigera commented once they found themselves deep within the lush, dripping forest, "that you do not permit the prospect of a prolonged stay on this asteroid to disturb you. But then you are a multitalented being, well capable of filling any number of productive roles, and I could not help noticing the presence here of many attractive females of your species . . ."

The joke was old between them. Scutigera's mating season was limited, requiring drastic physiological changes before it became even mechanically possible. Like all sapients he had excellent memory, however, especially for pleasure. Despite his usually high tolerance for differing customs, he envied those capable of recreational mating. It was a measure of his fundamentally good nature that, rather than resenting what he saw as an immutable fact of life, he teased his friends among the more fortunate species about it.

A flock of pink, long-legged birds of a kind Eichra Oren had never seen before flew over, making an absurd racket. Gripping the weapon which was his honor and burden, he shook his head, knowing the gesture would be visible within his friend's 360 degrees of peripheral vision. The topic of females was a bit tender at the moment and might remain so for some time, so he pushed it out of his mind. If the ride atop the giant arthropod was slippery, it was smooth, taking place as it did on so many points of suspension. From the timbre of his voice, he might have been speaking from an armchair.

"Life serves its purpose simply by being lived," he replied, "and to me, it doesn't much matter where. As you probably know, Mister Thoggosh required my services here as an assessor. . . ."

"One could hardly miss an event that generated such heated debate," the giant centipede replied. No Elder, nor any among the many species associated with them, could abide an unpaid moral debt, especially one owed by himself. It was customary to resolve personal and business disputes, and to examine one's own conscience periodically, with the aid of professional assessors wise in the half-billion-year-old philosophy of *p'Na* and capable of prescribing measures to restore the balance. This didn't often require literal use of the assessor's sword, but it was there if need arose. "I collected over a year's income in gold and platinum, wagering on your decision with unfortunates less well-informed concerning your habits of mind. Although considering how it ended, perhaps I oughtn't to admit to such crassness."

Eichra Oren laughed. Whatever they'd accomplished on their own before discovery by the Elders, Scutigera's folk, like many primitive societies, had never reconciled what they imagined to be moral perfection—altruistic self-sacrifice—with personal material gain. This contradiction had resulted in the downfall of countless otherwise admirable civilizations, and was taken seriously by the Elders as a symptom of potentially fatal social disorder. Adopting *p'Nan* ethics had solved the problem at a conscious level for the centipede people, yet Eichra Oren knew that with cultures as well as individuals, it is the oldest, most self-destructive habits that die the most lingering deaths.

"Even the Americans have a proverb about an 'ill wind,'" he said. "Or was it 'insider trading'? In any case, the task is done, thanks to *p'Na*. I'm glad someone benefitted by it. Now I've set out to accomplish what may prove far more difficult: understanding my fellow humans and the bizarre, twisted culture they've created."

Antennae waved in agreement. "They *are* a strange people, Eichra Oren."

"You said a mandible-full!" Sam volunteered, sounding out of breath. The man knew that he regretted not accepting a ride, although how he'd have stayed atop their friend's slippery carapace defied speculation.

"Stranger than you can possibly imagine," Eichra Oren told the arthropod. "You know that their *leaders*"—the alien concept had to be rendered in English—"somehow obliged the expedition's members, in such a manner that many of them felt they must comply even if it meant dying, to drive us off this asteroid by force, despite Mister Thoggosh's unquestioned prior claim and our obviously overwhelming numerical and technical superiority."

"So I gather," Scutigera answered. "I was warned when they first arrived that a collective willingness to condone outright thievery, and an individual capacity to ignore the facts of objective reality, are considered indispensable civic virtues in American culture. Or perhaps it was religious virtues—it seemed so absurd at the time that I don't remember clearly now. How could such a people have survived the rigors of natural selection?"

"Civil *and* religious. They've acquired a reflexive aversion to the plain, inconvenient truth; they're ready to vote away anybody's life, liberty, or property—even their own—if that'll help them pretend the truth doesn't exist. In any case, through this mysterious power to impose ridiculous obligations, these *leaders* caused a murder. Apparently it was intended as a provocation to general violence, although why they thought it would serve that purpose, I still don't fully understand. It makes no sense to blame a whole people for the actions of a single individual. But now, as the Americans say, it's academic—"

"Telling us much," Sam offered, "about their educational system."

"Since even their *new* leader has abandoned them," Eichra Oren finished.

Scutigera chuckled. "I reiterate my question about natural selection."

"Now for the really confusing part," the man mused. "Horatio Gutierrez, another of these leaders—although in some way he reminds me of Mister Thoggosh—seems almost relieved to be abandoned. More, I think, than can be accounted for by any last-minute cancellation of the hostilities I don't believe he ever planned to commence. He even makes jokes about it. Comprehending that alone ought to fully occupy my time here . . ."

Scutigera slowed the pace. "And?"

"And there's no deceiving you, is there, old friend?" He shook his head. "All right, I find I'm not overly eager to go home. There remain aspects of this recent assessment I must think through. For one—although I haven't a doubt that I executed my office correctly—I find that I don't look forward to telling my mother about what happened. I'm uncertain why. So for the time being, I'm content—"

"Ask if *I'm* content!" interrupted Sam, tired of keeping up. "How many females of *my* species have you seen hanging around this free-floating dungball?"

Again Scutigera chuckled. "It was always my impression, Otusam, that you prefer females of the human species."

"—and confident," the man ignored the byplay, "that

we'll get home eventually, when and if the Elders ever
stumble across whatever it is they're looking for here. By
the way, old friend, you wouldn't happen to know what it
is, would you?" Here, Eichra Oren thought, trying not to
be seen holding his breath, was the most fascinating and
annoying mystery of all. The challenge of solving it, despite
his employer's determination to keep him in the dark, was
a primary reason he didn't mind staying on 5023 Eris.

"You weren't informed?" The arthropod's tone was ironic.
"It pains me to say that if I did know—and I don't say
either way, *old friend*—I couldn't say. Conditions of the
strictest secrecy were agreed upon in the first clause of
the contract I signed with Mister Thoggosh."

Eichra Oren was silent. Proprietary secrets were certainly
no novelty in the Elders' free-trade society. Nor was it
impermissible, within bounds of *p'Na*, for others to ferret
them out and make what use of them they might. Still, this
was an enormous undertaking even for them to keep under
wraps, involving (he hadn't needed the numbers before this,
now they scrolled past his mind's eye via his implant)
thousands of beings on this one asteroid alone, plus how
many more—that many?—in support roles back in the
home universe.

How often had he heard Mister Thoggosh say that two
can keep a secret as long as one of them is dead and the
other frozen in liquid nitrogen? Shrugging, he blinked away
the display.

"Slow down, old friend, this is where I want to stop."

THIRTY
The Scene of the Crime

He'd dreaded this moment for what seemed like weeks.

In fact, it had only been a couple of days, yet Eichra Oren knew that the exercise, which was how he thought of it, however difficult or painful it proved, was necessary to his peace of mind; a matter of tying up loose ends. Not long ago he'd remarked that life consists of little *besides* loose ends and that often they were the only thing that gave survivors a reason for going on. The way things had turned out, he'd said it to someone who *hadn't* survived.

A great distance overhead, he spotted a tiny black dot against the yellow canopy, one of Scutigera's "flying bagels," coming from the direction of the human camp toward the Elders' settlement. Wondering idly who it was, he slid, sword in hand, from Scutigera's back, landing lightly on his feet (given his training and condition, he'd have landed lightly anyway) in the low gravity.

Neither noticing nor caring whether his friends followed—a heroic feat of shutting out the world considering that one of them was a talking dog and the other nine meters from antenna-tip to toe-claw—he pushed a curtain of leafy branches out of the way, each motion of his body stirring memories burned into his brain by later events, to cross a little creek he recognized, and began working his way upstream along its low bank. The air felt cool and moist, laden with the oddly mixed perfumes of fresh growth and decaying forest debris. For a few heartbeats, an iridescent blue-green dragonfly hovered over his shoulder like a singing jewel before darting off on some predatory errand. In the end, he came to a miniature waterfall that broke the stream's course at the sprawling foot of an enormous canopy tree.

Not more than forty-eight hours ago (although he realized all over again that it seemed much longer), he'd stood on this exact spot with a peculiar object in the palm of his hand, knowing it would resemble an undersized golf ball to the person he was showing it to, complete to color and texture.

"My office and personal quarters," he'd told her, "at least it will be in a few days. It's a seed with engineered genes. Be careful not to drop it or it'll try to take root. When it matures," he remembered saying with a glibness that made him feel a bit ashamed now, "it'll cantilever out over the stream and I can fall asleep listening to the waterfall."

Drawing sustenance from the tree (equally engineered to tolerate the process), the new growth jutted out now like a shelf mushroom, still many days away from its intended size and shape. All nautiloid construction on the asteroid had been accomplished this way, by living things designed at a molecular level to grow to a certain shape and size and die, leaving skeletons of titanium or plastic as coral leaves a skeleton of calcium—preconceived, rather than prefabricated. On the way here with Sam and Scutigera, he'd persuaded himself that he wanted to check the progress of the seed he'd planted. He was weary of his impersonal temporary quarters in the Elders' complex, wearier still of the forced companionship they necessitated, at meals for example. A need for solitude throbbed within him like a toothache. But at this particular moment he couldn't imagine dwelling on this spot. He had more compelling reasons for being here.

He and his guest had found a mossy place to sit at the base of the tree. Listening to the waterfall—in the clearer, deeper water a meter away, a handful of silver minnows darted and gleamed—he'd explained that the site he'd chosen was exactly halfway between the human and the nautiloid camps. This seemed appropriate, since it more or less described his own position. Had circumstances been different he'd have gone on to say that, as a human brought up with the outlook and values of the Elders, he'd felt a bit lost since coming to 5023 Eris and at the same time caught in the middle.

Had circumstances been different, he'd have asked her . . .

Instead, he'd accused her of a series of terrible crimes, tricked her into confessing, and dealt with her in the customary manner of a moral debt assessor, assisting her to pay the token price (it could be no more than that) for three lives she'd taken with far less concern than he was showing her. And now the thought of living and working here—but that was pointless. Suppose somebody lived as long as Mister Thoggosh—or his own mother—indulging in the kind of fetishism which made him avoid every place where something painful had occurred: eventually there wouldn't be anyplace he could go, anything he could do, that wouldn't carry with it some unbearable association.

"So the criminal does *return to the scene of the crime!"*

He turned, startled not so much by the presence of another person as by the fact that he hadn't noticed her until now. The first thing that impressed him about Doctor Rosalind Nguyen, here in the deep, kilometer-tall forest, was how tiny she looked. She wasn't the least bit frail; at the moment she seemed the most solid thing here. Her eyes were huge and dark, her skin the color of antique gold. Only as an afterthought did he open his mouth to protest the injustice of her words. Stepping toward him around the canopy tree, hands in her trouser pockets, she cut him off simply by raising her eyebrows.

"Forgive me, Eichra Oren, that was unkind and untrue. I just—well, it was there inside me to say." She scuffed at loose leaves lying on the ground and smiled, her eyes crinkling at the corners in a way that appealed to him. If his culture had used the same symbolic conventions as hers, he'd have described her face as heart-shaped, its lines beginning with a small, almost pointed chin, sweeping upward through pleasing curves and angled cheekbones to a broad, intelligent brow. Her hair was black as space and unusually fine in texture. "Now that it's said, at least I don't have to think it any more."

They'd spoken several times in camp, but never like this, out of sight of the others. He was unaware that, like many Asian English speakers of even the third or fourth generation, she spoke with something that wasn't quite an accent, a lingering habit of family speech or even some minor difference of structure that nobody but a physical anthropologist would know or care about. What he heard he might have called a lilt. Sensitive as he was to language and the sound of words, he only knew that he enjoyed listening to her.

"What are you doing here?" He cleared his throat. The question hadn't come out as he'd intended, but like his idea of a police interrogation.

She shrugged, unoffended, a pretty gesture he surprised himself by hoping was uncalculated. "Trying to figure out what happened here—not the facts, I know them all too well—just how I feel about them, what they mean. Yours is a strange culture, Eichra Oren. It prefers its charity and brutality in unmixed portions."

The statement was so full of false assumptions that he didn't know where to begin setting her straight. She'd have done the necropsy, of course, and that would be influencing her. She was standing beside him now, looking up into his eyes, close enough that he caught the clean scent of her hair. That and the way she'd said his name suddenly made it difficult to think. Reille y Sanchez had had the same effect on him. What was it about American women?

"I—"

He wanted to argue, to tell her that whatever favors the Elders had done for her people, they hardly constituted charity. And more importantly, that the act of judgment—of justice—he had committed in this place had been the *opposite* of brutality. Somehow the words wouldn't come and he dragged himself to a halt at the first stupid-sounding syllable, unwilling to compound inanity.

Again she smiled. "Don't misunderstand me, Eichra

Oren, that's not a criticism." She lifted a small, slender hand as if to lay it on his forearm, then let it drop. He saw, with the involuntary eye of a reflexive observer, that it had that look of transparent parchment—not as unattractive as it sounded—which came from a physician's practice of washing dozens of times a day. "At least I don't believe it is . . ."

He'd noticed before that Americans had characteristic reflexes of their own. At the moment, she was looking around to make sure they weren't being overheard, completely unaware that she was doing it. He encouraged her with a nod.

She got it out in a rush: "It might even result in a happier world."

That was the very point he'd come here to ponder, although he found, somewhat to his chagrin, that he was less interested in what she was saying to him than in how she looked as she said it, the way she moved, the way her mouth, her lips, her tongue, her small white teeth had with the words they made.

"That's interesting. Tell me why you think so."

"You have to understand," she was still tentative, "that everything about life the way we humans lead it—"

"You humans?" He suppressed an impulse to step back. What was implied by that phrase, even unintentionally, disappointed him. But at least, as she struggled to deal with her own awkwardness, he had a chance to catch his breath, regain his conversational bearings again.

"I mean . . ." She looked down at her small feet, keeping her eyes on the mossy ground, obviously feeling as self-conscious as he did. It was easier for her to speak to him this way, focused on battered Kevlar and neoprene rather than his face. " . . . those of us from Soviet America, from the United World Soviet, from our version of Earth. Everything about life there has always felt, to me, sort of murky and diluted at the same time—"

He bent, tilting his head to look up into her eyes, resisting an urge to reach out and lift her chin. Aside from the effect her small, well-shaped breasts and slender waist—contours easily discernable under her soft, well-worn ship-suit—seemed to be having on his endocrine and circulatory systems (how could this be happening so soon after what he'd just gone through with Estrellita?) she was the first of these people who promised to make anything resembling sense. He didn't want to spoil it.

"What do you mean, 'everything,' Dr. Nguyen?"

"Nobody here but us Rosalinds." She looked up at him. "Anyway, I seem to have left my doctorate—and any wisdom I ever managed to acquire with it—back in camp. Or back on Earth, maybe. I don't *know* what I mean, Eichra Oren, the moral atmosphere, I suppose."

She shrugged, this time with tension and frustration, folded her hands and pressed the heels of her palms together. The tips of her left fingers were calloused. He remembered seeing a stringed instrument in camp and guessed—in his profession guesses were as important as deductions—that she seldom played for others. It wouldn't suit her character. Whatever music she made would serve her as a means of relaxation, meditation, even therapy.

"*Polluted*," she went on, "and at the same time lacking enough oxygen. At home all of our favorite homilies condemn seeing things in black and white. But that's the way I see them, Eichra Oren, the way I always have. I must, doing what I do, or people who are counting on me die. That's why I think I understand what happened here. There's a cleanliness in the way your people address moral issues, as if they were engineering problems, a genuine aspect of reality, that I find—whatever it reveals about me—exhilarating, like a mountain breeze blowing away the cloying humidity of a swamp."

He grinned at her. "Or the miasma of Marxism?"

"Nobody believes in that superstitious rot any more," she protested. "But somehow it seems to lead a life of its own no matter what anybody believes. And whenever anything important has to be done, we spend half of our precious time and energy giving it lip service, frightened to death that the other guy will turn out to be orthodox and expect it of us."

He searched his recently acquired memories. "Comrade Grundy?"

She smiled. "She's probably trapped just like the rest of us. The awful part is that you can never tell, nobody wears a sign, and the price for guessing wrong is terrible.

Even once that's settled, we waste the other half of our time and energy trying to find ways around the constraints imposed by the belief-system itself. You should see the contortions our geneticists have to go through, just because Saint Karl backed the wrong theory of evolution!"

"Not to mention your economists. You're saying that, with the exception of the occasional dangerous believer, you're all compelled to live with Marxism the way your Western civilization was compelled to live, however uncomfortably, with Christianity for what . . . twenty centuries, wasn't it?"

She gave him a reevaluating look. "That was long before my time, Eichra Oren. As the saying goes, I'm an atheist, thank God. And 'our' Western civilization aside," her eyes twinkled, "my ancestors were all Buddhists."

Whatever he'd intended to say never got said. They turned at the sound of someone, something, crashing toward them through the dense underbrush. When he saw who it was, Eichra Oren realized that the racket had been a deliberate, polite warning.

It worried him when Sam was polite.

"Hiya, Doc. I hate to break this up, Boss, but the reluctant crustacean says he has klicks to go and promises to keep. And His Majesty Thoggosh the First is paging us again. Anyway, you two don't have as much privacy as you think. Rubber Chicken Alvarez has been watching you from the bushes."

"Garbage grinder, practical joker, and Peeping Tom." Rosalind shook her head. "Somehow it doesn't surprise me at all."

THIRTY-ONE
Water Music

Gazing through the liquid medium he breathed at the pale, soft-bodied creature before him, Mister Thoggosh shuddered. The varied, adventurous life he led threw him into contact with sapients of many species, yet sometimes even he felt overwhelmed by the unlovely appearance of his intimate associates.

This was among the worst. He was unaware that the revulsion he felt was akin to that experienced by a mammalian sapience at having turned over a rock to see what squirms beneath it. Where, he thought, were this thing's graceful, powerful manipulators, its firm shell, striped and colorful? Its stubbed limbs were obscenely jointed, terminating in a clutch of grotesque wrigglers that reminded him of the linings of intestines. Instead of a pair of large, thoughtful, bronze-colored eyes, slit-pupiled, with reflective retinae, two hard little buttons glittered at him from a death-white mallet of a face. Nothing about them, nor of the alien countenance they were set in, conveyed any hint of the intelligence he knew—although at present he had difficulty *feeling* that he knew—resided behind them.

His moment of revulsion ebbed as it had a million times

before. Again he merely saw humanity sitting before him, no more inherently evil, stupid, or disgusting than any other sapience, every bit as capable of decency, brilliance, and nobility. He reminded himself that it was kin, albeit through some seven hundred fifty generations, to his dear friend Eneri Relda and that fearsome hatchling of hers.

It was the first chance he'd had to interview this particular specimen, although he'd wanted to from the moment he'd first heard of her. Until now, there simply hadn't been time. Complications seemed to arise of their own accord, one after another, in this enterprise he was attempting to direct on what some called "5023 Eris." Adding to his burdens was the difficulty of achieving a reasonable balance between kindness and justice in his relations with these beings who'd shown up on his property without having been invited.

Someone—perhaps his assistant, Aelbraugh Pritsch—had informed him that Eris was an ancient human deity associated with confusion. That seemed appropriate. He'd immediately adopted the name for an asteroid which heretofore had only been known by a serial designation.

"I *am* a trifle curious about one thing," he continued a conversation which had been going on for several minutes without getting much beyond the pleasantries both species were accustomed to, "if you don't mind my asking..."

This small, frail-looking female was considered timid even by her own cosapients. He realized that he must be a rather imposing sight, resembling as he did "a giant squid with eyes the size of banjos." (He must remember to ask Aelbraugh Pritsch what that meant; it had been excerpted from one of the reports Gutierrez had sent Earthward.) Add to all of that his sinuous luminescent tentacles, not to mention an exoskeleton as large as a small personal vehicle of the previous century which his language software rendered "peoplecart," still greatly beloved by these humans for some reason. He was gratified (and surprised) that he didn't seem to frighten her.

"Not at all, sir." Perched on the edge of a wire-mesh chair, Toya Pulaski absently snagged a strand of floating hair and tucked it back into place. Her earlier misgivings, he thought, over breathing the oxygenated fluorocarbon filling his quarters (for the benefit of nonaquatic visitors, he remembered with a trace of annoyance), seemed to be subsiding. "The more we all know about each other the better."

Under a low ceiling, the walls of the long, wide room were lost in the low light he naturally favored, having evolved from abyssal organisms. Kelp plantings here and there gave the place a homey feel; he'd brought several favorite tactiles from his sculpture collection. Even to his own discriminating eye they appeared abstract, yet each was completely representational, playing on differences between touch and vision—in a manner analogous to human art based on optical illusion—to produce the kind of object he most enjoyed, that which appeared formless until physically engaged.

He laid one long tentacle over another. "I agree. And it occurs to me, Sergeant Pulaski, that our respective species have somewhat more in common than might first be expected. After all, I'm obviously a marine creature. And your species, of course, has a unique aquatic heritage all its own."

"Unique?" She sat up straight. "But Mister Thoggosh, *all* life on Earth—on our Earth, anyway—began in the sea."

"I refer, my dear sergeant, to the millions of years that your evolutionary predecessors spent paddling about the lakes and streams of Africa—having been driven from the trees by bigger, stronger monkeys—before they became formidable hunters of the veldt."

Pulaski sat back with an expression of disappointment. "Elaine Morgan, *The Descent of Woman*. I'm afraid it's just an old theory, Mister Thoggosh, and not very—"

"Ah, but *look* at yourself." He upturned another tentacle. "A mammal without fur except where it protects the head and shoulders from sunlight and water-reflected glare—or prevents small swimming organisms from entering bodily cavities? A land animal with the subcutaneous fat reserves and respiratory reflexes of a cetacean? A female whose breasts—my dear, how can you stand naked before a mirror and doubt it?"

Pulaski blushed furiously. "I never stand naked before a mirror."

"What a shame," the giant mollusc lied gallantly. "Yet any appreciation for beauty in others must begin with—"

"Mister Thoggosh, don't con me." She folded her hands. He saw her knuckles whiten, understanding what it implied. "I wonder what you really know about us, or whether you can even tell individual human beings apart. I'm not sure I can tell individual nautiloids apart. Don't we all look alike to you?"

Having dealt with members of her species long before Pulaski's ancestors had rediscovered bronze, he found he learned more about them by listening than by talking. His experience told him that something—he wasn't certain what, perhaps his very nonhumanity which made him, in her eyes, a nonjudgmental neutral—was about to plunge her into a self-revealing mood. He wasn't about to interfere with it; there was still too much to learn. Even had he been inclined to answer, he didn't get a chance as she rushed on.

"Well, we don't look alike to each other, and whatever anybody tells you, Mister Thoggosh, looks count. When I was younger I remember hearing Somebody-or-other's Law to the effect that no woman is ever satisfied with the size of her breasts. Those with little ones want big ones and those with big ones complain of the inconvenience. Those in the middle—I don't know why I'm talking about this, but let me tell you, I would have been happy just to have more than what my dorm mates used to call 'fried hummingbird eggs.'"

"As you put it yourself, Toya—if I may—the more we know about each other . . ." He laid a gentle tentacle atop her hands, which appeared to be crushing one another, gratified that she didn't flinch from his cold, molluscoid touch. "You're certain you don't care for something to drink? I'm having beer." As he withdrew (trying not to feel too relieved about it, himself), she shook her head, causing more of her fine, brown hair to float free.

"No, thank you, Mister Thoggosh."

To the left, his prized and beautiful songfish warbled sweetly in a cage suspended between floor and ceiling. He considered throwing something at it, wondering why he suddenly felt so irritable.

True, Pulaski was the subject of his next talk with Eichra

Oren, but no one had forced him to ask Scutigera to delay the debt assessor so that he might have her flown here for a preliminary interview. Perhaps this was the source of his annoyance. Mister Thoggosh regarded himself as an essentially simple being (which would have amused anyone who knew him) who pursued his goals straightforwardly.

He sent his separable tentacle for beer, knowing, as Pulaski watched the specialized limb detach itself from his body, that it wouldn't be the shock to her that it had been to the first American, General Gutierrez, who'd witnessed it. As it swam to the wall-cooler where he kept his kelp beer and returned with a container trailing a long sipping tube, he pushed their conversation onto the course he'd planned earlier.

"Toya, I've studied several hundred of the entertainments you call motion pictures. They have equivalents among my people and tell a stranger much about the culture that created them." He sipped his beer, enjoying it as he always did. "Hence the trifling curiosity I mentioned earlier. With but rare exception, I've noticed that those among you with their reproductive anatomy hanging unprotected between their locomotory extremities—"

Her face reddened. "You mean men?"

"—nonetheless seem to prefer garments consisting of two fabric cylinders which don't properly allow for their anatomy. Not one cylinder, mind you—not even three, which would make sense. Those among you *without* this anatomical liability, however, and who might better tolerate such attire, customarily wear only one cylinder."

Pulaski almost giggled, whether from tension or amusement he couldn't tell. She inhaled deeply, just as if she were breathing air. "There *are* Scotsmen, Mister Thoggosh. And women have been wearing trousers for quite a while, now." She brushed a hand down her patched and faded jumpsuit.

"Contrary to a verbal irrationalism in which you humans persist, exceptions neither prove the rule nor explain it." He took a sip of beer. Although his organs of speech and ingestion were independent, he'd acquired the useful habit of pacing his conversation from his air-breathing associates, and often wished he could smoke a pipe. "Similarly irrational, and vastly more hazardous, is this preference your male gender manifests for a wheeled transportation rack—"

"Give me a second, now . . ." She frowned, then smiled. "You mean bicycles?"

"—with a horizontal structural member in exactly the right position to inflict maximum damage to the most vulnerable part of their bodies." He shuddered, imagining it. "Analogous female conveyances, however, feature no such hazard."

Several heartbeats passed, his slow and ponderous, hers sounding to his acute hearing like the clatter of a small combustion engine. "I think it has less to do with . . . well, comparative anatomy than with the way men and women are expected to behave." She took a breath. "Traditionally, men are more active and aggressive. A man's bike needs that horizontal . . . member because harder use will be made of it. At the same time, a woman's bike has to accommodate the difference in clothing you spoke of."

"Rather than a difference in anatomy." He saw that his guess was correct: she was more at ease in his presence than she was among her cosapients. Curious about what caused such an attitude, he couldn't help wondering what advantage might be made of it. He lifted a tentacle in encouragement. "Kindly elaborate."

"As far as clothing's concerned, one cylinder might provide for the . . . difference. But it would catch on things and get in the way. Imagine a cowboy or a steelworker in a skirt." She giggled again. "And it's confining. Would you like a cloth cylinder wrapped around your—" She stammered to a stop, clearly realizing for the first time that Mister Thoggosh was naked.

"'Tentacles' is acceptable, Toya." He set half a dozen wiggling before her face. "I'm no more embarrassed by it than you by mention of your fingers."

She swallowed. "I never visited before with anyone who had tentacles."

"I see," he replied with a tolerant chuckle, then let his voice assume a more serious tone. "You failed to mention the emotional discomfort your species experiences with regard to its reproductive function. One-cylinder garments conceal it. Two-cylinder garments disregard it altogether.

An active male wearing one cylinder would be in constant danger of humiliating exposure."

She closed her eyes and grimaced. "I'm just about the worst person you could ask about this, Mister Thoggosh. In the first place, my primary interest is paleontology, not social anthropology, and in the second . . ."

"In the second," he observed, "discussing physical differences between the male and the female of your species embarrasses you."

"It does," she almost whispered. "It's just the way I am."

"It's just the way you were brought up, my dear, to deny the very aspect of your life which offers greatest gratification." He took a long draw on his beer, weighing his next words. "It's the same with many primitive cultures. Control that in a person, through repression and guilt, and what you call 'society'—religion or the State—needn't control one other thing about you in order to control you altogether, to bend you from your own healthy, natural inclinations toward its own, which are invariably less natural and considerably less healthy."

"People need direction," she protested. "You can't have them chasing any old selfish whimsy, living empty, meaningless lives. Isn't it better to serve some higher purpose, larger than yourself, than no purpose at all?"

"The concept of purpose," he replied, "is just that, Toya, a concept, an idea, a product of individual sapience. It didn't exist before sapience evolved. It's meaningless applied to a random, inanimate universe. Similarly, it's irrelevant—life having arisen from that randomness—to nonsapient organisms governed by simple tropisms and instincts generated in the trial-and-error process of mutation and natural selection."

"But—"

"If you seek purpose, employ your own sapience to look within yourself. Your life has only one purpose, my dear, to be lived as *you* wish. Beware anyone who claims otherwise: the mystic, the altruist, the collectivist. One life isn't enough for him; he wants to live his own, and yours as well. His pleading and demands are baseless assertions thrown in the face of billions of years of evolution—itself without purpose, yet in response to natural law, invariably and inavoidably culminating in greater capacity, greater complexity, greater individuation—the very pinnacle of which, its crowning achievement and ultimate triumph over entropy, is self-directed intelligence.

"But this is small talk; I'd a more practical reason—a *purpose*, if you will—for asking you here."

She appeared relieved and at the same time wary. "What's that?"

"Among other things, to benefit from the human—the Soviet American—point of view on a number of difficult questions which presently confront me." He lifted a tentacle in a negligent shrug. "For example, I'd like very much to know whether my guesses about your general's thinking are correct."

Now she frowned. "Why don't you ask him?"

"Because he's a busy sapient at the best of times and right now he has a headache on his hands. (Can you say that? What a remarkable language.) I must know what his people are thinking, how well they see his reasons for doing things. I demand no betrayal, Toya, you needn't answer unless you wish to. But just now, General Gutierrez is thinking about the future, isn't he?"

"I suppose," she nodded, beginning to be interested, "we all are."

"And foremost among his thoughts must be this." He took a last sip and set the container aside, resisting the temptation to send for another. "If the United World Soviet has truly abandoned you, what's to become of thirty-odd surviving Soviet Americans on 5023 Eris?

"After all, you're completely dependent on alien monsters."

THIRTY-TWO
Under the Microscope

"Alien monsters," Mister Thoggosh repeated, his tone gentler now. "You needn't be self-conscious about thinking it, my dear, nor deny that you do. With the best of intentions, I fear that I often think it of people like yourself. However in your case, they're monsters whose present kindness—"

She interrupted with a head-shake. "What bothers me, sir, is that your 'present kindness' seems to contradict this 'Forge of Adversity' philosophy of yours, at least as we understand it."

"It's scarcely an impenetrable notion," he answered thoughtfully, "nor some arbitrary superstition you are compelled to accept as you might some primitive tribal custom of diet or attire. It's simply that, for millions of years, we've understood—based on scientific reasoning open to reexamination at any time—that, as the product of eons of brutal weeding and pruning by natural selection, all sapients are the children of suffering and struggle."

"That's certainly grim." She gave him a brief, humorless smile.

"Not necessarily, Toya. After all, we've *survived* the

process, something I think we're entitled to celebrate. And since successful struggle is what enabled us to become more than we were, hardier and brighter, we realize that shielding an individual or a species from what your poet termed 'the slings and arrows of outrageous fortune'—from being shaped and hardened in what we ourselves somewhat lyrically refer to as the 'Forge of Adversity'—however kindly the intention, represents the ultimate cruelty, depriving them, as it does, of their only motive or opportunity to transcend themselves."

"'That which doesn't kill us makes us stronger.'" She pursed her lips in disapproval. "Nietzsche, social Darwinism, dog-eat-dog, kill or be killed. Some humans have thought well of that philosophy. The Nazis, for example."

"Do you blame Nietzsche or Darwin for having been willfully misinterpreted—after their deaths, when they couldn't defend themselves or their ideas—to serve the political ends of villains?" Mister Thoggosh gave her the equivalent of a resigned nod. "But I see that—like these Nazis of yours—you're going to read into my words whatever you will. That being so, you must be wondering how long our 'contradictory' kindness can be counted on. And what will happen if it eventually runs out?"

"'*That* is the question.'" She folded her hands in her lap, embarrassed. "Sorry—you're the one who started quoting Hamlet."

"Still, we approach the topic I wished to explore, nothing more than your general is asking himself this very moment: succinctly, in the otherwise hospitable environment of our terraformed asteroid, will you ultimately be allowed to starve to death where you sit? Or might you find yourselves evicted altogether, to suffocate or freeze in the depths of space?"

Pulaski shivered. "I wonder about that, myself."

"I'm sure you do." Mister Thoggosh paused to listen to a message coming over his implant. "Another matter: what of his authority, if the government it derives from has truly disowned you? It's a measure of his character, as I understand it, that this won't occur to him until he's considered the more urgent subject of his people's survival—Toya, please excuse my momentary inattention. I've received word that Eichra Oren has arrived and will presently be joining us. That is, if you don't mind."

"Why no," Pulaski answered, blinking. "Why should I?"

"Indeed." He noticed her countenance reddening again. Was this merely a demonstration of mammalian volatility or had he missed some nuance? Was his task about to prove easier than he'd believed? He had a deep distrust for things which came to him too easily.

"To continue, then, speculating upon your general's many concerns: authority would appear to be the lifeblood of your civilization, and this raises a number of questions. For example, is it exigent, in the absence of Earth-supported authority, that your expedition reorganize itself? If so, how is that to be accomplished?"

With a perplexed expression, she opened her mouth to reply.

"*In America*," a familiar human voice offered as, instead of speaking, Pulaski turned in her chair to see Eichra Oren and Sam swimming toward them through the fluorocarbon haze, "the law requires everyone to vote or suffer fine and imprisonment. And the franchise, as they call it, was an attractive and powerful custom long before it became compulsory." Man and dog back-paddled, settling to the floor. "Despite that fact—or because of it—Americans haven't had a truly free election since the early twentieth century."

Mister Thoggosh chuckled. "A cynic might amend that to the nineteenth century, citing the view of William Marcy Tweed, infamous boss of Tammany Hall and New York's Democratic Party, that he didn't give a damn who did the voting as long as *he* did the nominating. Good morning, Eichra Oren, Otusam, it's gratifying to see you at last. May I offer you something? I'm having beer."

"Coffee, thanks." He waited as a chair descended from the ceiling, then strapped himself in to avoid floating. The tentacle brought him a container. Unlike the beer, it was surrounded by mirage from the heat of its contents. Sam wasn't equipped to deal with a sipping tube. He sat beside Eichra Oren's chair, wedging his hindquarters under one leg in lieu of a seatbelt.

"They say—" the dog remarked, "and on Toya's Earth,

mind you—that if voting could change things, it would be illegal."

"Doubtless." Mister Thoggosh sipped his own drink. "The question remains, will the Americans here hold an election to reconfirm the general's authority, or choose a new leader? Will they consider it conducive to their survival?"

Eichra Oren grinned and glanced at Pulaski. "When has authority ever been conducive to anyone's survival?"

Sam looked up. "I was going to say that."

"I'll have some coffee now, if it isn't any trouble." Pulaski had overcome her shyness. "I also want to say that if you've heard of Boss Tweed—I remember the name myself, from high school, mostly because of Thomas Nast, the cartoonist who introduced the elephant and the donkey—"

"As well as the Tammany tiger." Her host sent his tentacle to the wall again. "Sugar? Milk? Cinnamon? Chocolate? Brandy? You'd be surprised at the things various sapients put in their coffee."

"But not that they all drink it?" She shrugged. "I guess I'll try milk and chocolate—thanks—but that proves my point, the Tammany tiger, I mean. You've been studying a lot more than old movies."

Mister Thoggosh returned to his beer. "I'm sure you realize that your radio and television broadcasts—have I mentioned that your culture is uniquely noisy in that respect?—have been received, translated, and sifted by our computers for whatever information they may yield about you."

Pulaski took a dubious sip. "This is good! I know you've broken all our codes and—"

He made a many-tentacled gesture of denial. "Not 'broken,' Toya, they're simply susceptible to the same protocols that sort out all those thousands of signals from one another, eliminate natural and mechanical interference, and enhance signal-to-noise ratios."

She looked up from her drink. "Don't we have any right to privacy?"

"You maintain that what you fling promiscuously into the air for anyone to receive is private? You're aware that we nautiloids have no voices in the sense you know. We communicate by natural, organic radio signals. At this moment, my words are being received, converted to sound, and relayed to you by those speakers against the wall. Must we stop our ears—are we morally obliged to—because someone else insists on shouting?"

Eichra Oren turned. "And exactly who do you mean 'we'? Your government? Only *individuals* have rights, Sergeant. Proving that is a *preschool* exercise in our world. On the other hand, as far as I can see, your government recognizes no individual rights of any kind, let alone one to privacy."

"Indeed," Mister Thoggosh agreed, "given the predilections of government, any eavesdropping we do seems more like turnabout to me, and therefore fair play."

She lifted a defiant chin. "It doesn't matter. I can't stop you."

"No," the nautiloid agreed, "you can't. What you, your general, or this Banker fellow have no way of realizing is that we know you even better than that, Toya. We have observed your species with the minutest care, since our initial unbeinged surveys of this asteroid, long before it was terraformed. We never interfered—although I confess that the temptation's been all but overwhelming at times."

She looked up again. "You're talking over my head, Mister Thoggosh."

"And if I told you that we returned to this universe—for the first time in fifteen thousand years—in the late nineteenth century as you reckon it? The 1880s, to be precise?"

"Our observations peaked," Eichra Oren added, "in the late 1940s."

"Just about the time," Sam lifted a hind foot to scratch contemplatively at one ear, "that you people started dropping dirty little nukes on one another?"

"Roswell." Pulaski's eyes widened with honest surprise before self-conscious disbelief swept across her face to erase it. "Flying saucers?"

"Interdimensional peepholes," her host replied. "The objective ends, if you will, of survey devices physically based in our universe, and rooted in the same technology which brought us to this place. In normal use, they're handled rather like the beam of a flashlight. As you know, the use of such energies entails side effects—secondary discharges, conspicuous coronal displays—hence an occasional awareness of it by your people, despite the fact that our devices usually created apertures no larger than—"

"Like a flashlight beam," she repeated. "No wonder they could do right angles at six thousand klicks an hour! I guess there always was a certain percentage of UFO sightings never properly accounted for."

The mollusc regarded her. "And a greater percentage misaccounted for, by nation-states reluctant to admit that they can't control every event within their borders. Yet all we ever did was watch. It's all we were capable of at the time, barring the odd accident—although the number of alleged landings and personal contacts we inspired among the more fanciful was, to say the least, instructive."

She nodded. "'Intelligences vast and cool and unsympathetic'?"

"By turns, as seems required of us. And I believe the proper quotation is 'intellects.' We can, of course, be quite as petty and irritable and sanguine as any species. However, unlike those Martians of Messrs. Wells and Welles, we've a perfectly good Earth of our own, and needn't regard yours or anybody else's with envious eyes."

"Also," Sam added, "we've managed to cure the common cold."

She and Eichra Oren laughed. "So what did all this . . . watching teach you about us?"

Mister Thoggosh considered. "In the main, that the less reliably an idea works, the more tenaciously you cling to it. Welfare payments drain your moral and economic vitality, so you approve more welfare. Criminal laws create crime where none existed previously, so you pass more laws. You defend yourselves from a tyranny you fear some foreign power may impose upon you, by imposing worse upon yourselves, then wonder why your freedom has evaporated. You brought Nazis into this, so you've no one to blame but yourself: Hitler's rise to preeminence took place in a manner fully reflecting the will of a legal majority. The ruination of your own country was achieved on precisely the same basis. Had half a billion years' bitter experience not prepared us to distrust majoritarianism, *that* would surely have done it."

"People get the kind of government they deserve," Sam grinned, "whether they deserve it or not."

It was Pulaski's turn: "One of our philosophers, Will Rogers, or maybe Winston Churchill, said democracy's a terrible system but it's better than anything else that's ever been tried."

"The Boss Tweeds of your world," Mister Thoggosh countered, "are very careful never to let the Will Rogerses or Winston Churchills try a *genuine* alternative to majoritarianism. They do exist, Toya, and they don't necessarily involve dictators or kings. Who says—what objective evidence supports the notion—that the majority has ever been right about anything, anyway?"

"More to the point," Eichra Oren put in, "what gives a majority its power to compel? Unless we're talking about brute force, why should anyone have to go along just because one over half of their fellow beings demand it?"

Pulaski blinked. "Because it's better than fighting?"

Eichra Oren grimaced. "It *is* fighting, Toya, with none of the satisfactions."

"Well, how about strength in numbers, then, or 'Two heads are better than one,' or 'United we stand, divided we—'?"

The nautiloid lifted a tentacle. "Toya, such attributes as virtue or intelligence aren't additive. It's absurd to maintain that two evil people can somehow be more virtuous than one decent person, or that two stupid people are brighter than one intelligent person. Why, then, does your culture assume that two people possess more rights than one?"

Her expression told them this was a new idea to her. She peered about with that reflex Eichra Oren had mentioned, as if she feared being overheard. At last: "I wish I could give you an answer, Mister Thoggosh. We're not encouraged to think about things like that."

"Whose interest does *that* serve?" He waved the rhetorical question away. "Never mind, Toya, skipping theory and fastening upon the urgently pragmatic, what if by some horrible—but typical—miscarriage of democracy,

Arthur Empleado, let us say, were chosen to lead your expedition?"

"I—"

"Alternatively, what would happen if you tried, individually or as a group, to join what you know as the Elders' culture? Other species have, and other individuals. Setting aside the question of whether we would permit it, certainly it won't be permitted by your superiors here. And are your leaders at home really out of it? This 'Banker' seems to have left certain contingencies open. If he should recontact you, which of the two—an unauthorized election, or an alliance with us—will he consider the more treasonous?"

"I don't *know*, Mister Thoggosh, you're raising points I hadn't even begun—"

"It might be well if you did, Sergeant. Difficult decisions will soon be required of you and your friends."

This was the principal point Mister Thoggosh had been working up to. He hesitated, knowing that if he succeeded now, it might save trouble for everyone in the near future.

"It had occurred to me, given your interest and expertise in paleontology—a subject of some importance to me at present—that I might hire you away from General Gutierrez. You will regard my terms as unprecedentedly generous. What would your general say? Do you care one way or another? What would *you* say, Toya?"

She blinked with surprise. "I think I ought to pretend that I didn't hear it—or any of the rest of this. I'm grateful, Mister Thoggosh, believe me. I wish I could accept. But if Mr. Empleado were to find out—"

Pulaski shivered.

THIRTY-THREE
A Policeman's Lot

"*Laika*," Mister Thoggosh chuckled. "Surely Mr. Empleado offered some comment on the general's attitude."

"Through clenched teeth, and at the top of his lungs." Eichra Oren grinned. "I imagine it must have hurt."

He willed himself off the chair-edge, trying to relax. Outside it would be afternoon by now. Pulaski had gone, presumably to ponder Mister Thoggosh's offer, although she'd made a pretense of turning it down. Sam, too, had run off on some errand. Furry sapients weren't very happy soaking in liquid fluorocarbon, however temperate and oxygenated. Eichra Oren looked forward to leaving as well, having had enough of the aqueous gloom the great mollusc regarded as cozy, but which the human often found depressing.

"I'm ashamed to admit that I enjoyed watching it," he told his employer. "It's slim return on the investment you're making keeping me around."

As they spoke, Mister Thoggosh stabbed button after lighted button set into the space before him that he used as a desk. In all fairness the atmosphere—at least the tempo—had changed with the amateur paleontologist's departure. She'd been a guest, while Eichra Oren was "family." A backlog of urgencies had accumulated during each minute spent entertaining Pulaski—with orders to Aelbraugh Pritsch that they weren't to be disturbed unless the asteroid was exploding (and a footnote to admit Eichra Oren whenever he showed up).

Enjoying a respite, the nautiloid lifted a resigned tentacle. "I'm aware that your services are costly, Eichra Oren, pray don't belabor the fact. Let it stand that it's preferable to the more dangerous and even costlier alternative of transporting you back home. With these Americans, I can't predict how soon I'll require your talents again, anyway, perish the thought. I assume that you're spending as much time with them as possible."

The man nodded. "For all the good it does either of us. The benefit of knowing more about events on their version of Earth than, say, than someone like Pulaski expects of me may be more theoretical than—"

"*Mister Thoggosh!*" The precise, fussy voice was that of Aelbraugh Pritsch, transmitted from his own nearby office. Feathered sapients cared even less for fluorocarbon bathing than furry ones. An image of the man-sized avian or dinosauroid (it amounted to the same thing) welled up in Eichra Oren's mind as his employer shared the incoming signal. "Nannel Rab reports another equipment failure at Site Seventeen. I'm afraid it's the drilling system again."

"I suspected as much." The nautiloid sighed, sending his limb off for another beer. "Have Nannel Rab follow the procedure we discussed. Keep me informed." He turned to the man. "You were saying that the benefit of knowledge is only theoretical?"

"*May* be theoretical," Eichra Oren corrected, failing to rise to the bait. "Despite the volume and quality of our data, there is much I don't understand about these inscrutable Americans and possibly never will."

"I see. That was to be expected, wasn't it? They have a lifetime in which to comprehend their civilization, and many of them fail, even so. What, in particular, is troubling you?"

"Many things." The human thought for a moment. "Just one item from the inventory as an example: where does the PRC really fit into the current world political picture?"

"The formidable People's Republic of China." Mister Thoggosh took a long drink. "You are perhaps acquiring a personal reason to be curious?" He transmitted another deep and (his organs of respiration and speech having no connection) thoroughly counterfeit sigh. "You humans are irrepressible; no wonder there are ten billion of them on this Earth alone. What an experience, to spend one's life swimming in a fog of hormones, gripped by perpetual coupling-frenzy."

Sam would have asked if it were envy speaking. He might even have suggested that Mister Thoggosh go couple with himself. Eichra Oren merely gritted his teeth and ignored the gibe.

"I've asked about them because I feel they're important. They've maintained a collectivist dictatorship for over a century—murderous and repressive even by Marxist standards—but have a longer history of private capitalism, which they show occasional interest in reviving. The World Soviet's afraid of that. They keep the massive Chinese population within its borders by brandishing the biggest, dirtiest nuclear weapons their science can devise. This encourages the PRC to revert to an isolationism they've been inclined toward readily enough on their own for thousands of years."

Eichra Oren was about to add something when Aelbraugh Pritsch filled their minds again. "I deplore interrupting, sir. Remgar d'Nod wishes to reduce power twenty-three percent while the matter-energy converter is serviced."

Had he been human, Mister Thoggosh might have rubbed a hand across his face. The tip of one tentacle made little circles in the thin layer of sand beside his working area. "May I assume that this is not another equipment failure?"

"It's routine scheduled maintenance," the avian answered.

A tentacle slapped the sand-pattern away in irritation. "Then why in the Predecessors' name does he bother me with it?" His tone changed as he cut the circuit and turned his attention again to Eichra Oren. "And the beautiful Rosalind Nguyen has nothing to do with this?" The mollusc possessed no eyebrows to raise skeptically at his employee, but managed to convey the impression anyway. "Perhaps not. She's of Vietnamese, rather than Chinese, extraction, isn't she?"

Again the man controlled himself, not without a struggle. An American habit he found particularly satisfying was their penchant for referring to an antagonist in terms of the terminal anatomical feature of the gastrointestinal system. Every sapient he knew of—excepting certain rare representatives of the plant kingdom—possessed such an anatomical feature, so the epithet could be appreciated universally. He predicted a brilliant future for it among those compelled to associate with the Elders.

Again Aelbraugh Pritsch interrupted. "Sir, I have a report of two humans wandering near the abandoned boring platform at Site Four." Eichra Oren had been occupied with other matters, but recalled this as another location where the subsurface geology had proven too much for nautiloid technology. Not for the first time, he wondered what they were drilling for.

"Was the excavation sealed?" his employer inquired.

"No, sir." Dinosauroid eyes rolled to an unseen ceiling as he consulted his organic memory or an electronic implant. "The crew was pulled off to another site. I'm sending a remote to see whether the bore collapsed on its own—unlikely in this gravity—or whether the humans might have discovered anything from examining the site." The remote, Eichra Oren knew, would be an aerostat like the one which had brought Pulaski here, under cybernetic pilotless guidance.

"Let me know," came his employer's weary reply. "And Aelbraugh Pritsch?"

"Sir?" The bird-being's down-rimmed eyes widened, pupils contracting and expanding as he gave the nautiloid his worried attention.

"Try to relax, my feathered friend. Even the end of the world isn't the end of the world. See whether you can find out who these humans were. That might tell us something."

Visibly attempting, with little success, to follow Mister Thoggosh's advice, he nodded. "I'll try, sir." Again his image faded from their minds.

"We were speaking," the nautiloid observed, "of China."

Eichra Oren lifted a hand. "All Dr. Nguyen says is 'We don't talk about the PRC.' 'We' meaning citizens of the American Soviet Socialist Republic, the Union of Soviet Socialist Republics, and the United World Soviet."

"Why do majoritarians invariably give their nation-states such awkward names?" Mister Thoggosh mused. "What was wrong with 'France' or even 'Bulgaria'? Never mind, please go on."

"She's ethnically Chinese, like many twentieth-century Vietnamese who fled the oncoming Communist wave by emigrating to America. Where they came from, they were a hated minority in any case, something like the Jews in Europe. In the end, they only escaped from one variety of repression into another. Perhaps because of her background, she appears to have difficulty fitting in among her fellow Soviet Americans."

"And as the sole non-Soviet human here," Mister Thoggosh suggested, "not to mention the only member of your species in our little group, you've developed more than a casual interest in her, is that it?"

The man frowned at what he felt was becoming a pattern of intrusion into his personal life. "You could say that."

"What is it this time?" His employer was speaking with the disembodied voice of Aelbraugh Pritsch again.

"Nek Nam'l Las in Logistics. They can't find sixteen pallets of extra boring coolant we brought with us and equipment failures have consumed more than planned. They want permission to send for more."

Mister Thoggosh was more than annoyed. "What does that pebble-counter think the transporter is, a tenthbit trolley? I discussed this with Nannel Rab and the other department heads yesterday, and thought it understood that we'll make do with what we have! Those pallets were moved from the equipment yard when space was required to disassemble the driver core damaged at Site Eleven. I knew some idiot would report them lost. They're stacked in the vehicle charge-and-storage bay at the north end of the converter. Tell Remgar d'Nod to move them back. Tell Nek Nam'l Las and everyone else there'll be no sending or receiving anything for another thousand hours! Turn down all such requests on your initiative. And one more thing, Aelbraugh Pritsch."

The dinosauroid gulped. Not only were his pupils bouncing from half to twice their normal diameter with each heartbeat, but ruffled feathers around his neck made him look as if he were molting. Reminded of his assistant's physiological sensitivity, Mister Thoggosh moderated his tone. "See here, I realize there hasn't been time for your remote to arrive at Site Four yet. Has Tl°m°nch°l managed to identify those wandering humans?" Tl°m°nch°l—whose name most sapients found unpronounceable—was an evolutionary relative of sea-scorpions, and Mister Thoggosh's chief of security.

"No, sir, he's trying a cyberscan-and-match." The avian's feathers were smoother now. "But he complains that all humans look alike to him."

Mister Thoggosh chuckled. "That's only fair, I suppose, since I'm sure his people all look alike to humans. They certainly do to me. Now hold all messages, if you please, while I finish my conversation with Eichra Oren."

Aelbraugh Pritsch blinked—"Yes, sir."—and faded.

Visibly preparing to issue more orders, the mollusc seemed to inhale and exhale deeply. "Eichra Oren: I sympathize with your resentment of my personal remarks, just as I admire the romantic inclinations that every human being I've ever known seems continuously inspired to manifest. I would prefer, however, that you forget Dr. Nguyen, however she may intrigue you. Concentrate on Toya Pulaski, who is in a position—something I doubt she realizes—to endanger a future triumph which will vindicate all of our past defeats."

"What do you mean 'concentrate'?" There was more in what he'd said that worried Eichra Oren, but this would do for the moment.

Mister Thoggosh lifted a tentacle. "Discover her likes and dislikes. Given her presumed heritage, normally I'd guess that she despises the current regime more than most; it's our misfortune that politics fail to interest her. We know she gave up her real love—paleontology—when drafted by the Aerospace Force. Here among sapient molluscs, sea-scorpions, dinosauroids, she must have trouble deciding whether she's in a waking nightmare or gone to her personal idea of Heaven. I'd hazard that it offers features of both." He curled the limb into a sort of fist. "*Stimulate* her political uncertainty. *Win* her over, if you can, to our point of view."

Eichra Oren's mouth compressed into a hard line. "If I had a clue what our point of view is. Is this a professional assignment?" He rose, clenching his own fists, determined to walk out.

"Sit down, Eichra Oren. I thought you understood that you were on the payroll the moment you arrived, and will remain so as long as you're here, in whatever capacity. Knowing humans as I do, I'm aware that Toya happens to be, by your aesthetic standards as well as those of her own culture, an unlovely thing. Although you'd gallantly have it otherwise, this makes what I ask all the more difficult. Be that as it may, given her interest in paleontology, she represents a threat to an achievement which will make good all of our past shortcomings. She must be turned aside. If you wish to add a surcharge, if it will make the task any less unsavory, by all means do so."

Eichra Oren stood beside the chair. Only at a time like this did it occur to him how small and frail human beings must look, how ridiculous he must appear, confronting a creature many times his mass, with ten powerful meters-long tentacles. "Before we change our minds about what profession I'm here to practice, you should consider my lack of credentials in the field, instead of haggling over my price!"

"This is American humor?" Mister Thoggosh asked mildly.

Disgusted with his lack of dignity (Eichra Oren was capable of winning a physical battle with a nautiloid and had done so more than once as a professional necessity), he stepped around the chair and sat again, arms folded across his chest, his mind seething with suspicion. "Better than nautiloid humor: hiring me to protect your little secret and not telling me what it is I'm supposed to protect."

"We come to it at last!" Mister Thoggosh laughed. "Dear boy, I acknowledge that you're stranded here as a result of a task I hired you to accomplish, one I confess you performed with astonishing alacrity, in a manner satisfactory to me. I'm obliged to see that you suffer no further for it, just as I would if you'd been injured in the line of duty."

Apparently surprised to find his container empty again, he sent his tentacle for another, bringing the coffee Eichra Oren preferred without asking. Knowing his employer, the man accepted it as the token of reconciliation it was meant to be.

"It is your fortune," the great mollusc continued, "for good or for ill, that you're free—as a kind of workman's compensation—to enjoy this time as a vacation if you wish, with no additional obligation. It is my fortune—and I regard it unreservedly as good—that you're not a man to whom idleness for its own sake is welcome. I'm grateful that you're willing to help me perform my solemn duties here, even at the confiscatory rates you deserve so well."

Eichra Oren did have eyebrows, and raised them. "But?"

"You ask too much. If the Americans—or worse, their *leader*—were to discover what we seek here, not learn what it is, but make the find before us, it would culminate in a disaster of unparalleled magnitude."

"If it's so serious, I'd like to help. You're willing to swear Scutigera to secrecy. I'm your friend, I'm Eneri Relda's son, I'm a *p'Nan* assessor for reason's sake! Why won't you confide in me?"

Mister Thoggosh thought long before answering. "I *need* partners like Scutigera; it can't be helped. I chose them as best I could. Even so, each morning I awaken hoping I've chosen wisely."

"I have some savings, make me a partner."

"Eichra Oren, I esteem your discretion above that of any sapient I know, excepting your mother. And at this point, I wouldn't confide even in *her*. The risk is unthinkable. If you wish to help—and for the sake of restitution which will repay every past transgression we ever made against ourselves, I hope you do—distract and occupy the attentions of Toya Pulaski!"

THIRTY-FOUR
A Shadow Among Shadows

Arthur Empleado was cold.

He hadn't thought it possible in these artificial tropics. At 390 million kilometers from the sun, 5023 Eris was a hothouse, every centimeter of the false upper surface provided by her biological canopy given to absorbing and hoarding sunlight. Yet he was chilled to numbness, almost to the bone.

It was possible that what he felt had less to do with temperature than with his exclusion from the group lounging around the campfire in the center of the hollow formed by the three shuttles. It had never been stated in so many words—no one would have dared, even given their isolation from Earth and the disrespect habitually shown him by the mission's highest-ranking officers—but as its principal KGB agent, charged with maintaining its ideological consistency, he wasn't welcome socially among its personnel, and he knew it.

On the other hand he was used to it. A likelier source for his present discomfort was the paper slip he fingered in his jacket pocket, a note left in his bunk earlier today. Now that he considered it, just the thought caused him to ache and shiver, shifting from one foot to the other in the shadows, watching his shipmates enjoy each others' company in a way forbidden to him, not only by current circumstances, but by a lifetime's habit and inclination.

dam oooo: wound my heart with monotonous langour

Ironically, he'd selected the code himself, expecting to hear it someday, planted in a transmission from Earth—never anticipating that he'd be reading it scrawled in ballpoint on a scrap little larger than a postage stamp. The historic phrase, lifted from an obscure poem and broadcast by the BBC 100 years ago, had informed French partisans, mostly Communists like himself, that the long night of fascist domination was about to end with the Allied invasion of Normandy. For him it meant orders were coming from the American KGB which would override every other duty and obligation. Assigned to the expedition as a civilian, he'd been secretly commissioned as an Aerospace Force general officer, the microfilmed documentation he carried dated retroactively to give him seniority over Gutierrez in the emergency which would constitute his only justification for revealing it.

He examined the gathering around the campfire with renewed professional interest. Among these unlikely candidates (and several others not present at this evening's festivities) who was his likeliest contact?

Lieutenant Colonel Juan Sebastiano was young to be commander—Empleado was annoyed at the untidiness of referring to a colonel as "captain"—of the *McCain*, or of anything else important. Empleado had always rated him as politically unreliable. He had a careless mouth with regard to authority and was personally loyal to Gutierrez. Empleado cherished plans for dealing with him when time and opportunity presented themselves. Of course the same apparent qualities might make perfect cover. Still, Empleado had a feeling for these things. He couldn't see Sebastiano as any sort of KGB agent.

Major Jesus Ortiz was a different matter. It was said that the new commander of the *Hatch* had ancestors, not all that remote, who thought it hilarious to skin the soles of a victim's feet and let him walk home across a broiling desert floor. He remembered reading that even the Apaches and Comanches were afraid of the Yaquis. Of course the rumor might be untrue. Empleado's personnel files, condensed for spaceflight, didn't go back that far, and Ortiz may not have inherited his forebears' sense of humor. That sort of sanguine ruthlessness wasn't the best test of an agent, anyway. He himself had a rather tender stomach when it came to the brute mechanics of interrogation, a failing he tried to make up for in other ways. Nevertheless, it wouldn't surprise him if his contact turned out to be Ortiz.

With the equivalent rank of major, there was his own subordinate, Roger Betal. The man was becoming a problem, his usefulness destroyed by a beating at the hands of this interloper Eichra Oren, and what had happened to his fellow enforcers Roo and Hake. Empleado had relied not only on Betal's martial arts, but his ability as a deceptively charming talker. Surprisingly, that ability was always less effective with female subjects than expected. Now he seemed to be avoiding Empleado, seeking the company of expeditionaries friendly with the so-called Elders and their pet human. Such a problem was best dealt with sooner rather than later—unless the whole thing was a brilliant ruse and Betal was the one who'd left the note in his bunk.

Empleado shook his head. This game he'd begun playing with himself was useless. The next person he considered was Rosalind Nguyen. As a physician, she was an ideal intelligence gatherer. And so were women, especially small, pretty ones. She saw crew members in their weakest moments and most vulnerable states of mind. Carrying the rank of captain lent her a measure of nonintimidating authority, while her ethnic origin and the political background it implied might lead them to believe she'd be sympathetic with their discontents, since she was ideologically suspect simply by being what she was.

He'd never say that the government of the ASSR was racially motivated—not within hearing of his superiors and at the same time hope to continue occupying a position within that government himself. It was wise to avoid the habit of even *thinking* it too frequently. But one look at personnel distribution, at the disproportionate number of Hispanics and Blacks and their relative ranks within the Aerospace Force, would convince anyone that it was more fashionable these days to lay claim to certain ancestors, or to possess certain surnames, than others.

Someone passed a guitar to First Lieutenant Lee Marna, life-support technician for the *McCain*. She let her fingers ripple across the nylon strings, singing of "the strangest dream I never had before."

There was an alarming number of amateur musicians with this expedition. If it were within his power he'd have forbidden it. A guitar was worse than a loaded gun. Home-made music, like homemade humor, was inherently sub-versive, especially made by an attractive young woman whose cornsilk hair and fair complexion—opposing the officially encouraged physiognomy he'd been thinking about earlier—drew attention to the performance. In the inter-est of state security, entertainment must be left to care-fully winnowed specialists. He'd always argued that the greatest danger to authority was laughter (or any unsanctioned happiness, for that matter) which the state had not provided as a reward for approved behavior and was not therefore in a position, as a punishment, to deny.

Empleado wasn't the only one watching the little blonde. Second Lieutenant Danny Gutierrez—now there was a thought: what if the general's son were the undercover agent? Young Gutierrez was a petty criminal, a smuggler and small dealer in forbidden goods. That would certainly provide him with credentials valuable to a covert agent of the KGB. What else did he know about the boy? He was Gutierrez's sec-ond son, the eldest having been killed in some particularly horrible manner during a recent unpublicized conflict in South Africa. Danny was a friend of Sebastiano's, to all appearances more the colonel's protégé than his father's. That placed him in position to keep an eye on Sebastiano, pro-vided anyone in power felt the colonel was important enough to merit it. Or it might just represent precaution on the general's part. Like racism, nepotism wasn't unknown within the ASSR, but blatancy was a far greater failing.

Whatever his real status, it was obvious the boy might

soon have another problem on his hands—and *only* on his hands, if he was lucky. He hadn't yet noticed the longing glances being cast his way by Demene Wise, making a first appearance in public since Eichra Oren had crippled one of his knees, possibly for life.

Before the mishap, Wise had been another of Empleado's informal "staff," with the equivalent rank of Master Sergeant. Empleado, preserving the tatters of the man's cover, hadn't visited him in the improvised sickbay and didn't know whether he'd show an inclination, like Betal, to avoid his superior. With that great cube of a head and his enormous shoulders, he still looked as if he'd been carved from basalt, but his sagging face had aged twenty years. The man had never seemed particularly bright, but in Empleado's present frame of mind, he considered sexual deviation as a KGB cover without rejecting it altogether. Wise's presence in the gathering was being tolerated, possibly for the doctor's sake. Aside from body language that belied his Herculean appearance, and his effeminate mooning over the general's son, he seemed to be enjoying the music as much as anyone.

As Marna played, firelight picked out the dark, bearded features of Staff Sergeant C. C. Jones, former TV star, now eyes and ears for *American Truth* and, rumor had it, an enemy of Horatio Gutierrez. Empleado wished he knew more about that. He always wished he knew more about everything. As usual, Jones was trying to steal the scene, lending conspicuous approval to whatever everyone else demonstrated they were enjoying, in this case, the pretty lieutenant's singing.

Of many types for which he had nothing but contempt, journalists held top position on Empleado's list, even above politicians. Anyone, from left to right, who'd ever been personally connected with an event that became news knew that they were incapable of getting the simplest story straight. Pre-Soviet American journalism had always gloried in its self-appointed role as watchdog over the rights of the individual. The truth was that during its long, self-congratulatory history, it had been more like a cur caught bloody-muzzled time after time, savaging the very flocks it had been trusted to protect.

No one knew better than the KGB that there is no such thing as "the news." Jones, his colleagues, and his predecessors peddled gossip, mostly in the form of horrible things happening to faraway strangers, things that might have happened to *you* and still might, unless ... More ignorant than the nine-year-old minds they pitched to, dirtier than the ward heelers they supposedly kept an eye on, they were nothing more than merchants of fear, parasites feeding on calamities that bred more fear, and an ever more powerful state, a state that grew by promising to keep everybody safe from everything. Since the universe is an inherently unsafe place, it was a profitable symbiosis. The media might single out this incompetent bureaucrat or that corrupt politician, they might favor those whose paranoia dwelt on domestic dangers rather than foreign, but they never questioned the paranoia itself, or the wisdom of erecting a security state to assuage it. Over three centuries, they had never once taken the individual's side against the growth of government power.

Of course Empleado approved of the security state, and recognized the importance of journalists in creating and maintaining it. That didn't make associating with them turn his stomach any less.

Reflected firelight from Pulaski's glasses caught his eye, distracting him. The idea that this gangly, bespectacled female—what was the old-fashioned word?—*nerd* might be a high-ranking undercover operative for the KGB was so ridiculous he refused to consider it.

For similar reasons, he rejected machinist Corporal Roger Owen. Empleado's father, Salvador, had been a machinist, dragging himself home with blackened nails, reeking of overheated solvents, slouching in a dilapidated armchair swilling rationed *cervezas* while Arturo's *mamacita* fried the evening tortillas and beans, watching propaganda on TV as if it meant something. How he'd longed to get out of that house—however well it reflected the proletarian ideal—out of that self-consciously blue-collar life, to do something that would leave his hands clean after a day's work, to get a glimpse of what lay behind the propaganda, to make something important of himself.

It wasn't that he hadn't loved them in his way. Father,

like son, was an ardent if naive Marxist, loyal to his union and the socialism it buttressed almost as solidly as journalism did. But Empleado distrusted all men who worked with their hands. They were too bound up in the concretes of life, unable to detach themselves from petty facts. They insisted that philosophy and politics make sense—dollars and cents—unable to see that nobody interested in accruing power had anything to gain by limiting himself to the mundane. Besides, he thought, if Owen had written that note, it would have been in soft pencil, with greasy thumbprints around the edges.

As Marna finished her song, Rubber Chicken Alvarez, last and by any measure least of the group around the fire, became the life of the party, impersonating Jerry Lewis, telling jokes he laughed at loudest himself. In other circumstances he'd have been wearing a lampshade on his head. Empleado was confident these would-be Robinson Crusoes would be weaving him one next week, of bean sprouts or whatever the corporal was cooking in his cast-iron pot. If he'd had to stake his life on it, Empleado believed he'd bet on Carlos the Clown, preparer of food, disposer of garbage, maker of practical jokes, as his spy. He fit his role as village idiot too perfectly. He played the fool too well.

dam oooo: wound my heart with monotonous langour

It could only mean "the dam at midnight." Glancing at his watch, he slipped from the camp, headed for his rendezvous. It didn't take him long to get there. "Dam" was an ambitious term for the barrier of meteoric stone (carbonaceous chondrite, comprising most of the asteroid, was too crumbly) piled across the stream where it came nearest the camp. The idea was to raise the level to obtain running water. Sebastiano, who'd taken charge of the project, still hadn't any idea what he was going to use for pipes—plastic provided by the Elders, or the hollow trunks of bamboolike plants.

The site had been chosen for more than proximity. Here also the stream passed through a gully which, once full, would make a natural reservoir. The gully itself was probably a deformed impact crater, a random feature of a terrain that had never been shaped by moving air or water until the Elders had recently created an atmosphere. At the moment, the dam was less than a meter high—Sebastiano's men were having to go further afield in search of suitable rocks to add to it—and the water less than half that depth.

Empleado heard a noise, turned, and was blinded by intense light. In the next heartbeat, someone was standing beside him turning a small, black, knurled-aluminum flashlight downward to shine on the thin slip of plastic which served each expedition member as ID and—with information retrieval equipment—a dossier on the person it was issued to. This one was unique, its back surface consisting of a hologram. Seeming to float above the card was the curved, elaborate shield of the KGB.

"Satisfied, Comrade?" came a whispered voice.

"You!" Empleado couldn't help gasping.

THIRTY-FIVE
Prostitution

Eichra Oren looked around at his audience gathered in the clearing.

"This morning," he told them, "if there's no objection, I'll communicate in the human language, English, for the benefit of those without cortical augmentation. Please adjust your implants to the appropriate translation channel."

The *p'Nan* debt assessor sat cross-legged on a blanket at the base of a huge canopy tree, sword lying across his knees. Sam lay nearby, tongue out, looking like an ordinary dog. Overhead and to the rear, the pearlescent fungoid growth which would soon be Eichra Oren's quarters jutted over the nearby stream. For a few seconds, only the murmur of that stream broke the silence, as sapients of many sizes and shapes briefly contemplated an inner reality unshared—*as yet*, the thought entered Toya's mind—by the small handful of humans present.

They were a mixed handful too, increasingly uncaring of position or rank. Betal was here, having appointed himself a sort of acolyte to the Antarctican. The general, behaving self-consciously toward her as he had since last night, sat beside her on a convenient fallen log. His son Danny leaned against a tree across the clearing, conversing with Sebastiano until the moment Eichra Oren spoke. Not far away, Ortiz glowered (that being his natural, relaxed expression) either at Wise—here for a therapeutic outing on his crippled knee—at his doctor (and everyone else's) Rosalind Nguyen, or at C. C. Jones, whom none of the officers seemed to like. Toya thought him handsome with his rugged features and salt-and-pepper beard. In the middle of the clearing, amidst the aliens, sat Owen and Marna. Even Rubber Chicken Alvarez had shown up. What interest that overgrown class clown had in these proceedings defied Toya's power of imagination. The only individual she missed was Empleado, and she didn't miss him much.

Aside from her own cosapients, it seemed to her that no two creatures among Eichra Oren's listeners were of the same species. Until a moment ago—the same moment Danny had quit talking—Dlee Raftan Saon, courtly surgeon of an insectile race, had been enjoying what may have been a professional discussion with Rosalind, although Toya rather doubted it. Raftan liked the ladies—of whatever species— and had once even "kissed" Toya's hand.

Llessure Knarrfic was here, too, which Toya found surprising since that individual was a busy executive in Mister Thoggosh's various enterprises and on top of that, a sort of potted plant-being resembling a giant rubber flower.

Remaulthiek, on the other hand, dispensed refreshments at Dlee Raftan Saon's infirmary. She resembled a big gray quilt in a plastic bag, being distantly related to skates and rays. She was always interested in anything to do with moral indebtedness. Her rather menial vocation was something of a penance she had long ago imposed on herself for some unknown transgression.

There was no sign of the sea-scorpions who provided security here, nor of Aelbraugh Pritsch, Mister Thoggosh's assistant, nor (as Aelbraugh Pritsch referred to him) of the "Proprietor" himself. Scutigera was rumored to be off on the other side of the asteroid, dealing with some technical problem which had been bedeviling the nautiloids. Toya did see a giant spider, three meters tall and strikingly beautiful in its red-and-sable furry pelt.

After a moment, Eichra Oren nodded. "Before we begin

this morning, let me help our guests understand what's about to happen. As many of you appreciate, the one debt assessment they've seen was unusual, and may have given them a false impression of what takes place under normal circumstances."

He shifted on his blanket, settling into a more comfortable position.

"For most of human history, disputes between individuals have been settled by professional arbiters hired by a government which they—the arbiters—rely on to impose whatever decisions they arrive at, by coercive physical force. Which is to say by threat of injury or death. Those among you unfamiliar with the concept of government will find it described among human customs on one of the supplementary information channels."

For reasons Toya could only guess, a mild disturbance sifted through the crowd. Eichra Oren let it fade before continuing. "Irrational assumptions, faulty logic, and politically expedient dispositions are the hallmark of such an arrangement. Trial by ordeal was common throughout many human cultures. Imperial magistrates in ancient China were legally empowered to torture testimony from unwilling witnesses, even those not criminally accused. It was left, I imagine, to a magistrate's personal integrity whether that process produced anything resembling the truth."

Another stir and Toya knew her guess had been correct. The nonhumans were scandalized at this description of human customs while the humans, feeling they were being slandered, reacted in a similar manner. Eichra Oren gave his listeners a moment to absorb the horror of what he'd told them. Meanwhile the nearby stream did more to preserve the resulting silence than to break it, its minimal white noise muffling other sounds.

"Greater individuation, however," Eichra Oren resumed at last, "is the inviolable rule of evolution. No despot, however draconian, has ever been entirely successful at stopping it. Over many centuries, the brute power of these false arbiters—'judges' they were called—came to be limited and more or less objective standards of evidence and procedure adopted. By the current civilization's nineteenth century, due to worldwide majoritarian influence, judges were generally held to be servants of the people. Even some of *them* believed it. Everyone involved pretended not to notice where these judges' salaries came from, and the malignant conflict of interest that represented."

Absently, he turned his sword up to rest on its scabbard-tip. "What was termed the 'rule of law'—meaning participation in the process by government, an entity beyond the reach of any law—distorted and contaminated every honest effort to balance the moral scales. Still, it is significant that, for a time, judges no longer appeared to wield absolute power in the name of some ruler, but nominally on behalf of those they were presumed to serve."

He fixed his gaze on Toya or perhaps on Gutierrez sitting beside her. "It isn't my intention to criticize the customs of our new acquaintances, but to clarify our own by contrast. Pragmatic or philosophical, any differences between those majoritarian judges and their authoritarian predecessors evaporate, compared to those between them and myself. My clients come of their own volition, seeking the benefit of whatever knowledge and skill I possess. I've no power to compel their presence, nor to compel the testimony of witnesses, nor even to compel acquiescence to any judgment I render. A culture in which people are forced to behave as if they were virtuous (however you define the term) can never know virtue, only sullen compliance and its concomitant: a widespread, furtive criminality."

Across the clearing, Danny laughed out loud.

"On the other hand," Eichra Oren told them, "when an individual's fortune rises or falls with whatever traits of character he manifests spontaneously, his culture discovers within him virtues neither he nor it suspected. My clients pay for my services themselves and these are the only conditions under which I can guarantee value. The power to compel would only make what I do harder, although it would be an easy way to cheat my customers, forcing them to accept the sight of my thumb lying heavy on the scales of justice."

Toya yawned, realizing it was an inauspicious start on the task she'd been given the previous evening (early this morning, actually). It wasn't her fault that her superiors had kept her up half the night briefing her (after questioning her endlessly about her conversation with Mister Thoggosh), but she also realized that, whoever was really to blame, she'd be held responsible for any failure. She would certainly never have asked for this duty, as a *spy* of all things.

"I know it's a bizarre assignment I'm giving you, Pulaski." She hadn't believed what she was hearing. Leaning against one of the pilot's chairs, Gutierrez had hesitated, almost shy, as he attempted to explain himself. *And he should be*, she'd thought, *considering what he's asking!* Her most heartfelt wish was the same as it had been since landing here, that they'd all just leave her alone to study the Elders and their odd companions.

Gutierrez had looked down at his hands. "I'm not certain I can legally order you to do it under ASF regulations."

"I can, Sergeant, I assure you." Empleado leaned forward in his lightweight folding chair, another of the Elders' puzzling gifts, emerging from an unlit corner of the command deck where he sat listening. The agent took a final drag on his cigarette—like others, he'd recently taken up the habit again—stubbing it out in an improvised ashtray turned out by Corporal Owen. "It's perfectly legal under KGB authority which, in case it escaped your attention, I happen to represent." He shook a finger at them. "That's the only consideration which should be important to either of you."

He sat back, features indistinct again in the shadows. Through the windows fireflies, a decorative domestic species someone had told her, with fat abdomens which made them the size of canaries, twinkled at the edge of the jungle surrounding the encampment.

Gutierrez shook his head. "It's important to me, Art, that the sergeant understand why I—why we're giving her these orders." He returned to her. "There doesn't seem to be another choice. You know our situation, Toya, as well as anybody. You also know that Mister Thoggosh is searching for something on this asteroid, more and more desperately, it appears to me. Perhaps we can make use of whatever he's looking for to get ourselves out of this mess."

Standing almost at attention, hard to do in the cramped conditions, she began to reply bitterly, "And I'm the only one you thought of—"

"I don't like it," he interrupted, showing her a palm, "and you may like it even less before it's over with. But we have to take advantage of the one card we've been dealt. You're in a unique position to find out what they're looking for, and I want you to do exactly that."

How frustrating! "I don't know why you keep saying that, sir."

"I'll spell it out. You've heard the rumor that Mister Thoggosh is looking for some sort of fossil remains beneath the accretion-crust."

"Yes, sir, from two of the *McCain* crew who spent all day yesterday poking around one of the abandoned drilling sites until an unmanned flying machine ran them off."

"Toya, you're the only one who'd recognize the significance of such a find if you happened across it." He hesitated, his words coming slowly, as if he were ashamed of them. "The easiest way is probably through Eichra Oren. Given what happened with Reille y Sanchez, he may be emotionally vulnerable right now, susceptible—"

Empleado leaned forward again, eagerly. "You must expend *every possible effort*, Sergeant, to determine what this Antarctican knows!"

Toya whirled, feeling the sudden heat of angry embarrassment rise in her face. "You mean I'm supposed to try to seduce it out of him?" She turned slowly this time, to face the general. "Is that right?"

Gutierrez didn't answer, perhaps thinking the question had been directed at Empleado. The KGB man, understanding that it hadn't been, that it was more of an appeal than a question, stepped in. "Tell her, General," he insisted, "that she must do more than just try."

Gutierrez shook his head. Gazing out the window into the darkness, he almost talked to himself. "I keep imagining how I'd feel if I learned that one of my daughters had been ordered to—"

"Prostitute herself for the State?" Arthur laughed

unpleasantly. "What higher purpose could any woman serve, especially one like her?" He observed her with a sneer, ostensibly addressing Gutierrez. "You merely want her to understand, General. I wish to leave absolutely *nothing* to her imagination. I rely on you to help: she is to do whatever it takes to accomplish her mission. Isn't that so?"

Empleado seemed to be enjoying himself. The general's face was still turned away, his attention somewhere outside the window. But he'd nodded, confirming the edict.

What they weren't telling her, she realized with a sinking heart, was how to go about transforming her rather drab self from the bespectacled nerd she knew herself to be into something resembling a Mata Hari.

THIRTY-SIX
Restitution

"Now then, who requires my services first?"

Like Pulaski and a handful of others, Gutierrez was among those drawn the next morning by an announcement of Eichra Oren's first public session as a *p'Nan* assessor. Moral debt had been much on the general's mind over the past few days, especially the past few hours, and especially in connection with the amateur paleontologist. He knew she was unhappy with the assignment he and Empleado had imposed on her. What she didn't know—what thousands of years of military tradition would never have allowed him to tell her—was that he despised himself for having given her the order.

"I do, Eichra Oren."

Something flowed from an edge of the crowd. Gutierrez's first impression was of a human stick-figure rendered in red-orange pipe cleaners with an extra leg standing in place of its head. His second, a product of hundreds of nature documentaries watched with half an eye and half a mind, was of a deep-sea brittle starfish with long, sinuous arms and a ceramic-looking pentagonal "torso" where the arms met. Its voice was human enough, even pleasant.

For the most part, the general's mind was elsewhere,

still focused on Pulaski. However reluctantly, he was acting on secret orders, direct from the American KGB, through a watcher-of-the-watchers code-named "Iron Butterfly," officially unknown to him until minutes before his meeting with Toya. "Officially" was a flexible word: Gutierrez had made it his business from the first premission training day to know his people, including the backup undercover agent charged with keeping an eye on the expedition's overt political officer, Arthur Empleado, as well as its first-string covert operative, Richardson. What he hadn't realized until now was that it was also Iron Butterfly's job to report to the Banker on everyday activities and attitudes of the expedition's thirty-odd surviving "heroes."

"Very well," the debt assessor replied, "and you are?"

The creature approached on two of its delicate limbs and suddenly relaxed onto the ground beside him. "I'm Clym Pucras."

"Greetings, Clym Pucras." Eichra Oren entwined an arm with it and released it. "Will you tell me your profession?"

"I'm a machine-tool designer."

Gutierrez also knew (never mind how, he thought) that Iron Butterfly was a bitter, twisted spirit. Contrary to the agent's official—and completely phony—background story, Iron Butterfly's homeland was a Caribbean satellite which had almost broken free from Russian influence just before America had willingly adopted Marxism, spoiling everything for the little island nation. That this should make Iron Butterfly a more zealous instrument of Soviet policy didn't make a lot of sense, but it was a common, extremely human reaction, reflecting a certain vindictive fatalism.

"Would you describe yourself," Eichra Oren went on, "as a sovereign individual of fully intact sapience?"

Clym Pucras lifted a tentacle and splayed the tip into a five-fingered hand. "Without undue modesty, I would."

"Does anyone dispute this?" The man lifted his eyes to the crowd. The muttering of a single individual—another starfish creature—arose and died without any real dispute being offered.

The general had every confidence that Empleado's sources kept him well aware of Iron Butterfly's machinations. He regarded Empleado as a tolerable moderate, unmoved by any humanitarian spirit but by a physical squeamishness which produced the same results. The tragedy (for the expedition, anyway) was that to keep himself above suspicion, he must now pursue his job with a zeal—and cruelty—he wouldn't otherwise have exhibited.

"That being established," Eichra Oren returned to his client, "where do you live, Clym Pucras?"

The creature waved a limb again, part of its body language, Gutierrez guessed. "I presently make my home on the south side of the uppermost branch level of the third tree west of the matter-energy converter."

"Within the Elders' Settlement on the asteroid known as 5023 Eris?"

"Yes, that's correct."

Thus, between them, Iron Butterfly, to whom brutality came naturally, and Empleado, fearful and ambitious, had already combined to make life miserable for Pulaski. Gutierrez feared that she was only the first such victim.

"So much for formalities," came the reply. "What can I do for you?"

Clym Pucras rose a centimeter or so, turned slightly, and resettled himself. Or herself, the general thought. Or itself. "I request that you render an assessment with regard to appropriate restitution, inasmuch as I've recently trespassed against the physical property of one Babnap Portycel, creating on my part a state of moral indebtedness to him."

"You committed this trespass willfully," Eichra Oren raised his eyebrows, "against that being's plainly expressed wishes to the contrary?"

"I'm afraid I did." Clym Pucras' limbs drooped.

"Babnap Portycel is also a resident of the Settlement on 5023 Eris?"

"Yes," Clym Pucras answered, "also of the third tree west of the matter-energy converter, on the south side of the uppermost branch level—save one."

The assessor looked at the crowd again. "Is Babnap Portycel here today?"

"He is," Clym Pucras told him.

Eichra Oren showed a palm. "Let's have him answer for himself, shall we? Babnap Portycel, will you identify yourself? Are you present?"

The former mutterer arose on wiry limbs. "Reluctantly, Eichra Oren."

"Wait a minute," Pulaski turned to the general, whispering. "It's the trespasser, not the property owner, who's bringing suit? Against himself?"

"Shhh!" Gutierrez answered impatiently.

Not having heard the byplay, Eichra Oren went on. "Your reluctance is duly noted. Clym Pucras, one more question before we begin. Do you object to your assessment being rendered in public, as an example to our human guests?"

"Not at all," answered the starfish-creature. "I intended it to be exemplary. I'd be honored."

Pulaski whispered again. "What does he mean 'begin'? This character has already admitted to the crime. What else is left but the sentence?"

"Shhh!" replied Gutierrez, the same as before.

"All right, Clym Pucras, you might start by telling me about the trespass in your own words. Try to be brief, but I want the whole story."

As if struggling against its own weight, it tilted itself until the pentagonal portion of its body, now diagonal, could be seen. "Gladly, Eichra Oren. I was pacing the balcony of my dwelling yesternoon, preoccupied with the repeated failure of certain plasma drills I had designed for Mister Thoggosh, when I missed my step—I'm not quite sure what happened—and fell over the rail. My species are somewhat frail of constitution compared to others—I make no excuse, mind you—and a fall of that distance to the ground would certainly have killed me. I took the only chance I had and seized the rail of Babnap Portycel's balcony as I passed it, one branch level below."

"I see," Eichra Oren told the creature. "Please go on."

"Babnap Portycel saw me from within. He rushed out complaining that I was on his property without permission and demanded that I let go the rail."

"In order to fall to your death." Gutierrez knew Eichra Oren well enough by now to see that he was suppressing some facial expression, although he wasn't sure which. "I gather that you didn't comply."

"I considered it, letting go the rail, thinking that I might stop my fall again on the next level below. But by that time

I had grown fatigued and feared that I might not be able to save myself that way twice. As I say, I make no excuse for my unprincipled behavior."

"That, too, is noted," observed the man, "although I suggest that you leave the final judgment to me. You're paying me to make it, after all. What did you do?"

Clym Pucras gave a shrug. "I pulled myself onto his balcony, entered his dwelling, and made my exit in a conventional manner, out his front door and up the spiral staircase which services all the dwellings on that tree."

"I see. Did Babnap Portycel resist you, either when you pulled yourself over the rail or made your exit through his apartment?"

"No, and I'm grateful. He continued to complain bitterly. I acknowledge that he'd have been within his rights to push me off or shoot me."

"Indeed he would." Eichra Oren nodded. "Did you linger in his apartment or proceed straight to the door?"

"The latter. Babnap Portycel's rather shrill voice was giving me pain in my auditory organs—although I concede that he was well within his rights."

Eichra Oren looked up. "Babnap Portycel—you needn't rise—has Clym Pucras accurately described what happened yesterday?"

Gutierrez happened to be closer to this member of the species and had a better view of it. Neither seemed to be wearing the transparent plastic moisture suits affected by many aquatic species, but they did speak through thin-film sound transducers affixed to their carapaces.

"He has, Eichra Oren, although now that the damage is done, I wish he hadn't bothered! He violated my rights! I don't *want* his restitution!"

"I don't suppose you do, Babnap Portycel." Eichra Oren's voice was suddenly weary, as if he'd heard it all a thousand times. "I suspect you'd find it far more satisfying to have him remain in your moral debt for the rest of his life. Well, as an assessor of the *p'Nan* school, I can't permit that, and I won't. Civilization rests on the ability and willingness of individuals to pay their moral debts to one another."

Babnap Portycel made a snorting noise which, despite

his utterly alien shape, reminded Gutierrez of Grumpy from *Snow White*.

"Now, Clym Pucras," Eichra Oren continued, "ordinarily I wouldn't ask this question and you're certainly not obliged to answer, but our guests may find what you have to say enlightening. If Babnap Portycel doesn't want any restitution, why did you come to me?"

"I want my other neighbors to know that, despite what I did to Babnap Portycel, I continue to respect their right to property and privacy, just as I respect his. I want them to understand that, like any decent individual, I'm willing to pay my debts in full, moral and otherwise. Also, Eichra Oren, I'd rather not remain indebted to a curmudgeon like Babnap Portycel."

This time the man couldn't resist a chuckle. "I can't say that I blame you. Anything else?"

"Now that you mention it. I feel self-conscious saying this in the presence of a famous debt assessor who deals with this sort of thing every day, but I was concerned about the precedent that might be set by Babnap Portycel's refusal to accept restitution."

"Nor can we force him, since that would establish an even worse precedent. On this Earth it's called 'eminent domain.' But I believe I know what you mean. Would you mind explaining for our guests?"

The pentagonal shape with five sinuous tentacles sprouting from its sides swiveled to face Gutierrez. "Thinking afterward, I was deeply troubled. It had been an emergency. But my use of Babnap Portycel's property, if it were to become generally acceptable, would inevitably be abused. The time is long past when anyone who lives among the Elders may assert his *need* as a claim upon the lives of others, as I gather is customary among humans. The word 'emergency' is subjective: people would begin cutting through a neighbor's property—mine, for example—merely for the sake of convenience. Such violations are habitual and progressive. Before long we'd be living like animals, reduced to the level of . . ." Clym Pucras swiveled to Eichra Oren, "I can't remember the human expression."

"'Socialism,'" stated the assessor, "and I fully agree. Your trespass was understandable in the circumstances and

Babnap Portycel's refusal to help at least unkind. But as one of the few great human philosophers once observed, one's need doesn't constitute a mortgage on someone else's life. Babnap Portycel was not morally obliged to tolerate your presence, let alone to help you.

"Now on one hand, the purpose of property rights in particular and of moral codes in general is to support the lives of sapients. On the other, they must support the lives of the specific sapients they belong to, or they're without meaning. You acted to preserve your life, something we can all sympathize with and, in a different context, even commend. However, as you say, should *need* become a general excuse for violating individual rights, then all of our lives, in effect, would eventually be forfeit, defeating the whole reason for having moral codes in the first place. Your concern was well-placed."

"Thank you, Eichra Oren."

He raised a hand. "Don't thank me yet. I also agree with your choice of words. Babnap Portycel is as curmudgeonly a being as I've heard of. Of course, that's his right. And curmudgeons, whether they intend it or not, do all of us a favor. In many cultures, miners take small birds into the earth to warn them—through their fragile metabolisms—of poison gases or a lack of oxygen. Curmudgeons are their moral equivalent. Any culture which fails to uphold the rights of curmudgeons, no matter how inconvenient, no matter how tempting it is to cut corners 'this once,' degenerates until no one has any rights, not even nice people.

"Now, Clym Pucras," asked the assessor, "how long would you estimate you occupied Babnap Portycel's property without his permission?"

"I'm not certain. Perhaps a minute, perhaps two."

"To be safe," declared Eichra Oren, "I advise that you offer him five minutes' rent on his rail, balcony, and dwelling at the most exorbitant rate being charged in that neighborhood. I estimate that this should come to five hundred copper sandgrains. Have you that much with you?"

"Yes, Eichra Oren, I believe I have." One tentacle held out five copper coins, another proffered a token of gold. "And enough to pay you, as well."

"You and I can settle later, Clym Pucras. Go ahead and pay him now."

Clym Pucras arose, approached Babnap Portycel where the latter now sat alone in a clear area in the middle of the crowd, and offered him the copper coins. Babnap Portycel slapped them from his cosapient's manipulator.

"I told you, I don't want your money!"

Clym Pucras turned expectantly to Eichra Oren.

The assessor nodded. "You've done your best, Clym Pucras. Babnap Portycel has refused restitution in front of witnesses. Go home now and see whether the neighbors whose good opinion you value don't agree that the moral balance has been restored."

"'Go thou,'" Pulaski whispered, "'and sin no more.'"

THIRTY-SEVEN
Selfsame Seducers

Finished for the day, Eichra Oren watched his audience and clients depart the clearing in apparent varying degrees of perplexity or satisfaction, depending on whether they were human or members of another species. Once more he felt he'd failed to help the former understand the latter, and had the whole task still before him to do over again.

Toward the opposite end of the little grassy spot, only Pulaski lingered, sitting at one end of the log she'd shared with Gutierrez, eyes downcast, fingers playing idly with a long stalk of grass. The assessor was suddenly conscious of what amounted to his orders to do his best to . . . what was the old-fashioned English expression? *Compromise* her.

Suppressing a sigh, he arose, for some reason stiffer in the joints than he was accustomed to being, thrust his hands in his pockets and, leaving his sword behind on the blanket he'd occupied, ambled toward the girl as casually as he could manage. He'd known that they would find themselves together after this session. Somehow knowing didn't make it any easier.

"Well, there you have it, a much more . . . 'normal' sort of procedure."

"No one beheaded," she glanced up briefly, "or impaled."

Not yet, he thought cynically as he reached to take her hand, surprised when she didn't flinch or withdraw. She was without doubt the most clumsy and unattractive young woman he'd ever known. Nothing he could say or do would change that. Despite hymns of altruism sung by the Soviet Americans, he was from a culture vastly more mature, and knew that feeling sorry for the other party was no way to begin a relationship. It occurred to him that he'd felt many things during his brief acquaintances with Estrellita Reille y Sanchez and Rosalind Nguyen, but he had never once felt sorry for either of them.

Letting go of her hand, he put his own at the small of her back above the waistband of her jumpsuit, guiding her across the glade to the blanket and sword he'd left behind. A dubious symbolism, he thought, groping for some inconsequential thing to say to fill the silent air about them. The words didn't come, and she was quiet, too. Soon enough they'd find themselves making love under the tree where his office and residence grew. Without saying it, both realized it was the same place where another woman had died at his hands. He thought of Rosalind and of a novelty postcard one of the Americans had told him about: "Having a wonderful time. Wish you were her."

By mutual consent, they remained standing, silence growing until it threatened to overwhelm them. "Let's climb a tree," Eichra Oren declared suddenly, trying to seize control of his existence again. "I've been meaning to take a closer look at what's happening with my house."

"Okay." There was relief and no small amount of gratitude in her voice as she surveyed the giant before them for a foothold. It wasn't hard, even for him, encumbered by his sword and the accusing blanket. The spot they'd chosen was rough and furrowed, the barklike covering of the great green stalk, and the way it spread to the roots, almost forming stairs. Before they knew it, they'd reached the first branch and were looking down at a broad, flat, off-white shelf formed by the mushroomlike organism Eichra Oren had planted here. Various features of the house-to-be had already become recognizable: partitions, deck railing, "built-in" furniture that looked closer to being half-melted than half-grown. At the back, nearest the trunk, sat the smooth-surfaced platform of a bed.

Eichra Oren tested the fresh growth with a cautious foot, and then stepped down solidly, taking Toya's hand—unnecessarily, in all likelihood—to help her down. She held on once she stood beside him and despite himself, he was gratified. He seemed, the cynical thought arose unbidden again, to be accomplishing the vile deed with marvelous dispatch; Mister Thoggosh would be delighted. Of course Sam, who picked up slang from the Americans at a dismaying rate, would have called it "shooting fish in a barrel." For his own part, everything he said to Toya or did with her made him feel like what they called a "heel." He knew it would forever afterward, whenever he thought about it, but what were a few moral consequences among friends, anyway?

What sickened him most was the way that he'd derided the obsessive American concept of duty. Now, it seemed that the same consideration was compelling him to make unfeeling love to this vulnerable young woman, and he could see with a pitiful clarity how the prospect seemed to fill her with equal amounts of joy and terror. *Great Egg, she's a virgin!* He was about to hurt her, and himself, for no reason that struck him as particularly worthy, which meant that somehow he'd been corrupted by his contact with collectivism—and so had Mister Thoggosh—and it was possible that he'd never feel clean again.

Toya gasped. The muscles of Eichra Oren's arms felt like oak where her shoulder blades lay across one of them as the other swept behind her knees to lift her off her feet and lay her down on the low platform. Fine hairs on the back of his hand glistened like gold wire as he reached to her throat for the toggle of her ship-suit zipper and pulled it as far below her waist as it would go. In an instant she lay exposed to his eyes and hands as she had never been to any man, naked from the over-prominent knobs of her collarbones to the first fair curls a handspan below her navel. A single syllable from her lips could make this into rape or something else. Whatever she said, it wouldn't stop what was happening, or change (very much) the way she felt about it.

She reached to lock her fingers into the thick bronze hair at the back of his neck as he pressed his mouth against a small, flat breast she was afraid might disappear altogether if she put her hand behind her own head. Even as she responded to his fingertips pressing their demands into her flesh, she was astonished at what she was doing. A warmth grew, somewhere between her knees and her waist, spreading upward and outward. Asked to describe herself, she'd have said "tech sergeant," and perhaps "amateur paleontologist" after that. "Woman" would never have been her thoughtless, automatic response.

He rolled aside and slipped a hand into her open coverall between her thighs, probing with a finger. A wave of shock and heat went through her, her blood sizzling in its wake as if it were carbonated. She felt limp, weak, about to slide off into sleep, but she was wide awake and focused in a way, and in a place within her mind, that she'd never seen before and never knew existed.

All of her adult life, until just a little while ago, it had been her expectation that she would always be a virgin and would die, at whatever age, in the same unenviable state. She'd never dared dream of this, of finding this kind of happiness. (And she realized as, step by step, he claimed her body in his methodical, relentless way, that she *was* happy.) It wasn't a matter of having tried and failed. The fact was, fearing humiliation, she'd never tried at all. Such a thing had never consciously occurred to her. If it had, she wouldn't have had the courage. Nor was it that she'd been rejected by men. They hadn't ever noticed her enough to reject her.

Now, on this little island in space, deep within an alien forest, all of that seemed to be changing. Toya never remembered how Eichra Oren got her arms out of her sleeves or the rest of the jumpsuit off her. All at once, he was above her and between her legs. She felt herself parting, felt pressure and a little pain, then wave after cool, white-hot wave of something wonderful and far beyond her power to describe.

Life, it appeared, was full of surprises.

✧   ✧   ✧

"Well that was certainly educational."

Sam approached Eichra Oren where the man sat once again at the base of the canopy tree, lost deep in what he felt was a miserable substitute for thought. He was more than a little surprised, given the circumstances, that he'd been physically capable of doing what he'd just done. He was especially disturbed about where it had been accomplished, if "accomplished" was the word. Too many memories, all of them bad, lived here.

Having made love to Toya three times and sent her, dazed and happy, on her way back to the human camp, he'd immediately begun to feel guilty and to despise himself both for the deed and for the feeling it evoked.

"Wonderful," he told the dog, using the language of his people and the implant of the Elders. To an eavesdropper, the two would have appeared to be contemplating one another silently. "Did you watch the whole thing?"

"Would *I* violate the privacy of a fellow sapient?" Sam sat down beside his human friend, then stretched at length on the grass. He sighed. "Despite your late success, this hasn't been a very lucky assignment, has it, Boss?"

"I feel," Eichra Oren shook his head, "that I've been forced by circumstances to revert to a more primitive philosophical state here."

His canine friend gave the little bark that served him as a laugh, "Bullshit."

"Thanks." Eichra Oren paused, thinking. "You're quite correct. It takes every scrap of honesty, integrity, character, and self-discipline I have, not to blame somebody else— say the Americans—for what seems to be happening to me here. What stings is that this is the very feeling my profession is supposed to help people overcome. Do away with."

Sam yawned, apparently unsympathetic, and rolled to scratch behind one ear. "Somebody told me the other day that California is the only place in the universe where people feel guilty for feeling guilty."

"More than that," the man ignored the dog, "I dread the moment when my assignment here is finished and I have to break things off and hurt her."

"And despite yourself, you're already mentally rehearsing the tragic scene?" The dog yawned again. "Gimme a break, will you? All you're doing is smelling smoke and looking for a fire escape. You can't help it, Boss, it's a reflex. Individuals of my species chew their legs off when they're caught in a trap. In your case, I guess you'd have to chew off your—"

"What rankles most," the man interrupted, "is that the damage I'm inflicting on Toya and myself is all for nothing. The one I'm really angriest at, besides me, is Mister Thoggosh. At him I'm *very* angry. And before you say a word, Sam, don't bother trying to talk me out of that minor satisfaction."

"Wouldn't dream of it. I know your opinion of the professional methods appropriate to this assignment, Boss. I share them. They don't include sucking face and parts south with a female you don't care for."

Eichra Oren grimaced. "They're corrupting you, too, Sam. That's about the most disgusting turn of phrase I've ever heard."

"For the most disgusting situation we've ever found ourselves in?"

"Well, it does seem that Mister Thoggosh is requiring me to play the game, as the Americans put it, with one hand tied behind my back." He plucked a blade of grass, put it in his mouth, and thought of Rosalind and Toya, Toya and Rosalind. "I can't protect the Elders' damned precious secret unless I have an idea what that secret is. On more than one occasion, I've all but begged that old bag of ink to be more open with me. He seems to regard this whole matter as something personal, something reserved exclusively to the Elders, something they apparently believe doesn't involve any other species."

Sam looked up. "Boss, have you ever suspected that your present 'assignment' is just a convenient way of keeping you out of Mister Thoggosh's figurative hair?"

"More than once," the man conceded. "On other occasions, I suspect that something even more sinister might be happening. . . ."

Sam grinned, "You show me your paranoia, I'll show you mine."

"Well," he spat out a bit of leaf and frowned, "you'll remember that we made as detailed a study of this culture as time permitted. And in the course of that study, we ran across all sorts of bizarre ideas either abandoned long ago by the Elders, or never invented by them in the first place. Among them, you'll recall, was this infantile tendency, present in most primitive cultures, which these particular humans don't seem able to outgrow. They believe things without sufficient evidence—often in the face of proof to the contrary—simply because they *want* to believe them."

The dog responded sourly, "We're talking Yahweh and Company here?"

Eichra Oren nodded. "That infantile tendency's most conspicuous result is the survival and proliferation of religions, long past the period when, in any other culture, they ought to have begun to wither and die."

Sam shook his head, a human gesture. "Looks to me, Boss, like the situation's worse than that—a matter of permanent, deadly fixation at the most primitive stage of cultural development."

"I don't think we contradict one another," the man said. "Look: with these people, mysticism forms—with altruism and collectivism—a tight, mutually supportive, impenetrable network of roots that bind the human mind and make its further progress impossible."

"And all you're hoping now—" Sam's tone fell to a sudden and uncharacteristically serious level. "Pardon the, uh, over-pertinent comment, Boss, but nobody could help observing your confusion and unhappiness. You only hope that the condition isn't as contagious as you fear it might be."

Eichra Oren closed his eyes, breathed in deeply, and exhaled, relieved to hear the words. "Something like that, yes."

"Ain't likely," the dog argued. "One thing separating you from your fellow apes here is the history of your people with respect to mysticism. How many times have I heard your own mother say that their most popular religion was pretty feeble and uncomplicated to begin with, and that it was already feeling the discouraging effects of early scientific progress by the time the Continent was Lost?"

"Yes, my fellow apes, as you charmingly put it, are comparing what they call 'Antarctica' with England in its early nineteenth century, when their culture should have started shedding its religions. I don't know what went wrong. For my people, the polar reversal and climatic disaster finished off anybody's faith in benevolent deities. And among those refugees who were 'collected,' exposure to the rational philosophy of the Elders did the rest."

Sam snorted. "Whereas it would probably have made these jerks even *more* religious. So what's the point, if you don't mind me asking—or even if you do."

"Nothing I can put a finger on, just the general feeling of a bad situation. I'm beginning to suspect our Mister Thoggosh—and you'll appreciate how deeply this dismays me, especially since it's none of my business—of something like a religious motivation. In every respect, Sam, this disquieting affair smells of the irrational. And that from someone with a nose a million times less sensitive than yours, my canine friend." He shook his head. "It's uncharacteristic of the Elders in general, and of Mister Thoggosh in particular."

"Religious motivation?" The dog looked him in the eye. "I'd say that rancid old mollusc's behavior is uncharacteristic of the normal relationship between himself and you, and *that's* what worries you."

Eichra Oren stood up. "One way or another, Sam, I've come to a decision. I'm going to ferret out the secret on my own. With respect to what Mister Thoggosh wants, that will put me closer, faster, to anyone else trying to do the same. Also, and this is no small consideration, it'll satisfy my professional and personal curiosity."

Sam got to his feet as well and wagged his tail. "Make that on *our* own, Boss, and you've got a deal!"

THIRTY-EIGHT
Four-legged Footwork

"Yes, Nannel Rab, I know, I know."

Having decided, Eichra Oren didn't wait. Before another hour had gone by, Sam was keeping an appointment—rather, he was spending more time than he cared to, cooling his nonexistent heels as the *appointee* attended to other chores. Eichra Oren was off on another part of the asteroid.

"Yes, yes, Nannel Rab, I know."

At the moment, Aelbraugh Pritsch was speaking with Mister Thoggosh's chief engineer, his words spoken into empty air while his thoughts traveled halfway around the little world via cerebro-cortical implant. He and Sam were in the building that served the scale-feathered being as office and quarters, a rambling structure which never seemed quite the same whenever Sam visited Mister Thoggosh's assistant. The plan was open, without floors or partitions. It was a multistory maze of crisscrossing stairways, perches, and swings unique to the warm-blooded avian dinosauroid species. Aelbraugh Pritsch delighted in rearranging it every chance he got, although it confused his nonavian, nondinosauroid associates.

"I know it isn't working. I merely observed that it meets the standards originally specified. I don't see how a debt assessment would help. We're here, the manufacturer's back home. We must make do with what we have."

Sam dreaded continuing the conversation. From long acquaintance, he knew that Eichra Oren's "disrespectful attitude" and "disorderly methodology" upset Aelbraugh Pritsch, a being capable enough in his own fussy way (although it pained Sam to admit it) but neither by personality nor inborn nature a particularly happy soul. Sam thought he understood why, although he'd never been able to persuade Eichra Oren. The species had descended from forms which, over the long course of their evolution, had given up their ability to fly. Flying being a biologically expensive strategy, flying creatures often found easier ways of staying alive: ostriches had sacrificed wings for size and running speed; penguins had followed the way of the seal. Giving up flight had freed dinosauroid brains—already well developed for the three-dimensional task of flying—to do other things.

Mostly, it appeared to Sam, worrying.

"Yes, yes, I'll ask about ion implantation. If it's within my power . . ."

In many respects, too, beings like Aelbraugh Pritsch remained creatures of the flock. In their world, they were used to hierarchy and predictability. Unlike humans (and dogs) they'd never felt at ease as Appropriated Persons, although they'd been collected in greater numbers than any other species, due to a habit of staying in large groups. The Elders' laissez-faire informality, a result of the molluscs' sophisticated history, went against the avians' bent as badly as Eichra Oren's personality which, to a degree, reflected it.

"The Americans? Why you're right, Nannel Rab. Their ships *do* show evidence of ion hardening. If in need of a dugout canoe, ask a savage. But you'll have to do your own asking, I'm afraid. My time is occupied."

It didn't help that Aelbraugh Pritsch was aware of all this, or that by avian standards he was a loner bordering on the psychotic. Avians tended to strike others as neurotic anyway. They, in turn, had long ago given up pointing to the difficulties that others experienced adjusting to life with the nautiloids. By all rights, he ought to have gotten along with the newly arrived humans—professed altruists and collectivists that they were—but by nature, they were no more creatures of the flock than he was an individualist. Sam had noticed he could hardly stand to be around them.

"Where were we?" Aelbraugh Pritsch had finished speaking with the engineer. "Doesn't Eichra Oren realize the risk that he incurs? He's supposed to protect the Elders' privacy. Yet someone—anyone—by staying one step behind him in the course of his investigation, would benefit from whatever he discovers."

"He wondered whether you'd been let in on the Proprietor's secret."

"I certainly haven't," came the answer, "nor, considering the terrible responsibility entailed, do I wish to be. I've too much responsibility of my own."

"Aren't you curious," Sam asked, "about why you came to 5023 Eris?"

"If I were, I wouldn't be doing my job, would I?" So there, nyah, Sam mentally completed the thought. "Need I add that those associated with the Elders are hardly monolithic in their views? They begin with the intransigence natural to them and then, thanks to the Elders, add half a billion years of disunion to that. Humans like Eichra Oren are unruly to the last cell of their bodies, incapable of acting as an unprotesting unit. From the moment of their arrival, it puzzled me that the Americans had ever talked themselves into socialism. Generations have passed, and still they spend each waking minute writhing in the discomfort of it, imposing it by force on one another. For all they've achieved, they might as well be pachyderms, flapping their ears and trying to fly."

Sam had seen an animated movie on that subject, but didn't mention it. "You complain that they're *trying* to be monolithic?"

"I complain that they act against their nature. I live among natural individualists and to an extent, because I'm sapient, have become one myself. Yet for my species, it isn't necessary to adopt an ideology, we naturally sort ourselves into a 'pecking hierarchy' and obey orders. To us it feels as if that's what we've chosen freely. Before the advent of the Elders, we had to *invent* a semblance of individualism, simply in order to advance. In that respect, I can sympathize with these 'Marxists.' Collectivism can't be any more comfortable for them than its opposite has been for my people."

"The difference being," Sam offered, "that collectivism fails to benefit them the way individualism did your people. But we've digressed."

"We have. I understand that any preference on my part that others be more like me is doomed. That's the danger I foresee in this scheme of Eichra Oren's. Like individuals everywhere, some among our party have looser tongues than others. Others disagree with the necessity of keeping undercover."

"Or the dignity," Sam interposed.

"Or the dignity. Have it your own way."

"I try to," the dog replied absently. A light had begun flashing in his mind at Aelbraugh Pritsch's last words, but he couldn't pin it down.

Tongues, loose or otherwise, had nothing to do with the Elders themselves, who spoke by radio produced by the same sort of cells that make some eels electric. Despite the fact that it was their expedition, few had come here besides Mister Thoggosh and the late Semlohcolresh. With Pulaski in tow, Eichra Oren made short work of interviewing half a dozen of them. Now the assessor was traveling all over the asteroid in search of answers.

At the moment they sat with a third individual on packing crates in a large tent overlooking one of the mysterious drilling sites that seemed to be the reason for the colony's existence, while a fourth, incapable of sitting, stood nearby. All about them were the scattered reminders—folded cots, stretchers, stacks of bandages, metal and plastic implements—of an emergency safely past.

"Dear me, yes," Dlee Raftan Saon told them. "When a piece of machinery that size comes apart at 150,000 gigavolts, there are bound to be injuries, no matter how hardy the species." He turned his triangular head to regard Nannel

Rab, a nine-foot spider covered in black and reddish-orange fur. Toya found the arachnoid engineer beautiful and repelling at the same time, although her beauty was marred just now by surgical dressings over a large area of her great abdomen. "I'm just grateful that no one was killed, thanks to Nannel Rab's quick thinking. She heard the plasma drill begin to fail and ordered an evacuation. Those I treated had dorsal shrapnel wounds, including Nannel Rab herself."

Nannel Rab waved a modest palp. "You are too kind, Dlee Raftan Saon. I merely performed as any rational being—"

"Perhaps, my dear," the insect-being replied before the giant spider could finish, "but there are too few rational beings in the universe."

"Yes," Toya put in impatiently, "but you haven't told us what they were drilling *for*, Dlee Raftan Saon."

He emitted wheezing noises she'd learned to interpret as a chuckle. "You noticed. That's because I haven't the faintest idea."

Eichra Oren shook his head. "And you aren't curious?"

"I'm *consumed* with curiosity. I'd hoped, somewhat unethically, to learn something from my patients under anaesthesia—you'd be surprised what we hear that way—although I'd never have repeated a word to anyone, of course. But we made do with topicals, so I'll have to wait until another time—may fortune forfend." He wheezed again.

"But you're a partner in this enterprise, aren't you?" Toya protested.

"You don't think I'd come here for professional fees?"

"Then how can you not—"

"Rather than promise not to divulge something I might find interesting to talk about, I refused Mister Thoggosh's explanation and trusted his judgment. Isn't it more fun," he lowered his voice and wheezed, "to guess?"

"Some fun!"

Eichra Oren grinned. "What have you guessed so far?"

"It's my impression," Dlee Raftan Saon scratched at a mouth part, "that it concerns development of sophisticated technology, involving unconventional application of certain philosophical principles."

The assessor blinked. "That's a hell of a guess, even if it's wrong."

"I'm a good guesser—that's what diagnostics is about, after all."

"In that case," Nannel Rab put in, "I had better obtain a second opinion. The most charitable speculation is that this mission is nothing more than an archaeological expedition."

Eichra Oren raised an eyebrow. "And the least charitable?"

The eight-legged giant peered down at them, its many eyes hard, glittering drops of obsidian. "That we look for treasure."

The physician gave an almost human shrug. "Well, some of it Mister Thoggosh told me in the first place to get me interested. As to the rest, I keep my eyes open. Like Nannel Rab, here, I haven't any choice; unlike yours, they have no lids!" He was still wheezing to himself as they left in search of their next subject.

Toya couldn't decide what Voozh Preeno was.

The creature was the result of impressive evolutionary divergence. He, she, or it (she hadn't learned much about the assistant logistics specialist) might be distantly related to anemones, urchins, even the starfish at Eichra Oren's session. On the other hand, Voozh Preeno might descend from organisms as diverse as fan corals, arachnids, even intelligent plants—its overall color was a pale green—like Llessure Knarrfic. Sam would say it was an extroverted hairball a meter in diameter. Observation revealed dozens of fibrous tentacles rising from an unseen center, branching into dozens of smaller appendages which branched into dozens more. The finest tendrils at the ends of all that branching were specialized. What kept Voozh Preeno from looking like a furry beachball was the fact that, as it moved, when it "walked" or "handed" her a drink she accepted for the sake of observing it, it appeared to split, revealing a coarser inner structure. She still wasn't sure whether there was any central body or if it consisted entirely of limbs.

"Truth is a valuable commodity," it informed Eichra Oren, "which we do not automatically owe to anyone. I am, moreover, honor bound to withhold it. That is more than you would learn did I offer you an engaging falsehood."

"Well put, Voozh Preeno," a fourth individual declared. "With eight legs, you might have been a Minister of the Royal Web."

Like Nannel Rab, Nek Nam'l Las was a spider of daunting proportion—arachnoids appeared to be highly successful across time, and these two didn't represent the only species of sapient spiders Toya had heard of—but that was where resemblance ceased. The engineer was black and red and furry. Nek Nam'l Las was a hardshelled blue-black from palp to spinneret. Nannel Rab was descended from solitary hunters. Nek Nam'l Las's ancestors had been gregarious web spinners.

"You flatter me, Your Highness—but I enjoy it."

Eichra Oren stood. He'd been sitting on the floor. "We thank you for that much, Voozh Preeno. Ready, Toya?"

"'Your Highness'?" Toya was confused: why was Eichra Oren giving up so easily? "I thought your society didn't have any government."

The sleek black form, a meter taller than the girl, pivoted on its legs to focus several eyes on her. "We haven't, my little warm one. Our noblesse oblige is *not* to rule, so that anarchy is free to reign without a power vacuum begging to be filled. Thus it has been for generations among my kind on our world, and among those of us caught in the Elders' web of power and transported to theirs."

"The Princess is the highest of her line among the Appropriated Persons," Voozh Preeno explained.

Toya shook her head, "And a humble logistics officer at the same time?"

The spider raised a foreleg. "Those who will not endure *social* equality condemn themselves to suffer the *political* variety in its place."

Toya set down a glass which had been filled with ordinary tomato juice—she hoped. These quarters seemed ordinary, too, their only odd feature being a vat of oily fluid in place of the usual sleeping platform. Looking closely at Voozh Preeno again, she played with the idea that perhaps the Elders had accidentally collected at least one extraterrestrial in all that sampling fifteen thousand years ago.

They were back at the settlement to question beings from a list Eichra Oren had made, having spoken with dozens more across the asteroid. The results weren't very different, she suspected, from those obtained on Earth by any conventional detective. This wasn't the first outright refusal they'd elicited, along with a mixture of unrelated facts, unsupported theories, and lies. Out of this mixture, the stubborn investigator was attempting to sift, one microscopic hint at a time, something resembling the truth. At least he'd been stubborn until now.

She got to her feet. "Thank you, Voozh Preeno. Sometime I'd like to speak with you about your people. I'm interested in evolution."

"And you wonder what I am, Sergeant Pulaski?"

"Toya. Yes, I hope you don't mind."

Voozh Preeno laughed. Toya didn't know where its voice came from, but it sounded human. "Other sapients often have trouble placing us. Your interest is generally shared in the culture the Elders have helped us create. It would be strange if this were not the case."

She nodded. "I suppose it would."

"To answer your question: you are distantly related to chordates, like sharks. Well, through an extremely indirect process which makes us a species rather younger than the Elders, my people are related to sponges. And before you ask your next question, I am both male and female, although I am gratified to say that we mate with others of our species rather than ourselves. That is biologically unproductive and also considered a perversion."

Toya nodded gravely and thanked Voozh Preeno for explaining.

"But stay, mammals." Nek Nam'l Las wheeled until she stood between them and the door. Toya felt a chill run down her spine. "I relish the odor of your blood. And you have not yet asked for *my* opinion."

Eichra Oren reached up to stroke the furry palp of the giant towering over him and another chill coursed through Toya's body. "I thought it more respectful, Princess, to wait until you offered."

Nek Nam'l Las turned to the girl. "The expression among your kind is 'in a pig's valise,' is it not? Eichra Oren, you have never been respectful of anyone. But I am subject to no promise of secrecy, and have heard it said that Mister Thoggosh seeks a faster-than-light technology called the 'Virtual Drive.' " She regarded Toya. "Now, was that not worth the risk of being eaten alive?"

"Your Highness," Eichra Oren touched her again, "I'll repay you with my firstborn child the second Thursday of next week. You'll find it a succulent tidbit for your web."

"Not if half as acerbic as yourself. Fare well, delicious friend, and you, as well, Toya Pulaski."

Hand shaking, Toya reached up to stroke the coarse fur of the creature's face, then hurried out the door. In the corridor, Eichra Oren turned. "You survived that rather well. What are you trying not to laugh about?"

Toya giggled. "Perversion. I don't know about going blind, but Voozh Preeno seems to have grown a lot of hair on its palms."

"And," he grinned back at her, "everywhere else."

She shook her head. "I like your cannibal princess. Where to next?"

"The infirmary," he told her, "and Remaulthiek."

Another thing Toya couldn't figure out was why Eichra Oren chose certain individuals to question. The creature Americans had first labeled a "walking quilt" dispensed refreshments at the infirmary and was also a partner in Mister Thoggosh's enterprise. Why Eichra Oren thought she'd violate the contract to tell him of the mission here, Toya couldn't guess. They found her, another of the chordates Voozh Preeno had mentioned (more closely resembling a ray than a shark), sitting beside her cart, having a meal on a lawn before the infirmary.

"Greetings, Remaulthiek, how do you do?"

"I do not return your greeting, but keep it for my collection. I do by eating as you see now, Eichra Oren, and by getting sufficient sleep."

The human shook his head. "I'm sorry, I didn't mean 'how is it that you exist.' I meant to inquire as to your state of being."

Remaulthiek, glistening within the covering which kept her gills moist, stretched to the cart for another sandwich.

"It continues," she told him, "as it has for some time now. This is one of the new ones?"

"Toya Pulaski. We've come to ask you questions, if we may."

"There are better answerers than I. What do you wish to ask?"

"I want to know why the Elders came to 5023 Eris. What—"

"I interrupt," Remaulthiek told him, "saving you much time and further effort. We are here because we seek after the Gods."

With a disappointed expression, Eichra Oren opened his mouth, but was interrupted again. "Gods?" Toya asked.

"The Great Ones who no longer choose to manifest themselves upon this plane of existence," came the reply. "Was not this made clear to you?"

The girl sat down beside the creature. "It's supposed to be a secret. Didn't Mister Thoggosh swear you to secrecy when you signed his agreement?"

"My kind make no agreement, human person, but do as we say and deny not reality. This is not so with other species. We respect the ways of others."

"I see." Eichra Oren's words followed a long silence while the creature contemplated her sandwich, "What happened to these gods, Remaulthiek?"

"They departed long ago. Know you nothing of unnatural history?"

"It's my place to seek the truth. How long ago did they depart?"

"Close upon the ninth order. We partners seek to follow them."

THIRTY-NINE
Two-legged Footwork

As the asteroid rotated into the night, and the canopy darkened overhead, Sam returned to the temporary quarters he shared with Eichra Oren, thinking about his unproductive interview with Aelbraugh Pritsch and of one or two similar conversations that had followed it.

Chief of Security Tl°m°nch°l was one of the sapient crustaceans Soviet Americans called "giant bugs with guns." Asked what he knew of the nautiloids' purpose on 5023 Eris, he had expressed a belief that, after a hiatus lasting fifteen thousand years, the Elders were again seeking other alternate-world beings. On the other limb, Clym Pucras, the machine-tool designer that Eichra Oren had heard in a professional capacity, argued that if the mission were seeking anything, it was traces of a vanished species of sapients even older than the Elders, now extinct in all known versions of the Solar System. Neither being had offered much in the way of evidence to support his position.

At the moment, Sam was wondering whether Eichra Oren had given him this unproductive assignment simply to keep him out from underfoot with regard to Toya. They would soon leave this impersonal apartment, he thought, and not a moment too soon. He wondered whether Eichra Oren would be coming home tonight. The dog was too proud—or he wasn't sure what—to contact the man and ask. When not actively assisting his human companion, he often succumbed to periods of lonely meditation. It appeared he might have another night of it ahead of him to look forward to.

"Hello, Sam."

Someone was waiting at the door when he arrived. "Hello, Dr. Nguyen. Eichra Oren isn't here right now, and I don't know when he'll be back." Sam liked her. She was small and soft and golden-brown. Despite a lingering hint of disinfectant perceptible only to his canine senses, she always smelled good. He waited for her reply before going inside.

"That's all right, Sam. It's you I wanted to see, anyway. I wish you'd call me Rosalind. May I come in, please?"

"Follow me." He was surprised and pleased. Scutigera's wry observation was correct to an extent. He preferred the conversation and company of human females to that of his own kind, although it had never gone further than that and never would, despite the centipede's innuendo. "Can I fix you something to drink?"

She was looking around, but it didn't take long because there wasn't much to see. "In a little while, perhaps. There's something I'd like to ask you about first, if you don't mind."

Another thing Sam liked about her was that she didn't ask, as many of her fellow humans had already, how he could accomplish something like fixing her a drink when he didn't have any hands. "I will if I can. Please find a chair." He hopped onto a corner of the bed, lay down on his belly, and crossed one paw over the other. "What's all this about—Rosalind?"

Across the little room she smiled, but her tone was grim and there was no relaxation in her posture. "Sam, there's a rumor going around about Sergeant Pulaski, that she's been given a special assignment by the KGB. You probably remember that Estrellita—Major Reille y Sanchez— was the last one to be given such an assignment. You're aware of what happened to her."

He nodded. "You worry that the same thing might happen to Toya?"

She bit her lip and nodded. "There's no end to the surprises on this asteroid. Startling, mind-altering discoveries. Why most of them should center on the only human among the nautiloids is more than I can—"

"You're afraid that, like her predecessor, Toya may make the *wrong* discoveries about Eichra Oren? That isn't what killed Estrellita, Rosalind, although I must admit that the private life and personal statistics of a *p'Nan* debt assessor—or of any human being if you ask me, no offense—are more bizarre the more you learn about them. Somehow I feel that isn't what you're getting at."

"It could be." She shook her head, contradicting herself. "Most of his friends and clients are such alien creatures. Like that giant centipede—"

"I was just thinking of Scutigera. And don't forget Sam the Wonderdog."

She went on as if she hadn't heard him, locking her fingers together and staring at the floor. "On the other hand, my life among sapients of only one species must seem narrow and dull to him. Until I began meeting his friends, this hadn't occurred to me," she concluded glumly. "And no, I'm not forgetting Sam the Wonderdog. It's icing on the cake that his best friend and assistant happens to be a cybernetically augmented sapient canine."

"Best friend and assistant. Watson to his Holmes, eh what? Let me tell you something about that—although I thought this was about Toya—but first I'd better fix you that drink I promised. What'll you have?"

"Nothing alcoholic, thanks." She smiled. "This visit is technically professional, and I'm on call."

"Nothing alcoholic coming up!" He nodded at a wall panel which melted away to reveal a shelf of glasses beneath a row of dispensers. A glass slid from one nozzle to another, filling itself with a brown, foamy liquid. The niche was closer to Rosalind than Sam. She rose and took the glass before the wall went solid and sat down again.

She drank, then looked up. "Why this is—Sam, the formula for this is supposed to be a trade secret. How—"

"Another advantage," he grinned, "of being able to crack

any code. I was about to tell you that my kind were intended by the Elders as nothing more than remote-controlled conveniences. I'm supposed to serve Eichra Oren the same way Mister Thoggosh's detachable limb serves him. But somewhere, the nautiloids' biological engineers made a mistake. I'm much more than that—all of my kind are— both to myself and my 'master.' "

"I can see that." She took another sip. "What do you mean, specifically?"

Sam gave it thought. "Well, I learned recently from you Americans about 'Seeing Eye dogs' for the blind."

Rosalind nodded. "A better analogy than you know, Sam." She hesitated, then: "You may have to be Eichra Oren's 'thinking-brain dog' for a while. He seems to be having trouble in that department himself lately."

"Bringing us to the purpose of this conversation?" He chuckled. "I can't say I haven't been worried about him, although if I were truly man's best friend . . . I'll settle for being his partner. It isn't always easy. In fact, I often find myself wondering . . ."

There was a long, empty silence.

"Wondering what?" Rosalind asked.

"Suppose the Elders had kept searching fifteen thousand years ago, through the infinite worlds of probability. Mightn't they have found some alternative reality in which the dogs grew hands, walked erect, and invented technology so they'd have more time to spend wallowing in self-doubt? You know, all of the things that make you human?"

She laughed openly and honestly. He liked the sound of it. "Sam, this is about you, isn't it? You must know that you're liked simply for yourself. That's especially true of us Americans who don't know anything about any role you're supposed to play in nautiloid society. It doesn't matter to me anyway, and I don't think any of us see you as a mere appendage, to Eichra Oren or anybody else. Besides, in that other universe you're talking about, you might not even recognize the evolutionary result as a dog. They might not recognize you. To those canine somethings somewhere, you'd be like a . . ."

"Like a chimp to your people? Somehow that fails to comfort me."

She raised her eyebrows. "Is that what it was supposed to do? I thought I came to ask you questions. Seriously, I'm curious about all sorts of things. For example, what's it like to be tied permanently into a sort of mental internet?"

He had to think for a moment before he realized what she was getting at. "You mean the Elders' implant network?"

"Yes, to me it's a real wonder, given that item of technology, that individualism has managed to survive at all among the nautiloids. I'd have expected it to be swept away by all that brain-penetrating machinery."

"Well, implants are analogous to something the Elders were born with and had several hundred million years to get used to. The Elder who invented what you'd call the Faraday cage—and mental privacy—is revered as the greatest . . . nautiloiditarian . . . who ever lived, sort of a combination of Thomas Edison and Albert Schweitzer. And even if what you say about the danger to individualism were true, there was no one with the political power to do any sweeping away. It wouldn't be the same on your world, would it?"

"There we agree. The fact is, *nothing* is the same here. Just as an example, and strangest of the strange: Sam, that burden which has rested heaviest on human shoulders throughout all recorded and inferred history has no influence whatever on you, or Eichra Oren, or any of your associates."

He cocked his head. "Now you've lost me."

"I know I have." She grinned and he knew that she'd been struck all over again by the contrast between their conversation and the kind of being she was having it with. "That's my point. And whatever else we may agree on, it makes for a fundamental difference between us. We might as well be from different species, people like Eichra Oren and myself. It's like a chronic debtor trying to imagine the world from the viewpoint of someone who has never had to worry about money."

"Well it's true that we're a wealthy culture, but—"

She shook her head vehemently. "I'm not talking about wealth—or I am, but not about money. Sam, in my experience—my people's experience—men and women are confronted from their first adult thought, maybe even their first waking moment, with the inevitable prospect of aging and death. I often heard my father lament that, just as he was beginning to acquire some skill at living his life, it was beginning to end. And as it happened, he died prematurely, even for someone of his time and place, at the age of fifty-nine."

"I'm sorry." Sam didn't know what else to say.

She looked down at her hands. "So was he. He hated it. No amount of talk about what's natural or normal ever made him hate it less. I feel the same way. It may be natural, but it doesn't feel *right*. I think that's why I became a doctor. Nevertheless, I've always lived with the fact that I, too, will grow old, get wrinkled, become feeble, and eventually die." She looked up at him. "Species associated with the nautiloids, however, everybody in the category 'Appropriated Persons,' enjoy extraordinarily long lives, don't they?"

Sam nodded. "Certainly by your standards. It was part of the Great Restitution the Elders made for having removed them from their native environments."

"That much I know. There were other benefits: cerebro-cortical implants, useful companions like yourself, full participation in nautiloid society, whatever that means. Somehow, knowing Mister Thoggosh, I doubt it has anything to do with voting. I'm certain it has nothing to do with taxes. But—" Her expression changed. Suddenly she was a small child wanting answers. "How *long* do they live, Sam? Until now, I haven't been able to find out."

"Probably because nobody knows."

She frowned, puzzled. "How can that be?"

"Well . . ." Weary of the position he was in, Sam slid onto the floor, stretched, then crossed the room. To Rosalind's left was a small table, and, beside that, another chair. He hopped onto it and sat. She turned to face him, both hands on the left arm of her chair. "The Antarctican disaster occurred fifteen thousand years ago, when the Earth's magnetic poles shifted naturally, as they do from time to time, disrupting the planet's climate. A civilization was buried beneath a fall of permanent snow. Soon that snow became three kilometers of glacial ice which still cover the continent in our time."

She was impatient. "I've heard this. What does it have to do with—"

"I'm getting to it, Doctor. Antarctican culture was cut off almost at the initial moment of its greatest achievements—"

She sat back, relaxing for the first time since she'd entered the room. "I've been told it was about where England was at the time of Napoleon."

"Seems about right," Sam agreed. "They had fair maps, good navigation, very good ships for all that they were wood-built and wind-powered. When the climate changed, some Antarcticans took to these sophisticated sailboats and escaped, to the place you call India. But a shipload was 'collected' by the Elders during one of their remote surveys." He paused, trying to think of how to phrase the next idea. "That happened fifteen millennia ago, long before the present civilization on Earth. But there are a few human beings still alive—in the Elders' universe—who personally remember it."

"*What?*" Rosalind sat up and stared at him.

"Eneri Relda, Eichra Oren's mother, for one, and sort of a living legend. She was a girl of seventeen or eighteen at the time, and still looks about that age."

Rosalind sat back again, shut her eyes, and marveled, "You're telling me that she's older than the sequoias, older than the bristlecones . . ."

"That's what I'm telling you. She's older than the pyramids, the tablets of Sumeria, and the legend of Gilgamish. She's three times as old as the entire length of recorded human history in your world—which, I suspect, says more about recorded human history than it does about Eneri Relda."

Rosalind was visibly stunned, but Sam knew she had the advantage of the best general scientific education her rather narrow and impoverished culture was capable of providing. He made some comment to that effect. Until now, she answered, she'd concentrated mostly on fields related to space travel—problems of freefall, acceleration, decompression, and radiation.

"Still, I have enough general biology to know there's no reason why the small handful of degenerative diseases we collectively refer to as 'aging' should forever remain incurable. Every one of them was arrested or slowed in lab animals in the twentieth century." She shrugged. "Having an imagination better than my education, I confess that I believe it, in part, simply because I want to."

"Exactly as Eichra Oren might have predicted." Sam sighed. Life, apparently, had never been so miserable for Rosalind Nguyen that she was unwilling to extend it. Maybe there was hope for these people, after all.

Rosalind blinked at him. "How's that?"

"I was just thinking out loud."

"Then so will I. Sam, I wonder what living a hundred and fifty centuries feels like. Does time continue to pass more quickly as you grow older? Do the decades seem to flee like weeks for someone fifteen thousand years old? Are the centuries beginning to seem like nothing more than years to Eneri Relda?"

"It isn't the kind of thing one asks, Rosalind. Maybe time reaches some sort of cruising speed and levels off, I don't know. I can tell you that Eneri Relda is unusual in another respect—it's why I brought her up in the first place. The average human living among the Elders has an indefinite theoretical lifespan. But in practical terms, that means a considerably shorter life expectancy than hers, although it hasn't anything to do with aging or disease, but with statistics."

"Oh?"

"Sure. People at home run the usual gamut from adventurers and athletes to what you call 'couch potatoes.' They have the technology to eradicate biological maladies. Even relatively serious injuries can be dealt with by nautiloid science. But sooner or later almost everyone among the Elders, including the Elders themselves, dies violently, simply because unpredictable catastrophes of one kind or another are the only thing left to die *from*."

Rosalind shuddered and wrapped her arms about herself. "What a prospect to look forward to. I wonder how they live with it."

"You should ask," Sam grinned, "whether the inevitable

prospect of violent death is too much to pay for prolonged life."

She blinked. "I find that easy to answer, Sam. If that's the price, it's cheap. How long could I expect to live, statistically?"

He reached up to scratch an ear. "A thousand years, give or take."

"A thousand years." She set her mouth. "And Eichra Oren?"

"I thought you'd never ask. He's a mere youngster, Rosalind. On his last birthday, as I recall, he was a mere five hundred and forty-two years old."

FORTY
The Predecessors

"Hang on, General! These things are supposed to compensate for gees, but—*whoops!*"

Toya slid against the tense form of Gutierrez as the electrostat they occupied banked suddenly to avoid one of the great canopy plants. The machine had no seatbelts—no seats at all, for that matter—no visible controls, and its smooth, sloping interior threatened to spill them out at any moment, dashing them against a tree or into the cratered ground at what the general estimated, between gasps, was 500 klicks per hour.

"That was *too damn close!*" Gutierrez squeezed his eyes shut and shuddered, suffering the pangs of an experienced combat pilot with someone else—in this instance, an invisible, electronic someone else—at the controls. What made it worse was that they didn't know where they were going. They'd been summoned by Eichra Oren only minutes ago, when the unpiloted and unannounced aerocraft had settled in the middle of camp and paged Toya through some sort of public address system. When she answered, the Antarctican had made a point of insisting that she bring Gutierrez along.

"Y-yes, sir!" Although she was unaware of it, Toya wasn't the first to observe that there was no end to the surprises 5023 Eris could hand them. She'd been shocked already by the discovery that Mister Thoggosh had left even Eichra Oren in the dark regarding his activities on the asteroid. She was convinced the Antarctican was being open with her about this ridiculous situation and had never been told the facts. It meant that the assignment Gutierrez and the KGB had given her was meaningless.

On the other hand, she didn't want to give up her newfound relationship and hoped perhaps she could get the answers her superiors demanded in another manner. Working together, with Sam's help, she and Eichra Oren had begun questioning other sapients, beings hired to accomplish parts of some goal which none of them, apparently, knew much about. The only reason they were here, aside from excellent pay and possible adventure, was a reputation Mister Thoggosh had earned for undertakings on a historic scale that nearly always turned out profitable. Like Eichra Oren, most had been left out by their employer. A few partners like Scutigera had been sworn to secrecy.

Eichra Oren reasoned, however, that each might possess a tiny piece of the puzzle, by virtue of various tasks and responsibilities he, she, or it had been assigned. He was determined to gather all of this "need-to-know" information and try to assemble it. So far, laborious questioning had only given the would-be detective a few leads—and probably a lot of disinformation.

"Look out!" Toya watched Gutierrez watching another giant tree whirl past at dizzying velocity and a stomach-wrenching angle. Before they'd quite gotten used to the little craft—this was the first such trip for the general and Toya's previous rides had been rather more sedate—it slowed to a hover, lowering them gently to the ground.

They found themselves in a steep-walled canyon choked with vegetation. At the bottom, a wide space had been cleared—the crisply singed tops of many larger plants hinted that something like a laser had been used—and promptly filled again with the same heavy equipment and bustling personnel Toya had seen at other drilling sites.

"Well, that was enough exhilaration for the next twenty

years or so." Gutierrez stood up and tested his legs, which seemed to be less wobbly than he'd expected. Sweat trickled from his hair, down the side of his neck, into his uniform collar. Even through the canopy, the sun seemed brighter, hotter, and the atmosphere noticeably thicker in the depths of the canyon. "Given that long—and a good enough supply of tranquilizers—I might even get used to it. Now that we're here, Sergeant, where do you suppose 'here' is?"

"No-Name Gulch, according to Sam, here," a familiar human voice behind them answered the general's rhetorical question. "Mister Thoggosh thinks it may be an impact fissure. Or his geologists do. It's the largest—and deepest—physical feature on 5023 Eris."

They turned. Eichra Oren and Sam were approaching the aerocraft, the former casually, with his hands in his pockets, the latter with bright eyes and his tongue hanging out. Toya and Gutierrez clambered through a section of the hull that melted out of the way.

"Somehow," the general replied, "I have a nagging suspicion that scientific sightseeing wasn't why you called us out here in such a hurry."

Eichra Oren grinned. "Well, General, in a way you could say it's scientific sightseeing. We came in almost as much haste as you did, summoned in almost the same way by Dlee Raftan Saon." The man hooked a thumb over his shoulder. "He's waiting for us now, at the field infirmary."

Together, the four walked toward the walled tent Toya had seen set up a day earlier, half a world away. This time there was no visible emergency. Inside, the insect physician was puttering with a bank of electronic-looking instruments arrayed atop a folding table. Hunched over his equipment, more than ever he reminded her of a praying mantis. Odd clumps of short, stiff bristles protruded from his joints, which were like those of a crab or lobster. Perhaps oddest of all, he wore a long white cotton four-armed laboratory jacket.

She recognized from her Aerospace Force basic training days the oddly pleasant and familiar smell of tautly stretched and sun-warmed canvas. The floor was canvas, too, lumpy and uneven underfoot. It seemed cooler and dimmer within the tent, although it brightened now and then as the doorflap blew open and shut in an impressive breeze funneling down the canyon.

"Here you are!" he exclaimed without looking up. "General, Sergeant, I thought you might be as interested to see this as our friends, here."

His head swiveled on his armored shoulders. He indicated Sam and Eichra Oren, then the electronics on the table before him. "What you see here, my friends, is a sort of instant antique I ordered constructed this morning, a little bit as if you, sir, were to ask your Corporal Owen to build you a crystal radio receiver. It's a giant analog to the cybernetic implants most of us wear snuggled against whatever we happen to use for brains, intended for use by people like yourselves who are bereft of cortical implants."

Toya could see that it looked sort of like a tabletop computer of the previous century, found in offices and homes, long since declared illegal. The computers aboard the shuttles looked entirely different. The thing plugged into a small, suitcase-sized box under the table constructed of some off-white plastic with smooth surfaces and rounded corners. The mythical tradename "Mr. Fusion" came to mind.

"It's so large and clumsy in part because, instead of addressing the language-forming areas of the brain as a proper implant does, it must perforce generate and interpret language for itself, before passing it on to us by rather primitive graphic means.

"You see," the physician told them, "I happened to be searching our records late last night for some technical clue that might prevent injuries like those I dealt with yesterday, when I made the adventitious discovery of an important fact about the Elders. I believe it has a bearing not only on our respective missions here but, I felt, on keeping the peace between us. So I summoned Eichra Oren and persuaded him that it must be shared with you."

"'Happened to be searching'?" Sam repeated cynically.

"'Happened to be searching.'" Dlee Raftan Saon nodded back toward the device, which immediately sprang to life. At least, Toya thought, it was implant-controlled. A series of brief messages translated into English began

scrolling across the monitor, sideways rather than
bottom-to-top. More than anything they resembled business and personal memos. In Soviet America, the age of
government tolerance toward private computer networks
and bulletin boards had ended long before she'd been born.
But the six-legged physician, it appeared, was far from
finished with his explanation.

"I was performing a key-concept search on the message
base, relative to these accidents we've been having, when
the system alerted me to the existence of a pattern I had
not anticipated." A faint, sweet scent, quite the opposite
of what she would have expected, exuded from his body.
"It's there, to be sure, but subtle and elusive, consisting
of tiny snippets, indirect references, asides in thousands
upon thousands of communications between Mister
Thoggosh, his fellow nautiloids, and certain beings such as
Scutigera."

"Doesn't this kind of snooping violate the privacy customs of your own people?" Gutierrez asked.

"Certainly not," came the reply, a bit stiffly. Huge iridescent eyes glittered and his mouth-parts worked nervously. "I was looking for purely technical conversations
among our people here. Everything I discovered was
'posted' publicly. The Elders simply aren't as discreet as
they may prefer to believe. They're also fully as unaware
of the revealing power of accumulated data as any human
who ever had his fortune 'read' for him by one of your
Gypsies."

"Well it serves the Elders right." Toya suppressed a
giggle. "They thought it was fine to intercept and
decode—"

"Accidentally decode," Eichra Oren corrected. "They
simply wrote their noise-elimination software too well."

"Whatever," Toya responded with sarcastic impatience.
"They were *our* transmissions to and from Earth, Eichra
Oren. *Private* transmissions. Mister Thoggosh brushed our
objections aside. I wonder how he'll feel about having the
same idea applied to him."

"Good question, Toya," the Antarctican told her. "I
remember other circumstances, other times, in which he'd
think it was funny."

"Yeah," Sam agreed, "but he hasn't been himself lately. I wish he'd get back to it, because nobody else wants the job." He leered and waggled his eyebrows.

"Sam, you've been watching old American movies again, haven't you?" Dlee Raftan Saon inquired. "Speaking of intercepting and decoding transmissions."

"Why," asked the dog, "are my Groucho-marks showing?"

"Ahem . . ." The surgeon turned to look again as messages continued scrolling. Toya noticed that a word here, a phrase there, were marked, set apart from the rest in different colors. "You see, my friends, for as long as anyone can remember, the Elders believed themselves the earliest species ever to have evolved sapience on any alternative version of Earth."

Sam had placed his front paws on the table-edge and was peering into the screen. He imitated the surgeon's voice. "Lately, however, they seem to have suffered an agonizing reappraisal of that opinion."

"Relatively so," Dlee Raftan Saon answered, unaware of the impersonation. "It's that plain? Dear me, I had to carry the process to the next step, myself." Another nod and the messages vanished, leaving only the marked portions, sorted out by color, which began to assemble themselves into a document of their own. "At any rate, now they seem to be searching desperately for some evidence of ancient sapient beings they call the 'Predecessors.' "

"It helps to carry a processing system around in your head, Dlee Raftan Saon." Sam looked up at Eichra Oren. "One of the reasons for all the secrecy is that the Elders appear to be humiliated."

"These Predecessors," Dlee Raftan Saon persisted, "were a species unknown even to the Elders. There is, on the other hand, plenty of evidence for their having existed. Their artifacts, misidentified by most archaeologists, seem to be lying about practically everywhere."

Toya interjected, "What do you mean, 'everywhere'?"

Although he was no taller than Toya, his long, bobbing antennae bent over her, almost touching the top of her head. "In each alternative universe the Elders discover, my dear, the Predecessors seem to have been there first."

Gutierrez chuckled to himself. "Kilroy was here."

"I've heard that before," the girl told him. "Corporal Owen said it when we discovered that the Elders were here ahead of us."

"Old joke." The general shook his head. "Later, Toya."

Dlee Raftan Saon raised a hairy manipulator. "In at least one reality—and there's reason to think it may have been more than one—they became Earth's predominating sapience long before nautiloids evolved. They rose to civilization, making every mistake any species makes, and like their 'Successors,' eventually discovered an infinity of worlds of parallel reality. Like their Successors, they learned the secret of interdimensional travel." That brought exclamations from everyone. "So far, they're the only others within the explored realm of probability to have achieved this impressive technical feat. It is that, of course, which makes our culture, the culture originally created by the Elders, so wealthy and diverse."

The doctor pointed to one series of message fragments written in blue-purple lettering. "The Predecessors seem to have taken another approach to multidimensional exploration, however. They never 'Appropriated' sapient inhabitants of other realities, for example."

"Ethics already. That has to be an item," Sam offered, "which galls our illustrious benefactors."

"Of course, there weren't as many other sapients then. Certain other differences exist, as well," Dlee Raftan Saon went on, "between the Elders and their unknown Predecessors, and their achievements. For one thing, the Predecessors enjoyed a lead of millions of years on their Successors.

"Which means they weren't as bright as the Elders?"

The physician ignored the dog. "For our culture, the culture of the Elders, interdimensional travel is still a risky, expensive, power-consuming undertaking, even after tens of thousands of years of research and practice."

"Which means the Elders aren't as bright as the Predecessors."

"Well, Sam," Dlee Raftan Saon acknowledged grudgingly, "it does seem to be a source of humiliation with regard to the Predecessors, who appear to have been adept at slipping from one continuum to another. They made easier, more frequent use of interdimensional travel than we are able to do so far. Before the end, it had become a casual, everyday mode of travel to them, like driving a car once was to you Americans. Naturally, they left tantalizing traces of their culture spread throughout many coextant Solar Systems."

Toya stepped toward the doctor. "And the end you mentioned?"

"My dear, despite their ubiquity, much time has passed and much has been destroyed by its passage. The Elders know little about the Predecessors, not even what they looked like. They have discovered one important fact—"

"They aren't around any more," Sam suggested.

"Apparently by their own choosing. Eons ago, if I read these messages correctly, the Predecessors departed the System en masse, for the stars."

Momentary silence was filled with the sounds, outside, of heavy machinery and vehicles, an undertone that may have come from the drilling, the shouting of workers in a dozen languages, the voices of a dozen species. Above it all, Toya heard the whispery sound of another aerocraft passing over the worksite.

"Oops," the dog observed.

"You put it well, Sam. This discovery, as you anticipate, came as quite a shock to the Elders. It is characteristic of their culture that such a thing as traveling between the stars never occurred to them, and I believe they've always been inclined to dismiss similar ideas in currency among Appropriated Persons as the petty aspirations of, well, superstitious primitives—although they're far too polite to put it that way, of course."

Sam agreed, "They didn't even bring any spaceships of their own to this rock!"

"Indeed," replied the insect. "This does not, I'd have you understand, represent a great failing on the part of the Elders. Humans have an interest in going to the stars which the Elders never developed. But you never—or at least very seldom—thought about traveling to other alternative universes."

"It's a matter," Toya decided out loud, "of a culturally shared mindset."

"What do you mean?" the general asked her.

"Well, sir, Europeans in the Age of Discovery thought mostly about trade, conquest, and religious conversion. Things like that never occurred to . . . well, to the classical Chinese at the height of their power. They impoverished themselves sending a vast fleet around the known world. But its sole purpose was to give gifts away to impress the local rulers with China's magnificence."

"In any event," continued Dlee Raftan Saon, "upon departing the Solar System, the Predecessors seem to have deliberately left behind the secret of their faster-than-light 'Virtual Drive.' "

"It is meant," declared a voice they all recognized, "as the inheritance of whatever Successor species eventually finds it."

Five beings turned as one to face the tent door. Through it slithered a glistening four-meter snake which spoke with the voice of Mister Thoggosh.

FORTY-ONE
A Certain Uncertainty

"I see I've made what I fondly hope is an uncharacteristic error," the snake told them.

It was a separable "messenger" tentacle, outfitted for an excursion on land with a transparent plastic covering. Like a snake, it arranged one end in a supporting coil, raising the remainder of its length to human eye level. Unlike a snake, it tapered from that base, as thick as Toya's upper leg, to a finger-slender tip. She could see the dark patch of a thin-film transducer that was the electronic source of Mister Thoggosh's voice.

Toya knew that originally a limb like this had evolved in nautiloids, as it had in other cephalopods, as a specialized auxiliary sexual organ that detached itself from the owner's body to carry sperm to the female. In the Elders (who, like human beings, had changed their reproductive habits about the same time they'd developed sapience) it had become a sort of built-in "gofer," controlled by the same radio waves the nautiloids generated for speech. It was the organ to which symbionts like Sam had been intended as an analog.

"So much," Mister Thoggosh continued, "for the well-laid plans of molluscs and men. I fear 'gang aft aglay' doesn't express the half of it. Preoccupied with what I foolishly believed my own safe secrets, I failed to perceive the figurative hot breath of two detectives on my even more figurative neck."

Sam looked to Toya. Toya looked to Sam. Both wondered which had been left out of the Proprietor's calculations.

"Three detectives, sir," Eichra Oren offered, turning a palm up. "You simply made a mistake nonscientists often do, of thinking of scientific facts as if they were some arcane ritual knowledge. You, more than anyone, should know that trade and defense secrets derived from objective reality never last very long."

Gutierrez grinned and shook his head, but kept comment to himself.

"Indeed. Good afternoon, Dlee Raftan Saon, General Gutierrez." The tentacle slithered closer to the little group around the table. "Toya, Eichra Oren, Sam, my congratulations to all three of you, then. Although I am scarcely to be blamed for such a mistake as you suggest if, in truth, I made it. Nautiloid physics and metaphysics have long been rooted in concepts which are often rather mystical sounding to other sapients."

The breeze blew the doorflap open and shut again, momentarily dazzling the eye. From somewhere outside, they heard the screech of protesting machinery, followed by the shouting of workers. It wasn't the first time they'd heard it, nor would it be the last.

"You're referring," the physician stretched three hands to the tabletop and switched his antique machinery off, "to the 'Twelve Elementals'?"

The tentacle-tip bobbed affirmation. "That I am, Raftan, although in point of fact, that magnificently breathtaking concept lies about as far from the realm of mysticism as it can and still relate to its primary context, the field of natural philosophy which our human guests call cosmology."

More mechanical and vocal noise filtered in from outside. Toya wondered if they were having another of the failures which had plagued Mister Thoggosh on this asteroid. Without being asked, Eichra Oren went to the back of the tent and began unstacking several folding objects of tubular metal and fabric which could be adjusted to support any one of a number of species. As soon as Gutierrez saw what he was doing, he went back to help.

"Refresh my memory on cosmology," the general asked over his shoulder, "if you don't mind."

The end of the appendage, bent over at an angle, pointed at him. "Gladly, sir. It's that field of intellectual inquiry concerned with the fundamental nature, especially the origin, of the universe. More than any other, it straddles the fence your people have mistakenly erected between the scientific discipline of physics and the philosophical discipline of metaphysics."

"We humans can't do anything right." Gutierrez placed two folding chairs near the table. To match his sarcastic tone there was a skeptical look on his face. "You think there's really something to all that nonsense about reincarnation, extrasensory perception, spirit mediums, and crystal gazing?"

The tentacle conveyed a shudder. "Dear me, I'd forgotten quite how badly contaminated certain words have become on your world. Metaphysics, my dear fellow, is an ancient and honored discipline rather like cosmology, except that it asks, and tries to answer, questions about the fundamental nature of reality."

"'Reality,'" Gutierrez sat beside Toya, "as opposed to 'the universe'?"

From Eichra Oren, Dlee Raftan Saon accepted a chair, folded in a different pattern to accommodate his insectile anatomy. He fished in a pocket of his lab coat and extracted an ordinary-looking briar pipe, stuffed it with what appeared to be tobacco, lit it, and puffed. Apparently, Toya thought, his species had outgrown spiracles. Aromatic smoke filled the tent. "The difference, General, is subtle, but significant."

Gutierrez grinned and pulled a pack of smuggled cigarettes from his own breast pocket. Giving it a characteristically American toss, he offered one to Eichra Oren, who raised a palm and shook his head politely. The Antarctican was sitting in a chair of his own, Sam on the floor at his knee as if he were an ordinary dog. Lighting his cigarette, the general said, "I'll take your word for it."

"Very well," declared the tentacle, settling itself lower on a second coil, "I suppose the place to begin, the first thing you should understand, is that the shrewdest among our philosophers who concern themselves with the origin and nature of the universe are presently in my employ. You might say I've recently taken a sort of 'crash course' in the subject myself, although I'm still attempting to absorb the more slippery concepts involved. In any event, according to them, the universe possesses only six *known* fundamental forces."

"Is this anything human physics knows about?" Gutierrez inhaled smoke.

The surrogate gave the general another nod. "Three are known as the 'Outer Forces,' familiar to you as gravity, magnetism, and electricity. Three more are the 'Inner Forces': the strong nuclear force, the weak nuclear force, and what is still to humanity a 'hidden' nuclear force often, and erroneously, referred to as the 'fifth' force."

Gutierrez exhaled. "Why erroneously?"

"The name, General, overlooks the epochal work of your own Michael Faraday, or at least its cosmological significance. For you, the existence of this force has been inferred from other data. For us, it is an essential part of the machinery that brought us here. Together the two sets of forces, Inner and Outer, balance one another, creating a harmonious whole which your theorists would call symmetrical or 'beautiful'. . . ."

"Beauty," Dlee Raftan Saon added, making clicking noises with his mouth parts which Toya knew signified amusement, "being in the optical receptor of the beholder." The insect-being drew on his pipe and exhaled a smoke-ring, making Toya think of the hookah-smoking caterpillar in *Alice in Wonderland*.

"Indeed," responded Mister Thoggosh with a trace of annoyance. "Likewise, General, the universe has long been known to possess six dimensions. Three are the familiar dimensions of space: breadth, depth, and height. Three are dimensions of time, the first and most familiar of which we call 'duration.' The second is 'probability,' along which we all traveled—all of us except your party—to arrive on this asteroid."

"And the third?" Toya startled herself by blurting the question. Embarrassed, she sank back in her chair, determined not to interrupt again. Beside her, Eichra Oren gave her hand a reassuring touch.

The snakelike object standing in for Mister Thoggosh was unperturbed. "The third, Toya, remains unknown, even to us. It is the 'hidden' dimension of time. Nobody knows quite what this last mysterious dimension might consist of, even (I might say 'especially') our philosophers, although they're certain it is something already quite familiar which everyone has overlooked."

"I'm not sure I understand, sir," Toya admitted, unable to help herself.

"Well, reconsider the second dimension of time. Didn't your people wager with one another long before Monsieur Pascal formally discovered the laws of probability? I assure you that they did in my version of reality."

"Mine, as well." The surgeon nodded, knocking his pipe out in an oddly shaped bowl he and Gutierrez had been sharing as an ashtray. Toya was sure it was some sort of bedpan. "In fact I'll wager that our guests would enjoy a bit of refreshment, perhaps even lunch. Is anyone else as hungry as I am?"

For a few minutes, the dissertation on metaphysics and cosmology was interrupted as their orders were relayed to the camp caterer via implant. The general put his cigarette out and asked for a cheeseburger, knowing it was a dish the nautiloids had recently discovered. Toya asked the physician to make it two. Sam and Eichra Oren sent their own requests. Whatever energy it drew from Mister Thoggosh's body, the appendage was incapable of refueling itself and continued lecturing while they waited for lunch.

"These two pairs of three forces and three dimensions comprise the twelve presumed 'Elementals.' Just as we have found the hidden nuclear force—as your scientists have not yet—we all fondly hope to find the hidden dimension of time on 5023 Eris. It is believed by some, having done that, that we may discover yet another set of six—or even twelve—'hidden' Elementals."

Before anyone could ask him to explain, the meal arrived

in insulated boxes carried by trainable insectile nonsapients. Except for the number of limbs, they bore little resemblance to the highly sapient Dlee Raftan Saon. Food was distributed as Mister Thoggosh went on.

"Which it will be—six, twelve, or none—is the subject of the most sanguine debate since those culminating in the Great Restitution. Careers are made, unmade, and remade every day depending on who's currently winning. Lifelong friends are known to stop speaking for centuries. It doesn't seem to matter that, so far, there are no hard facts to base an opinion on."

"Just like academics back home," Gutierrez observed around a bite of burger. Like Toya, he held the plastic container on his lap. The sandwich had come with lettuce, tomato, onion, and a pickle. Nor were French fries forgotten. A tall glass of lemonade stood beside his elbow on the computer table.

"Regrettably so. I even know of a duel fought over the subject."

"Now *there's* an idea for establishing priority!" Gutierrez laughed. Toya was unsure what he found so funny. "What do you think it is, six or twelve?"

"I've no idea whatever, General. However it turns out, these new Elementals are likely to be arrayed in either two or four subsets of three Elementals each, bringing the universe into full symmetry. These extra Elementals, like the hidden time dimension, can possibly be inferred from the workings of the Predecessors' Virtual Drive, our understanding and operation of which, it seems, depends on accepting an even more bizarre idea."

He waited for some reaction. Eichra Oren's attention seemed to be on his food, some unrecognizable but vaguely Chinese-looking dish. Sam was eating the same sort of thing from a container on the floor. Toya's hamburger was better than anything she'd ever had back home. She couldn't bring herself to examine too closely whatever Dlee Raftan Saon was sucking through the tube he'd inserted in one side of his food container. She was certain that all three were in fact focused intently on the nautiloid's words.

"Mass, as such, my associates inform me, doesn't really exist. Unlike the question of how many Elementals there are, nobody in the philosophical community seems to disagree with this idea, which, I confess, seems ridiculous to me. Subatomic particles, they say, are merely probabilistic ripples on the matrix of space-time. This includes, of course, those particles comprising sapient beings who wish to travel from place to place."

Sam looked up from his plate. "How's that?" It was the first time Toya had seen him eating and she understood now why he was shy about it. Lacking hands, he was reduced by the process to the animal nature he'd otherwise transcended.

The tentacle leaned over to address the dog. "As I understand it, Oasam, quantum physics holds that these particles are no more statistically likely to do their rippling in any one place than in any other. However intelligent and curious one may be, the concept almost makes one's brain ache."

"In other words," the dog offered, "if some particle can exist 'here'—"

"By which I take it you mean the traveler's presumed point of departure . . ."

"Right—then why not over 'there'?" Sam lowered his head to lap some liquid from a compartment of his plate.

"His intended destination?" The tentacle assumed a twisted posture, then relaxed. "According to physics, the two phenomena amount to the same thing. In theory, getting 'there' should be no greater a problem than simply staying 'here.' And after all, people and other objects seem to do the latter on a regular basis without difficulty, don't they?"

"Zen teleportation." Eichra Oren spoke for the first time in a while. "What you're saying, sir, is that the Predecessors traveled from one place to another more or less simply by changing the way they looked at things."

"And a pinch of pixie dust," Sam suggested.

Mister Thoggosh's answer began with a long pause. "One of the difficulties I find with this concept, gentlebeings, and I assure you that I find many, is that it sounds suspiciously like a free lunch. Over the course of a long career and an even longer lifetime, I've learned to distrust such propositions."

"Still, if it were true," Dlee Raftan Saon mused, "it would be a wonderful thing, brimming with possibilities."

"Indeed it would, Raftan. The concept, you see, doesn't involve real acceleration or its concomitant, uncomfortable, and rather inconvenient inertial and relativistic effects. It seems to be a matter of avoiding the speed of light, rather than exceeding it."

"Better yet," Sam suggested, "from a businessman's point of view, the process consumes no fuel."

"That thought had occurred to me, yes," replied the mollusc. "These would all seem to be costs of complying with what now look like merely local laws of physics. However, theory to one side for the time being, and from a strictly practical standpoint, things haven't been going smoothly for our enterprise here, which is why I've decided to tell you all the full truth and enlist your aid."

"About damned time!" Sam exclaimed, then looked up sheepishly at Eichra Oren. "Sorry, Boss."

"Don't be, Sam. I was about to say the same thing myself."

FORTY-TWO
Hope of Redemption

"*Geronimo, John Galt*, this is *Laika*. Check your throttles again. My line feels slack, regardless of what the tension readouts tell me. Over."

Horatio Gutierrez, former Aerospace Force Brigadier General, officer in charge of the American Soviet Socialist Republic's expedition to the asteroid 5023 Eris, still captain of the twice-refitted and renamed space shuttle once known as the *Honorable Robert Dole*, peered out the left seat window at two other spacecraft, identical to his own, where they strained under their respective loads against a star-flecked background of blackest velvet. He'd never have believed it possible two weeks ago, but it felt good to be in space again, even if it meant resuming command of the small fleet of "Polish bombers" which in so many ways were the exact opposite of the sleek American Soviet interceptors he'd spent most of his life flying.

"*Geronimo, here*, Laika. *We copy*." The voice of Major Jesus Ortiz, captain of the former *Honorable Orrin Hatch*, issued from a speaker overhead. "*This goofball of ours claims we're three hundredths of one percent over-throttled. I repeat, zero point zero three. I'm attempting to correct now. Over.*"

"John Galt *to* Laika," added Lieutenant Colonel Juan Sebastiano, captain of the former *Honorable John McCain.* "*Our goofball's telling the same story. I'm not sure our control's that fine, but we'll give it a try. Over.*"

The "feel" Gutierrez had referred to was more a matter of how the modified engines sounded to him than of any tension reading or velocity indication. He was too preoccupied even to spare a glance at the computer, one of three onboard which struck him now as primitive.

Projecting from it, the alien interface Mister Thoggosh had supplied (the same casual way his chemists had cooked up the needed fuel) looked like a head-sized gray-green fungus. It had been created to help *Laika* and her sisters complete a mission which, like the expedition itself, they'd never been designed for. Hooked into the nautiloid cybernet, the "goofball," as his crew was calling it, performed calculations necessary to insert a miniature moon into orbit around the miniature planet. His own goofball told him, through a telltale on the already-crowded control board, that his adjustments were perfect.

Gutierrez didn't trust it.

Trailing on impossibly slender cables ten kilometers behind the craft (although in another sense they were trailing it as it preceded them in orbit) was a mountain of silica which would have been a kilometer in diameter had it been remotely spherical. To Gutierrez it resembled nothing in particular, "potato-shaped" in much the same way that every kind of unfamiliar meat is said to "taste like chicken." It was about twice as long as it was thick, and peppered with tiny impact craters. One curving surface was almost smooth except for a large elongated astrobleme (he'd thought craters weren't supposed to form like that) which was the most remarkable feature of the unremarkable rock. What was important was that it was the correct mass and composition. They'd found it, as Aelbraugh Pritsch had suggested they would, within a thousand kilometers, the average distance between asteroids in this region of the Belt.

Had it only been a week since Mister Thoggosh had confessed, during that remarkable conversation in Dlee Raftan Saon's tent, how weary he was of equipment failures and other technical problems associated with a ground-search for the Predecessor artifacts he was looking for? Looking back, it seemed much longer. What he wanted to do, he'd told the general, was place a smaller asteroid in a polar orbit around 5023 Eris. He'd reassured Gutierrez that, given the technology available to the Elders, such an undertaking was by no means impossible. There was no lack of small rocks circling the sun in this orbit and many were within easy reach of the nautiloid establishment.

"In aid of what, I suspect you are about ask," the appendage had responded to the general's upraised eyebrows. "Quite simply, I plan to establish an unbeinged base on our semi-artificial moonlet. At that range, it can be directed quite as efficiently as one of our aerostats."

Gutierrez had grimaced, then laughed. He'd ridden here aboard one of the machines Mister Thoggosh was talking about. So had the tentacle, for that matter. Both bagel-shapes were parked just outside the door. Gutierrez had long since gathered that, had some calamity happened to the appendage, the mollusc could grow another, however long it took or painful it might be. He'd have a much tougher time growing himself a new Horatio, he thought with a morbid grin.

"It's the next step, General, no more impossible than the rest, I assure you, which takes one's intellectual breath away. We have in our possession certain instruments, new even to our science, which collect and interpret the galaxy's natural background neutrino-flux. They were imposed upon me at the outset of our expedition by certain individuals with a greater and more detachedly scientific interest in this affair than my own. They believe that each alternative universe has its own unique neutrino pattern. Now I'm rather grateful they were so adamant."

Gutierrez had listened as Mister Thoggosh explained to Dlee Raftan Saon (whose specialization lay in areas other than physics), that neutrinos were subatomic particles so small and swift they could pass through anything, including an entire planet, almost as if it weren't there. During the course of this explanation it had developed that the word "almost" (statistically a few neutrinos would be stopped or slowed by denser objects they attempted to pass through) was critical to the scheme.

"As these elusive particles pass, or fail to pass, through the world we occupy, which possesses roughly the same surface area as the region of your world known as 'Texas,' these captured neutrinos will create, in effect, a spiraling X-ray or CAT-scan of the entire globe. This three-dimensional pattern of relative transmission and absorption will be detected on our little moon and relayed to our imaging and translating computers." The latter were devices which had "accidentally" broken Earth's most sophisticated military codes, having mistaken them for naturally occurring interference. "Since neutrinos are very small themselves," Mister Thoggosh had concluded, "resolution should be excellent."

"Giving us a peek," Dlee Raftan Saon suggested, "at what's inside."

"Precisely." Bent at the tip, the tentacle had given the impression it was turning to look at each of them. "I cannot bring myself to believe that the Predecessors, having taken care to leave so many tantalizing clues behind, would have made the task of recovering their technological legacy as difficult as it's seemed. Such a scan should reveal any great masses beneath the surface, including the object of our search, and possibly a method of getting to it. I can stop wasting my time, my investors' money, and the colony's dwindling supply of equipment on all this confounded blind drilling."

At this point the surrogate had turned to Gutierrez. "I believe this plan to be effective, General, but it's hindered by a lack of spacecraft to move the requisite small asteroid. I confess it was not a necessity I anticipated when I planned this expedition a century ago."

Gutierrez had nodded. "I assume you can't just send for a spaceship."

"Well, sir," Mister Thoggosh replied, "I've always been reluctant to employ, without the direst necessity, the expensive and somewhat unreliable facilities for interdimensional transport we have at our disposal. In this instance, both the difficulty and the expense increase as a function of the fifth power of the longest dimension of whatever's being sent."

"So it's especially dangerous to bring something as large as a ship?"

"And expensive." Even through a voice transducer, irony was audible in the nautiloid's chuckle. "What made the task appear absolutely insurmountable, however, was the utter impossibility I anticipated of accomplishing what I believe necessary under your watchful eye, sir. Thinking of you Americans, however, gave me an idea. You have the spacecraft, even if—I, er, that is . . ."

"Even if they're primitive by standards you're used to?"

Again the chuckle. "You've said it, sir, so I shan't have to. Might it be possible, I thought, given appropriate consideration, to borrow one or two of your craft and the crewbeings necessary to operate them?"

The general had laughed. "It wouldn't be unprecedented. It would be like people from our civilization borrowing a canoe from Pacific natives to recover the nose cone of a downed satellite. But you couldn't do it, could you, without giving the purpose of the search away?"

The transducer had transmitted the sound of a deep sigh which Gutierrez knew to be an affectation. The marine mollusc, a relative to the squid and octopus, breathed silently through gills. "I confess, Horatio, had I been human I'd have shaken my head with the futility of it all. The canoe analogy occurred to me. It appeared to have ominous implications. If I recall correctly, primitives who use them are likely to be headhunters or cannibals."

It was the first time Mister Thoggosh had called him by his given name and it felt friendly even if it was a sales pitch. Gutierrez had been about to reply that he'd never cared for calamari, but wasn't sure how it would be taken.

"From the long, terrible experience of my own people," Mister Thoggosh had continued, "I knew that there's more than one kind of cannibalism. Sapients are as easily consumed by taxation or conscription as in a black iron stew pot. I shuddered—indeed I still shudder—to think of the immoral and insapient uses your governments might make of the Predecessors' impressive technology."

"Yet datum by datum," Eichra Oren had interrupted, "you realized you were inevitably losing the hopeless struggle to maintain secrecy."

Sam had added, "You weren't surprised at all by our uncovering your secrets, were you, you old fake?"

"Only by how quickly it was done. No need to be so harsh, Otusam, put yourself in my place. I was aware that, with your help, against my explicit wishes, Eichra Oren was continuing his investigation." The appendage had swiveled back to the general. "The stubborn fellow defined learning my secrets as a necessary part of the task I'd assigned him. I was forced to concede, to myself, that he'd a measure of logic and justice on his side."

"Logic and justice," Eichra Oren observed, "are the same thing."

"Well," Mister Thoggosh had gone on, "there wasn't much I could do short of firing him. Not only would that involve me in the difficulty and expense of shipping him home, but his mother, an old and esteemed friend, would likely never speak to me again." Mister Thoggosh had sighed once more. "On the other appendage, whatever Eichra Oren discovered, an observant and rather *frightened* Sergeant Pulaski would soon learn, as well."

Sitting up suddenly, Toya had opened her mouth in reflexive denial. Mister Thoggosh had ignored her.

"She, I knew, reports directly to you, Horatio. This saves a shy and nervous little female the emotional strain of dealing with less sympathetic superiors. You, sir, report to the American KGB's own Mr. Empleado. He, in turn, reports to the mysterious secret Russian agent, 'Iron Butterfly.'"

This time Gutierrez had laughed and slapped a knee, shaking his head in surprised amusement. "I only regret that Art isn't around to hear that!"

"But he is," Mister Thoggosh had corrected, "just outside, at the back of the tent. What *he* doesn't know is that Iron Butterfly is watching him through binoculars from the rim of the gulch. No matter: the time lag represented by this layered method of communication was less than a couple of your hours. Left to itself, a quiet but rather desperate race would soon develop between our two groups, human and nautiloid. Despite any superficial cordiality we somehow managed to maintain between ourselves, it would be an all-out struggle. Who would find, understand, and employ the Predecessors' Virtual Drive first? And it was this string of expectations which made my mind up."

Ignoring an almost irresistible urge to run out and

drag both damnable secret operatives from the bushes—
he wondered who they'd hitched a ride with—Gutierrez
had fished in a coverall pocket for his cigarettes, pulled
one out and lit it. "A while back you said 'given appropriate consideration.' Did you have anything specific in
mind?"

It was Mister Thoggosh's turn for a thoughtful pause,
although he lacked the excuse afforded by a cigarette.
"Well, sir, as you know, we're reluctant to deal with your
governments—let's make that 'unwilling'—whatever the cost.
Nevertheless, each of our groups has motivations of its own,
rather I should say that each of us as individuals does, and
sometimes they're shared by others in the group—consistent
with our own peculiar necessities."

Gutierrez had looked at the messenger shrewdly. "And?"

"And those referred to as 'the Elders,' including myself,
feel a degree of humiliation by what we now see as our
lack of imagination and progress."

The general had leaned forward. "I'm not sure I follow you."

"You will, Horatio. I'm being as open with you as I know
how to be. True, we independently inferred the existence
of alternative realities. Using this esoteric knowledge, we
invented (or with reference to our Predecessors, I should
say unknowingly *re*invented) interdimensional travel."

"Okay so far." Gutierrez had grinned, struck with the
necessity of reassuring an ancient and accomplished being
who suddenly seemed hesitant and doubtful. "Watch it on
the corners, though."

"I shall. We even have a healthy interplanetary commerce
in our version of the System, mostly carried out, I'm chagrined to confess, by Appropriated Persons. For millions
of years we've had astronomers and are well aware of the
size, shape, and composition of the galaxy around us. Yet
it never occurred to us to physically explore interstellar
space."

Gutierrez had asked Toya, "The cultural viewpoint thing,
right?"

The girl had nodded back, shyly.

"We fervently hope," Mister Thoggosh had told them,
"to redeem ourselves by following in the Predecessors'

wake. I feel I can trust you to help us, because I believe I know what you want."

"And what," Gutierrez had asked him, "is that?"

"With what you learn here, you exiled Americans simply hope to buy yourselves a ticket home."

FORTY-THREE
Fear of Confrontation

Aimlessly, Mister Thoggosh wandered through the garden of tactile sculpture he maintained in the forefront of his office, letting his tentacles trail across each piece without feeling the contours beneath them.

Filled with a quantity of metabolic carbon dioxide, the great color-striped shell which housed his body hovered a meter above the sandy floor. A less ponderous being than he appeared, he had always been lighter on his metaphorical feet than he let the Americans realize. Now he wondered if he should drop that pose for the benefit of his next visitors.

The truth, he thought bitterly, doesn't always set you free. He'd realized, following the conference in Dlee Raftan Saon's tent, that he'd soon find himself with an angry moral debt assessor on his metaphorical hands. He'd decided that when it happened, it would be his own fault, a price he had to pay to attain his ultimate objective. That it had taken Eichra Oren a week to make this appointment—ostensibly because he must help his fellow humans rearrange their camp so the shuttles could be used to capture a moon—only served as a measure of the man's annoyance.

Eichra Oren had every right to be annoyed. Security restrictions on the scale that Mister Thoggosh had initially imposed here were unheard of in the world of the nautiloids and their many associates. They'd long since proven more expensive (economically and in a sense that went beyond economic consideration, crossing into personal dignity and liberty) than anything preserved by them. Having imposed them nonetheless, he couldn't, in all justice, blame Eichra Oren for resenting their sudden and complete abandonment.

His implant chirped a message from Aelbraugh Pritsch. His guests had been processed through the air lock—they had filled their respiratory systems with the same oxygenated fluorocarbon liquid he swam in—and were waiting outside his office. Sending an assent, he pivoted in midfluid, intending to return to the area that served him as a desk, then thought better of it and decided to break all precedent by greeting them at the door.

It wasn't the only broken precedent. When the pressure-panel slid aside, in addition to Eichra Oren, he saw Sam (whose furry coat usually made him hate plunging himself into the liquid that filled Mister Thoggosh's quarters) and Toya Pulaski. At his invitation they preceded him toward the back of the office and sat in chairs—all but Sam—which lowered themselves from the ceiling while he arranged himself behind his "desk."

Behind him, against a starry background incongruous in the depths of his live-in aquarium, a wall-display set up for the benefit of his Soviet American visitors showed the progress of the mission in space from the vantage of Gutierrez's flagship, the *Laika*.

"It's good to see you here, my—"

"Skip the amenities, Mister Thoggosh," Eichra Oren declared. "I came to hand in our resignations, mine and Sam's. We might work for an employer who lies to us. 'Truth is a valuable commodity you don't automatically owe to everyone.' But we won't work—I won't work—for someone who gives us a job and then undoes it himself without any warning."

"Me neither," Sam added.

"I see," replied the nautiloid. "What will you do instead?"

The Antarctican frowned. "We'd go home, but I understand your reluctance to use the interdimensional transporter too casually. My quarters are on your land and grew
from a seed you provided. I suppose, until enough good
reasons accumulate to use the transporter, I'll vacate them
and throw in with Toya's people. Don't worry, it isn't your
obligation any more."

Mister Thoggosh lifted tentacles in a sinuous shrug. "I
believe you're mistaken. I promised I'd compensate you
whether you worked or not, until I get you back to our
continuum. Your quarters are a part of that compensation.
I'll keep the rest of my promise if you'll permit me."

Eichra Oren opened his mouth to protest. Mister
Thoggosh hurried on before he could utter a word. "I'd
like to ask you a procedural question, however. You feel
you have a grievance against me. I'll concede it for the sake
of discussion. If I wished to make appropriate restitution,
Eichra Oren, how would I go about it, since you're the only
debt assessor on the asteroid?"

"Watch it," Sam warned, "he's soaping it up to stick it
to you!"

The man leaned back and put a hand under his chin,
"You could wait until this is over and we can settle the debt
back home."

Not for the first time, Mister Thoggosh wished he
could shake his head. "If we succeed here, I may not
return. Besides, the Americans have a saying: 'Justice
delayed is justice denied.' You'll acknowledge that this
applies to a moral debtor who wishes to rebalance the
scales as much as to any creditor?"

"For the sake of discussion. What do you suggest?"

"That, in absence of another debt assessor, I rely on your
faculties in an attempt to explain my actions. Possibly you'll
feel afterward that I don't owe you a debt. If not, I'll accept
any judgment you care to levy."

Eichra Oren raised his eyebrows, "Any judgment?"

"Did I speak too softly? *Any judgment!* I'll abandon this
project and take everyone home if you insist. I'll have
myself sliced up, breaded, and deep-fried, just the way the
Americans like it. You have my solemn word of honor."

Eichra Oren was visibly taken aback. "I'll listen."

Mister Thoggosh laid one tentacle over another and began to relax for the first time in days. "Very well, you heard something of my concerns last week when I spoke with General Gutierrez about borrowing his spacecraft. Primarily I feared that a human government might get hold of Predecessor technology. That, you can appreciate, is something to be very much afraid of."

"*Mister* Gutierrez," Sam corrected. "His commission expired when he agreed to help you. The reason his people didn't replace him, or have him sliced up, breaded, and deep-fried, is that they're all as fed up with their government, most of them anyway, as he is, and agreed with him it was a good idea."

The nautiloid suppressed annoyance. "I was under an impression that military rank would be retained as an aid to efficient operation. But I was explaining myself." He turned to the Antarctican. "When I gave you your assignment, I did not wish to burden a valuable employee with my deepest fears. I worried that it might affect your, er, spontaneity, interfere with your all-important attempt to get to know the other humans on this asteroid better. Especially," he gave Toya what he hoped was a look of appreciation, "the increasingly knowledgeable and dangerous Sergeant Pulaski."

"That much," the man responded guardedly, "I understand."

"Also, there was the embarrassing matter of what I felt— still feel—are the historic failures of my own species. Perhaps I fell short of candor, but I wasn't anxious for others to know just how dull-witted the 'Elders' have been."

With what the humans might have called a sinking circulatory organ, the nautiloid suddenly realized that everything he was saying sounded perfectly idiotic. He hoped Eichra Oren would see through that to the real message he wanted to convey. He allowed the empty spaces in his shell to fill with air, gradually rising until he floated a few inches above the floor. To his right, at a signal from his implant, the door to his personal quarters slid aside.

"But come—I've something that should be of particular interest to the sergeant. We can continue our conversation under pleasanter auspices."

He encouraged them to follow him through the door and, with an enthusiasm he knew was transparently proprietary, welcomed them into his apartment. He'd adjusted the light to suit them. To him, descended from deep-sea creatures as he was, his familiar quarters were filled with glare, as if they were arc-lit, and his pupils had shrunk to fine vertical lines barely visible, he suspected, to the others. There was little any human being would have recognized as furniture. In one corner stood a high-sided bed of carefully cleaned and sifted sand where he slept. On a sort of night table he'd set his favorite piece of tactile sculpture. It bore no visual resemblance to anything real (this being an important part of the artistic effort), but was immediately recognizable to nautiloid tentacles as a particularly seductive female of his own species.

"I've brought you to see my collection of Predecessor artifacts."

Scattered about were the more mundane objects Mister Thoggosh had everyday use for, books in different media, writing implements of various kinds, portraits of his friends and relatives, personal weapons. Instruments for cleaning and grooming himself sat on a shelf below what humans might have recognized as a mirror, had they been capable of seeing in the same spectrum of frequencies nautiloids used. Even to Eichra Oren, who knew what it was, it looked like a dully polished sheet of metal. Their host invited them to sit on the floor, deeply covered with yet another grade of soft, fine sand.

"One reason," he continued as before, "I kept my search a secret for so long was out of simple consideration for others. The last thing I wanted was to get everyone unduly excited about the possibilities here."

Sam yawned pointedly and settled to the floor, "Gimme a break."

Mister Thoggosh ignored him. "It wasn't just a matter of the gamble I had persuaded Scutigera, Semlohcolresh, and the others to take with me. They were highly sophisticated investors, well aware of the risks involved in any such undertaking. It was a much more intangible matter of the morale of an entire civilization—I needn't add that

the self-esteem of the nautiloid species is involved, as well."
He lifted a tentacle. "Just look at the objects in this display case and you'll see what I mean."

"Excuse me, Mister Thoggosh," Toya asked, "but what
display case?"

He laid a tentacle on what Eichra Oren had taken for
another mirror. "What's transparent to one eye may not be
to another." He opened the panel and removed a couple
of small objects which he passed to the humans.

Eichra Oren nodded without comment as he accepted
one of the objects and Toya examined another. Everything
Mister Thoggosh handed them appeared delicate. Each
appeared to have been formed randomly of some ceramic
substance, yet, at the same time, seemed made for some
specific purpose.

"That's a common sort we find everywhere on various
versions of Earth, although this one's from here. A kind
of wrench, I think," Mister Thoggosh told Toya. "The irreg-
ular taper within the crescent fits a knob seen on larger
artifacts. We've never been able to turn those, with our
own tools or even with tools like this, but such devices
applied to simulations turn them without effort, as if there
were a motor inside. I think it's a sort of lever to convert
whatever force you apply to rotary motion. It's all of a piece
and contains no separate or moving parts. It also makes
musical noises when subjected to anything over six tonnes
of torque."

"Six tonnes?" Seated on the floor with her legs crossed,
Toya looked up at the Elder. "But it seems so fragile."

"Do anything you wish, my dear. Such remnants prove,
under all but the most strenuous tests known to mechanics, completely indestructible."

Eichra Oren held his own object up, a disk four centimeters in diameter, transparent to the human eye—he
wondered whether Mister Thoggosh knew that—with extensions of the same material, shaped a bit like antennae. It
looked as if it were made of lace—glass lace—two millimeters thick, yet he couldn't bend it, let alone break it.
Deep within its illusionary center, there appeared to be
vague movement and light.

"We don't know what that is," confided Mister Thoggosh,

"except that it must be locked away. It interferes with certain radio frequencies and some chemical reactions refuse to occur in its presence. You'll appreciate that I don't look forward to sifting the soil of 5023 Eris a cubic meter at a time for any more such. Yet if we hadn't solved the drilling problem, that's exactly what we'd have had to do."

Drifting over the bed, Mister Thoggosh settled himself. "There are other objects in the cabinet if you care, but they're all trivial so far. What might yet be discovered is without precedent in the history of known civilization. Only the exploration of alternate worlds fails to pale by comparison. Had I disappointed everyone, I might have incurred a moral debt to them. I wasn't certain anyone knows how to pay such a unique debt, or that even a *p'Nan* debt assessor would be able to figure it out."

Having grown up in the same culture as Mister Thoggosh, Eichra Oren shared his ethical values, along with the uncertainties they sometimes produced. For that and other reasons he was beginning to see some sense in Mister Thoggosh's explanation. Such an attitude was easier to assume, of course, now that he knew his employer's secret anyway.

"We've known each other a long time," the mollusc told him. "All of your relatively short life, in fact. I've known your esteemed mother, Eneri Relda, even longer. We've been friends the majority of her remarkable fifteen-thousand-year lifespan. We were first introduced when she was a girl just snatched from disaster, and I little more than a freshly hatched egg."

The dog yawned. "Is all this ancient history headed somewhere?"

"Dealing with humans, I often ask myself what Eneri Relda would do. Since my secret would soon be out—I'm relieved no longer to have the burden of protecting it—and there was no way of getting it back, I thought it of paramount importance to reach some sort of agreement as quickly as possible with General Gutierrez which would preclude his government's interference."

"Hmm." The assessor looked at the paleontologist. "What you don't know, what I didn't see any reason to tell you since you were holding out on me, was that Toya and I came to a similar agreement. She's decided she prefers the society created by you Elders to the one she grew up in."

"Yes," the girl responded diffidently. "I remembered your offer, Mister Thoggosh. I found myself regretting that I didn't take it. I decided I'd tell them nothing which might endanger your project, whatever it was. Or your culture's ability to defend itself from the United World Soviet."

Eichra Oren grinned. "I thought Toya's attitude was sensible. I told her I'd do my best to find a place for her when this was over with. She believed we could trust Gutierrez. He seemed to be coming to the same conclusions she had and wouldn't pass on dangerous information to the KGB."

Mister Thoggosh grunted. "I can't say I blame you for failing to allay my fears. Our mutual trust of the general is borne out by his cooperation, and in the way he renamed his spacecraft and allowed the others to be renamed by their respective captains. Geronimo I've heard of, but you'll have to fill me in on the other, Toya. Who is John Galt?"

She shook her head. "Colonel Sebastiano won't tell anybody." She still hadn't lost the American habit of glancing around to see if anyone dangerous was listening. "I think it's from some TV series that was suppressed."

"I see. Well, it's time we came to an agreement ourselves, Eichra Oren. May we assume that something resembling peace exists between us once again?"

Eichra Oren nodded. "I think we can assume that, yes."

"Because, unlike Toya here, and General Gutierrez, some Americans have yet to reach a resolution to their problems. First and foremost, especially for individuals like Mr. Empleado, is the question of survival. I want you to make sure that, whatever solution he arrives at, it doesn't imperil our own."

FORTY-FOUR
Of Streetlights and Matches

Away, away, we're bound for the mountain,
Bound for the mountain, bound for the mountain,
Over the hill, the wildwood's acallin',
Away to the chase, away, away!

"I seem to recall," Rosalind remarked as she scuffed through the leafy debris of the forest floor, "that the name of that song is 'Cumberland Mountain *Deer* Chase.' I thought we were hunting wild pigs."

Betal grinned back and slapped at the pistol thrust into his coverall pocket. "Yes'm, but I don't rightly know no pig-huntin' songs."

A few paces behind, Danny and a companion enjoyed the good-natured banter. "Each day it's harder to believe that Betal was a KGB thug."

"One of Empleado's enforcers?" Dlee Raftan Saon asked.

"Yes, Doctor, that beating seems to have done him a world of good."

"Call me Raftan. Today I am not a healer, but a hunter. For my part, I find it equally hard to believe that your delicate-looking physician insisted on coming with us for more than merely medical reasons."

Danny laughed. "She grew up on her grandfather's tales of stalking tigers and monkeys and God knows what else in the 'old country.' Now she wants to try it herself."

He doubted whether the Marine-issue Witnesses she and Betal both carried were adequate for the boar described by their "native guide." Glancing at the stainless .44 magnum in his own hand, he realized he didn't have much confidence, either, in the stopping power of the short-barreled S&W his father had left with him. But they were going to have a hell of a good time finding out, and maybe bring back some roasting pork as a bonus.

It was hard to tell who was in charge. Dr. Nguyen relied for whatever authority she needed on her medical degree. Danny couldn't remember whether that rated her bars or oak leaves. Betal had a commission but it was probably classified. Marna was next in line but she'd signed on as a techie and, like most of the party, had never hunted before. She carried a Mini-30, the same Ruger-designed carbine, in 7.62x39mm Russian, they'd been issued in basic training.

"You're right to wonder," he told Raftan. "In our culture, hunting's sneered at and discouraged." By an aristocracy of wine-and-cheese snots, he thought to himself, who'd converted America into a Marxist state a century ago and continued to rule it from the top down, despite their claim that it was the ultimate democracy.

The physician chuckled. "Only someone who has never gone hungry disdains hunting."

Well, Danny thought, the one promise socialist egalitarianism had kept was that everyone had the same chance—slim and none except for the Volvo nomenklatura—at three meals a day.

"In our culture," Dlee Raftan Saon added, "it's valued, among other reasons, because it's the only thing, besides sapience itself, that all of our species have in common."

Danny felt his eyebrows lift. "Even mobile veggies like whatshername?"

"Why do you think they became mobile? For a number of excellent reasons, all sapients begin as predators."

That would bear thinking about. It certainly explained, Danny thought, why things like wild boars had been included in the terraforming process. In part, this asteroid was a game preserve!

As a second lieutenant, he supposed he came next in rank, but any claim he made to bossing this effort would seem silly beside the credentials of its three lowest-ranking members. It turned out that his nominee for Most Useless Crewman, Staff Sergeant C. C. Jones, had actually done a lot of hunting, illegally, growing up as a country boy. That was probably reflected in his choice of weapon, one of the mission's Remington Model 1100 twelve-gauge semiautomatic riot guns, now loaded with enormous solid slugs. Corporal Roger Owen, another individual of rustic background, carried a Mini-30. Corporal Carlos "Rubber Chicken" Alvarez, cook and garbage disposer, rounded out the trio of experienced hunters with another Remington.

As the party made its way through the woods the three betrayed their past crimes another way, swapping yarns about the power and ferocity of wild pigs they'd hunted before. For Owen it had been javelina in New Mexico, "almost too fast to draw a bead on." Jones and Alvarez had hunted—and apparently been hunted by—things called "razorbacks," capable of absorbing dozens of bullets without damage and hamstringing opponents with their sharp, side-reaching tusks. Danny had always thought of pigs as cute little pink things with curly tails who tended to stutter when they got excited.

"There's no finesse to this," Owen had warned him. "These animals are territorial and mean as hell. We'll just spread out, stomp through their front yard, and when they show up to eject trespassers—pork chops!"

"Or long pig." Alvarez had chuckled.

Jones had nodded. "Always that possibility." He almost seemed to relish the idea. Danny had gulped and done his best to look intrepid.

The three conferred with Tl°m°nch°l, who had already hunted here and acted as their guide. He seemed to have a few yarns of his own. No one minded that the humans had begun supplementing their rapidly dwindling rations by foraging in the "super kudzu" forest. Mister Thoggosh, making the point through his assistant, had insisted that they hunt only with guides at first. Otherwise, they might kill and eat some sapient no human had ever seen before. There was no lack of individuals willing to "sacrifice" themselves—on company time—by hunting with the humans to prevent such a tragedy. Tl°m°nch°l carried a boxy-looking weapon on his equipment belt. His companion, introduced as Dr°f°rst°v, was trying his luck with a Mini-30, like a human hunter opting sportingly for a muzzle-loader or a bow.

But, as Danny explained, there was more involved in this trip than sport. "Since arriving on the asteroid, we Americans have enjoyed what amounts to an all-expense-paid vacation. Without lifting a finger, we're supplied with adequate water, warmth, shelter, and more than ample elbow room."

"Sweet streams flow freely," the physician replied, apparently quoting something, "and the air—"

"Is unpolluted," Danny suggested, "unlike that of the world most of us wish, perversely enough, to get back to."

"While overhead, the Elders' canopy protects you from the rigors of space. All of this bounty, my friend, is a simple, unavoidable by-product of arrangements which the Elders and their friends have provided for themselves."

"Yeah. So I understand."

Until now, for protection from weather under the canopy, they'd had the venerable spaceships—and the shelter beneath their wings—which had brought them here. For the time being the ships were gone, lifted in the baskets that had lowered them to the surface, on a mission to give 5023 Eris a moon. But even the Elders' makeshift was better than Earth's best. In addition to the cargo bay passenger inserts, removed from the shuttles to make room for internal fuel tanks and set up in the encampment on the equivalent of concrete blocks, tents, self-heating and self-cleaning, now stood in their place. Everyone now had the privacy they hadn't enjoyed since taking off from Earth—in some cases, since they'd been born. That was probably why two or three of the women were whispering about missed periods and tender breasts, although

Rosalind maintained that it was too early to tell. Few seemed unhappy about any of it, pregnancy included. Eventually, they'd been promised, they'd get their precious ships back. Aelbraugh Pritsch had told them they could keep the tents, as well.

"Although Owen's making noises about building a log cabin."

The insect chuckled again. "So your needs are taken care of by individualistic, capitalistic aliens better than any socialist regime on Earth has ever been able to do."

"That's right. We're getting a free ride on their incidental surplus."

"Let me tell you, young friend: as you've observed, the Elders enjoy a half-billion year lead in areas philosophical as well as technical. They don't view 'free riders' as a concern. Theirs is much more than the negligent generosity of a people who've always had enough to eat. Among other factors, they know from experience that it costs more to collect from free riders than it's worth."

Still, as his father had put it on a rare occasion when he'd had too much to drink, socialism at its unclean root is no more than the politics of envy, collectively expressed resentment of achievement. A century of the oppressive poverty it always caused hadn't prepared them to appreciate what they were being given here. It even caused a few to question it.

"If the tables were turned," he told the doctor, "there are plenty of us capable of resenting free riders. And precedents to show that we're willing to waste resources trying to do something about it."

"And it is these individuals who worry most about survival here. How long, they ask, can this suspicious generosity last? Why don't the Elders do what any right-thinking human would in their place? Their education hasn't prepared them to look for what you call the 'bottom line,' the ethical aspect of any economic situation."

"And what might that be?"

"To us, Danny, ethics is far more than a conflicting laundry list of free-floating rights and arbitrary wrongs. It's a discipline which asks—and in a healthy culture tries to answer—the question, 'What is the good?'"

"Well, you're the doctor, Doctor. What is the good?"

"Self-ownership, self-responsibility, whatever you wish, provided it doesn't interfere with someone else's notion of the good. This is why the Elders never worry about free riders. When someone installs and pays for a street light, the benefit he seeks, if he's rational, is the light itself."

"Sounds vaguely Masonic. As opposed to what?"

"As opposed to the dubious satisfaction of denying it to those who don't pay but may incidentally benefit. Didn't one of your own thinkers, Robert LeFevre, observe that a truly ethical person will even blacken a portion of his light so that it won't spill into the window of an unwilling beneficiary?"

Danny laughed. He seemed to be doing a lot of that lately. "It's true that nobody in our group understands why we're being helped."

"You find the Elders' generosity perplexing?"

"You could say that."

"You've never observed that it's the capitalist society, rather than the workers' paradise, that gives away matches, food, soap, and other commodities. The catch—if you can call it that—is that a producer advertises on the matchbook, or may be handing out samples trying to get you to buy more."

"And what's the catch on 5023 Eris?"

"Mister Thoggosh is probably trying to think of one right now. Of course you have loaned him your spaceships. . . ."

"It's a point in our favor." Danny knew that his father was reluctant to continue depending on the charity of strangers. Despite his socialist background, he tended, in character and principle, to value self-sufficiency and independence. Maybe he'd acquired this antisocialist trait during his training and experience as a pilot. Maybe it was just that somehow the American spirit had survived in him. In any case, the Elders' philosophy regarding the "Forge of Adversity" had been hovering constantly at the back of the general's mind. Danny tried to explain that to Dlee Raftan Saon.

"It seems to me that they're contradicting what they claim to believe in. I've never been sure how much is metaphorical and—I mean, does their philosophy describe reality as they conceive it, or does it prescribe action?"

The physician considered. "What makes you feel vulnerable is that your education—that is, your compulsory government indoctrination—leads you to expect social Darwinists to be less considerate of the needs of others, although another of your philosophers, Charles Curley, once defined capitalism as encouraging the survival of the most helpful."

"I'm just afraid that their ideals won't let them deprive us of a chance to overcome our difficulties and transcend ourselves."

"So that, from a kindness you feel misplaced, the Elders may deny you further help at any time, leaving you to be tested on the Forge and perish."

"Something like that. Don't think I'd be good at perishing gracefully."

"Therefore, in your view as well as your father's, survival depends on seeing to your own needs as completely and as soon as possible."

"At least these guns my dad didn't want to bring are good for something."

"Danny, in an ethical society, no one is ever *placed* upon the Forge of Adversity. We stand upon it every instant of our lives. The greatest point in your favor is that you are here, doing what you're doing."

"Hunting?"

"Those who make a habit of free rides do not survive in the long run."

"I don't know, Raftan. Tax collectors have been around a long time."

"They strive like any parasite. Still, we attach different meaning to the phrase 'long run.' You speak of hundreds of years, I of millions. Tax collectors didn't survive in our civilization. The two, tax collectors and civilization, cannot coexist—*watch out!*"

Without further warning, a gray-brown blur of feral tusks and bristles crashed from the underbrush and hurled itself in their direction. Danny had a fleeting impression of a flat black snout and amber eyes insane with rage. Lost in the moment, he clamped his gun in both hands the way his father had taught him and Basic Training hadn't. His right hand held the rounded rubber grip, his left hand the right hand. Left arm bent, elbow pointing downward, he tipped his head as if his right arm, stiff and straight before him, were a rifle stock, and kept both eyes open.

The pig was a growing, fuzzy blob, the sharply focused orange insert of the front sight his entire world. He pulled the trigger. The chrome-frosted hammer rose and fell. The short-barreled S&W roared and bucked. He neither heard nor felt it. A ball of blue flame at the muzzle lit the woods for yards around. Danny didn't see it. All he knew was that the big silver slug had plowed a furrow in the leaves behind his target. The wild pig kept coming, straight for his legs the way they'd said it would.

He fired again, to no visible effect, then leaped at the lowest branch of a nearby tree he hadn't consciously realized was there. Scrambling until he straddled the limb, he saw the animal below him shaking itself as if it had crashed headlong into the trunk. He regretted missing that.

Aiming carefully with one hand as his other held him steady in the tree, he shot the pig between the shoulder blades. This time he felt the impact of the .44 magnum in his palm and saw the muzzle bloom with fire, although he couldn't remember hearing the report afterward. The pig went down as if a safe had been dropped on it and didn't even quiver afterward.

"Congratulations, my boy!" From the branch above him, he heard the voice of Dlee Raftan Saon. He turned his head. The physician clung upside down to the tree with four limbs. "Low gravity's a wonderful thing, isn't it?" The insect being laughed. "You've shot a razorback sow, much hardier and more tenacious than the boar."

"Tell me about it!" Danny grinned. He dropped to the ground, his hands shaking a little as he reholstered the revolver. "Tonight *I'm* bringing home the bacon!"

FORTY-FIVE
Of Swords and Plowshares

Rosalind shot another wild sow before nightfall with a single well-placed bullet to the lungs as it charged an empty jacket Owen had tossed in its path. They would eat well over the next few days.

The veteran hunters—humans returning as empty-handed as their scorpionoid bretheren—were delighted with their pair of freshly blooded novices. The pigs were field dressed on the spot, slit from crotch to breastbone, the breastbone split, and the insides—except for the liver and heart—left for carrion-eaters. Danny, stained and sticky to the elbows with his part of the task, shouldered one end of the pole his pig was tied to and grinned every step of the way back to the camp until his jaws hurt. Now he knew why some men in the nineteenth and twentieth centuries had become professionals at this "sport." He wanted to come out again tomorrow.

"Funny," Rosalind told him as she strode beside him carrying the organ meat in a plastic bag she'd brought for the purpose, "I don't feel the way I always thought I was supposed to feel about killing an animal. Certainly not sad or guilty." She gave her head a toss in the direction of Alvarez and Betal, who'd demanded the honor of carrying her trophy home. "Instead, I feel like singing."

"And why not, dear colleague?" Dlee Raftan Saon called to her over what would have been his shoulder if he'd had shoulders. "It's what three billion years of evolution have prepared you for!"

Rosalind smiled and curtsied to the other doctor, her service pistol incongruous on her hip. *Hooray for evolution*, Danny found himself thinking, *and for the wild frontier*. Their expedition had been colonial in concept, its members undesirables, embarrassing presences, outcasts, exiles. They'd been ordered to make a permanent home for themselves among the asteroids. Whatever they discovered they were stuck with; no resupply was planned for the foreseeable future because the Earth had no more ships. There had always been vague talk of a new fleet, but no resources. The present effort was expected to return the investment it represented to America's failing economy, in part by becoming self-sufficient as quickly as possible. Well, they'd made a good start today—perhaps their first.

Something concealed in the gathering darkness hooted at him, making him jump and reminding him that he was still an amateur at this wild frontier business. He shook his head. What had he been thinking about? Oh yes. Nobody had talked about it, nobody had needed to. Their leaders hadn't wanted to mention it and those ordered to go hadn't wanted to hear it. But if things didn't pan out, the ASSR was rid of a lot of misfits. Later—much later— if they proved successful, new ships might be built to relieve the first arrivals. Earth had plenty of unwanted characters to be sent hundreds of millions of kilometers away. Now that Danny had discovered that he could feed himself and his friends, none of these considerations seemed as grim— or even as important—as they had before. He had learned a lesson socialism never dares teach: the joy of individual independence.

The hunting party hadn't strayed far into the forest, so it wasn't long before they reached camp again. It looked much as it had from the beginning. In the flickering firelight even the new tents fooled the eye for a moment, standing beside the offloaded passenger modules in place of the shuttles.

There was no lack of shoulders to relieve Danny, Betal, Alvarez, and Jones of their burdens. Despite the absence of the general, Ortiz, Sebastiano, and their minimal crews, the camp seemed crowded. In addition to the American expeditionaries, temporarily commanded by Empleado, Mister Thoggosh was present, completely in the flesh, colorful shell and everything, to greet them this time, along with his assistant, Aelbraugh Pritsch. One reason, perhaps, that the camp seemed crowded was that Scutigera—who took up a lot of room all by himself—had come with them.

"Auspicious beginnings!" the great centipede declared in a booming voice. "Congratulations! I shouldn't have thought your weapons adequate to the task."

Danny grinned up at the enormous being who, for once, wasn't making him feel like the next dinner course. "There's little, sir, in this or any other world that a .44 magnum isn't adequate for."

He didn't mention that it had taken him three shots to get the job done, or that Rosalind had killed her pig with a single, less powerful 11.43x23mm Lenin—about the same power level as a .357 magnum. He was about to speak of her achievement when he was shouldered aside by Andre Valerian, one of the agricultural specialists included in all three shuttle crew-complements. Danny was fairly certain that the Russian was what he appeared to be, and not just another KGB agent traveling incognito. With him was Captain Guillermo, a soil geologist, and Major Ortega y Pena, another scientific type, a botanist, whom everyone referred to (behind his back) as "Pinhead."

"*Corporal Owen!*"

The machinist ducked out from the crowd of well-wishers and welcomers to address the major. "You rang?"

"Take a look at this." Ortega held out a metallic object, indistinct in the darkness. "How do you explain it?"

"I don't know, Major. It would help if I could see it better." Before the indignant botanist could reply, Eichra Oren was beside the corporal, shining a powerful light down at the object in Owen's broad hand. Sam was at the Antarctican's knee and Pulaski was within an arm's length. It took a moment before Danny realized that the "flashlight" was the plasma pistol, a multipurpose tool with which Eichra Oren had held off one of Empleado's thugs after they'd first arrived on the asteroid. "Okay, that's the nosepiece of the plow blade I made for you aggie people, and it's sheared off. Pretty neat trick, Pin—I mean, Major. It's graphitic tool steel, hardened to sixty-five on the Rockwell 'C' scale. How'd it happen?"

Ortega sniffed. "I expected you to tell me, Corporal."

Owen ran his fingers through his black, bushy beard and hair. He'd neither shaved nor had a haircut in months and often looked like a wildman to his fellow humans—God knew, Danny thought, what he looked like to the aliens— the lieutenant often thought of him as the world's biggest hobbit. "Gee, Maje, I expected to win the state lottery someday, too, but it never happened—got sent here, instead. Life's full of disappointments, isn't it? Let's go sit by the fire and talk. You used the winch with this?"

The group adjourned to the center of the camp, where logs had been laid as seats around what had become a permanent fireplace. Several people took charge of the pigs. There were compartments within the tent walls in which food never spoiled, even though it remained at ambient temperature and was subjected to no detectable radiation.

The experts had started a little garden under a sheet-plastic greenhouse. Among the expedition's most important supplies were fast-growing high-yield seeds of various kinds. Twentieth-century experience with Lunar soil samples had led this mission's planners to expect fast growth and high yield in uneroded carbonaceous chondrite despite the fact that less sunlight was available beyond the orbit of Mars. Before taking off on a hunting expedition of his own, General Gutierrez had decided it was time to put both experts and supplies to their intended use.

At Ortega's order, some of the personnel had begun laying out a plot next to the encampment. Various individuals from the nautiloid establishment had come from time to time to observe the quaint agricultural practices of the barbarians. Thanks to a nearby stream and the soft rains that fell almost every night, there was no lack of water. A shallow ditch had been scraped to divert a little of it to the garden. Everyone had expected that the soft,

crumbly carbonaceous chondrite soil would work easily.
If the Lunar soil experiments were any guide, all one had
to do was shove the seeds into the ground, sprinkle on
some water, and jump back out of the way.

The experts had assured everyone that, despite the
canopy, there was more than enough light to grow crops—
just look at the jungle growing all around them. Danny had,
and began to wonder why it was necessary to plant their
own crops, when more food than they could ever use
seemed to be hanging wild on every tree and bush. Owen
had spoken of little else all the way back to camp, wondering aloud if the local equivalents of tomatoes, garlic,
mustard, and onions they'd already discovered would make
suitable barbecue sauce for pork. He'd spoken with Raftan,
Tl°m°nch°l, and Dr°f°rst°v about obtaining vinegar and
brown sugar. Danny hadn't had the heart to remind him
that at any moment they might be cut off from that kind
of largesse, especially since Marna, who outranked him, had
joined the conversation, arguing for sweet-and-sour instead
of barbecue.

However, if everything else went as it should, they would
soon have their own food supply, and if somebody didn't
happen to like broccoli, cauliflower, or Brussels sprouts,
it was just too bad. The trouble was, Danny grinned with
ironic appreciation, *he'd* never liked broccoli, cauliflower,
or Brussels sprouts himself. On the other hand, he thought,
when, since they'd landed on this asteroid, had anything
gone as it should? This, of course, was yet another thought
which, like the political opinions he shared with his father,
was best kept to himself.

Owen had asked Ortega, "You used the winch with this?"

The botanist bobbed his head as if he were the corporal and Owen the major. "As you instructed." Since the
expedition was shorter on available labor than on land,
they'd adopted a semimechanized plan to make their furrows radial instead of parallel, each terminating at a common point. There, Owen had set up a powerful electric
motor and steel cable to drag the plowshare through the
dirt from the far ends of the furrows to the center.

After each furrow was completed, the plowshare would
have to be carried out to the end of the next furrow by

hand, but that was the full extent of any physical labor involved.

"It appears that the topsoil in the chosen location is only centimeters deep," Valerian told the machinist, glaring at the soil geologist, Guillermo. "Almost immediately our rig hit impermeable bedrock—we couldn't stop the motor in time—destroying the blade."

Running a thumb over the jagged edge, Owen raised his eyebrows. "And what about the spare blade I made you?"

A long-suffering Guillermo polished his glasses and sighed, "I'm afraid this *is* the spare blade, Corporal."

"Well," replied the machinist, "before we left to go hunting, I was working on a third blade, cobbled together from carbide-edged titanium alloy, but I'd like to see this bedrock of yours before I finish it. I can't guarantee that it won't meet the same fate."

"I can guarantee that it will," declared a familiar voice. They turned to watch Mister Thoggosh drag himself into the firelight. Covered in plastic that kept his body moist, the mollusc glistened. "It's exactly the same problem I've been having, and the reason I came to visit you tonight. You may wonder why none of us is amused at your mishap. I observed what you would-be farmers went through with sympathy. You see, I've been making—rather the scientists and technicians in my employ have—a series of bewildering discoveries about this troublesome asteroid. If you'll accompany me to the place your agricultural implement failed, I'll tell you about some of them."

"I just suggested that," Owen told Mister Thoggosh. "Got a flashlight?"

He was answered by a burst of blue-green brightness and a loud, hollow-sounding hiss. Behind Mister Thoggosh, Llessure Knarrfic, looking, as she always did, like a six-foot rubber flower, held one of the expedition's Coleman lanterns. "Excellent, Lieutenant," the plant-being declared to Marna, who stood beside her blowing on a burnt-out survival match. "It has a nice, piquant, after-dinner flavor I've never experienced with artificial lighting before, heady, but with just a touch of mellow smoothness."

Marna grinned and shook her head. "Can I cook, or can I cook?" Several people turned to listen.

"I thought you were supposed to be a carnivorous plant," objected Danny, who'd been content to watch until now. "That's what Raftan told me, anyway. He said your people hunt—just like we do."

"That's what I told him," the insect physician confirmed, his faceted eyes glittering in the lamplight.

The enormous flower swiveled her blossomlike face to look at him. "Because I'm a vegetable, did you think I have to be a vegetarian? That's the animal thinking process for you. Of course we hunt, young person. But we're also fully photosynthetic, like any proper org—er, plantlife. And by the way, Corporal, I believe that I agree with Lee: sweet-and-sour sounds much better than this bar-bee-queue you suggested. Shall I kill a pig of my own? I'm looking forward to the feast. Now, are we going to see this tragic furrow of yours, or not?"

Owen laughed and led the way. A rather large, slow procession wound between two of the tents in the direction of the stream, its pace set by Mister Thoggosh, who didn't have the option of buoyant levitation that he enjoyed in his own quarters—and had decided to continue concealing what agility he did have. As he drew himself along with his tentacles, theatrically dragging his shell behind him, he continued his explanation.

"I already knew there was something strange about this planetoid's composition," Mister Thoggosh told them. "I'd have been surprised had it proved otherwise. I was attracted to this asteroid in the first place because it had no equivalent in any other parallel universe."

They found the "tragic furrow" when Demene Wise, still hobbling on crutches, stumbled into it. Rosalind rushed forward to get him on his feet again. The man, another former KGB ruffian, even managed a self-deprecating laugh, something he'd have been incapable of only days before. Whatever difficulties the asteroid presented, Danny thought, being here seemed to be good for some people.

Mister Thoggosh went on. "It persists in destroying my custom-designed drilling equipment at various sites, deep in what you call the super-kudzu forest. Understand that we're speaking of nuclear plasma bolides now, not tool steel.

I've just learned, with the help of your father and his associates, Lieutenant Gutierrez, that it also renders the asteroid opaque to neutrino-scanning."

"What?" Several people gasped the word at once. Small insects began to be attracted to the light, and somewhere, deep in the forest, a night bird made a gobbling noise, mocking them.

"Indeed," the nautiloid replied, "and this, as we all know, is quite impossible—unless 5023 Eris were as dense as a collapsed star."

Owen was down on one knee in the furrow, brushing soil away from the infamous bedrock with the aid of Llessure Knarrfic's lamplight. Danny leaned over and watched as the machinist ran his short, blunt fingers over a surface which looked to the lieutenant like the dried peel of an orange, highly magnified. He wasn't disturbed to feel the tips of Scutigera's long, sensitive, tapering antennae slide past his neck like armor-covered snakes for a look at the ground below.

Owen had other ideas. "Petrified dinosaur hide," he declared. "But the whole asteroid can't consist of material as dense as you say, Mister Thoggosh; its gravity would exceed that of Earth."

"I'm certain," Mister Thoggosh replied, "that the astronomical-minded among you have followed much the same line of thought, Corporal. It can lead to one conclusion only, not one that I like much, but consistent with what we know. This asteroid's impermeable surface—"

Danny interrupted. "Is nothing more than a hollow shell!" His words seemed to die as soon as they were spoken, absorbed by the nearby woods. A breeze stirred its leaves before Mister Thoggosh spoke again.

"Quite right. And to account for the low gravity, it has to be a relatively thin shell, at that. As fantastic as it seems, 5023 Eris appears to be—"

"A giant spaceship!" Toya almost screamed the words which caused another round of gasps among her fellow humans.

"Go to the head of the class, my dear. It would appear that the Predecessors *constructed* 5023 Eris, dwarfing any of their previous artifacts."

FORTY-SIX
Hinges of Hell

"More like a space station than a spaceship. No exhaust ports, no nozzles, no engines."

Horatio Gutierrez strode from the forest margin where he'd been all but invisible in the darkness. Looking worn and tired to his son, he stepped into the blue-white circle of the hissing Coleman. Behind him loomed the shadowy forms of Sebastiano and Ortiz.

"As far as we can tell, anyway." He glanced at the small crowd gathered about the furrow. "What's in the hole—and why do I have a feeling you haven't all turned out to welcome homecoming spacemen?"

"Dear me!" Aelbraugh Pritsch squawked. "Back already! If you'd let me know, General, I might have arranged transportation for you and your—"

"It was a nice evening for a walk." Gutierrez grinned wearily. "We left our ships upstairs," he lifted a thumb, "parked on the outer surface ready to be lowered. The rest of our crews stayed behind in your area to have dinner on Mister Thoggosh. You can arrange transport for them, if you like. Some of them may not be walking too well before long."

Aelbraugh Pritsch glanced at his employer for confirmation

and received it via implant. "I'll do that, General. Would anyone care to return with me now?"

Scutigera, too large for any flying machine available, excused himself anyway, saying he'd intended to go back to his quarters before now. Llessure Knarrfic and the scorpionoid guards accepted the offer of a ride. Sam, too, declared that he had a personal errand and disappeared into the woods.

Wise had begun to weave on his crutches. Sweat trickled down the side of his neck although the night was cool. Rosalind ordered him to bed and took him that way under escort.

Marna declared that she wanted to look to the shuttles' life-support systems before they were powered down. Alvarez volunteered to go along as an extra pair of hands, but not before he gave Betal and Jones detailed instructions in preparing the wild pigs for the meal he planned tomorrow.

Owen, conferring with Ortega and Valerian, decided there wasn't any point in repeating the plow experiment until Guillermo found an area nearby where the soil lay deeper over whatever 5023 Eris was made of. The first two said good night. The latter stayed to continue the discussion. The machinist ambled off to put his winch away.

Danny noticed that Empleado wasn't around any more, having vanished without a word, which seemed appropriate for the KGB.

Ortiz and Sebastiano excused themselves to try out the showers with which the tents had come equipped and, before retiring, check on members of their crews who hadn't gone on the capture mission. As spacecraft captains under the tutelage of Gutierrez, each took new responsibilities seriously.

Danny could see that his father needed rest, too, but knew he wouldn't take it until his own duties were discharged. That included discussing Mister Thoggosh's revelation, and it was to this that the former general steered the conversation as he led the handful who remained to the tent that was still lighted.

"So if it's a Predecessor ship, why is it still here in orbit around the sun?" He went to a table, poured coffee, and found a chair. Eichra Oren, Pulaski, Guillermo, Dlee Raftan Saon, and Danny followed his example. "Why didn't it disappear a long time ago to wherever they went?"

Mister Thoggosh abandoned any final pretense of helplessness out of the water, since he couldn't drag his massive shell across the tent floor without pulling rumples in the fabric. Looking like a misshapen spider, he took advantage of the low gravity to rise up on the tips of his tentacles and step delicately into the center of the room, where he settled.

"We've no significant argument, sir—"

"Although," Raftan interjected, "I meant to ask the general where the exhaust ports or rocket nozzles of one of his culture's nineteenth-century Yankee clipper ships were to be found."

"We're in agreement that the place is artificial," Mister Thoggosh went on. "And knowing as little as we do of the Predecessors' impressive accomplishments, who's to say there aren't any engines?"

Eichra Oren nodded, looking to Pulaski for support, perhaps because she was the closest thing they had to an archaeologist. "Given their technology, they might turn out to be the size of a walnut."

Raftan agreed. "Mister Thoggosh, I suspect that your assistant, were he here, might hold that since 5023 Eris floats freely in space, circling a sun rather than a planet or moon, it must by definition be a spaceship, because—"

"I must be getting tired, Doctor," the general interrupted, "you've lost me."

Mister Thoggosh lifted a resigned limb. "In this context, the distinction between space station and a spaceship is pointless. We argue to no purpose, as is often the case where fresh facts fail to present themselves, and I, too, am a trifle fatigued." He glanced, wistfully, Danny thought, at the coffee pot. "To any extent I care, I hope it's the latter. The idea of a spaceship the size of a world, even a small world, rather strikes my fancy."

"The idea of owning the Death Star *would* appeal to you," Eichra Oren suggested. "And machinery powerful enough to move a world—even a small world like this one—would be extremely valuable."

Mister Thoggosh shrugged. "Well, I only hope it isn't a *defective* spaceship."

"What?" That from several present.

"The general said it, himself. Why is it still here? What if, at the last moment, it was abandoned as flawed?"

Raftan nodded. "It certainly betrays every manifestation of abandonment, even to having acquired an outer coating of natural asteroidal material."

"Not substantial enough to suit my ag people." Gutierrez paused as if in thought, then grimaced with resignation and asked his son for a cigarette.

Danny leaned toward his father to light it, then lit one of his own. "Sir, all this carbonaceous chondrite might be meant to disguise the true nature of 5023 Eris from casual observers."

His father agreed. "It would also be cheap protection from radiation and meteorites—except that this place doesn't seem to need it. It would be like covering a tank with a protective coating of Silly Putty."

"Or, as Raftan suggests, it might be the inevitable effect of ages spent orbiting among real asteroids," Mister Thoggosh argued, "since they're seventy percent carbonaceous chondrite. The inference can be taken either way. It's just another question no one knows the answer to."

"With no way of finding out," Danny added.

"On the contrary, Lieutenant. Eichra Oren, show them what we brought. They're what you'd call 'hardcopy' from the neutrino scan. I'd like to have your experts, in addition to those among my party, examine them."

The Antarctican unrolled a great sheaf of what appeared to be photographs, printed on some sort of heavy white plastic rather than paper. In them, the asteroid occupied the entire frame. The canopy was invisible, as was the jungle. The Elders' buildings—and in one picture certain features of the human camp—seemed transparent, ghostlike. The asteroidal layering, whatever its origin and purpose, formed a kind of second skin underneath which the impermeable core of 5023 Eris lay flawless and unbroken. The humans took turns peering at the photos, searching for a clue to the mysteries the asteroid continued to generate.

"Well, here's a small apparent flaw." It was Guillermo,

pointing to a section of the asteroid's otherwise armored hull. Four feet away, Danny couldn't see the feature he referred to. Mister Thoggosh slid forward.

"I see what you mean. If you'll excuse me . . ."

Guillermo backed away, watching. The nautiloid placed a slender tentacle-tip on the map where the captain's finger had been. The image on the plastic sheet swelled and acquired more detail. "I quite agree, Captain. It might be a small meteor crater, but there should be a great many more of them if it is. It looks to me as if it might well turn out, upon examination, to be a large, well-buried door. Or perhaps that's only wishful thinking on my part. What do you say, General?"

Gutierrez leaned over the map, then compared it with several of the other documents. "Looks like it's about five meters below the natural carbonaceous chondrite surface—and, wouldn't you know it, on almost the opposite side of the asteroid from here."

"So it is," replied Mister Thoggosh, beginning to sound excited. "Now to rush my weary and exasperated drilling crews to the site. Here at last is something they can get their teeth into. Will you be joining us, sir? I'll call for another electrostat."

Gutierrez sighed. "Call for two. I'll bring Danny along as my aide. Our physician and machinist should come." He looked up at Toya, as usual of late, standing as close as she could to Eichra Oren. "Also our resident paleontologist. And I suppose I'd better invite Arthur and Sgt. Jones or there'll be hell to pay." He turned to Guillermo. "Hector, in the absence of the late Dr. Kamanov, you're our chief geologist. Go round up whatever you need, notify the people I just named, those who aren't handy already, and get back here five minutes ago."

Guillermo grinned. "Yes, sir!"

"General," there was concern in Mister Thoggosh's voice, "you're in need of sleep. It will take hours to dig that far. Rest and join us later."

Gutierrez stood up straight and stretched. "Thanks, Mister Thoggosh, I'll sleep in the aerocraft. At this point, it couldn't keep me awake if it flew around this world upside down and backwards!"

✧   ✧   ✧

For once, to everyone's amazement, everything worked.

Placing Sebastiano in charge of the camp, the general got his much-needed in-flight nap and more opportunity to rest once they'd arrived at the broad green meadow on the dayside of 5023 Eris corresponding to the small feature the sharp-eyed Guillermo had discovered on the neutrino map.

At Rosalind's suggestion, they'd detoured into the treetops above the nautiloid settlement to retrieve half a dozen spacesuits from the shuttles. If the asteroid were hollow as they had come to believe, and artificial, then hundreds of millions of years of corrosion would long since have removed any breathable oxygen from whatever atmosphere still lingered after seeping into space, molecule by molecule.

Mister Thoggosh ordered a pit dug, five meters deep and thirty in diameter. Looking more like recoilless artillery or giant bazookas than industrial equipment, his mining machinery—which had proven useless against the obstinate material of the asteroid itself—hissed and roared on its supporting framework amidst unbearable brilliance, clearing soft soil off the impenetrable substrate in a matter of minutes, almost vaporizing it, and somehow compressing it into glassy bricks which were used to support the sloping sides of the excavation.

In due course, they found a huge triangular hatch with rounded sides and corners—"trochoidal," someone called it—ten meters on a side. After their earlier troubles, it wasn't even locked. Instead, despite its being a meter thick and composed of the same material as the rest of 5023 Eris, it lifted on counterbalancing pivots. An unlit chamber of unknown dimensions and contents awaited. Not knowing what to expect, nervous explorers, human and otherwise, suited up and prepared to descend into the cavernous interior.

The initial party would consist of Gutierrez and his son, Owen, Rosalind, Pulaski, and Eichra Oren in a borrowed NASA suit. Mister Thoggosh had ordered light, transparent gear manufactured to fit the humans (and a canine suit, as well), and the next explorers would be more comfortable, but no one wanted to wait until this new equipment was available. Tl°m°nch°l, two others of his species, and Nannel Rab, the spiderlike chief project engineer, completed the group, wearing spacesuits of their own. Given the density of the surface material, communication with those remaining behind would have to be by wire, trailed behind them. Several individuals, not just humans, pointed out the similarity between this situation and that of old-time "hardsuit" deep-sea divers.

Representing Mister Thoggosh, Eichra Oren was the first to duck beneath the uptilted corner and drop a full ten meters to the floor of the triangular chamber. One by one, he was followed by the others, the giant spider squeezing through last. The human popped up again to deliver a distressing report to Mister Thoggosh and Sam (who was already upset at being left behind) while hanging onto the edge by his fingertips.

"It's an idiot-proof airlock," he told them, pushing a gloved thumb over his shoulder toward the point, beyond the massive pivot, where the large counterbalancing end of the triangular hatch tilted downward. "And guess who the idiots are. The next door below swings into this chamber, and right now it's blocked by this one. It won't move a centimeter until this hatch is closed and out of the way."

"Ingenious," his employer answered. "Which means that if you go on, we'll lose contact with you."

Gutierrez joined Eichra Oren. Hanging there, the would-be explorers looked like oddly dressed swimmers chatting poolside with friends. "That's about the size of it. Corporal Owen says this slab fits to a ten-thousandth. I don't know if he meant millimeters or inches, but it'll shear any wire we try to leave behind."

"Or jam on it," Sam offered, "and we'll never get you out."

Eichra Oren grinned inside his visor. "Now there's a cheerful thought. I don't see that we have any choice about it, though. We're as well prepared as it's possible to be, and the sooner we get on with it, the better. Watch your fingers when the lid comes down."

With that, he let go of the edge. The general dropped beside him. They strode across the chamber to their waiting comrades. Danny and Corporal Owen stretched themselves and leaped to give the rear edge of the hatch cover a shove. It would be meters beyond their reach once it was back in place, but the single push was all it needed. It pivoted and settled with a thump, plunging them all into darkness.

Several light beams sprang into existence. With the interfering upper hatch out of the way, the inner hatch swung aside as if it had been made of balsa wood and had been used just the day before, instead of millions—perhaps even billions—of years ago.

FORTY-SEVEN
Looking for Pellucidar

"Holy shit—" The voice was Danny's. Sheepish at his own outburst, he added, "—Batman."

It would have been pitch black without their helmet lights and the handheld lamps the scorpionoids had brought. In their yellow beams they observed that they'd entered a half-sphere forty meters in diameter, the hatch they'd come through set in the flat side. The curved surface underfoot was broken every few meters by a yawning trochoidal tunnel mouth, giving the impression that they stood within an enormous colander.

Perhaps "stood" wasn't the word. They found themselves half-swimming in the chamber, the local gravity they'd come to regard as normal no longer pulling at them. It was an indication of the density of the shell they'd penetrated, and how much it contributed to the total mass of 5023 Eris. In spite of that, it appeared that the asteroid wasn't hollow like a basketball, as they'd imagined. Each of them grimly visualized thousands upon thousands of kilometers of dark, twisted passageways worm-riddling what they still thought of as a natural body despite the fact, Danny realized, that it was as artificial as the battered ASF-issue Timex on his wrist.

It was cold, just above zero, Celsius. Nannel Rab and the scorpionoids (it amused Danny that they sounded like a rock group) carried instruments to sniff the contents of the chamber. They reported that it consisted mostly of vacuum—one millibar, about the same atmospheric pressure as Mars, a thousandth of Earth normal—but with traces of nitrogen, oxygen, carbon dioxide, numerous hydrocarbons and, intriguingly, fluorocarbons.

Pulaski peering over his shoulder, Owen examined the walls, built, or at least lined, with a seamless plastic, ribbed for traction. A scratch with the Czech Army knife he always carried showed that it was almost as indestructible as the asteroid's surface. Others peered into each of the tunnels without entering any, shining their lamps down them until their vision was obstructed by a curve or the light was absorbed by sheer distance. Gutierrez and Eichra Oren conferred about the order of march and chose the entrance nearest the center.

They made an impressive party. Seven humans in bulky suits, who might appear frightening to a nonhuman race. Three outsized lobsters and a huge red-and-black spider in almost invisible outer skins. Despite every sign that the place had been deserted thousands of millennia, no one had tried to talk them out of arming themselves to whatever their respective species used for teeth. 5023 Eris had already presented them with too many surprises.

"We ought to leave some kind of markings as we go," Guillermo observed, "like bread crumbs or Huckleberry Finn's ball of twine."

"Tom Sawyer," Owen corrected, although no one could remember whether he or the geologist was right.

Eichra Oren chuckled. "Sam wouldn't let me come without these." From a suit pocket he extracted a package, took something out, and flattened it against the wall nearest the chosen tunnel. When he took his hand away, he'd left a glowing spot. "Powered by background radiation. They should last several centuries."

"I wish you hadn't said that." Through the glistening substance of Tl°m°nch°l's suit, Danny heard the speech-sounds he made, like an old manual typewriter. "I didn't know I was claustrophobic until now. Going down that tunnel will be like crawling through the intestines of some unspeakable giant."

"I wish you hadn't said *that*!" Pulaski told the scorpionoid.

There was no more reason to put it off. The general led the way, followed by Danny, Nannel Rab, and Eichra Oren. Tl°m°nch°l, his comrades, Guillermo, and Owen were the rear guard. Rosalind and Pulaski were sandwiched between, fear of the unknown prompting an unconscious return to chivalry. Danny noticed that both women gravitated toward Eichra Oren when the going was especially scary. It gave the man a look of distinct pain, even through his helmet. At the same time, mutual repulsion seemed to be at work between the women. It was almost as interesting as the physics of the asteroid itself.

The corridor they entered, like those they'd rejected, was low and wide, built for original occupants who'd been neither humanoid nor nautiloid. Nannel Rab, the giant among them, had a difficult time, but refused, given a chance, to return to the surface. After the first curve, a hundred meters from the entry, the path branched at a spherical junction. They had to choose from dozens of alternatives. Eichra Oren marked the tunnel they'd come from. Gutierrez chose another which seemed to lead toward the asteroid's center. The Antarctican slapped a glowing patch beside it.

Geometry dictated, Guillermo maintained, that it wasn't possible for all the tunnels to keep branching this way. As they made their way deeper, the atmosphere thickened, the temperature rose and, after several junctions had proven Guillermo wrong, they began to see what appeared to be pooled remnants of the same liquid fluorocarbon that filled Mister Thoggosh's office. To some of the explorers, that meant the previous occupants had been marine creatures.

"Hold on," Gutierrez argued, "is there any indication that the Predecessors needed fluorocarbons to deal with non-marine sapients?"

Pulaski shook her head, the gesture lost until she spoke

aloud. "There's little indication that other sapients even *existed* when the Predecessors did."

"Score a point for the ship theory, then," the general declared, picking his way around a large puddle clinging to the wall they'd arbitrarily decided was the floor. "This stuff, if it once filled the whole place, would have transferred momentum rather nicely, increasing the passengers' tolerance for acceleration."

"It might just have been a way of transferring garbage," Nannel Rab suggested. "It wouldn't be the first open sewer system I've heard of in so-called civilized realms. Who can outguess another species?"

Owen grunted. "Especially one that's been extinct a billion years."

"Whatever its original purpose," Rosalind stated, leaning over an instrument the giant spider carried, "over the time it's been here, it's lost any oxygen it ever carried and turned foul. This stuff has a nasty color. I'm glad we can't smell it."

According to Guillermo and Nannel Rab, the pools of artificial liquid shouldn't have grown larger and more frequent the way they did as the adventurers burrowed deeper. They also grew uglier in color and consistency, although the principal ingredient remained a fluorocarbon similar to the one they were familiar with. As they groped from one tunnel branch to another, they never knew what to expect. In some places the remaining chemical "atmosphere" lying on the "floor" (despite Nannel Rab's suggestion, that was what they continued to believe the stuff was) had deteriorated or become contaminated until it was opaque.

"Holy mother of God!" Gutierrez was the first to come across a chamber filled with the stuff. Its condition had awakened a childhood verbal reflex.

"What is it?" several voices responded at once.

"You have to see this to believe it," he told them in disgust, "and we don't have any choice about wading through it."

By that time, Danny had caught up to his father and saw what he was talking about. The once-liquid contents of the chamber had gelled into a mass into which Gutierrez had stumbled. He'd managed to back out, but it covered his suit in putrescent-looking brown slime marbled with streaks of black. Danny switched his transmitter off and risked touching his visor to his father's. "Dad, it looks like you've been spending too much time with the KGB."

His father chuckled. "I've been in deep shit before, but—"

"General!" Rosalind pushed past Danny, her helmet mostly hiding an expression of disgust which her tone betrayed. "I wanted to warn you about removing any part of your suit before its exterior is sterilized. There may be dangerous microbes here that have been multiplying and mutating for eons."

Gutierrez nodded. "Understood, Doctor. That goes for everybody, I want individual confirmation that you heard it, starting with you, Lieutenant."

"Yes, sir. What do we do, scrub down with peroxide?"

"We'll leave that to Rosalind. For now, we all have to slog through this gunk, and I want her warning understood. Hector? Corporal Owen?"

One by one they replied, including the nonhumans. Hoping this chamber wasn't the start of an entire asteroid filled with filth of the consistency of dirty Vaseline, Danny needlessly held his breath and took the plunge, following the senior Gutierrez. Crossing that chamber was the most revolting task he'd ever faced, but his worst fears failed to be realized. After twenty meters of it, his faceplate broke through, not into thin air, but into clear, healthy-looking fluorocarbon which quickly washed the slime from his suit. His father waited and the rest of the party soon emerged.

Once past that unpleasant chamber, the corridors widened as if intended by the original occupants to be gathering spots. Here the ancient ship or station appeared even better preserved. To their astonishment the walls glowed with a light rather like that of the contrastingly colored adhesive spots Eichra Oren was still leaving behind them.

"I guess," the general declared, "this is what we came to see."

After orienting themselves as best they could, the explorers got started by examining various rooms they had begun to find branching off from the corridors. All had heavy, tight-fitting triangular doors without anything like a lock. Some were clearly residential. Others might have been offices, laboratories, physical-plant control rooms, infirmaries, or eating places.

What might have been sanitary facilities they tentatively identified merely by endless ranks of grotesquely shaped low-standing ceramic objects bolted, without partitions or any other attempt at privacy, to the floor. If that was what they were, Danny wasn't sure he ever wanted to meet the creatures they'd been designed for. On the other hand, they could as easily have been the equivalent of slot machines or feeding troughs.

And what were they to make of a huge domed chamber in which there stood a construct over a hundred meters tall that called to mind a great radio telescope or directional antenna connected at its base to a lighthouse, complete with a glassed-in booth at the top, but which pointed nowhere but a curved, blank wall of solid, plastic-covered, super-dense metal?

Another find was even more peculiar. The room was the size of a football stadium. Its ceiling, however, was only a little over a meter high and they had to stoop to explore it. It was filled with precise rows of featureless solid metal cubes half a meter on a side, capable of sliding easily across a floor that seemed to Danny like greased Teflon—although it provided perfect traction for their booted feet. Any cube, once moved and released, glided sedately back into its place, others getting out if its way if necessary before resuming their own positions.

It was a frustrating experience. What was the purpose of the dozens of gimbaled, dust-filled cylinders they discovered, five-meter drum-shapes lying on their sides, embedded in the floor, and resembling a geologist's rock tumbler? (For all the explorers knew, they might have been car washes or torture chambers.) Pulaski shyly suggested that this was how the Predecessors cleaned and polished their (hypothetical) exoskeletons. If so, how they had kept from injuring themselves? And what had the polishing medium been, long since wasted away to nothing?

The great majority of rooms and fixtures couldn't be

identified even that far, or guessed at credibly, either by
the humans or the species accompanying them. "But what
will future archaeologists make," Guillermo asked his companions pointedly, "of one of our rooms back on Earth,
half-filled with brightly colored Ping-Pong balls?"

"Forget future archaeologists," demanded Tl*m*nch*l.
"*I'd* like to know what humans do with a room half-filled
with brightly colored Ping-Pong balls. Something suitably
salacious, I trust."

"What sort of creature is a Ping-Pong?" Nannel Rab
asked, "Poor things. Are they good to eat?"

In all their explorations, the fascinated, frustrated party
discovered nothing like written records. Visible technology
was sophisticated enough to have made the equivalent of
a library or computer unrecognizable. Few of the smaller
artifacts of the sort Mister Thoggosh collected seemed to
have been left behind.

At the widest points in the passageways the walls were
adorned with textured areas with raised borders. To human
eyes, everything about them was a burnished golden-
bronze. "Paintings or sculptures," Pulaski guessed, "maybe
both."

"Abstracts," Rosalind agreed, "intended for senses different from ours."

Owen grinned. "I'll bet they all say 'Eat At Joe's.'"
Nobody laughed; it was as good a guess as any.

"Whatever they are," Eichra Oren observed after running his gloved hands over them, "they don't seem representational." He explained the tactile sculptures that
Mister Thoggosh fancied. These were rather like certain
items in the Proprietor's collection back at home, he said,
perhaps intended to please and amuse those who passed
by them in the corridors.

"General! Eichra Oren! Come look at this!"

In the center of the next "square," Nannel Rab had
encountered a large representational metal statue. Struggling against the drag of the liquid fluorocarbon atmosphere, Gutierrez hurried. "Why, the damned thing's
bronze-colored," he observed, puffing inside his helmet,
"like everything else."

The others were close behind. The object was four

meters long, three meters tall and about the same width. It squatted over a broad pedestal on what might have been a traffic island in a shopping mall. There was no way of telling whether it was realistic in scale or heroic, but judging from the corridors around them—if it portrayed the sapients who had made it—it had been rendered in true-to-life proportions. "It's possible," one scorpionoid observed, "that this indicates the physical nature of the Predecessors. It's consistent with the size and shape of the doorways."

"Otherhandwise," Owen argued, "a thing like this may tell us nothing."

"Beyond something of their aesthetic preferences," Pulaski noted.

"Right," the corporal continued. "Humans are fond of sculpture and a lot of it depicts other species. There was a famous sculpture of a seagull once in Salt Lake where the Beehive Commune later put up the statue of Geraldo Rivera. And a real good one of a moose," he added, "in St. John's, Newfoundland. And what about that Picasso thingamacallit in front of Communist Party Headquarters in Chicago?"

"Or all the renderings," added the paleontologist, getting into the spirit, "of seven-foot-tall mice in the Disneylands."

"A month ago," the general answered, running a glove over the sculpture, "I wouldn't have believed in nautiloids or hyperthyroid spiders." The thing depicted here was long, wide, flat, segmented, and possessed many short, jointed legs. In some ways it was rather like the sowbugs— roly-polies—children like to play with. "If this thing is representational, I won't have a lot more trouble believing in giant, sapient trilobites."

For want of better reaction, each of the explorers ran eyes and manipulators over the object, shrugged in his own fashion, and moved on. The ancient spacecraft may have been odd, but not completely incomprehensible. One by one, they managed to identify practical installations—life support, communications, and an impressive array of what looked like weapons systems—the appearance of which was dictated more by function than aesthetics. Although they'd yet to find the weapons themselves—or discover how they operated through the impenetrable barrier of the hull— it began to seem that 5023 Eris might have been a battleship of some kind.

"Yeah, but the Death Star," Danny muttered, "was supposed to have been fully operational." He gazed down from the "balcony" of what they believed was a fire-control gallery, a vast, dimly lit auditorium dwarfing any opera house he'd ever heard of. Only their spacesuits kept his voice from echoing.

"A good trick," his father observed, standing beside him, "since, so far, we've discovered nothing resembling any sort of engines or drive."

"It was a station, then, intended to cover the Predecessors' retreat. But from what? Maybe we could find out if we activated some of these systems."

"I agree," Eichra Oren offered. He leaned against a rail, his back to the endless stepped ranks of consoles far below. "Our first object might be to rid the ship of these stagnant fluorocarbons. I wouldn't be surprised if fresh liquid from reservoirs deeper down began to displace those that have spoiled."

"Neither would I," replied the general, "Still, would you be willing to take your helmet off and try breathing this stuff?"

The man was about to answer, but stared instead in the direction they'd come from. *The implant look*, Danny thought, although they'd already confirmed that radio wouldn't carry through the structure of the asteroid and their plan to string wires to the surface had been canceled by the way the air lock worked. "It's Sam," Eichra Oren told them, amazement in his voice. "He'll be here any second."

"I *am* here," the dog corrected, half-swimming out of the nearest corridor in a transparent suit. "A little out of breath. I wanted to surprise you, but you caught me swearing at that room full of *gunge* back there. My message'll be surprise enough. There's another party of 'human interlopers'—Aelbraugh Pritsch's words—threatening to arrive on the asteroid. Seems there's been another change of policy following the recent shift of regimes, and a small fleet, cobbled together in haste, has taken off from the Soviet Union."

"Why the hurry, Sam?" Danny asked. "It'll take them a year to get here."

"Somebody's been keeping secrets, Lieutenant," the dog replied. "They're fusion powered, and constant boost. They're coming, they've announced for our benefit, to claim the United World Soviet's share of the fruits of a 'joint cooperative mission.'

"The flagship, we're informed, the *USSR Lavrenti Pavlovich Beria*, has somebody onboard that Juan Sebastiano calls 'the Banker.' "

FORTY-EIGHT
Midnight Sun

By the time they all made it back to the surface, there was more news.

"*Five-Oh-Two-Three Eris, this heah's ASF Fleet Admiral Dan Delacroix aboard the flagship* ASSR John Reed. *I wanna speak with, uh . . .*" The drawling voice paused as if its owner were reading from a memo. "*Gennul Horatio Z. Gutierrez. You-all copy down theah?*"

"This is Gutierrez." From the excavation site he'd hurried around the little world into the treetops over the nautiloid settlement and out through a ribbed plastic tube connecting 5023 Eris with his ship. Innocent as yet of any newly arrived fleet, the sky held only stars shining down on an unending mustard plain of polymerized leaves. Work crews swarmed over all three vessels, preparing them for another unanticipated mission. Sam and Eichra Oren were with Gutierrez on the command deck. They still wore their suits and had been warned to seal them again while the hull was penetrated for installation of another nautiloid-designed control system. Workers overhead made pounding and drilling noises. The general bent the suit mike to his lips.

"I've heard of you, Admiral." What he'd heard was that Delacroix made a deceptive and dangerous enemy. Behind his carefully cultivated Louisiana accent, he concealed a ruthless shrewdness honed at Harvard and Annapolis. "I don't know of any *John Reed*. I thought I had our only three spaceships here. Over."

"That's what you s'posed to believe, Gennul. The USSR ain't the only power buildin' spaceships. I'm told you got a fourth y'self, that the whole damned asteroid's artificial! Ovah."

My tax dollars at work, he thought—for the KGB. "Yes, Admiral, I've just returned from an initial survey of the interior. 5023 Eris is some kind of ancient space vessel. Over."

The man paused as if absorbing an unlikely truth. The noise conducted through the hull grew worse. Added to changes in engines and fuel systems which had made the asteroid capture possible, something was now being done about their ability to defend themselves. It had taken Gutierrez five minutes to consider and approve the plan.

"Then we-all got ourselves a problem, Gennul. Mah orders're t'prevent anybody else takin' 5023 Eris or learnin' its secrets—includin' ouah Russian friends. I'm here t'seize it, or see it destroyed. It's all up t'you folks down theah. Y'all copyin' me, Gennul? Ovah."

Dazzling against a star-flecked backdrop of blackest velvet, a space-suited figure made signals at him through the windshield. He should seal his helmet and gloves. Eichra Oren complied, helping Sam. Gutierrez shook his head and made stalling motions. "Not altogether, Admiral. Over."

The radio crackled. *"Horatio, like we say back in Baton Rouge, it's time t'fish or get off the pot. Yo' earlier orders're rescinded. Yo' people will return t'Earth, to a hero's welcome an' substantial raises in pay and benefits, if they'ah willin' to—hold on a minute."*

Again the radio fell silent. Inside his helmet, Eichra Oren blinked in response to a sudden implant message. He put a hand on Gutierrez's shoulder. The general closed the end of his mike tube with his thumb. "What is it?"

"Mister Thoggosh asks me to inform you that there are now *three* armed fleets in orbit, Russian, American, and

Chinese. An Admiral Hoong Liang is talking with him now, from *his* flagship, the *Dee Jen Djieh*."

This time the name of the ship seemed vaguely familiar. Gutierrez had no more than nodded before Delacroix was back. "*Horatio, it's gettin' crowded out heah. May be hard t'keep that promise—amnesty, a hero's welcome, pay an' benefits—shockin' how little store folks set by international treaties. I asked this heah Chinaman to explain himself, an' he said he's savin' his explanations for 'the Elders.' That make any sense to you? Ovah.*"

It should have made sense to Delacroix, or he should fire his Intelligence people. Gutierrez explained that the Elders were their nonhuman hosts. Outside, signals to seal his suit grew more frantic or irritated, depending on how much respect he believed was being accorded his rank. Delacroix thanked him in ominous, gracious tones, replying that with two hostile fleets to watch now, he had "choahs." He'd recontact the "gennul" as soon as possible.

Gutierrez unhooked his carrier from the console, plugged it in inside his collar, and had just settled his helmet when another voice sounded in his ears: "*Greetings to the expeditionary party on 5023 Eris. This person is Admiral Hoong Liang of the Celestial Fleet of the People's Republic of China. Have I the honor to address General Horatio Gutierrez?*"

Unable to resist peering out for a sign of the latest arrival (he saw none), Gutierrez replied in the affirmative. Through repeaters set up in camp, thirty-odd other humans listened. At news of a coming fleet, they'd debated the course they should follow while Gutierrez's party was still underground. They'd failed to reach a conclusion, nor would they have been entitled to act if they had. He'd given no one except Sebastiano and Ortiz, who must pilot the other ships, his reasons for allowing the shuttles to be armed. They'd agreed as he'd known they would and now sat in the lefthand seats of their own craft, *John Galt* and *Geronimo*, awaiting orders.

"*I've explained to Mister Thoggosh,*" Hoong replied, "*that my government, unlike certain others, is satisfied merely to keep the great ship you've discovered out of the exclusive hands of its potential enemies.*"

Gutierrez was suspicious. "You're saying you don't want it?"

"*Only the knowledge it represents.*" Hoong was amiable. "*I am confident that the Elders will someday share their own technology with us, whatever they find here. Perhaps they can be persuaded to establish regular trade with the Chinese People's Republic. In any event, as long as no nation has a monopoly on that knowledge and technology, we are content.*"

"Meaning what?" Both overhead observation windows chose that moment to pop from their frames, the round-cornered panes fielded by Eichra Oren as they drifted to the deck. This was the reason for insisting that they suit up inside the *Laika*, although no more than a heartbeat passed before the windows were replaced by mounting plates for the new weapons systems. Workmen trooped inboard and heavy cables soon extended into the command-deck computers.

"*Meaning,*" replied Hoong, "*that the Elders and your expedition are free to do what they wish without interference. I am authorized to help guarantee that freedom, should you desire it.*" Admiral Hoong would be unaware that Mister Thoggosh's mining equipment, basically electromagnetic cannon firing plasma "torpedoes" of unthinkable brilliance and heat, was a better guarantee than any he could offer. It had failed to penetrate the secrets of 5023 Eris, but that didn't keep it from being installed on the shuttles and used as weaponry more effective than any Earth had yet developed.

"*I'm impressed,*" Mister Thoggosh's voice was on the line, "*with your expression of self-interest, Admiral, so refreshing coming from a human. I daresay I haven't the faintest interest in trading with any Chinese People's Republic. I might, however, be persuaded to trade with Chinese people.*"

Chinese *people*, Gutierrez noted, not *the* Chinese people. He, too, was amazed by the admiral's offer, although he remained wary. The PRC was a mystery to generations of Americans. In an odd way it was a reversal of her classical policy of closing out the world. The world—at least its leading Marxist nations—had closed her out. Nobody in Soviet America was supposed to know what went on there, any more than what was happening in Switzerland, NeoIsrael, or South Africa, all polities which had refused—in terms expressible at times in body counts or megacuries—to join the United World Soviet.

"*Mister Thoggosh,*" Hoong replied, "*I am humbled by your—*"

Whatever else he had to say was drowned in static as, through the shuttle window, Gutierrez watched a new star flare to life and wink out. No one was ever certain who had launched it, but a missile of about a kilotonne's yield had been fired at the *Dee Jen Djieh*.

The instant its blip appeared on that vessel's radar, a dozen or more computer-controlled Gatling guns spewed tens of thousands of projectiles at it, in this instance failing to destroy it, but slewing it off course. When the missile's warhead, fused for impact, struck something solid—probably a chunk of orbiting debris—and ignited, it was hundreds of kilometers off-target. Fortunately, it had missed 5023 Eris, as well. The asteroid's organic canopy, where radiation rained down upon it, turned blue-purple for an instant, then slowly returned to its original butter yellow again, absorbing furious energies and protecting the asteroid's many tenants.

"Ortiz, Sebastiano, heads up!" Mindful to avoid the asteroid's unnamed artificial moon, Gutierrez—with the old fighter pilot's sizzle in his veins—ordered his ships aloft, their blunt noses aimed (the actual calculation was more complicated) at his estimate of the missile's launch-point. Eichra Oren slammed into the right hand seat, assisting as if born to it. Asteroids are wonderful, Gutierrez thought, for all the things they don't have, like significant gravity. Shuddering dramatically, which only made the overall effect that much better, the *Laika* took off horizontally, just like the rocket ships in an old Flash Gordon serial.

The word "orbit" had been abused to describe the locus of Earth's spacefleets, but the gravity of 5023 Eris was too negligible for that. The flotillas were disposed about the asteroid at roughly 120 degree intervals, keeping their eyes on both the surface and their rivals, but fuel—reaction mass, he reminded himself, these ships were fusion-powered—was being expended to keep them there. He didn't know whether the missile had been Russian or American. His copilot informed him that the Elders didn't know; everyone had been rattled by that first shot. As his own ship clawed its way into the sky, he expected to be blasted any second and thanked somebody's lousy reaction time when it didn't happen.

"This is the Erisian Space Patrol," he told his mike and got a grin from Eichra Oren (he'd been looking forward to saying that for hours). "All alien fleets will withdraw to a distance of one hundred thousand klicks or be destroyed." He'd had no idea of tactics when he'd ordered the launch, just a pilot's reflexive need, with their base under attack, to get his planes off the deck. Might as well be hung for a sheep, he thought, as for a lamb.

Delacroix had the same preference. *John Reed* chose that moment to fire several missiles. Gutierrez suspected that they were going to MIRV into dozens of smaller nuclear-tipped weapons. He couldn't tell whether they were aimed at the asteroid or at the shuttlecraft. He nudged the attitude control to drop the nose and slew it to starboard, lined up crosshairs painted on the windshield, and slapped a panel duct-taped to his seat arm.

A ball of eye-searing brilliance flashed toward the American fleet at a respectable fraction of the speed of light, catching the incoming missiles before they could disperse and enveloping them in a cloud of incandescent gas. As the wave front, attenuated by an intervening fifty kilometers, caught the *Laika*, he knew the critics were wrong to nitpick space operas for their battle scenes. Explosions in a vacuum are perfectly audible—when they create their own temporary atmosphere. His ship buffeted by a man-made storm, he wrestled with the attitude controls and primary thrusters.

Whenever his makeshift sights brushed across the fleet again, he stood his thumb on the trigger-panel and bore down. Distracted and confused, which was perfectly normal in combat, he never felt the blade sink into his neck until Eichra Oren leaped up to grapple with the assassin. Imprisoned by his seatbelt and unable to leave the controls in any event, the general could only watch—and listen—as whoever had attacked him caromed off the walls of the command deck with the Antarctican and his dog.

Sam couldn't use his teeth. Handicapped by his suit, he had to settle for springing from wherever he found himself, crashing into the struggling men, hitting Eichra Oren as often as the killer he fought. Eichra Oren, hampered by his clumsy NASA outfit, wasn't up to his martial best. It was all he could do to control the long, slim knife, still slippery with the general's blood.

The general's attention was elsewhere. So far, the intruding fleets had not engaged each other further, but were concentrating their energies on the three ancient but far from helpless shuttles. Gutierrez, one hand on the flight controls and the other on the firing panel, couldn't check to see how badly he was cut. He had to keep both eyes on the sky. Outside, one of Earth's ships exploded, spewing air and broken bodies.

He shook his head to clear it, which didn't produce any better results than it ever did. His own wound was beginning to hurt now as air whistled from his punctured suit into a cabin that was only partly repressurized. The blade had glanced off the metal ring which formed the suit's collar and had entered, almost at right angles to the original thrust, driving between his collarbone and shoulder. Deep enough and he might lose a lung.

A flash of light somewhere behind him put an abrupt stop to the wrestling noises. Gutierrez risked a brief glance. Eichra Oren had his fusion pistol in his hand and a torn thigh pocket to go with it. Half the assassin's body lay against the deck. The lower half was missing. Where it had been was a waist-thick cauterized stump.

Gutierrez turned his attention to the battle again, just in time to sear another flock of missiles.

With effort, Eichra Oren pried the helmet from the attacker's head.

"Alvarez," Sam said. "I've been keeping an eye on him. What'll you bet he's Iron Butterfly, the one who probably summoned that fleet out there?"

"No bets," the general answered over his shoulder. "Take a look at that!"

One of Gutierrez's automatic follow-up shots had fetched the *John Reed* a glancing blow on her starboard wingtip. He could see her now, along with a pair of escorts, hypersonic aerospace planes considerably larger than the shuttles, a fanciful design once meant to carry more than a thousand paying passengers across the Pacific at many times the speed of sound. To his knowledge, the idea had been abandoned as pointlessly expensive and the craft never built. Now here they were, three of them—probably more out of sight—fitted up as warships and carrying a swarm of smaller craft which they'd released just before the *John Reed* was hit. The plasma explosion had vaporized half a wing and set the Soviet American flagship spinning like a badly balanced top about her yaw axis.

"They seem to have skimped on attitude controls," Sam observed as the ship failed to slow and began breaking up with centrifugal stress. Ignoring her, the smaller ships, lifeboats or landing craft, the general wasn't certain which, began jetting for the asteroid. Getting handier with the plasma cannon, he picked as many off as he could until the angles changed and the asteroid was within his field of fire. The defenders on the surface were about to get very busy.

Gutierrez had ordered Sebastiano's *John Galt* toward the five-ship Russian fleet. To him they were mere dots on radar, which, after a single multimissile salvo and a mass launch of their own small vessels, began to withdraw. Sebastiano's cannon, spectacular even at this distance, batted the attack aside. The colonel's victory whoop—which he'd have expected sooner from Ortiz—rang in the general's ears, but Gutierrez didn't have the heart to reprimand him. One errant missile, still intact, seemed to impact without harm on the asteroid's borrowed moon.

Another volley, similar to that which had destroyed the *John Reed*, was less successful. The Russians had observed that the plasma weapons' speed far outstripped the reaction time of human or computerized gunners. They'd begun firing their Gatlings in the direction of Sebastiano's ship the instant they released their missiles. The resulting stream of projectiles was only partly effective at breaking up the ball of plasma streaking their way, but it saved the Russian flagship and the Banker with it. Damaged, the *Lavrenti Pavlovich Beria* withdrew at top velocity.

Gutierrez, one hand holding his ripped suit closed now, thought about picking up survivors from the *John Reed*, but the remaining American ships beat him to it. He thought about examining his own wound, but pushed it out of his mind. Ortiz, following a longer assigned course toward the PRC fleet, demanded attention. *"Don't look now, fellow space cadets,"* he remarked, *"but we're flanked!"*

The major was correct. Instead of firing missiles, the *Dee Jen Djieh* and three auxiliaries stooped on the asteroid like birds of prey, releasing hundreds of smaller objects. The Yaqui officer described them as spacesuited figures who landed on the surface and disappeared. They seemed to have some easy means of penetrating the canopy. Mister Thoggosh denied via implant having anything to do with it. His property was being invaded, he told Gutierrez through Eichra Oren, and he was sending security forces to deal with the intruders.

Before the general could give Eichra Oren a reply, a harsh light flared in the sky again. An unexpected interaction had occurred. Mister Thoggosh's unbeinged orbital station, with its automated neutrino-detector, was ablaze with dazzling white-hot thermonuclear fire. The nearby burst of a Russian atomic bomb had somehow ignited the little moonlet.

The bizarre result was that a tiny, artificial sun now brightened the sky of 5023 Eris.

FORTY-NINE
Sleeping Dragon

When PRC forces began appearing near their camp, the Americans were treated to a surprise. Not one was wearing anything describable as a uniform. Their leader (and all the rest as it turned out) spoke perfect colloquial English.

"Hi there!" A young oriental in Levis and flannel shirt greeted Owen, the first person he encountered. "I'm Colonel Tai of the People's Republic Extra-Special Forces. Could you direct me to the officer in charge? I've orders from Admiral Hoong to place myself under his or her command. We're the cavalry, arriving in the nick of time."

Sweating in the double-shadowed light of one sun too many, Owen looked to his companions, Danny and Tl°m°nch°l. Amidst the sound of faraway gunfire, the two men were trying, with scorpionoid assistance, to defend this sector of their perimeter. They'd already had a bit of sporadic shooting, nothing anyone would call a firefight, with Russian or American intruders (they weren't certain which) deeper in the forest. Whether this had produced any enemy casualties was something else they weren't sure of. They themselves were unscathed.

Owen inspected the young PRC officer who, despite his casual clothing and a kerchief he'd tied to a branch, wore a large autopistol slung under one armpit in a black nylon harness, and an even larger knife suspended handle-down under the other. "That'll be General Gutierrez," Owen told him, shifting the shotgun on his shoulder and lifting a broad thumb toward a canopy much brighter than when they'd first arrived. "He's busy right now and so are his seconds, Colonel Sebastiano and Major Ortiz. I'm Corporal Owen—" He gave Danny a nudge. "This is Lieutenant Gutierrez."

It was Danny's turn to blink, realizing that *he* was the officer in charge. "I suppose you're stuck with me, Colonel."

"Fine by me," the officer responded. He lifted fingers to his lips and whistled. Men and women in civilian clothing, more heavily armed than their leader and with a startling variety of what were clearly personal weapons, began melting out of the forest. They formed up loosely around the two surprised and skeptical Americans.

The scorpionoid laid a foreclaw on Danny's shoulder and did his best to imitate a whisper with his voice simulator. "Why do you and Roger not take Colonel Tai with you. I will stay here with his people."

Danny saw the sense of it. "Good thinking, Tl°m°nch°l, but all alone?"

In the distance, a grenade *crumped*. Chitin-armored manipulators rattled on Tl°m°nch°l's synthesizer where it hung beside his pistol. "No, Lieutenant, my people are scattered throughout these woods and are alert. We encircle them, should this prove to be a trick. Show the colonel your camp, I'll wait here."

"Okay." Danny turned to the young officer. "Colonel, I can't bring your whole unit back with me. If they'll wait here with Tl°m°nch°l, we can go see Mr. Empleado or Pin—I mean, Major Ortega y Pena."

Tai glanced at Tl°m°nch°l as if he were used to seeing aliens every day. "Okay, Lieutenant. One question: what do you want done with these?"

At a gesture, several of his troops dragged half a dozen figures forward, arms bound behind them, and threw them at Danny's feet. It was less cruel than it might have been at full gravity. Danny looked down at two Russian *Spetznaz* officers in battle dress and four bruised and disgruntled ASSR Marines.

"—estimates from my experts that our artificial sun will be short-lived, merely lasting a couple of thousand years. They're readjusting the temperature and humidity as we speak."

At camp, Mister Thoggosh was more in charge than anybody else. He'd returned with the general from the dig, but had decided to direct his own defenses from here, drinking beer through a plastic tube in his protective suit. Sporadic, faraway gunfire could still be heard as the PRC, the American expeditionaries, and the party of the Elders' people continued mopping up invaders.

"I'm impressed, Colonel Tai," the Proprietor admitted once a kettle had been set on the fire for tea. "We and our allies—with individuals from the ASSR expedition— welcome your support with gratitude. We nautiloids are amateurs in a field in which humans are the acknowledged experts."

Adjusting his weapons harness, the colonel settled by the fire despite the warmth overhead. He glanced around at the tents and other evidence of people roughing it on the terraformed asteroid. "And that would be?"

"War, my dear Colonel. 'Killing people and breaking things.' We haven't fought one in thousands of millennia. And in this particular battle, I'm afraid, nobody has the proper equipment or is altogether certain what to do. It was pure good fortune that our canopy was 'smart' enough to filter out the radiation from atomic weapons. Which reminds me—would you mind telling me how you got through it?"

"I'm pretty curious about that, myself." Still in his spacesuit, Gutierrez strode into camp with Sam and Eichra Oren. Toya rose from the fire to stand at the latter's side. Rosalind, who'd started to get up, sat down again. Danny suspected that Eichra Oren was about to have trouble. "Before anybody asks, the shooting's stopped upstairs, at least for now. The Russians and Americans have withdrawn amidst ugly muttering and threats from the Banker. Ortiz and Sebastiano are still out there patrolling, backed up by Admiral Hoong. My ship's refueling, so I can relieve them."

The man looked drawn and pale to his son and held his head at an angle. Perhaps only Danny understood that there was more to it than refueling or his father would have stayed with his ship. The PRC fleet was out there which meant that, having long avoided it, the rest of the expedition would now be forced to choose sides as the shuttle commanders had. It was a situation unlike any they'd faced before. In his mind were old movies about West Point on the eve of the War Between the States.

"Enzymes," replied Colonel Tai. "Your first reports were analyzed and, well, passed on, both to Russian and Chinese intelligence. I believe we arrived at the solution first, but . . ."

Gutierrez laughed. "Your secrets are as volatile as everybody else's?"

The colonel grimaced. "In any event, spray-application opened the canopy and closed it so that little air was lost. You've seen our prisoners?" He indicated the Russians and Americans, squatting in a row against one of the modules removed from the shuttles to make room for fuel. "We captured these Marines on the ground, having killed many of their comrades, but the Russians were trapped halfway through the canopy like flies in amber. These are the survivors. Their aerosol spray was too dilute."

"Russian quality control—or somebody's brother-in-law watering the stock to make an extra ruble." Gutierrez shook his head. "Very well, Colonel, what do you intend doing now?"

"Whatever you ask, sir, consistent with my nation's interests. I'm to assist under your orders. This group's one of twenty-three of which I'm in command. Altogether we are five hundred twenty-nine." He tapped an earpiece he was wearing. "I'm told we now have a great many more prisoners, too."

The gunfire did seem to be tapering off. The general whistled at the prospect of his command increasing more than tenfold. "Thanks, Colonel, I'll get back to you. If you'll excuse me . . ." He turned to Danny. "Lieutenant, have the company fall in, those not engaged in essential tasks."

"Sir!" Danny snapped a salute and began gathering the shuttle crews together. Perhaps the others had anticipated what was about to happen; the task was accomplished in only a few minutes.

It was obvious that Mister Thoggosh was satisfied. Rounding up personnel, Danny overheard him tell Eichra Oren—without benefit of implants—that it was a sign that "these organisms" were "learning to think for themselves. Despite Aelbraugh Pritsch's contrary urging," he told the Antarctican, "I intend to refrain from offering them any advice. As I informed my assistant, if they can learn to do the right thing, perhaps even bird-beings might learn to relax a little." Eichra Oren glanced at Toya and chuckled. Sam said something about Hell freezing over. Danny assumed the message had been meant for American ears although he didn't know why he'd been chosen to hear it. He'd pass it along to his father. The assembled company was asked to sit on the ground.

"So far," the general told his people, "events haven't left us much time for choices. The arrival of three fleets from Earth was a surprise even to the Elders, and we were fired on without warning. All we've done is defend ourselves. It may take some fancy legal work, but if anybody's interested, I'm willing to bet the offer from Admiral Delacroix is still open, and that the Banker will be willing to talk a deal, as well. Now that we've bought the time, we all have some thinking to do."

Gutierrez reminded his fellow human beings of everything that had happened here on 5023 Eris. On one hand, he pointed out, there were the Elders who, in their gruff, perplexing manner, had befriended them. They owed their lives many times over to these odd beings from a parallel reality. On the other hand, there were the governments of their own planet, made up of human beings like themselves. Did the expeditionaries owe them any special loyalty?

"Loyalty," Rosalind spoke aloud—and yet almost as if she were speaking to herself—"is supposed to be a two-way street."

"Excellent point," answered the Russian agriculturalist, Valerian. "Have these institutions ever done anything but exploit those of whom they demand loyalty—and in our case, betray and abandon us?"

"General Gutierrez, I demand that you put a stop at once to these disgusting amateur individualistics!" It was Empleado. "Our duty is clear! This talk is treason, not just to our government but to humanity itself!"

"Blow it out your ass, you KGB cockroach!" Danny watched his father carefully avoid seeing who'd said that. Some time passed before similar replies, mostly obscene, began to taper off. As his father continued, Danny found that his own choice wasn't all that hard. It was true that, if he sided with the Elders, he might never see his family—mother, brothers, sisters—again. His father had to be aware of that, and of the fact that the government might take his defection out on his wife and children. Danny also knew that this didn't make them different from anybody else here.

Although he couldn't say why, he felt that making the right choice was the best way he could help his family. He also knew that his father faced another problem. Despite his opening remarks, which had represented nothing less than the truth, the general wouldn't want, even by implication, to make choices for others. Wasn't the whole point of this situation the right and necessity to do that for oneself? This probably meant that Danny, too, should wait until the last minute before declaring himself, so as not to tip the balance. As it was, the others seemed to be having more difficulty than their commander and his son.

"I worry most," Gutierrez told them, "that after all we've been through, we'll find ourselves peering at each other over gunsights." He looked at his audience, most carrying weapons as they had since the initial misunderstanding with the Elders. "At the same time, you can bet the Banker's preoccupied with his own great fear that we might use Predecessor technology to defend ourselves. He may not know it, but his concern is groundless."

The crowd gave him a disappointed groan. Many of them, who hadn't helped explore below, had been harboring hopes of a miracle.

"Sorry, but it'll be years before we'll understand what 5023 Eris is capable of, let alone take advantage of it. Of course that hasn't stopped Nikola Deshovich from trying to prevent it. What he didn't count on was that, even with the Predecessors' systems still inactive, we're far from helpless."

"What do you mean, General?" the geologist, Guillermo interrupted. "I thought we were surrounded."

Gutierrez sighed. "Hector, there's a lesson here if we're smart enough to learn it. Back home, we delegate personal defense to the authorities."

"So scum like Deshovich," Danny was unable to help himself, "end up running things."

His father shrugged. "Fair enough. By contrast, the nautiloids are accustomed to personal weaponry." From a pocket, he pulled the tiny Kahr 9mm pistol he'd carried since finding it on Richardson's body. "And to tell the truth, I've sort of gotten used to it myself. Eichra Oren's little hypervelocity steam gun typifies the potency of private arms available to the Elders. The point is that each of these beings controls his own destiny."

Ortega y Pena snorted. "Small arms against nuclear weapons?"

"Excuse me, Horatio, I didn't intend to interrupt." Mister Thoggosh drew himself toward the group. "You mentioned a lesson to be learned. This Banker of yours doesn't want to destroy his enemies so much as steal what belongs to them, is that correct?"

"Not *my* Banker, Mister Thoggosh. Otherwise, you're right."

"Still, his purpose would be lost in destroying what he wants to seize."

The botanist nodded. "Which is probably why he's withdrawn for the present. A wise barbarian loots *before* he burns. The only way he could do that was to come down and fight at a level where small arms are effective. And there, he lost."

"For the time being, Federico, as you say," the general answered. "The nukes he brought are an empty threat. His manpower, drawn from World Soviet 'peacekeeping' forces, came expecting to assault wholly undefended territory." He indicated the prisoners. "Doctrine gave them no preparation for an armed population. Makes for an effective defense policy, doesn't it? But at a price no government today is willing to pay—"

"Limitations on its own power," Ortega y Pena offered, "set by the same armed population."

Mister Thoggosh chuckled. "They *are* beginning to learn, Horatio."

"Back on Earth, too," declared Colonel Tai. "Before we ran into Corporal Owen, we, well, *asked* our friends over there some leading questions."

Toya gasped. "You tortured them?"

Tai laughed. "We didn't have to—Pulaski, is it? They all gave themselves mental hernias thinking up information to swap for their lives. Some would have gone home for more, if we'd let them, and come back to give it to us. The point is, there are scattered uprisings all over Earth. The effort to seize this asteroid exhausted the resources of both Russia and America, weakened both governments, and deprived their leaders of any remaining credibility."

"So it's over."

"I'm not sure I'd go that far, General. If the Banker survived the battle, doubtless he'll continue to be the first-class nuisance he's always been."

"And what will your people do?"

"After things are squared away here, you mean? Well, some of us are preparing to return to Earth. If your people are concerned about events at home or worried about their families, they're free to return with us if they wish—and if you permit, of course."

"I appreciate the courtesy, but anybody can go back who wants to—including prisoners. Won't that make a crowded trip back for you, though?"

"Not for me, General. Many of us have elected to remain. After all, there's so much to be learned from the Elders."

"All right, welcome to 5023 Eris, then. Danny, please dismiss the company and let them do their own thinking." For the first time, he lifted a hand to his wounded neck. "Rosalind, can I see you a moment? I've got a paying customer for you—me."

FIFTY
Unfinished Business

Eichra Oren was sweating.

An artificial sun burned through the canopy, sharpening the shadows without raising temperatures. New friends and old enemies had departed for mankind's homeworld hours ago. Order was being restored to the motley communities of 5023 Eris.

By anybody's estimate, his professional tasks were probably over with. Now he steeled himself to attend to personal business. It was necessary, he told himself, and yet something he'd dreaded for weeks.

His relationship with Toya Pulaski, as artificial as the second sun shining overhead, had been imposed on him. From the first it had troubled his sense of ethics. The simple fact was that he found the woman about as unattractive as a human being could be. He felt guilty, but there was nothing he could do to hide it from himself, nor, knowing what he did of sapient psychology, would he have tried.

Just to make things even more complicated, he *was* interested in Rosalind Nguyen. It seemed to him she was everything that Toya could never be: graceful, beautiful, confident, even a little mysterious; the one similarity between the two was their intelligence. Rosalind, however, was unafraid of hers, and used it to accomplish things in the real world, rather than as a refuge from it. Still, before he could do anything about that, he had a debt to pay, and it was possible that it might spoil whatever chance he had with Rosalind. But as a man, and as a debt assessor, he couldn't afford to abdicate. He must tell Toya the truth about his assignment by Mister Thoggosh. Try as he might, in his 542 years of experience, he couldn't think of anything he'd ever looked forward to less.

After literally searching the world over—his legs ached from being folded under him in the electrostat he'd requisitioned for the purpose—he found her near the yawning triangular entrance to the asteroid's interior. A canvas awning had been put up on poles to protect its occupants from whatever weather 5023 Eris had to offer. Beneath it, a large table had been built from neatly sawn logs.

"Did you have a chance to talk with Colonel Tai about his personal background?" she was asking her companion. "I hear that the Chinese who came here are the result of endless batteries of personality tests as children who then underwent decades of isolation and cold-blooded conditioning."

Since the fighting, there had already been another subsurface excursion. Toya was examining Predecessor artifacts of a technical nature, spread out on the table before her. Nearby lay solvents, soap and water, and brushes of various sizes and stiffness. Bending over the table beside her, the machinist, Owen, was attempting to identify each of the pieces as it was cleaned off.

"What kind of training? Hello, Eichra Oren."

The Antarctican nodded back. Owen's beard was freshly trimmed and he was wearing what Eichra Oren was certain had recently been a clean uniform. He was shocked at this miraculous transformation. He hadn't seen an ironed uniform during his entire acquaintance with his fellow human beings on the asteroid, and Owen was the last individual he'd have expected to be wearing one. Sharp creases and pocket folds were still visible, although he and Toya were covered, head to toe, with several eons' accumulation of dust and dirt. It was clear to any observer that they were having the time of their lives.

"Hello, Eichra Oren," Toya echoed and went on. "Well, some subjects he mentioned were 'Elementary Practical Jokes,' 'Intermediate Intransigence,' 'Advanced Profanity,' and 'Postgraduate Greed.' "

"All of them meant," Eichra Oren told them, "to mimic the rugged individualism they feel was once characteristic of Americans and made you a great people. You began to decline—Tai's words, although I agree—when 'team-play' and other forms of soft collectivism became the order of the day. 'Ask not what your country can do for you,' et cetera, et cetera, et cetera."

"You're saying it was Wall Street and Madison Avenue that ruined us," Owen asked, "rather than Marxism?"

"I'm saying—or Colonel Tai is—that Marxism would have been laughed out of existence without Wall Street and Madison Avenue doing its advance work. However the kind of rugged individual the PRC most admires and tries to emulate isn't Rambo or John Wayne—although it's true that warriors are useful and comforting to have around—but the technically oriented 'nerd.' "

Toya started. Owen repeated, "Nerd?"

"Sure. Tai pointed out that the Japanese, to name a bad example, lost their technological and economic lead over that very issue. Not once during the twentieth or twenty-first centuries has that country ever suffered from mischievous computer hacking or lost a single person-hour to a domestic computer virus."

"This is bad?" There was a twinkle in Owen's eye.

"The PRC thinks it's bad for any culture. Like the lack of crime in England—because they haven't got the gumption for it—the Japanese lack the requisite individualism for such pranks. It's beaten out of them at an astonishingly early age, along with any real creativity, by their schoolmates, with the full approval of authority. There's a name for it that means 'Hammering down the nail that sticks up.' All they have left after that is a dull, placid conformity—and some really serious pathologies."

Owen nodded. "Therefore they lacked the resources—

call it the mental capital—for maintaining their otherwise impressive mid-twentieth-century gains."

"That's about it. The PRC belatedly decided to close its own potential 'nerd gap.' They built whole villages, high in the mountains or deep in the deserts, where individualism was practiced as if it were a foreign language. It was their hope that someday their experimental subjects could leave the villages to spread that 'language' among the rest of the people."

Toya shook her head. "But instead they risked everything to preserve the international balance of power? That doesn't make much sense."

Eichra Oren shrugged. "The whole effort would have been for nothing if the Russians or Americans acquired exclusive control of an overwhelmingly advanced technology." He cleared his throat. "Pardon me for changing the subject, Roger, but I need to speak with Toya, if you don't mind."

Before Owen could speak, Toya astonished them both. She blinked and looked at Eichra Oren. "I know why you're here and we don't have to make a big deal of it. There isn't anything we can't say in front of Roger."

Owen pointed a stubby finger at his own chest, silently mouthing the word "*moi*?"

Toya ignored him and continued speaking to the Antarctican. "I've been dreading this moment, having to tell you the truth, for weeks. I was assigned—against my will—by General Gutierrez and by Arthur Empleado, to 'distract' you and learn the Elders' secrets. I want to make it clear—no, no, please don't interrupt me, or I'll never get this out—that I have nothing against you. I enjoyed what happened, and I hope you did, too. It didn't just make me feel like a woman, it made me feel like a full-fledged human being for the first time in my life, and I'll always be grateful to you for that. But Eichra Oren, let's be realistic: I had my orders from the KGB, and I'll bet you had yours, too, from Mister Thoggosh."

Eichra Oren felt like imitating Owen, but she didn't give him time.

"Now I have my own interests." He knew that she meant something other than intellectual interests. Her gaze directed itself at the overweight, grease-covered machinist standing next to her. "And from the way you look at Dr. Nguyen and the way she looks at you, I'd guess that you have yours, as well. Over the past few weeks, I've learned to value you as a colleague and as a friend, Eichra Oren. Why can't we just leave it at that?"

Heretofore, Owen had been a dedicated bachelor, the expedition character. The lives of the Soviet Americans had often depended on his ability to fabricate whatever they needed. Laying a grimy hand on Toya's, he looked up from his work and grinned man-to-man at the assessor. Something about that grin told Eichra Oren he was more than he appeared to be. Not knowing what else to do, Eichra Oren grinned back, nodded at Toya, left the pair to their archaeological research, and stumped back the way he'd come to his waiting aerocraft.

To his surprise he found anger bubbling up inside him and knew he had some thinking to do before he could call his mind his own again.

It wasn't that he'd wanted the girl. She was right. His interests, like hers, lay elsewhere. Yet his ego felt bruised by rejection and he was dismayed to discover such a childish reaction lurking within him. It was another phenomenon he felt reluctant to tell his mother about. He knew from experience that this was a danger sign. He'd never been anything resembling a mother's boy. Eneri Relda, an active individual with "interests" of her own, would never have permitted it. But she was also a person of acute judgement who'd lived 15,000 years. He'd always valued her advice even when receiving it was painful or embarrassing.

By the time he reached his aerocraft, he'd had time to consider further and realized, with gratification, what had happened. As usual, the Elders' ancient *p'Nan* philosophy was proven correct. On the Forge of Adversity, Toya had transformed herself into her own person, self-confident and autonomous. And almost pretty, in a way, now that he came to think of it. It pleased him to believe he might have had something to do with the change.

Relieved—and free—he went to look for Rosalind.

BOOK III:

THIRD AMONG EQUALS

THIS BOOK IS DEDICATED to Dr. Jorge I. Aunon, to the faculty and staff of the Department of Electrical Engineering at Colorado State University, and to the CSU chapters of HKN and IEEE, in token payment of the only *other* kind of moral debt that is essentially unpayable.

FIFTY-ONE
Cocktails for Two

"But they're *vertebrates*, Doctor, they're *apes*! The fact is, they only qualify as predators on a technicality!"

"Yet qualify they do, my dear Chief Engineer, or they'd scarcely have evolved into sapient beings."

Running the soft grooming bristles growing along the undersides of his foremost pair of arms over his huge satiny-transparent eyes, Dlee Raftan Saon was barely aware of the gesture, which was reflexive. It always became more frequent when he was agitated. He'd have greatly preferred the comfortable ritual of filling, lighting, and tamping his long-stemmed briar pipe, but his companion's respiratory system, with which he had considerable professional acquaintance, was severely irritated by tobacco smoke.

"I beg you, Nannel Rab," he pleaded mockingly, "please tell me that you haven't acquired that pernicious habit of theirs, of judging others strictly by appearances."

Across from the doctor, Nannel Rab was as close to sitting as she ever came. Even as she tried to relax, the hairy palps either side of her mouth stirred restively, and she bounced a little on the eight furred, color-banded legs folded beneath her mass. On a low table between them, tall drinks of diluted grain alcohol (his flavored with honey, hers with dipteroid blood), gathered drops of moisture from the surrounding air.

Other voices came to them, muffled by a rough-textured ceiling, thick carpeting underfoot, soft upholstery, and an array of air curtains designed to provide privacy. Through a window close by, they could see into another lounge where marine sapients swam in liquid fluorocarbon charged with oxygen, breathable by the land species keeping them company. If her eight eyes, shiny black and of assorted sizes, had possessed lids, Nannel Rab would have blinked at what Dlee Raftan Saon had suggested. Even translated electronically, her voice was heavy with incredulity.

"Raftan, it has been my lifelong habit to judge people—of any species—only by what they do. These creatures began by intruding here unannounced, uninvited, disputing our claim to this asteroid—"

"Which only exists," he interrupted, "in their alternative version of the Solar System." He lifted a manipulator, forestalling any indignant retort on her part. "Nannel Rab, I don't question the justice of our claim here—rather, the claim of Mister Thoggosh—nor our right to be here, exploring. But it's wise to recall that we're the interlopers in this particular reality, and very far away from home."

"What is this American Soviet Socialist Republic anyway," she grumbled on as if she hadn't heard him, "but a coercive and collective state the likes of which more civilized versions of the Earth have not suffered in eons? Raftan, these people actually take orders from each other! I tell you, they're little more than savages!"

The doctor shook his head, a habit he'd learned from the very species under discussion. Given his exoskeletal configuration (he'd been compared by humans with a praying mantis a meter and a half tall), the motion came in short, hesitant jerks, his triangular face, mostly taken up by his eyes, swiveling on a nonexistent neck.

"Courageous savages, I daresay, to make what was for them a very arduous and dangerous voyage in three broken-down spacecraft left over from a previous generation—rather badly designed spacecraft, I might add, never intended for anything more ambitious than low Earth orbit, and unused for the better part of a century."

She snorted. "They were desperate."

"Still, it was a desperation with roots stretching back well before their time. Collective states are constitutionally incapable of reliably producing anything but corpses. Invariably, they use up whatever economic health they may have inherited from previous regimes even faster than they use up people. And in the end, they all come to pin outrageous hopes for recovery—asteroidal wealth in the present instance, or petroleum reserves in the past—on unreal expectations, in order . . ."

"In order to avoid abandoning the idiotic belief-system which made them desperate in the first place!"

"I know, I know." He nodded. "And so it was with our new human friends, although I gather that many of the individuals who were assigned here were disillusioned to begin with—and sufficiently indiscreet about saying so, perhaps, that they wound up being sent on this mission. Certain others among them seem to be learning quickly. Which means that they're rather intelligent savages, as well."

"Possibly too intelligent for their own good—certainly they are for ours!" The giant spider leaned forward, lifted her frosty glass, inserted its sipping tube past her complicated mouth-parts, and took a long, deep drink. "Consider the closely guarded secret of this asteroid, and Mister Thoggosh's high-flown ambitions for it. Look at the way they winkled *that* out of our esteemed partner-cum-employer. Human *friends*, you say? Raftan, are we speaking the same language?"

In fact they were not. From long association, each understood a smattering of the other's speech; neither was capable of generating the noises required for conversation. Nannel Rab had not said "winkled." Belonging to a species notoriously limited to a liquid diet, she'd used a verb-complex meaning, "draw blood for nutritional purposes." Dlee Raftan Saon's personal computer was well aware that a literal translation wouldn't have carried her intended meaning, since his ancestors had devoured their prey in chunks. For his benefit, it selected phonemes implying, "glean tidbits from one's seizing-claws." (Licking one's fingers was an equivalent habit, but that would have failed to convey the thought.) Only information-storage-and-retrieval devices implanted within the nervous systems of many simian, ursine, or dinosauroid/avian sapients would have chosen "winkled," meaning, "prise small scraps of meat from shellfish."

The physician followed the engineer's example, finishing his drink and mentally ordering another via the electronic network connecting his own cerebro-cortical implant with every other on the asteroid. As his order was brought by something resembling a large, glossy snake (it was actually the "messenger" tentacle of a bartender belonging to the same squidlike species as their associate, Mister Thoggosh), Dlee Raftan Saon patiently endured Nannel Rab's continuing diatribe.

"—their revolting mating habits, Raftan. That snoop Eichra Oren, coupling with Toya Pulaski merely for political purposes!"

Like everyone else in the small, isolated community who felt that they had little enough to amuse themselves with, both had followed recent gossip about the young human female who had been forced by her people's secret police to seduce Mister Thoggosh's only human employee in order to discover what was being searched for on an asteroid which, following human practice, was now being called "5023 Eris."

At the same time, Mister Thoggosh—the entrepreneur who sought a hoard of ancient Predecessor artifacts here—fearing what Marxist governments might do with such advanced technology (rumored to include a faster-than-light spaceship drive), had made similar demands of Eichra Oren, hoping to keep track of what the girl learned.

Dlee Raftan Saon made the dry, rustling noise that served his species as a chuckle. "I know your species marries for love, Nannel Rab. Mine, too, although we both have nonsapient relatives who tend to confuse their suitors with a midnight snack. I'll point out that Nek Nam'l Las is an arachnoid we'd both consider highly civilized. Nevertheless, her species never weds for anything *but* politics, and only stopped devouring the groom on the wedding night with the promulgation of her world's Sanguinary Edicts, a mere seven and a half centuries ago."

The mantis and the spider both paused to shudder over the strange customs of aliens. The culture they shared had

consisted of little else for 15,000 years, since the Elders—
an ancient species of spiral-shelled, sapient molluscs of
which Mister Thoggosh was a leading member—had begun
traveling between parallel universes. Until convinced that
the practice was unethical, the Elders had "collected"
millions of sapient beings (including mantises, spiders, and
Eichra Oren's human forebears from preglacial Antarctica)
from thousands of alternative versions of Earth. Even so,
there were still times, for specific individuals, when mutual
tolerance came somewhat less than easily.

"In any case," the doctor offered, "Toya has since shifted
her attentions to Corporal Owen, the machinist, who shares
her interest in paleontology, while Eichra Oren increasingly
seeks the companionship of my professional colleague,
Rosalind Nguyen. Left to themselves, perhaps they prefer
mating for personal reasons, after all."

"What they prefer is theft, rape, and murder! Having
abandoned space for a hundred years, it was only that incen-
tive which moved them to follow up their preliminary intrusion here by assembling not just one armed space fleet but
two—American and Russian—the latter commanded by that
butcher, what's-his-name, Nikola Deshovich, the one they
call 'the Banker,' for invasion of this asteroid!"

"Only after we'd discovered that 5023 Eris is no natural asteroid, but a giant spaceship, a technological prize too
glorious to ignore. And it was *three* fleets, my dear. You
have excluded mention of the Chinese People's Republic."

"Advisedly." She sniffed. "They came to rescue us. They
had no way of knowing that it was unnecessary, between
our technological superiority on the one manipulator—"

"And the fact that each of us makes a personal habit
of going heavily armed, on the other . . ."

"Not to mention Mister Thoggosh's last-minute refit of
those three American shuttlecraft."

Dlee Raftan Saon laughed. "Giving him something to
do with his otherwise useless mining equipment."

Had she been physically capable of it, Nannel Rab might
have blushed. As the Elders' chief engineer for this project,
she'd felt personally responsible for the failure of those
nuclear plasma devices—until they'd eventually discovered
that the artificial asteroid was covered, under a thin layer

of accreted topsoil, with a metallic skin so dense that not even neutrinos could penetrate it.

"Of all of the humans I've encountered so far," the giant spider offered, "excepting Eichra Oren and his mother, of course—" With her mention of the latter there was no sarcasm in Nannel Rab's voice; Eneri Relda was an original Antarctican, vastly long-lived even in the Elders' culture, "—only the Chinese are worthy of admiration."

"My dear Nannel Rab, the PRC Extra-Special Forces only came here hoping to obtain politically what they couldn't take by force. And Chinese history—from Temujin to Tien Anmen Square—is every bit as bloodsoaked and collectivized as any—"

"Yes, Doctor, but at least they had good sense enough to try to *simulate* individualism in order to restimulate their technical and economic progress."

"Certainly—by conscripting tens of thousands of bewildered and unwilling peasants, isolating them in mountain villages, and forcing them to be free at gunpoint." The doctor laughed again. "I must say, Nannel Rab, that your attitude surprises me. I was under the distinct impression that you *liked* these humans. You've always been civil to them, even pleasant at times."

"Those who try," the words came grudgingly, "to act like sapients. I suppose that you're right, that they can't help being what they are. Besides, we may well have been like that ourselves—our respective species, I mean—before we discovered real civilization. It was so long ago that nobody remembers."

"Nobody *cares* to remember." The physician nodded. "Except the Elders. They never forget anything."

"Thank the Egg," Nannel Rab sighed, unconsciously referring to the myth-system of an altogether different species that both were well acquainted with, "that all three fleets departed or were destroyed. We still have the humans from the first expedition and a few leftover invaders, but the excitement's over and done with."

"Yes," Dlee Raftan Saon agreed, raising his glass, "thank the Egg."

But they were both wrong.

It had only begun.

FIFTY-TWO
Gossip

"Trog Base, this is Trog One, do you copy?"

Something stirred in the darkness. Silent for uncountable millions of years, disturbed by trespassers only recently, briefly, then abandoned once again, the endless twisted passages now whispered with the echoes of a kind of movement which their builders had once made.

Within them, something—perhaps even someone—had ceased to be oblivious to her surroundings.

"We copy you five-by-five, Comrade Agriculturalist Valerian. What can we do y'for?"

Beneath the massive shield of her great body, the hardened ends of more than a hundred small limbs—locomotors and specialized manipulators—rattled and clicked as, pair by pair by pair, they slipped over the edge of the low pedestal on which she had stood sleeping for so long. Her most recent coherent memory was of having been placed there by her creators. It was the last thing she had been fully aware of—if such an expression was applicable under the circumstances—before losing her awareness for incalculable ages.

"We are still standing within the air lock, Colonel

Sebastiano—I mean, Trog Base. The outer door is down, as you can plainly see since you are standing almost on top of it—and apparently the new gold-foil antenna is working, or you would not be hearing this. The fruits of yesterday's capitalism should never be underrated. We have now swung the inner door aside and for the first time, Comrade Colonel, I myself truly believe that 5023 Eris is of artificial construction."

Her first new awareness had been of a short, broad-band burst of radiation exceeding that which was normally to be expected from cosmic rays and similar incidental energies. It could have been a nova in the near stellar neighborhood, even an unusually powerful solar flare. More to the point, its apparent proximity and magnitude had trembled on a threshold she had been constructed to interpret as potentially threatening to her own existence, and therefore to even more important values that she and she alone had been trusted to preserve.

"*I copy you, Andre. Glad to hear you're enjoying the sights. Please keep us advised of what everybody's doing down there, just in case something goes wrong, so the next bunch of victims will have some idea of what they're up against.*"

With enormous difficulty, she slewed and slithered down into the walkway running past the base of the pedestal, seeking traction, and attempting to point herself in the direction she knew to be correct. She was a superb thing of her kind. It was probable that no other sapient species could have brought anything even remotely as durable and reliable as she was into existence. Nevertheless, she had not moved from her place of waiting for an unimaginably long time, and her internal mechanisms for maintenance, regeneration, self-repair, and buoyancy control were slow responding to her needs.

"*I understand, Trog Base, like dismantling a bomb in the movies—and here was I, believing that you simply enjoyed chatting with me. We are about to start into the hemispheric chamber where the many tunnels diverge, and we can see the fluorescent adhesive markings Eichra Oren left behind just before our glorious United World Soviet attempted to steal this place from Mister Thoggosh. Do you copy?*"

Soon, in addition to her other difficulties, there was a problem with the medium she'd been propelling herself through. By rights it should have remained a thin, transparent, chemically neutral liquid. Certainly it had been that way when she had surrendered consciousness unthinkable ages ago. Now instead, having forced her way through a semi-hardened plug of the stuff into what appeared to her broad spectrum of sensors to be a near-vacuum filling the corridors all around her, what was left of her original environment seemed to lie congealed in thickened puddles on the floor.

"Copy, Trog One. Lay off the politics if you can, Andre. It isn't that I don't agree with you wholeheartedly—most of us do. But this little world has seen enough trouble recently, without your bringing up the late, lamented invasion by the combined—"

"And somewhat pathetic—"

"Yeah, and somewhat pathetic battle fleets of Earth. Tell you what: just be satisfied that they all went home in a snit, and stick to the travelogue you signed on for, okay, buddy?"

Perhaps "awareness" was not the proper word for what she felt. Perhaps "felt" was equally inappropriate. The fact was that, in the combined vocabularies of 100,000 sapient species scattered throughout an equal number of alternative probabilities, no entirely accurate expression existed to describe a phenomenon that was the transient manifestation of a highly complex process which could not be called thought, which was not exactly feeling, but which was far too sophisticated to compare with the dull-witted adding-machine workings of electromechanical computing devices. Nor was vocabulary the only barrier to fully comprehending, across a yawning gulf of time, space, and conceptuality, the precise nature of what was going on inside her.

"Okay, you got it, Comrade Colonel, sir. Please to inform Eichra Oren that his fluorescent patches glow very cheerfully in the darkness where he slapped them onto the walls— but that regrettably they are beginning to peel off. I believe that the surfaces are either too slippery, like Teflon, or that perhaps there is some sort of volatile substance hanging about in the atmosphere, attacking the adhesive."

*"That's a big roger, Trog One. And you're telling him
yourself, since he's standing right here beside me now, along
with Colonel Tai, late of the PRC's Extra-Special Forces.
Eichra Oren advises that it's probably a little bit of both—
slickness and solvent. The lovely Dr. Rosalind Nguyen, also
here I'm glad to say, warns us, solventwise, that you'd
better keep your helmets sealed up down there or your
offspring just might need two of them per suit."*

The recent radiation surge had been detected, not upon
her own immediate surface, here within the eternally night-
blackened corridors she had somnolently inhabited for inex-
pressible eons, but on the surface far above—for which she
had also been constructed to "feel" responsible. For her—
known to her long-absent creators as well as to herself, as
"Model 17"—the discrete location of any such disturbance
didn't matter, tied in as intimately as she was with the vaster
artificial organism of which she was a part. What she "felt,"
with regard to the disturbance, might have been compared
to a tickle or an itch. And her reflexive "instinct" to scratch
it was growing stronger and more irresistible by the nanosecond.

*"I am rogering the hell out of that, Col . . . wonder
what . . . must be doing to our . . ."*

*"Trog One, this is Trog Base. Andre, you're breaking up
down there, do you copy?"*

Model 17's second awareness was that something had
intruded here again *recently*. That expression, too, failed
adequately to express what was conveyed by the dense cas-
cades of fleeting subatomic particles that served as nerve
impulses for an entity accustomed to calculating the passage of time in substantial fractions of the life cycle of an
entire universe. The latest trespass had occurred within the
last seventy-two hours, vastly less than an eye-blink to
Model 17. Whatever the intruder's nature had been, it was
not the kind of being she "thought" of as her own kind.
Even worse, it had left its untidy, alien traces everywhere.

"Trog One, Trog Base. Do you copy?"

More than anything else, this particular response, bordering on the emotional, was sufficient reason to think of
Model 17 as "she." She had been created in the precise
image of her makers, each and every one of whom had

been a fully functional, if parthenogenetic, female. Her sense of what was proper and fastidious exceeded even theirs—exactly as they had intended—and her inclination to nurture and defend that for which she had been constructed to feel responsible was no less pronounced.

"Trog One, this is Trog Base! Andre, do you copy?"

"Very sorry about that, Trog Base. Complications have arisen. Please to give us just one fucking minute."

"Sorry, Doc! Hey, watch it, Trog One, there's a lady present. Will you please tell us what you're doing? Do you copy, Trog One?"

In part, Model 17's creators had bestowed upon her such powerful maternal inclinations because that accurately reflected their own underlying nature, unconscious and virtually uniform throughout the species. In part, the exercise had been deliberate. As they had conceived it, hers was a monumentally maternal task. To her creators—and now to Model 17— it was absolutely without question the most maternal task ever undertaken.

"Copy, Trog Base. This is Roger Betal, the new, improved Trog One, stuck here in the branching-chamber for the duration, according to plan. We all got started down that marked tunnel and lost you, Colonel, so now there's a Trog Two, for whom I'll relay."

In Model 17, the mere awareness of recent trespasses generated nothing resembling alarm. Even "heightened alertness" would probably have put it too strongly. Model 17 simply performed according to her technical specifications, doing exactly what she had been constructed to do under the presently governing circumstances by her far-sighted builders, exactly as she had remained dormant under the previously governing circumstances for more than three quarters of a billion revolutions of the planet she "regarded" as her home world, about the star she "thought" of as the Sun.

Now, reoriented and restored to an acceptable percentage of her fullest capacities, she began making her difficult way along the offensively filthy corridor (even in conditions approaching free fall, it seemed unnatural to her to be crawling, centimeter by centimeter, along the bottom of a passageway instead of jet-propelling herself through its center) upward, slowly, toward the surface.

"Roger, Trog One—I mean 'copy,' Roger. And will you kindly lean on them a little, down there, to keep us up to date? I know it makes me a boring person, but we'd prefer not to be left with any unsolved mysteries up here. Do you copy?"

"Copy you, Trog Base. I'm sorry to say that we've got a Trog Three now. C.C. Jones has been appointed Trog Two, stationary, and isn't liking it much. He's relaying to me. I sure wish we had some more of that gold foil to string along these corridors as an antenna. These little suit radios are the only good equipment we were issued, but the rest of the party only made it about seventy-five meters before I lost them. Some kinda stuff this place is made of."

"Copy, Trog One. If it stops neutrinos, it'll sure as shit stop radio—sorry, Doc. Keep us advised."

Model 17 crawled onward and upward, ignoring all clutter and decay now, having just received indication that two separate parties were descending toward her, following different routes. Whether her makers had intended her to operate in precisely this manner was questionable. Perhaps they had built better—or at least more thoroughly—than even they realized, emphasizing certain aspects of her fundamental programming to the detriment of certain others.

"That's a roger, Trog Base, and so am I—I always wanted to say that. Trog Three made it to the place we were warned about, where the fluorocarbon's congealed almost solid. Now I don't feel quite so bad about being left out of all the fun. They're making extremely rude remarks down there with reference to Vaseline and Jell-O. Also, we now have a Trog Four—made it almost three hundred meters that time, believe it or not—and it's Remgar d'Nod's turn in the barrel. The suggestion is that the tunnel must be acting as a waveguide. Do you copy?"

"I copy your copy, Trog One, Remgar d'Nod is at Trog Three, saving him the trouble of having to wipe Vaseline and Jell-O off of all eight feet. You can reassure Trog Four that they should be getting into cleaner stuff any time now."

Perhaps it was only that she had been built to reprogram

herself on the basis of new data: the noise and heat (which she was ill equipped to recognize for what it was) of a battle raging briefly over the surface of the asteroid; or an awareness that the trespassers were returning. Whatever the case, restoring her environment to original specifications would now be her second priority—immediately after she attended to these latest alien invaders of her realm.

"With due respect, Colonel, sir, it's getting kind of creepy down there, and I think they've got better things to worry about than my repeating what they heard at this morning's briefing. Hold on, we've got a Trog Five at another five hundred fifty meters. I don't know who's relaying traffic at Trog Four. The whole process is starting to take time and I'm not sure how accurate all these repetitions are. Wasn't there a party game like this, called 'Gossip'? You copy?"

In any event, Model 17 understood that it was her duty, crafted into every molecule of her being, streaming through conductors relaying data to her central processor, charging each returning particle which served her in place of will—to meet these invaders.

"Well excuse me all to hell, Trog One. We—"

"Break, break, break! We got a bulletin, Colonel!"

"Copy, Trog One, go ahead."

"You know that statue they told us to watch out for, the one that looks like a giant trilobite?"

"We copy, Trog—hey, watch the fingers!"

"Sorry, Juan. I, er, copy you, Trog One. This is Eichra Oren, Roger. What about that statue?"

"Well, you can tell all of its many admirers that it must be off on a museum tour."

"What?"

"Trog Five is at the traffic island where they told us to look for it—and it's gone!"

FIFTY-THREE
Eight Little Indians

Impatiently, Dr°f°rst°v rattled his claws on his equipment belt.

He was waiting for the humans to catch up—as usual.

For a while he'd hoped that the rest of those soft-bodied, slow-moving, overly fragile creatures would be left behind one by one, just as Valerian, Betal, and Jones had been, to relay communications to the asteroid's surface—until Tl°m°nch°l and Major Jesus Ortiz, jointly commanding this foray, had agreed to leave Remgar d'Nod at yet another point where the signal had begun fading. It had been a terrible decision, Dr°f°rst°v thought, and therefore probably Ortiz's idea.

Arachnids . . . now, they were worthwhile companions when going in harm's way. Despite their relative shortage of limbs they were almost as strong and adroit as his own people (whom certain unmentionable others called "sea-scorpionoids"—as if humans would enjoy being called "ape-oids" all the time). Remgar d'Nod was rather on the smallish side for a civilized spider, standing only about three quarters of Dr°f°rst°v's own height—no more than half that of a human—the majority of sapient arachnids was

considerably bigger, at least twice Dr°f°rst°v's height. However, even Remgar d'Nod's modest proportions seemed to
shock the humans, who had fondly imagined that kind of
size impossible for invertebrates to attain.

Yet in many alternative probabilities (including that which
had given rise to Dr°f°rst°v's species), an evolutionary turning point had been reached long ago when arthropods
developed a better sort of carapace, composed of long-chain
proteins stronger and more resilient than the crumbly
calcium carbonate or brittle chitin they'd begun with. Ironically enough, it greatly resembled the fibrous
silicon-petroplastics from which the humans had fabricated
major sections of their three primitive spaceships. With that
change, exoskeletous organisms could now grow large
enough, against the pull of gravity which had elsewhere
mandated internal skeletons, to support the extensive
neurological complexity necessary for sapience.

Dr°f°rst°v gave the synthesizer at his belt another
irritated drumroll while twiddling the small appendages
that served him as thumbs on his second and third pairs
of arms. It never occurred to him that he and Tl°m°nch°l
found the going easier because they were the only beings
who had been inside the asteroid once before—knowing
the territory did confer a certain advantage—or that the
organisms who had designed this place might have been
a bit like sea-scorpions themselves.

It was bad enough—it was positively nauseating if he
gave it any real thought—that these creatures wore their
bones on the *insides* of their bodies, with the squishy parts
outside for all the world to see. No wonder they moved
so cautiously: they must be in constant fear of injury! He'd
never seen the sense of being any kind of vertebrate. A
person might just as well have no skeleton at all.

"Hey, Driffer-stiff!"

Ortiz's breath steamed the inside of his helmet as he
waddled toward the sea-scorpionoid in his bulky spacesuit.
To Dr°f°rst°v, he looked like a nonsapient primate wrapped
in dough, ready for baking—one of his favorite dishes. He
would have been appalled to learn that Ortiz was equally
fond of broiled lobster. Major Federico Ortega y Pena, one
of the human scientists, puffed along right behind him.

And that was another thing, Dr°f°rst°v thought, he was thoroughly sick of hearing his name badly pronounced. Didn't any of these mammals have an ear between them? On the other claw, to be perfectly honest, no sapient he knew of—mollusc, avian, vegetabloid, even arachnid— seemed capable of saying his name right, and not even the Elders' translation software could manage it. He and his people carried vocal synthesizers, not merely to convert their own cheery click-rattling speech for the benefit of others, but to sift and strain the mumbling of those others into something understandable by beings accustomed to decent elocution.

Shrugging to himself, he let his claws rattle over the keyboard, "That's 'Dr°f°rst°v,' Major Ortiz. I'm sorry, was I traveling too fast for you and your companion?"

"Droverstove." The Yaqui officer frowned, concentrating hard. The sight of the man's expression was almost too horrible for Dr°f°rst°v, he had to acknowledge, hardened veteran though he was, even softened by the fogged plastic of the man's face-bubble. He'd never want any of his hatchlings to see it. "Drufferstuff. I'll get it right yet."

"Perhaps you will, Major, but not this time."

"Dr°f°rst°v!"

Another synthesizer sternly demanded his attention. The devices had been invented in the first place because V°bl°f°tz°r, Dr°f°rst°v's own name for the version of Earth his ancestors had been taken from some 15,000 years ago, had been broken up into thousands of—well, tribes wasn't the word, and neither was kingdoms—each with its own distinctive language. The Elders claimed that Dr°f°rst°v's species had generated more different tongues (both species speaking figuratively) than the remainder of all known sapients put together.

"Will you kindly stop giving that poor mammal a hard time and—" the speaker suddenly, and politely, switched to English, "help me find some trace of that blasted missing statue?"

"Yes sir, Tl°m°nch°l, sir." Dr°f°rst°v's touch on the keyboard, using a trade-speech their two cultures shared, was flavored with irony, "To hear is to obey. I live to grovel." In English: "Do you suppose it was stolen during the battle?"

Ignoring Dr°f°rst°v's sarcasm, Tl°m°nch°l made a gesture translatable as a shrug, "Well, it's true we haven't accounted yet for every one of the invaders, and it's possible that one or more of them managed to get down here. The airlock is larva's play to operate once you understand how it works. But if that statue was stolen, why?"

"And by whom?" Ortiz added.

"When did looters ever need a reason to loot?" asked Dr°f°rst°v.

"I don't know," replied Tl°m°nch°l, "but it makes me nervous, all the same. I wish we hadn't had to leave half of our party behind, just to retain contact with the surface."

Ortiz agreed. "Mister Thoggosh has promised that the next group will have automated relays they can place along the way. Meanwhile, we'll just have to suffer. Look, I'll check that battle-planning room Eichra Oren found, if you or Dreversteve here—" by now Dr°f°rst°v suspected the man was mangling his name on purpose, just to get under his carapace, "—want to start looking elsewhere."

And so it was.

On the previous sortie Dr°f°rst°v had done his share of cautious exploration and bemused speculating. Passageways, roundly triangular in cross section, branched interminably before them, disappearing into the unplumbed depths of the asteroid. They'd been forced to exercise extreme measures not to get lost. Corridor after endless corridor, unmarked as far as they could tell, had admitted them to countless rooms—administrative complexes, scientific facilities, janitoria, food services, surgeries—arrayed in no intelligible order, every one with massive, tightly fitting doors that swung at a touch on hinges still limber and silent after what, a billion years?

It sent an eerie flush of warmth through Dr°f°rst°v's gills just thinking about it.

Not even rooms which were unmistakably residential had locks. It was as if those who used them, unimaginable eons ago, had never developed a need for personal privacy. (Nor, to all appearances, had they invented bulkheads in case a section of the ship were damaged.) Huge chambers with long squatting rows of smoothly grotesque ceramic shapes attached to the deck reminded Dr°f°rst°v of stories humans told of communal lavatories during their military training days. His own people were fastidiously private about their eliminatory processes.

At all times, Dr°f°rst°v was careful to leave an open door between him and the remainder of his party, since signals from his implant wouldn't penetrate whatever the artificial asteroid was made of. That was another trouble with the humans. Not coming from the culture of the Elders, they were compelled to communicate through crude devices external to their bodies, built into their environmental suits. Fortunately, their signals could be received by his own equipment.

"Federico, Tlamanchal, Drafferstaff," the electronic voice of Ortiz came to him. "Be advised: Valerian at Trog Four says Remgar d'Nod just told him that Jones can't raise Betal at Trog One, so I guess we're cut off from the surface. He thinks it's just a temporary glitch of some kind, but I think we should all be ready to pull out damned fast if it isn't—and keep our powder dry in the meantime."

It had been a thousand years since Dr°f°rst°v's folk had used chemically powered weapons—and longer since they'd taken deities and damnation seriously—but he understood what the man had meant. That was his personal policy in any case. He helped search room after room again, looking for the vanished statue while preoccupied with increasingly uneasy feelings. It was a hopeless task anyway. They might poke around down here a thousand years or one hundred thousand, not just the four of them, but the entire personnel of both expeditions, human and that of the Elders, and not see a fraction of what was here to be seen.

It wasn't just the daunting volume of the asteroid. Half of what they investigated didn't have any discernible function. What was the purpose of a house-sized room, for example—its walls pierced at several levels by a dozen doors—filled to the ceiling with a resilient plastic, most of it removed again by boring millions of tiny tunnels through it, each no bigger across than his foreclaw?

And what should they make of the great free-turning cylinders—there were many more of these than of the bathroom-auditoriums—which one of the humans had aptly compared to an outsized geologist's tumbler for polishing gemstones?

Or of the enormous low-ceilinged chamber with its almost military ranks of large, polished metal cubes which could be pushed across the floor as easily as if they stood on ball bearings—but which sailed sedately back if left alone?

Absently he listened to Ortega jabber irrelevancies about the incomprehensible "artwork" decorating corridor walls. What would a soil specialist know about art? Meanwhile, Tl°m°nch°l and Ortega found what appeared to be a fresh fluorocarbon reservoir. Good: maybe they could get the place cleaned and oxygenated. Then they could stop wearing the protective suits (his own, unlike those of the humans, was of lightweight transparent film, but it chafed him and rendered him clumsy) which made exploring down here so arduous.

"Dr°f°rst°v!" This time it was Tl°m°nch°l's voice, although he could also hear Ortiz relaying the message to Ortega. "Valerian reports that Remgar d'Nod has lost contact with Jones! I don't know what's going on, but I want you to rejoin us where we first saw the statue. We're going to withdraw from this place immediately!"

"You needn't tell me twice," Dr°f°rst°v responded, consulting a map which had been growing in his memory as they explored. He'd planned to upload it onto the Elders' network for collation with his colleagues' similar maps, for use by anyone who wanted it. "I'll cut through the next chamber, since the path appears shorter."

"Hurry, Dr°f°rst°v, and be extremely wary! Now Valerian can't raise Remgar d'Nod!"

Senses on edge, Dr°f°rst°v pushed past what seemed like his hundredth door into a place he hadn't seen before but which had been described to him, a darkened hemisphere like an astronomical theater, occupied by two objects standing on a common, irregularly pentagonal base and raised about the length of his own body. Elsewhere, softly glowing walls had offered sufficient illumination. Here he must depend on what now seemed a feeble light that he carried at his belt.

Throwing bizarre shadows on the curved wall behind it, the taller of the structures, twenty or thirty times his height, was smoothly cylindrical except for a stepped section near the base. It reminded him of the observation tower at a flyport, even to the compartment at the top, a flattened cone consisting entirely of windows. What its occupants were supposed to observe here was unclear, since the walls around it were a featureless off-white, some almost indestructible synthetic laid over the same impervious metal as the asteroid's surface.

Standing beside it was something even more curious. Four or five body-lengths from the tower, a large pipe rose to twice his height, bent at a right angle, and ended in a ball joint straddled by a pair of massive bars rising to half the height of the tower. In the gloom, Dr°f°rst°v could just see that the bars were capable of lying parallel to the floor instead of standing as they did now, or of occupying any position between. At the middle they were connected by some kind of machinery. At the other end they held another ball joint forming the end of yet another angled section of pipe. This was flanged and attached off-center to the back (at least he thought it was the back) of what might have been a huge mirror, although the great disk-shape, as large in diameter as the pentagonal base it stood on, didn't reflect any frequency of light that he was capable of seeing.

"Hurry, Dr°f°rst°v," Tl°m°nch°l begged, "we've lost touch with Valerian—and Ortega no longer responds!"

"I'm almost there—another few dozen body-lengths, Tl°m°nch°l."

Silence was the only answer he received.

"Tl°m°nch°l!"

"I'm still here. Sorry to have frightened you, but Ortiz went to find Ortega, and now I can't contact either of them. Get back here as quickly as you can, my friend."

Ordinarily he might have objected to the word "frightened." Now, feeling very much alone, he crossed the chamber until he could see the blank, concave upper surface of the great mirror. On the floor behind the structures, somewhat concealed by them, lay a smaller mirror hinged at one edge to a complicated stem and a sort of streamlined collar that looked as if it might fit over the top of the tower. Close by moved a humped, oddly familiar-looking shadow.

Dr°f°rst°v shouted over his implant before he knew what he was doing and snatched his plasma weapon from its scabbard. The sighting-field above its boxy receiver rippled with the image of the small mirror and support structure which seemed to be wrenching itself across the floor. Panning to the shadow at one end, he was startled by the presence at his elbows of Tl°m°nch°l, also with weapon drawn.

"Greetings, Peerless Leader." Dr°f°rst°v had learned that from Owen. "Observe the lump over there, dragging stuff across the floor. We've found your missing statue."

"You'd entertain at your own interment." Tl°m°nch°l was annoyed. "I'd prefer to find our missing friends—and I worry that they may have found the statue before us."

"On the contrary," Dr°f°rst°v answered. "It found them."

He pointed to a place low on the wall where the vague, dripping forms of six limp bodies, five human and one arachnoid, hung upside down. Abruptly the humped object stopped its fretful tugging on the structure, turned, and started toward them.

FIFTY-FOUR
One Bug to Another

"Molluscs, you say? I don't *believe* it! Would either of you care for more tea?"

"No thank you, Model 17," Dr°f°rst°v answered. Tl°m°nch°l had curled both pairs of long, graceful, jointed antennae in a silent but articulate grimace of negation with which he completely sympathized, himself. A little tea went a long, long way, he was discovering. Any sanitary relief their suits afforded was of limited capacity, and no other facilities seemed available at the moment to match their anatomy.

"I assure you that it's true, however. As far as anybody is aware, the Elders—who are nautiloids and therefore molluscs—are the first Successor species to your own."

All three understood that Dr°f°rst°v was speaking figuratively. Model 17, as she had asked that they call her, no more typified those who had constructed 5023 Eris than the two sea-scorpionoid explorers did. She—it appeared females had been even more dominant among her creators' species than was the case now among most arachnoids— was a trilobitic robot rather than a proper trilobitoid. The trilobitoid sapients in whose image she had been created

444

had vanished utterly from the Solar System eons ago, leaving only her behind.

"Indeed," Tl°m°nch°l agreed, "sea-scorpionoids like our ancestors rose to sapience directly after the nautiloids, and only then, of course, on an entirely different set of time-lines. We've found that this is the way it usually works."

"It's absurd," objected Model 17, "and on top of one absurdity, you present me with yet another: you actually expect me to believe that some of the putatively sapient creatures you have brought with you are land animals— mammals!"

"And they call us giant bugs." Tl°m°nch°l's swimmerettes stirred in a resigned shrug. "If you live long enough, you discover that interspecies revulsion is relative."

"Speaking of relativity, Model 17," added Dr°f°rst°v, "as one bug to another, Trebla's Law of Relative Probability holds that, from the unique perspective of each individual universe of alternative probability, it will inevitably appear that that universe, and only that universe, represents the highest likelihood of having developed, and that all others are less probable—many absurdly so."

At the moment they occupied a small room ("parlor" was the word that came to Dr°f°rst°v's mind) just off the larger hemisphere where he had made his horrifying discovery.

Light and power had been restored here and the room refilled, Model 17 assured them, with clean, well-oxygenated fluorocarbon kept separate from the outer room by a transparent membrane they could walk through, if they wished, as easily as if it weren't there at all. This room, too, had a circular floorplan, its single enveloping wall composed of cabinets without conspicuous handles rising to the ceiling and of countertops no higher than the risers on a flight of stairs. For want of better furniture, they sat on the floor.

Model 17 had explained that this was one of several hundred such convenient sanctuaries scattered throughout the asteroid which she used as offices, workshops, storerooms, and to the degree she needed them, personal quarters. Several hundred million years ago, she had kept a few supplies here for the benefit of her creators, who had often come to consult her and check on her performance prior to their departure. Appearing eager now to impress the sea-scorpionoids as a hostess, she had offered them tea brewed in a sort of pressure cooker which they sipped from tubes, having taken the risk—being no less eager to be decent guests—of peeling back the faces of their flexible helmets.

The liquid atmosphere had an ancient, musty flavor which began to fade almost as soon as it was noticed.

It had been a matter of sheer evolutionary good luck that Dr°f°rst°v and Tl°m°nch°l had possessed organs of speech extremely similar to those of the Predecessors. The language they were presently employing was a common sea-scorpionoid trade-speech which Model 17 or some subordinate device of hers had been recording and sorting through ever since they'd arrived on the asteroid.

It was good luck, too, that they had managed to establish contact with the trilobitoid robot before they met the same grim fate as the remainder of their party. The shocking sight of those half dozen bodies glistening in the lamplight, their distorted shadows dancing on the wall behind them—and the way he'd felt about seeing them hanging there—would stay with Dr°f°rst°v for the rest of his life.

If he lived that long.

"Even so," Model 17 replied, "these nautiloids, these molluscs you speak of . . . they may be your metaphorical Elders, but they are most assuredly not mine. Nonetheless, my fine new friends, I am very grateful to have been awakened, whatever the nature of the beings who awakened me. You see, self-evolved organic sapience has always been something of a mystery and a marvel to me. I inevitably feel the most profound respect imaginable in its presence—although, of course, I realize that that is precisely what I was *programmed* to feel."

"Respect," Dr°f°rst°v replied graciously, "is a learned attitude in all sapient entities, Model 17, be they living or cybernetic. In point of fact, you could even say that my parents programmed me—although no doubt with considerably greater difficulty—in exactly the same way your creators did you."

"How generous of you." Her armor-segmented dorsal

area expanded and contracted in what appeared to be a sigh. "All the more reason, I fear, to regret my tragic error."

"Now, Model 17 . . ." Tl°m°nch°l waved a sympathetic feeler.

"I offer no excuse, gentlebeings, but simply explain that I am something more than the mere servomechanism you presently see before you, and at the same time, something less. I am not so much a self-contained device as I am an extension of this vessel's entire computer complex. Deeply preoccupied with bringing billions of systems back online for the first time in many ages, I was not yet operating at full efficiency. As a consequence, it was all over long before I realized that your friends were the representatives of various unanticipated Successor species, rather than the agents of our mutual enemy, the Eldest."

"Error, too," Dr°f°rst°v paraphrased himself gallantly, concealing his sincere relief that it would be Tl°m°nch°l's responsibility, rather than his own, to explain to the so-called Proprietor of this enterprise, Mister Thoggosh, what had happened to the others, "is characteristic of organic and mechanical entities. Except, of course, that unlike mutual respect, no one ever seems to have to learn it."

Model 17 had already implied that the sea-scorpionoids were the Successors her creators had really had in mind when they'd built 5023 Eris. Nor was this the first time she'd mentioned "the Eldest," whoever they were. They'd asked her about this earlier, and then backed off. Either she knew nothing more about the Eldest or would say nothing more. At this point, especially if she were indeed the key control-device for the asteroid, they were disinclined to press her.

"You are indeed kind, Draferstiv," Model 17 replied, proving no more capable of pronouncing his name correctly than any other being he'd ever known. "I was extremely worried that you might overestimate my capabilities and come to count on me too much. I am, after all, only a working prototype, the seventeenth in my line, to be precise, and the first to be deemed even marginally satisfactory by my makers. But they were hurried toward the end, by their preparations for departure, and may have been overly optimistic in their estimate, especially of my ability to survive all this time without significant deterioration.

"Are you sure you won't have more tea?"

Dr°f°rst°v cringed. "No thank you, Model 17, I think we've both had quite enough." He pointed toward the door they'd come though. "You might explain the machinery you were working with out there when we met—that is, if you don't mind."

"Not at all, Driferstav, that is the primary function I was originally programmed for, having been built to serve my creators' eventual Successors—molluscs, you say? I still find that very hard to credit. The machinery in the chamber next door—"

"It's a tachyon telescope."

The words were in English. Ortiz pushed through the membrane from the room outside, making scrubbing motions along his spacesuited arms and drawing his EAA Witness to make sure nothing interfered with its operation. Thumbing the catch at the root of the trigger guard, he slipped the magazine out to inspect the top cartridge, drew the slide back far enough to see the chambered round glittering back at him, moved the slide forward again, let the hammer down from its half-cocked position, reinserted the magazine with a slap of his palm, and holstered the weapon. He still wore his huge NASA helmet and they were hearing him over their implants. He put his hands on his hips and looked around.

"That's what our resident power engineer, Remgar d'Nod, has to say about it, anyway. Me, I'm just an old jet-fighter jockey who wouldn't know a tachyon from—"

"Tachycardia," Remgar d'Nod supplied, having followed Ortiz through the membrane and into the smaller room. He still looked a bit unstable on his eight furry legs. "Which is what our mechanical friend here gave me a healthy dose of when she—"

"There, Tleemeencheel, Droofoorstoov, you see?" Model 17 swiveled away from the newcomers just as Ortega y Pena joined them. "That releasing enzyme may work slowly after all these millennia, but it remains effective. If there were even the faintest trace left of the cyanoacrylate adhesive I used, so very regrettably, to attach these gentlebeings to the wall outside, I would be able to detect it instantly as a fluorocarbon pollutant on my life-support monitors."

She turned toward her erstwhile victims. "Major Ortiz, Engineer Remgar d'Nod, Doctor Ortega, I tendered my most profuse apologies to you while you were still, er, attached to the wall. Now I tender them again, with an equal sincerity. There is sufficient ambient oxygen in this chamber that you may safely remove your environmental coverings if you desire. May I offer you some tea?"

"Tea?" Ortiz repeated. "No, thanks. I'll keep my helmet on, too, if you don't mind." He hooked a gauntleted thumb toward the slim pack on his back, rather different in style and color from his bulky spacesuit. "This molecular recycler we got from the Elders works pretty damn well and so far I've avoided doing fluorocarbon with Mister Thoggosh. You wouldn't want me to spoil a perfect record, would you? I don't know about that releasing enzyme, either, Model 17. I still feel sticky all over."

Ortega nodded weary, wordless agreement, apparently still stunned by his recent experience. Unlike the major, the sea-scorpionoids knew, he was no rough-and-ready combat veteran by training or inclination, but a soil chemist. Despite the room's liquid buoyancy and the asteroid's almost nonexistent gravity, he sat down heavily on the floor and stared at his knees, staying out of the conversation.

"So do I," Remgar d'Nod agreed. "Model 17, you've brought a new meaning to the term 'glue gun.' It's one of the more effective weapons I've encountered—certainly enough to make any web-spinning arachnoid turn purple with envy. Hoist by my own petard, as it were—although I must admit I've never understood that particular turn of phrase. Isn't 'petard' French for 'one who farts'?"

Ortega lifted his head, opened his mouth to explain, then, appearing too tired, closed his mouth and waved it all away. Ortiz grinned. "You people must have more efficient spacesuits than we do. The expression makes *perfect* sense to me." Ortiz had found this whole episode nothing but funny, lending credence to the theory that he'd inherited his sense of humor from his Yaqui ancestors.

The mock trilobite rippled one edge of her carapace to expose a modified limb ending in a small nozzle. "My 'glue gun,' Remgar d'Nod, is strictly a utility meant for effecting emergency repairs. It hadn't occurred to me to employ it as a weapon until I felt compelled to improvise. The selectively permeable membrane you've passed through should have removed any lingering traces. Perhaps the residual stickiness you're experiencing is psychological in character."

"Perhaps," the spider told her. He, too, had his weapon out, a plasma pistol much like the one Eichra Oren carried, and was inspecting its heat-blackened blast orifice. "I'll risk breathing your fluorocarbon, and I'd appreciate a flask of tea—and anything stronger you put in it—after what we've all been through.

"Where are the others?" Tl°m°nch°l asked.

"Oh, they'll be along," replied the spider, sliding his little gun into a holster slung from the underside of his thorax and methodically proceeding to groom each of his spacesuited legs in turn, using his gloved palps. "For some reason, it seems to be taking their glue a little longer to finish dissolving than it did ours."

"It had been polymerizing somewhat longer," Model 17 began to explain, "since I came across them in the companionways above, shortly after finding the other . . ."

She broke off suddenly, turned, and lumbered to a low counter, preparing tea for Remgar d'Nod. As they had with regard to the Eldest, both Tl°m°nch°l and Dr°f°rst°v noticed her peculiar behavior and filed it away for future consideration.

"Also," she said, going on as if she hadn't suddenly interrupted herself and changed the subject, "I had to take more care for the safety of your friends Valerian, Betal, and Jones—just as I was with Major Ortiz and Doctor Ortega. The releasing enzyme threatened to attack the substance of their environmental coverings, which seem to be of somewhat lesser quality than your own."

She turned again, bringing a stoppered plastic flask of hot tea to the spider. "Remgar d'Nod, I've fortified this with a small amount of pure ethanol and trust you'll find it as much to your taste as my creators always did. While we are waiting for your friends outside, I'm pleased to inform you that the entire structure of this body you call

5023 Eris is capable of use as an antenna in your frequencies. Would you care to have communication with the surface restored?"

Ortiz laughed. "Does a chicken have lips?"

"A chicken?" Model 17 made a puzzled noise. Ortiz explained what a chicken was. "Then as I understand it," she replied, "chickens do *not* have lips. Does that mean—"

"He means," Remgar d'Nod put in after a long sip of fortified tea, "do nautiloids squirt luminous ink?"

Dr°f°rst°v recognized the game from his study of Earth culture, a new hobby he shared with many of the nonhumans. "Yes, in other words, is a bear Catholic?"

"And," offered Tl°m°nch°l, "does the pope—"

"Ah, it's the old jokes that are best," Ortega spoke at last, loosening the metal ring which held his helmet to the shoulders of his suit. Exhaling, he lifted the helmet—a huge air bubble drifted to the ceiling like a silver balloon—and took in a huge breath of fluorocarbon. "That's much better. I believe I'll try some tea now—just like Remgar d'Nod's—if you don't mind, Model 17."

"And meanwhile," Dr°f°rst°v offered, "you might explain what you look at with a tachyon telescope."

FIFTY-FIVE
Missing Matter

"I'll be morally indebted if I know!"

As with Tl°m°nch°l and Dr°f°rst°v, Remgar d'Nod's vocabulary had never included the expression—or more importantly, the concept—"to be damned." Unlike quite a number of other species with which he was familiar, his own people had achieved their place at the pinnacle of evolution relatively slowly and gracefully, suffering less damage in the process than those, like humans, who had virtually exploded into that awareness of self-awareness which is sapience. They had never (and the "therefore" was strictly Remgar d'Nod's opinion) felt a need for the buffer against harsh reality that religion represents.

Disgusted nevertheless, he cautiously regarded what seemed to be a solid, meter-square block of steel before he gave it an idle push with two of his right legs. There were, he estimated, some 1249 other meter-square steel cubes here exactly like the one he was playing with, lined up in neat rows of 50 by 25.

The object resisted his attentions at first, then it began to slide soundlessly, almost effortlessly—the humans had used the expression "greased ball bearings on Teflon"—

across the alleyway, also about a meter wide, separating it
from its nearest identical neighbor. Although Remgar d'Nod
carried an effective weapon, was not alone at the moment,
and his eight eyes gave him a full 360 degrees of peripheral vision, the low lighting and even lower ceiling in this
peculiar place were beginning to make him feel extremely
nervous.

"Model 17 started to explain what this place was for,
but then got bogged down somehow—not the first time
that's happened with her. In the end, she insisted that even
the Elders lack a sufficiently sophisticated understanding
of basic physics to comprehend what she was trying to tell
us!"

He made a trilling noise through the spiracles along
his abdomen, the arachnoid equivalent of a scornful snort.
It was one thing, he thought, to be insulted directly and
deliberately. It was another—and far more difficult to
countenance—when the insult was casual, accidental, and
delivered almost in passing.

The apostrophe-symbol in what he thought of as his
"trailing" name stood modestly for a lengthy collection of
syllables listing various praiseworthy achievements of his
ancestors, many of them scientific in character. When he'd
accumulated a list of praiseworthy achievements of his own
to be modest about (such as surviving this dumb expedition and maybe even distinguishing himself) another apos-
trophe might be inserted in his "leading" name. At the
moment, the prospects for such an honor didn't seem
particularly bright.

"Look at it this way," his companion replied mildly, crossing his eyes. Uncrossing them, he added, "That's why our
esteemed employer, Mister Thoggosh—addressed by those
who are overly impressed by authority as 'The Proprietor'—
brought us to this asteroid in the first place, isn't it, to gain
a better understanding of physics?"

Unlike the other rooms Model 17 had brought back to
life over the past several hours as she went through the
process of reactivating the entire artificial asteroid, the light
in this one had remained dim, tinted a deep, eerie blue.

The large, white, furry canine variously known to friends
as "Sam," "Oasam," and "Otusam," moved to sniff at the

metal cube in front of him and lift an irreverent hind leg—before he appeared to remember that he was still encumbered by his transparent environmental suit. Remgar d'Nod was well aware that it was an old joke his friend never seemed to tire of repeating, but exactly like crossing his eyes in the presence of sapients whose optical organs happened to be faceted, it was invariably lost on most of his nonhuman companions.

"In that respect at least," the dog continued, "I think we can afford to give Model 17 the benefit of the doubt. How would you like to try to explain the underlying principles of the dimensional translocator which brought us here, say, to one of our new American acquaintances? I'll bet you'd have better luck conducting a seminar for them on the practical application of evil spirits. By the way, did she ever reveal what the tachyon telescope is for?"

Remgar d'Nod kept pushing the cube until it almost touched the next one in line. He felt another hint of resistance, no greater than before, then there were two cubes—still not quite touching one another—moving along in front of him.

Although he rather liked the sapient dog, the arachnoid engineer found he resented being interrogated this way. Just now he didn't really want to think about physics, the Americans, Model 17, or his employer, Mister Thoggosh. All he wanted at the moment was to get out of this fluorocarbon soup, spin himself a nice tight, dry, little overnight cocoon somewhere, go to sleep, and dream the lucid dreams his people always dreamed, about his wives and children back home in a friendly universe that seemed further away to him every day.

Even more than Tl°m°nch°l, Dr°f°rst°v, and the other sea-scorpionoids he knew, Remgar d'Nod was the descendant of a hunter-warrior race whose nomadic yet highly technologized existence was a continual source of embarrassment to academics and scholars who maintained that, in order for true civilization to develop, a people must first tie themselves to a piece of land, preferably through the practice of agriculture. The culture his immediate ancestors had disappeared from some 15,000 years ago had ranged freely over two planets and three moons in their mechanized wanderings. They'd turned Mars into a hunting garden, been in the process of terraforming Venus, and made everyday household use of catalytic fusion.

And perhaps, Remgar d'Nod thought, because they'd never beaten their swords into plowshares—the latter demanding greater brute strength and sexual dimorphism from their wielders than the former—they were unique among arachnoids in that females were neither morphologically nor socially dominant. Most other sapients had difficulty distinguishing the males of his species from the females.

Remgar d'Nod stood twice as high as Sam at the shoulders and was covered with a soft tan-brown pelt shading to a creamy color at the rounded crest of his carapace and almost to black at the dainty tips of the plump legs curled beneath his body. His eight eyes were of assorted sizes, every one of them bright with intelligence, curiosity, and humor. An arachnid biologist would easily have spotted the tiny, alert jumping spider in his evolutionary past, slightly wider than it was long, little more than a ferocious little ball of fur and fangs.

A hundred million years of evolution had not left his species unchanged. For one thing, they were much larger than their ancestors—although small as sapient spiders went—having benefitted from the same mutational chemistry that made that sort of size possible for sapient arthropods elsewhere. They still spun fiber useful for hunting, fishing, and making shelter (although domesticated non-sapients kept by his people did it better and there had been a flourishing synthetic industry in his home universe, as well). But they ate solid food and gave live birth to blond-pelted bright-eyed children who clung easily to the thick fur of either parent, the females producing a fine, soft, easily digested silk for the young which other species sometimes compared to spun-sugar candy.

"The tachyon telescope?" he repeated Sam's question at last. "Certainly she explained it . . . sort of. In that polite, matter-of-fact way of hers, she informed us ignorant savages that it was for seeing anything out in the galaxy, beyond the Solar System, that happens to be moving faster than the speed of light."

"Hmph." The dog sat on his haunches between two stationary cubes. "How much would there be to see?"

"From what she said, more than you might guess." Experimentally, he applied sideways pressure until his cubes not-quite-collided with one to the left. He then pushed all three on an odd, unpredictable diagonal. "She told us that the universe—any universe—is full of natural objects moving faster than light, but that they can't be seen by anyone moving slower, which makes a crazy kind of sense, I guess. She says that's where we'll find the so-called missing matter astrophysicists worry about so much. She implied even more—an entire mirror-universe in which tachyons are basic particles like quarks or photons, complete with the analog of stars, galaxies, and living ecologies—but wouldn't go into any detail about it."

"As if we didn't have enough universes on our hands, already." The dog chuckled, a very humanlike sound coming from his suit transducer. Unlike many of Mister Thoggosh's land-dwelling employees, he didn't care for swimming in oxygenated liquid fluorocarbon even under the best of circumstances and had refused to take his filmsuit off down here. "Personally, I'd guess that anything moving faster than light would stir up a pretty visible racket, especially whenever it happened to smack into something going slower than light. Did she happen to say what she intended to look for with that thing? Or why it was so all-fired important to get it operating right after she came out of hibernation?"

At last Remgar d'Nod let the cube go, watching it and its displaced companions slowly reverse themselves and begin drifting back to their proper places. The fascinating thing, the reason he'd pushed them off sideways, was that any stationary cube which happened to be in the way would politely move until the displaced cubes had passed, then go back to where it belonged. Why, he couldn't say.

"I'm afraid she didn't, Sam. I have half an idea she wants to see what became of the Predecessors. If it works like a radio telescope, maybe she can even consult with them."

"'A radio for speaking with God,'" Sam quoted in a French accent. The citation was lost on the arachnoid. Probably another old American TV show he'd dredged up.

"She does seem extremely disappointed for some

reason," he told the dog, "that the Successors turned out to be molluscs, rather than arthropods." All three metal blocks were back in place now, and he had exhausted his patience. "Listen, Sam, I don't want to be rude, but I have work to do. Is there some point to all this?"

The dog appeared to lift an eyebrow. "I certainly hope not."

"What?"

"Look, Remgar d'Nod old buddy, it wasn't simply to annoy you that I asked you to step into this square-balled billiard parlor for a little chat with me. In the light of certain disturbing facts we've already uncovered, my boss was worried by the reports you and the others sent back of your initial interview with Model 17. That's why we hustled down here after communications were restored."

The spider focused his full attention on the dog. "Certain disturbing facts such as . . . ?"

"Consider the implications." Somehow the shaggy white creature managed to convey a shrug. "In our explorations so far, we've yet to find a single door—not even to what are clearly personal quarters—with a lock on it. And if we're right about the bathrooms, not one has a partition in it or a private stall."

"That's what's so disturbing?" Remgar d'Nod snorted again. "Sam, I know of many peoples, certain tribes among my own species, without much sense of privacy or property—"

"Okay," the dog persisted, "how about this: we've discovered several medical facilities aboard this overblown bowling ball. What you may not know is that Rosalind—Dr. Nguyen—says they're all just Band-Aid emporia for minor wounds, the school nurse kind of thing. Dlee Raftan Saon agrees: no equipment or supplies for dealing with major trauma, nothing at all to cope with disease."

"Interesting." The arachnoid thought about it. "No, I hadn't noticed that. Maybe the Predecessors had eradicated disease altogether. Judging from their engineering, they were pretty advanced. But what if they hadn't, Sam? What does it prove?"

"Not a blasted thing. But it gives us a very unpleasant idea." Sam lifted a hind foot to scratch behind one ear and was again impeded by his suit. "My boss thinks he knows what those big rock tumbler things are for. He thinks they're for grinding up the bodies of dead—or maybe just injured and useless—trilobites. Have you noticed how close they are to the kitchen facilities?"

Remgar d'Nod swallowed uncomfortably. "Ugh."

"I'll see that 'ugh' and raise you a 'yech.' Add it up yourself: no personal privacy, no heroic medicine, presumptive evidence of cannibalism. Model 17—"

The spider interrupted. "You think she's dangerous to us?"

Sam shook his head. "Not directly, perhaps, but Model 17's a cybernetic device constructed and programmed by a race of apparently antlike sapients—and that contradiction's disturbing enough—who never got around to inventing individualism. She was created to serve Successor species, yet unavoidably the Predecessors will have built into her many of their own values and prejudices."

"Well," the arachnoid argued, thinking of the robot's repeated apologies to Valerian, Betal, Jones, Ortega, Ortiz, Tl°m°nch°l, Dr°f°rst°v, and himself, "once she got the idea who we were—or weren't—she seemed to treat each of us as individuals."

"She's a very talented device. Her builders knew she'd be dealing with beings who possessed viewpoints quite different from their own. But she was constructed hastily, according to what she told you, and shut off before any extensive testing."

"Meaning what?"

"Meaning nothing—we hope. But deep down, she reflects the values of her makers. Even if we're only right about the locks, the infirmaries, and the bathrooms—not the tumblers or the kitchens—she inherently needs to be part of a tight-knit community of beings identical to herself. Now she's unique and alone. And she's been conscious long enough for the isolation to begin driving her insane."

Remgar d'Nod would have shaken his head had he been capable of it. "Can a machine go insane?"

"You haven't seen *2001 a Space Oddity*?" Sam peered suspiciously around the corners of the cubes to his right and left. "What worries Eichra Oren and me most is something else you may not have noticed. We're keeping quiet about it, so far. At the air lock, we've found what could be evidence of comings and goings during the late lamented unpleasant-ness with this Earth's gaggle of governments. Either some of the troopies got down here, which we doubt, or some-thing from down here got up there. If it was Model 17, why didn't she mention it?"

The spider sighed exasperatedly. "Why not ask her?"

"I'm here because I use my implant for more than com-municating. You might even say I *am* my implant. My boss thought I might see things from Model 17's point of view better than a natural sapient. If I had fingers and she had a nose, I'd try the Vulcan mind-meld. But I haven't asked because she isn't here now. She left after we came down, saying she had maintenance to perform. Eichra Oren was right: it sounded phony to me. She didn't say where or to what, but she trundled off, deeper into the asteroid, like a bat out of New Jersey."

"Which is why you asked me about the tachyon tele-scope. Well, I've given you everything I know, Sam, plus my unsubstantiated opinion that she wants to see what became of the Predecessors and maybe even talk with them. What else can I do for you?"

Sam peered around the cubes again, in imitation of the Soviet Americans, making sure they weren't being over-heard. "You realize there's another, more ominous possi-bility."

Remgar d'Nod flapped his palps in an impatient ges-ture. "And what might that be, my mammalian friend?"

Sam looked around again and lowered his voice. "That if it's dark outside, before putting your car in gear it's always a good idea to turn on the headlights."

"You mean—"

"I mean a tachyon telescope might be how a faster-than-light starship sees where it's going. Maybe we're all about to take a little trip, whether we want to or—!"

Without warning, the metal blocks Sam sat between sud-denly slammed together, snapping the dog's ribs, crushing his pelvis, and fracturing his spine.

FIFTY-SIX
More Restitution

"I, and I alone am responsible for what happened to your friend Sam, Eichra Oren."

"Now, Model 17—"

"Others of your friends have told me that you are a professional expert in matters of personal guilt. Is there anything I can I do to restore the moral balance?"

"I—"

English being the language they had in common, that was what they spoke. Momentarily speechless, Eichra Oren drew a ragged breath and shook his head. His experience with what amounted, metaphorically, to an amputation was much too recent for him to control himself any better than that. The sword he'd done the literal amputation with lay across his knees, still bloody from the ugly job.

Finally, he spoke: "Model 17, I'm too personally involved, I'm afraid—and on that account professionally disqualified—to be of much assistance to you. For whatever informal reassurance it may be worth, I can't see how you're to blame for what happened in any case. It's exactly the kind of horrible accident that was bound to occur sooner or later whenever people start experimenting, fooling around with an unfamiliar piece of equipment. In principle, it doesn't matter whether it's a simple handtool or a gigantic spacecraft."

Before Model 17 could reply, a creature resembling a manta ray wrapped in transparent plastic, walking on its rear corners, pushed a cart past where the human sat on a bench extruded from the sidewalk. Pausing along the way, she greeted Eichra Oren by name in his native Antarctican, tendered her sincerest condolences, and offered him and Model 17, who squatted beside him, a doughnut and a cup of coffee.

Each refused politely, for different reasons.

"That was Remaulthiek," Eichra Oren nodded in the direction the manta creature had trundled, "who probably knows more about matters of guilt than I ever will."

Everyone on 5023 Eris was aware that Remaulthiek was working her way through some kind of self-imposed penance for a moral debt she'd incurred long before anybody could remember. What Eichra Oren didn't know, nor did anyone else he was acquainted with, was exactly what she'd done and to whom. It was characteristic of the culture he'd grown up in that no one ever thought to ask her and never would.

"Nonetheless," the ancient trilobitic robot insisted, "it was my personal responsibility. It matters little whose mind or manipulator lay upon the controls. I was specifically constructed by those you call the Predecessors, and left behind when they departed, for the purpose of accomplishing two equally important tasks."

The man nodded. "And those were . . . ?"

"My first task," she answered, "was to warn possible Successor races of an impending catastrophe too unspeakably terrible for any organic sapient to contemplate sanely. Eichra Oren, forgive me, but I must reiterate that the threat to all sapient life, in every version of the Solar System, represented by the Eldest is—"

"Excuse me," the *p'Nan* moral debt assessor found that he was interrupting the robot as gently as he could. Something she'd said intrigued him, although he couldn't place a finger on exactly what. "What was your second task, Model 17?"

There was an empty moment where a living, breathing creature would have put a sigh. Like any sapient being, she was beginning to pick up phrasing and other nuances of language from those she associated with. "My second task appeared much simpler, much more straightforward than the first when I was initially programmed. Now I am not so certain about that. I was to be in total control of this gigantic spacecraft, as you call it, prepared in every way to assist less-technologically accomplished beings with its eventual management."

"Well," Eichra Oren answered thoughtfully, "these things don't happen all at once, do they? You're supposed to warn us all about the Eldest, and you're supposed be a—I don't know, a flight instructor, or purser or helmsbeing, maybe. It seems to me that you're somewhere in the middle of getting both of those jobs done."

"See how well I have accomplished either!" Making scrabbling sounds with her many feet, she swiveled around like a small tank, so as to avoid looking at him or being looked at.

Eichra Oren was profoundly surprised. Having lived among technologically advanced sapients all his life, well over half a millennium so far, even he would never have guessed that a machine, however sophisticated, might be capable of voicing sarcastic bitterness or what appeared to be genuine self-deprecation. Model 17 actually seemed to be experiencing guilt. This was a startling new phenomenon to him, or at least he believed it was. It had never occurred to him that the friend he grieved over at this very moment had been at least partially a machine himself—just as he had never thought of Sam as an animal.

Model 17 had told him that this was her first excursion onto the asteroidal surface, which had never been meant by its builders for habitation. Each of them had already expressed a wish that the circumstances of the occasion were more pleasant. At the moment, words having failed to take them any further, they simply kept each other company, the man sitting on his bench and the robot sprawling on her countless legs, waiting beside a main-level thoroughfare in the Elders' settlement. While Model 17 contemplated some inward guilt-distorted landscape, Eichra Oren stared upward into the great trees and the environmental canopy they formed overhead, reconsidering his evaluation of her.

At a sudden harsh noise, they both turned to listen. A little way down the busy street a shrill-voiced sapient whose species had obviously evolved from deepwater starfish had set up shop while they were preoccupied with their own problems and was now selling flowers, balloons, the equivalent of greeting cards, and similar gifts and souvenirs from a pushcart exactly like Remaulthiek's.

Eichra Oren returned his eyes to the canopy and his attention to his earlier thoughts.

The artificial environment which the Elders and their allied species had arranged for themselves here on 5023 Eris was simple in conception, but it was a simplicity born of great and ancient sophistication. Following the initial remote surveys of the asteroid—and the one and only universe of alternative probability in which it could be found—beginning in what Americans reckoned as the late nineteenth century, the seeds of a unique species of plant, genetically engineered to germinate and prosper despite the freezing vacuum of space, had been carefully scattered across its carbonaceous "topsoil." These had sprouted relatively quickly into what one deeply impressed Soviet American arrival had compared to outsized California redwoods and another with more imagination had later labeled "super kudzu."

Obtaining a predetermined maximum height of about a kilometer above the impact-cratered surface, the great trees had branched and leaved, spreading luxuriantly, intertwining at the tops with their nearest neighbors. Reacting to ultraviolet and other spaceborne energies as they had been designed to do, their overlapping leaves had fused with one another, finally forming a strong, translucent, air-tight sphere about the entire asteroid, capable of resisting further meteorite damage, absorbing harmful radiation, and retaining warmth, air, and humidity which the trees themselves and other organisms, subsequently planted, had begun generating.

The nautiloid settlement itself consisted of an airy and fanciful cascade of broad, interlocking platforms attached to the great trees and arrayed at various heights, most of them no more than a meter or two above the ground, some soaring into the uppermost branches. They, too, had been cultivated from engineered seeds, drawing nourishment which the trees were equipped to provide during an initial period of growth. Similar seeds had produced buildings of one or two or three stories resting atop these decks, affording ample space for offices, workshops, laboratories, residences, and commercial establishments which served the community of scientific pioneers, consisting of members of more than a hundred individual sapient species.

The resulting ambience was that of a small university town on the Earth where Eichra Oren had grown up. Most of the traffic hurrying past him and his cybernetic companion proceeded on foot or some analogous organ. High on its protectively shod tentacle-tips in the asteroid's low gravity, one of the automobile-sized, squidlike, colorfully snail-shelled molluscs called the "Elders" strode by, looking like one of the asteroid's spiders wrapped in cellophane.

Several genuine spiders of at least three species could be seen as well, along with a member of an insectoid race that strongly resembled large praying mantises, and many insectlike creatures who were actually more closely related to crabs and lobsters.

Here and there, a handful of three- or four-wheeled contraptions provided transportation for environment-suited marine organisms without legs. Overhead streaked an occasional circular aerocraft, miniature sister craft to those which, during the Elders' later surveys of this particular Solar System, had helped inspire "flying saucer" reports on Earth for more than a century.

A handbell rang.

What appeared to be a large, blunt-tailed snake rode by, wrapped about the upright portion of a unicycle. This was no independent organism, but belonged to one of the Elders who had dispatched it on some errand. Watching it turn a corner, and assured that it wasn't a messenger-tentacle sent to fetch him by his erstwhile employer, Mister Thoggosh, Eichra Oren discovered that despite himself he'd been considering the question of the robot's guilt in the back of his mind.

"Model 17," he asked suddenly, "can you say, in all honesty, that you've done your best to accomplish both of the tasks you were programmed by the Predecessors to perform?"

He waited through a long silence before she answered. "Why, I suppose I can. Although, with perhaps one exception so far, I've been unable to persuade any of you to accept what I say about the Eldest with a sufficient degree of seriousness. Eichra Oren, hear me out. In the Cometary Halo, what some of the Americans call the Oort Cloud, far beyond the orbits of the outermost planets—"

He shook his head. "Model 17—"

"—the Proprietor's unrelenting search for the Predecessors' Virtual Drive, or perhaps the recent violent struggle against the Soviet Americans' home planet—and originally yours, if memory serves—as well, both of them involving the modest but easily detectable release of thermonuclear energies—"

"Model 17—"

"—is absolutely certain to have awakened that nemesis which even the mighty Predecessors themselves feared. Unless we rush to meet it on its home ground, before it is prepared, I tell you, Eichra Oren, trillions of hideous, disgusting—"

"Model 17—"

"—indestructible and dismayingly intelligent organisms of the sort you call Precambrian will have begun to writhe and stir for the first time in nearly a billion—"

"Model 17!" He put up a palm. "We'll get back to that, I promise. I, for one, do take you seriously, believe me. But it's not my department, and it's always best to tackle only one thing at a time. You asked me about guilt, which is my department. My point now is to establish that you've done your absolute best to accomplish everything the Predecessors demanded of you."

There was another long pause.

"Gitcha cute, fuzzy, little stuffed toy animals here, while they last!" cried the pushcart vendor. "Gitcha flowers an' balloons! Gitcha cards of sympathy an' condolence!"

Finally: "Yes, Eichra Oren, I have, indeed. But certainly that cannot excuse—"

Satisfied at last, he nodded. "Model 17, an individual simply can't do any better than the best that he or she can do. Please think about it. It's a metaphysical impossibility." Before he'd thought about it himself, he'd reached over and given the unhappy machine a reassuring pat on her broad, metallic carapace. "And sometimes it works out, and sometimes it just doesn't."

Somebody made throat-clearing noises. "That sounds an awful lot like 'shit happens,' to me."

The intruding voice belonged to one of the Soviet American group, Second Lieutenant Danny Gutierrez, son of the expedition's commanding general, who had sauntered up quietly without either of them noticing him and stood now, leaning against the wall behind them with his legs crossed casually at the ankles, smoking one of his smuggled cigarettes. His supply of them seemed endless.

"In my experience, shit usually happens because some shit-head *makes* it happen."

"And I am the, er, shit-head," the trilobitoid robot intoned sadly, turning away again.

Danny drew on his cigarette and exhaled it at her back. "Well, Model 17, if the shit fits—"

Eichra Oren leaped up from the bench, seized the young man by the front of his coverall, and shook him until his arms flailed. "What the hell would you know about it?" For an instant, he loosened his grasp. "For that matter, what would I know about it, even after all these centuries as a moral debt assessor?"

Suddenly, the badly strained fabric bunched under his powerful fingers again and he pulled the lieutenant to him until their noses almost touched. "I'll tell you what I do know: what's left of the best friend I have in all the universes put together is lying in there smashed to a bloody pulp! And I don't give a damn who's responsible! Having someone to blame won't undo what happened!"

"My new friends, please—!"

At some time during his emotional outburst, Model 17 had closed a restraining metal claw around Eichra Oren's thigh. Feeling the pressure, the man froze, then turned slowly, looking down at the trilobitoid machine. The deeply serrated manipulator was obviously capable of shearing his leg through cleanly. Danny froze as well, his eyes bulging and startled, the tattered and ridiculous remnant of his cigarette dribbling its load of unburnt tobacco onto the pavement.

"I plead with you, Eichra Oren," the robot begged. "Do not add moral responsibility for such disharmony among your people to my numerous other shortcomings!"

Eichra Oren released Danny. He stood with both fists clenched and his eyes closed for a long moment, breathing deeply in a complex rhythmic pattern, then opened his hands and eyes. "You're quite correct, Model 17, and I thank you."

He turned to the other man, looking at him directly, and spoke formally. "Danny, I have initiated physical force against you, which happens to be the most serious violation of *p'Nan* ethical philosophy possible. Happily, I did not injure or kill you, although as you know, I might easily have done so. In any case, I have incurred a moral debt to you. What restitution would you have of me?"

With a wry expression, Danny regarded the ruined cigarette in his hand. Abruptly, he began looking around for the still-burning coal which had fallen off somewhere, finally found it at his feet, and stepped on it. In a high-pitched, silly voice, he said, "You must bring me a *shrubbery*! No, no, I'll tell you what, Eichra Oren. For starters, you could really listen to the lady here about these Eldest boogie-things. She's giving me the creeps with all that talk."

"Agreed." Eichra Oren nodded gravely. "I accept the commission."

Danny put up a hand. "I'm not done yet. I wish you'd find out exactly what happened to poor old Sam and why—and who, if anybody, was actually responsible. If you were yourself right now, you'd realize that it'll do us both good."

"Very well," Eichra Oren replied.

"And it will do me good, as well," offered Model 17. "Is there some way I can help?"

They both turned to the robot.

Danny grinned lopsidedly, nodding toward the pushcart salesman who'd continued his pitch, uninterrupted. "Do you think that guy might have a souvenir ashtray?"

FIFTY-SEVEN
The Great Leap Sideways

"Well, here goes nothing."

C. C. Jones ran a damp palm over his close-cropped, graying beard a final time, gave up any further pointless scrutiny of the glittering golf ball in his other hand, threw a tiny switch concealed in the base of its handle, which was too short for human fingers, and turned his professional attention on his subject.

This odd object he'd been given by that bird-man Aelbraugh Pritsch would either work or it wouldn't. For his purposes, it wasn't important at all that the damned thing didn't bear even the faintest resemblance to a TV camera or a microphone.

He cleared his throat.

The slight slur he spoke with, which had faded over twenty years, and the ropy scar concealed beneath his beard between his lower lip and chin, which hadn't, were both the result of an argument he'd had with Horatio Gutierrez, then a young lieutenant colonel in command of what would someday be the famous Redhawk Squadron.

He cleared his throat.

Four months in a military hospital after having had his

teeth dashed out by Gutierrez, wielding a heavy steel fire extinguisher, plus the resulting slur and scar, had cost him his network anchor position, his marriage, and had led him through an endless, nightmarish series of increasingly demeaning and obscure jobs with the wire services, news magazines, and newspapers—to here.

He cleared his throat.

"Lieutenant Colonel 'Chuck' Tai Chiao," he intoned, nervousness and preoccupation disguised perfectly by a deep, melodious voice which had once been familiar to the people of an entire planet, "is the commander of the PRC's 'Extra-Special Forces' on 5023 Eris, a military arm of the supersecret—and some would say bizarre—'Great Leap Sideways' program cobbled together in the late nineties."

Thinking back now, Gutierrez had been right. Antisocialist guerillas had planted a fuel-air bomb aboard one of his fighter-interceptors being used to suppress resistance to American sovietization. Television lights and cameras had not only made defusing that bomb a great deal more difficult, they'd also made brightly lit targets of the men trying to do a job which was deadly dangerous even under the best of conditions. However, even after all these years, Jones couldn't bring himself to like the officer, now a brigadier general and an exile just like himself, who had ruined his brilliant and promising career.

He probably never would.

He cleared his throat and looked up at the individual he was talking about, hoping that the omnidirectional image recorder was doing its job better than he was doing his own.

"Colonel Tai, since it's no longer much of a secret to anyone on 5023 Eris, at least, could you tell us something about the Great Leap Sideways?"

"Better call me Chuck." Walking beside Jones as they ambled through the woods between the American encampment and the Elders' settlement, Tai nodded and grinned. "Well, at the time it began, Deng Xiao Peng, better known around the world as the 'Butcher of Tien Anmen Square,' had just died of natural causes—after all, it's only natural to die when you've been force-fed several dozen grams of arsenic—and two related matters were perplexing our newest leaders in Beijing."

Jones nodded, but his thoughts were still elsewhere. It had been bad enough working for *American Truth* in the first place, and worse to be given a dead-end assignment like this. But he'd been absolutely horrified to discover that Gutierrez was commanding this expedition to nowhere. The likelihood that the general probably didn't remember him, after two adventure-filled decades, or the violent incident which had so disastrously changed his life, only made things worse.

Tai was going on. "The first was a continuing hostility exhibited by the people of the world, despite a demonstrated willingness on the part of their governments to pretend otherwise, because of what had happened in Tien Anmen Square and afterward. Beijing felt that many modern states had done worse on considerably less provocation, and couldn't figure out why it was being treated differently."

"I see," Jones answered, trying to focus his mind on business. This was the only fresh break he was ever likely to get—even if the whole damned underpopulated planet was only the size of Texas and his employer looked like something on sale at a bait shop—and he'd better not blow it. "And the second?"

"Increasing depletion of technical and economic vitality on the part of the Japanese, whom the PRC had broken its back to emulate over the previous decades. If Japan, Inc. could falter and stagnate, what of Beijing's hopes?"

"And the Great Leap Sideways," Jones asked rhetorically, "was an answer to that question?"

"Well," Tai replied, "an argument was put forth, I believe at Hong Kong University, using Japan as a bad example. Japan had been nominally democratic since World War II, but remained stratified and anti-individualist. It's simply not possible, went the theory, to foster economic and technical progress over the long run without corollary increases in individual political and social freedom."

Jones grinned. "Most of our nonhuman audience would probably agree with that. They might also be interested to know that Hong Kong was a city-sized free market enclave which had just been reabsorbed into the PRC after a long period of relative independence. And what was the reaction to this idea in Beijing?"

"Naturally, it was bitterly denounced by the older politicians who had risen to power under Mao Tse Tung and believed that his methods, by some standards the most vicious the world had ever seen, were fully vindicated by what they viewed as excesses committed by the advocates of democracy in Tien Anmen Square."

"I see." Jones had found the tone that had made him a star. "Make that fifty or sixty million murders on one side of the ledger, as opposed to a few banners and a styrofoam Statue of Liberty. But the younger pols felt there might be something to Hong Kong's theory?"

"Right. So it was decided to be very Western indeed, and conduct a scientific experiment—"

"A scientific experiment in personal freedom?"

"The whole thing could be aborted if it proved a mistake. Even the old guard felt they might learn something— like the parameters involved in extracting maximum effort from individuals while giving minimal freedom in return. To everyone this seemed very American in character, and that became the basis for the experiment."

"Er, um, yes. Please go on."

"Young peasants and workers in their early teens were rounded up from all over and sent to newly built villages in remote locations. Often no two spoke the same dialect. That was remedied by a teaching cadre educated abroad under previous regimes, who introduced their pupils to American English and the American way of life as they understood it, aided by a store of data including novels, old TV shows, and movies."

"What sort of movies?"

"Anything, as long as it showed something of everyday American attitudes. Movies like *The Shaggy Dog*, *American Graffiti*, *Some Kind of Wonderful*, *Sixteen Candles*, *A Christmas Story*, *Back to the Future*, *My Best Friend's Wedding*, *Stand By Me*, *Beetle Juice*, *Honey I Shrunk the Kids*."

"*Beetle Juice*? You'd get a pretty distorted view of American life from that, wouldn't you?"

"They were working with what they had. Even a movie like that gives some idea, say, about how American teen-agers relate to their parents. Anyway, when some criterion had been met, most of the teachers made an exit, leaving the subjects more or less on their own. A few remained as 'village elders' to keep the program on course."

"How did you come into the picture?" Despite a life-time of professional habit, Jones had begun to be fascinated with this man's story. He was forced to struggle, overcoming a reflex to suppress it and remind himself that Aelbraugh Pritsch had told him this was just what Mister Thoggosh wanted—humanity, enthusiasm, understanding, most of all, intelligence—none of the self-consciously detached, unjustifiably superior attitude which, with its resulting air of slightly bovine stupidity, characterized news reporting back on Earth.

"My four grandfathers and grandmothers," the colonel answered, "were among the young peasants and workers who were expected by Beijing to become Americans over-night. They suffered many hardships, mostly psychological in nature, but their children—my parents' generation—fared better. As a consequence, I grew up in a 'village' in east-ern Mongolia meticulously patterned after what Beijing believed to be a typical town in the American southwest."

"What was it like?"

"Well, its American twin could have been found anyplace from Laporte, Colorado to Clovis, California—two proto-types that were used. It was code-named 'Calumet'—"

"Because of another movie." For this, Jones was pre-pared. He imagined his former employers keeling over from strokes and aneurisms at what he was about to ask. It was a good thing this interview wouldn't be sent back to Earth. Maybe. "After the little community which resisted Russian invasion in John Milius's *Red Dawn*?"

"Cuban and Nicaraguan invasion. Believe me, it was equipped for the task it was designed to accomplish. We had a local MacDonald's, a Safeway, a Starbuck's, a Baer garage, a laundromat, a dry cleaner, two bars, a little one-horse shopping mall, three restaurants—"

"One of them Chinese."

Tai laughed. "That's right, a synagogue and two churches,

one Roman Catholic, used by Manchurian peasants shipped in to simulate a minority population. The other you might call generic Protestant—all Western religions look alike to Beijing. We had a movie theater and a radio station offering rock music and farm reports. Internet communication was limited to other villages in the program. TV was piped in from Japanese, Swiss, and South African satellites."

"Why not American satellites?" Another question he'd never have been allowed to ask back home.

"Because by then, American TV no longer reflected individualistic values which the program's directors were interested in. As a matter of fact, it hadn't for some time."

"I see. Well, tell me more about Calumet, Colonel Tai—Chuck. What else did it have to offer?"

"We had a video rental, a bank, even a gun shop—I was a grown man, an officer in the Red Army, before I knew how remarkable that was. On Sunday mornings the streets of Calumet would be filled with Ford and Chevy pickups with Norinco copies of Winchester and Marlin rifles hanging in their back windows. We even had one freelance prostitute living in a small frame house at the edge of town. I always believed she was PRC Intelligence, reporting directly to Beijing."

"And what about your life, growing up in Calumet?"

"No complaints. I was educated in an American-style community-oriented school system. 'I pledge allegiance to the flag of the People's Republic of China, and to the collective for which it stands . . .' I took Mandarin as a second language, along with Spanish. My folks belonged to the PTA and taught Sunday school. I was a Cub Scout, Boy Scout, Explorer, 4H, Junior Red Cross, and played clarinet for a while in my high-school band. I had to quit because I made the football team—my 'sports collective,' as Beijing called it—the 'Wolverines.'"

Jones laughed at another reference to Milius. "How did your hometown interact with the rest of China?"

"Not much. Calumet was surrounded by mechanized, American-sized farms owned by the farmers, which served as a source of supply for the program and as a cultural buffer. Outside the farms was a forested zone, ringed with barbed wire, guard towers, and mine fields, which could be crossed only with permission from Beijing. Among the kids of Calumet, it was known as the 'Lost Cojones Wildlife Preserve.'"

"I see—"

"That wasn't the only thing lost there—the first time I got laid was in those woods, in the shadow of an automated gun emplacement. No attempt was made to deceive us— we knew we were Chinese, living in China under special circumstances—or to deny us news of the outside world. Nor was any attempt made to indoctrinate us, either in Marxism or Chinese socialism. We had been placed where we were to see what developed. Our job was to be as classically American, to live as much like classical Americans, as we could."

"Which meant what?"

"Well, the program's directors couldn't be certain exactly what elements had most contributed to America's two centuries of almost unbroken prosperity and progress. They were terribly afraid to leave out anything, for fear it might prove important. So every aspect of American life, at least as we knew it, was copied in the most painstaking detail possible in Calumet and her sister villages.

"Our diet, which we largely supplied ourselves, was scandalously high in protein by PRC standards. Bureaucrats were always complaining that we swam in caffeine and nicotine, but they even allowed us a 'statistically valid' amount of marijuana, sold by the lady I mentioned in the frame house at the edge of town."

"What was that about Calumet's 'sister villages'? I hadn't heard about that before."

"In a way, you Americans really ought to be complimented—Calumet was only one of several artificial environments, each as American as . . . well, as America had been before it turned itself into a socialist republic. The Great Leap Sideways created eight or nine midwestern— 'Smallville,' I think they called it—southern, northwestern, and southwestern towns. The only typical American environment deliberately excluded by the program was that of your East Coast: New York, New Jersey, Connecticut, Massachusetts, and so forth."

"And why was that?"

Tai shrugged. "The directors felt that they too-closely

imitated Europe, producing the same human sheep, and contributed negatively to individualism. It's true, isn't it, that the northeast was the first American region to begin sovietizing itself?"

"Who's interviewing who here?"

"Who's interviewing *whom*. Our towns, on the other hand, were intended to close the 'nerd gap,' to assure the social and technical progress Beijing came to feel were a natural outgrowth of untrammeled individualism. Aside from the obvious travel restrictions, the only limit was that the advocacy of collectivism was discreetly but firmly discouraged."

"Collectivism? Discouraged how?"

"Well, a newspaper editor I recall—we had a little weekly and the high-school paper wasn't bad—wrote a couple of editorials demanding confiscation of all the guns in town. Shortly after the second—I figure he must have gotten a quiet warning lecture about the first—he moved away and was never heard from again."

"All because the directors weren't certain what elements had contributed to American prosperity and progress, and were afraid to leave out anything, including private gun ownership."

"Exactly. They still aren't certain, especially since you people wound up destroying everything I was brought up to believe had been constructive and decent about America."

"Hmm. Well, now that you're here on 5023 Eris and the Great Leap Sideways is no longer a secret, what of the program's future—and that of the people you left behind?"

"Oh, it'll stay a secret. The program was always controversial in Beijing and that's truer now than ever. The third and fourth generations have begun to chafe under restrictions imposed on them by the outside world—consisting of a communist dictatorship. Beijing has never forgotten the hideous propaganda blunder committed by Deng, so they'll step lightly, but they're afraid of all these uncontrolled and uncontrollable individualists they've created—"

"Is there a particular reason for that?"

"Aside from general principles? Sure: they made a terrifying discovery in the second generation and never quite got over it. At first, Calumet and her sister villages were merely prosperous. After a subsidiary experiment abolishing taxes and internal economic regulation, they began producing huge surpluses, overwhelming the economies of the districts where they were based. The directors were afraid to reinstate taxes and regulation for fear of wrecking the program. Unlike American politicians, they understood the danger of interfering in a culture schooled in the spirit of the Boston Tea Party and Concord Bridge. However, they were equally afraid to acknowledge the actual economic effects—as opposed to the widely advertised and purely mythical benefits—of taxes and regulation."

"And that was a generation ago. How did it all work out?"

"Beijing decided to buy whatever surplus we produced. The old guard argued that it must be destroyed to avoid further disruption. This would have defeated the whole purpose of the program, but it would have been the Chinese thing to do.

"Younger politicians, not so young by now, argued that the program should be allowed to generate the benefits it was designed to generate. I suspect some were benefitting individually, on the black market. Anyway, we're on permanent probation, just as we've always been. In a sense, our group, the PRC Extra-Special Forces, has been sent here for much the same reason yours was."

"And that, specifically, is . . ."

"Well, if we accomplish anything positive out here for Beijing, that's fine. If not, at least Beijing is rid of some of us in a sanitary manner. Perhaps they'll wind up sending the rest of us and wash their hands of us entirely. Who can say?"

"Well, Colonel Tai, on that sobering but hopeful note, we'll end this. Thanks very much. I'd also like to thank Mister Thoggosh personally for giving me this opportunity. As a former network anchorman and a stringer for all the most prestigious American newspapers, this may be the first honest reporting I've ever done.

"Given a chance, it won't be the last.

"C. C. Jones, reporting for the Elders' Cerebro-cortical Network."

FIFTY-EIGHT
The Cybernetic Samoyed

Eichra Oren had returned to the low-ceilinged chamber of moving metal cubes and unearthly blue light.

Somehow he knew it was a nightmare. In some corner of his mind he was aware that he was still keeping his vigil with Model 17 on a street bench just outside Dlee Raftan Saon's surgery in the Elders' settlement, just as he knew that he had been completely exhausted by the disorienting shock of losing what amounted to his symbiote.

Knowing that didn't help him wake himself up as he was usually able to, or keep him from reliving the last few terrible moments of Sam's life.

He'd heard the dog screaming (a gut-wrenching sound that couldn't be described any other way) from an adjoining passageway at the same time it came to him over his implant. He didn't remember how he'd covered the intervening distance in the interval of a heartbeat. Sam had been so badly hurt that it hadn't mattered.

In any other context, it might have made the very picture of absurdity. As the arachnid engineer, Remgar d'Nod, stood by helplessly, Eichra Oren had found the terminally injured animal almost standing on his hind legs, his head

477

sticking up like that of a comic decapitation victim from between two of the massive metal blocks—blocks now set apart by the space of less than a centimeter.

The worst part was that Sam's mind was still working. He could still communicate his agony electronically. What leaked from around the circumference of the crack between those blocks—a fleeting impression of blood-soaked fur was all the man permitted himself now—hadn't borne close examination, and Eichra Oren had been grateful for the low, off-colored light. It had been obvious enough, both to him and to the dog, that from the neck down Sam was already dead.

Thinking fast and acting even faster, on a desperate inspiration which hadn't formed within his conscious mind, Eichra Oren had drawn his razor-sharp assessor's sword—even now he could hear the ringing, steely whisper of the double-edged blade as it leaped from his scabbard—and struck off the dog's head, level with the tops of the blocks. Wrapping what was left of his friend in transparent plastic from the environmental suit Remgar d'Nod had shucked off and shoved at him, he'd rushed it to the surface, another journey that he failed now to remember clearly, although he did recall that it had seemed to go on for days.

Similarly, he didn't remember the flight from the excavation site to the Elders' settlement at all. However long it had lasted, it had lasted far too long. In the end, his desperate gamble to save Sam had failed. Instead of keeping his best friend alive, he had taken away his last few minutes and mutilated him in the bargain.

Now, a familiar, disembodied voice echoed inside his skull. *"Trust the Force, Boss."*

"What—!" Eichra Oren shook his aching head, certain he must still be asleep.

"And never let 'em tell you that major wounds don't hurt. Boy, I'd like to find the dickless wonder who thought that one up and squish his gizzard in a vise!"

"Sam!" The possibility that he had gone insane entered the man's mind. "Is that you, Sam?"

"Obi Wan Doggie, himself. I'd make that 'in the flesh,' but it would be a base canard—or maybe just a baritone

canard. While we're on the subject, Boss, let's discuss beheading as a first-aid technique."

Eichra Oren opened his eyes to discover the American TV reporter, C. C. Jones, with Colonel Chuck Tai, late of the PRC Extra-Special Forces, bending over him where he'd fallen off the bench onto the sidewalk. Squatting between the newcomers, Model 17 had extended a cold, hard, but commiserating feeler of some sort and was stroking his arm. Danny Gutierrez leaned on the wall behind them, the usual cigarette smoldering in his hand.

"Hey, I wouldn't get too close, you guys," the lieutenant wisely observed, "just in case he wakes up fighting!"

"My poor, unfortunate friend," Model 17 exclaimed, "I do not know what convulsions are supposed look like in your species, but I believe that you were having them a moment ago, which may account for Lieutenant Gutierrez's rather thoughtless and unsympathetic remark. Are you quite all right now, Eichra Oren?"

"He could start a business called 'Thoughtless and Unsympathetic Remarks Are Us.'" Eichra Oren levered himself to his feet, sat down on the bench, and pressed both palms to his eyes. "You wouldn't think I was all right if I told you the dream I just had."

"Why don't you try us anyway?" suggested Danny, dropping the cigarette and crushing it out with his heel. He walked over to put a hand on the debt assessor's shoulder. "I let you sleep, O shamus of shame, because you looked like you could use the rest. You've been dead to the world, snoring at ninety decibels, for over an hour."

"Tell 'em all to go away, Boss," the voice inside his skull demanded, sounding more and more authentically like Sam. *"Tell 'em we're busy. We gotta talk."*

This time, Eichra Oren almost jumped off the bench. He started to reply, then looked up warily at Danny, the American reporter, the Chinese officer, and the robot, knowing that even if he wasn't losing his mind, none of the four had cerebro-cortical implants—which seemed to be the source of Sam's voice—couldn't hear what he was hearing, and would assume he'd gone insane. If they hadn't already.

"Mr. Jones," he began carefully, "I understand from

Aelbraugh Pritsch that you've been interviewing Colonel Tai about his military unit for the implant network."

"That's right," the reporter replied. "We just finished and were headed to Nellus Glaser's for a beer."

Eichra Oren nodded. "Well, I may have another story for you, but I don't know whether the headline should read—" he glanced up at Danny "—'Guilt Gumshoe Goes Ga-ga' or 'Deceased Dog Discourses.'" He looked from one face to another and back again, then cleared his throat. "I seem to be hearing Sam over my implant."

There was a long silence.

All three men looked down at him with their hands thrust in their pants pockets, tossing occasional brief glances up and down the street as if to reassure themselves that this embarrassing conversation into which they had somehow fallen wasn't being overheard by strangers. To his chagrin, they were wearing expressions he'd never expected to see directed his way. The black face showed impatient skepticism, even mild contempt, while the yellow seemed inclined to pity. The brown face, Danny's, shook from side to side with an unreadable smile.

"Boss, that's only because I managed to upload all my personality and memories at the height of the excitement downstairs, first into the electronic areas of my brain— which kept overflowing, by the way, giving me full-chip warnings and scaring the bejabbers out of me—and then onto the information storage and communications network."

"In the name of p'Na—"

"Hey, it wasn't any big deal—except that it does constitute the first genuine out-of-body experience ever documented. I'm the document, in fax! At three hundred thousand klicks a second, I was here at the surgery before you—and my head—were."

"Eichra Oren." Model 17 touched him on the arm again, shyly. *"If you have been driven mad,"* she told him electronically, *"then at least you are not alone, for I have attuned my self-contained electromagnetic communications circuitry to the Elders' network, and I, too, can hear your recently deceased friend."*

"Eavesthinker!" Sam's tone was bantering.

Eichra Oren laughed out loud, transforming Jones and

Tai's skeptical and pitying looks into expression of alarm until he began to explain what had just happened outside their hearing. Danny understood immediately and began to grin from ear to ear.

"Tell him—tell him I'm glad he isn't dead!"

"Actually, it's nice to hear you, Model 17," Sam declared, the robot relaying his words to the astonished Jones and Tai through a transducer on her carapace. *"Danny. For that matter, it's nice to be hearing anything, considering the alternative!"*

"You'd be in a fix," the lieutenant replied, "if Model 17 hadn't rigged communication with the surface."

"Yes," Tai agreed, "this would be a religious experience instead of an ordinary conversation."

Eichra Oren turned to the colonel. "Tell me one thing ordinary about it and the drinks are on me, Chuck."

"Try and relax a little, Boss. I'll be my old self again in no time at all. Dlee Raftan Saon and Rosalind held onto my head—which you'll notice I'm not exactly using right now—and are presently extracting tissue from it to clone me a brand-new body. Not a pretty sight, believe me, but I guess the Elders' medical technology is good for something after all, besides helping nautiloids live too long!"

"I believe a highly cogent argument could be made," replied a new voice, "that our friend Sam never did have much use for his head. In the end, that's probably all that saved him. The operation was a failure, but the patient lived."

Dryly chuckling, Dlee Raftan Saon emerged from the dilated door of the clinic with a tired-looking Rosalind Nguyen behind him. The insect physician used all four hands to fluff up the hanging fabric strips of which his clothing was made and sat down, as near as his species ever came to it, on the bench beside the man.

"I'm here to tell you that there's nothing, on this world or any other, quite like laboring for hours performing delicate surgery with an obnoxious patient as a backseat driver!"

Rosalind smiled but said nothing, a look of understanding sympathy in her eyes for Eichra Oren. Wearing surgical greens from Soviet American expedition stores, she pulled the cap off, shaking her hair out and running her slim fingers through it.

"*C'mon, now, Doc,*" Sam complained electronically, "*it couldn't have been as bad as that. Why, most of the time I wasn't even there. I was elsewhere, practicing a newfound aptitude for astral projection. Okay, half-astral—I had to say it before any of you did. For example, I heard Eichra Oren here promise Danny he'd really listen to Model 17's story about the Eldest.*"

"You heard that?" Eichra Oren turned back to Model 17, still addressing Sam. "And you let me go on worrying myself to—why didn't you say something?"

"*Unaccustomed as I am to public reticence,*" the animal replied, "*I wasn't all that sure myself that I was having a real experience. Or, to be honest, that I was real, myself. It's what comes of reading too many of Heinlein's later novels. Anyway, it was necessary to take a while and sort myself out, if you see what I mean. I used to wonder whether I was a dog with a computer-enhanced brain or a computer in a dog-enhanced cabinet. Now I'm just a former computer or a former dog who doesn't know whether he's a program or a database.*"

"You mean whether he's kibbles or bits." Danny ground a cigarette on the pavement at his feet—Eichra Oren hadn't even seen him light this one—and immediately lit another. "Sorry about that, an old commercial I saw once. Speaking of that promise, Eichra Oren, is there any reason you couldn't begin keeping it now?"

The Antarctican looked a question at the two physicians. "At this point, we've done all we can do," Rosalind answered. "The rest is up to automated equipment."

"And Sam's fragile will to survive," Dlee Raftan Saon added, provoking general laughter. "I could use some sleep, myself, but I'm far too . . . what's the expression?"

"Keyed up," supplied Rosalind, "and curious—speaking for myself."

"And curious," the insect doctor agreed, "speaking for both of us." He turned to Tai, doing a fair imitation of a human American southern accent. "You bein' the only cunnel heah, Cunnel, may Ah suggest that we-all repaih to mah office—where we kin all sit on the floah as comf'table as we can on the sidewalk out heah—for brandy an' cigahs?"

Eichra Oren stood up, stretching. "Good idea, Raftan, only make mine coffee, with a Turkish accent."

"In the name of the Grrreat and Merrrcifool," replied the insect, "kindly walk this way, Effendi."

"*If I tried to walk that way—*" Sam's disembodied voice began.

"I'd wind up in traction!" Danny, Jones, Tai, and Rosalind finished for him in unison. Together they entered the surgery and found places to sit in the doctor's office—only Model 17 sat on the floor—while their host ordered coffee and other refreshment, found a chair for himself, then filled and lit his pipe.

Jones pulled the glittery golf ball from his pocket.

"By this time, I'm curious, too," Eichra Oren told the robot. "Please feel free to satisfy our curiosity, Model 17. You have the audience you wanted."

"At last." Model 17 began, "How much do any of you know about slime molds?"

"Yech!" That was Danny, about to take a bite of ice cream covered with butterscotch syrup.

"*About as much as I ever wanted to,*" Sam replied through the same speaker she'd used. "*Practically nothing. I know they're like the Rio Grande, an inch deep and a mile wide.*"

"More on the order of a meter wide and a few dozen millimeters deep," corrected Dlee Raftan Saon. "To borrow Sam's unique manner of stating things, a slime mold is—well, more of an animal than a plant, that doesn't seem to know whether it's one big single-celled organism with thousands of nuclei, a single multicelled entity, or thousands of separate creatures which look rather like tiny worms. At one time or another, depending on temperature, available food or moisture, or maybe just its mood, it can be any of the three—or convert itself into a fine, dry powder and simply blow away on the wind to a better location."

"God," Danny gulped, "it sounds like something Spock and Captain Kirk would have to fight!"

Rosalind laughed. "Yes, but they're real, and just about as mundane as any living thing ever gets. People scrub them off their shower curtains every day without knowing it.

They're a very ancient kind of organism—Precambrian—one of the first ever to evolve."

"And in at least one universe, the first to evolve intelligence," declared Model 17 with an electronic shudder. "They are the only Precambrian organisms ever to do so."

"And yet they left no traces of it," Dee Raftan Saon mused.

"The Eldest constructed no artifacts that we know of," Model 17 explained, "but created whatever they required out of their own substance, and perhaps even their thoughts. In all the myriad alternative worlds of infinite probability, neither they nor their soft-bodied nonsapient ancestors left any fossil record."

"I see."

"Nor," she continued, "does it appear that they could be killed in any way we know the term."

"*What do you mean they couldn't be killed?*" Sam demanded, "*They're slime mold. Enough household disinfectant and—*"

"So what happened to them, then?" Rosalind asked.

"In their own universe—the one we presently occupy—after a bitter conflict lasting millions of years, of which I feel fortunate to have been given little useful memory, my builders believed they had imprisoned the Eldest in eternal frozen sleep in the absolute cold of the Cometary Halo. Even thus contained, the Predecessors greatly feared that the Eldest might somehow be awakened accidentally."

"So greatly," asked Eichra Oren, "that they invented the Virtual Drive just so they could flee the Solar System?"

"Yes," Model 17 answered. "I am afraid that correctly states the facts of the matter."

"And now," the Antarctican persisted, "the Eldest *are* awakening?"

"Yes, Eichra Oren." She gave him one of her almost-sighs. "I have just seen indications of it by means of what the Soviet Americans call my tachyon telescope."

Dlee Raftan Saon blew multiple smoke rings from the spiracles along the sides of his abdomen, forcing the humans to revise some of their theories about his respiratory process. "I'd like to see that myself, Model 17, very much."

"You are most welcome to at any time, Doctor."

"Thank you. Some of my colleagues here believe that your fears regarding the Eldest are an expression of mass paranoia among your builders induced by fundamental contradictions between their natural collectivism and the sapience they evolved into."

Model 17 was less capable of facial expression than the mantislike doctor or she would have nodded. "This is why they were reluctant to take my warning seriously?"

Laying a gentle hand on Model 17's carapace, Rosalind hunkered down beside the robot trilobite. "I'm one of those colleagues Raftan mentioned, Model 17, and I won't deny that I still believe that the contradictory beliefs he refers to can have dangerous consequences both to those who hold them and everyone around them. Except by way of contrast, intelligence and socialism don't even belong in the same sentence, let alone the same belief system."

"I am most sincerely grateful for your honesty, Doctor Nguyen," the robot answered her.

"That's about the most polite way I've ever heard of telling somebody to go to hell, but you're welcome anyway, Model 17, and I am willing to listen seriously about the Eldest. If they're stirring out there, what will you do about them?"

"What I shall do? Some of it I am already doing, preparing for the conflict inevitably to come. The rest depends on how easily I convince you and your companions to travel aboard this vessel with me to the Cometary Halo, where I hope to reimprison—or even destroy—the Eldest while they are not yet fully awakened."

FIFTY-NINE
A Bird in the Hand

"Drat!"

The aerostat looped at half the speed of sound, hurling its occupants to the floor of the passenger compartment—temporarily the ceiling—before righting itself to resume course. A flock of large, pink, long-legged birds it had swerved to avoid flew on, unaware of how closely death had brushed their wingtips.

Preening his own feathers indignantly, Aelbraugh Pritsch levered himself back to a sitting position beside Horatio Gutierrez, who was cursing quietly in Spanish. No one knew better than the bird-being himself that the nautiloid Elders he'd served all his life—particularly including his employer of the last couple of centuries, Mister Thoggosh—were imperfect creatures. The vehicle he and the American general presently occupied provided ample illustration of their fallibility.

One of the engineers, the arachnid Nannel Rab, had described it as a "floored torus," which seemed to put any humans who heard it in stitches, reciting arcane phrases like "found on road dead" and "fix or repair daily." They called the aerocraft which served the nautiloid community "flying bagels." For his own part, Aelbraugh Pritsch thought they bore a greater resemblance to red blood cells.

Only a few meters across, their operating principle was foolproof and simple, befitting the sort of rough camping which the colony on 5023 Eris represented. They had no moving parts. A layer of air molecules next to the surface was continuously ionized and drawn to zones of opposing polarity which "flowed" over the surface themselves, creating currents which lifted and propelled the craft in any direction at speeds of several hundred kilometers an hour.

Controlled by cerebro-cortical implant, each aerocraft automatically obeyed the will of its operator. Concealed behind an emergency panel were manual controls, but suitably forewarned, no one in his right mind would consider going into the air in one of these machines if the cybernetics had failed for some reason.

Within the padded passenger compartment, no seats had been provided. Too many different species used these machines, of too many different shapes and sizes. A constant airflow like that on the outer surface created a dynamic windshield and, in a sense, served as seatbelts (he'd never tested this himself), blowing any potential accident victim back inside before he could tumble out—for example on a tight, looping high-speed turn such as they'd just experienced.

With considerable trepidation, Aelbraugh Pritsch sat up straighter and, as an exercise of character, forced himself to peer over the machine's softly rounded edge at the ground.

"It isn't the fall that kills you," Gutierrez joked in English, "it's the sudden stop at the bottom!"

Aelbraugh Pritsch gulped bile, glaring resentfully at Gutierrez, although he doubted that the man would recognize a resentful avian glare when it was aimed at him. He agreed with the general's sentiment, although he didn't understand why it was supposed to be funny. There were many items like that which no one had ever been able to explain to him. Often he sat up all night with references, trying to figure them out. If his texts on sapient behavior had been printed on physical pages, the sections on humor would be the best thumbed by now. He was aware that

even his symbiote, a nonsapient reptile, had a better sense
of humor than he did.

Nonetheless, he could appreciate how the general's
feeble jest might apply as a metaphor to their current circumstances. It wasn't so much this flight from the human
encampment he deplored as what would inevitably happen
at its end.

From the corner of an eye, he saw Gutierrez looking
him over and wondered how he must appear to someone who had never lived among other sapients. About the
height of the average human being, he was a typical
member of a race descended from the "missing link"
between birds and dinosaurs—except that the link wasn't
missing; the ancestral form was well known to
paleobiologists not only of his own world but to those of
many others—who had survived whatever catastrophe had
wiped them out in a majority of other universes.

Why this should be, nobody knew. Iridium traces hint-
ing at an asteroid collision with Earth sixty-five million years
ago lingered in his world's soil, as they did in almost everybody else's. Perhaps his forebears had taken to living in
caves, as was often suggested—scavenging the remains of
species that had perished, displacing mammalian scaven-
gers whose offspring came to dominate other worlds—long
enough for the atmosphere to clear and the sun to return.
Birds had survived elsewhere. Only in his world, as far as
he knew (and in this area his knowledge was considerable)
had they arisen to sapience.

For whatever reason, the straightest path to sapience,
unlike the preposterously circuitous route followed by
humans, had in his people retained a birdlike form.
Some exigency of natural selection had halted the full
development of feathers, fusing individual fibers to form
light, flexible armor. As his species' diet became
omnivorous—and dependent on manipulative ability—the
beak had flattened and softened until it formed a convex
inverted shield below his eyes, concealing elementary
teeth which were still a subject of controversy among
avialogists. Were they descended from the primitive teeth
most birds had given up or were they another convergent development?

His legs and feet were birdlike, resembling those of an ostrich. The wing-claws his ancestors shared with other primitive pre-birds—and at least one contemporary species on many versions of Earth—had come to dominate the upper limb structure until they formed hands similar to those of humans, although he could still set the air in an entire room in motion with his broad, pseudofeathered arms.

The representative of a more fanciful people might have tried flight here, where the air pressure was kept at Earth-normal and the gravity was a tenth of that exerted by his homeworld. Such an idea had never occurred to Aelbraugh Pritsch.

His symbiote was a tiny, blue-green jewel-scaled lizard of a type his ancestors had originally brought from their home time line. They'd been kept as decorative pets which made sweet trilling noises and helped their owners control parasites in their plumage. As part of the Great Restitution to all Appropriated Persons, they'd been enhanced the same way Eichra Oren's Sam had been, through selective breeding, genetic engineering, and the addition of sophisticated electronics to their nervous systems. The result was a companion species just below the borderline of sapience, useful for many tasks.

But they no longer sang.

Each Appropriated species had been given symbiotes. This had worked more or less well, depending on the species. One never saw symbiotes with sea-scorpionoids, for example, who had been barbarians when the Elders discovered them. Aelbraugh Pritsch suspected that their erstwhile masters had eaten them.

In the case of Eichra Oren and his fellow humans, it had worked altogether too well. The necessary enhancements, performed on a breed of large white dog found aboard the original sailing vessel escaping the Antarctican catastrophe, had been carried too far, creating symbiotes who were sapient themselves.

The craft dipped abruptly, plummeting toward the nautiloid settlement and skidding to a landing on the platform which served as a foundation for dozens of buildings set a few meters above ground level. Climbing out with the feeling of unfocused gratitude he always experienced, Aelbraugh Pritsch turned to the general.

"Mister Thoggosh will be waiting for you in his office. Will you need my help finding it?"

Gutierrez shook his head. "Once I've been to a place, Aelbraugh Pritsch, I can usually find my way back." He grinned. "Thanks for the ride—I think."

It was one of those rare occasions when the avian understood and shared the feelings of another sapient. He would have grinned back if he'd been physically capable of it.

"You're quite welcome, General. I must be getting along to my own office, then. I'll be available, when you're ready, to transport you back to your encampment."

"Try not to be too disappointed, Aelbraugh Pritsch, if I decide it's a nice day for a walk."

They shook hands, a purely human custom almost everyone on the asteroid had adopted, and parted, the man to his appointment, Aelbraugh Pritsch to his office to observe remotely, as requested, the conversation between human and nautiloid.

By the time the bird-being reached his desk, Gutierrez had descended a dozen steps from the main platform level to Mister Thoggosh's sunken quarters, inhaled the oxygenated fluorocarbon with which they were filled, entered the air lock, and been greeted by his giant host. Relayed by the nautiloid's cerebro-cortical implant, images of the Proprietor's office filled Aelbraugh Pritsch's mind.

As usual, the first thing the human seemed to notice—besides the imposing sight of Mister Thoggosh himself—was the Proprietor's colorful and highly prized songfish, warbling in a cage hanging beside the area of the floor, swept clear of sand by a carefully calculated current, which served the great mollusc as a desk.

"Ah, General, it's good to see you again." The nautiloid lifted a long tentacle, offering Gutierrez a chair. "Would you care for something? Perhaps a hot flask of coffee? I'm having beer."

"Thanks, coffee will be just fine. And it's not really 'General' any more, Mister Thoggosh. I've resigned from the American Soviet Aerospace Force. Horatio will do nicely—

which reminds me of something I've been meaning to ask about since we arrived here."

In its hanging cage, Mister Thoggosh's songfish trilled sweetly in the momentary silence. From his office a few dozen meters away, Aelbraugh Pritsch watched Mister Thoggosh send his separable limb away to fetch refreshments, gratified that the sight no longer seemed to startle the humans. "And what might that be, Horatio?"

Gutierrez shrugged. "Well, I understand that your civilization has been free of government—"

"Of coercive authority, Horatio. We practice individual *self*-government. As nearly as I can tell, the only purpose served by the State—yours or any other—is to deny to the average individual the benefits of the Industrial Revolution."

"Somehow," Gutierrez grinned, "they neglected to point that out to us that in high-school civics."

Mister Thoggosh grunted. "Look closely enough at the structure of the State and what it resembles is a network of plumbing designed to drain the lifeblood from the productive class, those willing to work for a living, and deliver it to those who won't—nor do I speak of the 'widows and orphans' whom the real beneficiaries inevitably prop up to justify their parasitism. Or have I said all this before?"

"If you have, it wasn't to me. It probably bears saying again." The man nodded. Aelbraugh Pritsch found himself wondering what he was working up to. "*Self*-government. And that's the way it's been with you for something like half a billion years?"

"More like 350 million. Here's your coffee." The nautiloid took a long, satisfying draft from the fluorocarbontight sipping tube of his own container. Gutierrez followed suit. "Even we did not create Utopia in a day, Horatio."

Gutierrez persisted. "And in spite of all that history, the boss-man here—I mean the head being—is still called 'Mister,' a title deriving from 'master'?"

The avian was scandalized at the personal nature of the general's question, and its relative triviality. Sensing his assistant's reaction, the giant mollusc chuckled. "I wondered how long it would take for you to ask about that. I noticed the similarity almost as soon as I absorbed a working personal knowledge of English and ceased relying on the translation software—which was never very good to begin with. It's a coincidence, Horatio. You may have noticed that most nautiloid names consist of four syllables, with stress on the penultimate."

"No, I haven't." The former general shook his head. "I haven't met that many nautiloids."

"I suppose not." The speakers behind Mister Thoggosh emitted something resembling a sigh—a transparent affectation, since his means of breathing and speaking had nothing to do with one another. Nautiloids used organically generated radio signals for communication. "There are dozens of us here on 5023 Eris, but we're a notoriously reclusive lot, I'm afraid. I'm regarded as something of an eccentric because I rather enjoy my contacts with other species. In any event, you'll recall my late friend Semlohcolresh; his name was typical."

"Toscanini." Gutierrez grinned. "Rumpelstiltskin."

"The latter would make a fine name for an Elder if it weren't laughably close to that of a certain common household appliance. I'm aware your people think of me as M-R-period-T-H-O-G-G-O-S-H. I'm afraid I've encouraged them, since it suited my purposes. But a more accurate rendering would be M-I-S-T-E-R-T-H-O-G-G-O-S-H, one word. As I say, the resemblance to a title followed by a name is pure coincidence. It is also irrelevant. The fact is, I asked you here today to discuss our plans for 5023 Eris, since they will inevitably necessitate choices on your part."

Gutierrez raised his eyebrows. "You mean Model 17's plans for taking us all on a little trip out of the nice, warm Solar System and into the frozen wastes of the Cometary Halo?"

Aelbraugh Pritsch gasped in astonishment. It seemed that this was to be his morning for surprises. Mister Thoggosh, meanwhile, was taken somewhat less aback.

"Ah, I perceive that the community kelpvine is up to its usual, highly efficient standard." He took another sip of beer. "I do indeed refer to those plans, Horatio. Model 17 informs me that the miniature asteroid which you kindly placed in orbit for us—and which was regrettably 'ignited' at the thermonuclear level by our brief space battle with Earth's legions—will accompany us. Not so regrettably, it will act as our sun, providing light and warmth to the canopy which protects our colony and to all beneath it. Please understand, my human friend, that you and your people need not be dragged along on such a protracted voyage as this promises to be, if you wish otherwise."

Leaving his own drink to float in mid-fluorocarbon, Gutierrez leaned back and interlocked his fingers behind his head, a casual posture Aelbraugh Pritsch would never have dreamed of assuming in the Proprietor's presence. The bird-being caught himself being scandalized again and, for once, felt amusement with himself.

He and his people were not entirely without their own subtle sense of the absurd; it was a natural and necessary concomitant to sapience. Were they not as famous throughout the continua for their humor doors—which told a visitor a joke while he waited to be greeted—as for their 'fireplaces' of electrically heated rock and their pleasant custom of grooming themselves in public as a social ritual?

"You wouldn't be trying to get rid of us, now," Gutierrez asked, "my nautiloid friend?"

"On the contrary, sir. I, for one, would sincerely appreciate having you along on such an expedition. You're a primitive people, it is true, with an undue respect for authority. But over the past few weeks you have proven yourselves resourceful and courageous. I simply didn't wish to volunteer you without your consent."

The general laughed. "Well, I, for one, am sincerely *not* interested in leaving—at least until the mystery of what happened to Sam is solved." Gutierrez leaned forward in his chair, suddenly excited. "I don't mean what was done to him or who did it. That's a mystery in itself. I mean what happened afterward. Mister Thoggosh, you've got a miracle here—a practical form of immortality!"

His host gave another electronic sigh. "We have other, more reliable means of life extension, as you know. Cybernetic salvation? Perhaps. If so, there are no shortcuts, Horatio. It's a miracle predicated upon five centuries of practice on Sam's part, slipping in and out of the data mode thousands of times each day."

"Just like anyone who uses an implant?" Gutierrez tapped his head with an index finger. Beside Mister Thoggosh, the songfish suddenly began to whistle *Eine Kleine Nachtmusik*.

"A point, I concede," came the reply, "But there's this: we're not certain if it really is Sam communicating with us over the implant network. He may be truly dead, you know, and this, er, manifestation merely a fair copy of his memories and personality."

Gutierrez sat back. Apparently he hadn't yet considered the possibility. "Well, why not ask him?"

In his office, Aelbraugh Pritsch had been wondering exactly the same thing, himself.

Mister Thoggosh crossed two of his tentacles in front of his torso. "Because he doesn't know, either, Horatio, don't you see? How could he? To be sure, he feels like himself, but if the copying were done correctly, accurately, then of course he would. No one would be able to tell the difference, not even Sam."

"I don't suppose he could, at that. Now that you mention it, I'll bet there's no way anybody can, or ever will. What was that I heard about Helen Keller falling in the forest? Oh well," Gutierrez shrugged and added in a doubtful tone, "as M-R-period-S-P-O-C-K put it, a difference that makes no difference *is* no difference."

"It might have made a difference to that entity which once inhabited Sam's furry body. As you say, we'll never know." Mister Thoggosh would have raised an eyebrow—if molluscs had ever evolved eyebrows. "Rather than quote James Blish, under the circumstances I believe I prefer your itinerant philosopher Steven Wright—'Somebody broke into my apartment, ripped off everything, and replaced it with exact duplicates'—or was that the Mullah Nasrudin?"

Gutierrez chuckled. "Sounds more like Robert Anton Wilson. Speaking of furry bodies—and the cloning thereof— how long will it be before Sam has a new one?"

Mister Thoggosh made a negative gesture with a wave of one long, slender tentacle. "I'm afraid you'll have to ask Dlee Raftan Saon about that. He's the medical expert, and with all of the respect due Sam, I've far too many other matters on my mind at present to meddle where I may lay claim to no expertise at all."

"Such as?"

"Such as." The mollusc's sighs, thought Aelbraugh Pritsch, grew more sincere and authentic sounding every day. "It isn't enough that I must contemplate taking command of the most ancient archaeological artifact ever discovered and—with a pilot at the helm I neither know very well nor entirely trust—flying it far beyond the edge of the Solar System, where no nautiloid has gone before."

"Mister Thoggosh, I'm surprised. And here I thought it was Sam who had been watching too many old TV programs."

"Pardon me, Horatio, you're the one who brought up Mr. Spock. No, before we even get underway, having just fought the combined battle fleets of the great powers on Earth, I am now confronted with shrill demands on the part of a newly formed Committee for the Preservation of Antiquities that I cease and desist all operations at once."

"Don't tell me," replied Gutierrez, "let me guess: Arthur Empleado."

SIXTY
The Burning Bush

"What?"

In another room, not far away, Aelbraugh Pritsch, who had heard nothing about any of this, sat up straight.

Elsewhere, in the sudden silence, the brilliantly colored songfish hanging in its cage beside Mister Thoggosh's "desk" began to warble the "Funeral March of a Marionette."

The nautiloid somehow managed to convey a nod. "That was another thing I wished to speak with you about, Horatio, once we'd established whether you desired to join us on this voyage. You are entirely correct in your surmise: it seems that your Mr. Empleado, finding himself no longer gainfully employed by the American KGB, has discovered a new way of keeping himself busy. I simply wanted to give you advance warning that I intend being rather abrupt with him."

"Fair enough."

"I look forward," the Elder added, "to using your own charming expression and telling him to piss off."

Laughing quietly, the man leaned back again. "Be my guest, Mister Thoggosh. Arthur isn't really *my* Mr. Empleado, anyway. He's Arthur's Mr. Empleado, which ought to be punishment enough for anyone. But why, er, be abrupt with him on this particular issue . . . ?"

"When in the past he's proven himself capable of so many other kinds of foolishness? I thought you might ask about that." The nautiloid lifted a tentacle and let it drop. "To borrow yet another phrase, it's the camel's nose under the tent-flap, Horatio. Switching metaphors in the middle of the conversation, it may even be the straw that broke the camel's back—the American camel, that is."

Obviously confused, Gutierrez shook his head. "A Committee for the Preservation of Antiquities?"

"Indeed." The Elder let a few internal compartments of his massive, brightly striped shell fill with metabolic carbon dioxide, lifted it a few dozen centimeters, and resettled himself more comfortably on the sandy floor. "Horatio, if I read the historic record correctly, America didn't become the last Marxist nation on Earth overnight. Nor was it done at a single, telling blow, a la Mr. Milius's *Red Dawn*. It happened in a series of nasty little collectivist revolutions pulled off while nobody else was looking, in this case, literally underground.

"In many ways, the nasty little revolution within archaeology strongly resembled a similar coup which saddled your people with the so-called International Law of the Sea."

"That sounds vaguely familiar." The general frowned, trying to remember. *Red Dawn*. He'd seen the interview with Chuck Tai, too, thanks to a computer setup Dlee Raftan Saon had sent to the camp.

"There's certainly no reason why it should. Your electronic mass media did their usual highly efficient job of keeping the whole thing out of public view until it was too late. The scheme was inspired by the Soviet Union and enacted into international law by certain Third World dictators greedy for the technological fruits—which they could never have produced for themselves and didn't deserve—of the remnants of your nation's intellectual and economic liberty."

"Such as it was," the former general remarked sadly, almost as if to himself. The most sobering thing about the interview, he thought, was that the PRC had been imitating an America which he'd never had the chance to see himself.

Mister Thoggosh made a sympathetic noise. "Such a battle could only have been waged, of course, such a travesty of law enacted, in the General Assembly of your United Nations. Ignoring the abuses which are inevitably visited upon collectively held assets—a phenomenon known historically as the 'tragedy of the commons'—they established your world's oceans as the 'common heritage of all mankind,' effectively forbidding private property claims and private enterprise beneath international waters and therefore any significant exploration, exploitation or, ironically, preservation, of those oceans. Another such treaty was only prevented at the last minute from damaging your hopes for the future in space."

Gutierrez nodded. "That's probably why I remember it. But what does any of this have to do with archaeology or committees for the preservation of antiquities?"

"Horatio, most of the enemies of liberty in twentieth century America were part of no real organized conspiracy I can find any lingering traces of. Yet they formed a cohesive social entity sharing a similar worldview and values. The UN collectivists had their counterparts, advocates of a parallel variety of collectivism, mostly among American academics, including those practicing archaeology, a field obscure enough that they could get away with practically anything they wished, long before anyone outside the field even took notice."

"I don't get it." Gutierrez shook his head, "Even if I accept your theory, how could they promote their cause in a field that has nothing to do with politics?"

"In a majoritarian society like yours, Horatio, *everything* has something to do with politics." Mister Thoggosh took a long, last sip of his beer before he went on. "These academic collectivists promoted their cause by helping to alter the unconscious assumptions on which your culture was based, and by setting certain precedents which could then be applied elsewhere. Under the noses of citizens kept ignorant by their comrades in the mass media, their political objective was to establish ancient artifacts everywhere and anywhere, discovered or as yet undiscovered, as the common heritage—and perhaps more to the point, the exclusive purview—of all *academickind*. Much of this transparently self-serving nonsense

already had the force of law by the final quarter of the last
century, and wherever it hadn't, new laws were being
demanded—and passed—every day."

"And so they got away with it," the man shrugged, "just
like they got away with everything else. But the world didn't
come to an end over archaeology, did it?"

"Great oaks from little acorns, Horatio." Without asking, the Elder sent his separable tentacle for more beer
and coffee. "The nation-states that passed these silly laws
had no more legitimate or natural a claim to objects buried beneath them ages ago than they did to seabed man-
ganese nodules they couldn't collect without Western help
or to Moon rocks they couldn't reach at all.

"Governments seldom have any historical or ethnic connection with the long-gone individuals whose abandoned
property they claim. In fact the same can be said for people
occupying a given geographical area in whose name governments usually make such claims. They're seldom
descended from those who left the artifacts. Frequently
they aren't even of the same race or speak any related language."

"*I'll give you Greece and Italy,*" replied a familiar voice,
coming through the same speakers Mister Thoggosh used.
By coincidence—or some inconceivable design—the
songfish abruptly broke off with whatever it had been
whistling and took up Lennon and McCartney's "Here
Comes The Sun." "*The people there are mostly descended
from barbarians who* destroyed *the ancient Greek and
Roman civilizations. But there are those who'll argue with
you over Mexico and China.*"

Mister Thoggosh responded, "Good morning, Sam, it's
nice to see you, if only in a figurative sense."

"*That's okay, Mister Thoggosh,*" the disembodied voice
answered. "*In the sense you mean, I'm only a figurative
dog at the moment. Hi there, General. I overheard my name
being taken in vain and thought I'd drop in cybernetically
and see what's up.*"

Listening from his office, Aelbraugh Pritsch groaned
inwardly. Life seemed to be heaping him with one burden after another lately. Sam had been a great enough nuisance merely as an ordinary talking dog. As a noncorporeal

entity capable of inhabiting—of *haunting*—the entire cerebrocortical implant network, he was going to be truly unbearable.

Gutierrez grinned. "What about Sam's point, Mister Thoggosh, on the Mexican and Chinese populations?"

The Elder harumphed. "I'll gladly concede any point where he's correct. However the salient issue, Horatio, is that ethnic and linguistic histories only serve as an excuse—exactly like those widows and orphans I mentioned earlier—for pedigree-waving academics attempting to assert some automatic and exclusive claim to the field, employing brute government force to back them up. A desire for knowledge is understandable and commendable, but it grants no monopoly. More importantly, it confers no right to beat people up and kill them—which is what law and government are all about, under any system of analysis."

Gutierrez shook his head. "Except that without the laws you complain of, Mister Thoggosh, all kinds of historically important artifacts and information could be lost to clumsy, inept, random digging by curiosity-seekers."

"And what is any scientist," Sam asked, *"but just another curiosity-seeker?"*

"Correct again, Sam." The nautiloid resettled himself on the sand. "And so, of course, is Horatio—in his way. Academic archaeologists do frequently charge that the unfranchised delver fails to preserve the historic context of his finds. That may even be true. And it's unquestionably better to reclaim the past methodically.

"But when were mere data more important than life and liberty? And how can anyone take proper scientific pains while worrying that he's about to be arrested or shot in the back because he didn't purchase the right paper from some corrupt official? If historic context is so blasted important, then why not take the more realistic step of persuading and educating amateurs toward cooperation—instead of coercing and brutalizing them in the name of some unenforceable prohibition?"

"I'll have to ask Pulaski about that." Gutierrez smiled, wishing the amateur paleobiologist were here, taking part in the discussion. "Toya's the closest thing we have to an expert in the field, and with due respect, Mister Thoggosh, I've too many other matters on my mind at present to meddle where I may lay claim to no expertise at all."

"For somebody without the advantage of an implant, General, that's an impressive memory you've got."

"For trivia." Gutierrez took the last sip of his coffee. "Call me Horatio, Sam. If you overheard the original comment, then you heard me say I'm no longer a general."

"And since I'm no longer a dog, that makes us even. Okay, Horatio, you're on."

"What I don't see," Gutierrez continued, "is why you're so worked up about this archaeology business, Mister Thoggosh. Talk about ancient history—what effect can it have three hundred million klicks from Earth? Arthur—and whoever is in this with him—can't represent any serious threat to what you're doing here."

The Elder lifted tentacles in a nautiloid shrug. "I suppose it's the hypocrisy of the thing I despise. Reading transcripts of their publications, as I have for some time, it's easy to see what really moved these jealous guardians of a history whose lessons they seem to have been incapable of learning—especially when they spent so much time and effort slandering the great amateur archaeologists whose contributions to the field even they couldn't entirely deny."

"Like Howard Carter," asked the former general, "who discovered the tomb of King Tut?"

"Or Heinrich Schliemann, for another example, the oddball who supposedly dug up Troy?"

"Schliemann was the prime example I had in mind, Sam, although, as you imply, his less-gifted and persistent successors claim he didn't discover Troy at all—"

"But another city of the same name in the same place."

"Quite. Whenever I hear adventurers of the past castigated for their methods, I recall that in those days the academics, when they dug at all, did their digging with dynamite, too. And not just over artifacts; they were known to conduct authentic Western-style gun battles over sites containing dinosaur fossils. It's arguable that the best methodology was worked out by these amateurs, often pursuing dreams and legends ignored or dismissed by the experts."

"It's always seemed to me," the human agreed, "that experts exist only to tell you why something *can't* be done."

"Just before some gifted and persistent amateur who doesn't know any better goes ahead and does it."

"My opinion exactly," Mister Thoggosh replied. "From the academic standpoint, of course, the most grievous sin of these amateurs was simply that of any amateur with regard to any established profession. They were self-appointed, self-educated, uninitiated by the guild, uncircumcised by the priesthood . . ."

"And therefore untouchable and unspeakable," Sam observed.

The giant mollusc made a chuckling noise over the same sound system the dog was using. "Whenever we speak of archaeology, Sam, amateur or professional, we must always remember that what we're really talking about is abandoned property—"

" 'Little bits of junk,' as Marion Ravenwood described it in Raiders of the Lost Ark—"

"Thrown away by their original owners who, in any case, couldn't take it with them. Whatever legislation is passed in an absurd refusal to confront that fact of pragmatic reality—"

"Among others."

"—those little bits of junk belong to no one until they're physically discovered and reclaimed."

"In other words," Gutierrez offered, " 'finders keepers'?"

"I like the way you put that, Horatio."

"In any case," insisted Mister Thoggosh, "the value of those bits of junk, like all material value, is subjective. Some, whose goal was treasure and glory, were reviled by academics as 'looters' and 'pot hunters,' pursuing that ultimate dirty word, 'profit.' In the end, even collectors came to be despised, although most were moved by the same thing that presumably motivates the professional: a fascinated curiosity with the past."

"You're right there," Gutierrez agreed. "Whenever I had time, and was stationed in the right place, I used to take my sons out to look for Indian arrowheads."

"Which makes you a pot hunter, Horatio, within the

customary meaning of the term. And certainly the pot hunter's right to satisfy his fascinated curiosity—"

"*Or any other itch.*"

"Indeed, Sam, or any other itch, is just as great as that of anyone with an academic degree, whose personal profit, if you will, consists of academic preeminence, scientific priority, prestigious publication, professorial tenure—"

"*And government grants.*"

"As opposed to something as clean and uncomplicated," asked the general, "as cash?"

"Precisely. Nor have I yet thought to mention the greedy, self-righteous museum directors who stuff their basements with booty forever to be kept from private hands and the public eye until one day in a distant century perhaps, it's dug up again by future archaeologists. . . ."

Gutierrez laughed.

"How," Mister Thoggosh went on, "do we avoid the inevitable conclusion that they and their colleagues were moved by a visceral, infantile, hypocritical hatred for the very concepts of private property and individual achievement, which had nothing to do with science?"

"I sympathize with your point of view, Mister Thoggosh," Gutierrez sighed, "but you still haven't explained how archaeology became 'the straw that broke the American camel's back.'"

"Forgive me, Horatio, but you Americans started with a nation-state in which any individual could make of himself anything he had the gumption for. Then you let it go a little bit at a time to minor trespasses like zoning laws and building codes—or the International Law of the Sea—until no one was at liberty any longer, even to dig with his hands in the dirt and keep what he found there."

"I think I see what you're getting at, Mister Thoggosh, but—"

"One state, Oklahoma, I believe it was, demanded a written inventory of each individual's personal belongings, everything from wristwatches to farm tractors—threatening to send its minions to break into people's homes and make the inventory themselves if it was not immediately forthcoming—and there was no revolt."

"But that was—"

"How about the federal judge during the same period who ordered local property taxes increased, despite the clearly stated wishes of the voters—and even their elected officials?"

"Your Supreme Court backed him up, Horatio, ending the last pretense to democracy in America—"

"And it never occurred to anybody to take him out and string him up like he deserved!"

"Now hold on, Sam, Mister Thog—"

Gutierrez's sputtering objections were waved away by more tentacles than the man could count. "Your government routinely denied any obligation on its part to defend your life, liberty, or property, Horatio, while simultaneously forbidding you the physical means of defending them yourself. At the same time, ludicrously enough, toward the end of the last century, animals had rights in America—"

"Nonsapient animals, he means."

"But human beings did not."

"Well, I—"

"Finally, a blatantly power-hungry pack of conservative congressman, elected on the promise of bringing freedom back to the people, instead forced 'emergency' legislation through, using drugs as an excuse, which suspended the Bill of Rights altogether, destroying the last vestiges of the system of which you Americans had been so proud for so long. Justifiably proud, I might add, considering the historic context. Your liberals 'responded' by adopting more and more of the tattered trappings of Marxism being shed everywhere else in the world. In the end, they were even able to create an enormous slush fund through the World Bank—using three gigantic pseudoscientific hoaxes as a pretext: acid rain, global warming, and ozone depletion—to finance and enforce the sovietization process."

"Horatio might be interested to know," Sam added, *"that the last capital offense on record in the Elders' culture—the last death sentence before they shed government altogether—was reserved for politicians caught lying to the public."*

"In particular," Mister Thoggosh agreed, "for public misuse of the word 'emergency.'"

"Which has what to do," Gutierrez sounded impatient, "with Arthur's group and archaeology?"

"It's all of a piece, Horatio, and I don't intend for a moment even to let it *begin*—"

Mister Thoggosh suddenly fell silent, listening to his implant. Somehow sensing the Elder's tension, even the songfish momentarily stopped its trilling.

Then: "I beg your pardon once again, my friends, but I've just received some extremely disturbing news. My assistant, Aelbraugh Pritsch, informs me that your three spacecraft, Horatio, the *Laika*, the *Geronimo*, and the *John Galt*—"

"*Have caught fire!*" Sam interrupted.

"And are burning out of control on the outer surface of the canopy!"

SIXTY-ONE
Canary Row

"Shitgoddamnittohell!"

Coughing fluorocarbon every step of the way, Gutierrez erupted from the entrance pool outside the Proprietor's quarters and ran for the foot of the nearest staircase.

Access to the outer surface—and to his precious shuttlecraft—was through an air lock, installed recently as a courteous afterthought at treetop level, which penetrated the mustard yellow polymer to hang beside a convenient canopy tree. Most of the community's buildings above ground level were supported like so many shelf mushrooms anyway, so it was not unusual to see a spiral staircase encircling one of the forest giants. In the asteroid's minimal gravity, the climb always turned out to be less daunting than it initially appeared.

What was odd about this particular staircase was that it worked like a high-speed escalator—the treads and risers even canted inward to avoid flinging passengers away—without benefit of any visible moving parts. In stolid silence and with gritted teeth, Gutierrez took the spiral journey which amounted to almost five kilometers but consumed less than a minute and a half.

"Horatio!" a familiar voice greeted him at his journey's end. "Sam told me you were coming. I got here as quickly as I could, myself. Tl°m°nch°l's on his way, too." He handed Gutierrez a small bundle. "In the meantime, see if you can squeeze into this!"

Eichra Oren, looking incomplete somehow without the talking dog who'd been his lifelong companion, had met the former general on the small balcony outside the hanging air lock. They were joined within a score of heartbeats by Mister Thoggosh's security chief, one of the sea-scorpionoids that the humans sometimes called "lobster people."

Both wore the lightweight, transparent filmsuits which provided protection for various species associated with the Elders in virtually any hostile environment. Eichra Oren had brought one for Gutierrez. His arms and legs slid easily into those of the suit. The midsection stretched to accommodate his own. Sealing the seam and pulling the flexible helmet and mask over his face, he would have appreciated the many advantages it had over the bulky armor his own people had inherited from NASA, if the situation hadn't been so urgent.

By comparison with the escalator, the lock cycled slowly, rising through the canopy as it did, giving Gutierrez time to adjust to his clothing. He noticed that Tl°m°nch°l had reslung his gun belt outside his own protective covering, that Eichra Oren even had his sword of office handy, slapping at his plastic-covered thigh, and realized that his own little pistol, the Kahr K9, was buttoned up under his suit where it couldn't do him any good. As the floor of the lock rose under them, carrying them outside, he nodded toward his companions' weapons.

"You really think we're going to need all that hardware? Seems to me our real problem is going to be figuring out how to fight a fire in a vacuum."

The elevator stopped; the door began to open. Gutierrez was aware that his feet were sticking gently to the floor. Staying put had been a challenge when they'd first arrived.

"On the contrary, friend Horatio," Tl°m°nch°l's clawtips raced across the keyboard of his vocalizer, "our real problem consists of figuring out how a fire *got started* in a vacuum!"

"Make that *three* fires, Tl°m°nch°l," corrected Eichra

Oren. "Horatio, I hate coincidences like this. And yes, they never fail to make me look to my arma—"

The man was suddenly speechless. Everywhere they looked, people of a dozen different species, in thin filmsuits and heavy NASA armor alike, were scurrying about like vermin whose comfortable log had just been kicked over. Although many carried fire extinguishers and other, less-identifiable equipment, they seemed to be accomplishing about as much as scurrying vermin, to Gutierrez's eye, trained for command.

Far out across the plastic plain, literally smooth as a billiard ball beneath two suns and a scattering of embarrassed-looking stars, all three of the venerable American spacecraft were belching thick, black, greasy smoke through their many hull penetrations. In the absence of any significant gravity, the pall surrounded them like an evil fog, hellishly lit, orange-red, from within.

Gutierrez set his jaw and turned to the Antarctican. "Eichra Oren, give me your sword!"

S°bb°ts°rrh was a happy being.

Although he was the only member of his species here not working in the security contingent, his position was important and remunerative. As a Small Artifactologist, it was his responsibility to supervise the excavation, handling, and disposition of whatever hand-carryable Predecessor discoveries were made. It was exacting work which he enjoyed, having spent most of a lifetime preparing for it.

That wasn't why he was happy at this particular moment, however. Earlier this morning, an entity he thought of as °rth°r°mpl°°d° had barged into his office in the Elders' settlement—it was pure chance the creature had caught him there, he was usually out in the field these days among new friends who shared his interests—claiming to speak for something called "The Committee for the Preservation of Antiquities, representing the unanimous opinion of the human community" nearby. Citing the fact, which nobody disputed anyway, that the asteroid 5023 Eris was located in an alternative version of the Solar System presently inhabited by its own species and none other, it had demanded that all exploration of the ancient spaceship halt immediately.

S°bb°ts°rrh had begun by calling °rth°r°mpl°°d° a liar. In the first place, there wasn't a sapient species in all of probability capable of unanimity in numbers much over three, and humans had proven themselves no different from anyone else in that regard. Dissent was the primary social characteristic of sapience. How could a species explore every environmental niche and avenue of survival—which in the last analysis was the function of intelligence—if they acted like copies of one another? In the second, some of his new friends happened to be human, and—T°y°p°l°sk° and R°g°r°w°n in particular—were as sanguine about exploring the asteroid as himself.

He'd begun by calling °rth°r°mpl°°d° a liar, but he'd hardly stopped there. As exacting with his insults as he was with everything else, he'd exhausted the invective vocabulary of twenty-three languages before going on to items of his own devising. In the end, °rth°r°mpl°°d° had stalked off, tossing vaguely ominous alien terms like *libel* and *slander* over his shoulder and threatening to *sue* S°bb°ts°rrh for what he'd said—a process the artifactologist gathered was akin to adversary proceedings before a moral debt assessor.

Determined to remain methodical, S°bb°ts°rrh was now on his way to the office of Eichra Oren between the Elders' settlement and the human encampment. He was no *p'Nan* professional, but he knew that, no matter how annoying it might be, moral debt cannot be created by a verbalism. Somewhere at the heart of every moral debt lay an act of initiated force, actual or threatened. He was certain that his judgement in this matter would be confirmed—which was why he was happy—and because this assessor happened to be human, the experience would add something to his understanding of the species.

Having decided to walk in order to prolong his enjoyment of the moment, he was mentally occupied with the delightfully delicate problem of preserving an actual Predecessor footprint in the dust, deep inside the asteroid, which had been covered over with more dust for a billion years, had just rounded one of the giant canopy trees, and was virtually within hailing distance of the assessor's home. Thus he failed to see his attacker until the final instant.

S°bb°ts°rrh's fleeting first impression was his last. What he saw as he drew the last molecules of air over his gills and snatched desperately at a weapon he carried on his belt—*beneath* his filmsuit—was an apparition three times his size belonging to no species he'd ever heard of. The thing's face may have been that of a mantoid, rather broad at the top, narrower at the bottom. Its principal features were a pair of rage-maddened eyes, two nostril penetrations, and a slash of a mouth filled with nasty-looking masticators.

The rest was worse, a patchwork of pallid flesh and haphazard plates. Some of the manipulators sticking out at odd angles around the edges appeared mammalian, others arthropodic. S°bb°ts°rrh didn't have time to be certain, but thought he saw an odd number of them, seven or perhaps nine. It was the last thought he had. Before it was complete, the entity swung a huge tool it held in a manipulator, bringing it down on S°bb°ts°rrh's head, crushing his pseudochitin skull, dashing his brains out on the grass, and ending his life.

Arthur Empleado, former head of the American KGB on 5023 Eris—in the same sense that Gutierrez was a former general—stood in the open air lock wearing someone else's discarded spacesuit, watching the efforts of several different species to fight the fire outside. A row of buttons blinking angrily on the panel told him that someone below was clamoring to use the elevator.

All three of the elderly shuttlecraft were ablaze. Each had survived many distinguished twentieth-century missions, more than three quarters of a century lying in mothballs in Florida, rededication in the names of heroes of the socialist revolution, and a three-hundred-million kilometer trip to the asteroid belt.

Soon they would be gone.

There would be no way his companions could avoid inferring that their precious spacecraft had been sabotaged. The only way to get them to burn was to fill them with oxygen instead of the plain air they'd been designed for. That sort of thing could hardly happen accidently, not to three ships separated by several hundred meters' distance.

In his mind's eye, Empleado could see the incendiary devices plainly. If he remembered right, they'd been invented by the French resistance during the Second World War. An ordinary cigarette could be placed anywhere, closed in a book of matches so that, once it smoldered down to the heads—five minutes in a normal atmosphere, probably less in oxygen—they'd go up in a sudden blaze, taking everything else with them.

Gutierrez had evidently arrived at the same conclusion. Empleado saw him seize Eichra Oren's proffered sword and run toward the nearest shuttle, the flagship *Honorable Robert Dole* illegally rechristened *Laika*, followed by the assessor and Tl°m°nch°l, the sea-scorpionoid he knew was Mister Thoggosh's chief of security. Raising the razor-sharp assessor's weapon over his head, the general hacked brutally at a spot on the shuttlecraft's hull just below the pilots' windows.

Before the man had taken a dozen such strokes, the unearthly alloy of the sword had found its way through the tough material of the hull and a sudden spark-edged tongue of flame shot outward as Gutierrez leaped aside at the last instant to avoid it. The beleaguered spaceship vomited smoke and flames for a couple of seconds, then the conflagration whuffed out as if someone had thrown a switch. Without waiting to see the results, the general hurried to the next ship.

If he'd planned repeating his Conan act, Tl°m°nch°l was too fast for him. That being drew its sidearm, aiming at the same spot on the hull of the *Honorable Orrin Hatch* (alias *Geronimo*) which the Gutierrez had attacked on the *Laika*. There was no report, but a head-sized ragged hole opened in the vessel's side, shot flames, and went black as the fire inside died for lack of oxygen. By that time, Eichra Oren had used his fusion-powered pistol on the *John Galt*, formerly the *Honorable John McCain*, and put her fire out, as well.

Inside his helmet, Empleado shook his head. He pushed a button on the panel of the combination elevator–air lock. The door closed, and the machine descended. He stepped out at treetop level under the canopy, where there was almost as much activity as topside. Several aerostats hovered directly below the points where the ruined spacecraft stood—for what reason the former KGB man couldn't say.

One carried Mister Thoggosh himself.

Half a dozen individuals, identifiable as aliens under their transparent coverings, gave him what he was sure was a dirty look as they stepped into the air lock he'd just stepped out of. Empleado shrugged to himself indifferently, put a foot on the first step of the spiral escalator, going down, and headed back the way he'd just come from the human camp.

Mister Thoggosh returned to his office/living quarters that afternoon, looking forward to the peace and quiet of his accustomed solitude—and the comfort of peeling off the environmental filmsuit he wore to protect his gills and other soft tissues in the desiccating atmosphere preferred by his land-dwelling associates.

Lightweight and transparent though it was, the absurd getup still made him feel uncomfortably confined, and restricted his movements. Moreover, it had been no help when it came to shielding him from the heat of the shuttle fire which had been perceptible even through the world-enveloping organic canopy beneath which he'd hovered—all day, it seemed—in his aerostat.

The heat had worried him most, not just for the craft—which would have come in handy exploring the Cometary Halo—but for the entire colony. The canopy had begun as intertwined branches at the tops of great trees that supported it a kilometer above the asteroid's real surface. Ultraviolet exposure had softened and polymerized it into a covering to hold the atmosphere on the planetoid and protect its inhabitants from the cold, vacuum, and radiation of space. Intense heat was one thing it had not been engineered to withstand.

All afternoon, he'd had disturbing mental images of the canopy melting, bursting, and spewing its contents, including thousands of sapient beings, into the void. Had it not been possible to put the fires out immediately, his people would have cast the stricken vessels off and let them burn several kilometers away from the canopy. Thanks to fast thinking and even faster action on the part of Gutierrez, that had proven unnecessary. The canopy had held. Cooled again, it appeared as reliable as it had been to begin with.

Dictating the hundredth memo of the day into his implant for transmission to the appropriate recipient, the nautiloid descended a flight of stairs into the fluorocarbon with which his apartments were filled, cycled the lock, and floated inside. A stand of housekelp waved a friendly, mindless greeting, and he began to feel at home.

"Princess of the Royal Web Nek Nam'l Las, Chief Logistics Engineer. Copy to her aide, Voozh Preeno, and to Llessure Knarrfic, Administration. Note her rank according to customs of her people. My dear Princess, colon, I transmit this for the record, comma, to commend you and your division on their energetic and brilliant assistance during the emergency connected with the destruction of the human spacecraft, period. Had it not been for your swift judgment and attention to vital detail, comma, in excess of duties for which you originally contracted, comma, there is no way to estimate the disastrous consequences which might have resulted, period. Paragraph. You will be gratified to learn that this exemplary performance will find a substantive reward in the form of a bonus in the amount of—"

The nautiloid stopped dictating abruptly, disturbed by a sense that something was out of place in his office. The tentacle which had begun reaching for the fastener of his filmsuit froze in place as he realized what it was: his prized songfish, which usually greeted him with its beautiful trilling, was silent.

Grateful to be away from what he regarded as the eerily inhuman environs of the nautiloid settlement, Empleado trudged through the forest, back toward the American encampment.

The bulky spacesuit he carried over his arm would have been a burden had it not been for the light gravity. Whatever it had cost him in nerve-strain and fatigue, it had been worth wearing the sweat-stinking armor and rubbing elbows with that nightmare menagerie. He'd had three objectives in mind, and seen all of them accomplished in half a day. His old superiors would have been proud of him had there been some way to report to them—and if they weren't busy preserving their own hides just now in a world turned politically upside down.

His way through the woods followed what was becoming a well-worn trail. Before he knew it, someone would be suggesting that it be paved. For some reason that annoyed him, and he left the path where it curved about the base of one of the great trees and took the other way around. The ground was reasonably clear of cover here, and the footing was no more difficult than on the path.

He hadn't gone another hundred yards when he saw something glistening between the spreading roots of another canopy tree, as if someone had been littering, discarding, of all things, a huge wad of transparent kitchen wrap. That thought suddenly made him freeze in his tracks, hair stirring at the back of his neck. There was only one thing on this asteroid that looked like kitchen wrap.

Someone had been littering, all right—and apparently trying to do his job for him in their clumsy, violent way. Pushed hastily between the barrel-sized roots was the dead body of one of the lobster people, its head smashed to a pulp.

In effect, Empleado realized, somebody had just killed a cop.

Mister Thoggosh was as angry as he ever got.

Almost anyone who knew the nautiloid Elder would have agreed that this was angry enough. His assistant, Aelbraugh Pritsch, had once remarked, when he thought he was outside his employer's hearing, that for a cold-blooded entity, the Proprietor was more terrifying in his hot-blooded wrath than any other being he'd ever met—or even heard of. At the time, the giant mollusc had felt somewhat complimented. Now what he experienced was a hostility toward whoever had done this to him, so powerful and implacable that he wondered how he could possibly contain it without bursting.

The brilliantly colored and beautiful songfish that had come with him on the arduous voyage to this alternative reality was floating belly-up in its little cage, eyes clouded over and scales fading to a deathly white. Its melodious singing would never soothe him again. Monitors built into his desk, which he usually relied on to tell him that the fluorocarbon surrounding him was sufficiently charged with oxygen, were flashing an infuriated red of their own.

He'd never been meant to see those monitors. The would-be murderer had assumed he'd pull his nearly invisible suit off as soon as he stepped through the door. He'd very nearly done that. Only his abstraction and fatigue, his concentration on the memo he'd been dictating, and a subtle feel of wrongness within his suite, had stayed his tentacle until he'd reached the area of the sandy floor at the opposite end of the room set aside as a desk. According to his instruments, the fluorocarbon had been contaminated with a lethal volume—it must have taken several liters—of an industrial solvent combining the attributes of carbon tetrachloride and dimethyl sulfoxide: highly penetrative and extremely deadly.

What made him angriest, having been in the midst of a commendatory note to one of his employees, was that it must have been someone he trusted. The door, for example, wouldn't open to just anyone, but employed a crude form of judgment based on information automatically derived from the day-to-day operation of his implant. In short, someone he trusted had tried to kill him, and it made him furious.

Terrorism, under which this incident must be categorized, was an interesting and instructive phenomenon in the abstract. His culture intelligently took its appearance as a sign of deep social maladies. Like political assassination, it was an ultimate check and balance, never to be altogether discouraged. Those who practiced terrorism functioned something like canaries in coal mines—or his poor songfish in its little cage—informing those who ran civilization that they were failing a few sensitive individuals at the fringes and were therefore in danger of failing less sensitive, more sensible individuals if they continued along whatever course had triggered the event in the first place.

That said, Mister Thoggosh was unable to view his own attempted murder quite so detachedly. Prudently, he believed, he'd already set automated devices to cleaning up the mess himself. He hadn't made it to his present ancient age entirely by accident. He decided to tell no one about this, with the exception of the closest thing his culture offered to a detective, the *p'Nan* moral debt assessor—and his good friend—Eichra Oren.

Someone was going to pay for this.

In blood.

SIXTY-TWO
Councils of War

"Boss?"

The familiar voice, sourceless and inaudible to the unaided ear, echoed within Eichra Oren's skull.

The Antarctican moral debt assessor had just returned to his office and living quarters, built in the forest between the American encampment and the Elders' settlement. Now he shrugged out of his transparent filmsuit and stepped into the shower. The suit had protected him from the flame and smoke of the fire and had dealt in its own way with the sweat and grime of his exertions, but he still needed hot, soapy water running over his body in order to feel clean.

He also needed to speak aloud, although it wasn't technically necessary. "What's up, Sam?"

"I hate to disturb your privacy, Boss, but we wondered if we could have a word with you."

The debt assessor's house drew its water supply directly from the veins of the great tree it was attached to. Even the energy required to heat the water had first fallen on a billion leaves as sunlight. Eichra Oren ducked his head under the shower tap, briefly enjoying the warm, gentle drumming on his scalp. " 'We'?"

*"Mister Thoggosh and I. For reasons he'll explain when
I give him a chance, he's sitting in a quiet corner of Nellus
Glaser's greasy spoon at the moment, having nine or twelve
beers and feeling extremely pissed off about being kicked
out of his own office. I'm hanging out wherever the little
dot goes when you turn off the TV. Boss, there's a pattern
starting to take shape that neither of us likes very much.
We thought you'd better know about it as soon as possible."*

Eichra Oren finished rinsing, willed the water off, and
stepped out of the spiral shower enclosure—an idea he'd
swiped from the Americans' most famous science-fiction
writer—which made a door or curtain unnecessary. Currents of warm air sucked moisture out of the enclosure and
would have dried his body if he'd let them, but he also
needed the feel of a rough towel on his skin. He'd rubbed
his face dry and was starting on his thick, wavy hair before
he replied.

"One incident, however spectacular and disastrous, hardly
constitutes a pattern, does it?"

*"Why, Boss! I wouldn't have believed it possible, but I
think you've hurt my feelings!"*

Another familiar voice, equally sourceless, amplified
Sam's complaint. *"Three incidents, my young friend. First
came the 'accident' that happened to Oasam, then the
shuttle fire. Afterward, when I returned to my quarters,
the fluorocarbon there had been contaminated with a deadly
poison. I'm gratified to say that I discovered this act of
sabotage before I removed my protective clothing."*

*"Otherwise we'd both be communicating with you from
electric limbo. Or is it purgatory? Anyway, who'd have
guessed there'd be a digital afterlife? Ain't seance wonderful?"*

Despite his present fire-blackened mood, Eichra Oren
chuckled to himself. He'd discussed all of the philosophical ramifications with Mister Thoggosh, Dlee Raftan Saon,
and Rosalind until he was tired of thinking about them.
Nobody would convince him that this wasn't his old friend,
but only a clever copy, talking inside his head.

Tossing his damp towel at a rack that would clean and
dry it, he strode from the bath into the bedroom where
a closet operating on similar principles had already cleaned

and pressed his clothing. For the moment, he felt a great reluctance to resume one of the Hawaiian shirts and the faded Levis he'd worn since coming to 5023 Eris. Originally selected to help the Americans accept his presence here more readily, they remained as alien-feeling to him as, say, Gutierrez might have felt in one of Raftan's "ghillie" suits of multicolored fabric strips.

Instead, he chose a lightweight, knee-length tunic from his native Elder-influenced Antarctican culture, although he did slip his feet into a pair of comfortable Japanese running shoes, sitting on the edge of the bed to tie them and thinking about the power laces he'd seen in one of the American movies Sam had come to love. Another thought passed through his mind—untransmitted to the beings he was conversing with—that he'd been on this asteroid too long and that it was past time to go home.

"All right, granted," he told them at last. "Three incidents does point to a pattern of some kind, and I don't like it any better than you do. We no sooner deal with one set of problems, culminating in the defeat of a military invasion, when somebody tries to cause us even more grief. What do you two suggest?"

"*Aside from my own determination, becoming manifest even as we speak, to combine the surviving structural elements of the three American shuttles into one undamaged, 'Elder-enhanced' spacecraft,*" Mister Thoggosh replied, obviously pausing to take a sip of beer, "*I understand that you're already trying to find out precisely what happened to Sam, at the request of Model 17, is that correct?*"

"Danny Gutierrez." The man nodded, then realized that the gesture would go unperceived, since he was unwilling to pass along everything he might be feeling at the moment, even to Sam. "Once I got my emotions untangled and my thought processes straightened out, I realized I'd be doing exactly that, even if nobody had asked me to. Not just what happened to Sam, but who did it and why. I haven't had time to make much of a start yet. And I'm going to need Sam's help."

"*Just what I always wanted!*" groaned the former dog, his tone only half serious. "*Oh well, on the other hand, I guess it isn't everybody who gets to investigate his own murder!*"

"No, it isn't."

Grinning, Eichra Oren took his sword of office from the bed where he'd tossed it, pulled it from its scabbard, and peered critically down each of its edges in turn, looking carefully for small nicks and scratches. The alloy the weapon was composed of lay far beyond the metallurgical abilities of the Soviet Americans, but their spacecraft had been constructed of an aggregate of rather odd materials and there was no telling what damage they might have done to his blade.

Satisfied that his weapon was intact, he nevertheless slipped a small white ceramic hone from a pocket on the back of the scabbard, sat cross-legged on the bed with the sword across one knee, and gently stroked its already gleaming edges, a gesture as unnecessary—and yet somehow needful—as his shower and rough toweling.

It seemed to be his day, he thought, for that sort of useless, necessary gesture, all around.

After a few minutes of this, he spoke again. "Very well, here's your pattern, gentlebeings. And after sufficient reflection, it becomes a reasonably obvious one. Somebody is trying to set the Americans against us, and vice versa."

"*Again,*" Sam added.

"*I was very much afraid you'd say that.*" Mister Thoggosh gave forth with one of his counterfeit electronic sighs. "*That was my thought, as well. You both know these Americans much better than I do. Politically speaking, how effective are their memories? Is it too much to hope that both parties have been through enough together by now, not to be manipulated again in such a manner?*"

"*Why don't you tell us?*" Sam demanded. "*You're supposed to be the wise and ancient being here.*"

"*Then I greatly fear, Otusam, that it is my considered opinion as the wise and ancient being in residence here, that unless we discover who's really doing all these terrible things—and stop him cold, or her—precisely the same tensions and mistrust which threatened to destroy us all once before will return. To that end—discovering and stopping this culprit, I mean—I should like to assign the task to you, Eichra Oren. That is, if you're willing.*"

Eichra Oren experienced a transitory glimpse through

Mister Thoggosh's eyes, of the interior of the restaurant he'd taken refuge in while his quarters were decontaminating themselves. He wondered briefly what he'd see if he looked through Sam's "eyes." So far he hadn't asked. He surprised himself, replying without hesitation.

"I'm willing, right enough, Mister Thoggosh, provided Sam is, too. And I suspect that we've already been presented with a clue of sorts. Our 'culprit' has to be somebody unattached to either group, human or nautiloid."

The giant mollusc made a sort of hiccuping noise of startled objection. *"That's rather a leap, even for you, my young friend. How did you arrive at this conclusion?"*

"Yeah," Sam asked, *"and who the hell does it leave?"*

"Excuse me, I probably should have said ex-Soviet American, rather than human, but even that doesn't say it quite right. I intended to exclude any of Horatio Gutierrez's people, even the former KGB agents among them. Whoever he or she happens to be, our villain has to be one of the most recent newcomers—Chinese, Russian, or American—not to have known about Mister Thoggosh's filmsuit, and that it would function as a layer of emergency protection against any poison."

The Proprietor took a moment to mull it over. *"It may be more a measure of my desperation than of objective reality, but that sounds reasonable to me. You're suggesting it's some straggling survivor of the recent battle, someone who didn't get rounded up by Tl°m°nch°l's security people or Colonel Tai's Extra-Special Forces?"*

Eichra Oren shook his head. "I don't know exactly what I'm suggesting, Mister Thoggosh, except that everyone who was already here—including members of Gutierrez's party— knows all about filmsuits and would probably choose some other way."

"The trouble with your beautiful theory, Boss," Sam pointed out, *"is that they have to be ignorant about filmsuits—and at the same time know how to manipulate the mechanisms down below that got me."* Somehow, Eichra Oren felt Sam shudder at the memory.

The nautiloid agreed with the dog. *"Yes, not to mention how neatly they defeated my security precautions. Yet another trouble with the idea is that the saboteur might well have counted on my removing my filmsuit before I noticed the poison. That's very nearly what happened, you know. If it hadn't been for my poor—"*

Mister Thoggosh was cut off as Eichra Oren gave him the cerebrocortical equivalent of a suddenly upthrust hand. Someone—it could only have been one of the Americans, of course, since anybody else would have simply "rung the doorbell" via implant—was outside shouting, pounding frantically on his front door.

Cautious in light of recent events, the moral debt assessor slipped the tiny silver-colored plasma pistol he always carried out of his tunic pocket. Although it weighed less than a quarter of a kilogram, it may have represented the most powerful type of personal weapon on the asteroid and was a popular choice, especially with many of the smaller sapients. Concealing it in his palm, he rose from the bed, mentally allowing the door to dilate slowly as he approached it.

Empleado paced up and down on the balcony outside, looking pale and shaken. "Eichra Oren! There's something—somebody lying over there in the trees! I mean a dead body! It's one of the . . . the sea-scorpions with its head all bashed in like—" Abruptly, the former KGB agent turned, bent over the rail of the balcony as if someone had punched him in the stomach, and vomited onto the ground below.

"KGB agent," observed Sam, watching through the assessor's eyes, *"tough guy."*

Without comment, Eichra Oren went back into the house for a fresh towel and moistened it. He returned to the balcony and handed it to Empleado, who was still bent over the rail making futile, retching noises. Eyes streaming, the former KGB man finally straightened, accepted the towel, and pointed a shaky finger at the base of one of the trees perhaps a hundred meters from the house.

Eichra Oren nodded, descended the short flight of stairs, and crossed the leaf-littered forest floor, headed in the indicated direction. The dead body Empleado had discovered wasn't hard at all to find—but it was impossible to identify.

For a long while, the assessor knelt beside the corpse,

lifting various portions of it with a telescoping stylus from his tunic pocket and peering down at it with much the same expression he'd displayed earlier, examining the edges of his sword.

"Well, here's a fourth incident for you," he muttered under his breath, addressing Sam and Mister Thoggosh, "to add to your pattern. I don't have any idea who it is, but from his weapon—and the fact that he was caught with it buttoned up under his filmsuit—I'll bet it isn't Tl°m°nch°l or any of his people."

Sam agreed. Both he and the Proprietor were observing the scene relayed by Eichra Oren's implant. *"They're a wholesomely paranoid bunch, all right. And our late friend here is living proof—or at least recently deceased—that paranoids live longer."*

"If it isn't one of Tl°m°nch°l's," Mister Thoggosh declared, *"then there's only one other individual it could be. S°bb°ts°rrh, our Small Artifactologist. Dlee Raftan Saon will be able to confirm that through external stimulation of his cerebrocortical implant, of course, and perhaps even get a picture of the killer. By why in an infinite number of universes would anyone wish to kill such a charming, harmless—?"*

"That's the really nasty part, I suspect." Eichra Oren was disgusted. "I don't think it mattered who got killed, as long as the body was found halfway between—"

A footfall on the dried leaves behind him made Eichra Oren stand up from where he'd been kneeling beside the body and turn, plasma pistol ready in his hand and pointed. Adjusted properly, the little fusion-powered weapon was capable of blasting man-sized holes in solid rock, and the Antarctican had it turned up all the way.

But it was only Empleado, walking a bit unsteadily and still dabbing at his mouth with the towel. Still preoccupied with the shock of his discovery, he didn't even seem to see the pistol pointed at him. "Do you know who it is, Eichra Oren?"

"Maybe." The *p'Nan* moral debt assessor pocketed his weapon. "We were discussing that."

"We?" Empleado repeated, glancing around.

"Mister Thoggosh, Sam, and I, via cerebrocortical implant.

Let me ask you something which you may recognize from your own experience as professional routine: after you found it, did you move this body or disturb it in any way, Mr. Empleado?"

Looking bewildered, the man shook his head vigorously. "Arthur, please. No, I didn't. I don't think I could have . . . Eichra Oren, I've got to admit something to you. To somebody. I never really thought of these things—all of the Elders' people, I mean, except for you and maybe Sam—as real people before this. If anyone had told me that I'd react this way to seeing one of them killed . . ."

At least partly sincere, the debt assessor placed a sympathetic hand on the man's shoulder. "I'm sorry it had to happen this way, Arthur, but it's a good thing to hear, nonetheless. It means you're growing up in a way your own culture never allowed you to. To answer your question, we're not absolutely certain, but we think it's one of the archaeology staff, an individual named S°bb°ts°rrh."

Apparently it was too much all at once. Empleado reeled with shock. "But . . . I was speaking with him only a few hours ago! We had an argument, a loud one in front of his subordinates. He—" The former KGB man shut up suddenly, displaying the reflex his people had to look around for anyone who happened to be listening.

Less sympathetic now, the Antarctican tightened his grip on the man's shoulder. "He what?"

"He insulted me, Eichra Oren, he really insulted me, in several different languages, I think, in front of witnesses!" Empleado took a deep, shuddering breath and let it out. "His clerical staff or whatever. Which makes me the principal suspect."

Eichra Oren released Empleado's shoulder with a vague look of negation. "Arthur, everybody on this asteroid is a suspect until I get a chance to begin eliminating them one by one. Anyway, as I say, we're not yet completely certain that it's S°bb°ts°rrh . . ." He paused, listening. "Although Mister Thoggosh informs me that S°bb°ts°rrh was the only sea- scorpionoid on 5023 Eris not associated with Tl°m°nch°l's security group. I'll have to call on Dlee Raftan Saon before we can—"

"That won't be necessary." A voice came from the depths

of the forest, followed by the sound of feet wading through dried leaves and other woodland debris. Before either man could respond, the aged insectoid physician emerged from the trees, dapper for one of his kind in the suit of long, multicolored strips Eichra Oren had imagined Gutierrez trying on. "I happened to be on my way to see you."

Dlee Raftan Saon stopped beside the sea-scorpionoid's body, hunkered down as close as his rigid arthropodic anatomy would permit, and began rummaging through the small black medical bag he always carried. Some things were the same in any universe. "Now where did I put that—ah, here it is! This will only take a moment."

"And it won't hurt a bit," added Sam, speaking sarcastically from recent experience.

Ignoring the dog's remarks, as he often did, the physician had removed a black-enameled metal object shaped like a small flashlight from his bag and was applying one end of it to the ruins of the sea-scorpionoid's chitinous skull. After a few suspenseful seconds, the object chirruped at him and Dlee Raftan Saon looked up, consulting information the device had just transmitted to his implant.

"It's S°bb°ts°rrh, all right," read the insect-being, "age: 323—too young to die, but then aren't we all? Current occupation: Small Artifactologist, originally with the University of H°rr°s°nf°rd where he had taught for—"

"That will do, Doctor," Mister Thoggosh interrupted. *"I have all of that information here. Thank you for identifying the remains—er, he is dead, isn't he?"*

The insect-being chuckled grimly. "I, physician Dlee Raftan Saon, do hereby attest and certify that our friend S°bb°ts°rrh is a *former* Small Artifactologist—if that's what you meant. Somebody did a pretty brutal job on him." Suddenly he leaped up and confronted Empleado. "Was it *you*, Mister Secret Policeman?"

Empleado took a startled step backward. "My God, no! I never . . . I mean I couldn't—" Again the physician chuckled, more good-naturedly this time, and his compound eyes, the size of grapefruit, glittered at the American. "Forgive me, Arthur, I've always wanted to try that, just once. Didn't work worth a dither, did it?"

"But I didn't have anything against him!" Empleado

wasn't listening. "We only disagreed about the importance of preserving antiquities in their undisturbed—"

"We'll get to that in a minute," Eichra Oren told the man. "I'm not sure I believe you really care about the preservation of antiquities. I think you've been—but we'll see." He turned to Dlee Raftan Saon. "What are the chances of an image of the killer having been recorded in the victim's implant?"

Dlee Raftan Saon inspected the readouts on his instrument and imitated human head-shaking. "Not good. It was rather badly damaged, I'm afraid."

"All right, then." Eichra Oren nodded. "What brought you out here in the first place, Doctor?"

Air rushed in and out of the row of spiracles along Dlee Raftan Saon's abdomen in the insect version of a sigh. "Rosalind Nguyen brings me, Eichra Oren. I've been taking care of minor casualties from the shuttle fire all day, and was looking for a little help. I started inquiring around about her—I do wish she'd have an implant installed—and apparently she can't be found anywhere.

"She seems to have disappeared!"

SIXTY-THREE
The Cosmic Collective

She awoke alone, in blackest darkness, without feeling in her hands and feet.

At first Rosalind thought she'd simply fallen asleep on the command deck of one of the shuttles, until she remembered that they were parked, at present, on the outer surface of the canopy. Nevertheless her hips and shoulders ached from lying on a hard floor in an uncomfortable position, and it was very cold.

Trying to move, she found that her arms were bound together behind her back and her legs tied at the ankles.

And she was naked.

With the greatest possible effort of will, she hammered back the terror threatening to overwhelm her and focused on the immediately practical. In the feeble gravity of 5023 Eris, she must have been lying here for a long time to feel this stiff and sore. Bound as she was, there was no gag in her mouth—be grateful for small favors, she told herself— and she was certain from its bone-numbing chill that the floor beneath her was metal. Despite that paralyzing cold, she also felt stifled somehow, as if the air were unusually humid.

It wasn't until a loose strand of her own hair floated past her face that she began to guess the truth: she was breathing poorly oxygenated liquid fluorocarbon.

She must be inside the asteroid!

No wonder she was cold! The drawback of fluorocarbon in general was that it conducted heat away from one's body more efficiently than air or even water did—this stuff she was breathing now had been hanging in the absolute cold of space for a billion years. Even the cold-blooded Mister Thoggosh maintained his office at close to mammalian body temperature. The invention of central heating, he'd once told her, had contributed as much to the rise of nautiloid civilization as the discovery of coffee—to which he credited the Industrial Revolution—had to her own.

Also, she was willing now to wager that her aching muscles had every bit as much to do with a marginal supply of oxygen as it might with gravity or lack of heat.

Something else brushed her face, almost shattering her resolve to remain calm. Whatever it was, it had been slimy, and colder than her own flesh. The sensation lasted only an instant, but she had jerked away, hurting her wrists and ankles.

"Aha, I see that you have awakened!" The voice coming to her out of the darkness was as liquid as the medium conveying it, even colder, and ominously familiar. "You will be interested, I suspect, to learn that you cannot be found by your friends and will soon be presumed dead—or in hiding. No one but you and I will ever know the truth, that you have been . . . what is the term they use? 'Appropriated'—to spend the brief remainder of your life serving the most whimsical desires of your captor."

Cautiously, Rosalind tested her own voice. "Is it necessary to gloat about it?"

"But that is one of the principal benefits of doing villainous deeds, is it not?"

Rosalind felt that she trembled at the edge of recognizing the faceless speaker. His English was unaccented, uninflected by any trace of emotion. His elocution was flawless and pleasant to listen to, even when he addressed unpleasant ideas.

"In time, of course, a gullible few will come to blame you for the brutal murder of that waterbug thing— disregarding the utter lack of any credible motivation on your part—and of the vile slug who temporarily commands this asteroid vessel."

She started again. "You killed Mister Thoggosh?"

"He's as dead as dead can be," the voice rose, almost losing itself in an inhuman, hysterical squeal, "with poison in his tea (would that read better, 'sea'?)—they'll find it in his pee, adding up to three for me! And now we two will see," the voice sank to an ominous, terrifying whisper, "what I shall do . . . with *thee*!"

Rosalind shivered violently and it had absolutely nothing to do with the cold. She'd recognized the voice at last, and the one thing that frightened her even more than the presence of Nikola Deshovich—dread master of both the Russian and American KGB, meticulous student of the most draconian methods developed by Joseph Stalin, implacable dictator of the United World Soviet, and infamous as "the Banker" for settling his old political debts "with interest"—was the presence of a Nikola Deshovich apparently gone stark, raving mad.

Involuntarily she spoke his name just as some soft, slimy object brushed her upper arm. Her muscles jumped. Whatever it had been wriggled away across her unprotected flesh.

"Yes," came the voice in a breathy, almost wistful tone. "It is I, Nikola Deshovich."

A terrifying silence ensued, during which Rosalind attempted desperately to concentrate on something other than her fear, to recall, for example, how she'd gotten here.

The last thing she could remember was being on her way to the house of Eichra Oren. She and the Antarctican were on the verge of some sort of personal understanding again, now that the ugly business with Toya was over— and who was she kidding, with this "verge" bullshit? She and Eichra Oren had been powerfully attracted to one another, almost since the first time they'd laid eyes on one another. No matter what had happened with Pulaski, or even with Estrellita, "some sort of understanding" between them had always been as inevitable and unavoidable as the sun rising in the morning.

All right, then, honesty taken care of, she'd been walking through the woods, almost within sight of the moral debt assessor's house, when she'd felt something brush past her face, a mist or perhaps cobwebs, she'd thought, and then—

Then nothing.

Then this.

Suddenly there was noise in the darkness again, an eerie and unrhythmic wheezing that disturbed all of her instincts as a healer. "In my present unenviable condition, I sometimes lose self-control to my . . . enthusiasms," Deshovich informed her. "Say rather that they sometimes gain control of me. You must forgive me. I assure you that it's only momentary and that I'm practically harmless."

Rosalind knew this last was a horrible lie. "Your present condition?" she asked, trying to keep her voice even, which was very difficult. "Tell me about your present condition, Nikola Deshovich. Perhaps I can help. I am a doctor, you know."

"You don't say." Again the wheezing noise. "I had no idea. I simply wanted someone, preferably a young boy or a woman, from the human camp. As you can see, I've settled for a woman. It was a worthy attempt, Doctor, but I'm afraid that even if I were to trust you, which obviously I cannot, there's precious little you could do for me, medically speaking, that hasn't already been done."

"What happened to you?"

"Quite an embarrassing series of events, really. My flagship, the *Lavrenti Pavlovich Beria*, was unceremoniously shot out from under me, practically the moment I arrived. I believe I have your famous General Gutierrez to thank for this, although I rather doubt that he had the satisfaction of knowing it at the time. Nevertheless, I intend to see that he goes down in history as did Benedict Arnold, Erwin Rommel, or Georgi Zhukov—posthumously, of course. I barely escaped with my life."

In the stifling darkness, the unseen speaker paused again for a moment, apparently to catch his breath, which continued to sound labored to Rosalind when he resumed.

"And that was only to begin with. We managed to limp away. I was superficially wounded, when the flagship began breaking up, by an ungrateful protégée of mine, a young woman who seized the tragic moment to exact her petty revenge."

Rosalind controlled her tone. "I see."

"Being a young woman yourself, you probably do. You're really all alike, you know. 'All pink on the inside,' as the saying goes. Then my escape capsule struck the outer covering of this asteroid, sticking fast and killing my perfidious little companion who, I regret to say, was crushed beneath me. I was a man of considerable substance at the time. This lifepod was equipped with an emergency spacesuit of sorts, really nothing more than airtight insulation, without supplemental oxygen or environmental control. I was farsighted enough to have obtained a supply of the solvent which our scientists had produced in order to get our Spetznaz forces through the canopy."

"Tell it to the Marines," Rosalind replied. "I saw how it worked: flies stuck in amber. Not a pretty sight."

"Knowing Russian quality control, I had taken the precaution to acquire a sample of the PRC formula. I emerged from the pod, which I suppose would have killed my young lady even if the fall had not. I sprayed the area around my feet with the solvent. The canopy quickly sealed again over my head and I climbed down one of those astonishing trees. It's simply marvelous what even a man of my former girth can accomplish without gravity to hinder him. Dodging troops of every stripe and occasional withering gunfire, as I once did escaping from Siberia to India, I eventually found my way to the excavation site."

"So I was right," declared Rosalind, perversely proud of her deductive ability. "We're inside the asteroid."

"Where else could we be?" the Banker acknowledged. "Although I must say getting down here all in one piece the first time wasn't quite as easy as I may have implied. You see, I hadn't survived the landing entirely without injury. The humiliating fact is that I'd broken an arm and a leg—which slowed me appreciably when someone threw a fragmentation grenade at me just outside the entrance. I fell into the air lock—and with an agonizing slowness, let me tell you as a former sitting duck—pierced through with a dozen rifle bullets, believing that for all practical purposes I was a dead man."

"It's too bad wishing can't make it so," Rosalind observed wryly. She was tired of this conversation in the dark, tired of being frightened, and beginning to get angry.

"Well, in a manner of speaking only partly metaphorical, my dear Doctor, that's precisely what I was." The Banker chuckled eerily. "A dead man. And still am, I suppose, despite my dubious good luck in being taken in and 'healed' by the benevolent trilobitoid automaton who so modestly refers to herself as Model 17."

"You said something before about three killings." She was reluctant to risk another hysterical reaction, but Deshovich was dangerously unpredictable whatever she did, and there was one question that had to be answered. "Was it you who injured Sam?"

"Sam? I don't believe I know any Sam, here on this—"

"Eichra Oren's dog. Large, white, shaggy?"

"Ah," the Banker wheezed. "An experiment of sorts. I was endeavoring to squash a rather disgustingly large spider at the time, but had only a partial understanding of the mechanisms involved. I don't believe Model 17 completely trusted me at that point. My only consolation was that the dog didn't die instantly."

Rosalind laughed. "He didn't die at all! He transferred his personality to the implant network. They're cloning him a new body right now. You lose, Banker, Sam is alive!"

Silence was followed by another of Deshovich's ominous chuckles. "And do you also believe in the tooth fairy, Doctor? There is no Sam. I killed him. Or I am Sam, if you prefer. His 'personality' as you call it, is my cleverest ruse so far, enabling me to communicate on an intimate basis with my enemies, and they're never the wiser. In the end, of course, their trusting nature will destroy them."

Rosalind would have gasped at the enormity of what the Banker had told her if the fluorocarbon had allowed it. Sam irrevocably dead and his cheerful surviving spirit a hoax? As it was, she remained silent, feeling stunned and defeated.

"Not that I haven't made mistakes," Deshovich went on. "I wasted days stalking something called a 'leeroo obeelnay' before discovering, quite by accident, that it was no more than a trainable domestic with the brains of a fruit fly. The maddening part of planning and executing these things is that it's so difficult telling who's who among all these damnable animals. Don't you find it so?"

"They're not animals, Nikola Deshovich, they're people!" she shouted, then, remembering her own helplessness, forced herself to calm down. "They only look like animals."

"Whereas," the Banker replied cooly, "animals of my acquaintance happen to look like people. I learned long ago that it scarcely makes any difference, in the end."

"A very convenient philosophy." The man sounded just like Empleado, except that Arthur was all theory on the outside, wrapped around a core of basic gutlessness. "Is that what let you murder a sea-scorpionoid and poison Mister Thoggosh?"

"Dear me, no. For the most part, I do these things because I enjoy them so much. I notice you neglected to mention destroying your shuttlecraft, but since I accomplished that after I took you, you've no way of knowing about it. Nonetheless, you can hardly understand what I'm doing here if you don't know about my setting fire to them. All three are no more by now than ashes and embers. And now that I'm about to work my evil will on you, Doctor, your friends up there will be at each other's throats, probably before the sun rises again."

This time, when something long, cold, flexible, and slimy stroked her legs in the darkness, to her amazement the adrenaline it generated helped her keep her head. "And Model 17," she replied, "unknown to the people on either side, and in violation of the basic instructions her builders programmed into her, is just going to stand by and let you get away with all these atrocities?"

"Model 17, my dear, suffers terribly from a number of internal conflicts." If it was Deshovich touching her this way, his voice gave no indication of it. "True, she's programmed to aid sapient beings of all species. However she was also programmed to an astonishing degree of paranoia regarding certain subjects. I happen to be something of a paranoid, just like any powerful leader. From the beginning, there was a sort of automatic sympathy between her and myself."

"That's right." Rosalind nodded. "The beliefs you share are completely unnatural for any sapient being.

Fundamentally, they arise from an extraordinary sense of personal unworthiness, giving rise to an insecurity which in turn produces an exaggerated and unhealthy fear of every known phenomenon. The mildest form was once called 'liberalism.' I've often thought that this, rather than any real threat, is what caused the Predecessors to flee the Solar System."

The Banker laughed. "I'm aware how deeply Model 17 fears return of the Eldest, if that's what you mean. That was the first thing she told me of when I regained consciousness. As much as I wished, I could not prevent her telling your people. I only narrowly succeeded in persuading her to conceal my presence. I argued that she and I stand for the same principle, the Cosmic Collective."

"Except that with you, it's an ideology, whereas with her it's an unintentional programming bug."

"How uncharitable—but I see that you grow restless. Perhaps you're bored. Or perhaps you're looking forward to what I'm about to do with you. I'm certainly looking forward to it, myself. To finish, I warned Model 17 that the intruders here included not only enemies and traitors to our common principle, but spies for the one power she fears beyond reason—the Eldest."

"But that's a lie!"

"My dear doctor—you know, I don't believe I caught your name—Model 17 took me in," he was beginning to sound hysterical again, "and I simply returned the favor!" His breath came to her again in a wheeze as he calmed himself. "But I've been an inconsiderate host. I forgot that you lack certain of my new-found sensory capacities, among them the ability to see in what you think of as the dark. Please allow me to correct my little mistake."

Light gradually began to fill the room, emanating evenly from the walls. Rosalind saw that she'd been bound with some sort of heavy, plastic-coated wire, now cutting into her flesh painfully. She blinked and looked up. Standing over her was something straight out of the worst nightmares of a madman.

The principal element seemed to be the humped, segmented carapace of a giant trilobite, like the hollow corpse—only hundreds of times larger—of a dead sow bug.

Flattened and spread across its inner surface, protected by the curve of the shell, were the internal organs of a human being, sealed in transparent plastic.

It was like a high-school exercise in dissection. A bewildering array of wires, and tubes filled with bubbling fluid, led from each organ to those of some other species, probably a trilobite, seemingly mixed at random among them, or to various electronic devices. Rosalind thought she recognized a pacemaker for the heart.

The spiked edge of the carapace was fringed with an indeterminate number of hairy, armor-jointed legs, each ending in a powerful claw. Two of these legs had been removed and the shell notched to make room for Deshovich's remaining unbroken limbs. His injured arm and leg lay buried among his internal organs, drawing sustenance from the gurgling plumbing. Perhaps they were in the process of healing. Perhaps they were there for good and would eventually atrophy away.

The sexual organ—Rosalind averted her eyes and gulped back vomit—cruelly barbed and armored, had a hundred tiny legs of its own. It seemed to be a living thing in itself, perhaps the nonsapient male component of a species otherwise consisting entirely of females. Tubes and wiring had made it a part of Deshovich. She had never imagined anything could be so vile, brutal, and obscene.

The head was almost as bad. Its back was shielded by a skull and face like Model 17's, worn something like a hat. What was left of the human face lay exposed on the underside, but was only partly flesh. The rest was a flexible substance like the leather between a lobster's joints. One eye was intact. The other was artificial, wired into what remained of Deshovich's brain. Even that had been added to with electronics, and with a bloody, pulpy mass, sealed in plastic, that might have been neurological matter from a trilobite.

"I was in a sorry state by the time Model 17 found me. She wasn't properly equipped to administer first aid to a human being, let alone major reconstructive surgery, so she used what she had: knowledge of her builders' physiology, certain medical supplies laid in for their benefit, equipment and parts provided for her own maintenance. The result is not exactly what you'd call pretty, but it works after its fashion. Modest creature that she is—and a billion years old on top of that—poor Model 17 is highly dissatisfied with her work. This is a stopgap, as she calls it, only good for a thousand years."

Rosalind's overloaded mind reeled. She hadn't regained control of it before the Banker spoke again.

"But I think before we begin, we should enjoy a light lunch. I'm sure you must be famished." One of his claws slashed out abruptly and plucked some living, squirming object from the "air." It was a squid, mottled black and green, eight or nine inches long. She couldn't believe that she hadn't noticed until now that the room was full of the creatures, swarming around like moths in the sudden light.

That had been what she'd felt touching her.

Deshovich stuffed the hapless wriggling creature into the ruins of his mouth and swallowed, making ugly noises. She'd heard that sound before and realized that the man had been catching and eating live squid all the time he'd been talking. She would have vomited there and then if her stomach had contained anything.

When he snatched another, crushed it to death, and pushed it at her face, that didn't stop her.

"Imagine," Deshovich continued, ignoring her as she doubled over in agony, "I need only spend a dozen lifetimes in this state until I am released to death!"

SIXTY-FOUR:
The Wrong Arm of *P'Na*

The Proprietor gazed across his desk at the massive artificial organism, almost as impressive in appearance as himself, who'd requested an appointment with him.

"I've come to report," declared Model 17, "that we're prepared to test this vessel's drive system."

Being a machine, she'd refused his offer of refreshment, and it had put him off his pace. He would have liked to have a beer himself, but felt it would be ungracious, since he'd insisted that his assistant, Aelbraugh Pritsch, squeeze himself into an environment suit—the bird-being disliked having his feathers wetted by liquid fluorocarbon—and lend his presence to the unusual occasion. Also, he missed his songfish more than he might have guessed.

"We?" he asked.

The robot stirred slightly on her many feet. "Yes, Mister Thoggosh. At your request, I have included personnel from all groups represented here in my maintenance and start-up procedures. They are now sufficiently familiarized with the systems—at an empirical, rather than a theoretical level—to assist me."

Mister Thoggosh lifted a tentacle and idly scratched the

area above one eye, a gesture he'd unconsciously picked up from several of the humans he knew. "Remarkable. I don't recall making any such request, although it is an excellent idea."

Aelbraugh Pritsch made throat-clearing noises, similarly acquired. "Er, I made the suggestion, sir, on my own initiative." He turned from Model 17 to his employer, obviously feeling awkward in the suit. "I hope I did right. I believed that such a demonstration of trust would help eliminate friction among us."

"Thank you, Aelbraugh Pritsch." The nautiloid laid a reassuring tentacle on the avian's plastic-clad shoulder. "Who are these representatives, Model 17?"

"Your power systems engineer, Remgar d'Nod. At the suggestion of General Gutierrez, the American spacecraft commander Colonel Juan Sebastiano, And, since there was no individual with the requisite technical background among the PRC Extra-Special Forces, their leader, Colonel Tai. The cybernetic entity referred to as Sam has also been observing and participating in our activities."

The nautiloid chuckled at the picture her words made in his mind. "Quite a motley crew, I daresay. And when do you purpose to begin testing—and what precaution should we take on the surface? Should we scour the settlement, fastening things down?"

"That will not be needful, Mister Thoggosh." There was a hint of impatience in the robot's tone which he could well appreciate. "What your theorists call the Virtual Drive takes no account of inertia—rather it binds everything within its influence into the same inertial reference. Certain inefficiencies exist, but I greatly doubt that you will even be able to feel the Virtual Drive in operation."

"That's a trifle disappointing, Model 17. Call me a romantic if you will, or merely hopelessly nostalgic, but I confess that I had expected us to stretch out and snap away to the Great Beyond, trailing streaks of colored light."

Model 17 turned a few degrees and looked at Aelbraugh Pritsch as if to ask whether the Proprietor were serious. With amusement, Mister Thoggosh watched the bird-being suppress a shrug. "I can arrange that if you wish," the robot replied, "but it will then be necessary to take the precaution you mentioned. As to when: the initial phase will be a short displacement of perhaps ten million kilometers which I'm prepared to initiate immediately upon your command."

The Proprietor was startled. "Oh? Very well, then . . . er, make it so." He'd always wanted to say that.

"Yes, Mister Thoggosh." A heartbeat. "It is done."

"What?" He was startled all over again. Even Aelbraugh Pritsch seemed to shiver at the robot's words.

"It is done," Model 17 repeated, sounding slightly irritated. "We are now ten million kilometers further from the solar primary than we were before you issued the command."

For a long moment, Mister Thoggosh was at a loss for words. Then: "Great Egg, as my loyal and trusty assistant would doubtless say were he not shocked into an entirely uncharacteristic silence. I find that I'm impressed after all, Model 17. How gratifying. How *very* gratifying. When shall we do it again?"

"In about twenty hours. I will need to take measurements and do some recalibrating. After that, we can go anywhere you care to, Mister Thoggosh, at any time you wish."

Unaware that he did it, the nautiloid muttered to himself, " 'Where no mollusc has gone before.' "

"Excuse me, Mister Thoggosh," Aelbraugh Pritsch asked diffidently, "what was that you said?"

"What?" He forced himself back to alertness, momentarily wondering whether such kelp-gathering wasn't a pathological sign of advancing age. "Oh, nothing of significance. Please carry on, then, with your measurements and calibrations, Model 17."

"Yes, Mister Thoggosh." The robot turned like an armored vehicle and started for the door.

He lifted a tentacle. "And Model 17?"

She paused. "Yes, Mister Thoggosh?"

He dropped the tentacle. "Thank you very, very much."

"It was my greatest pleasure, Mister Thoggosh, if I understand the word, and the only justification for my existence." She turned and faded into the hazy distance of the liquid-filled room.

"Mine, too, Model 17," the Proprietor of 5023 Eris muttered to himself, "mine too."

❖   ❖   ❖

The forest was as colorful and brilliant as a thousand-ring circus going on in a tent with ten thousand poles, and almost as noisy. Trees, bushes, and flowery undergrowth of every hue imaginable gave food and shelter to screaming scarlet birds and chattering monkeys with painted faces— and backsides—while the littered woodland floor rustled with a small, warm, gray- and brown-furred life of its own.

Eichra Oren neither saw nor heard the performance going on all around him. Exercising an almost inhuman capacity for concentration, he shuffled slowly through the forest litter, half bent over, intent on discovering a tell-tale broken twig, a torn leaf, an upturned stone, or a patch of toe-scuffed moss. The only things missing were his famous predecessor's brass-bound magnifying glass and deerstalker cap.

Somewhere at the back of his mind, set aside and ignored just like the forest beauty surrounding him, the reason he was here boiled and churned like a sour stomach.

"For a celebrated thinker of elevated thoughts, you're having a hard time with your anger, Boss."

The man straightened abruptly, startled at the voice inside his head although he'd spent most of the day with his semideceased canine partner, searching for traces of the Vietnamese-American doctor and what everyone seemed to be assuming was her unknown abductor.

"Oh. Sam." Now that he allowed himself to notice it, he discovered that his back ached. "I'm afraid you may be right."

The disembodied voice that only Eichra Oren could hear at the moment had an irritable edge of its own. *"You know goddamned good and well I'm right! Boss, we've been together for five centuries. I know what you're thinking before it gets processed through your implant. First the lovely Estrellita Reille y Sanchez, whom p'Nan principle— and a need for self-defense—compelled you to kill."*

Eichra Oren raised an eyebrow, electronically conveying the unique sensation to Sam. "Whom?"

The dog seemed to ignore him. *"And then the not-so-lovely Toya Pulaski, whom you never really cared for in the first place and* whom *you were ordered to betray in the second. And now Rosalind Nguyen, as lovely on the inside as the outside—the foregoing was an unsolicited testimonial—this time, gone before you two even had a chance to—"*

"Sam!" For once it was Eichra Oren, rather than one of his KGB-fearing American friends, who glanced around nervously to see if anyone was listening. Recalling suddenly that Sam's words would have been completely inaudible, even to someone standing right beside him, only made him angrier. When he realized how irrational a reaction that was, he took several deep, cleansing breaths and attempted to calm himself. "Sam, you're the only one I'd ever permit to say things like that to me."

"Like the plain truth? Gee, Boss, that kinda gets me right . . . right . . . now where did I put that pesky organ?"

"Asshole. I only meant that I trust you. Just don't wear the privilege out, all right?"

"Feeling a bit touchy, are we? And on top of that, we get a dead body planted in our front yard, and El Mollusco Supremo gets slipped the ultimate Mickey, and me—"

The man made a snorting noise. "And you, as usual, go all the way and get yourself *murdered!*"

"Oh well, who was it who said 'anything worth doing is worth overdoing'?"

Eichra Oren made a face. "Charles Manson."

"Well the experience is worth it, Boss. Basically, I'm a self-modifying program. I can go anywhere, do anything, even be in two places at once. And you wouldn't believe *the colors! We'd be rich if I could bottle what I'm seeing and drop it on sugar cubes—as long as I get a chance to help you hunt down the moron who committed possibly the most imperfect murder in the history of crime!"*

The man laughed. "Not that we aren't entitled to an occasional nervous breakdown, but I suspect both of us are letting our emotions get in the way of our work. For instance, I shouldn't have accepted the assumption, right from the beginning, that Rosalind has been kidnaped. It's just that knowing her as I do—"

"It's the likeliest possibility? Me, too, Boss. Rosalind is all right. Practical and intelligent. And she smells good. I

*can't see her stumbling into a gopher hole and breaking
a leg—*"

"Or running off somewhere to 'find herself'?"

"*Or taking it on the lam after bludgeoning poor old
S°bb°ts°rrh into anchovy paste.*"

"Lobster bisque," the man corrected. "Then again it's
possible that to someone with a little more detachment,
the other matters you mentioned—S°bb°ts°rrh and Mister
Thoggosh—should be assigned a higher priority than
we've given them."

"*Especially our esteemed employer? Don't listen to the
Americans, Boss. A century of state capitalism has left them
soft in the gray matter. The trouble with making the right
moves and climbing the corporate ladder is that it doesn't
go anywhere you want to go, and you're unfit for anything
but cutting out paper dolls by the time you get to the top.
What the hell, we've done what we've done.*"

"I agree." The *p'Nan* assessor bent over and began his
slow, searching shuffle across the leaf-littered clearing floor
again. To his urbanized eye, completely unpracticed at
detecting in the out of doors, it looked as though no one
had been here since the beginning of time. "And I refuse
to make excuses, even to myself."

Sam simulated a rude noise. "*Hooray for us and three
cheers for our personal integrity. I hope you've been keeping up the premiums on our unemployment insurance. Not
that we've accomplished much of anything with our day's
inattention to duty.*"

"How could we, Sam?" He stood up again and waved
a frustrated arm around, indicating the ground he'd just
covered a square centimeter at a time. "I've known all along
exactly where Rosalind was supposed to be at the time she
vanished, because I asked her myself to meet me at the
house after our meeting with Mister Thoggosh. That was
before we heard about the shuttlecraft fire, of course."

"*—I understand, Boss. At least we're not a total loss as
detectives. We managed to find out that she was seen entering these woods by several human witnesses.*"

The human camp had been the first place they'd
searched, aided by thirty-odd Soviet Americans shaken by
the destruction of their only way home, and as worried

about their doctor as the Antarctican and what somebody had called his "virtual dog." It had taken all of the moral debt assessor's persuasive power to keep the whole mob from similarly "helping" him to comb the woods, at the risk of destroying fragile physical evidence that might lead them to her.

Eichra Oren added, "And by our friend Scutigera—"

"*Ha! That wily old crustacean—*"

"He's not a crustacean, Sam, but a giant centipede and you know it. You only call him that to annoy him, and he's not here now, so lay off. He says he saw her halfway between the house and the camp. She'd have missed me at the house—we'd responded to the emergency by then— but Rosalind is hardly the type to flounce off over something like that, and we'd have gotten together eventually."

"*Sounds like the story of your life. What beats me is that there's no sign she ever made it to the house.*"

"Right." Eichra Oren looked at the ground around him in disgust and frustration. It may have been thickly littered with dead leaves, broken twigs, seed cases, and all sorts of bugs, but it was barren of information to his untrained eye. "I even sent a message home from Mister Thoggosh's office, telling her about the fire. She would have headed straight for Raftan's infirmary when she let herself in and read it. But according to him, and to the terminal I had installed for the benefit of those without implants, she never received it."

"*Lift that hand again, Boss, will you? That's what I thought—it's shaking. Is that worry about Rosalind or simple fatigue? Have you eaten anything today?*"

The man grinned. "A little of both, probably. Sam, you sound like my mother—which is something of a coincidence. I had an odd hallucinatory experience myself, if you could call it that, earlier, while you were off tormenting Scutigera."

"*Crustaceans don't torment, Boss, they can take care of themselves. What kind of odd experience?*"

"If you tell anybody about this ... I thought I saw my mother. Strike that, Sam, I *did* see my mother, although whether she was really there is another question. I was pushing through a thicket. When I got to the other side, there she was in one of her billowy party gowns, about forty meters away, across a clearing."

Sam was silent for several seconds. *"I think you need a good meal and a lot of sleep."*

Sensing his friend's concern, Eichra Oren nodded. "That's exactly what I think. I also think I've been cracking up ever since we came to this blasted asteroid."

"You've said that before, Boss. I don't believe it."

"Then account for what I saw, Sam. I didn't just get a vague glimpse of her. She turned and looked at me and winked—my mother! Then she slipped between some bushes and there wasn't any more trace of her afterward than we've found of Rosalind."

"Hmm. You don't suppose it could be some kind of feedback from what I'm going through, could it?"

The man lifted both eyebrows this time. "I hadn't thought of that. She surely didn't come here the way we did, through Mister Thoggosh's dimensional translator."

"That we'd know about. On this little world, it's the light show to end all light shows. I can still see and hear the tropical storm we caused arriving here."

"So can I. I like your feedback theory. Let's consult one of the implant network technicians about it."

"In our copious free time. Meanwhile, I see that our trusty scouts have come back empty-handed."

Together, through Eichra Oren's eyes, they watched a pair of armed men trudging toward them, looking every bit as worn out as the debt assessor felt himself. One was relatively short and broad, the other tall and black. Each carried an ASSR-issue Mini-30 semiautomatic rifle chambered for the obsolete 7.62x39mm cartridge, and some sort of pistol on his belt. When they'd come close enough for the gesture to be seen, the short, broad one, Major Jesus Ortiz, shook his head. He and the implant network's newest reporter, C. C. Jones, had taken up hunting several times a week, to feed the American expedition.

Eichra Oren shrugged back at Ortiz. Within minutes they were joined by the soil geologist, Captain Hector Guillermo, and Major Federico Ortega y Pena, the expedition's botanist. They, too, were familiar with the territory, and had been searching from the opposite side, with no more apparent success than Ortiz and Jones.

"*So here we are,*" Sam observed. "*From the place Rosalind was seen by Scutigera, to the place she was supposed to have been, not a single clue, not even to the woods-wise senses of Davy Boone and Daniel Crockett over yonder. Which leaves only three alternative possibilities, each of them more depressing than the other two.*"

"Thousands of offices, residences, businesses, warehouses, and other structures in the Elders' settlement," Eichra Oren agreed. "Or thousands of kilometers of endless, twisting corridor, down below, constructed by the Predecessors."

"*Or the rest of this stupid asteroid's surface,*" Sam finished the list, "*a geographical area equal, I've been told by those who know, to the American state of Soviet Texas.*"

"Yippee-ki-yo, motherfucker!" the man quoted with uncharacteristic sarcasm. His knees had begun to shake like his hands.

"*I admire the way you always know the right thing to say, Boss,*" Sam replied. "*For what it's worth, my money's on the interior—the deeper the better.*"

"You don't have any money, Sam."

"*I've been meaning to discuss that with you.*" Eichra Oren could feel Sam shrug. "*I don't have anything right now, except myself, but do you hear me complaining?*"

Bone weary with this futile searching, the debt assessor sighed. "Do nautiloids squirt luminous ink?"

SIXTY-FIVE
Persephone, If You Please

"Now what, in heaven's name, is *this*?"

Toya Pulaski looked at the object in her hand and shook her head. Under a brittle crust of fossilized fluorocarbon contaminants, she could see that it was similar to—but much larger than—something she'd once examined from Mister Thoggosh's personal collection of Predecessor artifacts, gathered from over a hundred alternative versions of the Solar System. The Predecessors had certainly gotten around, she thought, and they were real litterbugs.

Roger Owen peered over her shoulder. "It's a hydrospanner. You know how the Predecessors used triangular bolt heads. Well, you apply lateral pressure to the grip extensions and the energy is transferred through internal counterrotating channels—if there's any fluid left inside—to the jaws, which rotate. See, it still works after a billion years. 'Takes a licking and keeps on ticking.'" He gave her behind a gentle pat, an intimate gesture of affection she was still trying to get used to. "Very handy in tight spaces and free fall."

She set the prehistoric tool down, turned, and regarded him suspiciously. "Roger, I never saw anything like that before I came to this asteroid. How do you always know these things?"

"What's to know?" He shrugged, spreading his broad, blunt hands. "I'm a machinist. I just wish it was half as easy to identify some of the rest of this junk."

Thrown together from the nautiloid equivalent of plywood and sawhorses, the rough table before them was heavy with paraphernalia they'd retrieved over the past few days from inside the ancient space vessel that was 5023 Eris. From time to time they'd checked with Model 17, to make sure that nothing they brought up here for scientific examination was vital to her own important work. As it had turned out, there were more than enough tools and other equipment down there for a million Model 17s or her organic progenitors, and her objections—always made politely—had been few and far between.

Until this morning, they'd also had the enthusiastic and competent assistance of S*bb*ts*rrh, the Small Artifactologist. Learning that the sea-scorpionoid was dead—had been horribly murdered, in fact—they'd decided to carry on with what they were doing out of respect for the little fellow. Besides, they'd received news of the shuttle fires at the same time, and neither of them, presumably, wanted to think very much about what that might mean to their futures.

A sudden flash of movement caught Toya's eye. She looked up to see that it was only the warm breeze playing gently with a loose flap of the makeshift plastic awning they'd rigged over their worktable to protect the artifacts they were studying—and themselves, of course—from the weather, which on 5023 Eris consisted primarily of diffuse sunlight and rain showers engineered by the Elders' environmental specialists to occur every evening as regularly as clockwork.

Briefly, she considered a third, more cheerful datum they'd had this afternoon by radio from the human encampment on the opposite side of the asteroid. Mister Thoggosh's wild entrepreneurial venture had paid off, at least technologically: Model 17's first prolonged run of the Virtual Drive had been even more successful—if as undetectable by the nervous system of any organic sapient—

than the ten-million-kilometer start-up test. No one, Toya thought, would guess from glancing at the butter-colored sky overhead that 5023 Eris, with its tiny artificial sun, was just about to cross the orbit of Jupiter.

Before she looked down again, one of the bagel-shaped nautiloid aerostats settled to the floor of the lush green valley where they'd found the entrance to the interior of the billion-year-old vessel, and where she and Owen had established their own personal—and private—headquarters for the past few weeks.

It was Eichra Oren, of all people, who stepped out of the little machine and strode toward them, nylon rucksack in one hand and sword in the other. As usual, he wore a splashy Hawaiian shirt, faded Levis, and battered neoprene and Kevlar running shoes. It was still strange to see the Antarctican all alone, and stranger yet to realize that his sapient dog Sam was dead—and not dead at the same time.

As if he couldn't wait, when he was still several dozen meters away, the debt assessor lifted his scabbarded weapon of office and waved it at the couple. But it was hardly the friendly greeting they were expecting that followed the gesture. "Rosalind Nguyen is missing," he told them with a grim expression. "We think it's possible she was kidnaped, and we're going down below to look for her."

"How can we help?" Toya and Owen spoke the words simultaneously. To the extent that they were capable, they understood the situation with Sam and the bizarre manner in which he'd managed to survive what had happened to him; neither of them bothered to ask what Eichra Oren had meant by "we". Nor did they ask why he and Sam believed Rosalind had been kidnaped, or what made them think that she was down inside the asteroid. Eichra Oren was the famous detective, after all—or as close as nautiloid civilization had come to producing one.

The man blinked. "I don't know. How *can* you help?" He tapped the side of his head. "We have a three-dimensional map of all of the areas we've explored so far down there. I have a couple of other technological tricks to try. And we're in constant touch by cerebro-cortical implant with Model 17, who's supposed to know where everything is whether we've gotten around to exploring it yet or not."

"You can always use an extra pair of eyes." Owen moved to one end of the worktable, rinsed his grimy hands under the tap of a plastic water reservoir, and carefully dried them on a roll of paper towels. He drew his regulation EAA Witness, a high-capacity service automatic originally carried by the ASSR Marines, a special-purpose variant with an oversized trigger guard for arctic use, which had proven useful with spacesuit gloves, as well. Seeing that the magazine was full and the chamber loaded, he reholstered his pistol, patted the pleated pockets of his Aerospace Force coverall where he carried extra magazines, and nodded. "Count me in."

"Me, too," Pulaski declared. She seized up an olive-drab canvas bag and began scooping up certain items she believed they might need, for the most part freeze-dried rations. Until this minute, she'd been embarrassed to have Eichra Oren see their untidy campsite—they'd been too busy to do housekeeping—especially the single sleeping bag airing out on a line stretched between two saplings. Now all that was forgotten in the light of Rosalind's disappearance and with the prospect of adventure ahead. "I don't have a gun, but I can see and hear as well as either of you two."

"So you can, my little chickadee," Owen replied, doing a terrible W. C. Fields imitation, "and I would be honored beyond my poor ability to express it if you should desire to carry my very own personal shotgun for the defense of your delicate—"

"I'd be more honored, Mr. Dukenfield," she grinned and shook her head, "if I weren't aware that that blasted Remington of yours weighs about nine pounds, fully loaded."

The corporal flicked ashes from his imaginary cigar and waggled his eyebrows. "But my little petunia, what does nine pounds come to in a mere one-tenth gravity field?"

"The same nine pounds of ungainly *mass* it comes to at one full gee." Toya watched Eichra Oren's face, knowing that he'd be surprised to hear her bantering this way with Owen. She couldn't help being proud of herself. She'd been a fairly humorless—and timid—old maid, she knew, when they'd first met. "All right, give me the damned gun, Roger. I'm no pistol fighter like you desperados, but at least I know which end of a shot-gun to point with."

Owen nodded, handing her the weapon, a semiautomatic twelve-gauge with extended magazine and short, riot-length barrel. "Before we descend into the abyss," he suggested to Eichra Oren, "there's something special I want you to see."

Toya trailing along, he led the man out from under the awning to a point behind a clump of bushes which almost formed a hedge. Propped over a small, smokeless fire stood a kettlelike vessel of raw copper with a long coil of the same material leading from the top. Its free end slowly dripped a thin, transparent liquid into an ASF canteen.

"Arthur Empleado would shit blood if he saw this," the machinist declared proudly, "if he weren't too busy sticking his long brown nose into Mister Thoggosh's business."

The Antarctican looked puzzled. "What is it?"

Both Americans gave him an unbelieving stare. "You've heard of Dutch courage, haven't you?" Owen asked.

"It was included in my vocabulary injections." Eichra Oren nodded. Toya wondered whether he was serious or had merely adjusted to the level of discourse. "A euphemism for liquor."

"And Southern comfort?"

"Yes, that, too."

"Well," the machinist proclaimed, producing three small plastic cups and pouring liquid into them from the canteen, "I call this 'Southern Courage.' Dlee Raftan Saon supplied the yeast. I hate to think what Dutch comfort might be—sounds like something you'd find advertised in the personals of small San Francisco newspapers."

He handed them each a plastic cup. Having had experience with the stuff already, Toya sipped at it cautiously. Eichra Oren took a much larger draft. He didn't quite burst out in a fit of coughing, as she'd expected, but his eyes began to water.

"Smooooth," he managed to croak.

Owen held his cup aloft, critically squinting at a bright spot on the canopy through the liquid. "Hold on, friends, we need to toast the enterprise we're about to undertake. Toya?"

"Me?"

"Sure, why not you?"

"Okay, a toast: let's go."

"Yeah, Boss," Sam agreed electronically, *"What she said. Enough of this debauchery."*

Without acknowledging a message the others couldn't hear anyway, Eichra Oren nodded, shouldering his rucksack and strapping his sword belt about his waist. He also made sure his little plasma pistol was handy—although after that one drink, he wasn't sure he wanted to touch it for a while. It served several purposes in addition to self-defense. One of them was as a flashlight.

Gathering a few more things—canteens, their own flashlights and spare batteries, and the transparent filmsuits Mister Thoggosh had recently given them—the two Americans walked with the Antarctican a short distance to the asteroid entrance, easily tilted up the huge bronze-colored metal slab which, lying flat, formed the outer door of the cleverly uncomplicated Predecessor air lock, stepped over the edge—a mere one tenth of a gravity was good for something, after all—and together dropped gently to the floor several meters below.

The machinist picked up a long fiberglass pole he'd left there for the purpose and tilted the slab back into place, plunging them into darkness. "Another labor-saving device from Owen Industries, where profit is the most important product. If the Predecessors put a light in here," he added, "we sure as hell haven't found it."

Working in the dark from memory, he and Eichra Oren pushed and swung another enormous metal slab, horizontally this time, on its concealed pivot-pins, opening the inner door. Even after a billion years, the process was smooth and soundless. Passing through into the asteroid's main entrance chamber, they shut the door behind them so that others from the surface wouldn't be locked out.

Penetrating the incredibly dense surface of 5023 Eris, which accounted for most of the asteroid's mass, they left the last hint of gravity behind. The entrance chamber was a huge metal bowl filled, since Model 17 had turned the power on, with sourceless pale light. They'd entered, in effect, from the middle of the lid. The bottom was perforated like a sieve with dozens of tunnel-mouths leading in all directions.

Those which the humans or the Elders' people had explored were marked, either with daubs of paint or fluorescent stickers.

"Well, Bwana, where to?" Owen asked, standing against the curved wall balanced on one finger.

"Yeah," Sam agreed. *"Do we have a plan here, Peerless Leader, or are we just going to search through thirteen million cubic kilometers of asteroid until we all drop dead of old age?"*

"You're already dead, remember?" Eichra Oren's reply got an odd look from Toya, and an even odder one from Owen. The Antarctican repeated Sam's question for their benefit. "In the first place," the debt assessor insisted, grinning at both of them, "Sam has always been a professional pessimist, and whether it was accidentally or on purpose, getting crushed to death hasn't changed that."

"Geez." Owen shook his head. "I don't expect that it would.

The debt assessor laughed. "Nevertheless, I don't think the situation's quite as bad as he paints it. As far as we know—as far as Model 17 has told us, anyway—there's only one way into and out of the asteroid, and Mister Thoggosh's excavation specialists had to dig down half a dozen meters to find it. I believe we should limit the scope of our initial search to passages and compartments which one person, dragging another one along involuntarily—or unconsciously—could get to before being seen by some third party."

"I don't understand." Toya blinked. "Why do you and Sam assume that it was only one person?"

"We don't, really. But I don't believe that changes anything, either. Two or three or four or five kidnapers would have to smuggle Rosalind down here without any of our explorers and researchers spotting them, and that's getting harder every day."

"Besides," added Sam, *"the more miscreants, the harder it becomes to remain inconspicuous."*

"I'd think it'd be impossible," observed the machinist, "with most of the population wired into each other cybernetically." Since they'd discussed it several times, Eichra Oren knew both Toya and Owen had been thinking about acquiring implants. Specific details—including cost—hadn't been worked out yet. It was relatively rare in the culture Eichra Oren came from for an adult to undergo a surgical procedure usually performed on children shortly after birth.

He shrugged. "There are plenty of built-in privacy safeguards in the system. And some people, members of the more bashful species and reclusive individuals, sometimes go for weeks without any contact with the network. I've done it myself when I was working hard and trying to concentrate without interruption."

Owen nodded, understanding.

"Rosalind isn't within view or earshot of anybody with an active implant," Sam informed the Antarctican. *"Not now, and not when she disappeared."*

Toya shook her head. "The question remains, how do four of us search such a huge volume?"

"To begin with, we use these." He reached into the bag he carried and extracted a thin, flexible disk about the size of his palm, which appeared to be made of coppery paper or plastic. "Courtesy of Clym Pucras, machine-tool designer and instrument maker. You may recall that I conducted an assessment for him not long ago."

"Wasn't he the little guy," asked Owen, "who sued himself for trespassing on his neighbor's property?"

Toya remembered that both Clym Pucras and his irascible neighbor, Babnap Portycel, had strongly resembled deep-sea creatures from her own world called brittle stars.

The Antarctican nodded. "He's the one, all right." He indicated the object from the bag. "These are like the audio transducers you've seen some of the marine species wearing attached to their filmsuits, only they're wired for both sound *and* pictures. I had them colored to match the interior materials of the asteroid, so they don't stand out and won't be avoided or removed. As we descend, we'll place them where we've been, so that nobody can sneak past us, up to the surface. Sam will monitor them for any trace of Rosalind."

"I wish they were wired for odors, too, Boss. I sure like the way Rosalind smells!"

Owen grinned. "So do I."

L. Neil Smith

Eichra Oren sent the machinist a sharp look—how could Owen have heard Sam?—but his eye was distracted by sudden movement and a flash of white deep within one of the many tunnels leading to the entrance chamber. He had just caught another glimpse of his mother, Eneri Relda, waving at him.

"*Boss, I see her, too!*" Sam was excited. "*If you're hallucinating, so am I!*"

Eichra Oren seized Owen's shoulder, pointing him in the right direction. "What do you see down there?"

The American squinted. "A young woman I don't recognize, waving at us. Looks about seventeen or eighteen, maybe a little older. Long hair, blonde as near as I can tell. Very good looking. She's wearing a long, white, floaty kind of dress."

Toya pushed between the two, straining for a peek, but by then the apparition had vanished into the darkness and she was disappointed. "Damn! Who was she, Eichra Oren?"

Severely shaken, the Antarctican took a breath. "I don't know for sure, but if my guess is right, she's a lot older than seventeen or eighteen—unless you're counting in thousands of years! I can tell you one thing, though."

"What's that?"

"Our choice has been made for us. This is the tunnel we're going to follow!"

SIXTY-SIX
Squid Pro Quo

Rosalind never got to see whatever it was the evil and demented Nikola Deshovich intended doing to her.

Not that time, at least.

In the first place, she'd passed out, something she'd have sworn, as a medical practitioner and a strong-willed modern woman, she'd be incapable of. True, she argued with herself inside a darkness having little to do with the absence of light, she'd gone at least two or three days without eating. She'd also just been kidnaped by the horrifying wreckage of what had been a pretty horrifying man to begin with. She'd spent uncounted hours tied hand and foot, breathing badly oxygenated liquid fluorocarbon of dubious purity at paralyzingly cold temperatures. She'd even had to listen while Deshovich gloated over the vile trick he'd played on poor Sam's grieving friends, not to mention the callous, despicably underhanded murder of a very wise and ancient being she'd come to respect and admire.

Finally, forced to witness the Banker's disgusting eating habits—and threatened with his other habits of a different nature—she'd thrown up. Still, she argued disappointedly, she'd always believed she had a lot more

character than to swoon away like a silly little schoolgirl
in a novel two centuries out of style.

Somehow it all proved something, but she wasn't certain what.

She never knew how much time she spent in this half-
contemplative, half-unconscious state. The next thing she
was aware of, she heard somebody else arguing—no, more
like *two* somebody elses, which made more sense than the
argument she'd been having—outside. With a little effort,
she discovered that she had a vague memory of
Deshovich—what was left of the son of a bitch, on the half
shell—interrupted in mid-villainy, hurrying from the room
where he was keeping her a prisoner, alarmed and angry
because someone or something in an adjoining corridor had
tripped his perimeter warning devices.

How Deshovich had left the room was another question. Four meters on a side, the dimly lit chamber she lay
in, tied and naked, consisted of six featureless walls—two
of which she arbitrarily decided were the floor and ceiling—
so bare she might as well have been inside a solid metal
cube that had somehow been turned inside out.

Even so, she wasn't alone. The place swarmed with hundreds of the little squid the Banker had been eating alive.
Seeing them now made her shudder; she'd never feel the
same about calamari again. They reminded her of the big
brown moths her family had called "millers"—because they
were dusty like medieval people who ground grain, she
supposed—only these were larger. And slimy instead of
dusty.

Somewhere, as if in the great distance, she could hear
Nikola Deshovich thundering away in Russian—she'd never
learned it herself, but there wasn't a single American who
didn't know what it sounded like—and someone replying
less passionately in the same language. Whoever it was, it
was a female, probably Model 17.

Rosalind hoped it was. Any trouble that arose between
the trilobitoid robot and the Banker, she reasoned, almost
certainly had to be good news for Rosalind. Just as the
disagreement outside of what she was beginning to think
of as her cell seemed to be reaching some kind of cre-
scendo, Model 17 herself crawled through the wall—where

there had been no visible seam or opening of any kind—and came to a multilegged rest beside the physician. Since the noisy discussion continued, Rosalind calculated blearily, it had to be somebody else out there with Deshovich.

During the entire time, Rosalind had been lying on her side, weak from hunger, numb with the cold, generally in great discomfort. She spoke to the floor now, without making the impossible effort of turning to look up at Model 17. "Well, are you here to rescue me, or are you just helping the Banker keep me prisoner?"

The trilobitoid robot stirred on her many mechanical legs again and courteously skewed around to face Rosalind. "You are here against your will, Doctor Nguyen?"

With a mental exertion that was painful in itself, Rosalind bit back a sarcastic answer that would have been wasted on the robot and may have been unjustified in any case. "Yes, Model 17, I'm here against my will. My people call it 'kidnaping.' "

The unblinking device hesitated in thought. "An odd phenomenon, this individual will, Doctor Nguyen. Inscrutable, if you don't mind my saying so. I've studied it profoundly every nanosecond I could spare and still I fail to understand. Among my creators, you see, no single organism could ever be imprisoned against her will, since, if the community desired her confinement, it would also be her will to go along. Likewise, no one organism would perform this act of . . . kidnaping you speak of, because the community wouldn't countenance it, and therefore neither would any prospective kidnaper. In either event, were you one of my people, you wouldn't be here."

"Is that so?" Rosalind shook her head, which had felt fuzzy to begin with and might never function correctly again after enough conversation with this mechanical entity. "If I were one of your people, Model 17, I wouldn't be here because they're all gone." Straining against her bonds, she tried sitting up and failed. "Just where is 'here,' by the way? And who is Deshovich arguing with?"

"To answer your first question, Doctor Nguyen, you have been here before. We are still very near the hull wall—which you interpret as the surface of the asteroid. Our outer location is the chamber in which the physical aspect of the individual called Sam was broken and destroyed just before his essence entered the cyberspatial realm."

Rosalind's head reeled worse than before. "My God, we can't be inside one of those little—"

"Our inner location is a storage facility created by folding space to generate a subcontinuum which—"

"Cut the Captain Video routine," Rosalind's sudden anger broke through her confusion, surprising her, "and give it to me straight, Model 17—those metal cubes that smashed Sam up were only about a meter across. This place is at least four times that size. Exactly what the hell is going on here? Did Deshovich shrink me somehow, or did you do it for him? How can I get back to my normal size?"

"You *are* your normal size, Doctor Nguyen; so am I. We remain whatever size we would be according to the specific, localized laws of spatial geometry. By the standard of our outer location, we might appear to be about one fourth our previous size, although no way exists for anyone to observe us from there. In any event, it makes no sense to measure anything except with regard to local conditions. You are no smaller, with reference to the laws of this subcontinuum, than you would be outside it, under a more general set of laws."

"Thanks a bunch, Model 17. Now, have you got an aspirin? You're telling me that as big as this asteroid is already, there are a zillion more cubic meters inside it than anybody could tell simply from examining its exterior?"

"I'm afraid I have no definition of 'zillion' in my vocabulary, Doctor Nguyen, but there are many cubic kilometers of storage within this facility—and many more such facilities scattered throughout this ship." The robot paused, then spoke again, somewhat diffidently. "Doctor Nguyen, do you truly wish your limbs to remain attached to one another in that manner? I deduce, from what I have learned of human anatomy and physiology, that it might be extremely uncomfortable."

Rosalind's heart leaped. "You're offering to untie me? I accept, Model 17, I accept! Er, just make certain that my limbs remain attached to *me*, will you?"

"That I will, Doctor." A specialized wire-cutting limb

emerged from beneath the robot's arched and armored carapace and made quick work of Rosalind's bonds. Freed, the young woman sat up against a wall, briskly rubbing circulation back into her cold-numbed hands and feet until they began to tingle painfully. As she'd suspected, the wall she leaned against was warmer than the liquid surrounding her.

"Great," she told the robot after a few minutes. Her mind began to turn now to thoughts of escape—and food— but for the time being she kept them to herself. "So here we are, still our normal size, but somehow stuck inside a hollow metal cube only one fourth the size on the outside that it looks on the inside?"

Model 17, a shy entity, had backed off to the opposite wall as soon as she had finished untying Rosalind. "The volume we occupy—I'm not happy with that verb—is solid, Doctor, not hollow. Nor do the dimensions of projected images on a screen have anything to do with the originals on the emulsion. It is equally unimportant what the screen is made of, as long as its surface characteristics lie within the correct range of reflective properties."

The physician thought the words through as carefully as she was capable of at the moment, almost having to tick off the points Model 17 had made on her fingers. "I think I follow you. But where are we, then?" She wrapped her arms around her knees and shivered, wondering what Deshovich had done with her clothing.

"We are precisely where I told you we are, Doctor Nguyen." This was as close as the robot, programmed by her creators to remain polite under any circumstances, ever got to displaying exasperation. "We are in a subcontinuum associated with the unique alternative reality in which the vessel 5023 Eris has its existence."

Rosalind frowned, concentrating hard against the overwhelming pressures of fear, cold, and hunger. At that, she reflected, arguing the whichness of what and unscrewing the inscrutable with a billion-year-old robot was better than cowering alone in terror. "I remember your saying something like that before, Model 17, but it didn't make any sense to me. I'm afraid it still doesn't."

The robot almost sighed. "Then perhaps an analogy will

help. It is the same analogy that I have adopted in order to understand the problem of sapient individuality."

Rosalind smiled. "Okay, I'm game."

"I take that to mean you wish me to continue. Very well, consider the mind of an individual sapient. In many ways it operates much like the other minds around it, following the same principles. Yet in matters of detail—which appear to accumulate until they become as important as those operating principles, if not more so—it is extremely different, even from the minds closest to it."

Rosalind nodded. "Okay, Model 17, I understand you perfectly so far. I even agree with you, based on personal and professional experience. But where does it get us?"

"I am coming to that, Doctor Nguyen, if you will kindly exercise whatever faculty you possess for patience. Please accept, for the sake of this discussion, that these minds are somewhat akin to the various worlds of alternate reality— touching at their borders, even communicating with one another with the advent of interdimensional translocation— yet separate, distinct. Often that distinctness is their most sharply defining quality. Do you accept this analogy?"

"Model 17, I can accept anything that will help me understand what the hell is happening to me." Despite her circumstances, Rosalind had to laugh at the idea of being given a lecture on the virtue of patience by a machine. "You're saying alternative universes are like different individual minds. I understand that you don't mean this literally, but simply as an illustration. Please go on."

"Very well, I draw upon what I have learned of your culture over the past several days, much of which remains as incomprehensible to me as this must be to you. Consider a fictional character or location created by an individual mind. If that mind works hard enough, if it dwells upon that character or location with sufficient concentration for a long enough time, does not that character or location begin to assume—if not reality, then an importance to that mind, and perhaps to others, comparable with that of real people and places?"

Rosalind thought about it for a long moment. Mostly she thought about Sherlock Holmes, Lazarus Long, Lord Darcy, Jim Kirk, and Win Bear. Model 17 was right: they were all more real to her, or at least more important, than, say, Abraham Lincoln, Calvin Coolidge, Herbert Hoover, Franklin Delano Roosevelt, Bill Clinton, or Tom Sellick. She knew more about them, and cared more about them, too. They were the intimate companions of her childhood and immortal, whereas the others were just dead presidents, in their own way more fictional than her childhood friends.

"All right, Model 17, but I still don't see—"

"Excuse me: in the sense that a fictional person—an artificial mind—may abide within the mind of a real individual, so, given the technology, may an artificial subcontinuum abide within the confines of a natural one. Such a subcontinuum requires an anchor, a point of physical focus in the originating universe, if it is neither to dissipate nor assume the qualities of a genuine universe itself. It is the function of these blocks to provide such a point of focus."

Rosalind's head ached, and her last reserves of energy suddenly seemed to have drained away. "That's interesting, Model 17, and I'd like to know more, right after the lobotomy. But how do we get out of here?" She thought of Eichra Oren. "My friends will be looking for me, sooner or later." Outside, they could hear Deshovich's angry rumbling, counterpointed by a higher voice, and Rosalind realized that the robot had never answered her second question.

"They already are," Model 17 declared. "Please watch the apparent surface of the wall you appear to be facing."

Rosalind shook her head at what all those apparent qualifications seemed to imply (now *she* was doing it), but turned her attention to the wall as instructed. What she saw was a colorful three-dimensional image of Eichra Oren, Toya Pulaski, and Corporal Owen, coming to her rescue, if Model 17 was to be believed. The trouble was that they were passing through an enormous room which she had never seen before and which had never been described to her by anyone, human or otherwise, who'd explored the asteroid's interior.

To begin with, the vast floor of the stadium-sized chamber was slanted, down and to her friends' left, nor did any of the walls intersect each other or the ceiling—several hundred meters above their heads—at right angles. It was amazing how disorienting a simple thing like that could be. In addition, the room was strung with millions of, for want of a better term, big rubber bands the thickness of her little finger, set parallel to one another no more than a handspan apart. In order to get through them, the three adventurers had to push them apart, step through, push the next set apart and let the first bunch snap back—sometimes with a painful slap at various portions of their anatomy—into place.

What this "facility" was meant for, Rosalind had no idea. It was far from the first time 5023 Eris had handed them such a mystery. Eichra Oren bore the hardship of traversing the room with a grimly set jaw and stoic silence, while Corporal Owen's language grew fouler with every meter. Toya, constitutionally incapable of imitating either of them, alternatively shrieked whenever one of the bands stung her and whimpered quietly to herself, but she kept going, nevertheless.

Abruptly, Rosalind was staring at a blank wall again.

"Your friends," Model 17 told her, "will arrive eventually. They have been delayed so that circumstances may be prepared for them. In the meantime, I am here to assure that no further harm comes to you, since this falls within the category of responsibilities for which I was programmed. I regret that unless it threatens the ship, I cannot take a greater hand than that in what is about to happen."

"You mean you can't get me out of here? What *is* about to happen, Model 17?" Rosalind sat up. "And who the hell is out there, arguing with the Banker?"

The robot's voice grew more solemn than before, if that was possible. "A conflict is taking shape between two, possibly three groups of Successor species. I was created to serve all Successors alike, and may not take part in conflict between them."

Rosalind nodded. "Which is why none of us saw anything of you during the invasion from Earth. I guess that makes a certain demented sense. But you can prevent the Banker from doing horrible things to me, for which I thank you very much."

"No need to thank, Doctor Nguyen, it is my function.

Had I known the Injured One intended to kidnap you, I would have prevented it. As it is, I now believe that he deceived me with regard to his purpose here, and will have to reevaluate everything else he told me."

"And is it also your function to avoid answering the question I've asked you twice already?"

"Who argues with the Injured One? No, Doctor Nguyen. Only . . ." It was the first time she'd heard the robot hesitate. "I'm uncertain I can credit the answer myself. She claims to be the maternal progenitor of Eichra Oren, who is called Eneri Relda."

SIXTY-SEVEN
Eneri Relda

"*Our friend Roger has an implant,*" Sam insisted, "*that's the only explanation!*"

Forcing his way through a tangle of giant rubber bands he'd privately decided had been built simply to provide a workout for sedentary trilobites, Eichra Oren muttered his reply under his breath. "That's totally impossible, Sam. The Americans are adopting many customs from the Elders' people, just as we're adopting some of theirs. But I believe we'd have heard if somebody from the expedition had gone ahead and done that. And why would he keep it secret?"

"*I can't explain anything these Soviet Americans do, Boss, any more than you can. Maybe he doesn't want his own people to know. Maybe it's against some regulation. The fact remains he heard me, and he saw your mother.*"

"Ow!" As he grabbed at the next one, the rubber band he'd just released slapped him in the back of the head. "Sam, we're not absolutely certain she's an illusion."

"*No, we're never absolutely certain of anything, are we? Maybe Eneri Relda simply materialized on this miserable,*"

564

stinking planetoid in a cloud of happy thoughts and pixie dust, without benefit of the dimensional translator. It's time to shave with Occam's Razor, Boss, the simplest explanation is always the likeliest. I caught a virus somewhere, passed it on to you, and now Corporal Owen's got it— which can't happen unless he has an implant. 'Q,' as they say, 'ED.' "

"Don't get yourself in a solipsistic lather." The man grinned, knowing his canine friend would share the sensation—and the annoyance. "What if we're simply hallucinating the evidence that Owen has a cerebrocortical implant?"

"Yaaaagh!" Sam replied.

"What the hell are you two muttering about?" The recent subject of their silent conversation tapped the moral debt assessor on the shoulder with a thick, heavy finger. "Do either of you get the sneaking feeling we're being watched?"

The Antarctican opened his mouth to reply. Somewhere behind him, Toya muffled a shriek of pain and fury as one of the elastic bands they fought their way through slapped her on the backside. "Whoever it is, I hope they fucking enjoy it!"

"Now that you mention it," Eichra Oren nodded, "I do." He continued in what he hoped was a casual tone, "We've no idea, of course, how well-wired this place is for observation. I suppose the signals could somehow be impinging on our implants."

Owen shook his head. "They're impinging where they always do, on the fine hairs at the back of my neck, and I don't like it one bit. It would help a hell of a lot if the goddamned floor were level. It feels like we've been at this for days. While you're supposing, how much further do you suppose this mess goes on, anyway?"

"Nice try, Boss," Sam responded, *"but score one for the corporal, aplombwise."*

Owen's question received an answer almost immediately, when they suddenly ran out of rubber bands. Toya gave a huge sigh of relief, but Eichra Oren wasn't quite so certain it was justified. Before them, a long, high wall angled away from them, fading away in the darkness overhead. At its foot it was penetrated by hundreds of the squat, trilobite-shaped doors they'd long since gotten used to, each of them spaced no more than two or three meters from its neighbors.

"I'll be damned," predicted the corporal.

Just as Eichra Oren was about to turn and say something to Owen and Toya, his mother suddenly appeared in one of the doors, fifty or sixty meters to their left. Unable to do more than stand and stare, he watched her beckon urgently at them without moving.

"I see her this time!" hollered Toya, more excited than the Antarctican had ever heard her.

"Then I guess you'd better do something, Sergeant Pulaski," Eneri Relda shouted back from the doorway. "If we leave it to the men, you'll still be standing there gawking, another billion years from now. Do hurry, dear—I'm extremely busy elsewhere at the moment, and I wasn't supposed to interfere, in any case!"

Sam's voice crackled in Eichra Oren's head. "*Boss, you heard the lady, get a move on!*"

Feeling his two American friends pressing eagerly at his back, the moral debt assessor stumbled forward, trying without much success to gather his wits about him.

"Please listen to Sam," his mother agreed, still beckoning. "I'm no hallucination, my dear, not by half. But I haven't got time to explain what's going on at the moment. Come this way before it's too late. Lovely Rosalind is depending on you!"

Somehow that was what it took to break the spell. In possession of himself once more, the Antarctican jogged forward toward the door, followed by the sergeant and a puffing corporal.

However, by the time they reached the doorway she'd indicated—and exactly as Eichra Oren had expected, somehow—the legendary Eneri Relda had vanished again.

"Enough of this nonsense, girl," the monster that had been Nikola Deshovich demanded, "get out of my way now, or you'll be the one I satisfy myself with!"

"Girl?" Eneri Relda sneered. "I happen to be more than fifteen thousand years older than you are, you twit!"

Considerably more than fifteen thousand years in one

sense, she thought to herself. Still, she couldn't help being the tiniest bit flattered. She'd maintained her appearance rather well over the millennia. No one would possibly guess, for example, that she was the mother of a fine, big, strapping fellow like Eichra Oren (always secretly her favorite), and more than a score both before and after him. Perhaps it came from spacing her children so far apart. Enjoying a baby no more than every quarter century or so always seemed to give her ample time to pull herself back into shape.

"As for satisfying yourself," she roared, feeling it appropriate, "you and whose Galactic Overlords, you vile, disgusting, smelly reject from a deli counter?"

Frothing with fury, the Banker lunged forward, countless claws and one remaining hand outstretched for her tender unprotected throat. It wasn't the first time he'd tried that sort of thing. Lifting the hem of her long dress, she extended a casual index finger and touched the merest edge of his grafted-on carapace. Deshovich reeled as if struck by a land vehicle, spun around several times, and fell backward, landing in a heap against one of the metal blocks that filled the room.

Shaking her head sadly, Eneri Relda rearranged her silky gown and sat on another cube, the one she knew presently served as a physical focus for the parasitic subcontinuum where her likely future daughter-in-law (or outlaw—after more than fifteen thousand years, one finally grew relaxed over ceremonial trivialities) was being watched over by the Predecessor robot, Model 17.

Slowly, and with many a groan, the remains of a human being which had been pasted on the inside of an artificial trilobite carapace, wired together electronically, and coated in protective plastic, rose from where the energy of his own anger had tossed him.

"I thought," Deshovich glared at her, "you weren't supposed to interfere with what happens here."

Eneri Relda shrugged. It was a very pretty shrug, she knew, because she happened to be a very pretty girl, small of stature, but slender enough and with sufficient presence to impress those who met her as much taller. Small-breasted and with narrow hips offset by an even narrower waist, she had sea green eyes exactly like her son, and the same fine, spun-golden hair, falling well past her shoulder blades. On one hip she even wore a tiny plasma pistol like her son's, a gift from him and Sam. All of that must have been annoying to the Banker, who believed girls in general and pretty girls in particular were only good for one thing.

Eneri Relda was good for that, all right—very good, in light of plain fact and unsolicited testimonial—but she was also good for about a million other things, as well.

A poet had once compared her beauty to that of a brightly colored songbird whose melodious trilling and brilliant plumage somehow translated across the aesthetic barriers between species to be appreciated by all sapients alike. She'd never cared for birds (or their sapient equivalent, if dreadful truth be told) but she treasured the remark because it had been made by Eichra Oren's father. Like most individuals associated with the Elders, he'd died violently, that being the only thing left, statistically—old age and disease having lost to science—to kill him. What made it particularly poignant was that it had been during one of Mister Thoggosh's beinged surveys of this system, during a squalid little mess the locals grandly referred to as World War Two, not far from the coextant location of their own home, at a place called Anzio.

"That wasn't interfering, you poor miserable excuse for a life-form. It may be successfully suppressed where you come from—that's usually the way with governments, I understand—but every sapient has a fundamental right to defend itself."

A glimmer appeared in Deshovich's good eye. "And if I refrain from any threat to you again, what can you do? I can do anything I wish, and you can't do anything about it except . . . I understand! You're stalling, aren't you? You're attempting to delay me until something else happens! Until somebody arrives who *can* interfere!"

"Why Nikola, darling." Eneri Relda smiled her sweetest smile, a smile which had been known to change the course of history in more than one universe on more than one occasion. "Of course I'm stalling. And it's worked pretty well so far, hasn't it?"

The once-human monster trembled with frustration, but

did not advance. Even if he hadn't had her to deal with, Eneri Relda knew, his plans for Rosalind might be thwarted inside the cube (she couldn't help thinking of it that way, although she knew it wasn't literally true) by Model 17. Then again, they mightn't—Eneri Relda wasn't certain—the trilobitoid machine was powerful and unrelenting, but had a spectrum of limitations of her own to work within, imposed on her by Creators who were well out of the current picture.

"I don't know who you are," rumbled Deshovich, "or where you come from, but I'm going to—"

An odd noise came to them both, much like the sound of something frying in a pan. She looked down and saw the robot, who (despite the real physics of the matter) appeared to be emerging from the surface of the cube Eneri Relda perched on.

Model 17 lashed out with a long, slender, jointed metal antenna even one of the sea-scorpionoids would have been proud to display. It stopped just short of the Banker's nose as it cracked like a pistol shot. "You are going to do nothing, you devious organism, except stand there and be absolutely quiet!"

She turned to Eneri Relda. "I've warmed the subcontinuum's fluorocarbon with my built-in welders and supplemented its oxygen from the same source. Doctor Nguyen has fallen asleep." As quickly as with the lightweight feeler, the robot threw a massive claw at the Antarctican woman, seizing her by one fragile-looking shoulder. "Now at last I have the time to deal with you, agent of the Eldest!"

"News flash! Mister Thoggosh relays word from Model 17—confirmed by observation on the outer surface—that 5023 Eris has crossed the orbit of Pluto. That's on the general implant system. What isn't onsystem is that Model 17 says she's detected the first traces of the Ancient Enemy, but doesn't go into any more detail.

"Mister Thoggosh has doubled the shifts rebuilding one space shuttle from the ruins of three, and has ordered all three plasma cannon mounted on her. He's also ordered several more drilling rigs converted for mounting on the

surface of the canopy itself. That's all for now from the Canine News Network, Cybernetic Sam reporting."

Eichra Oren repeated what Sam had told him for Toya and the theoretical benefit of Corporal Owen. Their roundabout path had finally led them to a familiar neighborhood within the asteroid. They were in the passage between what appeared to be an amphitheater filled with desktop computers and the room where Sam had been hurt.

Owen raised an eyebrow. "Benevolent Mister Thoggosh, censoring what goes out over the network?"

The Antarctican shook his head. "Until he releases it, the information is his property, to do with—"

He was interrupted by what sounded like a gunshot coming from the room with the metal cubes, followed by somebody shouting. "You are going to do nothing, you devious organism, except stand there and be absolutely quiet!"

Drawing *p'Nan* sword and plasma pistol, the moral debt assessor rushed toward the sound and pushed through the door to the chamber, followed closely by the two Americans who had their own weapons at the ready. They arrived just in time to see Model 17 seize Eneri Relda by the shoulder and shout an accusation at her. "Now at last I have the time to deal with you, agent of the Eldest!"

Eichra Oren's sword made a dull, chirring noise as it sliced through the fluorocarbon surrounding them and continued completely through the robot's arm, severing the limb cleanly and leaving behind an angled, mirror-surfaced cross-section.

"Owch!" Model 17 complained.

"Take your claws off my mother!" Eichra Oren shouted, a bit off with his timing.

Eneri Relda plucked the inert portion of the robot's anatomy from her shoulder, handed it back to its owner, and ruffled the sleeve of her gown to remove the crease. "Be gentle with her, dear. You know she's absolutely correct—I am an agent of the Eldest."

"What?" That word came from several sources—her son, the robot, the Americans—even the Banker, who almost seemed to have been forgotten in all the uproar.

The woman gracefully hopped down from the cube and turned slowly, looking each of them in the eye in turn. She continued to address her son, but it was the robot whose eye she caught and held. "That's right, dear—it's so nice to see you, by the way! I do hope Sam's still making you eat right—the only respect in which Model 17 is incorrect is that the Eldest are not malignant."

The robot rattled forward a step, looked down at the stub of her missing claw, gave Eichra Oren a resentful glance, and rattled back into place. "Of course they're malignant! What do you hope to gain by telling such a lie, Eneri Relda?"

Eneri Relda shook her pretty head. "No, dear, they're just so mighty and extremely long-lived that until 'recently'—the last few million years or so—they scarcely even noticed the existence of all these lesser beings we call Predecessors and Successors."

"But," Model 17 objected, "my Creators defeated them, forced them to retreat!"

"What your Creators, the Predecessors, mistook for a military retreat," the woman explained patiently, "was simply a planned migration by the Eldest to the Cometary Halo. In fact, the Eldest weren't even aware they were being fired on at the time. The Predecessors just misidentified a desire on the part of the Eldest to enjoy some peace and quiet. All they really desired—the Eldest, I mean—was to have eternity just to think about, um, the 'whichness of what,' as somebody recently put it. It was their attempt at that which the Predecessors mistook for an eternal frozen sleep which was forced upon them. It wasn't."

Eichra Oren examined the edge of his sword before resheathing it. It had cut through the robot's arm without apparent damage. "But now all that's changed, is that it, Mother?"

Eneri Relda smiled sweetly at her son, and meant it. "Well, dear, those weren't the only items the Predecessors were wrong about. As you and your fellow investigators—by the way, hello, Toya and Roger, it's so nice to meet you at last—anyway, as you're about to discover, even their pronouns were wrong."

Toya, beginning to sense something momentous in the

offing, squinted at the Antarctican woman. "How's that?"

"The Eldest is a single three-billion-year-old sapient entity, my dear . . .

"And I'm it."

SIXTY-EIGHT
The Eldest

"That being the Predecessors called the Eldest," Eneri Relda gave them all one of her world-destroying smiles, "is a solitary collective entity, a single sapience evolved—and not very different—from common, ordinary slime mold."

Like the inside of an old shower curtain. Eichra Oren was the only one of them with the faculty, a subsidiary discipline of *p'Na*, of shutting off his emotions. There would be a price to pay, but hearing what his mother had just said, it was his only chance for survival.

"A solitary collective entity." He gulped his feelings and managed a coherent reply while others around him were still stunned. "Isn't that a contradiction . . . Mother?"

"No more than for any multicelled organism, dear." The beautiful Antarctican matron laid a gentle hand on his arm. "One difference is the need for mechanical proximity. The Eldest is comprised of countless man-sized amoebalike 'cells' capable of operating at great distances from one another. Some have been disguised and placed among the younger races as . . . well, observers, the same way the

Elders employed what Americans call 'Unidentified Flying Objects' to observe their system."

Model 17 was as outraged as a mechanical device could be. "This confirms what I am now convinced the Injured One thought merely a clever lie—there are spies among us!"

Eichra Oren hadn't taken his eyes from his mother's. How could Eneri Relda be nothing more than an amoeba, part of a giant slime mold? Couldn't he remember when she read him bedtime stories? He couldn't remember nursing at her breast, but Antarctican women were not shy, and he'd watched several little brothers and sisters at it. Couldn't he remember her kissing him better when he fell and hurt his knee? Was he a giant amoeba, too, who simply never knew the truth about himself until now?

"Despite its multicellular nature," she continued, "the Eldest is a single, vast organism, just as each of you are. But another difference, one that may seem like another contradiction until you see it working, is that each of those cells operates more autonomously than yours, while at the same time, I . . . *the Eldest* exercises more conscious control over them than you do over yours."

"Mother, I don't understand. . . ."

Eichra Oren had meant the statement more generally than Eneri Relda took it. "Very well, dear, let's attend to a bit of overdue business we all seem to have forgotten, then we'll take a look at one of those cells. . . ." As if she were someone's fairy godmother, she raised a hand and gestured. Eichra Oren felt something brush, then seize, his ankle. He looked down to see a human hand protruding from the metal block he stood beside. It was a familiar hand, golden brown, slender-fingered, with the shiny look that comes from being washed too often.

"Rosalind!" He knelt down beside the block and grabbed her hand. It was cold to his touch and closed hard on his fingers. He pulled, and the hand was followed by a wrist, a forearm, an elbow, an upper arm and shoulder. Eichra Oren reached through the apparent surface of the block, got both hands under Rosalind's armpits, and lifted her out into the light. Her lips were blue and her teeth chattered, but she blinked up at him, taking in Owen, Toya, and Eneri Relda, as well.

"I never thought I'd see any of you again," she croaked. "Is this your mother? Nice to meet you. Anyone feel like calling out for a pizza—and maybe ten or twelve dozen cheeseburgers?" She slumped back and closed her eyes. Toya pulled a blanket from her bag and wrapped it about the physician's shoulders, not knowing how much good it would do in the liquid fluorocarbon that surrounded them. She began to feed Rosalind from the bagged emergency rations she'd brought along.

Eneri Relda made another gesture. In the square formed by two pairs of nearby blocks, a glowing, fuzzy patch of vapor began to form. Before they were entirely aware of it, the patch had grown to man-height, solidified, and assumed a shape they all knew.

"Well, it's about time, isn't it?" declared Mister Thoggosh's dinosauroid assistant, Aelbraugh Pritsch. "Let me tell you, I've been looking forward to this for *centuries*!"

With that, the creature began to shed what he explained had been a form of hot, uncomfortable camouflage—although he seemed to retain many of his nervous mannerisms. What was left, once its scaly feathers were on the floor or drifting through the fluorocarbon around them, resembled something usually seen under a microscope. Standing before them was a glistening, transparent, pear-shaped object two meters tall. Through its surface, Eichra Oren could see organelles, he supposed, busy with functions similar to those performed in other beings by mitochondria and such subcellular objects. The entity's boundary seemed to pulse as it talked, and the whole thing jiggled like a gelatin dessert.

"It's a welcome relief," it informed them, still using the voice of Aelbraugh Pritsch, "to have all of my mind back. Now I can relax and freely communicate my thoughts as the Eldest—rather than that silly bird-thing which never knew what it really was—to all the sapient beings aboard the wonderful 5023 Eris!"

"How did you—I mean Aelbraugh Pritsch—get down here so quickly?" Owen demanded.

"Yes," added Model 17 suspiciously, "and please explain why you've been spying on us!"

The amoeba-thing that had once been Aelbraugh Pritsch twisted itself around to the American. "Owen, comma, Roger, corporal, Aerospace Force, one each: I believe, sir, that you have too many secrets of your own to be as anxious as you seem to disclose the secrets of others too quickly. As a single example among many, I'm tempted to fetch that distillery of yours down here and sample what you're brewing. At least three minds among you tell me it would be an interesting experiment."

Owen grinned and spread his hands. "Be my guest, Eldest."

"Another time, perhaps. In one way, you disappoint me. Transferring Aelbraugh Pritsch from the surface was a much less impressive accomplishment than another you all seem to take for granted. I suppose you'd prefer to hear, given your scientific prejudices, that Eneri Relda appeared suddenly aboard 5023 Eris, whisked across space, time, and probability, courtesy of some variation of the Virtual Drive."

"Somebody," replied Owen, "said something about happy thoughts and pixie dust, as I recall."

"That sounds like Sam." The giant amoeba gleamed and jiggled. "He was closer to the truth than you might believe. Try this with me: concentrate on your smallest left toe. That's it, place all your attention there, all your consciousness. *Be* in that toe. Now, employing the same concentration, switch the locus of your consciousness to your right ear. That's how Aelbraugh Pritsch and Eneri Relda got here."

At mention of his canine friend, Eichra Oren called to Sam through his implant, but received no answer. The upper third of the Eldest turned again, its surface showing twist marks until the rest flowed around and caught up. "You're a fine thing of your sort, Model 17, you've nothing to be ashamed of. Any error you may feel you've made was that of your Creators, programmed into you.

"For myself, I'd protest that I was content for many eons to be alone, without external irritants. But I realized that, sooner or later, evolution would provide me with company whether I wanted it or not. Thus I stationed 'spies'—small portions of myself—among the more promising species, to be certain I had sufficient warning of their impending sapience. Otherwise, I did not interfere with them, and I most carefully refrained from doing them harm."

"They all say that," Toya declared, but without feeling. Eichra Oren suspected she was beginning to like the Eldest and knew why. The ancient being reminded him of Mister Thoggosh, too.

"Indeed they do, my dear Sergeant—Toya, if I may—but I had a good, selfish reason to be circumspect. You see, I found I had grown lonely." The moral debt assessor nodded to himself. He'd also suspected that the Eldest felt that way and had actually been looking forward to what he called "company." "I must say that the trilobites, once they arose to sapience, were rather a disappointment. In the first place, they seemed to possess no sense of humor, whatever."

Eneri Relda caught her son's eye and laughed. "Above all, a sapient needs a sense of humor!"

"In the second," the Eldest went on, "when they invented interdimensional translocation—and discovered that the first alternative world they explored was already inhabited by an organism vastly older and (it is profoundly to be hoped) wiser than themselves—the poor darlings were struck absolutely numb with terror."

"You are speaking," stated Model 17, who shared the Predecessors' disability, "of yourself."

"I suppose it might have been that way with whatever sapience they ran across first. Among their other somewhat odd reactions, they began to feel a protective, almost motherly urge toward their own presumed Successors. It never seems to have occurred to them that this was a contradictory and rather destructive attitude. All the pitiable things being of one mind—quite literally, I'm afraid—they had no one to disagree with them and point out their error."

"That, of course," added Eichra Oren's mother, "is the ultimate problem with any form of collectivism."

Toya shook her head, unable to decide whether to address Eneri Relda or the thing that had been Aelbraugh Pritsch. "But you're a collective organism yourself, aren't you?"

"Yeah," Owen asked, "what makes you immune to error?"

The Eldest laughed. "Oh, I'm not immune to error, not at all, dear me. Nor am I a collective organism in the same sense as the trilobites. To be sure, the distinction is subtle. I spent a million years pondering it until I arrived at my present opinion."

"Opinion?" Wrapping the blanket around her shoulders, Rosalind struggled to her feet. It must have been warming her; she sounded angry. "The oldest, wisest being in the System spends a million years pondering a problem and all he has to offer us in the end is an *opinion*?"

"I'm glad you've sufficiently recovered to feel belligerent, Doctor—may I call you Rosalind?—but isn't that all any of us offers? Each of us may feel certain that he or she possesses answers which are absolutely true. Perhaps some of us do. To others, they can never be more than opinions, which is why it's important that no one ever be given authority to impose his or her opinions on others by force. As long as they all agree on that principle— and the right to defend it using any means that come to hand that do not contradict it—then sapients of all opinions can live together and cooperate freely to their mutual benefit, in peace."

Eichra Oren laughed. "That's *p'Nan* philosophy! Nautiloid civilization didn't really begin until they discovered that principle and put it to work. It took them fifty million years!"

"More like a hundred and fifty million," replied the Eldest. "That's one reason I've been so lonely, don't you see? And highly interested in any sapient species that came after me? It's why I took a purely metaphorical hand in their development—so that perhaps I wouldn't always be lonely."

Eichra Oren nodded, understanding. "'And God divided himself into a myriad of parts, that He might have friends.'" The quotation was from one of pre-Soviet America's most important—and viciously suppressed—philosophers.

"And enemies," the Eldest added. "They're every bit as necessary as friends, you know. In terms of one's physiology, I suppose they're good for the circulation."

Owen remained suspicious. "What do you mean, 'a metaphorical hand in their development'?"

"Yes," Rosalind agreed, "I thought you said you didn't interfere with other sapient species."

"He said he never harmed them," Toya offered quietly, "but that's only an opinion, isn't it?"

"And speaking of enemies," Model 17 demanded, "who else do you have spying on us?"

"Dear me," sighed the Eldest, enjoying himself thoroughly, "whatever have I gotten myself into now?"

Eneri Relda gestured. In answer to Model 17, Aerospace Force Major Jesus Ortiz, former captain of the *Geronimo*, materialized between two metal blocks, shed his human skin, and melted into the shimmering entity that had been Aelbraugh Pritsch. This performance was duplicated by the appearance—and disappearance—of Andre Valerian, the expedition's Russian agricultural specialist. The large amoeba was now even larger, about three meters tall.

Pushing the thought away from himself as quickly as it came, Eichra Oren kept expecting his mother, the exquisite Eneri Relda, esteemed and legendary survivor of the Lost Continent, to perform the same vanishing act. Instead, the Eldest extended a pseudopod for a gesture much like Mister Thoggosh might have made.

"I believe that pair of demonstrations will be more than sufficient, at least for the present. And I solemnly promise you all that I will answer the remainder of your many questions later. In the meantime, a certain matter has come to my attention which—"

"*How about answering one more question, right now?*"

"Sam!" Eichra Oren shouted the name out loud.

He heard a canine chuckle. "*None other than. I've been topside, Boss, with the World's Foremost Authority, watching this clambake as it happened, courtesy of your implant, among others. I thought I'd better get down here right away, because—*"

"You're quite right, Sam," the Eldest acknowledged. "I apologize for not thinking of it sooner. Sam anticipates that you, Eichra Oren, have been wondering exactly what the hell (his words, I fear) all of this makes you. That fact is," the entity declared proudly, "you—or, more properly, your lovely mother here—were an experiment, and a very successful one, I might add, in something akin to—"

"*Where the flaming fuck is Deshovich?*" Owen's shouted question caused them all to look around the chamber anxiously. None of them saw any trace of the Banker.

The Eldest sighed. "I suppose he took our preoccupation with one another as an opportunity to escape. Not to worry—I don't believe he can get far in his regrettable condition."

"There isn't any place he can go that I can't find him," Model 17 vowed grimly.

"In any case, Nikola Deshovich has an appointment to keep with destiny," Eneri Relda told them, looking from Eichra Oren to Rosalind and back again, "in the form of my son."

"*And may God,*" added Sam, only partially sarcastically, "*have mercy on his soul.*"

SIXTY-NINE
Chase to the Cut

Rosalind gasped.

What came into her lungs, instead of oxygenated fluorocarbon, was dry, fresh—warm—air. In a twinkling, she and her companions had been transported to the asteroid's surface.

Her first reaction was indignant. This kind of blink-of-the-eye stuff was fine, she supposed, in old movies and TV programs. She found it disorienting and annoying in real life—although she had to admit that it appealed to her sense of efficiency, especially since it hadn't been necessary to cough the liquid up before breathing air.

Looking around, she corrected an earlier thought to "*most* of her companions." They were in Eichra Oren's living room, halfway between the Elders' settlement and the human encampment. Standing with her in the middle of the room were Toya, Owen, Eneri Relda, even the amoebic entity which had been Aelbraugh Pritsch—plus Ortiz and Valerian—and which now spoke as the Eldest. They'd apparently been joined—Rosalind wondered if a similar sleight of pseudopod had been pulled on them—by her insectile colleague Dlee Raftan Saon, the plant-person Llessure Knarrfic, arachnoids of two different species, Remgar d'Nod and Nek Nam'l Las, and . . . the Proprietor himself, Mister Thoggosh!

Apparently, rumors of his demise had been greatly exaggerated.

Of their theoretical host—and Model 17, as well—no trace was visible. Rosalind felt an urgent need to warn Eichra Oren about . . . something to do with Sam.

"Welcome, Eldest!" the nautiloid proclaimed. "Please sit . . . er, make yourself comfortable. Do you care for anything to drink? I'm having beer." Some of this was planned, she thought. Mister Thoggosh would never take that kind of liberty in someone else's home.

"Mister Thoggosh, I am always comfortable, thank you. It's one of the few advantages to being an amorphous blob." The surface membrane of the Eldest, Rosalind noticed with professional interest, seemed to have thickened and was less transparent, presumably to protect him from the air or solar radiation. "And I would indeed enjoy a beer, if you'll permit me just a moment to form a vacuole for it."

The offer was repeated all around. Instead of sending a tentacle for drinks while everyone distributed themselves about the room, Mister Thoggosh had refreshments brought by several of the large, nonsapient insects used as servants. As might have been expected, Rosalind found herself sitting beside Raftan with a tall drink in one hand and a ration bar in the other, when the Proprietor addressed her.

"Doctor Nguyen," he told her, "this will be the most important gathering we've held on 5023 Eris. We already have three Americans here, but perhaps you'd feel more comfortable if we invited someone from your expedition with more authority."

Rosalind considered. "That would be fine, Mister Thoggosh. I'd suggest the general to begin with, and Colonel Tai . . ." She hesitated. "And I suppose you'd better ask Arthur, too."

Owen scowled at her, then shrugged, resigned.

Mister Thoggosh turned to his guest of honor. "Eldest, in the vernacular, you're the man with the hoodoo."

"Only too happy," replied the giant amoeba.

In the middle of the room, in a space which everyone

had vacated earlier, former Aerospace Force Brigadier General Horatio Gutierrez appeared stark naked, dripping wet, the lower half of his face covered with lather, and a safety razor in one hand.

Somebody whispered, "Oops!"

Gutierrez looked around at the crowd, managed a brief, "We've got to stop meeting like this," and vanished.

Empleado appeared in midair where Gutierrez had, in a horizontal position two feet from the floor—the height of one of the American camp cots. He fell with a dull plop into the puddle his superior had left and shouted himself awake. By the time Rosalind had calmed him down and explained what had happened, the general reappeared in uniform, dabbing at a cut on his cheek, along with Chuck Tai, who'd been forewarned and was awake and properly attired.

The human physician stood up from where she'd been kneeling beside the still-angry KGB agent. "Well," she said, "it's just like one of those murder mysteries, isn't it, where they drag everybody together at the end? The only thing we're missing is the detective, his semiloyal assistant, and the principal suspect."

"It's amazing how quickly friends abandon you when they find out you're the son of a slime mold."

"Grandson, Eichra Oren," the trilobitoid robot corrected him politely. "You'd be the grandson of a slime mold."

The Antarctican glanced around the empty chamber with its hundreds of metal blocks, then down at the one visible companion he had left. "Still here, Model 17?"

"I am, Eichra Oren. It's my purpose to remain with you and help you hunt down Nikola Deshovich."

"Oh?" The human raised one eyebrow. "I picked up the idea somewhere that you generally try to remain neutral in disputes between Successor species."

There was a prolonged silence while Model 17's hundreds of clawed feet clattered quietly on the decking. A human being would have been looking down, scuffing a reluctant toe in the dirt. "Ordinarily, I would, Eichra Oren, but you are not a true Successor. Quite the opposite, in fact. You represent the Eldest."

"Hmm. I suppose I do, at that. This must be his subtle way of engaging my putative talent as a *p'Nan* moral debt assessor. Ordinarily, like you, I wouldn't accept a commission offered like this. But under these particular circumstances . . ."

"*I'm still with you, too, Boss,*" Sam broke in. "*The others have been whisked magically back to the surface by the Wizard of Ooze. Matter of fact, they're at your house right now, having a party. What y'wanna bet they trash the place?*"

"And besides," Eichra Oren continued to address the robot, "you're sore because the Banker fooled you."

Model 17 swiveled around to face the man and levered herself up so that her foremost third was almost as high as his face. It was the first time he'd seen her do anything like that.

"Eichra Oren, he is not a true Successor, either, but the very sort of phenomenon my Creators warned me about. They believed the danger lay with the Eldest, whom they greatly feared, but I have learned that they were grievously mistaken and have had to realign the parameters of my programming—not a comfortable feeling. Nikola Deshovich is a threat to all productive sapient life everywhere."

"*No different from any other head of government, past or present,*" Sam told her blandly.

Model 17 was angry. "You deal with everything as if it were a joke, you self-perpetuating disembodied programming error, don't you? But I am serious about this!"

"*What have we got here, Boss? First Model 17 displays righteous anger at the Banker, then she shitcans her programming because she decides her Creators were a bunch of goofs. Now she recognizes a joke when she hears one, and it pisses her off!*"

Eichra Oren discovered that he'd been holding his breath, which seemed appropriate in the presence of a miracle—or the birth of a child. "What we have here, Sam—are you listening, Model 17?—is true sapience emerging."

"This cannot be!" the robot protested. "I am a servant of my . . . oh, I see. They *were* a bunch of goofs, sad but true all the same. Does this imply what I think it must, self-ownership, the freedom to do with myself—with my life—whatever I wish?"

"*It means you're the queen of the bug-bitches, baby,*" Sam cut in before the man could reply, "*and I love every square centimeter of what has to be the ugliest body on the asteroid! Welcome to the world, Model 17, such as it is! And listen, thinking for yourself is always painful—that's why so few people bother.*"

Eichra Oren laughed. "Would it be in accordance with self-ownership and the freedom to do with your life whatever you please, if we started looking for Deshovich?"

The robot placed her front legs back on the floor. "I sense him even now. He has headed inward, downward. I believe I told you earlier, human friend and possible grandson of a slime mold, that's why I'm here. And Sam, what the Eldest did was not magical, it was merely an application of advanced technology."

"'Any sufficiently advanced technology will resemble magic,'" Eichra Oren quoted.

"*Yeah, Boss, but any sufficiently advanced magic will probably resemble technology, too!*"

"There is no such thing as magic," Model 17 protested, "only technology!"

"*Everything is magic, Model 17, including technology! I oughta know that if anybody does!*"

Still arguing the point, and enjoying themselves enormously, the human and the dog inside his head followed Model 17's lead, out of the chamber of the metal blocks, into the corridor outside, and down into the center of the asteroid.

At first, Arthur Empleado was delighted.

Although he'd long since grown cynical about it—as who wouldn't given the history of the last century, let alone events he'd lived through recently himself—he was one of the few orthodox Communists who remained on 5023 Eris. On being introduced to the Eldest, he'd experienced a brief surge of renewed fervor—somewhat like the "Christmas spirit" usually felt at that time of year by the most apathetic Christian—at encountering a collectivized mass-being.

After a while, as he waited for his soggy uniform to dry and sat in one of Eichra Oren's bathrobes watching and listening as the Eldest explained himself to the various beings gathered in the debt assessor's living room, he was a bit less sanguine. His head began to ache, and the tall, cool drinks flowing freely at the Proprietor's command didn't seem to help as much as they usually did.

Initially Empleado suspected that, deep down inside, what he feared was confronting a living God the existence of whom he had always denied. At first blush, this amoeba-creature seemed the very embodiment of Marxist-Leninist idealism, a perfect model for what the human race might have become under that doctrine.

Then, in a burst of crushing pain that narrowed vision to a dim tunnel and made his stomach churn, he suddenly knew that what dismayed him was discovering that the trillions of semiautonomous "cells" the Eldest claimed to be composed of meant little or nothing to him in terms of his identity. No matter how many aspects there may have been—he may have generated—to his overall personality, the Eldest considered himself a single, highly individualistic entity.

Moreover, the Eldest demonstrated little interest in any of what Empleado considered the important issues of existence. Political theory was a mystery to him—a mystery too irrelevant to bother solving. Even worse, admittedly wise and ancient as he appeared, he was the first to inform them all that he was far from infallible.

"After giving it concentrated thought over more millennia than you can possibly conceive," he told them now, "I've come to the conclusion that my sole purpose in the universe—self-assigned because there's no one else to do it for me—is to have fun."

That last was too much. For the second time that day, Empleado passed out on the living room floor. When he awakened, he would be a very different Arthur, indeed.

Model 17 waved her long, flexible antennae and pointed to their left. "Thirty-three kilometers."

She pointed to their right. "Thirty-three kilometers."

She pointed forward, backward, and down into the heart

of 5023 Eris, just as she'd begun this exercise by pointing over their heads. "Thirty-three kilometers."

"*It seems to me I've heard this before.*" Sam yawned. "*Next she'll be telling us that each of these oversized garbage cans generates one point twenty-one gigawatts.*"

"Rather more than that, I suspect," responded Eichra Oren.

"Some twenty-seven orders of magnitude," Model 17 agreed, "more than that. My friends, behold the work of my Creators. It is as if we stood at the heart of a small sun."

The ancient spacecraft's engines, as it turned out, were not the size of walnuts as one of the Americans had predicted early on, based on an estimate of the Predecessors' advanced technology. Although the asteroid's Virtual Drive units—Sam insisted on referring to them as "hyperdrive motivators" when he wasn't calling them garbage cans— were closer, individually, to the size of the *Graf Zeppelin* or the *Hindenburg*, Eichra Oren was disinclined to discount that technology.

With the dog watching figuratively over his shoulder, he stood beside the trilobitoid robot on a railed gallery seventy kilometers deeper within the asteroid than any of the newcomers had come so far. They'd taken what Model 17 had insisted was the only possible route, sealing themselves inside a streamlined projectile and blasting along an evacuated tube to reach this area. Although they'd chosen theirs from a rank of dozens of vehicles waiting silently since the departure of the Predecessors a billion years ago, the robot had maintained that this was the very machine Deshovich had taken before them.

Inside, the remains of more than a dozen half-eaten squid they'd found tended to support her argument.

Before them now, across a gap of a hundred meters as they stood on a gallery that dwindled in perspective and disappeared in the distance to either side of them, they regarded one of the gigantic power plants. It was basically a cylinder another hundred meters high, with what they assumed came to six enormous vertical flutes running halfway upward from the base. Between the tops of each pair of flutes, a relatively small, straight-sided notch had been cut as if by a titanic mill. Above these, almost at the cylinder's top, more flutes, horizontal this time and with one square end, stretched around the circumference.

But it was not this enigmatic construction, nor the massive scale on which it had been accomplished, that impressed the Antarctican moral debt assessor. Either side of the great cylinder stood another cylinder, and another. Above it, and below, stood yet another, and another. Model 17 had pointed in every possible direction and spoken the same three words: "Thirty-three kilometers."

The light was tinged with purple and subdued. A gentle current wafted through the fluorocarbon around them. There was no noise or other indication of the unspeakable energies being generated and put to work here, although the robot assured them that reactivating this complex had been her primary task since she'd awakened. They were here to insure that Deshovich didn't try his evil best to sabotage it.

"Released improperly," she observed, "the available power could destroy the Solar System."

Still, they were nowhere near the asteroid's center and no closer to catching up with the Banker.

SEVENTY
Icarus Was a Pisces

Together, in a figurative sense, they took another brief high-speed subway ride.

From the way he felt pushed back into the cushioned floor of the vehicle—which had been the rear wall to begin with—Eichra Oren estimated that the car's acceleration was about five times the normal force of gravity. After weeks of one tenth gravity, the pressure on his lungs alone was almost unbearable. In only a few seconds they'd exceeded the speed of sound and in a few more, twice that velocity.

"That's just about what I make it, too, Boss," Sam agreed. From the vantage of his presence in a world that was real in a different way than the one Eichra Oren and Model 17 currently inhabited, the dog had been plotting their swift progress into the depths of the artificial asteroid, employing the highly sophisticated calculating and mapping facilities of the cerebrocortical implant network. *"Those trilobite babies were tough customers!"*

Pinned flat on his back by acceleration, Eichra Oren glanced over at the stolid, armor-plated creature who had volunteered to act as his guide and partner, indicating silent but sincere agreement with Sam. He never figured out how they wound up arriving at the next subway terminal with the rear of the vehicle now in front. He certainly hadn't felt the car flip, which it ought to have, before it began decelerating. All he knew was that the apparent five gravities never let up. However it had been accomplished, the ride was soon over with and they exited into a facility identical to the one they'd just left.

He spent some minutes massaging feeling back into his upper arms and thighs. On foot again, they soon reached the dead end of a broad trilobite thoroughfare, where they ran into a bulkhead of a different style and much heavier construction than anything they'd seen so far. Huge beams crisscrossed the metal panel, which was at least five meters square, and there was an elaborate, massive locking mechanism featuring a small panel with a row of multicolored lights.

"We near the end of our voyage, gentlebeings," Model 17 told them, extending a built-in cable to the controls set into the bulkhead. The cable plugged into a socket. "My sensors don't extend into this area, but it's the only place the Injured One could have wanted to go. Among other things, it is a place of great healing. I haven't been here myself since a brief orientation shortly after I was constructed. And I've never been all the way to its center."

"*What's down here?*" Sam demanded.

There was an unaccustomed dramatic tone in the robot's voice. "You have but to wait, my cybernetic friend, and you will see such wonders as you have never beheld." Suddenly the bulkhead boomed, creaked, and began sliding, very slowly at first. Beyond it, all they saw was a metal chamber filled with the same oxygenated liquid fluorocarbon that filled the rest of the asteroid.

Eichra Oren felt Sam stoically suppress one of his sarcastic remarks as they stepped in and let the bulkhead close behind them, plunging them into absolute darkness.

In just a moment, a tiny pinpoint of light sprang into existence as a miniature gooseneck worklamp sprouted from between the robot's eyes. They heard her fumbling at the far wall as she'd done with the bulkhead outside and felt a dull thump and a creaking sound.

The inner door began to slide aside.

A golden illumination flooded the chamber.

Eichra Oren gasped and felt a similar reaction from Sam. Before his conscious mind could gain control, his most basic reflexes took over, screaming that they were standing in midair over a drop of at least forty kilometers!

Model 17 moved quickly. Somehow sensing the man's panic—with a liquid medium surrounding him, Eichra Oren, and Sam right along with him, were suffering attacks of claustrophobia and agoraphobia (or was it acrophobia?) at the same time—she pushed him toward the lip of the door, which he clung to like a frightened child.

"My apologies, dear friends, for startling you. I merely wanted you to be surprised."

Eichra Oren was incapable of a coherent response. "*We were surprised, all right!*" Sam told her. His tone quavered. He was in nearly as bad shape as the man. "*I swear I'll never give anybody a hard time again for being afraid of heights!*"

"That's quite all right, Model 17, I understand perfectly." The Antarctican took a long, deep breath, and then another. "What is this place, anyway?"

He'd never suffered fear of heights or enclosed spaces before this and his mind was under control again—and utterly fascinated. At that, his first impression had been correct. He seemed to be looking straight down no less than forty kilometers through the crystalline synthetic waters to the brilliantly glowing heart, obscured by sheer distance as much as any liquid haze, of 5023 Eris.

"Here, in effect" she explained, "is the residential area of the great ship you call 5023 Eris. It is the reason, I believe, that my Creators, whom you call the Predecessors, never became especially fond of their day-to-day working quarters nearer the surface. Perhaps it is also their reason for having constructed me, so that they were not required to leave this place more often than necessary."

Clinging to an outsized doorjamb, Eichra Oren peered out into the waters, wondering what it was, in the asteroid's center, that lit the enormous liquid-filled cavern so brilliantly.

"My dear friends," Model 17 announced, "we stand upon

the one shore, so to speak, of the Great Communal Sea, which is the Daughter to the Mother of us all!"

Mustering all his courage and determination, Eichra Oren pulled himself up over the edge—the real direction was down, of course, toward the center of the asteroid—and onto the "bottom" of the sea, which was actually its ceiling. What had been an open door in the wall before him now resembled a large hole in the floor.

"This reminds me of the way you kill a polar bear," Sam told him, *"with a can of peas."*

Not accustomed to being frightened of anything or anybody, Eichra Oren grunted and kept his eyes locked determinedly on the sandy ocean bottom lying "beneath" him, attempting desperately to reorient his much-abused sense of direction.

"For *p'Na*'s sake, not now, Sam!"

"Touchy, touchy, Boss."

"Please understand," Model 17 continued meanwhile, swimming along beside the man with delicate fluttery motions of her countless appendages, "that I had no responsibility for this area, myself. It is a perfectly balanced ecology, self-contained and self-maintaining, as it has been for a billion years."

Having convinced himself that the surface he lay across was *down*, Eichra Oren levered himself to his elbows and looked around. It might as well have been a landscape from an alien planet, he thought, but it was Earth, all right—of a billion years ago. To his inexpert eye, it looked just like one of those museum holoramas he'd loved as a kid, but it was all around him, and it was real.

The Midcambrian period of a billion years ago, he knew, was supposed to have been dominated by arthropods—above all, trilobites, but also crabs and shrimp of a thousand different varieties, including the primitive ancestors of sea-scorpions.

To Eichra Oren, it looked like the Age of Sponges.

It also seemed to be the Age of Animals Masquerading as Plants. There were huge ground-covering collections of complicatedly branched porifera in shades of yellow, red, and orange. Some clung to the sand like moss, while others reached toward the distant light like trees and bushes. The delicate glass sponges looked more like transparent balloons than living things. There were skeletal organisms which reminded him of the mesquite growing around his mother's house, and others that occupied niches ultimately taken over by coral on Earth.

It was the sponges which gave the underwater scene such an alien look. To the modern eye, the colors were all wrong. There was very little of the green and blue which made free-diving in the Elders' version of the Mediterranean such a cool and relaxing experience.

One item the museum holoramas seemed to have omitted, probably for the same reason that displays of Precambrian life were sometimes so misleadingly barren-looking, was the algae. Everything he saw around him now was matted with it, including any number of the animals that moved. Apparently algae-eating animals had not yet evolved to their present level of efficiency. In any case, it, too, was the wrong color. It had taken a mass extinction—not the one that eradicated the dinosaurs, but an earlier and even bigger one—to change the look of algae.

There were also jellyfish—now why hadn't the Elders ever run across a sapient species of jellyfish?—and elaborately fringed worms that looked like caterpillars bred for show, and snails, *millions* of snails. Something struck the Antarctican as extremely peculiar about the snails. One species resembled a five-sided pyramid, another was like a Chinese hat half a meter in diameter.

"Snails! Why did it have to be snails!"

"Lay off, Sam, I'm trying to think!" The man picked up a handful of sand, colored yellow and pink and black in layers, let it strain through his fingers to resettle on the bottom, leaving a cloud of tiny shrimp suspended, darting off to find new hiding places.

"Those clam things over there are brachiopods, Boss, a type of shellfish thought to be extinct!"

The man shook his head, concealing a grin. It wouldn't be the first time that the dog's annoying and persistent sense of humor had salvaged his sanity. "Yes, Sam, I'm just as well acquainted with paleobiology as any member of the

Elders' civilization, and I can even retrieve cerebrocortical implant data as well as you can."

"*Not quite—*" came an electronically simulated sniff fully as insincere as one of Mister Thoggosh's sighs. "*I am cerebro-cortical implant data, after all, Boss.*"

"It takes one to know one." He laughed. "Of course you realize what's missing here, don't you?"

"*A decent supply of horseradish—okay, okay, I'll cut it out! Of course I do: it was as broad and populous a group as mammals, and even in a ghost town where there aren't any people, you'd expect to see a kangaroo rat or a prairie dog.*"

"That's right, Sam. There are no trilobites down here of any size or description. Which brings me to another point I wanted to ask about, Model 17."

"Yes, Eichra Oren?" A shadow flowed across the man as the robot settled to the sand without disturbing it.

"Did I hear you right, that this area wasn't shut down with the rest of the ship, but has been warm, active, and alive like this for the whole billion years?"

She would have blinked had it been possible. "You heard correctly. That is what I said."

He stood up, completely oriented now, his mind comfortably at work on a problem. "Life on Earth *evolved* over the same billion years, Model 17. How come it hasn't here?"

There was a long silence. "An intriguing question, now that you mention it. It had never occurred to me before, although, as I say, this area lay outside the range of my normal responsibilities. I'm afraid that I don't care for what it implies."

Eichra Oren raised his eyebrows, wondering whether Model 17 had come to the same somewhat disturbing conclusion he just had. "And what might that be?"

Sam interrupted the robot before she could answer. "*For one thing, Boss, an absolute lack of radiation capable of producing mutations. Remember the way the hull of this asteroid even strains out neutrinos? Mutation is kept at a standstill here.*"

For once, Model 17 was ahead of the cybernetic animal. "Excuse me, Sam, but that was not my idea. It is a very good idea until you measure the radiation coming from whatever that thing is up there." She pointed an antenna at the apparent sun.

For once the virtual animal was taken aback. "*You mean that you don't know what it is?*"

"Did I not say only a few minutes ago," she grumbled, "that I had never been all the way to the center? If not, then I say it now. Please record and save it for future reference this time. I don't know what that object above our heads is, except that it is reputed to be the center of the healing powers of this place."

"*You don't mean . . . ?*"

"Yes, Sam," she interrupted, "I do mean. In order for Eichra Oren and me to capture and revenge ourselves upon Nikola Deshovich, we must now swim up to the center—and the Sun."

SEVENTY-ONE
The Evolutionary Imperative

"If we're trying to decide where we're going," explained the Eldest, "it's a help to have an idea where we came from, where we are now, and how we got here. This is a very big subject—almost the biggest subject there is—but buried within it is an even bigger idea, an idea so big that sometimes it frightens even me."

At his last five words, a stir went through the crowded room.

"Some six hundred million years ago," he went on, "life wasn't new to the Earth. Living things had already been around for 2500 million years. Yet the number of existing species was but a tiny fraction of those living today, and they made their living very differently from today's species, absorbing chemicals directly from the water around them, taking energy from the sun, scavenging the dissolving remains of their fellows. It all sounds rather boring, doesn't it? But it's what life was like, *had* been like, for twenty-five million centuries, right up to the line dividing the 'Precambrian' from the 'Cambrian' eras."

Since this "most important gathering" at Eichra Oren's house had begun, the giant amoebalike being had turned out to be extremely voluble. Perhaps, Empleado thought, this was what came from spending millions of years with nobody else to talk to. In any case, had anybody been inclined, it would probably have proven difficult to shut the remarkable organism up.

"Notice what was missing," the Eldest continued. "It was a period utterly without conflict, the very Utopia of non-violence many urge on you today. There was no predation, no exploitation of one species by another. So far, it had never 'occurred' to any organism that it might liven up its life—not to mention its diet—by absorbing another organism *before* it rotted away to its constituent chemicals.

"In short, no living thing had ever eaten another."

Empleado had more pressing affairs on his mind. During the recent battle with Earth he'd been ordered—through an agent planted among the Russian drop troops they'd captured—to disrupt nautiloid activity on the asteroid until the bitter end. His heart had never been in it, but the command had come from the *Lavrenti Pavlovich Beria*, indicating the highest possible KGB priority. In that moment, the Committee for the Preservation of Antiquities had been born.

"Nothing would be the same once this 'original sin' had been committed," the Eldest continued. "From that moment on, all life would feed on the death of other life. This evolutionary Big Bang is called the 'Cambrian Explosion' by some. Compared to the dull, empty eons preceding it, competition and progress increased a millionfold—along with the number of species found in the strata of that time. No longer content to scrape dead slime from sea bottoms, life-forms began evolving better ways to grab unwilling food, resist if they were on the menu, run away, disguise themselves, or hide. They had no other choice except to die. Life began to proliferate—to differentiate—to fill up every available niche that nature offered."

Along with his unwelcome orders, Empleado had been handed a big black Heckler & Koch P9S—yet another relic of a more prosperous century—and a pair of seven-round magazines with it, crammed full of 11.43x23mm Remington

185-grain hollow points marked +P. An extra cartridge had
even been included for the chamber. Empleado had never
liked guns and carried them in the line of duty only when
he couldn't avoid it. The handle of this one was so big that
his index finger barely reached the trigger.

"Others might say that the first hammer-blow had been
struck upon the Forge of Adversity. The sparks are still scattering today."

Empleado shook his head in disgust. That was a nautiloid idea, this goddamned Forge of Adversity, part of the
p'Na garbage the squid-things were always going on about.
It amounted to little more than dimestore Darwinism, the
notion that individuals and whole species "transcended
themselves" when they were mortally stressed. The trouble
with that theory was that it produced casualties—wouldn't
work, in fact, unless it did—and Empleado felt he was
about to become one of those casualties. Frightened at the
thought, he tried to focus his attention on what the Eldest
was saying.

"Given the nature of language, which may reflect the
nature of a species better than it does reality, it's hard to
consider the process of evolution-by-natural-selection without lapsing into teleology, an unintended implication that
the random motions of inanimate nature are somehow
meant to arrive at a predetermined goal."

"That difficulty is associated," Mister Thoggosh agreed,
with a wave of his tentacles that humans had learned to
take for a nod, "over the history of a thousand sapient
species with every absurdity from belief in deities to movies
about talking animals."

"Indeed," replied the Eldest. "Likewise, when one con-
templates a sweep of billions of years, it's difficult to remain
focused on the heart of the process, which is brute simple.
Bundles of data, protein chains called deoxyribonucleic acid,
order the birth, growth, and to an extent, the behavior of
organic machines which carry it prior to its self-replication.
If the nature of the machines is such that they carry it long
enough, and in the proper circumstances, to replicate, then
it gives rise to yet another generation of carrier-machines."

God, it was like listening to talking bookends! Across
the room, Empleado could see Rosalind Nguyen sitting next

to the bug-doctor, Dlee Raftan Saon, both of them nodding, agreeing with the Eldest and the Elder as they spoke. For some reason he refused to examine, it made him want to smash their faces in, human and bug-thing alike.

"If a machine fails to survive, then replication can't occur, and to any extent the data the machine carried were at fault—having given rise to an inefficacy—they're erased from the overall body of data we call the 'gene pool.' This is natural selection. One may not approve of the criterion, but it's fundamental to life. Complaining about it is like complaining that parallel lines never meet."

"Or that planned economies don't work," the woman put in, making everyone—except Empleado—laugh.

"Chemicals, radiation, or microorganisms may interfere with the replication itself. When it occurs, it is often imperfect. In most cases, mutations—changes in the data—either prevent birth of a carrier altogether, or don't affect its efficacy one way or another. In rare instances, mutation enhances a carrier's chances of survival. Science once believed this process occurred in tiny increments, as single molecules, or even atoms were rearranged. But evidence prevails that evolution occurs in large steps as sections of DNA are knocked out, inserted in the wrong place, or even turned end-for-end."

Dlee Raftan Saon raised a forearm. "Nonetheless, the overall process remains very slow."

"Quite so, Raftan," the Proprietor responded. "I often suspect that it's nothing more than a dull-witted inability to conceptualize the gulf of time involved that keeps otherwise intelligent beings from accepting it for the truth it represents."

Llessure Knarrfic, the plant-being, waved one of her odd number of leafy branches. "But Eldest, haven't you left out the effect of an organism's surroundings?"

"You're quite correct, my dear," the amoeba-thing told her. "No question regarding efficacy can be answered without reference to the organism's environment. A mutant polar bear born without hair dies at birth. A hairless tropical bear may well survive to reproduce. A bear belonging to a hypothetical species already trending toward a marine existence—the path followed by porpoises and seals—may enjoy certain advantages over its 'normal' fellows.

"Some species, notably those to which we all belong, alter the impact of the environment. This stratagem has proven so successful that, through the feedback inherent in such a process, evolution often accelerates fantastically in such species. On discovering fossil evidence of this acceleration, some observers even begin to doubt the theoretical basis for evolution."

"Although a better understanding of biophysics, and the selective power of factors such as language-use, inevitably reverse that first inclination," replied Dlee Raftan Saon.

"At least it is to be hoped," the Eldest agreed. "Let us see now how the process works in application. About two hundred thirty million years ago, three quarters of all life on most versions of Earth, animal and plant, marine and land species, died—whether on a geologic timescale or literally overnight remains unclear—for reasons that are still a source of controversy in scientific circles."

Pulaski sat up straight. "You're speaking of the Permian-Triassic Extinction."

"Indeed I am. Theories, naturally, abound to account for it. One holds that a nearby supernova bathed the planet in radiation, another that a meteor or comet struck it, filling the atmosphere with dust that blocked the sun, plunging the world into centuries of winter. Others claim a great volcano erupted, accomplishing the same thing or that continents drifted together, eliminating enough coastline to upset the balance of marine life and altering the over-all ecology."

"Maybe they adopted one too many Five Year Plans," Owen laughed, "and died of starvation."

Gutierrez shook his head. "Or maybe they declared war on drugs and arrested so many of each other that nobody was left on the outside to keep things going."

"It isn't that I don't share your sympathies," the Eldest told them, "but what concerns us most is what happened afterward. The planet had once teemed with life in abundant variety occupying every possible niche, making a living in every conceivable manner. Now most of it was gone. But a previously insignificant group, now deprived of natural enemies and competitors, began to proliferate and differentiate until, within a short span, they filled all the empty niches."

"Dinosaurs," Pulaski declared.

The transparent entity bent slightly, giving the girl a polite nod. "Few know what killed their predecessors or why they survived. One surmise, and it happens to be correct, is that they were different somehow from the seventy percent that died. They had different habits, lived in different places, were awake different hours, ate different things, required different atmospheric gases, had different muscles, different nervous systems, different organs, or different skin. It's not my function to be the back of the textbook. I don't intend giving you the answers. You'll profit more by finding them yourselves. Whatever the difference, it kept dinosaurs alive while almost everything else around them perished."

Mister Thoggosh lifted a glistening tentacle. "Life went on because they *were* different."

"Precisely. Because they were different. Roughly one hundred seventy million years later," the Eldest continued, "sixty-five million years ago, a large fraction of all life on Earth died out for reasons that remain unclear: a nearby supernova, a meteor or comet, a great volcano, drifting continents."

"The Cretaceous-Tertiary Extinction," Pulaski stated. "It's the disaster that everybody talks about, although it wasn't as bad as the earlier Permian-Triassic."

"This time," declared the Eldest, "the dinosaurs of most worlds weren't so lucky. They died, while a previously insignificant group, different in some way from those who perished, began to proliferate and differentiate just as the dinosaurs once had, until, in a short span, they filled up all the empty niches."

"Again," responded Mister Thoggosh.

"We call them mammals." Pulaski nodded.

Owen grinned. "And they are us."

"Some of us, anyway," added Remgar d'Nod.

The Eldest was persistent. "In any case, it should be clear by now that differentiation is the ultimate form of life insurance. Evolution by itself has no plan, but proceeds through random changes winnowed by the exigencies of harsh reality—as if the output of a million typewriting monkeys were edited to eliminate the gibberish, leaving something that *looks* purposeful. Call it an optical illusion of the mind's eye, but it's what makes each generation— barring an occasional Permian-Triassic or Cretaceous-Tertiary super-disaster—harder to kill. It has preserved life itself for three billion years, even *through* those super-disasters."

The Chinese commander—what was his name?—Colonel Tai spoke up. "Are you implying—?"

"That there's an overall pattern to evolution after all, one that might be expressed as a single 'Commandment'? Perhaps, Colonel. If so, then it's the same sort of conceptual illusion, but one which explains everything. The Evolutionary Imperative is this: for life to prosper, living things mustn't only be fruitful and multiply, they must be as *different* from one another as possible."

Tai shook his head. "But as far as human—I mean sapient beings are concerned, doesn't that—"

The Eldest interrupted again. "Thoughtful individuals often seek a meaningful distinction between sapient and nonsapient life: 'nautiloids are the tool-using animal,' they say, or 'sea-scorpionoids are the language-employing animal,' or 'insectoids are the fire-making animal,' or 'arachnoids are the time-binding animal,' or 'humans are the problem-solving animal'—"

"So much," observed Rosalind, "that when they run out of problems to solve, they're unhappy until they make new ones." General laughter suggested that this was not a condition unique to Homo sapiens.

Seeing where they were headed, Empleado grimaced. He didn't think he could take one more of the mind-boggling events which had marked his stay on this asteroid. One by one, each of the values for which he'd fought all his life had been confronted here, defeated, and dismissed, with nothing to replace them but excuses for the blatant, self-interested profit-seeking he'd always believed unspeakably evil.

"Permit me to propose the vital distinction: the real difference between sapient and nonsapient organisms is that what nonsapients do as species—be as different from one another as possible in order to fill every niche—sapients do as individuals. Political regimes that limit this natural urge represent a mortal danger to individuals, to species, and to life itself. My nautiloid Successors are correct: a single prohibition maximizes the differentiation possible to individuals living together in civilization, without imposing any real limits on them. It is this: nobody has a right to *initiate* physical force against another sapient for any reason."

SEVENTY-TWO
The Back Door

"I take it," the Proprietor asked the Eldest, "that you approve of what my species has accomplished?"

Empleado shuddered. If the nautiloids were right in what they believed, then how could he go on living with all the things he'd done over a lifetime's service to the KGB?

"I wouldn't wish to embarrass you, Mister Thoggosh," the Eldest replied, "nor myself. But I confess that I find your people rather stuffy. There are," he conceded, "certain adventurous individuals among them who represent a significant step toward perfection of evolution's highest possible level, the fully autonomous individual."

"But what about the Predecessors?" someone else wanted to know.

The Eldest dismissed the question with contempt. "In their own way, those poor bugs," he told the group, "are as silly and hysterical as the dinosauroids. Even now, I shudder at the thought that I was once Aelbraugh Pritsch. I shall have nightmares about that bird-costume I have now so gratefully discarded. I'm afraid neither the trilobites nor the avians are much of an improvement."

"Who *do* you approve of, then?"

"Well, from my admittedly limited point of view, I must say I rather like sea-scorpionoids and humans. All of the arachnoid species are very bright and attractive. Now that I've seen one, I entertain certain hopes for dogs. The fact is, with the possible exception of those termite-minded trilobites, I regard every one of my Successors as superior beings, vastly more admirable and successful than myself. Evolution has created, in each of their species, a greater number of complete individuals, in a shorter time, and in much smaller, more efficient packages.

"I also admire them personally. It is relatively easy to remain an individualist when you are the only one around. However, to accomplish it in company—in a crowd—requires concentration."

Empleado hardly heard the talk going on around him. More and more, he realized, each day he awoke, he felt he had less to live for. He caressed the smooth, hard bulge of the H&K P9S in his coverall pocket. Perhaps, the thought came, he would use the pistol after all.

And one round of the ammunition.

Together, they swam toward the light.

Increasingly, it was like swimming through a mist that had caught fire. Eichra Oren tired after the first few kilometers and, at her invitation, climbed on the tireless Model 17's broad, armored back. Even so, each hundred meters they gained was more difficult as the amount of algae suspended in the oxygenated liquid fluorocarbon multiplied until it made breathing impossible.

"*Hey, Boss,*" Sam's voice cut through the Antarctican's clouded mind like a knife. "*Better break out the filmsuit, don't you think? Your lungs weren't made for straining vegetables.*"

"Hunh? Oh. Yes, Sam, I think you're right. Do you mind stopping for a moment, Model 17?"

"Not at all. I shall use the time to clear the intakes of my jets, which are becoming clogged with the same material." She paused. "Eichra Oren, I do not believe that things here are as the Predecessors intended."

The man pulled the suit from the rucksack he carried. It made a bundle little bigger than his palm. Unfolding it, he slipped both legs and both arms inside, sealed the midseam from crotch to throat, and pulled the hood and flexible mask over his head. In a few moments, he could breathe again and his head began to clear.

"What do you mean, not as the Predecessors intended?"

"This algae," she replied. "If it bothers me—interfering with my propulsion system in this instance—then like you, they would have found it most unpleasant indeed."

"It's like every aquarium Eichra Oren ever tried to keep," Sam told her. *"You're the trilobite expert, what do you think it means?"*

"I'm not certain. Perhaps only that they ought to have had someone like me to maintain—what's that?"

Dark forms loomed out of the dazzling fog, headed straight for them. As they came nearer, Eichra Oren could see that they were like Model 17, only smaller. He counted half a dozen of them before he noticed that their claws were extended.

"It is the Predecessors!" Model 17 shouted. "My Creators have returned!"

"Yeah," Sam told her, *"and they're pissed!"*

Rosalind shook her head. "How can you be sure that's true for every different sapient species?"

Being careful not to disturb the others—they were all raptly paying attention to the Eldest, anyway—Empleado arose and quietly left the living room by the front door, descending the balcony stairs and going around the house into the woods behind it. Laid over a random pattern of small impact craters, the ground here was far from level. On a rise well back of the house, he sat down cross-legged, took several breaths, and pulled the big black pistol from his pocket.

"The combinations and permutations which make for mere physical appearance," explained the Eldest, "are virtually limitless, determined by genetic chance and by the selective exigencies of differing environments. Through more of my 'spy' cells, for example, I've been following the interstellar progress of the Predecessors, and they've yet to encounter anything that looks at all like organisms evolved on Earth. Evolution simply is not that convergent.

"On the other hand or claw or tentacle or pseudopod, intelligence is a specific quality bounded in its needs and capabilities by natural law. Each of you has already encountered, in each other, not to mention myself, minds fully as alien—and not very alien at all, as it turns out—as any they will ever meet among the stars."

Empleado could still hear the giant amoeba through a large open window. Its voice had amazing carrying power, possibly because its entire surface vibrated to produce words. What he didn't hear was the stealthy approach of a human being behind him.

"If you would care for a concrete example, simply consider what I sincerely believe is the finest invention of all the Successor races: the crossword puzzle."

"What?" That from at least half a dozen voices.

Empleado put the cool steel circle of the H&K's cavernous muzzle to his forehead.

The manipulator that slashed its way toward Eichra Oren's face met the edge of his assessor's sword, instead, and sheared away. The claw-end sank rapidly out of sight. It had been made of metal, rather than the armored flesh of a living trilobite.

Astride the larger, more powerful machine that was Model 17, he followed the defensive stroke of his blade with a thrust, probing the insides of his attacker, tearing wires and tubes, showering them all in short-lived sparks. The device, whatever it was, began to swim in wider and wider circles until it disappeared into the haze.

"Behind you!" How Sam could have seen their next assailant—after all, he could only see things from the Antarctican's viewpoint—was a mystery Eichra Oren didn't stop to ponder. Instead, he aimed with the pistol he held in his left hand, which he couldn't remember drawing, and delivered a bolide of plasma straight into its face. Unfortunately, the blob of energy cooled before it reached the machine and he had to shoot again as it drew closer.

This time, the pistol worked. The front end of the artificial trilobite vanished—he felt the heat of it wash over him—leaving exposed parts dangling.

It sank without another twitch.

Meanwhile, Model 17 had seized a third machine, taken the edges of its carapace in several dozen of her claws, and heaved with all her strength, ripping the luckless device straight down the middle. The remaining three dithered for a moment, hovering several meters away in the hazy liquid, then turned tail and vanished.

Man and robot hung silently in the mist for several minutes, catching their literal and figurative breath, respectively. Sam, too, was speechless for a surprisingly long time.

Then: *"I hate this, being helpless this way! I wanted to sink my teeth right into those—"*

"Had you done so, Sam," Model 17 observed, "you would no longer have had any teeth."

"He doesn't have any now," countered Eichra Oren. "Besides, those robots were only doing their job. I suspect I know why this area hasn't evolved over the past billion years."

"I believe I agree," Model 17 told him, "I think those things were mutant-hunters."

"You mean they're designed to attack anything that doesn't meet the local building code?"

"That's exactly what I mean, Sam," declared Eichra Oren. "If it isn't on their list of approved life-forms somewhere, they're supposed to kill it, preserving the Midcambrian ecology. Model 17, those things must be controlled by a computer. Do you think you might be able to communicate with it and ask it to back off?"

"I don't know, Eichra Oren, but it may not be necessary. During the fight we drifted upward, being somewhat buoyant. If you look ahead, I think you'll see an island."

The man stifled a retort at this absurdity. Through the haze he could just make out something solid, floating in the midst of all this liquid, under the apparent sun. Not only did it seem solid, but if he looked hard enough, he thought he could see trees growing on it.

"I thought that 'Committee for the Preservation of Antiquities' had a KGB stink to it!"

Empleado twisted around painfully to see Colonel Chuck Tai pointing an enormous nickel-plated revolver at his face. His own pistol suddenly seemed very small and redundant somehow, so he let the hand that held it fall to his lap. "Planning to assassinate someone in the house, Mr. KGB, like the Proprietor or the Eldest?"

"Oh dear," came the voice of the latter from inside. "And just as everyone was basking in a self-congratulatory glow. But I stand by what I said. I greatly enjoy crossword puzzles and have even added to the art, if I may say so, creating cubed and n-dimensional specimens. The point is that all of you—those who do the proper sort of writing— invented them because you all think alike. You must. If you did anything else, it couldn't be called thinking."

Empleado shook his head. "You don't understand . . . I wasn't planning to hurt anybody but—"

Before he could finish, a bizarre figure hurtled from the woods, charging straight for the back of the house. Both men recognized the half human, half trilobite immediately and lifted their guns. Tai fired his long-barreled weapon first, each of his six shots, inexpressibly loud, paced evenly, almost in rhythm. The heavy slugs splashed off the Banker's carapace without seeming to do any harm.

By the time Empleado began shooting, Deshovich had almost reached the big window. His first seven shots and the eight that followed had even less effect.

Tai was on his feet immediately, and somewhere Empleado found the strength to follow and keep up. The Chinese officer hurled himself at the nightmare form just as it crashed through the window. The thing which had been Earth's dictator seized the man by a thigh and tossed him back outside where he fetched up against a tree with a hideous dull thump. He fell to the ground, motionless.

Abruptly, Empleado found himself back in Eichra Oren's living room, facing the Banker with an empty pistol in his hand. Before he or anybody else could move, Deshovich raised a clawed mechanical manipulator and punched it through the KGB man's body.

Empleado's last conscious act was twisting around to see the clawed arm, syrupy with bright red blood, protruding from his back.

SEVENTY-THREE
The Propoganda of Action

"Keep it there and press!"

Rosalind rushed to the fallen Empleado, horrified at the amount of blood the man had already lost, practically arcing away from his terrible wound in a fountain. On her knees, she seized a sofa cushion, slapped it over the entrance wound, and ordered the nearest available individual, Corporal Owen, to maintain the pressure.

"You got it, Doc!"

She was about to turn Empleado over to deal with the exit wound when something seized her by the wrist. She looked up and realized that Deshovich was standing over her. She hadn't even thought about the Banker once she'd seen her comrade fall.

"No you don't, bitch! When Nikola Deshovich kills somebody, he *stays* killed!"

Another metal claw reached for her face and she felt the serrated jaws begin to close on her cheekbones. She raised a hand to protect herself, but it was slapped away.

Owen was near enough to touch Rosalind but helpless, now holding two pillows to Empleado's body, unable to reach his weapon. Beside him, Toya was unarmed, having

left her shotgun, which had materialized on the surface of
the asteroid with her, by the front door. Others in the room
were armed and had even drawn their weapons, but were
afraid to fire for fear of hitting the doctor.

Only Horatio Gutierrez, fumbling in his pocket for the
tiny Kahr K9 9mm pistol he carried all the time now, rose
from where he sat, and strode to confront the Banker.
However the former general was interrupted in midstep
by a familiar voice.

"Release her or I'll let you live!"

The command was Eichra Oren's, although his form was
hidden from Rosalind by the Banker's bulk.

To her astonishment, Deshovich did let go—the threat
had been unique and appropriate—and whirled to face the
man, insane fury boiling in his remaining eye. Time seemed
to stand still. Oddly aware of her surroundings, Rosalind
watched Model 17 across the room, her many legs twitching
strangely. Through the window, she even had a brief
glimpse of Colonel Chuck Tai, still alive somehow, crawling slowly toward the house with murderous determination on his face. In another moment the giant centipede,
Scutigera, would reach him.

Despite her age, both real and apparent, Eneri Relda's
expression was exactly that of any mother watching her
favorite son about to throw himself into harm's way. Everybody else in the room seemed frozen, unspeaking and
unmoving as a photograph.

"And who might you be, little man," the Banker roared,
breaking that silence, "to determine whether anybody lives
or dies?" As the flesh-and-blood hand he had left made
nasty, involuntary grasping motions, he lashed out with
another mechanical claw toward the Antarctican, who stood
his ground without so much as blinking.

There was a ringing sound, as if someone had struck a
tuning fork, and the claw fell with a thump on the carpeted floor, its wrist-end sheared flat, reflective as a mirror.

"I'm a *p'Nan* moral debt assessor," Eichra Oren answered
in a relaxed and even tone. He even gave the Banker a
small, sympathetic smile. Stepping back a little for more
room, however, he gripped his gleaming two-edged sword
high on one shoulder, like a batter getting ready to hit a

fastball. Rosalind noticed, perhaps irrelevantly, that he was wearing his transparent filmsuit—its hood and faceplate pulled down onto his chest—which seemed to be covered with a light green powder of some kind, beginning to flake off onto the carpet.

"It is my judgment, Nikola Deshovich," the assessor's tone was formal, almost ritualistic, "and a matter of my firsthand experience—that you have incurred many serious moral debts, on this asteroid and to all appearances long before you arrived here. I refrain from mentioning what you did to my friend Sam; that's strictly personal and I'm professionally constrained. I'm here now to help you offer the customary token for those debts, like that owed to your murder victim S°bb°ts°rrh, which are inherently and profoundly unpayable."

"You can't be serious!" the Banker roared.

"They can be discharged in only one way under the philosophy and discipline of *p'Na*."

"Such a pretty speech!" The Banker leaned backward and laughed at the Antarctican. "But thanks to my Intelligence operatives, I know something of this cant, little man, and you may not strike except to save a life—or unless your victim invites it. Put down your toy. It will all be over soon enough anyway."

"Why do you say that?" the Proprietor demanded, having sensed something ominous in Deshovich's words. Gutierrez scrutinized the Banker, too, waiting for him to drop the other shoe. There was also a look of concern on the face of Eneri Relda, standing between the giant mollusc and the amorphous form of the Eldest.

The Banker laughed again, his voice beginning to trail off hysterically. "School's out, as we used to say, for all of the little vermin on this rock who've been masquerading as real people! You freaks! You slimy, obscene freaks! The joke's on you!"

"Say what you mean, fool," the tone Mister Thoggosh used, one Rosalind had never heard before, would have struck fear into anybody who was sane, "and be done with it!"

Even Deshovich's reply was somewhat calmer. "At my insistence, Model 17 has employed that tachyon telescope of hers to send an emergency message to her Creators—"

"What?" The word had been the Proprietor's but everybody else around him contributed their full share to the feeling of increased tension in Eichra Oren's living room.

"—warning them that the Eldest has awakened! It is vulnerable, she's informed them, and can be destroyed, along with its multitude of variously shaped disgusting subcells— if only the Predecessors will return quickly enough and do it!"

Eneri Relda shook her head. "But that's a lie."

"What a charming and attractive creature you are. Of course it's a lie. In fact, it's two lies."

That the Eldest could be destroyed, Rosalind thought, despite the fact that apparently he was spread out over several alternative versions of the Solar System, and that all of the different sapients on 5023 Eris were merely parts of him.

"You lied to me about Mister Thoggosh being dead, and about Sam, too, didn't you?" Rosalind demanded, a feeling of relief flooding through her even before she received the Banker's answer.

"Pray don't begrudge me a falsehood or two, my dear. It's my chosen art form and practically the only weapon I have left."

"Except to deceive whole peoples into making war on one another!" It was the sapient plant, Llessure Knarrfic.

The Banker heaved a deep, dramatic sigh. "The likeliest outcome by far is that you and the so-called Predecessors will do the universe an enormous favor and exterminate each other. In the meantime . . ." He twisted around again to leer at Rosalind. Hating herself for it, she was afraid. "I intend simply to walk away from here. Perhaps we'll continue this another day—if we have time!"

"No!"

Despite his condition, the gravely wounded Empleado snatched the Witness from Owen's belt and immediately began pulling the trigger, emptying it into the great bowl formed by Deshovich's carapace. This time, unimpeded by the Banker's armored back, a dozen .45 caliber bullets, traveling just above the speed of sound, found vulnerable targets in the plastic-covered vital organs laid out within the circumference of the trilobite shell.

"You traitorous son of a bitch!" Deshovich staggered back, outraged, then lunged forward, clawing for Empleado's face with several of his metal manipulators. As the autopistol's slide locked back on an empty magazine, Rosalind, with help from Owen and Gutierrez, rolled the injured man out of the Banker's reach. Rosalind was vaguely aware of some small, heavy, chrome-shiny object falling to the floor as they pulled and pushed at the KGB agent's body, but whatever it was, and whoever had dropped it, it failed to register fully on her consciousness.

At the same time, Eichra Oren ducked underneath half a dozen outstretched artificial limbs, interposing his own body between the maddened Deshovich and his victim.

"Pick on someone your own size, Marxist scum!"

Injured though he was, and nearly insensate with rage, Deshovich's timing was still good—or Eichra Oren's luck was very bad—for as the Banker furiously flailed a dozen or more of his arms, still determined to redden his claws on Empleado, he somehow caught the flat of the moral debt assessor's sword with the back of a manipulator and slapped it out of the startled Antarctican's grasp.

The razor-edged assessor's weapon sailed straight across the room and, with a low, clear tone resembling that of a church bell, suddenly stood quivering in the wall a few centimeters from the Proprietor's slit-pupiled left eye.

The instant the sword left his tingling, impact-deadened fingers, Eichra Oren was struggling to get at his little plasma pistol, but the Banker seemed to forget Empleado and seized the Antarctican instead, using several claws, and picked him up bodily, intending to dash him to the floor or crush him against the ceiling.

Abruptly, just beneath the assessor's body, a storm of gunfire erupted as several individuals began shooting at once, some few to good effect, others inadvertently striking Deshovich's hardened parts, creating noisy ricochets which caused still others in the crowded room to duck and flinch, screaming profanities and protests.

In a window-rattling voice, the Proprietor shouted for them all to cease fire at once.

Meanwhile something—a bullet fragment or a bit of secondary shrapnel—had struck Eichra Oren in the forehead.

Blood flowed instantly, blinding him as against superior strength he vainly applied every martial technique he knew to free himself.

Suddenly a sinuous, heavily muscled tentacle slapped one of the Banker's claws away from Eichra Oren's right arm as another slapped the grip of his sword back into his hand.

One velocity-blurred slash of that blade, ending in a metallic peal, and the man had freed his other arm.

Another and he was standing on his own feet again, confronting the once-human monster.

The Banker roared defiance.

Eichra Oren roared back and lunged.

For the first time in his long career, the debt assessor wielded his sword of office with relish.

SEVENTY-FOUR
The Jabberwock

"He left it dead, And with its head, He went galumphing back."

"Ogden Nash," guessed the Eldest.

"*No, it's Robert Service,*" argued Sam. "*Don't you know anything about American literature?*"

"It's Lewis Carroll," the Proprietor corrected, "and Robert Service was Canadian, Sam. Only there's no 'back' to galumph to in any event. We're still right here where the whole thing happened. Nevertheless, I shall be happy to say, 'Come to my arms, my beamish boy,' if etiquette absolutely requires it of me."

"I don't think that will be necessary," Eichra Oren answered. Absently, he fingered a smooth, oddly shaped object in his trouser pocket. The old fellow was right about still being here, though. The carpet hadn't finished absorbing the blood.

"*You have the arms for it, Your Molluscitude,*" Sam observed, "*but I think that's Rosalind's line. Too bad she isn't here to say it. Maybe you'd better give this relationship some thought, Boss. A doctor's mate is in for a pretty rough ride—*"

The Antarctican sipped his tall, cool drink and laid two cautious fingers on his forehead, feeling the patch of gauze taped there. Underneath it lay a minor cut, two stitches, a small amount of antiseptic, and a kiss. He'd just returned from the infirmary.

"No more so than any moral debt assessor's mate, I should think. I wish she were here, too, but for the moment, it'll be worth it if she and Raftan can cobble poor Arthur back together." He turned to Mister Thoggosh. "Tai—who didn't even have a cracked rib, it turns out, to show for his run-in with the Banker—tells me Arthur was working up his nerve to kill himself out there."

"Dear me," exclaimed the Eldest, "now that I understand the concept, I find the idea of death—"

"It couldn't have happened to a nicer guy! Listen, Eldest, since we're understanding concepts here, you want to tell me how come we—I mean Eichra Oren and Model 17— ended up on the surface of this dungball when they were headed for the core?"

Somewhere within the gallons of protoplasm comprising the Eldest lay the cerebro-cortical implant which had belonged to Aelbraugh Pritsch. He was perfectly capable of hearing the dog. "You mean," the giant amoeba replied, "you haven't asked her?"

"Model 17 hasn't been much of a conversationalist since you brainwashed her." As he spoke, the robot sat by herself in a corner of the room, for all purposes inert.

"Sam, you exaggerate again, simply to annoy me. Scutigera warned me. I take it as a compliment, since he also told me that you only do it to those you like."

"If you say so."

"I do. But I didn't brainwash the poor thing—or then again, perhaps I did. Basically a liquid entity, I 'dissolved' myself into Model 17 and, becoming physically and mechanically at one with her, resolved her preprogrammed contradictions and repaired her. She has a few little things to sort out for herself yet, but she'll be her old self, or even more so, before you know it."

"Yeah, and in the meantime, I notice you didn't answer my question."

"About the center and the surface? I didn't know it was

my place to answer you, Sam. In the first place, I'm not omniscient, and in the second, I didn't build this place."

"5023 Eris," declared the Proprietor, "isn't a sphere, Sam, although it looks that way from our limited point of view. It's a six-dimensional torus. I'm not sure why the Predecessors built it that way, nor is Model 17, but we'll find out eventually. It may have something to do with the Virtual Drive. Eichra Oren and Model 17—and you with them—simply took a turn around the rim."

For a moment, Sam was stunned into uncharacteristic silence. Then: *"Oh yeah? Then how come nobody I know about has gone for a walk in the woods out there, where we popped up at the end of our swim, and stumbled across the Great Communal Sea?"*

"I can answer that one," Eichra Oren told him. "For exactly the same reason people attach doors to their houses and put glass or plastic in their windows. It's a one-way trapdoor, so that air and fluorocarbon can't leak out but the Predecessors had easy access to the surface without traveling all the kilometers we did."

"So you can't get there from here?"

"That's right, although you can get here from there."

The assessor let go of the round metallic object in his pocket, gulped his drink, and ordered another.

"I have a question of my own, Eldest, and you'd better not dodge it like you just did Sam's. My mother told us that she's a part of you. In fact, she claimed she *is* you. You said that she and I were some kind of an experiment. I want to know what in the name of *p'Na* that makes me? She's helping Rosalind at the infirmary at the moment, and won't answer me in any case. She said I should discuss it with you. I feel completely human. I have for over five hundred years."

The Eldest chuckled. "Aelbraugh Pritsch felt avian. He never knew he wasn't until he did."

"That's helpful!" Again he felt for the palm-sized device he'd picked up from the floor after the Banker's body was removed from his living room. Its contours were irresistible.

"I'm sorry, my dear boy, I couldn't resist a final jest. You and your mother are part of an ongoing experiment in recombinant genetics. I wanted to see whether selected combinations of my own genes and those of younger, more vital species might not produce something superior. In a way—although the mix is actually more complicated than that, you might say I'm your maternal grandfather."

The man swallowed. "You mean I'm not a . . . a . . ."

"A slime mold? As if that weren't a perfectly fine thing to be." The Eldest chuckled, jiggling his jellylike substance. "Nor are you a giant amoeba about to shed your skin—and neither is your mother, the eternally beautiful Eneri Relda. You're both quite human, with just a little something extra added—me. You're an autonomous individual, but biologically immortal and virtually indestructible. These are traits I believe you can pass on to your own offspring."

"Interesting," declared a new voice. Rosalind entered the front door and joined them in the living room. Sitting down beside him, she gazed at Eichra Oren speculatively. "I can't stay. Arthur's in therapeutic stasis and we have to check on him from time to time. I just walked over here to tell Sam that we're ready for him now—and also to escort him back, figuratively speaking."

"*Aw, Ma, do I hafta?*" Eichra Oren passed the dog's remark on to the physician.

"You will," Eichra Oren advised, "if you don't want to remain as useless as those zinkies and ferns the Americans are fond of talking about." He began to explain to the Eldest that these were slang terms for baseless currency, but the parts of the being which had come to the asteroid with the ASSR expedition already knew.

"Before you all go," Mister Thoggosh told them, "there's a final item I wish to discuss briefly—but before that, what is that object you're fooling with, Eichra Oren? I've been watching you at it for half an hour and it's driving me mad!"

Eichra Oren laughed. "It's a plasma pistol, similar in function to mine, but of a design completely unknown to our civilization. And I have a pretty good idea who it belongs to."

"Well put it away, for pity's sake." Preoccupied, Mister Thoggosh lifted his ponderous shell and settled so that he faced the Eldest directly. "If Deshovich was telling the truth about chivvying Model 17 into contacting her Creators—"

"He was," replied the Eldest, nodding toward the robot. "That was the first thing I looked into."

"Then we find ourselves," Mister Thoggosh persisted, "confronting the possibility that thousands of hostile space-craft, loaded with heavily armed, paranoid trilobites, are already on their way back to the Solar System. I'm willing to entreat you, sir, to intercede, if that's what it will take. Can you not call them off? You do, after all, have cellular spies among the trilobites, do you not?"

"Yes," the Eldest answered wryly, "but how can I do what you ask, Mister Thoggosh, without betraying my own cells, portions of my being, as agents of the Predecessors' ancient Enemy?"

"*Whom the Predecessors won't believe in any event, once they find out who they are?*"

"That's correct, Sam," observed the Eldest.

The giant cephalopod was indignant. "But—"

"And besides," the Eldest asked, "aren't you big enough by now to take care of yourselves?"

"I don't understand," responded Mister Thoggosh.

The Eldest sighed. "Isn't this something that will just have to be hammered out—on that Forge of Adversity you nautiloids are so fond of lecturing others about?"

EPILOGUE
The Watchers Watched

The man with sandy-golden hair, Hawaiian shirt, Levis, running shoes, and a broad-bladed, two-handed sword alighted from the disk-shaped electrostatic aerocraft. The sword he carried in its scabbard, tucked casually under one arm. At his knee trotted a large, white, shaggy dog with a perpetual black-lipped smile.

Together they crossed the little green valley which, as far as they knew, contained the only way to get *into* the billion-year-old Predecessor starship still known as 5023 Eris. They—and everybody else presently living on what had originally been thought to be an asteroid—now knew there was another way of getting out.

Near the entrance stood a fabric awning on a pair of poles, shading two human figures and a table which had earlier been scattered with Predecessor artifacts. Now the ancient objects were divided into two piles, one large, and one rather smaller. Beside the small pile was an even smaller collection of fabric bags and plastic boxes containing the personal possessions and clothing of two individuals.

"Going somewhere, Corporal?"

A heavyset man with curly black hair looked up as Eichra

Oren and Sam approached the lean-to. The Antarctican didn't give Owen time to answer, but thrust a hand into his front pants pocket to remove an oddly shaped chrome-shiny object with edges and corners that were softly rounded and a tiny orifice in front blackened by terrible heat. "You'll want to take this."

Standing with Owen, Toya gasped and stepped behind him.

"Yeah," Sam added in a voice that anyone could hear, presently laden with sarcasm. "Leaving it behind is probably a violation of the Prime Directive or something."

Owen threw back his shaggy head and roared with laughter. "The Prime Directive was a fictional device dreamed up by liberals to keep the populations of Third World countries in their place. My people believe in acts of capitalism between consenting adults."

He blinked with the reflexive gesture of a person consulting his implant, probably to see what time it was.

"Tell you what, Eichra Oren: you can give me back my plasma gun, or give me yours and keep mine. Make one hell of a souvenir, won't it?"

"I'll say." Aloud, Eichra Oren read what had been stamped on the side of the little weapon: "B&G 'Hornet' 5.0 Megawatt Fusion Pocket Model Pistol, Borchert & Graham Energy Weapons, Ltd., Anson Springs, New Colorado, Galactic Confederacy."

"I had that new," Owen told him, "a long time ago. It's seen a lot of light-years."

Toya did glance at her ASF-issue wristwatch. "We have five minutes." She turned and began moving their containers into a line a few feet away from the tent.

Returning the B&G Hornet to his pocket, Eichra Oren grinned and extracted his own plasma weapon—boxier and a bit less powerful, but considerably smaller—and handed it to the corporal. Then he went to help Toya, as did Owen.

"Any time now," Owen told him, and as he did, an impossibly brilliant tiny blue speck appeared in the air directly over the luggage and instantly widened into a fiercely blue-edged circle.

Behind it, Eichra Oren saw what looked like the lobby of a small, modern hotel—except that the plan was circular, and through the windows on the opposite side of the room, he could see stars against the night black of open space. In the great distance hung an object like the top quarter of a titanic orange, painted a searing white.

"Safety first!" The "corporal" hooked a thumb over his shoulder. "This probability broach is open on a small auxiliary vessel about the size of one of General Gutierrez's late lamented shuttlecraft. The ship you see out there beyond the windows is eight and a half miles in diameter, one of the Great Ships of the Galactic Confederacy.

"My real name is Owen Rogers, staff praxeologist aboard the *Tom Paine Maru*."

"Staff what?" Sam demanded.

"Look it up," replied Rogers, touching a sleeve of his filmsuit. Its surface clouded and resolved into a glaring plaid. "We have to be going, me and my war bride." He grinned at Toya who blushed and grinned back. "But I left most of the Predecessor stuff for Mister Thoggosh, and there's a message for him if you'll deliver it."

Eichra Oren nodded. "Of course."

"Tell him that we're friendly, but that he should be aware from now on that the Elders aren't the only ones watching all the alternative worlds of probability."

Within the aperture, a nonhuman—a chimpanzee, Eichra Oren thought—became visible, reaching through and grabbing boxes and bags. "Get a move on, Owen, we haven't got all day!"

Rogers shrugged, took Toya's arm, stepped through onto a carpeted deck, and flapped a hand in a gesture of farewell. Toya blew the debt assessor and his assistant a kiss.

The circle closed to a blinding dot and popped out of existence.

"Hmm."

"I'll see that, Boss, and raise you a whatthefuck. I wonder how the all-seeing, all-knowing, all-confused Elders missed *that* universe in their survey fifteen thousand years ago."

Eichra Oren shrugged. "They didn't. I think it must have diverged historically since then. Let's get back and deliver our message. And maybe Rosalind will have some free time."

"I certainly hope so, Boss."

Eichra Oren frowned down at the dog. "Why?"

"I wanted to thank her."

He sat on his haunches, held up a paw, and spread the toes. One toe on the outside spread further than the rest and turned to touch the tips of each of the others in turn.

"Thumbs!"

DAVID WEBER

<u>The Honor Harrington series:</u> *(cont.)*

Flag in Exile
Hounded into retirement and disgrace by political enemies, Honor Harrington has retreated to planet Grayson, where powerful men plot to reverse the changes she has brought to their world. And for their plans to succeed, Honor Harrington must die!

Honor Among Enemies
Offered a chance to end her exile and again command a ship, Honor Harrington must use a crew drawn from the dregs of the service to stop pirates who are plundering commerce. Her enemies have chosen the mission carefully, thinking that either she will stop the raiders or they will kill her . . . and either way, her enemies will win. . . .

In Enemy Hands
After being ambushed, Honor finds herself aboard an enemy cruiser, bound for her scheduled execution. But one lesson Honor has never learned is how to give up!

Echoes of Honor
"Brilliant! Brilliant! Brilliant!"—*Anne McCaffrey*

Ashes of Victory
Honor has escaped from the prison planet called Hell and returned to the Manticoran Alliance, to the heart of a furnace of new weapons, new strategies, new tactics, spies, diplomacy, and assassination.

continued ☞

Got questions? We've got answers at
BAEN'S BAR!

Here's what some of our members have to say:

"Ever wanted to get involved in a newsgroup but were frightened off by rude know-it-alls? Stop by Baen's Bar. Our know-it-alls are the friendly, helpful type—and some write the hottest SF around."
—**Melody L** *melodyl@ccnmail.com*

"Baen's Bar . . . where you just might find people who understand what you are talking about!"
—**Tom Perry** *perry@airswitch.net*

"Lots of gentle teasing and numerous puns, mixed with various recipes for food and fun."
—**Ginger Tansey** *makautz@prodigy.net*

"Join the fun at Baen's Bar, where you can discuss the latest in books, Treecat Sign Language, ramifications of cloning, how military uniforms have changed, help an author do research, fuss about differences between American and European measurements—and top it off with being able to talk to the people who write and publish what you love."
—**Sun Shadow** *sun2shadow@hotmail.com*

"Thanks for a lovely first year at the Bar, where the only thing that's been intoxicating is conversation."
—**Al Jorgensen** *awjorgen@wolf.co.net*

 Join BAEN'S BAR at
WWW.BAEN.COM
"Bring your brain!"